Татьяне Б[...] [...] [...]
уваж[...]

MW01102656

[signature]

MIDGET

Symphony of the Ocean

KATE VALERY

Order this book online at www.trafford.com
or email orders@trafford.com

Most Trafford titles are also available at major online book retailers.

Print information available on the last page.

ISBN: 978-1-6987-0416-6 (sc)
ISBN: 978-1-6987-0418-0 (hc)
ISBN: 978-1-6987-0417-3 (e)

Library of Congress Control Number: 2020925532

Trafford rev. 12/23/2020

www.trafford.com
North America & international
toll-free: 844-688-6899 (USA & Canada)
fax: 812 355 4082

TO MY ENDLESS LOVE OF CLASSICAL
MUSIC AND SYMPHONY

ACKNOWLEDGMENTS

I would like to thank my dear daughter, Inna August, for suggesting that I finish this book, which was half-done in 2006. It was a brilliant idea to occupy myself during the coronavirus pandemic, when I, as many others, lost any chance to travel more and to explore the world as I did during the passage of those previous fourteen years. However, I also gained a lot of experience during that time, and I am now kind of happy that I neglected my *Midget* for all those many years. The book would never have been done on the same emotional and spiritual level as it is now had I finished it in 2006.

Also, a huge thank-you to my beloved granddaughter, Martina Dominique, a student at Victoria University in British Columbia and a published author of poetry, for editing the first part of my *Midget* in 2009. Sadly, she wasn't able to do the rest of it now.

And the biggest thank-you to my dear boyfriend, Robert E. Butler, who was by my side since 2015 and helped me with editing my *Midget* during the summer of 2020 twice. Because of the pandemic, we can't travel now. But we were sitting in the forest, in the shade, breathing in fresh air, enjoying the birds singing and little rabbits jumping around. We worked on the book together, discussing every word, sentence, and paragraph. He inspired me and taught me how to improve my English at the same time as he admired the story and got fascinated by it. It is my hope to convey here my huge gratitude for his priceless help.

Love you all, my dears.

PART 1

THE WHITE RAT

CHAPTER 1

n the middle of the night, Jim Bogat was suddenly awoken by a strange loud sound. It seemed as though somebody downstairs had slammed the door. Still sleepy, Jim rolled over in his bed toward the window and pulled the curtain open. With difficulty, he opened his eyes and began to rub them, trying to wake up completely. Now through the window, he could see the dark November sky studded with stars and the huge full moon hanging right above a notched coal-black line of the forest. The smoky moonlight penetrated into the room, making visible a clock on the opposite wall that showed the time—a few minutes to three.

Would somebody go out at this time? Jim thought. *It's strange.*

He was new at the group home—it was just his third night here—so he wasn't sure about the rules and regulations, written and unwritten. Despite this, the sound troubled him greatly. Jim was sensitive to sounds, and now he felt uncomfortable. He didn't want to sleep anymore; he remained on his bed quietly and continued to listen.

Some minutes later, Jim heard what sounded like someone being hit and then a woman's scream and the noise of something small and hard, like a marbles or little stones, falling to the hardwood floor and spreading. He heard an angry man's voice shouting, and then the door slammed again. Jim's heart began to beat faster. He realized that something terrible was happening downstairs. Could it be a robbery? Or was it something else that he had never seen or heard in his life before?

His grandma, who had raised him, had always protected him from anything harmful or bad—even things in the books he read and the movies he watched—and did her best to create a warm and safe atmosphere for him. She loved him dearly, but as a result, his soul was left open and unprotected, and he was much more vulnerable to the realities of life—with all its dirty sides.

All the other residents at the group home were sleeping quietly, unaware of any noises. Maybe it was because they were on medication, but Jim wasn't. He was in his right mind and now lay on his bed, gazing into the darkness with wide eyes and feeling feverish.

Then Jim heard the sound of footsteps. Someone large and heavy had run just beneath his window toward the garage. The gravel rustled under the person's feet.

"Barry, Barry, don't do this, please!" Jim heard a woman's pleading voice and recognized surprisingly that it belonged to Mona Lainer, the owner and manager of their group home.

"Shut up, you fucking bitch!" the man shouted with fury. "You're an evil thief! You're a hypocrite! Holy shit! I don't want to go to prison with you! I'm not gonna do anything with you anymore! Go to hell!" The man, obviously Mona's husband, slammed the garage door, opened the overhead gate widely, started his van, and drove away.

Jim heard Mona's quiet steps on the gravel as she went back into the house. She sobbed but covered her mouth with her both hands so as not to make much noise, trying not to wake anybody. Then there was silence.

Jim felt such pity toward Mona. She was a nice woman, but she wasn't beautiful. Her hair, eyebrows, and eyelashes were so light that they looked almost colorless. Her slender face and long nose gave her the look of a rat (with her lack of color, a white rat), but in spite of what she looked like, she was kind, friendly, and full of care for all the residents. Mona was always smiling; her brows were jumping, showing people how much she really loved them. She was an excellent cook, read the handicapped residents stories and fairy tales in her pleasant voice, and together with four nurses—two men and two women—ensured that their medical needs were taken care of. However, the nurses came for work in shifts, one couple from 8:00 a.m. until 2:00 p.m., another couple from 2:00 p.m. until 8:00 p.m. During the rest of the day and night, Mona and her husband were the only people who lived in the home and carried out all aspects of the residents' care.

During his first three difficult days here, Jim received a lot of help from Mona and noticed that she was like a mother to all the handicapped. Now he felt sorry for her, seeing that she had problems with her husband—a rude-looking fat, bald man, Barry. It was sudden and sad and bothered Jim a lot. He had never known family problems and didn't expect that they could be so hurtful, so horrible.

It's not my business, of course, he thought. *But I really want to help Mona. I want to say something nice to her.* Jim slid from his bed carefully, pulled on his small pair of blue jeans, and slowly walked to the door, holding himself up against the wall with his hands so as not to fall down.

Jim was a midget. He had a small body and tiny feet and hands, but his head was of normal size for a man of thirty-two years. His head was quite heavy, and it was not easy for his little body and feet to carry it. During the first fifteen years of his life, he couldn't walk because of it; but later, his grandma hired a medical rehabilitation specialist and a physiotherapist to help him. They trained him for two hours every day. It helped. In a year, he was able to walk—slowly and with difficulty but on his own. It was his first true victory, and he was so thankful to his grandma for pushing him to do it.

At the same time, Jim was very handsome. He had refined features— large brown eyes with long dark lashes, delicate lips, and wavy dark brown hair. The dimple on his chin gave him a particular charm. It gave him sex appeal. His eyes shone with cleverness and allowed his spiritual nature to shine through. They were so deeply temperamental that he could probably have been a movie star if he weren't so badly handicapped. It was a tragedy, but he was a survivor and had already overcome the challenges that life had placed in his path during his teen years. Now he was accustomed to his condition and didn't care anymore, but the eternal deep sadness would remain in his heart forever.

Jim wasn't very happy but was able to tolerate being alive. He found a lot of interesting things to do, create, and think about; they held him in check psychologically. His outside life was simple—all he had to do was just take care of his little body and survive physically somehow. But his inner life was immersed in creativity. It enveloped him and filled his heart and soul with satisfaction in his existence. It stayed in him, in his mind, along with his childish naivety and inexperience of most aspects of the surrounding world. It was quite unusual—the whole of Jim's look was very unusual as well. In spite of his deformity, he was a warmhearted and kind person who liked the people around him, especially when they were happy, smiling, and laughing. The accidental witnessing of Mona's family scandal hurt Jim painfully, and he yearned to right this wrong.

He opened the door of his room and stood still for a while, listening to what was going on in the house. Everything was quiet on his floor. All doors were closed. No light could be seen from under the doors, and it seemed as though everyone was sleeping. Jim walked to the stairs, sat on the top step, and slid down on his bum step by step, like what little kids usually did. For him, it was the fastest and most comfortable way to get downstairs.

The living room and the large dining room were dark. However, in the kitchen—on the linoleum floor—he noticed reflections of the light that was on somewhere behind the storage room door. Jim passed the kitchen, opened the door, and walked into the storage. This room was quite long and full of shelves, and it was gloomy as the light was off.

At the other end of the storage room, Jim saw that the next door had been left wide open. Behind it was a short hall with a hardwood floor, and there, the light was on. There, Jim finally saw Mona. She was sitting on the floor in the doorway, between the storage room and the brightly lit hall behind her. She was crying soundlessly, her head in her knees.

When Jim came into the storage room, Mona quivered and looked at him in horror. She grabbed the kitchen towel from the lowest shelf she could reach from her sitting position and threw it onto the hardwood floor into the next room behind her. Then she turned back to Jim and stared at him with bulging, water-filled eyes. They were begging, wet, red, and desperate. "Sorry to bother you," Jim said sympathetically. "I just heard you crying. It's so sad. Can I help you somehow?"

Mona shook her head; her short blond ringlets swung. She looked weak and helpless. "No, Jim. Thank you. It's so nice of you, but you can't help. It's private. My husband is mentally ill. He is very difficult to deal with. Sometimes he has hallucinations and sees things the wrong way. He doesn't understand what's going on and accuses me of problems that do not exist in reality. It's nothing except his illness. You shouldn't worry about it. I'm used to it. We've already been together for twenty-five years, and it is always the same."

It's strange that the person who is supposed to take care of the handicapped, most of whom are mentally ill, is mentally ill too, Jim thought. He didn't say anything to Mona, of course, but approached her and petted her hair with his tiny hand. Her hair was so soft and fine like down. That surprised him. Never in his life had Jim touched somebody's hair except his own or his grandma's. Now it was a very different feeling.

Jim's little fingers ran through Mona's hair gently. He just wanted to express all his pity toward her, but suddenly, he quivered and jerked his hand back. "Sorry, Mona," he said, smiling coyly. "I've probably no right to touch you. It's just sympathy."

Mona smiled and looked attentively into his eyes. She was a tall and slim woman, but while she was sitting on the floor, her face was on the same level as Jim's, who was standing beside her. It was easy for them to stare into each other's eyes. "It's okay, Jim," Mona uttered slowly. "Don't worry, I'm like a mother here, and all of you are like my kids. I love all of you and hug and kiss everybody sometimes like a mother is supposed to do. The group home is an official institution, but it's your home and family at the same time. We should have a close family relationship here. It's our goal to keep all of you happy."

"I really don't know what a family relationships is," Jim commented sadly. "I never had a mother. My grandma was always nice to me, but even for her, I was an adopted child. I have no experience in relationship between people at all."

"It's a difficult area, believe me," Mona noted, continuing to stare into his eyes. "But I'll help you. For me, you look like a very smart person, and I'm sure you'll understand. Did you go to school?"

"No . . . but I studied a lot. I got my diploma by correspondence. Then I took courses at college and at university, also by correspondence— history, philosophy, languages, and computer science. Then I took music at Juilliard School in New York. I even got a master's degree in music."

"Did you? Really?" Mona sounded surprised. "Can you play an instrument?" She looked at his little hands and tiny fingers with uncertainty.

Jim caught her glance and smiled bashfully. "I can a bit. Mostly, I compose music on the computer. I'll show you later when my luggage arrives. I have a digital piano with the whole computer system."

"Oh, that's why I was told to give you the biggest room," Mona twigged with visible interest. "Of course, you need the room to place all this stuff. It's amazing. I'll help you get settled. Or will somebody else be coming to help you? Relatives . . . or friends?"

"No." Jim shook his head. "I don't have anyone else."

"Poor guy," Mona drawled, fondly putting her hand on his shoulder and smiling at him. "You're so smart and so handsome. You seem very special to me. I guess that you don't see your own value."

"My value?" Jim smirked. "I don't think I have much. What could be the value of a midget?"

"Oh no, Jim, forget it. Here, we don't use words like that to describe your conditions. We're one loving family, and I'm your mother, your teacher, and your closest friend from now on. You can trust me fully."

While saying that, Mona spoke in a sensitive whisper and put another hand onto Jim's other shoulder. Now he could smell her amazingly sweet perfume. It made him dizzy. It confused him because never in his life had he seen or felt a woman so close. His heart sank, and he stood still, not knowing what to say or do.

Mona pulled him closer to her, continuing to gaze straight into his eyes. She touched his neck and slowly moved her lips to his. Jim became shaky, feeling her warm breath on his face. Then she kissed his lips fondly and carefully in the beginning and then more and more passionately, plunging her tongue inside his mouth and sucking him madly.

Jim was dumbfounded. Without realizing it, he closed his eyes so as not to see Mona's rat face and tried to concentrate on his feelings that were amazing and absolutely unusual for him. He became hot and drank, as if it were champagne, which he had tried a couple of times in his life.

Mona hugged him amorously, pressing his tiny child body to her chest. Her lips slid over his face, sucking his nose, eyes, and cheeks, tenderly biting his ears, which made him moan. Jim put his little hands on Mona's shoulders, holding himself so as not to fall down. He couldn't stand for so long; his feet and legs got tired and weak, and he was about to collapse.

Mona noticed. "Are you tired, my baby?" she whispered lovingly. "Don't worry, you can lie down." She carefully lowered him onto the floor, bent over him, and tore away her T-shirt. Her small breasts were hanging up above his face. They were quite droopy as she was over fifty years old, but Jim had no idea what they were supposed to look like in reality. He was overwhelmed.

"Take it, Jim," Mona demanded in a hushed voice. "I'm your mother now. You never knew that, but you should. Everybody has gone through this experience to become a man. Take it with your hands and suck it. Every person in the world has done it."

Jim touched her breast and ran his tiny fingers around its soft and hot surface with uncertainty, amazed at how silky her skin was.

"More, more, my dear," Mona moaned. "Touch them more . . . with both hands . . . scratch, squeeze them . . . kiss them . . . suck them . . . I'm your mother, and you are my child. You are not lonely anymore . . . you are not alone in this world. Do it. Do it!"

Jim didn't know what to do, but his nature awoke somewhere deep inside his tiny body, and his man's brain took over. He took each of Mona's breasts with each of his hands, pulled them to his face, and sucked them lustfully in turn, surprised that her nipples were hard and sweet like candy.

Mona groaned with ardor and bit her lip to avoid making noise. Her hand moved over Jim's little body slowly and smoothly. She unzipped his jeans, hoping to discover if he had something what every man is supposed to have in this area and wondering what size it could be—normal like his head or tiny like his other parts? Mona was quite sure that he would be okay because he was shaving, and his voice sounded like a regular man's.

At that moment, the door between the storage room and the kitchen suddenly opened, and Jim heard someone walk into the storage room slowly, shuffling on the floor with large slippers. He jerked in horror and tried to free himself from Mona's hands, but she just glanced quickly toward the door and smiled at him. "Don't worry, baby," she said quietly. "It's just Maggie. She doesn't understand anything. Actually, there is no one in the house now who has a mind, except you and me."

Maggie came closer, and Jim noticed that she was young but very abnormal. From a distance, she looked like an old woman. Her swollen face was expressionless and her stare empty. Holding a plastic cup, she extended her hand toward Mona. "Sue . . . Sue," she mumbled, shaking the cup. "Wawa . . . wawa."

"She wants her nurse. She wants to drink. Could you wait a minute, my darling?" Mona whispered to Jim and kissed him tenderly on his forehead. "I'll be right back."

She stood up, pulled on her T-shirt, approached Maggie, and took her under her arm. "Let's go to the kitchen, sweetie," she said softly. "There is water." Slowly, they went through the storage room and left for the kitchen together.

Jim turned onto his stomach, stood on all fours, and then got up on his feet, holding himself steady against the shelves. It wasn't easy for him to stand up fast, but he tried to do it as quickly as he could. Shaky and finally beginning to be aware of his reality, he zipped up his jeans.

Jim didn't want to go back through the kitchen and to see Mona. He guessed that there should be another entrance somewhere and went into the brightly lit hall with hardwood floor to look for it as fast as he could. There were two more doors in the hall. One of them was open. Jim peered inside and saw that it was Mona's office. Another door was locked. There was no exit, and Jim had no choice, except to return to the storage room.

Hobbling back toward the storage room door, Jim stumbled over the kitchen towel that Mona had thrown and was lying on the floor. He jumped in surprise and accidentally leaned against the nearest wall, trying not to fall down. Jim noticed that it was not just a wall but the door to a giant safe. It was painted the same color as the wall so as not to be visible. The safe door was open just a crack, and there was a lot of stuff inside, but Jim had no time and no interest in looking what was there. His only wish now was to run into his room and be alone.

As he entered, the kitchen towel that Jim had stumbled over was lying on the floor. At first, he didn't pay any attention to it; but now stumbling over it and kicking it accidentally with his sneaker, the towel slid aside. Shiny, sparkling stones, which had been covered by the towel, scattered around on the hardwood floor, and he saw a stunningly beautiful necklace broken into pieces.

That's what I heard, Jim realized. *During their dispute, this is what Barry broke.* He noticed it unconsciously, automatically. It was nothing to him. He didn't care. He only craved to find a way to escape from this evil place. But there was no other way except through the kitchen, where Mona was now with Maggie.

Jim didn't want to see Mona anymore. Scared that she'd be back soon, he trembled and felt dizzy; his teeth chattered as if he had fever. He walked, passing the long dark storage room, and suddenly discovered a large box with paper tissues right beside the entrance to the kitchen. Jim squatted to hide behind it.

Mona appeared some minutes later. She had already given Maggie a drink and seen her off into her bedroom. "Where are you, my little darling?" she called in a pleasant voice, smiling, even though she couldn't see Jim. She was sure that he was joking with her and hiding somewhere to let her look for him. He was flirting, she thought. Mona was glad to play this game, but accidentally glancing ahead, she saw that the towel on the hardwood floor in the hall was moved, and the broken necklace was visible.

Mona raced to the hall, knelt, and started to pick up the pieces of the necklace with her shaking hands. She gathered them into her palm, whispering, "My goodness. Oh my goodness." She was almost crying again.

She was so busy with the necklace that Jim was able to sneak into the kitchen, unnoticed by Mona. He passed the kitchen and then the living room and climbed up the stairs on all fours like a child again. When he entered his room, he turned around to lock the door and saw Mona downstairs, running out of the kitchen into the living room. "Jim!" she called. "My baby! Where are you? Come here, my sweetheart!"

Ignoring her, he locked his door, threw himself onto his bed, and buried his face in the pillows. Jim lay still, motionless, holding his breath. His angst was so deep that he was completely lost and confused and didn't know how to live now. He was frustrated; he felt dead.

Mona looked for him everywhere and soon grew worried and upset. She didn't expect such a reaction from him. Not finding him downstairs, she tiptoed to his bedroom and touched the doorknob. The room was locked and the light off. Mona knew that Jim wasn't sleeping but simply pretending to. She thought it would be better not to bother him now but, rather, let him calm down.

She was curious about him. The short time that they were together was enough for her to understand his sensitivity. *His lips are fantastic,* Mona thought. *His tiny fingers are capable of doing an amazing job. It makes me dreamy. He may be a nice thing to use. Maybe I was too straightforward tonight. I need to find the right rule of the game with him. Let's look at his background. What was his family like? Where is he from?*

She went to her office, unlocked her desk, and found Jim's folder easily. It was on the very top of all the other folders—he arrived just three days ago, and his paperwork hadn't been completed yet. Mona sat back in her armchair, crossed her long thin legs, and started to read.

JAMES EMMANUEL BOGAT

Date of birth: *March 12, 1970*
Place of birth: *Los Angeles, California*

"No exact address?"

Original background: *Italian*

"Hmm . . . must be hot tempered."

Date of adoption: *March 15, 1970*

"Just three days later? So quick? It's not usually so fast. Normally, there is a long way to wait, especially for a handicapped child."

Place of adoption: *Pennsylvania, Farm Luhoway, Range Road 236*

"So deep in the country? That's strange."

Parents of adoption
Father: *Phillip Bogat, farmer, 65 years old.*
Mother: *Cathy Bogat, housewife, 50 years old.*
Original background: *Ukrainian*

"From Los Angeles to a Ukrainian farm? At the other end of the country? Just in the first three days of his life? That's unbelievable. There must be more to it."

TOP SECRET:
Biological parents
Father:

"What? No. Hmm . . . could this be a namesake?"

Mother:

"What? No, that's impossible. Is that right? No, no way, it couldn't be them." Mona couldn't believe her eyes. She jumped from the armchair and threw the folder. "No, no!" she exclaimed. "I saw her last week on the *Larry King Live*! There was a question about kids! She said she never had children. Was it a lie? She was lying! Oh my goodness!"

Mona grabbed the folder from the table and read it again and again; then she closed the folder, kissed it affectionately, and began to laugh with excitement. She pressed the folder to her chest and carried it into the hall with the hardwood floor. There, Mona locked it in the safe beside the broken necklace that was wrapped in a napkin.

CHAPTER 2

O ver the next few days, Jim tossed and turned in his bed, hallucinating in a state of delirium. He refused to leave his room for breakfast, lunch, or dinner. He was unwilling to eat, even when nurses brought the meals into his room. He couldn't calm himself down and shake himself out of it.

Mona's long-nosed and bleak face seemingly hovered over him. He was scared of her and didn't know what to do, how to escape, or where to hide if she came into his room and tried to kiss him again or simply to persuade him to eat. Mona, however, wasn't in a hurry to appear.

All day and night over the next few days, music sounded in Jim's sick, fevered imagination. A mad stormy ocean reverberated in his ears. It was a vortex of huge sea-colored waves that foamed at the tops and fell down onto his head with a thunder. He sank in this great ocean and died; then he was revived and flew up in the waves almost as high as the sky.

The music overwhelmed him. It was everywhere as the entire universe buzzed, growled, and sang around him with thousands of vocalizations. It was a symphony of the ocean that echoed with the sound of amazing, miraculous voices and left him spellbound. Jim was elated that the music that he had missed for the last two long months after his grandma's death had finally returned to him. He really needed it. Usually, it helped him, enveloped his soul smoothly, and soothed him.

The first time Jim saw and heard the ocean was when Grandma Cathy took him to the Atlantic coast for a week. He was only eight years old and was sitting in a child-sized wheelchair. The experience of the ocean was fantastic. It dumbfounded him. Upon Jim's first glance of this sublime endless, eternal water, music began to sound in his mind. However, he was too little and didn't know what to do with it or how to express it. He simply cried.

After that, Jim couldn't stop thinking about the ocean's music. He tortured his grandma with endless discussions about his feelings and the sounds he heard. He asked her questions that she couldn't answer until, finally, she grew tired of it all and hired a music teacher to keep him busy. Jim began to learn to read and write music. He immersed himself in these classes fully, and one of the major emotional difficulties of his childhood was solved.

Since that time, Jim pressured his grandma to visit the coast every year. Even when she had begun to get older and feel weaker, she hired somebody to go with Jim on this trip so he wouldn't miss it. The ocean music stayed with him forever. Of all the things he had in his life, this was dearest to him—it was his greatest love and most valuable treasure. It always came to help and support him when he was in trouble.

It was sad to recognize, but Jim's life was full of enormous challenges and difficulties right from the beginning. He had survived numerous tragedies and bouts of the blues that had squashed and almost annihilated him mentally. Music was the only thing that gave him the ability to regenerate spiritually. Now lying on his bed and burying his face into the pillows, he remembered his childhood, reviewed all his experiences, and tried to find the right way to go. But nothing he could think of resembled today's situation.

At the Luhoway farm, Jim led a secluded life with his grandma Cathy. She didn't want to show him much of real life and didn't let him go to school, thinking that other kids might hurt him—maybe physically but mostly mentally. Jim never played with children and never even saw them around. He only knew the adults—the nurses and doctors who took care of him; the teachers who taught him; the delivery, maintenance, and service people; and, of course, his grandma, who was with him all the time, fed and washed him, read fairy tales to him, and sung him lullabies.

The trip to the ocean was the first time in Jim's life when he left the farm and saw the city—streets, shops, restaurants, and the airport and airplanes. However, nothing surprised him as much as the sight of other children; these were real, live children, not simply those portrayed in books and movies. "Who are they, these little ones?" he asked, astonished.

"They are kids, same as you," Grandma Cathy answered.

"They are not like me. Why are they walking, jumping, running? Their legs and arms are longer than mine. Why can't I be like them? Why can't I do the same things?"

"You are different, Jim."

"Why? I don't want to be different."

It wasn't easy for Grandma Cathy to explain to him that he was handicapped from birth, that something went wrong during his mother's pregnancy, and that it disturbed his normal development, causing him to be born as a freak of nature. Jim didn't understand much; he just felt the horrible, devilish unfairness of the situation and the endless despair due to the impossibility of changing anything about it. He cried for hours in pain, and only seeing and listening to the ocean could finally soothe him.

Grandma Cathy wasn't educated much, but she possessed a grandmother's wisdom. She liked to analyze life and teach Jim her understanding, her point of view, and her simple philosophy. "As you can see, my little one," she always said, "all people are different. Some people have big ears, some are bald, some are blind, some are deaf. There are those who only have one hand or one foot. Some are little, like you. It doesn't matter. All of them are people. All of them have feelings and are the same as they all eat, sleep, breathe, cry, suffer, and experience pain or happiness. Everyone has his shortcomings, but everyone has his achievements as well. Everyone can improve, advance, and grow physically or mentally. It's all part of being human.

"Look at life. Look at nature in our garden and grove, read books, watch TV, and think about it. You'll find out that everybody is different and special. The person with big ears could be an amazing comedian. A bald person might become a banker, and then everybody will respect him and not pay any attention to his baldness. Blind people are often good musicians. Deaf people have the potential to be talented artists. The person with just one hand or leg could be a great scientist, a university professor. You, little one, can develop your brain because you are very smart, and I see the potential you have. Thank God I have enough money to help you.

"There's no reason for you to be in despair. Yes, you are different, but you can be different in your mind too. You are special, you are gifted, and I see that. Nature never took everything away from one person. It always gives a balance—someone who is weak in one area will be great in another. You can't run, and so you can't be an athlete or a cowboy or a truck driver, but you can be a scientist or a composer or an artist or a chess player. Just think about it. Listen to the voice of nature, listen to your own mind, and you'll know what you are capable of. Believe me, my little one. I love you dearly, and I'm telling you this from the bottom of my heart."

These kinds of conversations were repeated many times. It didn't matter that Jim was still a child. He understood Grandma Cathy. Her thoughts and ideas settled finally in his head bit by bit, and the feelings spawned by the ocean music helped them integrate into his mind. Jim began to set big goals for himself.

By his teenage years, he had already familiarized himself with a great deal of scientific information, but he still liked to watch cartoons. He saw them as fairy tales and didn't take them seriously; they were plain fun. Grandma Cathy didn't expect that they might cause him any trouble that, anyway, couldn't be completely avoided. Once, Jim saw himself in the nice story of a small deer, Bambi, and suddenly realized that it was natural for everyone to have parents. "Where is my mom?" he asked. "Where is my dad? I should have parents. Or was I cloned? Am I a scientific mistake of cloning? How did I come to be alive? Don't hide anything from me, Grandma. I want to know the truth."

Grandma Cathy took a deep breath. She felt sorry that she couldn't fully protect him from life. "I expected this question," she said dolefully. "You'd begun to know too much. I knew that, one day, you would get this far. I can't lie, but I can't tell the truth either. I really don't know anything. I was just told that your father was dead and your mother was alive when we took you. Many years have passed since that day. Maybe she is dead too. Who knows?"

"Can I find her?"

"I don't think so."

"Why? We could go to the social services office and find some information about her."

"I don't think we can. But even if we could, we shouldn't do that, Jim."

"Why?"

"The fact that your mother gave you up for adoption means that she doesn't want to know you. It's very sad, my little one, but it can't be helped. Forcing the issue will not work in this situation. What would be the point of making a contact with her against her will? What could we hear from her? Just 'go away' or 'I don't want to see you'? There's no reason to hear that again. Forgive me, please, my darling, for saying such things to you, but you should forget this idea forever. Shut it out from your mind. You need to realize that you are an orphan, and I am your loving grandma. We've been happy together for many years already, and we really don't need any changes or stress."

Grandma Cathy didn't tell him anything about her suspicions. She wasn't completely sure, but she guessed that Jim's mother had taken some kind of medication or drugs while pregnant, hoping to get rid of him. In Grandma's opinion, this was why he was born so badly handicapped. She considered his mother to be an evil enemy, a traitor who—unconsciously or on purpose—hurt and mutilated him and condemned such a beautiful and talented child to live his whole life as a cripple. Cathy Bogat felt pity for Jim and loved him so much that she hated this unknown woman for her deeds and would never forgive her. She didn't want to know or hear anything about Jim's mother.

After this, Jim spent a long time crying. He was already a teenager, but it was only now that he was finally aware of his mother's betrayal. In his opinion, she should have been his protector and the dearest person in his life. That he had been betrayed as a tiny and innocent baby was so hurtful to him. It was unforgivable. Just the thought of it drove him mad. He didn't want to live in this despair. He would rather die.

This time, it was the music of the ocean that saved him and returned him to life once again. He finally overcame his suffering and continued to focus on his studies. He began to compose.

For the most part, Grandma Cathy raised Jim alone. Phillip Bogat died from cancer when Jim was just three years old. Jim didn't remember Grandpa Phil; he only saw him in the framed pictures in Grandma's bedroom.

The Luhoway farm was big but run down and neglected. Phil and Cathy were very ill years before they adopted Jim, and they didn't have enough money to run the farm properly. The adoption officers promised them money if they took Jim, and they agreed because there was no other chance for them to correct their financial situation.

After Phil's death, Cathy sold most of the fields, farmyards, and cattle. She kept only the house to live in with Jim, the garden for him to play in, and a birch grove to walk with him in. At first, she had taken Jim in just for the money; but strangely, it turned out that she really fell in love with this smart and charming child who was so unhappy from his birth. Grandma Cathy loved him very much and spoiled him. He became her baby and the only meaningful part of her life.

She didn't care much about her property, usually dressed in a very simple manner; and most of her possessions, such as household items and furniture, were old, plain, and cheap. However, she was honest and not greedy. She never took a penny of Jim's money for herself. It was a great pleasure for her to do everything possible for Jim; he always had everything he wanted and needed.

Grandma Cathy hired the best doctors and nurses to take care of him, the best teachers and coaches to train him. Every year he had the most expensive newest automatic wheelchair until he started to walk. He had the most beautiful and expensive toys and books, VCR, record and CD players, TV, computers, digital cameras, and pianos. By correspondence, he took courses at prestigious schools, colleges, and universities.

After Jim took courses in computer science, history, philosophy, and languages (English, French, Italian, and Ukrainian), he began to study music in university and then composition at Juilliard School. At that time, Grandma Cathy even hired a group of computer programmers to customize a program that would allow him to create musical compositions on the computer. Jim's piano was connected to the computer through the special system, and when he slowly played a melody with his tiny fingers, the music was instantly written on his computer. Then he pressed some buttons to add other elements such as harmony and orchestration; afterward, he could listen to the music he had just created, make corrections, and add any nuances of the sounds and harmonies he wanted. Jim liked the florid style, full of changes in pitch. A special printer was also connected to the system. It made it possible for Jim to print notes and lines of music on regular paper, and Jim already had shelves full of folders with both completed and unfinished compositions.

Jim immersed himself in music fully. He wanted to make music around the clock for the rest of his life. He realized that there still was a long path ahead, that he needed to improve and refine his skills to create the musical composition of his dreams, *The Symphony of the Ocean*. Jim worked and learned restlessly. He planned to add vocalizations to his symphony and spent hours carefully studying the voices of all the best singers in the world to choose the right one. He aimed to contact symphony orchestras in different countries, present his complete compositions to them, and find someone ready to perform them.

Almost an adult, Jim dreamed about his future concert and, like a child, built castles in the air. He imagined the huge hall full of thousands of people enjoying his music, cheering and whistling with excitement and singing along. They would have tears in their eyes; they would understand the feeling of the ocean, the feeling of the greatness of spirit that he wanted to open them to. This was what Jim lived for. He was immersed in his joy of creation and had no time for nor interest in anything else.

Meanwhile, years passed, and Grandma Cathy realized that Jim was getting older. He was becoming a man, and that worried her. She guessed that, one day, Jim would have an interest in women, love, and sex, but nothing like that had seemingly occurred. To prevent these problems, she even consulted with a psychologist and asked him to talk to Jim as she didn't dare touch this subject herself.

After the psychologist left, Jim called Grandma Cathy and hugged her. "You're so sweet, Granny," he said, laughing. "Thank you, but you're worrying about things too much. How could you think that I don't know anything about sex and love when I spend so much time on the internet? Of course, I have seen some pornography, but I don't care. I know that it's not for me. Anyway, I'll never have anything of this. Why try to find out more? I just forgot about it because it means nothing to me. It's not interesting. I'm too busy with much more important things. I need to finish my symphony. This is my life."

This answer was a relief for Grandma Cathy. "I was worried, my dear, because I am too old to explain such things to you," she confessed to Jim. "Almost thirty years have passed since Phil's death. I didn't have another man in my entire life. My experience is limited. In my family, nobody cared about love or sex, which I see nowadays on TV. We just got married to be together and have kids, to work on the farm, and to continue this way of life. I don't know why Phil and I didn't have children. Maybe one of us was not healthy enough, maybe both.

"Now my only love is you. My only interests are your education, your health, your mental balance, and your ability to walk. I am happy and proud that I taught you how to do take care of yourself, even shave, even though you do it slowly, and it isn't easy. I think about what will happen to you when I die. I am still not sure that you can live all by yourself. I thought we might find somebody to live with you instead of me. Maybe we could find a wife for you."

Jim laughed sincerely. "Granny, are you kidding me? What an idea! Forget it. I'll be with you forever."

Three months later, Grandma Cathy died in her sleep. It was a serious loss for Jim. He loved her very much, and he knew that she was the only person in the world who truly loved him. Any other person who helped take care of him did it just for money. They didn't like him and didn't care about him in reality; they were just doing their job. He never felt any warmth from them, only fake, polite smiles. Cathy Bogat had special feelings toward him—he was her dearest grandson, and she devoted her whole heart and soul to him.

Why am I so angry about Mona? The sudden thought came into Jim's mind now while he was lying in his bed and remembering Grandma Cathy's death. *Who else in the world loved me? Mona is the only person who said that she likes me, that I'm special for her. It seems that her feelings to me are sincere, not just artificial like other people's feelings. Something didn't seem right, but maybe this was normal for a man, not a child. That's what she told me. Why am I making a problem out of this? Actually, it was a real pleasure to be with Mona. Am I sure that I don't want it anymore? Am I confident, however, that I can have it in full?*

Jim felt ashamed of himself. He realized clearly that his insane madness and anger toward Mona were based on fear—he wasn't sure if he could be a man; he wasn't sure if his genitals were normal and capable of doing what this part of a man was supposed to do. He never thought about it before and never even tried. He cut thoughts about sex from his mind. He told himself that love was impossible for him. Jim reckoned that it was easier to live this way. Mentally, it was comfortable and calming.

Mona had suddenly turned everything upside down in his head and made him scared and confused. Jim tried to push away all the nagging thoughts about her. He was completely lost now, almost as much as he was lost when he discovered that Grandma Cathy was dead.

Grandma's death was horrible and unexpected for him. Her health was not bad in the days before her passing; she felt old but still maintained a decent level of vitality, and Jim never guessed that she would die soon. He lost the only person whom he loved and had been used to. He was left alone in his existence now. Nobody could replace his grandma. It was especially difficult because Jim didn't know how to live without her. He felt as if the ground was slipping out from under his feet.

Jim's life was so quiet and comfortable; he was provided for financially before Grandma's death. Now everything had fallen apart, and the biggest difficulty of all was money. Jim had no idea about Grandma's bank accounts, bill payments, credit cards, loans, and mortgages. He was never interested in the source of her money or how much he had cost her. He was just excited that everything he wanted appeared right away and didn't need to know how high the price of everything was. Jim never had his own bank account and never gave it a second thought. Such things didn't interest him at all. They weren't any of his business.

Grandma Cathy was quite careless about these things too. She never complained and never said a word about money; she never mentioned debts and money problems. She never prepared Jim financially for the possibility of her death.

Luckily, Jim found the phone number of her lawyer in Grandma's notebook and called him when he discovered that she was dead. Otherwise, he wouldn't have known what to do. The lawyer gave Jim good advice, telling him where to call and how to organize the funeral, but Jim had no idea how to pay for it and with what. It was a blind spot in his education, maybe even more serious and important than his blind spot in sexuality, at least for now.

All previous tragedies that Jim had faced were only mental and spiritual. The shock of Grandma Cathy's death was more terrible because it was material—Jim had almost nothing to eat and didn't know where nor how to buy food. He just knew that Grandma usually ordered grocery by the phone, and everything was delivered to their home. There was no visible end to this problem. Grandma left no will, but even if she did, there was nothing to be left to Jim. She was completely bankrupt.

Jim was frustrated and terrified until, finally, the social workers—whom the lawyer had called—came to help him. They explained to Jim that there was absolutely no way for him to stay on the farm; it would be sold with the garden and the birch grove altogether. He could only keep his personal things—clothes; books; audio, video, and piano-computer systems; and the folders with his compositions. The social workers helped Jim pack his things and were ready to move him to the group home in the deep forest outside Minneapolis–Saint Paul, quite far away from the farm where he was raised. As a handicapped person, he was eligible for a small sum of money, which would go straight to the group home account.

The moving preparations required a lot of paperwork from the social workers because Jim was moving to a new state—from Pennsylvania to Minnesota. Jim didn't understand and didn't care why. He just let them to do their job. The whole moving procedure took a couple of months, during which Jim still lived at his grandma's house. Twice per day, the home care workers came to help him with his household.

Jim was in such despair due to the collapse of his life that he even forgot about music and the computer. It was strange for him, but music disappeared from his mind. It didn't come to help anymore. He didn't feel it and didn't hear it. His soul felt dry, empty, and dead, like Grandma's, and his mind was paralyzed like a zombie's. Jim took sleeping pills and tried to sleep all the time to avoid thinking about his future. This reduced his suffering a bit but not much.

The disappearance of music added more despair to Jim's condition. He was scared that he had lost his talent forever and that he was now approaching a dead end. If he couldn't compose, he didn't want to live anymore. Jim called the psychologist and consulted with him on the phone about his composing inability.

"It will return," the psychologist urged, trying to calm him down. "You're just going through a tough time now. When everything settles, you'll feel better. You'll look through your compositions, review them, and remember everything. Surely, your talent isn't gone forever. Also, it can help probably . . ." He paused in uncertainty as if wondering whether to continue. "If you have a woman that you like beside you, maybe just a good friend . . . maybe a sister or some kind of . . . someone should replace your grandma for you. Remember, Jim, I'm not pushing you. I'm just giving you a suggestion. Romantic feelings in one's soul are usually very helpful with the creation of poetry and music, believe me."

What could Jim answer to that? He remembered this advice now, lying on his bed in the confusion and astonishment and listening to the ocean music in his mind. *Maybe fate had sent me Mona on purpose to heal me after the loss of Grandma*, he thought, *on purpose to return me my music, on purpose to find out what's really going on in a relationship between a man and a woman, on purpose to know more about life and to be a man finally, not just Grandma's baby. Of course, Mona is not beautiful and not attractive. She is even pretty ugly, but she is a good and kind person. Being full of loving care, she is the only one in the whole world who sincerely likes me. Mona is so lonely now, her husband left her, and she needs help, care, and love as well. Maybe helping her would make me happy.*

Jim tried to recall the moment some days ago, the moment when he first met Mona. While moving into the group home, Jim was worried. He was nervous and scared; it was as if he had a bad feeling about something, but reality surprised him nicely.

The beautiful two-story building was about thirty years old but fully renovated. Jim's bedroom on the second floor was large, sunny, and furnished with new and charming but tiny furniture. His own bathroom with a little toilet, a bathtub, and a sink was adjoined to the room. It was much more comfortable than at the old farmhouse. It looked like the room had been specially prepared for a diminutive person and his needs. Such particular care amazed Jim and gave him a reason to feel better.

Mona greeted Jim warmly and introduced him to her husband, Barry, and the staff—two of four nurses who worked during this particular shift on that day and two cleaning ladies who, like the nurses, didn't live in the building but came for work daily. Everything seemed okay to Jim, just new and unusual. He calmed down and felt good and thankful for everything during his first three days at the new place, until he was woken up in the middle of the night by Mona's family scandal.

Now he was lying on his bed, and the ocean music played a soft lullaby for him. It was not a storm anymore; it was a quiet, calm silver surface of the evening ocean that reflected the pink-orange colors of a sunset and melted them into eternity. It was bliss. Jim really enjoyed it and suddenly realized that he was hungry—so hungry and so happy.

He slid from his bed and approached the table where the nurses left his meal. He ate a bit, piece by piece, slowly chewing, smiling, and rolling his eyes in pleasure. His body was very little and didn't need a lot of food. Jim usually didn't eat much and never really enjoyed eating. He considered it just a boring necessity, but Mona's cooking was so good, and he was extremely hungry now, so hungry that he could really appreciate the value of the tasty cuisine.

Then Jim went to the bathroom. He took a shower, shaved, washed his face with cold water, brushed his teeth, combed his hair, got dressed, and looked at himself in the mirror. He was still a bit sleepy and tired after the stress he had endured during the sleepless days and nights that had just passed. There were dark circles under his eyes, but they did not spoil his look but rather added more mystery and sexual allure. His face was still handsome, and his appearance satisfied him. It was the first time in his life that he paid attention to his own look and examined his own face. He usually wanted to be clean and proper but didn't ever bother to be good looking. There was no reason for it.

It was already evening when Jim left his room and slid down the stairs into the living room. All the other residents of the group home were sleeping as usual; only Mona was sitting at the big dining table and reading a book. She heard Jim's steps and turned to him. "Hi, Jim," she said, smiling nicely and raising her eyebrows in acknowledgment. "How are you feeling? Better?"

He came closer to her and put his cheek on her knee. "I'm sorry, Mona," he whispered and looked up into her eyes, begging. "I'm really sorry, but I want it again."

"What?" she asked, pretending that she did not quite understand.

"This game . . . where you're a mother and I'm a child. I want to know everything . . . about that . . . I want you."

Mona put her hand on his head and passionately brushed her fingers through his hair. Instantly, her facial expression changed to reveal her haughtiness, but Jim was so excited that he didn't notice. He stood still in breathless expectation of her answer. "You make me happy, darling," she said playfully, grinning victoriously. "Let's go."

CHAPTER 3

They went through the kitchen, the storage room, and the hall with the hardwood floor. Mona led Jim by the hand like a child, squeezing his tiny trembling fingers. Her long dry palm was right beside his face, and he suddenly believed that its clutch resembled the grasp of an eagle's talon. Jim found this thought unpleasant and made an effort to push it away, reminding himself that Mona was sincere and friendly to him.

They stopped by the locked door. "Here is my suite," Mona explained, smiling at Jim. She took a key from her pocket and unlocked the door. "I always keep it closed. No one has ever been inside. This is my private territory."

"What if your husband returns suddenly?" Jim asked carefully. "Does he have a key?"

"No, baby, don't worry. He won't return. He's staying at our daughter's house and will probably be there forever. We plan to divorce."

"I'm sorry to hear that," Jim noted politely. He found the news to be a relief. To have an affair with a married woman would be dishonest. Unconsciously, he recognized himself as a man and a woman's keeper. He wanted a woman whom he loved, one who belonged only to him.

They entered the suite, and Mona turned on the light. Jim looked around. The furniture in her small living room was quite plain. It was clean and simple but old and seemed cheap. It almost resembled Grandma Cathy's farm. "Don't be disappointed, my darling," Mona said, noticing Jim's embarrassed glance as he observed the room. "I'm a very poor woman. I'm only rich spiritually and intellectually."

"Don't worry, that's the most important thing to me," Jim assured.

"I hope so, my sweetheart. Can you imagine how much the salary is of a couple of social workers running a group home?"

"No idea." Jim shook his head.

"It's very little, unbelievably little. It's the lowest salary in the U.S. The only treasure I have is my necklace, the one you saw. It's broken. It was my wedding gift from Barry. He bought it for $12 at a thrift store. It costs nothing now. It just helped me keep my beautiful memory of our life together and of our past love. That's why I was crying. It hurt a lot to realize that it's broken forever. Nobody will be able to fix it. The jewelers usually refuse to fix that kind of cheap costume jewelry because repairing it will cost much more than buying a new one."

"I am really sorry that I am not a handyman," Jim said sympathetically. "If my fingers were bigger and worked better with little things, I would be happy to fix it for you."

"Thank you, Jim. That's so nice of you." Mona laughed playfully and changed the subject. "I see that you're still a bit tense. You need to relax. I'm your closest friend, and I want to give you pleasure. Let's try something that men usually like."

She opened the glass door of a china cupboard and took a small flat bottle of whiskey and two tiny liquor glasses. "Have you ever tried it?" Mona asked, pouring a drink for Jim and one for herself as well.

"No . . . I've tasted champagne though."

"It is a different flavor, but the result is almost the same. However, you need much less whiskey, just a few drops." Mona raised her glass to Jim's. "Cheers and congratulations, Jim. We're celebrating the first night of our love."

Jim smiled at her and bravely swallowed his whiskey, almost chocking, and coughed several times until tears appeared in his eyes. Breathless, he put his empty glass on the table and covered his mouth with both hands, continuing to cough.

"Sorry, baby, sorry!" Mona exclaimed worriedly. She sat on the floor in front of him, hugging him. "I should have told you to be careful and not to drink it all at once. It's a very strong drink. It's my mistake."

"No, it's okay, I like it." Jim calmed her down and had stopped coughing, finally, but was still breathing heavily. "It was just unexpected. Maybe it's too strong for me. I'm getting hot."

"That's what I want. It will make you more excited, brave, and relaxed. We came here to love each other, and nothing else in the world matters. Nothing else exists for either of us anymore. Okay, my dear?" While saying that, Mona stood up, pulled him into the bedroom, and sat him on her bed, which was covered with pretty flowered sheets. She turned off the light and switched on a small reading lamp to give the room a romantic ambiance. Then she knelt in front of Jim to be at the same height and hugged his neck.

Jim felt himself heating up. The whiskey scorched him inside; his face reddened. "I . . . never . . ." he whispered, biting his lips nervously.

"I know, my love. I understand everything," Mona answered ardently, quickly covering his face with tender, impatient short kisses. She unbuttoned his shirt and moved it down from his little shoulders, stroking and kissing them.

"I'm not sure," Jim moaned, shaky.

"Forget it, honey. There are hundreds of ways . . . to make a man happy. If you can't use a simple one . . . we'll find . . . something else." Mona kissed his lips and gently pushed him down on his back. Jim hugged her and closed his eyes, allowing himself to be swept away by the sensations.

It was an endless kiss. They rolled over in the bed, hugging each other. They couldn't tear their mouths from each other, biting and sucking each other's tongues and lips crazily. It wasn't as shocking for Jim as the first time. He already had had the experience, even if it was short. He liked kissing. It excited him. The stupefying aroma of Mona's perfume aroused him and drew him in, and the whiskey intoxicated him. He felt a frenzied power arising from within him, almost bursting from his little jeans. Mona tried to unzip his pants, but it was very difficult to do because they were so tight. Finally, with great difficulty, she was able to tear Jim off herself.

"Wait a second, baby," she whispered, sitting beside him. Holding his belt with one hand, she plunged her other hand inside and pressed his erect penis to his stomach, making space to free the zipper. Now it was possible to unzip it.

"Wow!" she cried. "Such an amazing thing! And didn't you know that? It's so sweet!"

Mona bent over and affectionately kissed its tip, strong and as resilient as a rubber, which suddenly exploded with a fountain of sperm straight in her face. "Oh boy!" she yelled and jerked back, but her cheek, nose, and lips were already covered with juicy white sperm that slid down slowly onto her chin and neck. The second and third explosions were shorter and squirted at her T-shirt and hands.

"I'm sorry, Mona!" Jim exclaimed in panic, looking in horror at what he had done. "I'm really sorry! Really sorry!" He was so ashamed that he was ready to cry. He wished the earth would swallow him up. Jim was sure that Mona would hate him after that. She would reject him, and his only love story would end in disgrace. His eyes filled with tears once again, and lips began to quiver. Jim turned around abruptly and hid his blushing face in the pillow like a frightened child.

Mona surprised him nicely. "Oh my goodness!" She laughed, taking a paper napkin and wiping her face. "You scared me, baby. That was so unexpected. Don't worry, my sweetheart, it washes away very easily. And it's actually the best natural treatment for wrinkles. You'll make me look young and beautiful. Now I just need to take a shower. Promise, please, not to run away anymore. You hurt me last time very much when you fled. That was not nice. Okay, darling?"

Jim just nodded, silently burying his face deeper into the pillow. He was tense from the start and now felt ashamed of what had happened. He couldn't hold back his feeling of embarrassment.

But soon Jim realized that nothing was lost; Mona wasn't angry at him and would forgive him for this sudden mess he made. He saw Mona's generosity and was graceful toward her for that. However, Jim felt that she was experienced enough to understand that this accident had happened because of his childish innocence and inexperience. The thought confused him. He dreamed of being a man and didn't want to look like a silly adolescent.

In spite of that, just a few minutes later, all things seemed to lose their importance. All his tension and fears slowly melted away and disappeared. He knew suddenly how tired and weak he was because he didn't sleep during the past three days of his "strike." He started to feel warm, relaxed, and dreamy. Feelings of bliss floated through his little body and smoothly enveloped his hot head, leaving him feeling carefree, lighthearted, satisfied, and sleepy.

After ten minutes, Mona appeared from the shower wearing a white terry robe with blue stripes. Her wet blond curls now looked much darker, but her eyes seemed to have deepened in color, blue like water. She had gotten a bit drunk too, just enough to be excited.

Mona lay down beside Jim and gently put her hand on his shoulder. "Baby," she whispered hot blooded, "please don't be upset. Nothing happened. You just need more practice, that's it. I can guarantee that, in a month, you'll know perfectly how to hold it, how to stop yourself, and how to keep your treasure inside for hours, even during intercourse. The more you practice, the better you get. I like to be a teacher. It's my greatest pleasure and favorite thing to do. Come here, my sweet boy. Let's study what a real woman is." While saying that, Mona impatiently removed her robe.

"You've already tried your mother's breasts," she moaned passionately, moving them closer to Jim. "It's time to repeat this lesson now and then go ahead to the next. Do it, please."

Surprised that he didn't respond, Mona turned him to her side. She looked intently into his face and discovered, finally, that he had fallen asleep. "Oh shit!" she cried out angrily. "Baby! Wake up! What the hell?" She became so furious and disappointed that she slapped Jim's cheeks in madness. Enraged, she grabbed him and shook him by the shoulders, but he didn't react. It was obvious that he had noticed nothing and continued to sleep. His eyelids opened a bit for a moment and closed again right away. He muttered something, but then his head fell back onto the pillow powerlessly. It was clear that he wouldn't wake up at any price.

Seeing that all her efforts were in vain, Mona left Jim alone at last. "My goodness!" she roared unpleasantly, squeezing her fingers into the fists. "What am I going to do now?"

Silly me, she thought, almost crying but trying to calm herself down. *What did I want from this child? It would take a lot to teach him. Hopefully, I didn't give him an alcohol overdose. Hopefully, he won't die. Oh my goodness! Who could guess that this thimble of whiskey would be so much for him? Stupid! I should have expected that he would sleep after such a huge ejaculation. Oh, poor me! You must spoil before you spin. Practice makes perfect—that's a rule I know. How come I made so many mistakes? Oh gosh, this baby is a very unusual partner. It's so difficult to deal with him, but his uniqueness is his greatest characteristic. I really want his innocent, beautiful fresh young cock inside me. This will need a lot of work, but I'm up for it.*

She looked at Jim's sleepy face, at his long eyelashes, hot pink cheeks, and beautifully outlined lips, which were slightly open and quivered every now and then as he breathed. He was so handsome, and his facial expression was so blissful and so innocent that it was impossible for her to feel offended by him for a long time. Mona forgave him for her disappointment, her lost pleasure, and her lost night of love. She was ready to forgive him for everything at the moment.

"I am too straightforward," she whispered to herself. "I need to be more understanding and more patient with him. I shouldn't be in a hurry. He will be mine anyway, and I'll do everything I want with him. He has no choice and no way to escape."

Mona stood up, put her dress on, and moved Jim to the edge of the bed. She wiped his sleepy prick with a paper napkin, hid it inside his jeans, and zipped them up. Then she fixed his shirt, buttoned it up, and took Jim in her arms as if he were a child. She carried him out from her suite to his room. It wouldn't be easy for her to walk up the stairs with such a load, though Jim wasn't much heavier than a three-year-old child, so she used the elevator to reach the second floor.

Mona put Jim on his bed, undressed him, and covered him with a blanket. She tucked him in carefully and fondly. Then she stroked Jim's hair and kissed his forehead tenderly. *I did not spend the evening in vain,* she thought. *Now I know for sure that he is capable.*

"Good night, baby," Mona whispered wistfully and left the room, quietly closing the door after her.

CHAPTER 4

The next day, Jim was awoken by an abrupt knock at the door. "Delivery!" he heard a husky male voice say. "Your luggage has arrived!"

Jim was so happy that he wanted to jump up and down—his piano and his computer would finally be with him—but he had a headache and was so weak that he couldn't move his head. He just moaned something, hoping to convey, *Come on in, please.* And he continued to lie on his bed sleepily.

The door opened, and two large men entered, carrying with them the smell of cigarettes. "Uh-oh," one of them said, observing the room. "There is not enough space for everything. Let's move."

They took Jim's bed and carried it into the corner. Then they moved his little table with breakfast on it, as well as the bookshelves. The biggest part of his room was empty now so they started to bring in the large boxes with Jim's piano, computer, TV, stereo system, clothes, books, and folders. The men worked fast, and just minutes later, the room was full of big boxes piled one on top of the other. Jim was lost somewhere behind them, but before he had even begun to think about how to get out of there, Mona appeared in the room.

"Good afternoon, my sweetheart!" she exclaimed cheerfully, kneeling beside Jim's bed and kissing his forehead. She smelled like a kitchen.

"Your stuff is here. Are you happy? I'm sorry that I can't help you unpack yet. The guys will arrive from work soon, but dinner is still not ready. I'm cooking. All the nurses are busy too. Anyway, I'll find someone to help you open the boxes. But this evening, I'll come and help you organize everything. It will be our evening. You are booked, my sweet boy. Okay?"

Jim mumbled something sleepily, aiming to communicate that he had no objection. Mona laughed playfully, touched his hair, waved to him, raised her eyebrows, and left to go for work.

About half an hour was enough for Jim to pull himself out of bed to shower and get ready. He found it refreshing, and it made him feel much better. His headache was gone; he was now in a good mood and even laughed, remembering last night's adventures. Then Jim heard a knock at his door again. "Come on in," he said and hobbled toward the door to open it.

There was a young man standing in front of him. He had dark skin, black hair curled in large rings, and an attractive, doll-like face. He looked East Indian. "Hi, I'm Ramah, the bus driver," he introduced himself to Jim. "Mona said that you needed help opening these boxes."

"Yes, but there is barely enough room for us both in here," Jim answered, uncertain of how to proceed. "I don't know how we can both work in here."

"Don't worry, I'll figure it out." Ramah entered the room and looked around. "Well, we need to cut the boxes open first and throw them away. We'll have much more room after that," he said and stared down at Jim. "Are you new here, little one? I haven't seen you before."

"I've been here for about a week. Sorry, I didn't introduce myself. My name is Jim." He pulled up his hand, which sank into Ramah's big strong palm.

"Nice to meet you, Jim. How long do you plan to stay here?"

"I don't know." Jim shrugged. "Probably forever . . . I mean, the rest of my life."

"Oh, that would be a long time. In this case, we should get you settled in for a permanent residence." Ramah took a small knife from his pocket and started to cut the boxes.

Jim realized that Ramah mustn't be hampered in his work. He took a cup of yogurt, a spoon, and a couple of cookies from the table and climbed on his bed to sit and eat. He had slept through breakfast and lunch and was very hungry now. At the same time, it was fun for Jim to look at his stuff, peeking out from the boxes. He really missed it and was happy to see it back. He felt as though his life had returned to him and impatiently looked forward to getting settled and starting to compose music once again.

Ramah pushed the door wide open and threw out the cardboard from the boxes piece by piece. The room was becoming much more spacious now, and it was possible to assemble Jim's piano. A screwdriver appeared in Ramah's hand, and he screwed the piano legs to the frame. For Jim, it looked magical. Then Ramah assembled the computer desk as well.

When everything was done, he let Jim choose the right spot for the piano, computer, table, shelves, and bed. Ramah moved all the furniture and organized it just as Jim wanted. At last, only Jim's clothes, books, folders with his compositions, and CD holders with thousands of musical disks were all lying on the bed, table, and desk, piled up like mountains. Ramah then brought in a vacuum cleaner that he borrowed from the cleaning lady and cleaned up the mess left by unpacking all of Jim's things.

While Ramah was working, he talked with Jim. They laughed and exchanged jokes, both feeling comfortable and friendly with each other. "Bye, Jim," Ramah said after about an hour, having finished the job. "I should go now, but you'll see a lot of me. Every day I drive the guys to work and back. Once a month, we go to shop. And another day, we go swimming. Sometimes I even drive Mona to pick up groceries and do her banking, so I'll see you for sure."

"Thank you very much for your help," Jim answered sincerely. "Tell me if I should pay you for the work. I really don't know the rules. Actually, I don't have any money, but I'm guessing that Mona can pay you on my behalf."

"Don't worry, Jim." Ramah laughed. "Everything has been arranged with Mona. You don't have to think about that."

Alone at last, Jim climbed the three little steps of the stool in front of the piano, sat, and opened the cover. He missed it so horribly that he was almost trembling with impatience, eager to play and to hear his music again. Jim petted the keyboard tenderly as if it were his baby and then carefully touched one of the keys with his finger. The sound echoed for a long moment, slowly dying away, and Jim closed his eyes to enjoy it. Then he moved his little hand to the right and tried another key and then one more. He needed to match the right keys to the notes that were resounding in his head during the last few days. This would be the closing to his symphony.

Most of the symphony was already finished. It was about two hundred pages. Jim wanted to compose one more part and then to add vocalization to the entire piece. He was stuck at this point as he had yet to choose a singer.

The final stage after that would be the orchestration that had not been completed either. Jim had tried to do it already on the computer, but the quality of the computerized work was quite standard and didn't satisfy him. There was nothing original or personal in it. He decided to do the orchestration himself manually when the work was finished. So there was a long wait before the symphony would be ready to be performed, but Jim felt confident. He was sure that about six months would be enough for him to accomplish his work.

The next spring, he planned to start looking for a proper orchestra and, at the end of the next summer, to have his concert, an event that would give meaning to his life and be his greatest triumph. What would happen after? Jim didn't care about that now. He was too preoccupied with today's plans, hopes, dreams, and expectations.

Jim continued to play, looking for the right key and setting the right pitch. He wanted to write down the music he had heard over the last few days but discovered suddenly that his computer system wasn't connected to the piano. Ramah hadn't connected it and probably didn't even know how. Jim knew how it was supposed to be done, but his little fingers weren't capable of putting the plugs in and turning the screws properly. "Oh God!" he moaned, frustrated. He slid down from his stool and slowly walked out of his room, holding himself up against the walls to look for Mona and to ask her for help.

Usually, Jim didn't leave his room in the daytime, and he was used to a quiet and sleepy atmosphere when he came out at evenings. Now he was really surprised to discover what an active life brewed in the house. During his first few days, Jim had already seen some of the residents and nurses but not all at once as he saw them now standing at the top of the stairs and looking down.

It was noisy downstairs. Dinner had just ended. Mona, wearing a white apron, loaded the dishes into the dishwasher. One of the nurses, a young Chinese lady, helped her by giving her the dishes from a small cart that she brought from the other rooms. A male nurse, a Filipino man, stood beside the table and refilled the glasses with water. He placed them gently on a tea tray beside the tiny pill bottles, all clearly labeled. He prepared the evening medications to be delivered to the residents.

Fat young Maggie with her abnormal face and another woman, Ella, sat on the couch in the living room, watching TV. Ella was in her forties, dark haired, and slender. She would have appeared completely healthy and normal if she didn't jerk spasmodically every minute. Her voice sounded loud and nervous as she explained to Maggie what was on the TV screen.

One man was quietly sprawled in a big leather armchair in the corner. He was quite good looking, about fifty years old with long white hair and a beard. His face and deep dark brown eyes, which contrasted sharply with his hair, looked dead and empty; his glance was directed at one single point. He was sitting in silence, motionless like a stone. It was possible to recognize that he was alive only by his breath.

Another man was seated at the dinner table and hummed something while playing solitaire. He was very tall with spots on his skin and had a bull's neck that occasionally jerked to one side. He did nothing wrong but looked scary perhaps because of the scars on his face, neck, and hands. His appearance resembled a killer from the Hollywood movies about the Mafia. Inside the house, he always wore a panama hat and earphones connected to a small radio that he constantly had in his pocket. Jim knew that his name was Todd.

Jim saw Mona. She was occupied, and he did not feel comfortable interrupting. He just stood silently, watching the people who were now supposed to be his family, instead of Grandma Cathy. All of them were very unusual, and all of them were strangers to him. Sadly, he remembered Grandma Cathy's lessons. "People are different, Jim. Some have large ears, some have one leg, some are bald, some are deaf." Now he could add "some are mentally ill" to her list.

It was wistful to realize that he would never see Grandma Cathy again. He could still hear her voice in his mind, in his dreams, and he could still remember her wisdom. "Bye, Grandma Cathy," he whispered to himself. "I'll try to love all of them, of course, if I can. Maybe each of them has his own accomplishments, like you taught me. We'll see. But I guess that the most difficult question is, would *they* love me or not?"

Jim stood unseen for quite a while until Mona suddenly noticed him. "Jim!" she exclaimed merrily. "Come over here. You know some of the guys already, don't you? I'll introduce you to the rest."

Jim wasn't a very sociable person; he didn't have much experience socializing with people, but he really tried to be friendly. He sat on the top step and slid down.

"Wow!" Mona exclaimed. "What an amazing trick! You're so creative, my sweetheart!" She approached him, bent over, and kissed his forehead.

"This is Sue, and this is Josef," she said, acquainting Jim with the nurses. "You can ask them for help anytime." Sue and Josef stopped working and looked at him with interest.

"This is Jim, guys," Mona continued, introducing him. "He is new here, and he's quite shy because of that. But I already know that he is very smart. I hope all of you like him. I don't think he'll criticize our service too much, will you, Jim?" Mona laughed playfully, leaving Jim confused.

Sue and Josef bowed, shook Jim's hand, and mentioned politely that it was very nice to meet him. Then they returned to their work. Sue walked up the stairs, carrying a pile of clean towels, and Josef followed her with his tray.

The group home residents didn't pay any attention to Jim, and that surprised him. He looked at Mona questioningly. She lifted her palms and made a wry face, showing to him her feelings of regret. "That's how it goes, Jim," she said in a quiet voice, a touch of sadness in her tone. "They aren't very sociable. They are on very strong medications, especially now in the evening. These four have an excuse. They're working at the furniture factory five days a week, from 9:00 a.m. until 2:00 p.m. They have to sand the wood. It's not easy, and it's tedious work, just moving your hand with a piece of sandpaper there and back, there and back, there and back along the leg of the chair without using your brain. Actually, they don't have one anyway.

"You are really lucky, Jim, that your hands are not capable of such a job. Otherwise, you wouldn't be able to escape it. These are our regulations. They have to do it as part of their therapy. Plus, they earn some money because their pensions are pretty small, and they don't nearly cover the cost of the service they're receiving. So they come home every day very tired and have dinner and take their medication right away. Now they are resting and relaxing. In about a couple of hours, they'll have some buttermilk and go to sleep."

"I already saw Maggie," Jim said, confused, remembering the funny situation in the storage room where this abnormal girl caught them.

"I remember too." Mona laughed. She raised her eyebrows and gave Jim a wink.

"One day I saw Todd. I also saw this lady, Ella, and even exchanged a few words with her when I had just arrived. She was here that day in the living room."

"She talks sometimes. As you see now, she is talking with Maggie. She just has an attention disorder, in addition to some other difficulties, so she didn't notice you."

"Does Maggie understand what she is talking about?"

Mona shook her head. "Absolutely not, my dear."

"But it looks like she is listening."

"It's just look like it. When we have reading time and I'm reading them stories, she looks like she is listening too. But it's just an illusion."

"It's sad," Jim noted. "Why do all these people live here? Do they have families, or are they just alone in the world like me?"

"You'll be surprised, but all of them have relatives, even those who stay in their rooms, except Victor." Mona pointed at the man with white hair and beard. "His family was . . . well . . ." She paused in uncertainty, doubting whether to tell Jim about this. "Okay, let's go up to the second floor, baby. I'll show you the other members of our group home family."

Jim turned to go toward the stairs, but Mona stopped him. "The elevator's over here, my darling. Let me show you." She led Jim into another small living room that was joined to the big one they had been in. This room had glass walls and ceiling and was designed to be a winter garden—full of live tropical plants. There wasn't any furniture except for two large armchairs in the corners under palm trees.

"Victor likes to sit here most of the time," Mona commented, pointing at the chairs. "He is very seldom in the big living room like today. Usually, he's here."

At the other end of the garden on the opposite wall were two doors. One of them was the elevator door. "Another door leads to the basement," Mona explained to Jim. "I'll show it to you another time. My animals are there."

"Really?" Jim said with surprise. "It's just great. It looks like a farm to me. You have a forest around the building, a garden inside, and animals in the basement. What kinds of animals do you have?"

"Just small pets. Come on in, Jim." Mona pressed the button, and the elevator door opened in front of them. They entered the elevator. It was upholstered with a dark brown carpet. After a minute, they were already on the second floor.

"It's funny." Jim smiled. "My room is just over there, and I didn't know that the elevator was in this corridor. Anyway, I prefer to use the stairs. It is good exercise when I slide down or climb up."

"Of course, my baby. The elevator is mostly for wheelchair users. Here is Ella's room on the right from elevator. On the left, there is Maggie's."

"Don't they share one room?" Jim asked. "I did hear from social workers that, in some group homes, people share rooms."

"That's right, baby, but that's not the case here. Maggie was born with a mental disability because her parents were alcoholics. She is actually very quiet and should be living at home, but her father didn't want to keep her. He is a senator, and to have a child like that would harm his political image. And he is paying enough for her to have a separate room. At the same time, Ella should be alone for medical reasons. She has schizophrenia."

"Does she? Is it dangerous?"

"It really is. She actually killed her husband. That's why she is here."

"What?" Jim said, dumbfounded.

"Don't worry, darling." Mona laughed, seeing his changed expression. "That happened a number of years ago. Now she is on such strong medication that she behaves well and keeps quiet. It's no danger for anybody, but I lock her door at night just in case. Next is Todd's room."

"Did he kill somebody too?" Jim asked, agitated. "He looks like a killer."

"No, my dear," Mona assured him, smiling. "He has the same kind of schizophrenia as Ella, but he is nice and not dangerous at all. It started when he was a teenager. He tried to commit suicide many times without any reason, maybe about ten times. Did you see his scars? Luckily, every time, he was rescued. Finally, his parents placed him here for treatment. Now he is okay. There is absolutely no reason to worry. But I lock his room so everyone can sleep quietly . . . because . . ." She stopped and looked at Jim meaningfully. "Because he likes Maggie. I caught him with her once."

"What's wrong with that?" Jim asked with uncertainty. "I don't get it. Are they in love? Could they be happy together? It would probably help their health conditions."

"Come on, darling." Mona shook her head. "Sex just makes mentally ill people worse. Love is not only physical but involves feelings as well. For them, it's just physical. It's blasphemy to talk about them and love at the same time. Forget it, my dear. Love can be just between us, you and me, but no one else in this home. They are just like animals and should be kept in cages."

Jim didn't feel very comfortable about this statement, but Mona pulled him farther, and he had no time to dispute her point of view.

"The last room at this side of the corridor is our laundry one. Here are two washers and two dryers. The cleaning ladies are usually doing the bedding for our guys and also could do your private laundry, if requested. It's really nothing special in there, but anyway, it's useful information for you to know. "On the other side of the corridor, the first one is Victor's room."

Mona pushed the door wide open, and with surprise, Jim saw that the room looked like a fitness club for a special weight-lifting champion. There were impressive-looking equipment in the middle of the room and dumbbells of different sizes and shapes on the floor. "Do these things belong to Victor? The one with gray hair and beard?" Jim asked, not quite sure. "The one who always sits motionless?"

"Yes." Mona nodded. "He is not as old as you would think. He wakes up every day at five in the morning and exercises for three hours, until eight o'clock. Then he has breakfast with the others and goes to work—all in silence, not one word. He is in a catatonic condition. It's sad to confess, but it's obviously going to last forever. He is a very nice man, but he witnessed a horrible tragedy that left him completely mentally paralyzed.

"He was a pretty big businessman, and some of his competitors killed his young wife and eight-year-old son, Johnny, right in front of him. There were probably some very powerful people involved. They didn't just shoot Victor's wife and Johnny but tortured and killed both of them slowly. I think the whole thing lasted a few hours. Victor was tied up and forced to watch. His hair turned white. They annihilated him mentally. He was toast. I talked with a police officer about his case. It's all very complicated matters, and the investigation is still not finished."

Jim felt feverish to hear that. He was appalled. He used to think that such things only happened in movies, not in real life.

"After that, he started to exercise," Mona continued. "His doctor insisted that we make it possible for him to do so and made sure we kept all the equipment in his room. I think that, subconsciously, Victor hopes to be strong enough one day to get revenge. He might know who they are but just can't tell anyone. But there is no evidence of that. Of course, I am only speculating. Sorry that I scared you, baby, but it's my job to deal with unique people who've survived pretty unusual circumstances. That's why some of them are now mentally ill, and I need to know their stories to take special care of them.

"I want you to know these stories too because all these people are your family now. They're like your brothers and sisters. It's good for you to understand their situations so you can communicate with them better. It will also help you realize that your tragedy is very sad, but there are people around who've survived worse things. You are mentally healthy, you're smarter, and you've risen to a higher level and found happiness. Compared with the others, you are very lucky."

Mona opened the door of the next room where Jim saw Sue and Josef working with two people to change their diapers. Those were very unnatural, anomalous people who were lying motionless on the two different beds by the wall, whining like dogs. "This is the only room that is shared because the people who live in here are brother and sister. Her name is Zahra, and he is Ali, but they didn't know even this. They are from the Middle East. Their story sounded like one of Scheherazade's *One Thousand and One Nights* fairy tales, just turned upside down."

"What kind of illness do they have?" Jim asked, traumatized by the sight of them.

"This is the most horrible paradox of life—they don't have any illness at all. They are healthy, but something is wrong genetically. It is nature's way of punishing people who don't follow her rules. The father of these unlucky guys was a very poor and uneducated peasant somewhere in the deep desert. He had no money to buy a wife. According to their rules, he must pay a girl's father to take possession of her. So he married his own sister because their father was dead, and nobody would ask him for money in this situation. Their blood mixed. It was incest, which is a crime, but nobody cared about it in the wild desert. She gave the birth to these two innocent pathologically abnormal sufferers, and he told her that it was her fault and divorced her. If something is wrong with the kids, it's always the woman's fault. Everything is against women. This seems to be a normal Eastern mentality. According to their laws, in case of divorce, children always stay with the father only.

"However, after this bad luck, Zahra and Ali's father suddenly had some good luck—the geologists found oil on his little sandy piece of property. He became a millionaire, married another woman, and immigrated with her to the U.S., taking these two freaks of nature with him. His new wife gave birth to five good, healthy, normal children, and they have a pretty united family now, but these two sufferers have been staying in our group home for about ten years already. Luckily, their father has enough money to pay for it. They are in a vegetable state, and there is no treatment for it at all."

Jim looked at Mona with wide eyes. She made his blood run cold. "Could it be something like that with me?" he whispered, terrified. "I'm healthy. I don't have any illness at all. Could it be that my parents are brother and sister too?"

"Come on, baby, forget it!" Mona protested excitedly. "What are you talking about? Incest only produces vegetables, but you are so handsome, smart, and such a talented guy. I can guarantee that it's not the case. Don't worry, my dear. I know this impression is shocking for you, but don't make any connections between their story and yours."

She squatted and kissed Jim's forehead. "Promise me you'll never worry about that, my darling," she whispered passionately, hugging him and looking straight into his eyes. "There was nothing dirty involved in your story, I'm absolutely sure. Believe me. I have a lot of experience. I've been working with the disabled for more than twenty years. I know everything in this area. If you're really interested, I'll try to find something about what happened to you but not yet, later. Okay, baby?"

Jim nodded, biting his lip.

"So now we are going to the last room, neighboring yours. There is a person with a multiple sclerosis whom you haven't met yet," Mona continued, opening the next door.

Jim saw a really strange creature sitting in a wheelchair and watching TV. Beside it was a coffee table full of bottles with cider, some of which were already empty. The creature was very slim and little, just a bit bigger than Jim, and was just skin and bones. It was very pale. The black hair on its head was cut short and spiky to make it look like a teenager. Was it a girl or a boy? It was impossible to say.

"Hi, Lily, how are you today?" Mona said. Jim was surprised to hear a woman's name.

She turned to Mona and looked at her unpleasantly with round doll eyes—big, blue, and beautiful. Lily's appearance and these amazing eyes made a strange combination. *Maybe Lily was a real beauty before she became sick*, Jim guessed, feeling regretful.

"I'm not very good," Lily answered sternly, shaking her head. "I'm angry and unhappy. Do you hear that noise on the roof?" She turned the TV off and pointed her index finger. "Listen! Can you hear it? It's so annoying!"

Jim concentrated, trying to hear something from above, but it was absolutely quiet.

"Here!" Lily shouted, pointing her index finger at the ceiling. "Something is banging. I complained yesterday, and still, nothing has been done. It's so noisy that I can't sleep at night. Please, Mona, you should fix it."

"Our maintenance person checked the roof. Everything is okay up there," Mona assured.

"Check it one more time, please. I don't like all this noise. It's driving me crazy."

"Will do, Lily. I promise," Mona said sadly. "If there is something wrong, it will be fixed."

"And there is wind outside. It's already November, and it's started snowing. I have a draft from my window, and it needs to be repaired as well. I have real bad luck with this place. There are so many problems here. I'm not satisfied with your service at all. I'll complain!"

"Sorry, Lily," Mona answered patiently. "I'll do everything possible for you. Your window is already taped. I'll do it one more time this evening."

Lily pulled her hand to take a bottle of cider from her table, eager to drink more, and suddenly saw Jim. "Who the hell is that?" she exclaimed indignantly. "I don't want any cripples in my room! How come you let him in without my permission? He looks like a man. I don't want to see any men, no place for men in my room! Yuck, yuck, yuck!"

"Sorry, Lily. Have a nice evening." Mona grabbed Jim's hand, and they left immediately. Closing the door, they heard Lily turn the TV back on.

"Uh-oh." Mona took a deep breath, already in hallway. "She is the most difficult person to deal with, much worse than schizophrenics. They take medication that holds them in check, but she doesn't."

"Why not?" Jim asked.

"There aren't any medications for her kind of MS. It's a horrible incurable disease, which harms a person's nerves and brain slowly until, finally, the nerves stop working properly. Usually, all these patients look like they have a very bad character, but it's just their illness. However, it's no picnic to work with them, especially with Lily. She hears all those noises because of damaged hearing nerves. All the drafts she feels are because of damaged tactile nerves. She doesn't understand that. It can't be helped.

"Lily's life is a real tragedy. She had a lot to lose. She was a ballet dancer, pretty famous, even prima ballerina—Lily Donovan, very wealthy and spoiled. She was a lesbian. Actually, she probably still is, but she hasn't had sex at all for many years, so it's not easy to say what she is now. I think she's just an unhappy ill, asexual creature on her way to death. Do you know what a lesbian is, Jim?"

"I read something about that." He nodded uncertainly.

"Our society is still quite judgmental about sexual orientation. Lily's family didn't want to recognize that and refused to associate with her. She had a lot of troubles with them, and that taxed her nerves. She also had a lot of injuries as a dancer and was even in some car accidents. I guess that these altogether made her sick, though officially scientists don't know the cause of MS. But these are just my guesses again.

"Being sick, she spent all her money pretty fast because her demands, as a spoiled, rich woman, were too high, and she went bankrupt. It was a dead end for her—all the services she needs should be paid for. And then her friends, lesbians, stepped in. They started to collect donations from their gay and lesbian community and paid us to take care of Lily. It was a real surprise for me when I found out. You'll see them sometimes. They come to visit Lily pretty often."

Jim took a deep breath. All these people and their horrible stories stressed him and made him tired and unhappy. He loved people, even though he didn't know them well, and really liked to see everybody around him content and smiling. Having a new family like this wasn't easy for him. With Grandma Cathy at the farm, he felt much more secure and comfortable.

"Don't be upset, my sweetheart," Mona said, smiling. "It's ghastly just from start. You'll get accustomed to all of them, and you'll make friends. You'll feel better later. The most important thing that will help you psychologically is our relationship—our love and close friendship. I'll replace your grandma, your mother, your sister, your wife, your friend, your lover—everybody. Trust me in full, please."

"Well . . . if our tour is finished . . . I don't want to be annoying like Lily, but I have one request," Jim begged. "Could you please help me connect my piano with the computer system and plug some wires in? My fingers aren't capable of that."

"Sure, my dear. Let's go and do that right away." Beside Jim's door, Mona stopped as she remembered something. "Wait a minute, baby. I'll be back soon."

She ran downstairs, took a camera from her suite, and returned to Jim's room. "Wow!" she exclaimed. "There are so many things in here now. It looks like Ramah did a good job of setting up your furniture. I'll help you organize the small things. Let's plug in your system first."

Jim showed Mona the spots where each of the plugs went, and she connected and fastened all of them easily. Then she helped him hang his clothes in a closet and place his books, folders, and CD holders on the shelves. "You have so much music," she noted surprisingly. "Usually, our guys only have a few CDs."

"I'm supposed to," Jim explained. "It's my profession. I'm not just listening to music because I have nothing to do. I'm studying the world's music and doing research. And it's actually my soul at the same time."

Mona looked at him, smiling, and shook her head. "Well," she said, "we'll return to a musical subject another time. Now I want to take some pictures. Your room looks much nicer since we've organized everything. It's clean and tidy. You just need pictures on the walls to make it cozier. Let me take a picture of you. I'll keep one of them for myself as a souvenir of our love and true friendship and will give you the others to put on your walls."

"I don't think I look good enough for a picture." Jim laughed. "Or for modeling either."

"Come on, baby, you'll be just great. I'll do a big portrait of your very handsome face. And you know that you're attractive, Jim. Don't be shy."

"I'm not shy. I'm just not very sure that anyone needs these pictures and will find a way to use them. I don't want you to spend your film in vain."

"We'll see what it looks like, Jim. Let's try. Maybe you are going to be a very famous person one day, and we'll sell your pictures to popular magazines." Mona raised her eyebrows and laughed playfully. "And you'll be very rich—rich and famous. How would that be?"

"Amazing! I hope!" Jim laughed sincerely, and Mona took the picture of his happy and smiling face. Then she took one more and then more from other angles, and at last, a couple of pictures were taken showing him standing at his full height.

"I'll bring them to you, and together, we will choose the best ones," she promised. "Sorry, Jim, but I should run to work now. It's almost eight o'clock, and the nurses will be leaving soon. I'll give all the guys their buttermilk and cookies and their medication, put them to sleep, and lock some of the doors. Then our time will begin. Do you want some buttermilk too?"

"No." Jim shook his head. "I already had some yogurt. But an apple would be great. I can play my piano while waiting for you."

"Okay, my baby. Then at ten o'clock, come to my suite and get ready for our night of love. I will leave my door unlocked. I want to make you happy. Are you okay with that?"

Jim nodded, smiling confusingly. Mona kissed his forehead and ran away.

CHAPTER 5

J im decided to continue playing and muffled the sound of his piano so he wouldn't bother anybody as it was getting late. His tiny fingers couldn't move fast enough; they couldn't move like the fingers of normal people were supposed to, but he had a fantastic musical memory and imagination that gave him a boundless ability to compose.

When Jim heard long passages in his mind, even of fifty notes or more, he could hold them in his memory for quite a while. He pretended to flick a switch inside his mind as if it were a button for playback in slow motion. In his imagination, he repeated the passage very slowly, and then stopped it. Unhurriedly, he moved his little finger, looking for the notes on his keyboard one by one, according to his ear for music. He had excellent sensory acuity.

Then Jim loaded the notes into his computer and saved them. He increased the speed of the music on his computer as he needed to match it to the initial speed of the passage he had heard in his brain before. After that, he would have the complex task of collecting every passage and piece of music and putting them all together. He had already mastered this skill and did it easily. When it was done, Jim liked to print it on the paper right away (in case the computer system crashed for some reason or all the data accidentally disappeared) and put the pages into the folder marked "Version no. 1." In the end, every part of Jim's symphony usually had about ten versions.

Composing was a serious and slow process that Jim loved deeply, feeling that it was his only real calling; it was what he lived for. The creative work demanded his full concentration; he had to immerse himself in his feelings, thoughts, and images. It was sheer pleasure.

During the move after Grandma Cathy's death, Jim dreamed about composing greedily—he craved it, he missed it, and he wanted it back, but there was no chance to do it. Finally, the time had come, but his date with Mona that night had disturbed his soul. Jim couldn't work calmly as he usually did. His thinking kept returning to Mona again and again. It was so irritating that Jim stopped working, turned off the computer, and lay down on his bed to relax. He was trembling, looking forward to the sensation of her kisses, but he wasn't sure if he wanted to go further.

However, Jim realized with sadness that he had no choice. He had to obey Mona because he was in her group home and under her control. His life depended on her. He wasn't free. She seemed to have fallen in love with him, and he felt he had to reciprocate. Otherwise, they couldn't live in the same house, but he had nowhere else to go. There was not one person in the world who could help him or protect him, and he had no way to escape.

Jim pondered, soothing himself with thoughts about all that Mona had done for him. He had no right to let her down; he should be thankful to her and didn't want to offend her. He liked the house and his room, which was quite secluded and would give him the good possibility to be alone and to compose his music. It was time to know a woman and to become a man. Jim felt it would be pleasurable to have sex with Mona and that it would be good for his body and soul. It would bring him balance and leave him healthy. Everything looked positive in the situation, and there was no reason to refuse.

Jim hoped that he would find out what other people meant by the word *happiness*. For him, happiness was making music. *I read and heard many times that love is the most amazing thing in life,* Jim thought. *But what kind of love? I know the love that Grandma Cathy gave to me. It was a mother's love, characterized by care and support. I also know my love of music, which could be called spiritual pleasure, excitement, or joy of creation. I know Mona's kisses. That was physical delight. What would love with a woman be like? A combination of all these? I really want to know. So I must go.*

At about ten o'clock, Jim stood before the mirror, preparing himself carefully, and left his room. He slid down into the dark living room and saw the reflections of light on the kitchen floor, which were, by now, well known to him. He realized that Mona had left the light on in the hall with a hardwood floor so that he could find his way to her suite.

Jim passed the kitchen and the gloomy storage room, and right beside the entrance to the next room, he saw something small sparkling like a star under the shelves, in the crack between the plinth and the floor. He stopped and watched it with interest for a while and then moved back. The glitter disappeared. Jim stepped forward again and saw it again—something twinkled in the same spot. He moved aside on purpose to check if it was real or just a hallucination. The scintillation ceased to be visible. However, when Jim returned to his first position, he saw it once more. He understood that there was something in the crack that was visible only from one angle and vanished from sight when he moved, even by an inch. No one who was taller than Jim could see it, of course.

Jim knelt down on all fours and crawled under the shelf. He touched the crack, put his tiny finger inside, and picked out a small piece of glass or a stone. It was quite narrow there, and he crawled backward with difficulty. Soon Jim arrived in the brightly lit hall with a hardwood floor and opened his palm to look at what he had found. It was a limpid stone the size of his fingernail, and it looked like a diamond. But Jim really didn't know anything about jewelry nor about stones.

First, he thought that he should give it to Mona, remembering her broken necklace on the hardwood floor, just a few feet from his find. There was no doubt that the stone belonged to this necklace—it had simply rolled pretty far away and stuck in the crack, so Mona couldn't see it and couldn't get it out either. The necklace contained so many similar stones that she didn't count them, obviously, and had no idea that one of them was missing.

However, another thought appeared in Jim's mind while he scrutinized the stone. *Mona said that the necklace cost nothing, and nobody would fix it anyway*, he remembered. *So it didn't matter how many stones were in the pile of broken pieces now. I can keep it as a memory about her. As far as I know from books and movies, lovers usually have little things to remind each other of their love, things they kiss in private. Actually, I can do this too, if there is true love between Mona and me.*

He took the stone with two fingers, kissed it affectionately, and put it inside his jeans pocket. Having the souvenir from Mona made him feel happy, proud, and brave, so he resolutely opened her door and entered the suite, guessing and impatiently expecting what was waiting for him there.

"You are late, my darling," Jim heard Mona's unpleasant voice say coming from the bedroom. "It's already twenty after ten."

"Sorry, Mona," he said quietly, not knowing how to answer if she asked him about the reason for his delay. He didn't want to tell her about the stone he had found, not yet at least, even though he never lied.

Luckily, she didn't question him, just demanded sternly, "Come here, baby."

Jim entered the bedroom, which was very gloomy—only a line of small flashing multicolored lights decorated the window. Mona was lying on the bed, covered with a blanket, but her shoulders and arms were bare. The aroma of her sweet perfume invaded the air. Jim already knew this smell and really liked it because it excited him. A little tray with two goblets of champagne and a small pail of ice was on the bedside table next to Mona.

"The bubbly is already getting warm. We need to add the ice now," she lamented, pressing and pursing her lips after each sentence to show that she was offended. "You gave me a lot of extra work, my darling. I was waiting for you so impatiently. I was suffering without you. I was melting in my love for you."

She expected that he would hug and kiss her, apologizing, as men would normally do, but Jim was standing before her silently, looking at the floor. He was still confused. He didn't like drinking and didn't want to drink every day as he feared becoming an alcoholic.

Mona's expression changed as she saw his uncertainty. "Drink your champagne," she imposed harshly, putting the ice cubes into the glasses. It sounded like an order.

She was educated in how to deal with the mentally ill. She knew that, after being nice, she needed to be strong and forceful to reach her goal; but she forgot that Jim was mentally normal and had his own character, his own way of thinking, and his own feelings. He had a personality and was never ever in his life forced by Grandma Cathy or somebody else. It was intolerable for him. He was not a child or a mentally sick patient; he considered himself a man—confident and free. He had a very high level of personal dignity.

However, now he had to break his own rules, and it wasn't easy. Jim knew that he should suppress his inner resistance and yield in this situation. This realization could produce only hate in his soul but not love. He narrowed his eyes, pressed his teeth together, and reluctantly stretched out his unsteady hand to take the glass.

Mona knew perfectly that, according to the *setup technique*, the next step after force should be softness. She bent over and stroked Jim's hair, affectionately kissing his forehead. "Careful, my love," she whispered passionately. "Drink with little sips, not all at once. I don't want you to choke like you did with the whiskey. I want you only to have pleasure with me. I'll give you a lot of delight tonight. You'll really enjoy it, I promise. You'll discover what it means to have sexual pleasure. You'll know that it's the best thing in our life and the power that rules the world." While saying that, Mona became more and more aroused. She took her goblet, drank her champagne quickly and greedily, threw the blanket aside, and sat on the bed completely naked.

Jim's breath was heavy. He was scared even to look at her and closed his eyes, continuing to drink his champagne sip by sip and trying to concentrate on its amazing taste.

"You should undress, baby," Mona said with an amorous hushed voice. "I don't need to expend so much effort to unzip your jeans, like last time. I want to have your body free for caresses and enjoyments."

Jim just finished his drink and put the glass back on the tray as Mona pulled off his T-shirt and jeans along with his underwear. Feeling doomed, he bent over and pulled off his sneakers and socks. He was cold and pulsating. Mona took him in her arms, sat him on her lap, and hugged him, pressing his head to her breasts. "You're so cold, my baby," she whispered. "Take my breast and suck it. This will warm you up."

"Could you kiss me first?" he begged, looking up and trying to see her eyes, which weren't visible in the semidarkness. They were in the shade and merely reflected the flashing lights on the window.

"Oh, you already have your own demands and preferences." Mona laughed playfully. "This is a big step ahead, my sweetheart." She reached over and slid her lips across Jim's face, seeking his lips. He threw his head back to let her find them quicker. He was impatient as well.

The kiss was a miracle. It was a fairy tale. Jim already felt hot and sweaty from the champagne. He realized that kissing would be his favorite thing to do from now on; he was ready to spend the entire night—a day, a week, a month, a year, an eternity—locked in a kiss with Mona. His lips were definitely too sensitive. He was sinking in pleasure; he was weakening and became excited. It was like a dream.

Hugging Jim with one hand, Mona caressed his little body with the other. She was playing with his tiny nipples; his stomach, tickling and scratching it with her nails; and his frenziedly erect prick, passionately sliding her palm over its wet tip.

Being drunk, Jim could break out of his shell, vanquish the shame, and cross the line that differentiated the possible and the impossible in his mind. He was shaking in Mona's hands, almost unconscious from the pleasure, while she turned and put him on the bed.

Jim didn't understand and was now practically unaware of what was occurring. He was completely drunk and lost control of his mind. He didn't even know what happened later and what Mona did with him, though he didn't sleep the whole night or just slept on and off. It was a strange time full of new feelings, discoveries, and realizations for Jim—full of the opposites. The bliss of heaven changed to the tortures of hell, wonders of a paradise to the dirt of reality.

It was the ocean again but not his—fantastic, great, and holy. In his ocean, Jim was always alone with his soul and his music, nothing else, and this was spiritual. Now in this black ocean, he was with somebody else—with a stranger's body he didn't know, didn't love but was supposed to explore, touch, and feel. He completely sank in this dark ocean of lust, feeling blood and sperm, rapture and delight, pain and dizziness—in turn or altogether.

There was the taste of maturity on his tongue. A child usually likes candy, cola, and ice cream. To discover, understand, and like the taste of mustard, horseradish, hot spices, caviar, and vodka, the person must be an adult. It takes time and maturity. To know the taste of a woman required maturity, which didn't come at once, so Jim couldn't grasp it yet, and it didn't matter that there was too much of it. This unusual taste just suffocated him.

Mona was a wild beast of prey, greedy and unstoppable in sex. She seemed ready to suck out not only Jim's soul through his lips but even all his sperm and blood, like a vampire. At times, he felt that he was dying from exhaustion, that he couldn't tolerate it anymore and wouldn't survive. She didn't give him a moment of rest and continued throwing, turning, screwing, squashing him like a doll almost until the early morning. She was hungry sexually and very happy to get the toy of her dreams finally.

Actually, it was too much for Jim—so little, weak, and inexperienced. He dreamed of being a man, but he wasn't yet. Jim was less than even a child—he was a handicapped person, an invalid. This night of such a crazy sex after the goblet of champagne turned out to be far too heavy, an unbearable load for his tiny body.

Unconsciously, against his will—which was paralyzed and lost at the moment anyway—Jim's body started to protest, opposing these burdens. Suddenly, he felt nauseous. An unknown power squeezed his insides and pulled them up toward his throat. He moaned and slid down from the bed, covering his mouth with his both hands. Jim realized with horror that he was vomiting, but he couldn't reach the toilet because he couldn't walk without holding the walls or someone's arm.

He jerked, jolting with seizures and crying helplessly, until Mona realized what was going on. She jumped up from the bed, grabbed Jim, and carried him to the washroom; there, she sat him in the bathtub and turned the warm water on.

Actually, there was nothing to vomit, just a little of a sticky, limpid liquid because his stomach was empty, but his tiny body tried to free and clean himself of the alcohol. The cramps were disgusting and painful. Jim cried from shame, splashing in the water, washing his face, mouth, hands, and whole body. He felt doomed. Every time he was with Mona, something was wrong. It looked to him like he couldn't have any sexual relationship, be with a woman, and make love. It was so offensive and so horrible for him that he couldn't hold back his tears, finding consolation only in the fact that water was around him. He was all wet, and Mona couldn't see his tears.

I've failed again, Jim thought in despair. *It's turned out to be a complete fiasco. What woman would tolerate me? I'm an idiot! I'm a loser!*

Mona brought a large towel, wrapped Jim in it, and carried him back to bed. She dried his body and his hair with the towel and then with a fan and kissed him lovingly. "You are like my toy, sweetheart," she said, smiling at him. "I feel with you as if I were a little girl playing with dolls. You rejuvenate me. It was my mistake again. I shouldn't give you so much champagne. So we must review our sexual program. First, not so much alcohol from now on, just a few drops. Second, no more entire nights of enjoyment, just a couple of hours, two or three times per week. That would be good for the first six months. Then you'll be a mature man, and we can increase the amount of hours and play our sexual games more fully, more dirtily. I'll teach you step by step. It's a good idea, isn't it?" She playfully gave him a charming wink of seduction.

Jim nodded, almost breathless. Mona seemed so generous to him, all-forgiving and so patient. He couldn't believe his own ears. Perhaps she was really in love with him. He felt happy, proud, and ashamed of himself—how could he hate her because of her rude, forceful orders she made last evening as he just arrived into her suite? Now she deserved real adoration and idolization from him.

Mona was probably just too passionate and too greedy for sex because Jim's lips were still swollen from her endless kisses, and his penis was in pain, even bleeding a bit, but he knew that these little problems would be over soon. He believed that Mona was truly in love with him. She was a real friend. "Thank you, Mona," he whispered and devotedly kissed her hand.

She laughed. Then she helped Jim put his clothes on and led him by the hand to his room. It was about four o'clock in the morning. "You should sleep, my baby," Mona said, stroking his hair. "You're tired. You deserve your rest. You're going to be an amazing man. You satisfied me so perfectly tonight, like nobody in my life before. I'm yours forever. Now I'll go to sleep too because I must start my work at eight. But I promise that nobody will bother you. You can rest and relax however long you want. Your schedule is free and completely different from that of the other guys because you are a preferred resident here. You're my favorite. Sweet dreams, my love."

As she left, Jim climbed out of his bed, took out the limpid stone from his jeans pocket, and put it on the desk. He placed his chin on the edge of the desk and looked at the stone closely. It shone and twinkled with different colors from somewhere deep inside—blue, green, yellow, and orange. It was fantastically beautiful.

"Sweet dreams, Mona," Jim whispered tenderly. "I'm not sure if what I'm feeling is love or not, but I'm really happy to have you in my life. I admire you." He kissed the stone, put it back into his pocket, and lightheartedly went to sleep.

CHAPTER *6*

November 12, 2002

Dear Madam,

I consider it to be my duty to inform you that your biological son, James Emmanuel Bogat, has been residing in the Fir Forest Group Home since November 1, 2002.

This situation seems to be wrong and obviously had occurred by mistake. Like other group homes of this profile in the country, our group home houses only people who are mentally ill.

Mr. James Emmanuel Bogat is uneducated and intellectually undeveloped, but he is fully mentally healthy. I am sending you a picture of him that can prove to you his normal facial expression. In his condition, he should live at home with his family. By force of circumstance, we have no right and no possibility to keep him here whether you like it or not. Such would be illegal.

At the same time, Mr. Bogat has been badly handicapped since birth and is not capable of any kind of work or even his own personal care. The second picture I have sent shows his full height and proves his condition. He requires special care, and staying at a group home would be good for his life and health. As we are compassionate people, we would be happy to make an exception for him and keep him here.

However, our service is quite expensive. After his adoptive mother's death (August 30, 2002), Mr. Bogat had no money at all because she was bankrupt. His disability pension from the government, which is transferred to our group home account monthly, is only $500 and does not even cover the most basic services we are providing. In addition, this amount does not cover the rent of his room that should be renovated and adjusted for an especially handicapped person's needs. The cost of this renovation (with special new furniture and exceptional washroom equipment altogether) would be about $100, 000. Altogether, expenses for Mr. Bogat here would be $200,000 just for now.

In our financial situation, we are unable to complete such a project now, and the government has informed us that we are not eligible for any kind of subsidy for your son's needs.

I regret to notify you that we can give you a grace period of only two weeks, beginning on the date of this letter, to voluntarily pick up Mr. Bogat. After this due date, he will be delivered to your residence by enforcement officers and be under your responsibility.

For more information, please do not hesitate to call or email me at any time. I am looking forward to hearing from you.

Sincerely,

Mona Lainer, Owner and Executive Director, Fir Forest Group Home
Official in Residence

Mona signed the letter and put it into an envelope together with the two pictures of Jim. "Could you mail this letter, honey, on your way home after you drop off the guys at the factory?" she asked Ramah, sealing the envelope. "It's very important. It smells like money."

"Sure, Mommy." He patted her behind, laughing playfully.

"And also, buy a couple of nice standard-sized frames. I'll decorate the midget's room." Mona turned and moved away from him. "Don't be so open, honey. Now we have a pair of smart eyes and ears between the idiots in our home. We should be more careful."

"What color of frame do you want?" Ramah asked.

"Black would be good. He has black piano and black computer desk. It will match."

"You care about him too much," he noted jealously.

"Come on, honey." Mona grinned. "He is a misshapen cripple. I have to care about everybody here if I want to maintain our reputation as the best group home in the States."

"But he doesn't pay anything for such special care," Ramah objected.

"Don't worry, he will and more than the others. You'll see. Anyway, thank you for your help. It's time for you to go. Look, the guys are already waiting by the door." She kissed Ramah's cheek and gently pushed him away.

As he left to drive the residents to work, the nurses started to care for the handicapped people who were staying in their rooms. The cleaning ladies, two deaf Vietnamese seniors, began to clean the empty rooms, kitchen, and living rooms; vacuum the hallways; and water plants in the winter garden. It was too early to begin cooking either lunch or dinner, and Mona, finishing her paperwork in the office, had some free time to see Jim.

She came up to his room, knocked at the door, and entered, not waiting for him to answer. She thought that he was still sleeping and wanted to leave his pictures on his desk as a surprise for him, but Jim unexpectedly was sitting in front of his computer. "Good morning, my sweetheart," Mona said fondly, stroking his hair and kissing his cheek. "I didn't think you woke up so early. It's only eight thirty. Are you already working?"

"Yes." Jim stopped what he was doing and looked into her eyes. "Good morning, Mona. I slept for two days after our crazy night. That was enough rest. Then I decided to organize my schedule because I missed more than two months of work. I want to make up for the lost time. I need to finish my symphony in about six months. It's a very big job. I have no time to relax anymore."

"But you can't work twenty-four hours a day," Mona objected.

"Of course. That's why I made my timetable. I'll wake up at eight o'clock every day to do my composing from nine till noon. Then I'll have a break until three o'clock to do my exercise, to have lunch, and to help you. From three till six, I'll continue composing. Then I'll have dinner, socialize with the guys downstairs, and watch TV. Maybe I'll go for a little walk outside around the building. From eight till ten, I'll listen to classical music, which I continue to study. So altogether, I'll compose for six hours per day. How is that?"

"Oh my goodness!" Mona exclaimed, laughing. "You're going to be such a busy guy! Just don't be too accurate and too organized because it could overload you. When do you plan on making love to me?"

Jim didn't understand her teasing. "As you said last time," he explained seriously, "twice per week, in the evenings from ten to midnight. I'll come to your suite and have sex with you."

"Jesus! Maybe we need to set up special days, like Monday and Thursday or Tuesday and Friday? Jim, you're so childish. What would you do if your prick were erect at another time? It's funny. Do you want me to break your schedule right now?" Mona knelt beside his chair to be at the same height as him, hugged him, and sucked his lips passionately.

Jim moaned and closed his eyes—it was impossible to resist his favorite pleasure. Mona took him from the chair and lowered him on the floor. They rolled over on the carpet, hugging each other and continuing to kiss almost breathlessly. About fifteen minutes passed when Mona felt that Jim's little hands were on her shoulders, trying fiercely to push her away. With difficulty, he tore his lips from hers, begging, "Stop! Stop, Mona, please! I can't! I really can't anymore!"

"I don't want anything right now either." She laughed and let him sit on the floor. "I just want to show you that such things are not always going on schedule. A sudden gust of passion is amazing sometimes."

They were both sitting on the floor, breathing heavily, fixing their hair and clothes, and laughing. "It's a good lesson," Jim said. "But anyway, I'll try to keep to my plan. Otherwise, I can't work productively. It's really important to me."

"Why? What is so important about this? It doesn't commit you to anything. It's only your hobby as I understand."

"Not exactly. It's something I must do. It's my calling from above. It's my soul. Even to a greater extent than that, it's my spirit. It's the meaning of my existence. I won't live without my music. I can tell you everything about this and show you my symphony, Mona, because you're my closest friend."

"Plus, I'm your mother and your wife. We are much more than friends," she added, smiling meaningfully. "It would be good if you showed me. I'm really interested in music. I can play piano, and I always dreamed of being a composer. However, my fate destined for me another life, but I gave the musical education to my daughter. She is now in her last year at Minneapolis University. She'll be a pianist, and she is composing a bit too."

"I didn't know that you had a daughter. Oh yes, I remember you told me . . . I was just too nervous and forgot."

"She is my daughter from Barry. Her name is Sharon. She is twenty-five. She lives in the city, and Barry stays with her now. She is a very talented and beautiful girl—an amazing girl but very poor as our whole family. You can't imagine, Jim, how much I dream to make her rich. It's my lifelong goal."

"So you'll understand if I show you my music, and you can tell me what you think," Jim continued without any interest toward Mona's daughter.

"Yes for sure. I could, and Sharon could be useful if you need some advice or help. You're really lucky to have met me, my dear baby. Show me, please."

Jim's eyes sparkled with happiness as he took a folder from the shelf and handed it to Mona. Then he started a computer program and turned the sound on. The music commenced, and he sat down still, listening and looking at Mona with spiritually excited big deep eyes.

Mona opened the folder and looked at the notes. She listened attentively, moving her finger along the lines, following the music. It was visible that she understood what she was doing. Jim read the expressions on her face that changed to admiration a few minutes later. She even began to look better in Jim's opinion and no longer resembled a rat as much as Jim noted when they met.

The first part of the symphony continued for about twenty minutes. The music was very unusual, overwhelming, and sharply plaintive. It breathed with magic and spirituality. It dumbfounded the listener, taking their soul in full, creating a holy feeling of a union, conveying a touch of spiritual beauty.

When it ended, Jim turned the sound off, and they sat for a few minutes, speechless. It would be blasphemy to pronounce even a sound and to disturb the sense of divinity that wafted in the air. They were spellbound. In about five minutes, this feeling subsided, and Jim looked at Mona questioningly. "It might be enough for today," he suggested in a whisper. "You're going to be tired from listening to so much. How do you like it?"

Mona took a deep breath. Her eyes blinked in uncertainty, making her jumping thoughts quite visible. Jim was too excited to grasp her facial expression. "Well," she said, "I . . . I could say . . . it's amazing, Jim. You're so talented! Jesus, it's unbelievable! You're like a goose who lays golden eggs. You just . . . just need some help. There . . . are some spots that didn't work out completely. I'm sure you need professional advice. It would be good if you could give me your folder or probably the disk with your symphony. I'll take a look at it once more in my spare time. Maybe I could help you make some corrections, or Sharon could too. Or she could show it to her teacher. It's a great idea, isn't it?"

Jim shrugged. "I'm not sure that I need any help," he said disagreeably. "I'm professional and educated enough. I'm absolutely capable of managing my creation myself."

"I'm sure you are, darling!" Mona exclaimed heatedly. "No doubt you can do everything yourself. But sometimes people are a bit blind about their own work and can't see some very tiny lacks. I just want to help you accomplish some small things superperfectly. Actually, I don't need to spend my time on you. I have too many things to do, but I'll do that for you as my favor because I love you. Did somebody already hear your symphony or see the notes?"

"Grandma Cathy. But she didn't understand much. I want to send the first part to my teacher from Juilliard, but I was too late. He died of leukemia quite suddenly. It happened after my graduation. His name was Dr. John Dangly. He was a very well-known teacher of composition. You've probably heard about him. Your daughter certainly has. He really liked me—I mean, my other compositions that were written before the symphony. He insisted that I get an honors degree after my graduation, but the examination board didn't agree with him because I can't play piano or any other instrument properly. So I got just a master's degree. Anyway, it's okay. I'm not career minded. It doesn't really matter. The most important thing for me was Dr. Dangly's recognition and professional assistance. He liked me and called me his 'little genius.' For me, it was funny. I felt happy with him, but then everything ended so unexpectedly. Yet nobody who is alive heard my symphony. You are the first one, Mona, because I trust you."

"Thank you, Jim. I'm very proud that I deserve your trust and your friendship. Hopefully, I'll deserve your love too," Mona said playfully. "So could you give me your notes?"

"Yes, of course," Jim agreed. "I can give you the three first pages. Anyway, you don't have time to look at the whole symphony at once. Then you'll bring it back, and I'll give you the next three. How is that?"

"Oh, it's just great!" Mona exclaimed cheerfully, widening her eyes. She felt furious, noticing Jim's stubborn resistance, but suppressed her feelings and showed Jim a fake smile. "I would really like to help you, Jim. It would be a great pleasure for me. I'm so ardently in love with you, my sweet boy. I actually have something for you as well. Look at this." She took Jim's picture out of her pocket and gave it to him.

"Isn't it amazing? You look like a model or a Hollywood star. You're so handsome, my darling," she said as she lovingly kissed his forehead.

"Not bad." Jim smiled coyly, scrutinizing his own face in the picture. "You're a good photographer, Mona. I actually can't believe that it's me. Thank you very much."

"You're welcome, my sweetheart. Later, I'll bring you two frames and some more pictures of yours, and we'll decorate your room."

"Wait a second," Jim requested, noticing that Mona took the pages of his music and was ready to go. "I'm not feeling very comfortable about bringing business questions into our friendly relationship, but I don't know whom else I can ask. I have a cell phone. I need to connect it and to be able to use it. And also, I need the internet."

Mona looked surprised. "Whom do you want to call or email, Jim? You told me that you're alone in the world."

"I don't have any friends or relatives, but there are some people I know. I can call the library and order books. I can call a video shop and order some movies. I should also order paper and cartridges so I can print my work. I have many places to call, for example, if I need to discuss something with my psychologist or lawyer. And for my musical creation, I really need the internet. I always had these things at the farm, living with Grandma Cathy."

Mona sat across from him and looked at him sternly. "We have a problem with that, Jim. Our group home was designed for the mentally ill who aren't allowed to use the internet or cell phones."

"But I'm not mentally ill, and you know that. I really need these things, and I want you to make an exception for me. Those things are so ordinary. Everybody has them in today's society, even out in the country . . . everywhere. It's nothing special. Why can't I have them? Grandma Cathy ordered them for me easily."

"I'm sorry, Jim, but Grandma Cathy spoiled you too much. She spent too much money on you, much more than she had, and as a result, you don't have anything now. Financially, she made a big mistake. You should know that all these services cost money, but you don't have any."

"Really? Why? I do have a pension," Jim objected.

"It's just pennies but not a pension. It's not enough even for your food. You should pay rent, bills, and all services. It must be about three thousand per month."

Jim scowled, not quite understanding and trying to catch Mona's thought. "Do you mean that I'm living in debt right now?" he asked worriedly. "How could I pay you for all these things?" He looked around the room, nervously biting his lips.

"Don't suffer, baby." Mona stroked his hair and kissed him tenderly. "You're living now because of my love, but I'm looking to find some sponsorship or some donations for you. We will hear about that pretty soon. I guess I can make some arrangements. You'll have your cell phone and internet as Christmas presents."

"I was thinking," Jim said pensively. "Maybe I can do some work and earn some money, like the other guys are doing, not at the factory, of course, but here in the house. I mean, your husband is not here anymore. I'm guessing that he used to shovel snow or other such tasks. I can help you instead of him. I shoveled snow pretty often with Grandma Cathy on the farm. She bought me a little plastic children's shovel, and it was quite easy. It was a good exercise for me. I'm not fast, but I can do it well enough."

"Shh, Jim." Mona pressed her index finger to her lips. "Forget it, please, that Barry is not here. Nobody should know about that. If one day inspectors come and ask you something, just keep silent. Your silence would look normal to them. They would think that you're one of the idiots. I'll tell them that Barry is here and that he just went shopping. Otherwise, they'll cut my salary in half because it's for both of us.

"I am so extremely poor and really need money, so I can't afford to lose Barry's part of the salary. It will not be fair to lose this money because I'm doing Barry's part of work myself. Why shouldn't I be paid for it? But here are the stupid rules. Oh, it's such a tragic woman's fate to be dumped by a husband. You must feel pity toward me, my little darling, and help me. Just keep silent about this. Promise?"

"We should usually obey the rules," Jim noted sadly. "But of course, I'll cover for you, Mona. I'm your friend, and I agree that it's not fair for you to lose money for work that you're doing. So I can't earn anything here, but please buy me a little shovel, and I'll help you voluntarily. I need it. The exercise and fresh air would be good for me. Promise?" He smiled, repeating her earlier question.

Mona nodded. "I have one more idea for you to help me," she remembered suddenly. "Voluntarily, of course. It's another part of the work that Barry usually did. You might think at first that it's a bit dirty, but it's really not because you're not touching anything with your hands, except a hose. Do you want to see it?"

"Sure," Jim said. "I've been sitting down for too long. Now I crave a bit of movement. Otherwise, I may lose my ability to walk. I need exercise. Let's go immediately. I'm dreaming of helping you daily during my breaks."

They left the room together, holding each other by the hand. In another hand, Mona carried the three pages of Jim's symphony. "Wait a second here, my baby," Mona said, leading Jim into the small living room—the winter garden. "I'll be back soon. Just leave your pages in my office."

She ran away quickly, and Jim climbed into the big leather armchair under the palm tree to sit and wait for her. It didn't take long—in a minute, Mona was back with a key in her hand. "I want to prepare you for what you'll see now," she said, sitting down on another armchair, "because it might look strange for you at first sight. There is my kingdom—the maintenance room. Nobody except my husband and our bus driver, Ramah, has the right to enter it, even the nurses. It's not for strangers' eyes. You'll be one more of my trustees from now on and my helper as well. Moreover, you'll have you own key. Okay, my darling? You see, I trust you. It's a special place, but I can rely on you in full. In the basement, we have our garbage removal 'factory.' I'm joking, of course. It's not a real factory. It's just . . . here, it's pretty difficult to get rid of garbage if you live in the country. You should know that. You're a boy from the farm."

"I have no idea how it was done." Jim shook his head. "Grandma Cathy always dealt with garbage. She usually called somewhere, and someone came and picked it up."

"Oh, she was so careless with money!" Mona exclaimed. "This is such an expensive service, and I, as a very poor woman, can't afford it. Our cleaning ladies usually sort garbage every day right in the kitchen. Leftover food and peelings are going in one plastic container, paper in another one, nonrefundable metal cans and glass in another, and so on. Refundable bottles and cans go in the boxes. Ramah usually loads all these into the elevator and takes them downstairs. There are also animals in the cage. They eat everything that is edible from the garbage. And there is a fireplace designed for burning paper, dry leaves, and branches from outside—in short, everything that is flammable."

"Do you want me to help with the garbage?" Jim asked, scowling with uncertainty.

"No way, my sweetheart. You're not a servant here. You're my lover, and you have preferential treatment, so I'll never allow you to touch any garbage even with one of your cute fingers. I need some other help—someone needs to care for the animals."

"Oh, I like animals." Jim smiled. "We had a lot of them when I was a child. I remember playing with a goat's kids and even baby lambs. They were so cute, but later, Grandma Cathy sold all of them."

Mona pursed her lips and shook her head, silently showing her complete disagreement with everything that Grandma Cathy had ever done. "Okay, my baby," she said, "let's go to the basement, and I'll show you what to do."

She unlocked a door beside the elevator and stopped at the entrance. A stairwell led down into a gloomy big room in which a red light was on. The noise of heavy-working fans, the explosions of boilers turning on and off, the sounds of big refrigerators, and something squeaking were heard from the deep underground and made Jim feel uncomfortable. In his imagination, the red light and flashes of fire resembled a hell full of blood from horror movies.

"Oh, no." Mona shook her head, looking at the steps in uncertainty. "You can't walk down there, baby. The stairs have no handrails. And you can't slide down like you usually do because it's made of cement, and you can hurt your sweet bum. You better use the elevator."

"Does it go down?" Jim asked, feeling a shudder ran over his spine.

"Yes, of course. We use it all the time. Down there is our loading dock and refrigerators in which I keep food that needs to be frozen and drinks too. When we buy groceries, we usually unload it all there. At the back of the house, there is a big overhead door that opens into the basement. Through this door, we load the boxes with refundable bottles and cans into our bus. Then Ramah delivers them to the bottle depot every couple of months. He also takes containers with debris and leftover garbage to a special station probably once every six months.

"It's a big job, baby, to keep this huge household well organized and in perfect working order. I'm working really hard and have already established the reputation of our group home as the best in the country. It's your home now. If you help me do my job, you'll help yourself and all of us. Life will be better that way, isn't it right?"

Jim nodded, not quite understanding how animals could live in such an underground hell and eat leftover food scraps. As far as he knew, animals should live in barns and eat grass.

Holding his hand, Mona led him into the elevator, and they went down. As they left the elevator, she turned on a light, and the maintenance room didn't look so scary anymore. On the right, Jim saw the cement stairs, leading up; on the opposite wall were three huge refrigerators and an overhead door leading outside. In the middle of the room were two enormous boilers, and on the left side, he saw a fireplace and a big cage hanging on the wall. The red lamp was located above the cage full of swarming white rats.

"What's that?" Jim exclaimed, looking at them in horror.

"They're my animals." Mona laughed, observing his terrified face. "There is nothing to be afraid of. They are cute and quite tame. They eat from my hands sometimes. Do you want to see?"

Jim couldn't say a word. Not waiting for his answer, Mona approached the cage door. She moved aside a metal bolt and opened the door just a crack, putting her palm under the opening. One of the rats, which was right beside the crack at the moment, slipped out onto her palm, sniffing Mona's fingers with its pink nose. Mona locked the cage right away and petted the white fur on the back of the tiny animal.

"Oh, look at this," she moaned joyfully. "It's tickling my palm with its whiskers. It's so nice and cute. It never would run anywhere. It'll stay with me because they like me. I tamed them. I feed them very well. They're always full and absolutely not dangerous because of that."

Jim made a wry face full of loathing. "I don't like these animals," he said squeamishly. "I actually hate them. They embody meanness, dirt, and malice."

"That's a big mistake, Jim. Only people who don't know them would say such things. They're cute, charming, and amazing helpers. They're carrying out our sanitation, eating all the edible garbage. Nothing is rotten or dirty in the house because of their help. And they work for free and are always happy to eat more. It's natural cleaning. To use them here was my own invention, and I'm really proud of it. Do you want to pet it?"

"No." Jim shook his head, moving aside. "Put it back, please."

Mona laughed again, opened the door, and let the rat slip inside the cage. "You don't like my friends, I see." She looked attentively at Jim's face.

"Absolutely not!" he exclaimed intensely. "I can't even call them animals. For me, animals are cows, lambs, and goats. Rats are just disgusting creatures with no brains and no feelings, just working jaws and stomachs. Nothing in life could be worse than them."

"I disagree, my baby. People are much worse."

"I don't know. I have never met bad people."

"Well . . ." Mona wanted to say sarcastically, *Do you think your mother who crippled you and then gave you up for adoption was better?* But the words stuck in her throat. It was too early for that. She still needed Jim. So she swallowed her words and kept silent. Then she found another example. "Well . . . Ali and Zahra's father who gave them such a horrible life, is he better?"

"These are incomparable things." Jim shook his head. "We can't say that he was a bad person. He was just uneducated. He didn't know what he was doing."

"That's no excuse."

"It is. He didn't want this. He did it unconsciously. He couldn't be guilty. It was just a terrible accident. We can call people who do mean things on purpose and absolutely consciously 'bad.' But luckily, as I said, I never met them."

"You would be a good lawyer." Mona laughed. "You'd beat every prosecutor. Anyway, my animals are not guilty, whether you like it or not. They're cheap and useful helpers who breed like rabbits. I bought just two couples a few years ago, and now here are more than fifty of them."

"Why is there a red lamp above them?" Jim asked with interest. "Does it help them breed?"

Mona nodded as he said, "You take such good care of them."

"Like everybody here." She grinned. "I'm a careful mother to everybody and everything, including the building itself. I've been here for twenty years. This group home is my creature and my baby. I like it, the entire ensemble—the building, the people, the things, and my animals, of course. All these together make up my business. It's my life's purpose."

"Well . . ." Jim looked at her with uncertainty. "Do you want me to feed them?"

"No, baby. You can't open the cage. They'll run out if someone inexperienced does that. Barry usually just washes them. We need to keep the cage and the floor under it always clean to avoid the smell. Look, there are droppings and food crumbs on the floor. It's very easy to do. Watch this."

Mona took the hose that was hanging on a big hook beside the cage, turned on a tap, and began spraying water right at the cage. The rats rushed into the corners, crowding and squeaking in horror.

"They don't like water as far as I know," Jim commented. "Usually, rats leave a ship that is sinking. They can smell it."

"You're right, baby, but these are *incomparable things* again," she teased, smiling at him. "Nobody wants to sink in the sea, but everybody takes a shower. They need to be washed daily. Look, the room is designed perfectly—the floor slopes toward the sewer hole, and everything goes down there. You don't need to touch anything, only the hose, which is clean. You won't even dirty your hands. Look." Mona turned off the water, put the hose back on the hook, and showed Jim her open palms.

"Of course, I can do it." He laughed. "I'm just not sure that I can hold the hose if the water gushes though."

"Don't turn it on too much. Let's try."

Jim took the hose with one hand, pulled the other to reach the tap that was luckily quite low, and turned it on a bit. Water started to trickle out. "More," Mona said. "Be brave."

Jim turned the tap a bit more, and water suddenly spurted, knocking the hose from his tiny hand. It fell on the floor, wiggling like a snake. The water spurted out like a fountain, making Jim and Mona both wet from head to toe.

"Oh my goodness!" Mona exclaimed, trying to catch the jumping hose on the floor. Jim bit his lips and looked with horror at his deed, unable to move. Finally, Mona found out what to do and turned the tap off. The water stopped, and she picked up the hose, almost breathless from laughter. "Oh, Jesus." She grinned, hanging the hose on its spot. "Baby, you're amazing. You're so cute. It's unbelievable. My God! You're soaking wet! Let's go. I'll change you. I'm wet too but not as much as you. Okay, we'll learn how to wash the animals next time. Today we had a shower instead."

She took Jim in her arms and carried him into the elevator. He was giggling as well, seeing that Mona wasn't angry with him. He hugged her neck.

"You are so funny." She talked while in the elevator, kissing his wet face passionately. "You brought so much light and enjoyment into my life. I'm so happy that you're here now, my sweetheart, and that we're friends."

"By the way," Jim said when they entered his room, "I have one more request—medical."

"Tell me. Dr. Mona can cure everything."

"I need some cream."

"What for?" She undressed him and seated him on his bed.

"It doesn't matter. Just give it to me," he asked coyly, putting a dry T-shirt on.

"You have an antibacterial gel in your first aid kit, on the shelf in the washroom."

"I didn't know that."

"It might be too high, and you can't reach it." Mona went to the bathroom and brought a tube. "I'll leave it here on the table for you. Just tell me, what do you need it for?"

Jim's face reddened, and he stubbornly shook his head.

"Tell me, baby. Otherwise, I can't leave it with you." She touched his chin and forced him to look into her eyes. "What happened? You shouldn't hide anything from me. I could guess. Is something wrong with your charming prick?"

"How do you know? I just have a little wound there, but it's quite painful."

"I know everything, my baby. I have very significant life experience." Mona laughed. "Your foreskin was broken. It happened because you lost your virginity. Congratulations! You're a man, finally. Wash it three times a day and put this cream on. Actually, I can do it for you right now."

"No, I'll do it myself," Jim protested actively, but Mona was already turned on and didn't want to listen to anything.

"Providing medical care for the guys is my job, baby, and the most pleasant part of it." She grabbed him, carried him into the bathtub, and washed his man's treasure with the foam of perfumed soap, sliding her hand over it tenderly and smoothly. "Do you like it, baby?" Mona asked impatiently, looking into his eyes while doing this. "Do you feel something? It's amazing, isn't it?"

"Yes." Jim made a wry face and moaned, biting his lips and tightening his face. "Just do it faster. It hurts."

"Sorry, sorry, my sweet boy. I know." She wrapped him with a towel and carried him back to his bed, laughing. "It's like playing with dolls. It's a lot of fun."

Then she opened the foreskin on his penis, putting gel around its head, and closed it again.

"That's why circumcision is so popular in the U.S. not only for Muslims and Jews but also for everybody. A men who's survived the same troubles as you doesn't want his sons to face the same things. But your grandma Cathy didn't know anything about that, of course. Whatever. It will be okay in several days. I'll come and check it, and then we'll make love again. See you, my darling."

"Mona!" Jim suddenly called her as she opened the door to go out. "Mona, wait, please!"

"What, baby?"

He took a deep breath. "Mona . . . I just thought . . . " He whispered thankfully, "I trust you. You can take some more pages of my symphony."

CHAPTER 7

During the following month, Jim's existence settled down slowly. He returned to his usual routine, accustomed to everything and everybody, and found the right way to deal with his new situation. The wound on his penis healed fast, and there was no more pain at sex time. However, he still didn't quite grasp neither the essence of sexual delight nor why the world was so crazy about it. He liked kissing, even though he found other things just pleasant, but no more than that—nothing to become obsessive about or addicted to.

Mona enjoyed it much more than Jim; he knew this, and this was the main reason for which he continued their relationship. He was grateful to her for her motherly care and wanted to thank her. His only benefit was an amazing feeling of pride—he owned the woman and gave her rapture and ecstasy, orgasm after orgasm; this meant that he was a real man now. It was only this realization that satisfied him in his relationship with Mona, a relationship that, for him, was more of boring obligation than an exciting experience. Sex required too much energy from his tiny body—usually, after each session, he was exhausted and did not recuperate easily.

Jim took much greater pleasure in his creative work. This was truly a source of elation for him. Regarding his schedule, especially its musical part, Jim was a persistent person. When he started composing, there was no power that could force him to stop (even if a bomb was dropped). Mona and the nurses entered his room a couple of times while he was playing his piano, but Jim reprimanded them so sternly that, later, nobody dared bother him during his creative hours.

The symphony went quickly and smoothly, and Jim expected to complete it in spring. Every week he gave Mona five to six pages for review. She made copies and put them into her safe. Then she circled certain spots in Jim's original version with a pencil and returned them to him in about a week.

"Sorry, I kept your pages so long," she usually said in an apologizing tone. "I absolutely had no time for them. You know how busy I am. It's so difficult to find extra time. I just love you madly, my darling, and do this favor for you in my few spare moments. So check my comments. I found some little mistakes. But anyway, you're so talented. You'll be rich and famous pretty soon. You'll get millions for this symphony."

Her eulogies forced Jim to laugh. He wasn't sure whether she was teasing him or really thought so. These praises were too funny and obviously blown out of proportion. He would be happy to receive some serious practical advice and didn't expect panegyrics.

Jim did not quite understand why Mona did it. She was not a music professional at all, and all the places she circled didn't contain any mistakes. He checked them; shook his head, smiling; and erased her marks, not saying a word to her. He guessed that it was important for her self-esteem to show him that she was a specialist in music too.

Jim noticed that having his pages was important for Mona and gave her this courtesy, trying to do something pleasant for her other than sex. He had no money and couldn't buy any presents for her, but he knew well (from the books and movies) that a real man was supposed to give gifts to the woman he's sleeping with. He gave Mona the possibility of being involved with his symphony, considering it as his gift.

Mona, in her turn, bought him presents—charming red rubber boots and a red plastic shovel too—both were suitable for a three-year-old child. "These are your Christmas presents, my dear baby," she said, kissing him. "But I'll give them to you a bit early because you need them so badly, and I know you can't wait. The shovel is so you can shovel the snow and get some exercise, and the boots are to wear when washing the animals to keep your charming tiny feet dry on the wet floor in the basement."

Jim laughed. These things were cute and gave him a sense of continuity of their mother-baby game. At last, Mona trained him to successfully deal with the hose, and Jim washed the rats, the cage, and the floor in the maintenance room daily during breaks from composing.

Jim's only failure was in his attempts to socialize with the other residents. Actually, there wasn't a single person with whom social contact was possible. Jim tried to talk to Victor, but he didn't react. Maggie didn't understand anything and didn't talk properly; Todd couldn't listen to him because his ears seemed to be incessantly plugged with earphones. When Jim attempted to make a conversation with him, he just gave a thumbs-up and sang his song louder. He also refused to share his card game and just told Jim to "go and find something to do" but in his deep voice added kindly, "Merry Christmas, child."

Nurses from both shifts were usually fully occupied with their work; the cleaning ladies were busy, as well as deaf and didn't know any English. The bus driver, Ramah, if he came into the house (which did not happen very often), was engaged with maintenance work in the basement, loading and unloading stuff. Ramah also shoveled snow but only during the day. In the evenings, when Jim walked outside with his red shovel, Ramah was already gone.

The only person who sometimes agreed to walk around the house with Jim was Ella. He found out that she liked to shovel snow too. She couldn't do it for a long time, being tired after work at the factory, but she was ready for a short walk. Ella was quite talkative but said mostly silly and meaningless things and didn't tolerate any objections. "Don't argue!" she would shout if Jim tried to give a different opinion about anything. So he shut up, remembering that Ella killed her husband during an argument a few years ago. Seeing a big metal shovel in her hand, he felt uncomfortable continuing their talks, walks, and shoveling. After that, he preferred to go for his outdoor promenades alone.

One day when Mona left to buy groceries, Jim walked through the hallway on the second floor during a break from composing. He noticed that the door to Lily's room was wide open. *She is the only person I haven't tried to speak to yet, aside from Ali and Zahra, of course*, he thought. *She is sick and has a bad character, but she is mentally normal. Why not try?*

He approached Lily's door and peered inside. He saw the strange little bundle of nerves sitting in the wheelchair, her back toward the door, looking out the window, and drinking her cider. Jim knocked carefully and asked, "May I come in?"

Lily turned her wheelchair and looked at him with her fantastic and unusually large blue eyes. "Who are you?" she asked sternly. "A man? No men in my room!"

"Why not?"

"'Cause you're dirty bastards!"

"I'm not," Jim objected, teasing her. "I take a shower every day, sometimes twice, depending on the situation."

"Shit! You're silly! I'm talking about another kind of dirt."

"I know. I'm just joking."

"This is not a good time for jokes. They're heating the house far too much. It's too hot in here. It's impossible to breathe. I already complained three times, but that old bitch Mona didn't do anything. I was forced to open my door for a draft, but there are men walking in the hallway. I don't feel safe."

"I realize that you're not feeling very well," Jim said sympathetically. "But this doesn't give you the right to be impolite toward Mona. She is taking very good care of all of us, and she is my friend."

"Friend?" Lily laughed hysterically until she finally choked and then began to cough. She coughed endlessly until she had tears; cider and saliva were drizzling from her mouth. For Jim, it looked like she was going to cough to death, and he wanted to go and call the nurse, but Lily finally stopped coughing and gestured for him to come in, still breathing with difficulty. "Friend?" she repeated. "How long have you been here, you little freak of nature?"

"A month and a half."

"Yes, yes, yes." Lily nodded. "She was my friend too . . . at the start. A very close friend! We were even lovers. She's a lesbian too. I had sex with her couple of times."

"What?" Jim exclaimed in disbelief. "That's impossible! She was a married woman and has a daughter! She can't be a lesbian!"

"Of course, she's not. She's just a bitch and cheated on me. Being a lesbian, it's a very spiritual condition. We're the most soulful and profound women in the world. I can say we're holy and don't allow the dirt in a relationship that comes from men. We are the superior creatures."

"Well, probably you're . . .," Jim said, turning to go. "Bye, Lily." He realized that Lily was not in the right mind either and didn't want to listen anything bad about Mona anymore. He had his own opinion.

"Wait, little one!" Lily called suddenly. "Look at me, please."

Jim stopped by the door and turned to her. "You remind me of somebody," Lily said, looking attentively at his face. "Could I have seen you before . . . somewhere?"

"I don't think so."

"How old are you, buddy?"

"Thirty-two."

"Maybe I'm mistaken. It was too long ago. I'm already fifty-two, the same age as your *dearest friend* Mona," she added sarcastically.

Jim gazed at her surprisingly. He didn't expect that this strange creature could have any age at all. It was similar to the impression he had when he saw her for the first time and thought she had no gender.

"You remind me of someone I saw quite a long time ago when I was a dancer. Even before I got my contract with the Metropolitan Opera as a ballerina . . . I was pretty well known. Lily Donovan! Ha! But I forgot . . . let me think." She frowned slightly, straining her memory. "I danced for variety groups . . . I was a teenager. It was the very end of the sixties. The groups got popular after the Beatles . . . no, you sure weren't born at that time. Actually, I can't remember. But I saw your face somewhere—in the movies, on TV, in newspapers. Yes, I saw it everywhere many times. I even have a feeling that I knew this person quite well. Jesus! Damn MS! It has completely messed up my head! But I'll remember eventually. I'll try. I promise. I'm just curious. It wasn't you for sure but someone whose face was just like yours. Your hair, nose, dimple on the chin, quite a rare thing, your lips and brows—everything . . . but the eyes were probably blue or gray, not as dark as yours."

Lily shook her head thoughtfully. "Who are you, little one?" she asked. "Where is your family?"

"I don't know. I was adopted by farmers and grew up on a farm."

"Ooh, that's pretty far away."

"Well . . . you intrigue me, Lily," Jim said. "I would be interested in finding out something about my parents, but it seems to be impossible. It might be that someone who looked like me was one of my relatives . . . but not exactly. There are so many similar people in the world. Sometimes doubles are living in different countries and not even in the same centuries—I read about that. Anyway, thank you. If you remember something that could be useful, tell me, please. Now I have to go. Have a nice day. See you."

"Bye, little one. I'll think about you," Lily said, turning back to the window and opening a new bottle of cider.

Wistfully, Jim came to the conclusion that Lily was judgmental, narrow minded, and impolite—for sure because of her illness. Her memories caught him by surprise, and he decided he would talk to her more another time. But he figured that it would be practically impossible to become friends with her. At this point, the situation at the group home seemed hopeless. There was no choice for Jim; he was doomed to socialize with Mona only.

He felt a bit dejected because this wasn't enough for him. He wasn't very sociable, but throughout his whole life, he had had contact with many people on his cell phone, especially on the internet. He really missed them.

Intellectually, communication with Mona was absolutely not enough (they didn't have time to talk a lot and to get closer spiritually); sexually, however, it was too much. Jim could tolerate it, but he wasn't very happy. His music and the creative work were still his only happiness.

CHAPTER *8*

Two weeks before Christmas, a heavy snowstorm rolled in during the night. Jim slept through it and only discovered in the morning that everything outside the house was covered with a soft blanket of white. Huge snow pillows hung off the branches of the fir trees, giving the forest an almost fantastic appearance. It reminded Jim of a fairy tale.

Gazing out the window, Jim felt impatient, wanting to play in the crisp-looking snow that sparkled in the sun. He decided to go outside during his break instead of washing rats. He had lunch as fast as he could, dressed warmly, took his shovel, and walked out of the house.

It was a sunny day. The snow was dazzling and made a squeaking sound under his feet. The amazing smell of winter, fresh and fragrant, wafted in the air, together with the light frost. Jim was in a very good mood and felt lighthearted.

In addition to blue jeans and sweater, he wore a leather jacket, skiing hat, scarf, gloves, and cute fur boots. He was well equipped for the winter. Grandma Cathy usually bought his clothes at very expensive children's clothing shops or from catalogs, and they were delivered straight to their farm. She spoiled him well. Now walking on the beautiful snow, Jim remembered his last Christmas, last winter at the farm, and in his thoughts thanked Grandma Cathy once more for everything she had done for him.

Jim noticed that, in the morning, Ramah had already cleaned the main entrance and the trail to the driveway where the bus usually came so the guys could reach the bus easily. Now he decided to shovel the backyard in front of the garage and slowly walk around the house, propping himself up on his red shovel. He started shoveling the driveway unhurriedly, accurately, little by little, thinking about the coming holidays and smiling at his own thoughts.

Jim liked to exercise and be active. He had spent many years in a wheelchair and was scared to return to one. His coach taught him that walking, exercising, and doing a bit of physical work were very important for him, and he did all these with pleasure.

It was very calm and quiet in the winter forest. Jim only heard the occasional caw of the crows, hopping from branch to branch or flying between the fir trees, and saw the snow pillows falling down with a rustle. Suddenly, the sound of an approaching engine broke the silence. *Could it be the bus?* Jim thought, surprised. *No, it's too early for the guys to return from work. Mona is at home. It's not shopping day today. Maybe some guests? But visitors' day would be tomorrow.*

Curious about who was coming, Jim stopped shoveling and walked to the corner of the house to take a look at the front driveway. He peered from behind the corner and saw a shiny black Mercedes 500 with tinted back windows parked pretty far away from the entrance, beside the garden. However, it was close enough for Jim to see through the front window; a gray-haired driver in a black suit, white shirt, tie, and white gloves sat in the driver's seat. Jim was shocked—a driver in white gloves must mean something very exceptional.

While he pondered about the car, the group home door opened, and Jim saw Mona running from the main entrance toward the car. She was wearing blue jeans and sneakers. As she ran, she pulled on her light blue jacket. It looked to Jim as if the sudden appearance of the car took Mona by surprise, but at the same time, he had the very opposite feeling—that this car was very special, and Mona had been waiting impatiently for it. It was quite strange, and Jim continued to watch with curiosity.

Mona was already halfway to the car as the back door opened, and a woman got out. She seemed quite slender, about the same height as Mona. Her long dark brown hair was twisted into a bun at the back of her head, making her look elegant, stylish, and professional. There was no smile at her well-tanned face. From the distance, Jim couldn't see her features very clearly. Leaving the car, the woman immediately put on the hood of her long light brown fur coat. It covered her hair and most of her face. In her hand, she held a black sports bag that didn't fit in with the rest of her appearance at all. The bag didn't seem very heavy but had a rustic look.

Mona ran fast, and Jim thought that she would jump on the woman and embrace her because she might be a relative—daughter, sister, or cousin. However, Mona stopped before the woman and bowed her head shyly, fawning on this mysterious stranger. They didn't shake hands, and it was visible that Mona wasn't even brave enough to make an attempt. She stood sternly in front of the lady. The enormous distance between them was obvious; this woman was definitely a stranger. They walked together over the snow near the bushes, moving far enough from the car so the driver couldn't hear what they were talking about. Then they stopped and continued their conversation.

Jim watched, practically breathless from the tension, feeling feverish. He couldn't suppress the thought that something very important was going on in front of him, but he couldn't grasp the meaning of the scene, though he knew well that it was something extraordinary.

Quite a bit of time passed until the women, still talking, slowly walked back to the car. The lady, with expression of disdain and disgust on her face, threw Mona the bag and sat in the car, not even waving goodbye to her. The driver started the engine, and a few seconds later, the car was gone. Mona went toward the house, carefully pressing the bag to her chest with both hands. She smiled victoriously and solemnly.

Jim hid behind the corner. He didn't want Mona to see him. Thoughtfully, he returned to the garage to shovel but couldn't work calmly anymore. The scene he had just witnessed bothered him. He wasn't sure if he had the right to ask Mona about it or even tell her that he had noticed something. He was painfully curious, and not knowing tortured him so much that he stopped working and walked home. He undressed in the little foyer, stomped the snow from his boots, and hung his clothes into the closet, continuing to think about the scene. Then Jim went up to his room, took the key from the basement, put his red rubber boots on, and went to wash the animals.

In about half an hour, he returned to the kitchen and saw Mona fussing by the stove on which dinner was boiling and frying, producing amazing smells. She wore her lacy apron and seemed very busy. Jim leaned against the wall, gazing at her attentively.

Mona felt his glance and smiled at him playfully. "Are you hungry, my love? In about ten minutes, everything will be ready. You could eat even before the guys arrive."

"Thank you, Mona," he said tensely, not smiling and continuing to stand silently.

Some minutes passed until Jim found the nerve to ask finally, "Who was this woman?"

"What did you say, darling?" It was quite obvious that Mona was just pretending not to hear his question properly, and he grasped it immediately.

"Who was that woman, I said," he repeated sternly, raising his voice. He didn't like it when somebody thought he was stupid.

"What woman, baby? What are you talking about?" Mona moved the stuff on the stove and, on the kitchen counter, opened the drawer, knocking around spoons and knifes, and narrowed her eyes, looking for something attentively.

"The woman in the black car who gave you a bag."

"Oh, that one. My goodness! How did you see? You were supposed to be in the basement. Oh, shit! I can't find a fork . . . this woman? It was . . . it was just Todd's mother. She brought some stuff for him. You sound agitated, baby. Why are you so worried about that? It's quite regular here—families bring things and presents for our guys."

"What is her name?"

"Hmm . . . Mrs. Spencer. You know, Todd's last name is Spencer, Jean Spencer."

"Are you sure?"

"Absolutely. What's the problem with that? Why are you questioning me? It's impolite, baby. Don't you trust me? Why are you trying to control me? You shouldn't spy on what I'm doing and then question me. It's not nice. I'm so busy and working so hard for you!" Mona exclaimed in a crying voice. "I'm so tired, baby. Of course, thank you for your nice help with shoveling and washing animals, but I never expected that you would be so rude to me without any reason—to me, who loves you so much!"

"Sorry, Mona. Maybe I'm just really hungry after my walk. That's it." Jim climbed up and settled on his high chair at the table. "I'm ready for dinner," he pronounced peacefully, trying to fix their relationship. "Maybe I have too much of an imagination. I didn't shovel snow at my regular time. I saw this woman accidentally, but her appearance bothered me somehow."

"We have many visitors here, my darling," Mona explained, calming down as well and pouring soup into Jim's little bowl. "And some of them are very high in society. For us, poor people like you and me, they look unusual and strange, but you'll get used to this later. There's nothing special about it. I have good news for you, my sweetheart. I found some sponsorship. Tomorrow morning, I'll make a couple of phone calls, and your cell phone and the internet will be connected. You won't even have to pay the bill. I'll do that for you. It's an amazing Christmas present, isn't it? You see, I'm keeping my promises."

"Yeah!" Jim exclaimed, making a thumbs-up. "Thank you, Mona! I really appreciate that. You can't imagine how grateful I am!"

"The very best thank-you for me would be if you would come and love me tonight." She flirted, and Jim realized that this Christmas present would be quite expensive, but anyway, he was glad. His disturbing suspicions about the scene he saw outside passed quickly, and he nodded in agreement.

Mona's soup was fantastic. Eating it and looking forward to enjoying the evening in her intoxicating embrace, Jim felt happy. All his problems and suffering were left in the past. Life in the group home seemed beautiful, and the future promised to be exuberant.

CHAPTER 9

The following Saturday was shopping day, and everybody was supposed to go, even Victor, who walked like a zombie, and Lily, Ali, and Zahra, who were in wheelchairs. The entire staff accompanied them—Mona, Ramah, Nurses Sue and Josef, and another couple of nurses, Andy and Rona. The last were both Americans, big, tall, and strong. They were brother and sister, both red haired and with the same haircut. Maybe they were twins because they looked so similar; they could only be told apart by Andy's bushy mustache and Rona's huge breasts.

"Why should we go shopping?" Jim asked Mona, not understanding the purpose of this outing. "It looks to me like a waste of time. What can I buy if I have no money at all? What can Victor buy if he's catatonic? Or Ali and Zahra? Or Maggie, who doesn't understand anything? It would probably be reasonable for you to go with Todd, Ella, and Lily."

"You're wrong, sweetie," Mona objected. "I'll buy things for the guys. Maggie, for example, needs new clothes. She's gaining weight every day and now has almost nothing to wear because of that. We're going to the Mall of America. There are a lot of nice things and lots of entertainments. Even if you don't buy anything, looking around and being in public is enjoyable. Christmas is such an amazing time—music and decorations everywhere. It helps sick people feel happier."

"It might help Lily but not Ali and Zahra, who are vegetables."

"For vegetables, it's not bad to be outside sometimes either. But for you, my darling, it will be a really special day. I'll go with you to the bank and open a bank account for you."

"What do I need one for?"

"The sponsors will transfer money for you, not a lot but enough, together with your pension for your living expenses and bills."

"Who are these sponsors?"

"What does it matter, Jim?" Mona scowled. "Some charitable organizations. It doesn't matter. I don't like your snooping. You're getting too investigative this time. You better think about your music and about our love than ask me questions about my business. Sorry, my sweet boy, but now I must pay more attention to other people. In the mall, you just walk beside somebody's wheelchair and hold on to it. That way, it will be easier to walk for you." She kissed his forehead and put on her backpack, ready to go.

Jim felt guilty and uncomfortable. He didn't want to bother Mona with his curiosity, but Grandma Cathy always answered his questions openly and never got angry because of them. He was accustomed to sincere relationships in their small family. *Why not ask now if I'm interested?* Jim thought. *Mona is probably right. The group home is a business, doesn't matter that she calls it "family." Like all businesses, ours has its business secrets as well. But I'm not a stranger. I'm her lover and closest friend.*

However, on the bus, Jim changed his mind and realized that this trip was not included in a group home program in vain. It was shocking to leave the rooms, the house, the forest and be immersed in the brewing life of the city, the people, and the country. It was a vortex of impressions—lights, colors, smells, and sounds that overwhelmed and excited everybody and made the residents feel animated, active, and to a greater extent healthy.

Everybody felt elated; even Lily started to smile. Moreover, Ali and Zahra turned their heads here and there, making cheerful sounds. Only Victor walked lifelessly, guided by the nurse, who held his hand. Jim held him by another hand, using Victor's motionless fingers so as not to fall down. This way, they were walking through the mall between the crowds of the people, crazily stimulated by Christmas shopping. It was another world. It was a living fairy tale. It was an escape from the boring and sad reality of the weekdays that overwhelmed psychologically not only the residents but the staff as well. This trip was a miracle.

While they were passing the bank, Mona found Jim, took him by the hand, and led him in. The rest of the group continued walking ahead. "Won't we get lost?" Jim asked her worriedly.

"No, my baby. We have a meeting point. The nurses know what to do. And you have absolutely nothing to worry about when you're with me."

Jim was surprised to know that Mona had previously arranged an appointment, and somebody was already waiting for them. The procedure for opening a bank account didn't require anything from Jim except his signature and a PIN, but Mona was so helpful and generous that she even chose for him the PIN and the telephone banking password. She also ordered the checks. Ten of them were printed out right away and given to her. The rest of them was supposed to be mailed to their address next week. Jim left a sample of his signature, which wasn't easy because his tiny fingers couldn't hold the pen; he wrote his name slowly in block letters.

Then Mona opened her backpack and handed the bank representative $2,000 in cash to put into Jim's account. Though Jim still didn't feel the value of the money, he considered her fine gesture as her love to him. In his opinion, it was so moving. At last, Jim got his bank card and was told that he could use it right away. He put the bank card into his pocket, and they left.

Mona took Jim to the food court, where the nurses and the residents made a stop for lunch. Everybody was already settled and had something to eat. The nurses were feeding Ali and Zahra. "Have some food, baby," Mona said, sitting Jim on the chair. "I need to go somewhere else and will be back soon. You wait for me or go with the group. Just don't get lost. Okay, my baby?"

Jim nodded and took a piece of a sandwich, which Nurse Josef had cut for him. Mona walked away quickly and disappeared into the crowd.

"How long do we plan to stay here?" Jim asked Josef, who was opening a can of cola for him.

"About an hour," the nurse answered, glancing at his watch.

"I'll walk around a bit. I'll be back soon," Jim said and slid down from the chair.

"Don't go far!" Josef shouted at his back, but Jim wasn't paying attention to him and walked away, holding himself up by chairs, tables, or walls.

Jim already had a little experience walking inside the mall. Last Christmas, Grandma Cathy took him to the city of Pittsburgh to walk in the mall and to buy some presents. It was their last Christmas together, and it was sad to remember it now. Jim felt so excited that he didn't want to concentrate on the sad feelings and just pushed them out of his mind. However, he knew that he needed to find the mall directory.

Some people passed Jim, looking at him surprisingly. He even heard a child exclaim, "Mommy, Mommy, look, this kid has such a big head!" Jim laughed. He absolutely didn't feel offended; on the contrary, people's mockery made him happy and satisfied. He liked it when people were smiling and was glad to pleasure and entertain them.

Finally, Jim found what he was looking for—a jewelry store. He knew that Mona liked jewelry, that her only necklace was broken. He decided to replace it for her—and not with something cheap but with a real gem.

There weren't many people at the jeweler's maybe because it was quite expensive. Jim entered and suddenly saw Mona. She was standing before the counter, and one of the shop assistants was serving her. Some jewelry was on the top of the counter. She touched and scrutinized each piece carefully; she talked, laughed, and flirted with the assistant at the same time. The counter was quite high, so Jim couldn't see the jewelry that Mona had chosen. He hid beside the entrance, behind a vase with a bushy, artificial plant. Luckily, he was so little that the plant kept him completely hidden.

Jim didn't mind spying on Mona; he just wanted to surprise her and thought that if she saw him close to jeweler's store, his surprise wouldn't work. He had no choice, only to hide. *Maybe she is buying a present for her daughter*, he thought, anticipating with pleasure. *But she would never expect a gift from me. I'm sure she would be on top of the world.* The idea to please Mona excited Jim so much that he could barely wait for her to finally leave the store. He fidgeted impatiently behind the plant, gazing at Mona from behind.

She put her backpack on the counter, opened it, and gave a package to the assistant, who bent over behind the counter and did something there for quite a while. Jim got tired of waiting. He couldn't see anything clearly and didn't understand what they were doing there. He was just happy when Mona took, at last, a long light gray velvety box, put it into her backpack, and left. The shop assistant saw her off to the door, fawning and almost bowing to her. She walked through the mall and disappeared quickly into the crowd. Knowing that she was far enough away and couldn't see him, Jim entered the store.

"How can I help you, sir?" the assistant asked, smiling at him courteously.

"I want to buy a diamond necklace for my girlfriend," Jim announced enthusiastically.

"Yes, sir," the assistant's face displayed a joyful smile. "You're in the right place. We have a great selection of them, perhaps the best one in the city. I'm sure you'll find exactly what you are looking for."

He led Jim to the same counter where Mona was standing just a few minutes ago, brought a stool for him to sit on, and helped him climb up. Jim looked through the glass and saw a lot of necklaces that were quite similar to Mona's broken one. "Are they high quality?" he asked.

"Of course, sir." The assistant laughed. "They are pure gems of the highest quality. Prices range between $50,000 and $500,000. They are arranged in order of price. What are you looking to spend, sir?"

Jim's face reddened. He coughed confusingly. "Two thousand dollars," he whispered.

The assistant feigned a cough but tried to remain professional. "Oh, I suppose that this exhibition is not what you need, sir, but I can suggest something really fine, beautiful, and charming as well."

He led Jim to another counter and put before him a large velvety holder full of little pendants with one, two, or three tiny diamonds. Jim smiled thankfully. Everything appeared so delicate, ethereal, and miraculous. He chose a cute heart with three diamonds hanging on a chain. The price of it was $2,124. "I have only $2,000 in my account," Jim said, frustrated. "I like this heart, but I guess I don't have enough money, and I can't buy it."

"Well, sir, we can give you a special Christmas discount," the assistant said, feeling such pity for this poor handicapped midget who was lucky enough to have found a girlfriend and so desperately wanted to make her happy. "We can't empty your account completely. I'll give you a deal—$1,998." The assistant had just made a sale to Mona a few moments ago and now was able to be charitable.

"Really?" Jim said with uncertainty. "It would be so generous of you. I really want to give this as a present. Thank you very much."

Five minutes later, Jim left the store with a little beige velvety jeweler's box in his pocket and the two dollars left in his newly opened account. In high spirits and proud of himself, he walked toward the food court and suddenly noticed Todd inside an electronic store. He was trying out new earphones, and when his ears were free for a moment, Jim approached him and pulled his sleeve. "Hi, Todd," he said, looking up at him. "Are you buying new earphones?"

"Oh, it's you, little one." Todd giggled. "I didn't know who was pulling at me. Yes, I'm buying a present for my father. I'm sure he will like it as much as I do."

"Did you already buy something for your mother?" Jim asked. "She sent you a whole bag of presents. What did you get for her?"

"Jesus!" Todd grinned. "Are you sick, little one? My mom died five years ago. How could she send me presents? You're crazy."

"Sorry, I didn't know that," Jim said politely. He was surprised.

There must be some kind of misunderstanding, he thought. *Did Mona make a mistake, or did I? Or did she do that on purpose?*

"Is you mom's name Jean Spencer?" Jim asked.

"Of course!" Todd exclaimed and plugged his ears again. It was impossible to talk to him more. Then Todd paid for his earphones, looked down at Jim, and laughed. The mischievous idea appeared in his head. He bent over, put his arms around Jim's waist, lifted him, and sat him on his shoulders as if he were a three-year-old child.

"Hold my hat, buddy!" he shouted.

Laughing, Jim grabbed Todd's hat as hard as he could. It was exciting to look around from such a height. He had never experienced anything like this in his life ever. From the top of a tall man's shoulders, life was completely different. Jim enjoyed it, roaring with laughter. Todd put his father's present into his pocket, grabbed Jim's feet with both hands, and ran. They arrived at the food court like this, causing a lot of laughter among the people on their way and granting unparalleled pleasure to other group home residents and staff. Everybody felt satisfied.

Now was not the right time to talk to Mona about Todd's mother. Almost everyone had already finished their shopping, and the group was probably going to walk back through the mall to the main parking lot, where their bus was parked. So Jim decided to clear up his misunderstanding with Mona later that evening during their date, when he planned to give her the present.

However, when he came at ten o'clock to Mona's door and knocked, it was locked, and she didn't open. Jim knocked again and again and then walked back to his room, guessing that Mona was probably tired after their shopping trip and went to sleep earlier than usual. Returning to his room, Jim turned his music on and sat in front of the window, looking outside. He felt melancholic, yearning for romance, looking at the white backyard, the black forest, and the dark purple night sky above them. The garage and the fence cast a dark blue shadow on the snowy surface. Jim enjoyed the music and, almost sleepily, gazed at the peaceful night view.

Then he suddenly realized that something was wrong with this usual evening picture he saw daily. The group home bus was parked in front of the garage. Jim had never seen it there at nighttime. It was weird. *How come the bus is here?* Jim thought. *Ramah always goes home on the bus and then comes back in the morning. Is he here now? No, that's impossible. As far as I know, we don't have any extra rooms here. Or am I wrong? Maybe we do. Or is he still working in the basement?*

Jim didn't want to go check and look for Ramah. It wasn't important to him. It was such a trifle. He noticed the bus only because it caught his eye. So he continued to sit quietly, watching the shadows on the snow until the music ended. Then he took Mona's pledge of love, the limpid stone, from his pocket; kissed it; and peacefully went to bed.

CHAPTER 10

Over the next few days, Jim saw Mona only briefly. She was extremely busy organizing and preparing things and cooking for the group home Christmas party. "You'll come and love me after the party, baby," Mona told him, kissing his forehead on the run, "but not during these crazy days. Okay?"

It was a really strenuous and hectic time, and even Nurse Sue stayed off her regular duty and helped Mona cook. In the evening, Todd, Ella, and Maggie decorated the living room walls and a huge live Christmas tree that Ramah had placed in the corner. Jim understood that at the moment, in such a rush, Mona would not be able to appreciate his present properly and decided to give it to her later, at the time they had set for their date.

So Jim continued to compose according his schedule, and during the breaks, he made phone calls from his newly connected cell phone. He wanted to say hello to some people he knew and to wish them a merry Christmas and a happy New Year. Jim spent one of his breaks visiting with Lily Donovan.

"Look, wee lad, what I bought when we went shopping," she said, showing him a box full of extravagant plastic toys and decorations. "All these are from a dollar store. They are presents for my girlfriends' kids."

"Do lesbians have kids?" he asked with surprise.

"Sure, most of them. Many girls get married, have children, and just then realize that they're on the wrong path. Men disappointed them, so they divorced and became lesbians."

"I could imagine that kind of disenchantment." Jim smirked bitterly. "Sometimes sex with a woman can be pretty unpleasant for me too. However, I would never agree to become gay."

"People are different, buddy."

"I know that. You sound like my grandma. That was her favorite expression. Do you have children too? From what I see, it seems you like them."

"Yes, I'm fond of them, but I didn't get a chance to have any. I'm one of the lesbians who was never married and never had any relationships with men. I prevented that according to my beliefs and convictions. But I really have a soft spot for kids, and I miss them. When my MS started, I left the Metropolitan Opera because I couldn't dance anymore on the level they required, but I was still able to teach for a number of years. So I became a dance teacher. It was great fun working with kids. I enjoyed it. Then my health got worse quite fast, and I had to leave that job too." Lily took a bottle of cider, opened it, and started to drink.

"Why do you always drink cider?" Jim asked. "Is it good for your MS?"

"I'm not sure. It contains a bit of alcohol, which I like, but it's better than liquor anyway. You know, I was an alcoholic a few years ago. Then I began treatment and stopped drinking because I got arthritis and osteoporosis in addition to my MS. The alcohol really worsened my condition. I'm much better now."

"Oh God," Jim said, shaking his head. "It looks to me as though you have the whole American bouquet—lesbian, alcoholic, MS, arthritis, osteoporosis."

Lily laughed briskly, choking on her drink. "You're not very nice." She grinned. "It's not the whole bouquet but just a part of it. For the whole bouquet, you need to add cancer, AIDS, and drugs, which I don't use. Your mother must have used drugs. That's why you was born so odd. Did she?"

"I really don't know," Jim answered, scrutinizing the toys in the box. "My grandma was quite sure about that because I'm absolutely healthy. I don't have any disease. I was just hurt somehow in the womb. Something must have happened, but nobody knows exactly what."

"Oh, by the way, I remembered something for you, little rascal, that face that looked like yours. I was acquainted with this man. I danced with his group for a number of months. He was very famous . . . I . . . I forget his name . . . something starting with an *S*, I guess. In 1969, I left their group for the Metropolitan Opera. Then he was killed. It caused a big, big stir. He was on TV all the time . . . oh, shit! It was so long ago . . . I can't remember the exact year . . . it was in the fall. It was September, I guess. Oh yes, September . . . for sure. I'll remember for you, teeny guy. I promise. I'll talk to you later about it—after Christmas or maybe after the New Year because, you know, these days I am so damn busy. I'll have so many visitors soon. All my friends with their kids want to see me. I'm also going to go on a little vacation for a few days. I won't have any time to think and to remember anything."

"Okay." Jim nodded. "Thank you, Lily. There is no rush. I'm just curious to know. I'll see you at the party downstairs."

"No way!" Lily shook her head. "I'm not partying with Mona. My first partner, Bertha, who is like my mom . . . she is taking me to a gay and lesbian community's Christmas party. It will be a lot of fun! Oh, good idea! I can ask Bertha for you. She is twenty years older than me. She was a mature woman at that time, not like me. I was a teenager with a head full of wind instead of brain, but she was an adult and smart, and she has a very good memory—fantastic memory. She knows everything."

"Don't worry, Lily. It's okay. Well, if I won't see you at our party . . . merry Christmas. It would probably be all right to give you a friendly hug, but I'm not sure that you'd like that."

"I'm sure as a hell would not, you little bastard!" Lily giggled. "No man has ever touched me. You're a man, aren't you? I'm not sure."

"Yes, I am."

"So merry Christmas, miniman. See you after the holidays then."

Jim left Lily's room smiling. Today she was cute and funny but not angry. This left a nice, friendly feeling with Jim, which was appropriate for the happy Christmastime. It felt like he might possibly have found a friend to communicate with.

Being in a really good mood, he had quick lunch, washed the rats, and returned to his composing. He had to work—it didn't matter that it was a holiday. His break for today was finished.

CHAPTER *11*

The Christmas party the next day was amazing. Jim had never experienced anything like it during his life on the farm with Grandma Cathy. She usually celebrated only Ukrainian Christmas on January 7. They always had a special dinner that she ordered from a restaurant, and then Grandma Cathy would hand Jim the presents. He, in turn, played for her his new music that was dedicated to her. Neither of them had anybody to invite to Christmas dinner. They were happy, quiet, and satisfied together but felt quite lonely.

At the group home, however, there was a big party. Everybody was invited—the friends, relatives of the residents, and even the staff and their families. But nobody from Mona's family appeared. Everyone knew her husband, Barry, well, and she announced to them that he was still sick and was being treated at the hospital. As the pianist, her daughter, Sharon, was on a Christmas tour in the eastern states of America and was supposed to return two weeks later.

Ella's mother and two daughters were present as were Todd's father, Maggie's grandmother, and even Victor's elder brother. Lily, as she promised, left with Bertha before the party began. All the nurses brought their spouses and children. Ramah came alone. He said that his parents were very religious and didn't celebrate American Christmas, but they gave him permission to come out of respect for his coworkers. For the same reason, nobody came to see Ali and Zahra, and they were given shots so they would sleep quietly in their room during the party.

Jim had nobody to invite. However, he didn't feel alone. He was friends with other residents and nurses too and could communicate successfully without feeling shy. The group home had become his home, and he was beginning to accept the residents and staff as his newfound family. He seemed confident, content, and elated.

The delicious dinner excited the guests. Then the folks took small presents from under the Christmas tree. Mona organized some games and other activities that caused a lot of laughter and fun. Everybody had a good time at the party.

When it ended, Jim came to see Mona. She was lying on her bed, tired and relaxed. Her naked body looked surreal—it appeared silver blue in the moonlight, which was streaming in through the window. A fantastic diamond necklace hung from her neck, iridescently shining in the gloominess of the room. It was the only thing she was wearing. Jim stopped before her in astonishment. The miraculous beauty of the scene overwhelmed him.

"Look, my sweet boy," Mona said in an amorous voice. "This is a present I bought for myself for just $16 at the thrift store. I was lucky to get it at such a price. Nobody believes that these are artificial stones, just polished pieces of a glass, because they look so perfect. I hope you will believe me, my baby."

"I do believe you because I trust you, Mona," Jim said sincerely. He really wanted to believe her.

I was told that there is nothing cheap at the store where I saw her, he thought, trying to find a reasonable explanation. *Maybe she didn't buy anything there. Maybe she just took a necklace to the jewelry store to be repaired for her daughter . . . or some other relative . . .and this one . . . maybe she really bought it at the thrift store on a different day. Maybe.*

"I want to thank you for the amazing party," Jim continued. "Thank you for everything, Mona. I want to wish you a merry Christmas in private, from myself only, and I brought you a present as a symbol of . . ." He stopped for a second, looking for the proper word. He didn't want to use the word *love* because he still wasn't sure what love was really.

After he thought for a moment, he continued, "Of my sincere gratitude."

Mona laughed playfully, sensing his uncertainty. "I'm still not quite sure. Are you too careful, too cunning, or too stubborn, baby? Why don't you want to confess your love for me? Who is closer in the world than we are? Anyway, thank you." She sat on the bed and looked at him questioningly, not seeing any present in his hands. Jim took a little jewelry box out from his pocket and handed it to her.

"Oh my goodness!" she exclaimed, taking the box. "I don't have enough nerve to open it. I hope it's not an engagement ring. I'm still not divorced from Barry, my darling, so I can't marry you yet." She opened the box but couldn't see clearly what was inside as the room was dark. Mona turned on a little lamp on the bedside table on which Jim noticed a bottle of champagne, two champagne glasses, and small bowls with whipped cream and sliced strawberries and pineapple.

"Dessert," she said, pointing at the stuff and giving Jim a wink. Then she took a deep breath, like a swimmer would right before a dive, and opened the box. "Oh Jesus!"

"This certainly isn't cheap, Mona," Jim said proudly. "I know that you like jewelry with diamonds, but you can't afford real gems. These ones are authentic diamonds of the highest quality—probably the first ones you've ever had. They're just tiny because I couldn't afford a bigger size yet. Later, if I get more money, I'll buy you more."

"Oh!" Mona didn't even know what to say but remained silent in awe. "Baby!" she exclaimed, hugging him. "I'm touched! I didn't expect anything like this. We have been together for two months already, but I still know so little about you. Thank you very much, my darling. I really appreciate your feelings toward me, and I sincerely love you, baby. You're so cute. But, darling, I need to explain something to you."

She undressed him, sat him on her lap, turned his face to her, hugged him, and looked straight into his eyes. "My sweet boy," she said, "it's nice to be generous, but you shouldn't be silly. I mean, you must understand the value of money. You were too spoiled by your grandma, and you don't know what life is really like. What was the price of this pendant?"

"More than $2,000, but they gave me a discount."

"So what's left in your account?"

"$2."

"Isn't that silly? How will you live this month?"

"I don't know." He shrugged as he continued, "I have everything I need. I don't need to buy anything for myself."

"But you need to pay your bills, rent, food, service, electricity, heating, TV cable, cell phone, internet."

"You said that you would pay for all that."

"I'll pay for you as a favor, to help you but from your account. Now your account is empty. How can I pay your January bills for you? That $2,000 that the sponsor gave you, in addition to your tiny pension, is barely enough to cover your living expenses. You have nothing left over."

"How did I live here in November and December?"

"You lived in debt, like I told you already, but now the sponsor paid your debt. Now everything from past months has been taken care of, but what about the coming months?"

Jim's face reddened. He bit his trembling lip. "So . . . it doesn't matter that you found a sponsor for me," he whispered. "I am still very poor. I still don't have an extra penny to give a Christmas present to my woman." He felt overwhelmed and tried hard to hold back his tears. He could not speak.

Mona smiled haughtily, seeing that he was humiliated enough. "Baby," she said, lovingly kissing his face, "you're not in trouble because I love you. I'll help you this time and pay all your bills, seeing that you love me too. Just be more prudent with money in the future. Don't buy anything without consulting me first."

"But I wanted to surprise you."

"I know, my sweet boy. You wanted to make me happy . . . that's why I'm forgiving you. Now I'll give you a chance to really pleasure me, and it will cost you nothing. You'll just enjoy time with me. Look, we're going to play a new game today. First, you probably need a couple of teaspoons of champagne to be more relaxed so we can start."

She poured a little champagne into his glass, and Jim drank it greedily, feeling that he really needed it at the moment to calm his nerves and to concentrate on Mona's body. Her sexual creativity frightened him, but he tried desperately not to reveal that to her.

Mona already knew perfectly well how to deal with him. She threw herself back on the bed, pulled him on top of her, pressed his small body to her chest, hugged him, and started to kiss him passionately. Jim moaned, giving in completely. His mind floated somewhere else.

It was easy for Mona to drive him slowly to the highest state; then she pushed him away, took a handful of whipped cream from the bowl, smeared her breasts, and garnished them with the pieces of fruit. "Lick it, baby," she said, smiling coyly. "It's tasty."

By now, Jim was so turned on that he couldn't resist. It was truly delicious, and even after all the whipped cream had been licked up, he still continued sucking her breasts, unable to tear himself from them. He lost control, and Mona delighted in it, laughing victoriously and reveling in her power over him.

I'll train you like a dog, my little animal, she moaned in her thoughts with a sadistic joy, wiggling her shoulders with excitement. *I'll squash you and step on you! Oh, I'll bring you down a level or two, my dear genius! My dear talent!*

She smeared more whipped cream on her chest and her stomach, growling with pleasure, giggling, and making a little trail of fruit down toward her pubic region, which was unusually well shaven today. Unconsciously, Jim followed this trail in a craze, sucking in and swallowing the fruit pieces and licking the whipped cream until his face ended up right where Mona wanted it. Jim did everything she wanted, not clearly realizing what he was doing. He acted like a zombie or like a rabbit that jumped voluntarily into the open jaws of a boa constrictor as if under hypnosis. He couldn't stop, and Mona, trembling and howling in ecstasy, held his head there, sliding strong fingers through his hair.

Only when all the whipped cream and fruit were finished and Mona had had multiple orgasms did she pull Jim up by his hair. She forced him into intercourse, and he entered inside her, kissing her sweet chest and adhering to it with his lips, cheeks, and wavy dark brown hair. Tonight he felt much hotter and full of lust than he usually did with Mona. It was the first time he started to finally realize what the words *sexual attraction* and *sexual desire* meant. He really wanted her and deeply enjoyed being inside her.

Then Mona brought him to the bathtub, and they took a shower together. She changed the bedsheets, which were all sticky after the crazy game; and then they rested, quiet and relaxed, on the clean bed. Jim put his head on Mona's shoulder and pressed himself to her side like a child, feeling so open and trusting of her, even much more than before.

"How do you like our new game?" Mona asked quietly. "It's my favorite. I'm hoping that you'll do that all the time for me, baby. That way, you'll satisfy me perfectly. I need to be satisfied. At my age, it's very important. The whole hormone system is changing now. I need your sperm for sure, but I need the pleasure from your lips and tongue even more."

Jim lay speechless. He felt too weak and too suppressed, even humiliated, so much so that he couldn't say anything. In spite of his fatigue, he didn't want to sleep. Some thoughts were bothering him. "Mona," he said finally in a hushed voice, "can I talk to you? I want to be closer to you."

"Aren't we close enough?"

"No, I mean, spiritually closer. I want more, much more. I don't completely understand you."

"You understood perfectly, baby." Mona guffawed. "That's what I wanted from you tonight."

"I want to talk about other things," he said, feeling offended.

"What kinds of things?"

"About that woman in the black car . . . who gave you a bag . . . I asked Todd. He said that his mother, Jean Spencer, died a few years ago."

There was silence for several seconds, and then Mona grinned. "Todd? He is schizophrenic. What could he say to you? Oh, you're silly, baby. There's no reason to talk to him. He's a total idiot. This woman is his mother. It's 100 percent true. Don't you trust me, my sweet boy? Why? I gave you everything . . . I gave you my whole body . . . and you're still asking me questions!"

"I trust you. I just want to understand. It's some kind of misunderstanding, I guess. Why was Todd's father at the party alone if his mother is alive?"

Mona laughed. "Jesus! Baby! They're divorced and are living in different cities and have different families. They don't want to have any connection with each other, but both of them love Todd. His father is visiting him and his mother, hiding, brought him presents another day. She didn't want to be seen by anybody. It's their private relationship and nobody's business. You shouldn't put your nose in this. Don't you agree?"

"Yeah," Jim agreed. The explanation about Todd's mother sounded convincing, but Jim still saw in front of his eyes the scene—the strange woman, with an expression of disdain and disgust on her face, threw the bag to Mona. It was not the way to pass Christmas presents for her son to his caregiver. "Why did Jane Spencer throw the bag to you instead of giving it properly into your hands?"

"Because she is a rich and arrogant bitch, but I am a poor, simple, hardworking woman. Isn't it clear, Jim?"

It could be, possibly, he thought. He had nothing to ask about this subject anymore.

"I have another question," Jim continued confusingly after some minutes of silence. "Why is Ramah sometimes here at night? Does he do some security work on top of his other duties, or—"

"Why are you asking that? He was never here at night!" Mona exclaimed indignantly.

"I saw Ramah's bus parked beside the garage a couple of times in the evening. Usually, he goes home on the bus after the guys came from work and returns in the morning to pick them up. Isn't that true?"

"Are you accusing me of sleeping with him?"

"For God's sake, Mona, what do you mean? I didn't make any guesses about you ever! I was just curious about why the bus was here, that's it!" Jim protested. "I'm used to understanding everything that's going on in life. Grandma Cathy always explained things that I was asking about."

"Why didn't she explain anything to you about money and banks? Why didn't she prepare you for today's society?" Mona teased sarcastically with a venom in her voice.

"Because I didn't ask. I didn't care. I lived in the forest," Jim replied heatedly, trying to protect the memory of Grandma Cathy from Mona's constant attacks. "Sorry if I hurt you. I don't see anything offensive in my question. You're the boss, and I believed that you should know why the bus is here at such an unusual time."

"Of course, I know," Mona said sternly, still seething with anger for Jim. "Sometimes Ramah needs a car when he goes on a date with his girlfriend. He asked my permission to leave the bus here and to take my car instead. We're friends with him, so I give him permission. It happens. What's the problem with that?"

"No problem, I was just curious."

"You're not a child, Jim. You don't need to be so curious. Curiosity killed the cat."

"Well . . ." Jim felt rejected seeing that his heart-to-heart conversation with Mona had turned sour. "It's sad that you do not really understand me. I didn't expect this. Even with Lily, it's easier to chat."

"With Lily? Did you talk to her after I introduced you?"

"Yes, I visit her sometimes."

"Really? That's strange. She usually never talks with men."

"She probably made an exception for me, not considering me a man. Maybe I look more like a child to her, and she loves kids. Sometimes she's quite rude and judgmental, but she knows many things that are unusual to me. She doesn't have a bad sense of humor, so we laugh sometimes. Underneath the surface, I can see a pretty soft heart. I feel pity for her. And it's amusing that my face reminds her of somebody she knew—a famous man who was killed many years ago . . . in September. She just can't remember his name, but she promised to consult with her friends and to find out for me. Isn't that curious? It looks like we have something in common." Jim felt that Mona's shoulder strained under his ear.

"I'm jealous, baby," she said with a fake smile, pretending to look at him playfully. "I don't like you talking with Lily. She's too sick and can have a bad influence on you. Did she tell you something bad about me?"

"Mm . . ." Jim didn't know what to answer. He didn't want to lie, but to tell the truth now would mean betraying Lily. She was open and honest with him, and he didn't feel he had the right to tell anyone—especially Mona—the information he had gotten from her. However, to keep silence would be ethically wrong as well because Mona could know that that meant the answer was *yes*. Jim had to say something. "No . . . nothing bad. Lily just told me that you were friends at the start."

"Yes, we were, but she's sick, you know. It was impossible to be friends with her too long. She wasn't responsible with her money, just like you. And pretty fast, all her savings disappeared from her account. That's understandable. It's exactly what should happen because she spent too much on entertainment. But her sick imagination in her ill head drew the picture of robbery or some other stupidity, and she started to accuse me. It was a lie. Her behavior was really rude and unfair toward me. She caused a couple of horrible scandals. After that, it was impossible for me to maintain our friendship. If I did, it would mean that I didn't respect myself. We're just officially cold with each other now.

Than thank God, her gay and lesbian community started to help her which calmed her down. That was good for me because Lily had finally refuted her idea to ask for an investigation into her missing money, which would have been dangerous—our group home and I as well could lose our perfect reputations. You know, in such a case, the media is usually involved and makes a big stir. It's very bad. I'm just happy that this is all over."

"How long ago did it happen?" Jim asked.

"About five years ago."

"No, Lily didn't tell me anything about that, not one word," Jim confirmed. "Actually, I don't have a lot of free time to chat with people. My schedule is quite full, but sometimes I need to relax and to talk. I don't visit her very often. You shouldn't worry about me. No one will be a bad influence. By the way, Mona, you're the same age as Lily. Maybe you could remember what happened in September . . . many years ago . . . probably in 1969. Who was this man who was killed and whose face looked like mine? Lily told me that he was everywhere—on TV, in newspapers, magazines. She promised to remember all the details of the story for me."

"She couldn't. Her memory is completely lost because of the MS."

"She'll ask all her friends to remember for me."

Jim felt that Mona was worried as she said abruptly, "No, baby, it's out of the question. First of all, this is Lily's sick imagination again. You don't remind me of anybody, absolutely not. Another thing, we live in America. Here is probably a part of our American culture. Every year, sometimes two or three times a year, a huge scandal occurs in which famous people are killed. It happens all the time. Hundreds of them are killed—Hollywood stars, singers, athletes, politicians, even presidents. It's absolutely impossible to remember all those scandals, and it would be silly to keep all of them in one's mind. I never watch such things on TV. I don't like them. They're disturbing. I don't want to worry or to suffer because of somebody. I have enough suffering in my own life—a mentally ill husband, divorce, really hard work, my daughter's poverty, crazy patients around, like Lily. I'm so unhappy and poor. The only happiness in my life is you, my sweet love. You're my light, my pleasure, my trust, my heart. You and your symphony are my only hope."

Mona turned to Jim and kissed him affectionately. "Thank you for being with me, baby," she whispered.

"You're amazing, Mona," he said, hugging her and feeling with his fingers the fine chain—she had already put her necklace away and put his present on. "I'm really sorry that I bothered you with my silly questions. I promise never to do that again."

CHAPTER 12

Quite a few days after Christmas, Jim was completely busy with composing. He missed a number of hours of it because of the shopping day, the party, and the other Christmas events and now tried to make up for lost time. He didn't even know if Lily had returned home after her trip or not. One day he finally decided to see her during his break.

However, when Jim approached Lily's door, he heard agitated loud voices inside. He stopped, recognizing surprisingly that the other voice belonged to Mona. Obviously, they were arguing, trying to hush their voices; but at times, they lost control of their emotions, and the words came screaming out, being heard even outside the closed door. "You have no right!" Mona shouted, banging her fist on the table so hard that Lily's bottles of cider clinked against one another.

"Why?" Lily screamed.

"'Cause I don't want it!"

"You're a piece of shit! I'll do what I want! I knew Emmanuel! I knew him well!"

"Leave him alone. Don't tell anything to him, or I'll shut you up!"

Jim's heart pounded. Both of them sounded so angry that it frightened him. He couldn't guess that his nice and quiet Mona could be so uncivilized and aggressive. Sometimes she was a bit bossy and manipulative, even with him, but not as much and not as rude as now.

Lily wasn't any better. They sounded like two mad tigresses or two jealously infuriated women who couldn't share a man and were ready to kill each other. Who was this Emmanuel? Jim had never heard of him except . . . except his own middle name was Emmanuel. However, Jim was quite sure that Mona's fight with Lily wasn't related to him. In his opinion, it was something between the two of them from their past.

"My God," Jim whispered, scowling slightly as he walked away as fast as he could. He didn't want to hear such things and didn't want the women to notice that he had heard. He went down to the basement and started to wash the rats and the cage, quietly humming some of the beautiful melodies from his symphony, trying to relax and not to think about the scandal.

A few minutes later, Jim heard the sound of the elevator coming down. The door opened beside him, and an enraged Mona barged into the basement. Not saying a word to him, she ran to the refrigerator, took out a box of cider bottles, and carried it quickly back to the elevator. Jim shut the hose off, trying not to spray her as she passed by. "Thank you, baby." She hissed to him. "I'm really in a hurry. Talk to you later. Keep working."

Jim continued working, realizing that the best way to behave now was to act as if nothing had happened. He promised Mona that he would suppress his curiosity, and he sincerely attempted to do so. Ten minutes later, Jim finished his task and took the elevator up to the main floor.

Mona was in the kitchen and was grinding something with a small brass mortar and pestle. The box of cider was on the table. It was open, and Jim noticed that some of the bottles were open as well. Their lids were on the counter beside the box. Mona seemed to calm down now. "Hi, baby," she said nicely as Jim approached her. "Sorry, I didn't pay much attention to you. I'm still horribly busy. I decided to make pancakes with whipped cream and discovered suddenly that we're out of icing sugar. I don't have time to go and buy more, so I started to use this cute little antique thing to pound cubes of sugar into a powder like in the good old days. Isn't it funny?"

"Not to me," Jim said. "I remember my grandma used it sometimes at the farm for the same purpose. We lived, like here, quite deep in the forest, and shopping centers were pretty far away. Are you drinking cider?" He pointed at the open bottles. "Like Lily?"

"No." Mona laughed playfully. "I just use it for cooking sometimes. It goes in many special recipes."

"Okay. If dinner is not ready yet, I can go to my room and play a bit more," Jim said, wanting to climb up the stairs.

Mona stopped him. "Darling," she begged, "could you please go outside and shovel the main driveway? It snowed after the guys left for work. It would be nice to have it clean when they returned. Would you mind doing that for me right now, sweet boy?"

"Okay." Jim nodded. "Of course, I can. No problem, Mona."

He dressed warmly, took his red shovel, and went outside. It was sunny out, and the snow cloud had already passed. A light covering of newly fallen snow sat on the steps and the pathway that led to the bus stop.

Jim started to shovel, which was very easy today. Actually, there wasn't enough snow to scoop up. He just played a bit, not quite understanding why Mona had asked him to shovel the snow when it wasn't really necessary. Anyway, he did it quite fast; and in fifteen minutes, he was already finished.

When Jim returned home, Mona still was in the kitchen, but the box of cider had disappeared from the counter, just like the mortar and the pestle. There was a plate with pancakes instead. More pancakes were frying on the stove. "Dinner is ready for you, sweetheart," Mona said fondly. "Do you want eggs and sausages too or just pancakes?"

"After working in the fresh air, I'm as hungry as a wolf but not as hungry as an elephant." Jim laughed. "So I only want two pancakes."

"Good, my baby." Mona put the pancakes on the plate for him and decorated them with whipped cream, blueberries, sliced strawberries, and kiwi. Then she placed the plate on the tray together with a cup of hot tea. "Enjoy, my baby, and remember how you were enjoying the same dessert when we were having sex. Hopefully, we'll do it again in a few days, won't we?"

Jim chuckled, took the tray from her hands, and went to eat in his room. He took the elevator to the second floor because he couldn't climb up the stairs with the tray in his hands. He spent the rest of the day composing and listening to music. He remained occupied in his room and didn't come out.

The next morning, Jim was awoken by a very unusual noise— somebody was running up and down the hallway. Rona and Andy, two nurses, were shouting something to each other and down to Mona. Doors and windows were slamming shut. Then he heard the doorbell ring, and a group of strange men arrived and went upstairs. They were speaking loudly and sounded agitated.

Jim peered out from his room and saw that the men were paramedics because they had a stretcher, which they left in the hallway beside the door to the next room. It was Lily's room, and Jim realized right away that something bad had happened. He remained standing and watching at the doorframe, feeling feverish, until Andy passed him, hurrying downstairs. "Andy, what's going on?" Jim asked impatiently.

"Lily died," the nurse answered quickly, not stopping for a second.

"What? How come?" Jim couldn't believe his ears. "Yesterday she was okay. She was so active," he whispered in frustration, remembering the scandal between Lily and Mona, but Andy didn't listen to him and was already gone.

The paramedics pulled the stretcher inside the room, maybe to put Lily's body on it. Then Mona appeared from Lily's room and pressed the elevator button. "Mona!" Jim called out with an unsteady voice. "How could this happen? I can't believe it's true."

She looked at him and scowled. "Things like this happen, baby," she said in a crying voice. "Usually, people with MS die suddenly. It's always like that. Believe me, I have experience. We've had many MS patients here during the last twenty years. You better stay in your room and not watch. She doesn't look her best. It's quite sad. It would be good if you could play some appropriate music."

Jim closed his door, ran through his CDs, and found the "Funeral March" from the *Piano Sonata No. 2* of Chopin, "Lacrimosa" from Mozart's *Requiem*, and then "Et incarnatus est" from Bach's *Mass in H - minor*. These were the best songs for a funeral that human beings had ever created in all history. The music conveyed the sound of tragedy, of holiness and had an air of deep spirituality so that it was impossible to hear it without tears in one's eyes.

Jim turned the music on, lay on his bed, and buried his face in his pillow. Lily wasn't his friend; he had only seen her three times, so he couldn't understand why her death moved him so deeply, probably no less than Grandma's Cathy death. He was in total despair and cried for a long while, playing the same music again and again.

Then he heard someone knock lightly at his door. It might have continued for a while, but he didn't hear it right away because his head was filled with music. When Jim finally realized that someone was knocking, he stood up, turned off the player, and walked to open the door.

There was a tall elderly gray-haired woman in front of him. Her hair was cut short and styled in a manlike fashion. She looked so masculine that Jim was surprised that she knocked so lightly. It would have been easy for her to break the door down. However, she was very quiet; her tear-stained red face was full of grief. In her hands, she held something wrapped in a paper towel. "Sorry to bother you," the woman murmured in a trembling voice. "I'm Bertha, Lily's friend. And you're Jim, I guess . . . I want to thank you for the amazing music you played in her memory. She was like my daughter."

"Come in, please," Jim said, moving back from the door and letting her in.

Bertha came in and sat on the chair beside the piano, which was the only chair of normal height. Whatever she was holding, she set on top of the piano. "I want to hand you this present from Lily. It is your inheritance, I guess," she continued talking while unwrapping the towel. Inside was a little statue of a very unusual shape made of gray marble. It was a young naked woman in a sitting posture, now placed on the edge of the piano top. Her legs were hanging down, and her arms were crossed on her knees. Her head was lowered so her face was not visible, but her long free hair hung down to her feet in front of her figure. Her body and hair created a circular shape. It was a masterpiece. The marble seemed to breathe as if it were alive, and the entire statue radiated an overwhelming sadness.

"Thank you," Jim said sincerely, gazing at the sculpture with excitement.

"To Lily, this figure was the symbol of true love," Bertha continued pensively. "She knew that she might die quite soon and made notes on each of her things, clarifying to whom she wanted each to be given after her death. I came to pick up all her stuff and execute her will—deliver everything to her friends. Your name was written on the sticker on this statue. Maybe Lily thought that only you could appreciate its true value. Maybe there was another reason why she wanted to give it to you. I don't know."

Jim didn't know too. He didn't expect this. He thought that Lily was just an acquaintance, and he felt he didn't deserve such a present from her. She always teased him and called him names.

"Lily Donovan left behind a lot of good memories in many people's hearts." Bertha took a deep breath, drying her face with a paper napkin.

"The only thing she didn't leave is money. Didn't she tell you what happened with her money a few years back?"

Jim shook his head.

"The woman who runs this place stole it all from her account. Lily trusted her. They were best friends. So Lily gave her everything—her PINs, her checks, a sample of her signature, complete access to her account—and Mona emptied it just like that. She is a beast! Lily called her a 'white rat.'"

Jim grimaced. He didn't believe her. "If something like that happened, why wasn't there an investigation?" he asked distrustfully.

Bertha waved her hand and continued to speak, weeping again. "This woman is smart enough. Everything was made to look as if Lily spent all the money by herself. Mona is a dictator here and does what she wants. Everybody knows that and keeps silent."

"Why?"

"Everybody is scared of her. She is an evil woman capable of anything."

"My God." Jim sighed, feeling frustrated. "Luckily, I only have $2 in my account. But really, Mona is so nice. She doesn't seem like the type of person you are describing." He choked suddenly, remembering Mona's fight with Lily yesterday and feeling anxious.

"Sorry about that," Bertha mumbled, sobbing. "Maybe it's not nice of me to say such things. I'm just too sad and can't forgive this woman for Lily's suffering. That's why I'm probably not impartial. Anyway, keep the statue, remember Lily, and be careful with Mona. That's my advice. I'm sorry I can't give you a hug. You know, I'm a lesbian too."

"Okay," Jim said dolefully. "Thank you for visiting and for the present. The figure is so spiritual. I'm sure I'll remember Lily forever."

After Bertha left, Jim turned the music on again and sat for a long time, looking at the sculpture. The marble girl expressed so much sorrow that her somberness matched the situation perfectly.

In a couple of hours, Jim finally found the willpower to hold his mood in check and to walk down to the basement to wash the rats. He was surprised to see Mona there with hose in her hand. A plastic box full of empty cider bottles was on the floor in front of her, and she was washing them. The water flowed around the room and dripped from the cage. The rats had already had their shower.

"Sorry, baby, I did your work myself today," she said, looking at Jim with a guilty, confused smile. "I just decided to rinse these bottles before taking them for a refund because they were too sticky and stunk of cider. So I cleaned my cuties at the same time. You lost a lot of your composing time today. You'd better go and work on your symphony. I can manage here. Okay, my sweet boy?"

Jim nodded, not quite grasping what was going on. He knew that Mona usually hated doing the washing. "Well . . ." He shrugged and went to go to his room.

"Baby!" Mona called to his back. "We are both so frustrated today. We need to caress each other tonight for sure. Come at ten this evening."

"Maybe we should have a date tomorrow?" he asked, turning and looking at her with uncertainty. "This day is too tragic. It would be sacrilege to make love at such a time."

"No, baby," Mona insisted powerfully, showing clearly that she wouldn't tolerate any arguments. "I want you too much, darling. Tonight! For our dessert game!"

Jim smirked as he nodded and silently left for his room. He felt embarrassed, unpleasantly realizing that he had behaved like a slave, but he couldn't do anything about it now. Jim believed that he wanted this woman too, he wanted to have sex with her, and he couldn't live without it.

CHAPTER 13

When Jim came to the living room and announced that Lily had died several days ago, nothing changed. He was surprised that this sad event didn't matter to the other residents. The absence of any reaction seemed strange to him. Jim had never seen mentally ill people during his life on the farm and had no experience in special techniques to treat them in the group home now. As a rule, he addressed them daily, considering them normal. Sometimes it worked; sometimes it didn't.

Jim tried to say something nice in Lily's memory, but it didn't work. Victor sat motionless. Todd went to listen to his music, humming. Maggie carried on watching TV. Only Ella did something different from usual. "How come you're talking to me, Jim?" she shouted angrily. "How do you know that I'm here? You can't see me!"

"Why not?"

"Because I'm not here. I'm in the forest, hiding behind a tree. And don't argue! Do you see my tree?" She took her hand from in front of her face and turned it toward Jim. Inside her palm, he saw a tiny Christmas tree. Now he realized what she meant. "I bought it on the last shopping trip," Ella explained, "just to hide behind it and have some privacy. I'm tired of all of you. Look at Maggie. She's getting fatter every day. There is almost no room for me to sit with her on the couch. I'm tired of this stony man who is always silent." She pointed at Victor. "But most of all, I'm tired of that pockmarked panama-head singer, pulling Maggie's breasts and squeezing her bum with his huge fingers, even at work. He doesn't even let her pass by. He catches her every time."

"I have never seen that." Jim was surprised. "Look, he is sitting pretty far away from her and playing solitaire. As far as I can see, he's busy with other things."

"Just at home. He's scared of Mona. She gave him a hell of a lecture already about touching Maggie. Now he's smart enough to do that in places where she can't see, like on the bus and at the factory." Ella sounded so agitated that, to Jim, it looked as though she was jealous and would have preferred that she be touched instead of Maggie. However, he didn't say a thing to her but only shook his head in uncertainty.

"I'm even tired of you, Jim, being so little. You're irritating me. I don't want to see you, and I don't want to talk to you. That's why I'm hiding behind the tree." She took her tiny tree by its stand with two fingers and held it right before her nose, pretending to hide.

"Sorry to bother you, Ella," Jim answered, feeling dejected but not offended. Ella's declaration didn't hurt him much because he had finally realized she was completely ill. "I just thought that you should know about Lily's death. She was your neighbor."

"Who's Lily? That lady in a wheelchair? There are too many of them. I don't like cripples. They bother me. I'm a healthy person and like to be around healthy people, like these guys over here. But even they drive me crazy. So I'm hiding, and I can't see you or them, and I'm not listening to you anymore. I'm in the forest."

"Okay, Ella, enjoy the smell of the fir trees. I won't disturb you anymore," Jim said unhappily and walked away.

He saw once again that there was nobody to socialize with, except for Mona. Afterward, Jim understood why he had unconsciously reached out to Lily—even with her "half-American bouquet" and difficult character, she was a mentally healthy person able to talk normally. There was a big difference between her and the other group home residents. He knew that he would really miss her.

Jim had no choice but to continue composing, maintain his relationship with Mona, and refuse forever the idea to find more friends inside the small group home community. But Jim didn't suffer a lot because of that; he just was a bit disappointed. At the farm, he was accustomed to being alone. Only his best friend, his music, was always with him—his symphony thrived, taking up most of his time and his soul. More than half the final part of his creation was already finished. So life continued quietly and regularly.

CHAPTER 14

One evening at the end of February, Jim went outside with his shovel to clear the snow as usual. There was quite a lot of snow outside, and Ramah had already shoveled it before dinner, but after he had gone home, it continued to snow for a while, so Jim had a bit of work left to do. Jim was surprised to hear the sound of a car approaching. It was quite late and an unusual time for visitors. Jim's heart started to beat faster. He guessed that it might be the mysterious woman in the black car again. In his mind, he believed Mona's claim that she was Todd's mother; but unconsciously, he sensed that something was wrong, and he yearned to see the stranger again or maybe even talk to her.

However, turning toward the driveway, Jim was disappointed. A bright red sports car, quite different from the black Mercedes of the mysterious woman, had stopped near the main entrance. A young woman got out of the car and swiftly walked to the main door. Though it wasn't windy outside, her long black coat flapped as if in the wind along with her red scarf and wavy dark brown hair. She looked conceited and arrogant as she passed Jim without even noticing him. When he went outside, Jim had left the door unlocked so the woman didn't need to buzz. She walked right inside as if she were entering her own home.

Jim stood outside for a few minutes in surprise, just gazing at the door that closed behind her and trying to guess who she could be. He guessed that she was Mona's daughter due to her confident behavior, but she didn't look like Mona at all. She was much shorter, dark haired, and in great shape. Her features were very different from Mona's—chiseled, much rougher. They looked like nature had used not tiny carving knives to work on her face but an ax. *Maybe she looked like her father, Mona's husband, Barry*, Jim guessed.

Her car was the only thing that seemed not to fit with this explanation. Jim had heard Mona say often that her daughter, Sharon, was very poor, but this bright red sports car appeared expensive to Jim. His investigative mind took hold of him once more. He forgot all the promises he had made to Mona to suppress it. He finished shoveling the snow as fast as he could, walked home, and looked the car up on the internet. It was an Aston Martin Vanquish S, which cost more than a quarter of a million dollars.

No, it's not Mona's daughter, he said to himself. *But who else would show up so late? The nurses are gone, and the guys are already in bed. Could she be visiting with one of them?*

While Jim pondered these questions, the young woman was sitting in Mona's living room and drinking tea. Mona, beaming with joy, put cookies and tea on the table. It had to be her daughter, Sharon, whom she hadn't seen for quite a long time and missed terribly.

"Tell me, how was your trip, sweetie?" Mona asked impatiently, smiling and looking into Sharon's brown eyes from time to time. She had already hugged and held her tightly, yelling with excitement as she came in. Now she wanted to hug Sharon more and more as she gazed at her, proudly believing that she was the most beautiful and most talented young woman in the world, like every mother believes about her daughter.

Sharon took her coat, scarf, and sweater off and relaxed in the chair. "Oh, it's getting hot," she said, sipping her tea and waving with her hand in front of her face as if to fan herself.

"Sorry, sweetie, I'll turn the heating off." Mona jumped up and ran to thermostat.

"It's okay, Mom." Sharon calmed her down peacefully. "Sorry, I didn't answer your question. Yes, the trip was good but extremely difficult. You know, there are too many good pianists around. The competition is big. To be the best, I need to play for twelve hours a day. It's the hardest work in the world. I'm tired of it, and I'm not really sure that I want do this in the future anymore."

"I want you to be famous so you can make more money from each concert," Mona explained. "In reality, your name means more than the music. With millions in your account, you can rest and relax . . . but not yet."

"I know, Mom, it's your concept. I can't say that I disagree with that. Of course, who doesn't want to be rich? But it's too heavy a task for me. I can't sit by the piano for twelve hours a day. I can't, Mom. Don't you understand? I want to have a personal life. I want to go out with friends. I want to go to parties. I want to find a boyfriend finally. I'm young. I want to live but not to work as hard as a horse through my youth. What's the use of being a millionaire if I'm old, ugly, and paralyzed?"

"Come on, sweetie. What do you mean? Why would you be paralyzed?"

"Because I'm sitting in one spot at the piano for so long. I get dead tired. It's impossible to sit for so long. When I finish playing, I can't stand up right away and have to stay slightly bent over with pain in my back and stomach. It's horrible, Mom. This life is making me handicapped. I'm sick and unhappy.

"This tour went well, but sure, it cost me. And at the last concert, I broke down. You know, it was Schumann's *Carnaval*, one of the most difficult pieces to play. I've always been scared to play it, especially at such an important event. I made a mistake. I stopped and couldn't play. I forgot everything. My mind was blank for minutes. It was a horrible moment. Everyone in the audience just held their breath. In the silence, I felt like my career was over. But I had no choice. I had to keep playing. I closed my eyes and surrendered to my fingers. 'God,' I thought, 'I've lost my memory. Just help me. Let my fingers save me.'

"Then I started to play the whole final again, not even knowing what I was doing. Maybe I was unconscious, but I finished successfully. It wasn't good. There was no soul in my playing. Obviously, my soul was dead at the moment. The public was too nice to me. They gave a standing ovation to encourage me. It was so generous that I cried tears of happiness, but Mrs. Thompson, of course, was not pleased afterward.

"She reprimanded me sternly, especially because I threw a Christmas party for all the students from my course. But I had to do it to be liked at school. I wish to be famous and well liked. I can't yet have the recognition as a pianist nationally, but I can be a popular, nice, generous girl at university. However, Mrs. Thompson said that time is running out, that I waste my practice hours. She just goes on and on. I can't do it anymore, Mom."

Mona listened patiently, looking at Sharon seriously. "Well," she uttered thoughtfully, "maybe the load all the years at university was too heavy for you. Maybe I was mistaken to push you to go there and to become a pianist. It was my life dream, but you can't carry this burden. Your young shoulders are too weak for that."

"That's exactly what Mrs. Thompson said to me. She said that I didn't have enough talent. She said that I don't have any talent whatsoever. That's why I need to practice so much. For a talented student, about three hours a day would be enough, she said."

"Hmm." Mona smirked, narrowing her eyes. "First of all, we need to disarm the panic-stricken Mrs. Thompson."

She walked to the bedroom, brought the little gray velvet jeweler's box, put it on the table in front of Sharon, and opened it. It was Jim's present—a heart-shaped pendant with three tiny diamonds on a chain. "It costs two thousand dollars," Mona said. "Take it and find out when Mrs. Thompson's birthday is or Easter or Victoria Day or something and bring her this present. I hope it will help her respect you more and appreciate your talent more. I think it will be enough, but if not . . . wait a second."

She stepped out of the suite, opened the safe, and brought another long velvet jeweler's box. "If not, give her this before your diploma concert." Mona opened the box.

"Wow!" her daughter exclaimed, looking at an amazing diamond necklace that gleamed so bright that it lit up the room. "Wow! Is it this one that Daddy broke when he left?"

"No, sweetie. I still haven't been able to fix the one that your dad broke because one of the diamonds is missing. I didn't notice at first. The jeweler discovered it when I brought the necklace in to be repaired. Your dad threw it on the floor so hard with all his might that the diamonds scattered around. One of them is lost somewhere. I need to find it so the necklace can be fixed, but it will be practically impossible to track it down. I could buy a new stone, but I don't want to. There is no solution for now. Forget it." Mona irritably waved her hand. "This necklace is new. I bought it as a Christmas present for myself. I got one hundred thousand for the renovation to the midget's room from his sponsor, so I bought this right away."

"Mom!" Sharon looked at her in confusion. "Are you sure that's safe? The sponsor might come and check if the renovations are done or not."

"Of course, sweetie. I'm surprised that such questions appear in your head." Mona grinned. "I know what I'm doing. The renovations were done in the last days of October, and our group home already paid for it. The room even still smells of paint. The furniture and bathroom appliances are new. I'm ready for any kind of inspection.

"So back to the point, this new necklace is not very expensive, only a hundred thousand bucks. And if the pendant doesn't work, I'm ready to give it away for Mrs. Thompson . . . to remind her that you have talent. After this present, your talent will appear just like that." Mona snapped her long fingers and gave Sharon a wink. "I want you to get your university diploma, and you'll get it at any price."

"Thank you, Mom. I'll do that," her daughter answered, still scrutinizing the necklace with excitement. "I'm sure there's no woman in the world that wouldn't be happy to get it. You're so generous, Mom."

Sharon closed the box with the pendant and the box with the necklace and put both of them in her purse. "It will help me get my diploma, for sure," she said, taking a deep breath. "But anyway, it doesn't completely solve my problem. Nobody has worked as hard as me, but all of them play much better. It's so much easier for them. I'm overloaded because I really have no talent. I'm on the wrong path, Mom."

"Sweetie!" Mona hugged her with a slight scowl. "I'm sorry. I didn't expect that you would have problems as a pianist. I was sure that you were a genius because you're my only daughter . . . so special to me. I have just one request—don't leave the university, please. There are only six months left until your graduation. Be patient, please. From now on, Mrs. Thompson won't be so stern with you. You must get your diploma. Then you can work as a piano teacher at a good college. That will be much easier than playing at concerts."

"I thought about that already, Mom. That's one possibility for me. But it's strange to hear that from you. You always wanted me to be famous. A regular teacher can't be famous. I knew that you wanted to see me as a star."

"You'll be a star, sweetie," Mona whispered fondly. "I found the way for you. I love you very much, Sharon. You're the only person in the world I really love. You're my flesh and blood, and I'm doing everything possible for you and will continue to do so in the future. I'll move heaven and earth for you and won't leave one stone upturned until I make you rich. You know, I have always helped you with money."

"I know. Thank you, Mom. I really appreciate that, but . . . I want to remind you . . . to be more careful. Daddy told me why he left . . . I mean, the last story . . . about my car."

"It's not the last story anymore." Mona laughed sarcastically. "What did he tell you?"

"He said that you had a handicapped man here. His name is . . . Val or Vell . . . I don't remember."

"Victor," Mona corrected her. "So what?"

"He was a big businessman and involved somehow with the Mafia, selling weapons to the Middle East. They killed his family in front of him. He was in shock and lost his mind for a couple of months, but then his mind began returning to him. For some reason, the Mafia still needed him and didn't want to kill him. They placed him at your group home until the investigation was finished, but they didn't want him to be a witness. They paid you to give him medicine to keep him brainless for even longer. You bought me the car with that money. The rest of it you used to buy the diamond necklace.

"Daddy was scared and unhappy that you started to deal with those kinds of people. You never did before. I know that you've always been creative and shrewd enough to get money from your wards' relatives but not as much as with this story. Daddy didn't feel safe with you. He got angry at you. He broke that necklace, took his van, and left forever.

"You know, he didn't even want to hear about reuniting with you and coming back. I tried to convince him that you belong together, such nonsense, but he said very abruptly that he won't take your crap anymore. You know, he's already started with the divorce procedures. This is another thing that made me nervous and unhappy and stopped me from concentrating on my piano playing."

Mona listened to her daughter attentively, frowning slightly and shaking her head a bit while Sharon was talking. "Your dad is a strange man, sweetie," she said finally. "He is quite rude. It's not nice to use such words, like *Mafia, kill, cash, weapon*. It sounds cheap. It's really a shame. You're not a teenager watching some Hollywood action movie. We are serious people on a very different level. I didn't do anything wrong at work. Officially, I have the right to give prescribed medications to my residents. It's my duty and responsibility.

"Yes, those guys, who are actually very intelligent and highly educated, rich people, have their own doctor who prescribes the special medication for Victor, but it's none of my business. I'm not a doctor, and

I don't know how it works. If a doctor prescribed it, it should be okay. I trust him, and I just follow his recommendations. That's it.

"Yes, they paid me something because it requires extra work. What's wrong with that? Extra work gets extra pay. It's obvious, isn't it? Yes, they brought the money in cash. I don't know why. Maybe it's the easiest way for them. It's understandable that I can't bring a full briefcase of money to the bank. It would look suspicious. So I bought you the car and the necklace for myself. What's wrong with that? I just got a bonus for doing my job well, and I spent it how I wanted. That's it. It's all fair and honest.

"They actually keep checking my work all the time. Their doctor came to our Christmas party to see how Victor was doing. I introduced him to our guys as Victor's elder brother. There's nothing wrong with that. They paid me, and they want the work to be done well. It's their right to do inspections sometimes, and that doesn't bother me at all because I'm a good worker and feel confident. Your father made a problem out of it, but he is wrong. He can divorce me, of course, but I'm still friendly toward him, and I'm still your mother who loves you dearly."

"I know, Mom, you're so sweet and full of care." Sharon stood up, walked around the table, and hugged her mother lovingly. "You're the smartest woman and the best mother in the world. I have always appreciated your way of life. Of course, it's Dad's business if he wants a divorce. I love both of you and always try to calm Dad down. I'm happy that he now lives with me in my house. He saves me from being lonely. I have been so terribly lonely these last five years since you bought me the house. This house is too expensive and too huge for me alone. That's why I always like to throw parties and invite a lot of guests."

"Sorry that the house is so big." Mona laughed, caressing Sharon's shoulders. "I couldn't find anything smaller for that amount. And I actually didn't have time to look. I needed to spend the money really fast because Lily Donovan, this rude ballerina with MS, started to make a stir. Oh, she was so difficult. She always put her nose in my business. You know, sweetie, how hard it is to work with mentally normal people. They understand too much, see too much, and know too much. Luckily, now we've gotten rid of her. This January, she died at last." Mona grinned victoriously.

"Thank God you're safe finally. I love you and admire your cleverness, Mom. You're just great." Sharon smiled and put her head on her mother's shoulder.

"So, sweetie, you have a lot of problems, I see," Mona said, fondly patting her back.

"Some of them are related to me. I pushed you to get an education, I bought you the house, I bought you the car, and I help you with money," she teased sarcastically, considering her husband's opinions. "Do I look like a bad mother and a bad wife like your father declared? I sure as hell don't. These accusations are not fair. I'm happy that you realize that and appreciate my care. Now I'll help you once more. Guess what? Fate has sent us a true gift that will make you very rich and famous. I found something. Look, I'll show you."

Mona went to her office and brought a folder back to the room. She put it on the table and opened it. Sheets of music were inside. "What's that?" Sharon asked in uncertainty. "Music?"

"Yes. This is a symphony that will make you a star. Here are your fame and your money, sweetie."

"Where did you get it?" Sharon turned the pages, looking through the folder distrustfully.

"God sent it to me in response to your sufferings."

"Mom, come on. You're not religious. I'm serious."

"We have a new resident, a midget. It's his room that was renovated. His name is Jim. He is a composer. He graduated from Juilliard and studied with Dr. John Dangly. You must know this name because I heard it from you. You told me that he's the best teacher in the U.S. He passed away recently. Could you imagine that Dr. Dangly called Jim a *genius*? Jim told me about that jokingly, but I took it quite seriously. I'm not a specialist in music, but for me, this music sounds special and unusual. I heard it. It's really divine."

"That midget? I saw him outside, shoveling. Oh, he's so ugly! Jesus!" Sharon exclaimed desperately. "Why does fate always send talent to someone disgusting who doesn't need it at all? It's not fair. He's such a piece of shit! He doesn't even deserve to live! Dear god, why did he get all the talent?"

Mona laughed with malice. "Yes, I hate him for his talent. It's not fair that he got it, sweetie, but we'll fix it. I have gained his trust. He's in love with me and trusts me fully. He gives me the pages of the symphony one by one as if I am his closest friend, but I copy them and keep the copies in this folder for you. Here is a bit less than three-quarters of symphony that's already done. Take it and show it to a composing teacher. Tell him that you started composing and that this is your symphony. Let him or her to tell you what they think of it. You'll see. If a professional told you that it's as good as I suspect, you'll take it and find an orchestra to perform it as yours. This would be your triumph." Mona giggled and added slyly, "And your money as well."

"But this ugly little guy will find out that his symphony was stolen. He could go to the police."

Mona shook her head. "Don't worry, sweetie. He wouldn't dare."

"How do you know?"

"When he finishes his symphony"—Mona pursed her lips scornfully—"I'll take care of him. The meaning of his existence is to create this symphony to make you rich and famous. That's what he lives for. You have nothing to worry about, sweetie. Remember that and be brave."

Sharon hugged her mother once more and put her head on Mona's shoulder. "Thank you, Mom," she whispered. "I'm so grateful to you, but it sounds a bit scary. You make me worry. What do you mean? What would you do to him?"

"It doesn't matter, sweetie." Mona laughed playfully. "It's none of your business. Everyone here is sick, and something could happen to any of them at any moment. And nobody would suspect a thing. Believe me, I know."

She walked to the kitchen, warmed up the kettle, and poured more tea for herself and Sharon. "You know, sweetie," Mona said, sitting at the table and sipping the tea, "to be more realistic, we should now go and visit that midget in his room. I'll introduce you. He's composing on the computer. You must know what the system looks like and its name because your teacher might ask you how you compose. You have to give the right answer. To use somebody's talent and creation behind his back is not very easy business. It's a big job, not much smaller than composing. Maybe we don't have a talent for music, but for making money, I have that talent for sure, as well as many other talents."

They both laughed proudly, feeling victorious. "You're amazing, Mom. I admire you," Sharon concluded.

CHAPTER 15

t was about 10:00 p.m. already, but Jim wasn't sleeping yet. He was relaxing in an armchair, listening to music, holding the notes in his hands as Mona opened the door of his room without knocking. "Sweet boy," she said, wincing, "aren't you sleeping yet? Oh, I see you're not. I have a visitor for you." She came in, pulling Sharon by the hand.

Jim looked at them without the slightest bit of excitement on his face, took a deep breath, closed his book of music, and pressed a button to stop the sound.

"This is my daughter, Sharon. I'm sure you'll be happy to talk to her. This is Jim, sweetie, my best and closest friend. He is an amazingly talented composer. He wants to show you the computer system that he uses to compose, don't you, my darling?"

Jim shrugged with a strange expression on his face. "Sorry, Mona," he said with a tone of uncertainty. "Isn't it too late?"

"No, my sweetheart, Sharon isn't able to come here often. She is a very busy pianist. She just returned from a highly successful tour around the States and is leaving pretty soon for another one around Europe. She only has this time to help you with your composition tonight."

"Actually, like I told you already, I don't need any help, Mona," Jim objected softly but adamantly. "If you want to know what my system looks like, Miss Lainer, I can show you, but it's quite ordinary. You can buy one at any computer store, I'm sure, or even on the internet."

Jim slid down from the armchair, walked to his piano, and turned the system on. "It's only my program that is special," he continued. "A group of computer programmers created it for me according to my personal specifications. It took them about six months. This program is really different from regular ones that you can buy in stores. With it, I can color and sharpen my music in a way that nobody else can. Basically, it's because of my hands. Because of them, I can't play properly. You don't need a program like this because you can play like a normal person, even perfectly because you're a professional."

Both mother and daughter moved closer to his equipment, observing it attentively, scrutinizing and touching everything, delving into every detail. Jim stepped aside, letting them look, and explained everything they asked about. "Do you have a disk for your program, baby?" Mona inquired finally in a cunning yet loving tone.

Jim nodded.

"You might have a disk with your symphony as well," Sharon added, making a charming yet fake smile on her face.

"Of course, I do but only the parts that I've already completed. My symphony is still not finished. I'll show it to you when it's done."

"Could Sharon have your disk, sweet boy?" Mona asked, kissing his forehead. "She wants to study composition from you."

"I'm not sure that I have the right to be a teacher. I don't know anything about it, and I don't really like teaching either," Jim objected. "I can certainly give you my disks when my symphony is finished but not yet. I don't want to show anyone a work that is incomplete, like I said."

"Well . . ." Mona's beast-of-prey eyes searched around the room and stopped on Lily's statue. "What is this, Jim? This wasn't here before."

"It's a present from Lily. She left it for me according to her will."

"Why? You weren't close friends."

"I don't know."

"Oh, my sweetheart, I'm getting jealous. Did you have some kind of relationship with her? I love you so much, and you are getting presents from another woman. Are you sure that you need it? Maybe you can give it to Sharon. She collected statues, but she is so poor that she has no money to buy them and can't increase her collection. Isn't that right, Sharon?"

"Yes, Mom," Sharon said with hesitation, giving Jim another artificial smile, even though she couldn't grasp what her mother was getting at. She didn't have any collection and wasn't interested in such things anyway.

"Excuse me, Mona," Jim said confidently. "I respect your daughter's hobby, but I don't give away presents I receive, especially in this case. I need something to remember Lily by."

"Well . . ." Mona's eyes had already found something else. She stood in front of two pictures on the wall. "Baby, how come you put these pictures into the frames I gave you? These frames are my present to you, and I asked you put your pictures inside . . . those pictures of you I took. But you put your grandma and your farm instead. You're stubborn, baby, and not doing what I told you to. It's not nice and hurts my feelings."

"Sorry, Mona." Jim shrugged. "It's my room, and I have the right to decorate it the way I want. There's no reason for me to look at my own face all day long. I can do that in the mirror if I need to. I loved my grandma, and I loved my home on the farm, so I want to have the memory of them and see them every day with me."

"I'm jealous again!" Mona exclaimed passionately. "You must put my portrait here and yours too because our love is the most valuable thing in your life! Isn't it?"

Jim lowered his eyes, biting his lips. He didn't know what to answer.

"Well, baby," Mona continued in a whiny voice, "think about your feelings toward me. I'll be waiting. And prepare your disk. Next time, Sharon will take it. She dreams of being your student and hopes to study composition from you. Isn't that right, Sharon?"

"Yes, Mom." The daughter nodded.

"Sweet dreams, my darling. Love you." Mona took Sharon by the hand, and they left the room, leaving Jim standing in the middle of it in a mix of strange feelings.

"What was all that about, Mom?" Sharon asked when they entered Mona's suite. "I didn't get it."

"It doesn't matter, sweetie. This little genius is stubborn, but I'll break him. Don't worry, in a few days, you'll have the disk. I'll call you when it's ready for you to pick up." She hugged Sharon and kissed her. "Do you remember everything about his computer system? Keep it in your mind when you talk to your teacher. It's already late. It's time for you to go, sweetie. Take the folder and show the music to your teacher. Then give me a call. Okay? I'll see you off."

"Thank you, Mom," Sharon whispered, putting her sweater, jacket, and scarf on and pressing the folder to her chest. "This symphony is probably my last hope for professional success."

CHAPTER 16

A couple of ordinary days passed until, one evening, Jim had just taken a shower and was standing in front of the mirror in his bathroom, shaving. Suddenly, he noticed something unusual in his appearance and stood motionless in bewilderment. He had never paid attention to his own body before, or if he had, it was only with regard to his health and walking conditions.

Now, however, he perceived himself as more adult and mature after four months of regular sexual relationship with Mona. His shoulders had gotten bigger, and his posture had begun to appear more masculine. He no longer looked so childish. Maybe the work he did daily helped on this point as well, but Jim could see that it was much more than that. It was to him as though something deeper was going on.

He had more hair on his chest, little arms, and legs, and the hair wasn't as sparse as before. It reminded Jim of a normal man. Now Jim had to shave his face daily, whereas while living on the farm he did it once every two or three days, and it was enough. Remaining in a child-sized body, Jim's hormones had finally developed into a typical condition for a man of his age. He had begun to feel the importance of a sexual life and wanted sex every day, fully realizing at last what lust was. Jim believed that Mona was right; it was the greatest power in the world. He craved sex with her more and more often, and when they weren't having it, he missed it deeply.

It was time already, ten o'clock. Jim dressed up, did his hair, and went to see Mona. But her door was locked. He knocked lightly, but nobody opened the door. Jim knocked again and again, thinking that Mona was probably sleeping. A few minutes later, she opened the door finally but stood at the entrance, not allowing him to enter. She appeared unhappy, and her reddened cheeks gave the impression that she had been crying.

"Oh, it's you, my darling," she said with a tone of surprise as though she wasn't expecting him. "What do you want, baby?"

Obviously, she knew perfectly well what he wanted. He looked up at her and whispered, "You."

"You know, Jim . . ." He noted that it was the first time since their acquaintance that Mona had called him by his formal name. It sounded so official. "I see that you don't treasure our relationship or our love. You didn't trust me, and it is very hurtful. It's painful. I've been crying for a few days. You broke my heart."

"Why?" he asked, not quite understanding.

"You don't trust me. I gave you everything. I trusted you with my body, my vagina, my heart . . . everything most valuable in my life, but you didn't want to give me even that little piece of plastic, the disk. These are incomparable values. I gave you everything, and you gave me nothing. You're greedy and uncaring with me. I was crying because of you! Oh my goodness! I'm so unlucky with men! My husband was so rude, and now you, the second man in my life, are so abusive again!"

"Sorry if I hurt your feelings, Mona," Jim answered, feeling guilty. "I really didn't mean to. It's just that my creative work is private."

"My vagina is private too!" Mona exclaimed heatedly. "We're the closest people in the world! We're in love with each other! I opened my privacy to you, and you should open your privacy to me."

"I have. I've given you the pages of my symphony."

"I want the disk as well. Right now, baby. Otherwise, I won't trust you anymore since you don't trust me, and you can forget about having sex with me! Go and look for another woman! You choose!"

Jim felt as though he had just been slapped in the face. He turned silently and walked to his room. He felt terribly hurt.

"I love you, baby." He heard Mona sobbing behind his back, but he didn't stop.

Jim entered his room and stood before his CD holder for a number of minutes thinking. He tried to understand what was going on inside his body and mind. He wanted sex so desperately that it was driving him insane. Jim realized clearly that his chance of finding another woman were slim. He was stuck.

With shaking hands, he took the disk out from the holder, the first version of the first part of his symphony only—a piece of his heart, a part of his soul. Holding the disk in his hand, he returned to Mona's door.

She was sitting on the floor with her head hidden in her hands, balling and hugging her knees. It was exactly the same position she was in when he met her the night after her argument with Barry. Her entire figure cried of suffering. Jim approached her and stretched his hand out toward her offering her the disk. "Take it," he said abruptly, almost feeling hatred for both her and himself.

Mona looked at him with tears in her eyes and smiled. "Thank you, my love," she whispered happily, grabbing the disk and putting it in her pocket. "You'll have the most fantastic sex possible . . . and right now . . . and as much as you want, baby."

She stood up, took him in her arms, and carried him to bed, already kissing him passionately on the way.

CHAPTER 17

After this frenzied sexual session with Mona, Jim regenerated very slowly and slept for two days in a row. At times, he would awaken and shuffle over to the washroom. He would have a drink of water and go back to sleep. He did not even have the energy to stand up or eat and could not bring himself to turn on his piano or computer. As a person, as a composer, as a soul and mind, he was dead—all that was human had died in him. He had become a small wild, dirty animal gone mad whose sexual rage had annihilated all other thoughts and feelings and had slowly killed him.

As a result, Jim was unhappy and dissatisfied, even though it seemed strange to him as he was having such an impressive amount of sex. Jim was clever enough to realize that he was sinking in the sea of darkness. There was no question about Mona's feelings for him or his for her.

He didn't love Mona; most likely, he even hated her, but he wanted her more and more every minute. Yet perhaps it was not really her he craved. Maybe he craved incessant intercourse forever with some imaginary partner. Jim was quite sure that Mona had replaced the emptiness in his heart because nobody else even desired such a role. But she insisted on it and seized it with the skill of a thief or the swiftness of a fierce predator.

Jim knew clearly now that Mona didn't love him either but was only pretending to. Why she was doing this was still unclear to Jim. Horrified by his own condition, he remembered an article he read some years ago.

A team of biologists had performed a series of experiments on rats. They implanted three electrodes into the brain of each rat—into the sexual center, into the food center, and into the play center. Then they connected these electrodes to large buttons and measured the frequency with which the rats pressed each button. The scientists wanted to know which kind of pleasure would be most desirable to the rats.

At first, the tiny animals—running and crawling inside their cage—would press the different buttons accidentally, getting pleasure from food, sex, or play at different times. However, after a few days, they realized that each button produced a different result. The rats began to purposely press the sex button more often. Then they forgot about the other buttons altogether and would spend their time just sitting beside the sex button and pressing it constantly. They didn't eat (though the food was in cage beside them), and they no longer played. They become obsessed with pleasure, and then they died.

The scientists believed that the rats died of hunger, but when they dissected the tiny bodies, they were surprised to find that rats died from heart attacks. Their hearts were overloaded with such an enormous amount of sexual delight that they couldn't handle it.

Jim was mortified that White Rat Mona had left him in the same position as the rats in the experiment, and he realized that her experiment seemed to have been a success. He was broken inside. He was her slave and had become addicted to the pleasure she provided.

It is just like being an alcoholic or a drug abuser, Jim thought. *The weak became addicted forever, but the strong could overcome their compulsion. I have to be strong. I must. Otherwise, I'll waste all my talent, my music, the meaning of my life! No way, Mrs. Mona. I will be strong. Yes, I'm little, but my willpower is stronger than that of three men put together. It's no coincidence that you are always calling me stubborn. My mind and spirit are stronger than these stupid hormones. I'll show you that I'm not an animal. I'll prove my character to you.*

Thinking back on how it had started, Jim felt he had made a big mistake. He should have refused Mona's advances right after the first kiss.

Of course, I suspected something strange about her behavior from the beginning, he thought regretfully. *But I was too stressed and lonely at that time. I dreamed of discovering what it was like to have a relationship with a woman. Now I know. What happened has happened. I wish I had thought about it before, but now it's too late to regret anything.*

Jim remembered what Grandma Cathy always said. "What God does always turns out for the best." Maybe, hopefully, if he could believe in God, he would be happy.

Anyway, thanks to Mona, he was a man now and needed to make a man's decision. He decided to put an end to his slavelike dependence. Jim was sure that it was possible because, naturally, he was a very organized person. He arranged his work on schedule and, for the most part, continued it diligently. He was capable of carrying out his decisions.

At the moment, thinking a lot about his situation, he made a commitment to regulate his body's wishes and impulses. To be a *person* but not a *slave*, Jim had no choice except to decrease the frequency of his meetings with Mona as much as possible—to slowly begin to have sex less and less often.

Convincing himself that he was a man of decision, Jim stood up, took a shower, prepared himself, and sat at the piano to compose. It was difficult to find the power to do that instead of lying in bed, relaxing, and dreaming about sex; but when he had just barely pressed the first keys, his mind became clear, and his soul floated right down to him. He could breathe easier and felt more lighthearted and quieter. The music was helping him once again. He continued his work on the symphony.

CHAPTER *18*

When another shopping day came, all the group home residents went on the trip. This time, Jim didn't need to buy anything. Valentine's Day had already passed.

There was no shopping trip before Valentine's Day, so he had had no chance to buy another present for Mona. Jim tried to get a gift for her on the internet but remembered that there might not be any money left in his account. Humiliated by his poverty, he made a gift for her; he designed a beautiful Valentine's Day e-card on the computer and sent it to her for free.

Mona didn't give Jim any presents on Valentine's Day nor for his thirty-third birthday on March 12. She didn't even organize a party. On both occasions, Mona merely kissed him lovingly and said, "I love you so much, baby, but I am sorry. I'm so poor that I have absolutely no money to buy you a present. I hope that you'll forgive me because my love, my sex, and my body are the best presents for you."

Jim thanked her and kissed her back, but deep inside his heart, he felt offended. Now he understood what poverty was, but he expected that Mona should at least send him an e-card. It would cost her nothing except a bit of time, but in Jim's opinion, it would show some attention and respect for him. But it didn't happen.

Grandma Cathy always bought him amazing things for his birthday, and they made him happy and gave the event a special meaning. She wasn't richer than Mona but always found a way to buy him something beautiful and expensive, something that was exactly what he needed. He sensed a great deal of sincere love and care in her presents. This year was the first time in his life that he didn't get a thing for his birthday, and it was very painful for his soul.

So on this shopping day, Jim didn't plan to buy anything. Easter was still quite far away, and he decided not to buy or make any presents for Mona in the future—ever. He was really hurt after his generous Christmas present, a diamond pendant for which Mona openly called him silly. Again, he didn't know if he had any money in his account and didn't dare ask Mona about it, no longer willing to hear about his *snooping* and *investigating*.

Jim had quite enough of this. After Sharon's visit, he had spoken out. "You said that your daughter is very poor, but she drives a car that costs more than a quarter of a million dollars."

"She is very poor, baby!" Mona exclaimed, seemingly offended. "You don't trust me still! She doesn't have a car at all. The car you saw was borrowed from a friend because she needed to visit me desperately. You're always spying on me and always coming to the wrong conclusions. Stop guessing about things! Please, stop! Stop! I cannot tolerate this anymore! You make my life so difficult!" She threatened Jim again, saying she would refuse him in sex and send him away to look for another woman. This statement made him even more motivated to end his slavery and no longer allow her to control him.

While getting ready for the shopping trip, Jim remembered these scenes. This recollection stopped him from asking Mona about his money. In reality, he didn't care, and he still didn't plan to buy anything anyway. So at the shopping time in the mall, walking slowly and meaninglessly with Victor and holding his hand, Jim felt bored. The mall was unusually quiet that day too. There was no music, no decorations, and practically no people compared with Christmastime, when the life was in full swing.

Mona just needed to buy more new clothes for Maggie, who had gotten so swollen and fat now that she had nothing to wear again. The other residents and nurses walked and did what they wanted or sat in the food court, where the meeting point was arranged once more. Ella and Todd left with Andy and Rona, two of the nurses, to watch the dolphin show. Ali, Zahra, and Victor stayed in the food court with other nurses, Sue and Josef. Jim decided to go for a little walk alone, like he did last time. He didn't have any special purpose. He was simply curious and wanted to look around since he had nothing better to do. *Maybe I can find some computer shops or a music store to see what they have*, he thought, *just to take a look.*

Jim found the directory, which he remembered from the last time; located the computer store; and headed there. He spent about half an hour at the computer store, scrutinizing the various new models and finally decided to try to purchase a box of CDs and a Kingston DataTraveler, something he had never had before. "I'm not sure, if I have enough money in my account," he said to the young cashier, placing a bank card on the counter. "Could you check it, please? If I don't, I won't be able to buy these."

"Let's try, sir." The girl smiled and slipped his card through the machine. She showed Jim the buttons to press and politely turned aside as he entered his PIN. The cash register buzzed and printed the check.

"Approved," the girl cheered. "So I guess that means you have enough money, sir. Congratulations. Have a nice day." She put the box of CDs and little case with the DataTraveler into a beautiful blue bag and handed it to Jim.

He stepped out of the computer store, still holding his bank card in his hand, smiling and feeling very happy with his purchase. Suddenly, Jim noted that the jeweler's store was right across the hallway. *Oh, now I know where I am*, he thought, remembering his nice Christmas visit.

Jim put his bank card into his pocket where his tiny fingers felt something little and hard inside. It was Mona's pledge of love, the limpid stone or polished glass. *Oh gosh!* Jim thought. *I didn't even know that I was wearing these jeans today.* He always kept the stone in the left pocket of his home jeans and never took it out so as not to lose it accidentally. Jim treasured it. This was the only meaningful thing he had from his relationship with Mona, this vague illusion of the true love he dreamed of.

If I'm here and the stone is with me by fluke, Jim decided, *I can show it to the jeweler and ask about Mona's necklace to see whether they can fix it or not. It would be nice for her to know.* He still was friendly toward Mona and cared about her, though she hurt his feelings and sometimes behaved strangely. He had the soul of a real man who felt responsible for the woman he slept with, even though Jim was not aware of this consciously.

Jim bravely entered the store and found the same shop assistant who had served him at Christmas, now dying of boredom. There were no clients around; he really had nothing to do. "Good afternoon, sir!" he exclaimed, full of excitement, recognizing Jim right away, even though almost three months had passed. He didn't see any other little people in the store very often. "How are you? Did your girlfriend like the amazing pendant you bought for her last Christmas? I'm sure she was happy, wasn't she?"

"Yes," Jim said, smiling at him back, still in a really good mood.

"Let me guess," the assistant continued playfully, rolling his eyes. "You want to buy an engagement ring now, don't you?"

"Not yet." Jim laughed sincerely. "Today I need a different sort of help. I need to fix some kind of broken necklace. But I'm not sure if you can do that."

"Yes, we can, sir. We can do any kind of repairs, anything you want."

"Okay, I just want to know. Could you fix a necklace that is made with about thirty pieces of polished glass like this?" Jim took the stone from his pocket and put it on the counter.

"Let's take a look." The shop assistant glanced at the stone and started to make a fuss about it immediately. "Oh yes, oh yes, sir!" he exclaimed. He brought a high chair and helped Jim to sit on it.

He took the stone and examined it attentively. Then he took a magnifying glass and scrutinized it once again. Finally, he took out a little device that reminded Jim of a pen, touched the stone, and pressed a button. It buzzed, and a red light in it started flashing. Then the assistant weighed the stone and looked at Jim, smiling victoriously. "Five thousand dollars," he announced. "Computer work, highest quality."

"Sorry?" Jim said, not knowing what he meant. "Five thousand dollars for what? For the repair? Or are you teasing me?"

"No, sir. I'm not talking about the repairs yet because I haven't seen the whole thing. But this gem is perfect quality. It costs five thousand dollars. That is what it is worth. Do you want to sell it? If you do, I'll give you the five thousand right away."

"No." Jim shook his head slowly, still not understanding. "Do you mean it's not glass? Or can glass cost that much?"

"No, sir. This is nothing cheap. It's a real diamond of the best standard."

"Could the necklace, which is made from about thirty diamonds like this, have cost $12 twenty-five years ago?"

"Absolutely not, sir." The assistant laughed, thinking that Jim was joking. "It's actually quite new, no more than five years old. This was made with modern technology."

"Are you sure?"

"I'm a professional, sir. And my device proves that it is a diamond." He touched the stone once more with the pen, and it buzzed and flashed red again. "Look at that. Aren't you happy about that, sir?" he asked with a tone of surprise, seeing Jim's face becoming gloomier and more dismal with each passing second.

"Thank you," Jim said abruptly, grabbing the stone. He jumped down from the high chair and walked away, not listening to another word of what the assistant had to say. Dumbfounded, he shuffled toward the food court like a zombie. His attention fixed straight ahead, totally oblivious to what was around him.

The "Barry's twelve dollars' wedding present" was a lie, Jim realized, pulsating with anger. *That it was a cheap thing was a lie. Mona knew perfectly well how much her necklace had cost. That's why she was crying and shaking while picking up the broken pieces of necklace. Actually, its real price does not matter at all. It's none of my business. I just want to know why she was lying to me. I didn't ask her a thing about the necklace. She lied to me for no reason. Why was she pretending to be so poor? Has she been lying all the time? Was she even lying in bed?*

Her daughter's poverty . . . Todd's mother . . . Lily's money and death . . . my money . . . my sponsors, Jim thought desperately, his heart pounding. *Rats in the basement . . . open bottles of cider . . . Ramah's bus at night . . . Mona's vows of love . . . her attempts to pressure me . . . her mentally ill husband . . . her teary eyes . . . her help to write my symphony . . . oh my God! Everything was a lie! Five months of lies! Round-the-clock lies! But why?*

There was darkness in Jim's eyes. He didn't even know how he found the food court. All the group home residents were already there.

"Where were you for so long, my sweetheart?" Mona exclaimed, beaming. But he didn't smile back. He just glanced at her angrily, noticing now for the first time how artificial her smile was.

Actually, it had always seemed fake. I only refused to see it, Jim remembered, agitated, looking at her with loathing. *Oh gosh! Silly me! I hoped to find a woman, a friend . . . trust . . . help . . . sincerity, and maybe . . . love. But it was all lies instead!*

"What's going on with you, baby? Has something happened? Oh, I see you bought CDs. Are they for your symphony?" Mona tried to make some kind of polite conversation for nurses not to see anything, but Jim couldn't stand it.

"I have headache!" he growled through his pressed teeth and turned his back toward her.

"Oh, darling, it's okay. I have pills with me. I can give you some." Mona nervously opened her purse, looking for pills and glancing askance at Jim's bag with CDs. She guessed that, while buying it, he discovered something going on with the money in his account.

"I don't want a pill!" Jim barked. "Leave me alone!"

He came to Victor, sat beside him, and hid his face on Victor's lap.

"Well," Mona announced in a cheerful voice, "it's all right, guys. It's time to go home now. You see, Jim is already tired. Let's go, my dears. You can go with Victor, sweet boy." She looked toward Jim with a forced smile. He didn't answer.

When they boarded the bus, Mona helped everyone on. She took Jim by the waist and helped him up the steps like a child. Pretending that it happened accidentally, she kissed his forehead and whispered into his ear, tenderly touching it with her lips, "Come to see me this evening, baby. My door will be unlocked." He kept silent, narrowing his eyes and biting his lips.

At home, Jim refused to eat dinner because he couldn't eat in such a nervous state. He stayed in his room and tried to play piano and compose, but he couldn't. His thoughts were confused, jumping crazily, and his little hands shook. Jim tried to listen to music but was unable to concentrate very well. The music forced him to cry, which he didn't want to do.

He merely lay down on his bed, motionless, and buried his face into the pillow. The feelings of anger and hatred toward himself and toward Mona suffocated him. Never in his life had he felt so humiliated and so offended. The illusion of happiness that he built for himself over the last few months made him bitter. Now this mirage had collapsed. He would be unable to fix it and would not be able to forgive Mona for his loss. His feelings had disappeared. His first love story had been lost, and there was no way to return it.

CHAPTER 19

In the evening, Jim finally found the power to hold himself in check and walked to Mona's suite to end things. He didn't look his best—his eyes had dark circles around them, they sparkled with anger, and his hair was matted. Jim didn't care about looking good on this night. He no longer had a lover for whom he wanted to look handsome.

Jim opened the door abruptly and went through the living room straight to the bedroom where Mona was, lying naked on the bed in the dimly lit atmosphere. Up until now, she was unaware of Jim's anger, but the sound of the slamming door clued her in. "Do you still have a problem, my darling?" she asked nicely and delicately in a hushed and amorous voice. "Come here, sweet boy, I'll make you happy."

Remaining silent, Jim turned a top light on, startling Mona.

"What the hell are you doing?" she exclaimed, jumping off the bed and wrapping herself in a bathrobe.

Jim had already noticed how wrinkled, flabby, and yellow her aging skin was; how ugly was her gaunt body with protruding bones. *How could I kiss it or touch it before?* he thought with disgust. However, it didn't matter to him now.

Jim put the diamond on the bedside table with such force that it made a loud sound. "Why did you lie to me?" he demanded harshly, pointing at the gem. "Why?"

"What's that?" Mona asked sleepily, trying to adjust her eyes to the sudden bright light.

"It's the diamond from your broken necklace. I found it on the floor. It costs five thousand dollars, and you know that. Why did you lie to me?"

"That one?" Mona moved her hand toward the diamond with uncertainty and picked it up. "This one? Oh my goodness! Where did you find it, baby?"

"Don't avoid the question!" Jim raised his voice as much as he could. "Why did you lie?"

"Sorry, my dear, you just woke me up. I don't really understand. You found the stone . . . what's the problem with that? Thank you. You made me happy. Why be so angry and rude to me?"

"You are lying to me! All the time! Every day! I don't believe you! I don't trust you! I won't give you my symphony anymore!" Jim turned and walked out abruptly.

"No, baby! No!" she shrieked in fear. She ran after him and collapsed on the floor in front of him, blocking the entrance. "No, Jim! Please! You're mistaken! This is a misunderstanding! I'll explain everything to you! I'll explain the situation!"

Mona grabbed him by the shoulders with her shaking hands, crying and hugging him, kissing and petting him, and pressing him against her breasts. "Don't go, baby! Just don't go!" she sobbed hysterically. "I'll tell you . . . I'll explain . . . I just . . . just . . . sorry, I was scared . . . please . . . please!"

Mona seemed so sincere that Jim felt pity toward her inside his heart. He didn't want to be as adamant as Othello in his distrust. He wanted to trust her, but he didn't want to listen to the lies anymore, knowing very well that she was an actress. "Leave me alone! You're a liar!" he exclaimed, pushing her away by her shoulders with all the power in his tiny hands. "You've been cheating me all the time!"

"Baby! Baby! Sorry!" Mona sobbed breathlessly. "I'll explain . . . just listen to me, please! Just listen . . . please . . . please." She kissed his face frantically, holding him tight and little by little pushing him back toward the bedroom. She felt some hope, sensing that he was giving up under her pressure. Without knowing it, he wanted to listen to her explanations and to trust her. If only he could believe her.

Finally, Mona pulled Jim into the bedroom and sat him on her bed. She knelt in front of him, hugging him and kissing his little knees. "I love you, baby," she continued, sobbing. "I love you so much . . . yes, I lied to you about being so poor . . . because I knew that you were very poor . . . I wanted us both to be equal. I didn't want to show you that I was rich. I was scared that you would refuse to have a relationship with me. I thought you might say you didn't want to be dependent on some rich old woman. I was scared to lose you . . . because . . . I really love you."

Jim knew perfectly well that she was lying again, but he couldn't find any comprehensible reason why. Why did she need him so desperately if she didn't love him? Just to use him as a toy? What else? He didn't have anything else. He had nothing at all . . . except . . . except his symphony!

"This isn't just about your necklace," Jim said agitated, continuing to push Mona away, even though she was much stronger than him. "It's about your constant lies. You lied about everything. I know it, and I want to know why."

"No, baby, I didn't lie about anything except the price of the necklace. And I explained to you why. It's understandable, isn't it?" she whimpered as she unzipped his jeans.

"No!" he exclaimed as he zipped them back up. "No, you're using me! I don't want this anymore!"

"I love you, baby!" she sniveled.

"That's a lie! It's ridiculous to even use the word *love* when talking about our relationship. It's a bunch of bull! *Mother's care*? It's a shame to say that! I hate you! I don't want you anymore! And no symphony! Remember that!"

Mona's face changed immediately as she realized that Jim was serious in his intention to end their affair. "Shut up, you little bastard!" she shouted angrily. "You're the thief who stole my diamond! You're a criminal, and I'll call the police to report you."

"I found it! You said it cost nothing, and I kept it as a memory of you," Jim protested.

"I'm not dead! You see me every day! You don't need any memory! What stupid things are you talking about? If you found the diamond, you should have returned it to me right away but not keep it. That's stealing! And you also brought it to be appraised, which is another crime. You infringed on my privacy! We have a privacy law. It's my property, and nobody should know how much it costs. The shop assistant could be a witness against you! I'll sue you! You'll go to prison, and the gangsters there will fuck your ass. You don't want me, the only one who gave you pleasure, but you'll have them, and they'll beat you and infect you with AIDS. Then you'll know what life is really about, you ungrateful pig!"

Jim looked at Mona, his eyes wide open, truly seeing her for the first time in his life. He didn't recognize her. It was not his nice, careful, and loving friend. It was somebody else—a stranger with the face of an evil rat. She was more infuriated than Jim had ever seen before. She revealed her true colors, and Jim felt only disdain toward her. It was too much. But she didn't scare him.

"How could you say all this after your love confessions?" Jim smirked bitterly. "Are you expecting me to beg for forgiveness and not call the police? Do you want to set me up? What for? Why? What do you want from me? To have me as your slave? No, I would never be your slave. I have enough self-esteem and pride. With your threats, it's clear that you lied to me about your love. Well, if you want to put our relationship in the hands of the officials, we can do that. It's your choice. But I would rather die in prison than let you touch my body ever again. And I won't give you one more page of my symphony. After all these threats, we can't even be friends. We will have official relations only. Sorry, Mona. I didn't want that. I better go and look for another woman as you suggested."

She threw her head back and guffawed and sobbed at the same time. "Another woman! Silly freak of nature! Look at yourself! Any other woman would be scared even to glance at you. My daughter was in shock when she saw you. Only me, someone accustomed to cripples, could tolerate you and be so kind to you. You should kiss my ass forever as a way of thanking me for sex. You will never have it again, never ever, ever! Forget it, you deformed talent! You ugly genius!"

Jim's face blushed, but he pressed his teeth together, squeezed his little fists, and didn't say a thing. He merely slipped down from the bed and walked to the door. This time, Mona didn't hold him.

At the entrance, he turned and glimpsed at her. She was still kneeling beside the bed, burying her face in the bed covers. He noticed that she wasn't crying anymore, only quivering a bit. "Don't lose your diamond again," he teased her sternly. "I don't want you to complain later that I stole it once more. And I might as well tell you . . . I wanted just to find out for you . . . the shop assistant said that they could fix the necklace. Be happy."

Jim left Mona's suite. On his way, he drank a half glass of cold water in the kitchen to calm himself down; then he returned to his room. He felt beaten up and exhausted. It was the first fight he had ever experienced in his life. It seemed so rude, ugly, and disgusting.

Jim never had fought or even argued with Grandma Cathy nor with anybody else. He was always nice and kind and was an easygoing person. He never had any problems in relationships with people. Now he was trying to understand himself. *How could I be so mad and so harsh with Mona? Was it my fault? Maybe Mona was the one responsible for our fighting since she was causing scandals with her deeds. Barry had a scandal with her and left. Lily had had a scandal with her and earned an enemy. How many other scandals had Mona been involved in during her years at the group home?* Jim couldn't be sure. He only knew that tonight was his turn.

Jim's eyes welled up with tears. He was mortified. However, what happened had happened. It was impossible to change anything now.

Jim still wanted to make clear to himself why his relationship with Mona had come to a dead end. He pondered this for a while but couldn't find any explanation. Then in despair, Jim took his cell phone and called his psychologist. He needed to pour his heart out to someone and, at the same time, wanted practical advice about what to do and how to live with this load weighing down on his soul.

It was quite late, but luckily, the psychologist answered right away and had time to talk. The conversation continued for about two hours until midnight. Jim told the psychologist everything about his relationship with Mona. He asked for an explanation of her every step, word, glance, movement, and face expression, and he got just what he wanted in full detail.

"This woman is definitely not your friend," the psychologist concluded at the end of their conversation. "She doesn't love you and doesn't respect you. She lied about her diamonds, guessing that you were a thief and would steal them. If she was really your friend, she would never do that. You should be careful around her, keeping in mind that she is not a friend but an enemy. Her threats about going to the police mean nothing. Don't worry. She may have many more reasons to stay away from the police than we can even guess.

"She is using you. But I'm 100 percent sure that sex is not her main interest. Be really careful about your symphony, especially because her daughter is a musician as well. I suspect there are also hidden motives, maybe financial. Keep an eye on your money and make sure to check your account regularly.

"Sorry, Jim. This is a difficult situation for you. But believe me, almost half of the husbands and wives in the world are living in the same quality of relationship. It's sad to realize, but it's true. I would advise you move out of this group home, but if it's impossible, just keep being careful. Stay away from this woman, but don't confront her and don't make the situation worse."

As Jim hung up, he looked through his CDs. With shaking hands, he took out Wagner's overture to *Tannhäuser*. He turned the player on, climbed into the armchair, and closed his eyes, breathing deeply and losing himself in the divine music. It carried him into the sky, up to the heavens. Jim bit his lips and sat motionlessly, quivering from a soundless cry that he did not even try to suppress. It was not his body that sobbed but his soul.

Grandma Cathy had made him accustomed to being surrounded by love, and now he couldn't exist without it. There was no reason to live—he couldn't compose without love. His creative world collapsed all around him with the end of his illusive love story.

"Oh, God," Jim whispered to himself, feeling the salty taste of his tears on his lips. He didn't dry them, only licked them, trembling, almost breathless. "Why did You do that to me? One more disappointment, one more loss. It's too much. I don't deserve this. Why? I would be happy to believe in You, dear God. I would be really happy. I promise, I would believe in You . . . just send me love. Send me a woman.

"My symphony is almost finished. Only half the reprise remains to be completed. I have to finish it. It's my calling. It's what You, God, created me for. But I can't do it without a woman in my heart. Help me, my God. Send me a woman who will love me."

Jim didn't know if God really existed and and listened to him, but he continued to pray, even though he had no hope, because he had nobody else to help him. "I don't need any beauty, believe me, God," he sobbed. "My demands are so modest. The woman can be very ugly, absolutely poor, horribly sick, old and worn out, even badly handicapped . . . it doesn't matter. It's not important. Just give her one thing—a kind, loving soul. It's the only thing I need. My dear God, just bring me someone to love."

Jim sat crying and praying the whole night, immersing himself in the same music that played again and again. He felt helpless. Only darkness was around him, and silence was his answer.

CHAPTER *20*

J im felt the result of his breakup with Mona very soon—right the next morning. He woke at about ten o'clock and was bewildered to see no breakfast waiting on his little table. Having missed dinner last night, he felt quite hungry and walked down to the kitchen to look for something to eat.

Jim asked Mona about breakfast, to which she answered politely but in a severe tone of voice and with a cold expression, "Excuse me, Jim, breakfast here is served at eight o'clock, and everybody who is not in a wheelchair needs to come down and eat in the dining room at the table. Now breakfast is over, and there is nothing left. The next time you can eat will be lunch at noon. If you miss that, then you'll have to wait until dinner at four thirty. After that, there is buttermilk and cookies at eight, and that's it, no exceptions for anybody."

"I usually had lunch at about three o'clock . . . before I work on composing on my schedule from three to six," Jim objected shyly.

Mona looked at him with her piercing eyes that seemed empty to Jim. "I do not care about your hobby schedule, Mr. Bogat," she announced sternly. "We have a schedule to follow around here too. I spoiled you from the start, which is not good. Now it's time to fix my mistake. You're a regular resident here, and you have to obey our rules and regulations if you want to continue living here. If you don't like it, you're free to break the contract and move out at any time." Mona turned her back to him and left to go to her office.

Jim didn't say anything but realized silently that a war had begun. What could he do to protect himself and to maintain his own schedule and creative life? He pondered for a moment and found the answer quite easily. Usually, Jim only ate small quantities of food. His portion was about one-quarter the size of a regular meal to which each resident was entitled at the group home. Here was the solution to his problem.

At noon sharp, Jim came down for lunch and asked Mona to give him a full lunch portion. He felt quite safe demanding this because two nurses, two cleaning ladies, and Ramah were having lunch next to him and Mona at the same table. In front of these witnesses, Mona couldn't object to a thing and would have to give a full meal according to the rules, which she did. Jim divided the meal into four parts and ate only one of them—an omelet with toast. Then he carried the rest of the food (an apple, a cup of yogurt, a bun, and a cane of fruit) into his room to eat for dinner that evening and breakfast the next day.

Now he had won; Mona couldn't refuse him. He was free again to wake up when he wanted and to work on his symphony according his own schedule. But Jim knew that he had to be very careful.

Mona's scandal with Lily Donovan hovered clearly in front of his eyes, like a sequence from a movie. He watched as an infuriated Mona took the box of cider from the basement before beginning to pound something with a mortar and pestle in the kitchen. He could remember the open cider bottles on the kitchen counter before Mona sent him outside to shovel, even though there was almost no snow. When he returned, there were no bottles in the kitchen; and the next morning, Lily was dead. Jim recalled that Mona was washing the cider bottles in the basement afterward and then remembered the story that Bertha told him about Lily's money.

Jim felt quite sure that Mona had indeed poisoned Lily, but he had no evidence at all and never would. Lily was cremated right away on the evening of her death. Jim's version of the events was merely speculation. "You can't say anything to anybody about me if you have no evidence. And if you do, I'll sue you," Mona once said to him when he asked her his nosy questions. "Your suspicions mean nothing without evidence. You should know this, my sweet baby."

Now he wasn't "her sweet baby" anymore. He was her enemy, "Mr. Bogat," "the cripple," "the midget." And he knew he had to be very careful, knowing what had happened with Lily. It was not easy to live with such a burden on his soul, but Jim had no other choice yet.

If my symphony is successful and I make some money, he dreamed, *I'll find an apartment somewhere and move. I'll hire a nurse or maid to reside with me to help me and take care of me. She will be nice, caring, and loving, and I will be happy with her. The only thing I need to reach this goal is to work very hard on the symphony and to accomplish it as fast as I can.*

Washing the rats that day, Jim continued to replay in his mind the movie of scandal between Mona and Lily. He tried to understand why this had all happened and suddenly remembered one strange detail. *I had told Mona that Lily said I reminded her of someone who died long ago. I had repeated to Mona what Lily had said, that she would find out for me who it was and ask her friends about the man who was killed at the end of the sixties. I recall that Mona refused to give me any information. It was as if she knew something and wanted to hide it*, Jim realized.

Silly me! I was just too excited with her love and sex games. I didn't pay attention to what was really going on. I trusted her at the time, Jim thought.

Then an idea came to him. *Emmanuel . . . maybe this man's name was Emmanuel.* As Lily returned from her Christmas trip, Mona came to see her, and the situation with Emmanuel occurred. And then Lily died so unexpectedly. Jim suddenly felt partly responsible for Lily's death.

I shouldn't have told Mona anything about my visits with Lily, he thought. *I shouldn't have told her what we talked about. Oh gosh!* Jim shut off the water, put the hose on the hook, and entered the elevator, feeling overcome with guilt.

Silly me again, he continued to think. *Why didn't I ask Bertha about this Emmanuel? Oh, no, she was too sad on the tragic day of Lily's death. She was crying. I guess it would have been wrong to ask her about it then. I had even forgotten all about it by then. But maybe I can find out about it now.*

Jim returned to his room, picked up the phone, and called the gay and lesbian community center. It wasn't very easy to find Bertha because he didn't know her last name, but he knew Lily's—Donovan. He talked with the receptionist for quite a long time. He explained everything he knew about Lily and Bertha, and finally, he was successful. He was given Bertha's email address.

Jim wrote a detailed letter to Bertha, asking about everything he wanted to know. The next day, he received a response. Bertha wrote him a nice letter in which she asked if he was enjoying Lily's statue. In response to his question, she informed him that Lily had not asked her to remember anyone from the past. Maybe Lily had forgotten to ask, her mind occupied by other things in the busy Christmas season. Or maybe she asked some other friends. She had seen many of them during her Christmas trip. Bertha wasn't sure.

However, she wrote that she did remember a very famous singer named Emmanuel who was killed. There was something about this on TV. But Bertha had forgotten his last name and couldn't remember what he looked like. She didn't remember the year in which this happened either, not even an approximate.

Jim was very thankful to her for this information. He tried to search for something on the internet, but to find the information he needed to know the singer's last name because there were thousands of them, he also had to pay. Jim was stuck. Finally, he decided to forget the whole story. Jim was aware that all his information had come from a woman who was ill with MS. Maybe all these were her imagination only. Maybe he didn't really look like anyone, and even if he did, this information wouldn't help him change anything in his life. There was no reason to spend time on this search. Far more important to him was to work to finish his symphony.

On the first days after his break-p with Mona, constant thoughts about sex bothered Jim. He didn't know what to do. It seemed like a problem with no solution because Jim had grown so accustomed to a regular sex life. Jim felt he needed it badly. He wanted so badly to be free from Mona, but it was as though he couldn't be.

The sex chapter of his life had come to an end, and Jim would have to find new ways of managing his impulses, which wouldn't be easy. *Everything was much simpler when I lived on the farm and didn't know anything at all about sex,* he thought. *I didn't care. Grandma Cathy used to worry about this much more than I did.*

As he remembered the farm, a sudden idea popped into his mind—Grandma Cathy. She had always told Jim to organize his time and to be reasonable in everything. "You must hold your wishes, Jim. The more you eat, the more you want. The more you sleep, the more you want." He laughed as he continued to think about this idea. *The more you fuck, the more you want it.* The idea was a perfect match for Jim's situation, but Grandma Cathy certainly had not expected Jim to apply it in this way.

How do people live in monasteries or on expeditions to the North Pole or in the deserts? Jim guessed the answer to this. *They see things from a spiritual perspective. They're busy serving the higher good—God or science. That's what I should do. I'm serving with my music. Grandma Cathy always believed that I would get it someday. This is my highest goal, and I won't let these stupid hormones stop me.*

Fight with hormones—Jim laughed again, imagining one more situation from the farm. They had a cat to catch mice. Sometimes in the spring, the cat would lie on the ground and roll, mewing passionately. "What's going on with her?" Jim asked with surprise when he saw this for the first time. "Is she sick?"

"No." Grandma Cathy laughed. "It's just spring. She had started to produce those stupid hormones. It's a shame. I really don't like it. Psst!" She waved at the cat threateningly, but it showed no reaction, immersed in its amorous feelings.

Then Grandma Cathy threw her slipper at the cat. It jumped with fright and ran to other end of the room. It lay down there and continued to wiggle on its back. "Oh my God!" Grandma Cathy grumbled. "We need to stop her. I don't want to have kittens every year and turn our property into a cat farm." She stood up, groaned, and approached the cat. She grabbed it by its back paws and carried it upside down right to the tub. She turned on the water, spread the cat's paws, and still holding it in the same position directed the cold spurt into the poor cat's little vagina. The cat screeched wildly, jumped down on the floor, and ran away, shaking.

"Now she's cooled down," Grandma Cathy announced victoriously to Jim, who was watching this scene, filled with horror and pity for the unhappy cat.

"That was quite mean, Grandma," he commented in a tone of disapproval.

"It is. I'm sorry. But we have no choice. It works."

Jim remembered this little story just in time and decided to make use this experience. When thoughts and sexual wishes began to bother him, he went to the shower and ran the warm water before he turned it abruptly to cold. He even shrieked at first, like the cat, because of this sharp temperature difference but stood bravely, gritting his teeth tightly, under the icy stream for almost two minutes. Then he dried himself with a towel until his skin got very pink and felt clean, refreshed and ready for loftier things, such as work on his creation.

Grandma Cathy was right, the cold water works perfectly, he thought. Considering this idea, Jim felt happy and confident because both of his problems, food and sex, caused by his breakup with Mona were solved. So Jim organized his mind, held himself in check, and persistently continued his work strictly on schedule, dreaming about a beautiful life and the nice woman he would possibly have in the future.

CHAPTER 21

S pring came this year to Minneapolis–Saint Paul very early. In the middle of March, all the snow had unexpectedly melted quite fast, and fresh, bright green grass began to sprout up everywhere. The need to shovel snow was gone. Jim only walked outside in the evenings, which were now lit by the waning daylight.

The decrease in Jim's group home duties changed his schedule a bit. He would only go downstairs to eat his lunch, wash the rats as quickly as possible, and then go back to his room (carrying the rest of the food with him) to continue working on his composition. This way, Jim could save a couple of more hours for his creative work, and the piano version of his symphony was finished quickly.

It was time to start the orchestration. Jim printed some large pages of lined paper and began to work manually. He put the paper on the floor and lay down on his stomach beside it. The notes—his piano version of the symphony—were in front of him. Jim wrote out the music from there in his imagination, sharing the melodies and accords between the different instruments, doubling or tripling some sounds when necessary. Then he jotted down the notes of the score according to the classical order of the musical instruments.

Unlike many modern composers, Jim liked the sound of classical orchestras. It satisfied him and gave him enough room for creativity and fantasy. He didn't need and didn't want to add any special new instruments or sound tricks like some other composers did. The orchestration work required the perfect knowledge of each instrument—to do it, one needed to be a professional.

Jim liked to perform the orchestration and was brilliant at it. He had an extraordinary sensitivity to sound and thought of this procedure as the painting of black and white pictures with colorful sounds. He breathed life into his music in the same way that a master craftsman breathed soul into the marble statue he had just created. There was something magical about this process, and Jim enjoyed it a lot. It was his favorite part of composing.

Jim had already sent emails to some of the orchestras in the United States and other countries, suggesting they play his symphony, but he didn't receive any answers yet. He guessed that promoting might turn out to be a problem. But he realized he needed to finish the symphony first anyway.

Another problem was to find an appropriate voice for vocalization. Jim wasn't even sure if he wanted it to be a man's or woman's voice. Every evening he listened to records of many singers and still couldn't choose one. He really liked some voices, like that of Maria Callas, but she was already dead. Jim needed someone alive who would agree to sing for him, who would find the time to come to the rehearsals, and who would be willing to work a great deal with the orchestra. This part seemed to Jim to be the most difficult to work out.

To organize everything with the singer and to promote the performance would be a special job that he wouldn't be able to do himself. He needed to hire an agent for this, but he had no idea how to do that and had no money to pay. For now, this seemed hopeless to Jim, but he refused to allow himself to think about it and concentrated on his orchestration work.

Each evening while listening to different singers, Jim stood beside the window and gazed out dreamily. He noted that, two or three times a week, Rama's bus was parked beside the garage at night. He knew Mona's explanations of that, but under the circumstances, he could guess that it was another lie. However, it didn't matter to him anymore at all. He didn't care. Everything related to Mona was dead in his heart.

Much more interesting for Jim were the changes with the group home residents that he discovered unexpectedly. Lily's room was fully renovated, and a new person, Basil, appeared there. At first, Jim didn't have a chance to see him but thought about visiting him and considered finding a new friend.

Another thing that caught his attention was Maggie's disappearance. One evening Jim noticed that she wasn't in the living room in her usual place, watching TV. "Where is Maggie?" he asked Ella, who was now enjoying watching TV alone and had even stopped using her tiny Christmas tree to hide from the others.

"She is sick," Ella answered, "and is sitting in her room. She isn't even going to the factory. She just stays home all the time. Do you know what her illness is? Fat. She is too fat now to fit on this couch with me. So Mona is keeping her in her room until she gets healthy again, until she loses weight. I made a joke about it. Listen, Jim. 'Maggie is too fat to fit in her own room so she sticks out the door.' Isn't it funny? I have an amazing sense of humor, don't I?"

"Yes, Ella." Jim nodded and walked away.

The situation sounded strange to him, and he decided to visit Maggie to see how she was doing. Jim went to her room and knocked on the door. He could hear the TV inside, the volume quite loud, but nobody answered. Jim knocked some more and then turned the doorknob, deciding to enter on his own. However, the door was locked, and it was impossible to open it.

Jim realized that Mona was now keeping Maggie under lock and key constantly and not only at night like before. To see her was impossible, and it seemed to be a mystery to the others too. But Jim, knowing Mona quite well, guessed that something was up. Jim knew that Maggie was alive because he could hear her through the door laughing loudly while watching TV.

Frustrated, he walked down the hallway and noticed that Lily's door was wide open. Jim peered inside and saw Nurse Rona changing Basil's diaper. Basil was a very deformed and badly handicapped young fellow. It was quite stinky there, so Rona opened the window and the door to allow some air to enter the room and sprayed it with a strawberry deodorant.

"Can he talk?" Jim asked sadly, already knowing the answer.

"No." Rona shook her head. "He just makes the sounds like a baby— oh-oh, uh-uh, aha-aha—but with no meaning. He was traumatized during birth. There was too much pressure on his head, and now he has cerebral palsy. Oh, Jim, you can't imagine how hard it is to work with him and with Ali and Zahra. But they pay us three times more than in the hospitals. That's the only reason that keeps me here."

"I understand," Jim said with compassion. "Sorry to bother you, Rona."

He walked back to his room with disappointment. His hope to have a new friend was once more in vain. "Instead of finding a buddy, I've discovered another of Mona's lie," he noted to himself with anger. "She told me that the salaries in group homes are the lowest in the U.S."

He already had too much of lies, and it didn't hurt him anymore but just added some further detail to Mona's portrait, which actually was already clear enough for Jim. So he returned to his usual things to do, trying to completely forget about her, but another story reminded him quite soon that she was still around.

CHAPTER 22

As a part of the regular group home schedule, every Monday when Ramah drove the guys for work, Mona went with him to buy groceries. Normally, they returned a couple of hours later and unloaded the purchases behind the house. Usually, Jim saw them carrying the pink grocery bags into the basement through the back door. There, Mona sorted the food, leaving part of it downstairs in the refrigerators and freezers. She and Ramah took the rest of the produce to the main floor and put them to the storage room behind the kitchen.

One spring Monday, Mona and Ramah returned from their shopping trip much later than usual. Jim heard the sound of the bus coming and looked out the window, expecting to see them smiling, content, and flirting as was customary while they unloaded the groceries. However, on this day, both of them were angry. Jim could see expressions of agitation on their faces and listened to them as they each talked with a tone of discontent in their voices. The food was in unusual bags—white ones instead of pink ones. Their facial expressions and behavior revealed to Jim that another scandal was occurring at the group home. It left him curious. After his breakup with Mona, he felt free to give in to his investigative nature once again.

Jim looked at the clock and gave them about fifteen minutes to unload. Then guessing that Mona and Ramah were already in the kitchen, Jim carefully opened his room door. Yes, they were there. Scraps of their worried dialogue downstairs caught his ears. He stuck by the door and stood still, listening more.

"I'm sorry, honey," Ramah begged. "But it's not my fault."

"It can't last this way any longer!" Mona exclaimed indignantly. "Look! Today we spent twice more money for these damn groceries than usual. There's nothing left for us. You have to persuade your father to change his mind. You must! Your father's grocery store was the reason why I hired you three years ago."

"Really? You surprise me, Mommy. I thought that you wanted to sleep with me," Ramah teased, patting Mona's bum to calm her down.

"Come on, it's just a joke . . . you know that, silly. Don't be a fool. And don't touch me yet." She slapped his hand. "Don't you see these stupid cleaners are still dusting the living room? They don't understand English, but they have eyes."

The plastic bags rustled as Mona emptied them noisily, throwing all kinds of packages and cans onto the counter. "I'm upset," she continued worriedly. "How could you make such a mistake? Why did you let your father check the bookkeeping? You should do it yourself! He didn't put his nose in your store for three whole years!"

"We had an accountant, and I paid him to cover everything so we'd be okay. Then my father retired. He had nothing to do and decided to take an accounting course so he could fire the accountant and do all the bookkeeping himself. As my father started his first review of the store, he discovered what was going on right away. He asked me where the rest of the money had gone."

"Why didn't you lie? He's your father. He must trust you."

"I did, but he was very angry and didn't want to listen to me. He shouted that we have never had a thief in our family. He prohibited me from touching anything in the store ever, and he said I was never allowed to set foot inside again."

"I hope you didn't tell him that we shared the money. He'll always forgive you as his son, but he wouldn't forgive me as a stranger."

"He doesn't know a thing about us, but he guessed. He said, 'I'm sure that this woman, your boss, dragged you into this affair, naive boy. Did you sleep with her?' Of course, I said no, but he didn't believe me. He said that he wanted me to get married and would start looking for a bride for me in our community immediately."

"So now should I shop at the supermarket and loose a couple of thousand dollars every month because of your stupidity?" Mona concluded, annoyed. "I can't handle this! How will I be able to live? You know that my salary is so small." She harped on the same old string in a crying voice. "I'm so poor!"

"Actually, none of us is poor," Ramah objected. "You can play these games with your cripples but not with me. I organized the grocery shopping for you quite well. It's not my fault that everything is ruined. It was just an accident. I'm sure you'll find a new way. You will think of new and creative ideas for how to deal with supermarkets. And stop accusing me. I have to listen to my father. It's our culture, our tradition, and our religion. If he said that our store is closed for you, honey, forever, I must respect his will. Sorry, but I can't do anything about that, even for you, even if I like our relationship."

Here, the conversation stopped. The cleaning ladies finished their work downstairs and noisily loaded their equipment into the elevator. Jim heard the elevator coming to the second floor. The door opened, and the cleaning ladies appeared in the hallway with their vacuums and went to clean the rooms.

Jim stepped closer to the banister and looked down. Mona and Ramah stood in the middle of the kitchen, hugging and kissing passionately. Then Mona took Ramah by the hand and pulled him through the storage door toward her suite.

Jim returned to his room and sat on his bed. He closed his eyes and took a deep breath, trying to come to terms with what he had heard and seen. Jim was quite astonished at this sudden, disgusting, and loathsome discovery. But he felt much less hurt than he would have expected.

Jim had never experienced anything like this in his life before. However, his own reaction surprised him much more than the encounter itself. He didn't feel anything that could be called jealousy and was completely indifferent.

Mona didn't belong to him; she never did. She was on her own. In Jim's opinion, she had the right to do what she wanted, and it wasn't his business.

The discovery was only partially hurtful as Jim had hopes that she sincerely loved him—if only for some time, if only temporarily—but now he realized that she never had. She had Ramah as a lover the whole time, during which her relationship with Jim blossomed. Her affair with Ramah had been going on for three years already.

This was a surprise for Jim, but at the same time, it wasn't. He had guessed something like this might be happening, seeing Ramah's bus at night much more often after his breakup with Mona. *Maybe this was one of the reasons why Mona's husband left,* Jim thought. *Could be. But she did not truly love Ramah either.* He understood that Mona was doing with Ramah exactly the same thing she had done with him and with Lily a number of years before and maybe even with others. Now he believed that what Lily had said was true. Jim was now aware that Mona just used people.

This was sickening and shameless, dirty and nasty, but it wasn't a shock. There was nothing unexpected. Unconsciously, Jim was already prepared for this. He had already heard the shouts of Mona's husband and then Lily's and Bertha's opinions, although he hadn't taken them seriously at first. He didn't trust gossip or someone's opinions about another and preferred to form his own point of view. Now he knew, however, that all those people were right. His personal experience proved it.

From Mona's conversation with Ramah, Jim was only affected by the part about their private relationship. Their stealing of the grocery money didn't bother him. *It is not my business at all,* he thought. *Mona's bosses from the social system should take care of that. Nobody at the group home is hungry. Mona cooks and feeds all of us perfectly. Why would I care about that?*

Jim was disappointed in himself at most. *How could I be so naive and credulous? Of course, I had no life experience, but I wasn't a child either. I should be more careful, especially with regard to my symphony.* With this decision, he ordered himself to forget about Mona altogether and continued quietly his intensive work.

CHAPTER 23

A few days later, Mona called Sharon, tired of waiting for her call. "Why haven't you called me for so long, sweetie?" she asked worriedly. "I'm so impatient about your maestro's answer."

"The symphony is good," her daughter explained without any excitement, "even too good for your first creative work. Maestro said that I'm very talented. He was really impressed. However, I'm in deep trouble, Mom. He said that it's very visible that I have a great deal of experience in composing and asked me to show him my earliest work from previous years, when I had just started. He wants to see how I was developing."

"Oh shit! It could be a problem . . . hmm." Mona bit her lip, thinking. "But I will do it for you, sweetie. I know the way. We'll find your first compositions. I promise."

"Maybe we better just stop it right here, Mom. I didn't expect such a problem. I'm scared that someone will find out that the symphony is stolen."

"No, no, no! Sharon, you should be brave. Remember that you're my daughter. I've never failed even one project that I had thought up. I'm always successful in my affairs."

"But this ugly bastard might notice something!"

"It's my business, my dear. When he finishes his orchestration, he won't notice anything at all ever. Forget it. I'll call you in a couple of days and let you know when his earliest compositions are ready to pick up. Okay, sweetie?"

"Be very careful, Mom. Love you." Sharon took a deep breath, still feeling uncertain and guilty and wanted to hang up, but Mona stopped her.

"Oh, by the way, sweetie!" she exclaimed. "I plan to fire my bus driver, but I don't want to pay for an ad in the paper to find another one. Would you mind doing a little favor for me, sweetie?"

"What do you mean, Mom? Do you want me to work as a bus driver for you? First of all, I have no time. Second, my driver's license is not good for driving a bus."

"Come on, my dear, how could you think that I'd ask you to do such a low-level job? For God's sake, never. I just wanted to ask you to make an ad and to put it on the board at the university or in the campus lobby. Maybe some of the students would like to work here. Group homes are paying pretty well, better than anywhere. I'm sure you know that. But I have special demands. It should be an immigrant—naive, inexperienced with very poor English, with no knowledge of our life, which would be just great. I need someone who doesn't understand much and will do whatever I ask. Do you mind doing this for me, sweetie?"

"Of course, Mom. It's such a trifle, especially compared with what you're doing for me. Of course, I will. Don't worry, I'll put your phone number up, and applicants will call you."

"Oh, no, my dear, please. I don't want everybody to have my phone number. You know . . . we are living in special circumstances. Better that you write your phone number there and choose someone suitable and then send him to me. Okay?"

"Okay, Mom, will do," Sharon promised and hung up, finally breathing with relief. She usually felt scared and uneasy to be involved with her mother's affairs but couldn't disclaim that it was true that Mona always won.

On this afternoon, Jim finished washing the rats and took the elevator to the second floor, heading to his room. As he exited the elevator, he was surprised to see Mona, slowly and carefully emerging from his room with a bag in her hand.

"Oh, here you are, my sweet boy!" she exclaimed cheerfully as she noticed him. "I was looking for you. I wanted to give you some interesting books to read." He heard a tone of meanness in her voice as she said the words *my sweet boy*.

"Thank you. I have no time for reading at the moment," Jim answered abruptly, eyeing her bag attentively. He was absolutely sure that she had stolen the ending of his symphony and that his notes were in there.

Not wasting any more time, he rushed into his room, locked the door, and grabbed his folders from the shelves fearfully. Jim checked every version of his work, every part of the symphony, turning the pages one by one with shaky hands. Everything was okay, nothing missing. Then he checked every disk and finally calmed down.

I'm crazy! I shouldn't be so suspicious, he thought, sighing with relief. *Maybe she really came in to bring me the books in her bag. Oh my, I'm going crazy like all the people here. I should relax. There is nothing to worry about.* Jim returned to his work, still feeling a bit guilty because of his accusatory thoughts about Mona, but then he sunk his head into his creative work, and the unpleasant feeling disappeared bit by bit.

The next day, Jim tried to wash the rats as fast as he could to return to his room as soon as he finished. He still felt tense, leaving his door unlocked.

As Jim rushed out from the elevator on the second floor and walked to his door, he turned his head and saw Mona downstairs with the bag. She just stepped down from the last step of the stairs onto the living room floor and walked through the living room toward the kitchen, heading to her suite. Jim realized that, once again, today he was late. "Mona!" he shouted agitated. "Stop for a second! Wait!"

He rushed to the stairs, crazily slid down, and approached her. Mona stopped in the middle of the kitchen, pursing her lips and looking at him indignantly. She put the bag on the floor beside her feet. "What's going on, Mr. Bogat?" she said sternly.

"Show me what is in your bag!" Jim demanded angrily.

"My bag is my privacy, Mr. Bogat. You have gone too far. You have absolutely no right to control me. It's illegal. I hope your question is only due to your mental illness. You need to be put on medication. I'll talk to our doctor about your condition."

Not listening to her, Jim unzipped the bag quickly and was astonished. There were only two books by Danielle Steel.

Mona looked at him victoriously. "So what?" she said. "You have infringed on my privacy, Mr. Bogat. You suspect me of stealing something from your room. You harass me with your suspicions. You steal my diamond some time ago—it doesn't matter that you return it.

You forced me into a sexual relationship with you, knowing well that I'm a married woman. Don't you think it's too much? I never could guess that you, so little and cute, could be a real criminal. Or you've gone crazy. Who do you prefer I call, the police or the psychiatrist?"

"Stop bluffing," Jim replied with annoyance and disgust, heading back to his room. He realized clearly that today Mona had returned to his room something that she had taken yesterday. That was why her bag was almost empty. But what? It was important to find out.

Jim looked everywhere, examining everything he had in his room; and finally, he found what he was looking for. The folders with his first composing works and his student's exercises, marked by years (1980–82, 1983–85, 1986–88, and so on), were quite messed up. It was visible that Mona was in a hurry putting the pages back into them.

Oh shit! Jim thought with fear. *Silly me! Why didn't I check them yesterday? They should have been empty last night. It was the evidence, and I missed it so easily. I was only concentrating on my symphony. I couldn't even guess that she might be interested in these old things. There is of little value there, just beginner work. I don't get it. But it's certain that she took them. They were well organized and couldn't have gotten so messed up without someone's help.*

The war continued. Restless and agitated, Jim paced back and forth in his room, thinking seriously about what to do. He had no key to lock his door when he went to work in the basement or walk outside. If he asked Mona for the key, she would surely want to keep a copy of it. Jim couldn't call a locksmith to change his lock because he had no money to pay. He felt helpless and couldn't even call his psychologist to consult any longer because of his lack of money. His situation was getting desperate.

It was also impossible to sit in the room all the time like a prisoner, remaining there only to guard the symphony. The constant fear and worry was beginning to get to him. Realizing that Mona might poison him as she had done to Lily, Jim decided to eat and drink only canned food and drinks, even if the mere idea made him sick.

Though I can lock my door from inside, Mona surely has a key. She could also come and smother me with a pillow in my sleep, Jim thought in despair, remembering that he had once seen something like this in a movie. *I must be stronger to fight with her. Maybe I'll have to borrow the smallest of Victor's weights to exercise and gain some weight and build some muscle. That might be the only thing I can do to protect myself.*

The next task was to protect the symphony. Jim saved all versions of it on the DataTraveler that he had bought on the last shopping trip. Jim was sure that the idea to buy it was no accident. He had thought of it at the perfect time and realized now that, obviously, it was fate.

There was still a lot of room left on the DataTraveler after the symphony was saved, so Jim decided to save all his compositions, beginning with the first. This was important now because of Mona's sudden interest in them. Then he put the DataTraveler around his neck and swore to himself never to remove it, not even at night. The only exception would be when taking a shower. Even then, it would have to remain beside his clothes in the bathroom, and the door would have to be locked from inside.

Once all of Jim's creations were saved, Jim spent the rest of the day hiding the disks between the pages of his books and workbooks, which were organized neatly on the shelves. He made a list of what was hidden where and saved it on the DataTraveler as well.

He changed the password on his computer and put the last piano version of the symphony under his mattress along with the completed orchestration pages. He hid symphony CDs into his closet, on the shelves under his T-shirts, jeans, and towels. Then Jim put all the extra copies of his symphony and of his earlier creations into a bag and slowly pulled it out from his room toward the elevator. The bag was quite heavy, and Jim couldn't carry it, but he was strong enough to pull it.

In the basement, he pulled the bag toward the fireplace, started the fire, and burned the pages of his heart and soul one by one. The tears slid slowly down his cheeks as he watched as the pages, enveloped in flames, turned brown and then black and finally were reduced to ash.

Jim felt as though he were an ancient man sacrificing his only child for his highest aim, though he was not yet sure what that aim was. He didn't know. But he knew that something had happened because his life completely changed at this point. It changed even more than after Grandma Cathy's death, and it changed forever.

"Dear God," he whispered, "I'm giving You everything I have to save it from this evil white rat. Just send me love. Send me a woman. I can't stand this war alone. I can't live in hate. It burns me inside. I'm accustomed to living in love. I need it. I crave it. If I can't have love, I am ready to die in this basement, to burn myself here, together with my music. But please, dear God, give me a chance to live, to create, to love."

Jim sat on the floor and watched as the burned pages scattered into ash inside the fireplace. It was his heart slowly dying in front of his eyes. It was unbearable, and he sat there, sobbing soundlessly.

He still didn't know if God existed and had no idea if He was listening to him. Once again, only silence was his answer except here, in the basement, he heard the sound of water in the pipes, the hum of the refrigerators and the boilers, and the noise of rats swarming, scratching, and squeaking in the cage.

God didn't send him a sign. Why? Did He not exist? Or was it simply not yet time? Jim had no idea.

CHAPTER 24

Some days passed until once, at lunch, Jim was surprised to discover that Mona and Ramah were absent. Not seeing Mona was a relief for him, but at the same time, it was quite unusual. "Where is she?" he asked the nurse Sue.

"Mona went to the bank," Sue responded happily. "Today is payday, and she's usually bringing all our money here for us."

That evening, returning from his walk, Jim saw Mona fussing in the kitchen. She ignored him, and he returned the favor, heading silently to his room.

The following day, Mona and Ramah were not at lunch once again. "Where are they?" Jim inquired of Andy, one of the nurses.

"Mona told us that something happened yesterday," he said as he shrugged. "I don't know exactly what."

The next morning, two policemen arrived to speak to the nurses. As Jim walked out for lunch, he saw them leaving with Mona. The policemen noticed Jim too but didn't ask him a thing. Perhaps they considered him one of the mentally ill residents with whom there was no reason to talk.

Ramah wasn't at lunch again, and dying of curiosity, Jim even couldn't eat. "What's going on?" Jim demanded of Sue and Josef. "Tell me, please. I saw Mona with the policemen. And where is Ramah?"

"Mona left to take care of some paperwork with the police," Josef explained. "Their bus was robbed, and all our money was stolen."

"Oh no! How come it happened?" Jim exclaimed in disbelief.

"Mona is the only one who knows. She went into the forest with Ramah, leaving all the money on the bus. Then she lost him in the woods somehow. Later, she found him, so they returned to the bus and found that it had been robbed. Mona guessed that Ramah had taken the money, so she fired him. He doesn't work here anymore," Sue added, lowering her eyes. It was evident that she felt uncomfortable saying that.

"Ramah? Come on!" Jim recalled the scandal between Mona and Ramah. Shaking his head, thoughtfully he commented, "No, I'm sure Ramah didn't."

"Maybe not. The police didn't even arrest him, but he's still not with us anymore," Josef said wistfully. "He was a very nice guy. I feel pity toward him. It's not a good time to lose a job. Actually, it's never good for anybody but for him especially. He told us that, this weekend, he's getting married. His wedding is already arranged and the guests invited. It will be a beautiful wedding and big too. The whole East Indian community is invited. Ramah's father organized everything . . . and, suddenly, such a problem. Gosh, it's bad for him."

"Did Mona hear when he told you about his wedding?" Jim asked.

"Of course. Ramah was so happy. He announced it to everybody. Actually, all of us are invited. Yes, Sue?"

The nurse nodded as she added, "I already got a present for him."

Jim now realized what had happened. *White Rat!* He shook his head with disgust, feeling bad for Ramah. *It's her revenge. How would she live now with menopause and without a lover? Look for a new bus driver? Or kill me and put a new handicap in my room to use him?*

"How about your salary?" Jim asked. "Will you be able to live this month without money?"

"Don't worry," Sue confirmed. "The social system will return the money to us and also provide for all the residents this month. I'm sure that Mona has insurance for the group home for cases like this. None of us have lost anything, just Ramah."

The news was unexpected and disturbing. It agitated the group home residents and gave the staff lots to gossip about. However, over the next few days, Mona was hardly ever at the lunch table. "Is she still doing the paperwork at the police station?" Jim teased sarcastically.

"No." Nurse Rona grinned. "Now she's driving the guys to work in her car. Actually, there are only two of them, Ella and Todd. Maggie and Victor are sick. And then Mona has many things to do in the city, like shopping, appointments, interviewing people for the bus driver position, and so on. She'll be back only after three o'clock when she brings the guys back from work."

That's perfect, Jim thought. *I still have the chance to visit Victor and to borrow some weights from him.*

"What happened to Victor?" Jim wanted to know.

"He's just got a cold," Andy explained. "Mona ordered him to stay home. She hates runny noses in her car. In a couple of days, he will be okay."

After lunch, Jim brought the rest of his food to his room, washed the rats, and walked to see Victor. He knocked gently on the door to be polite, knowing well that he wouldn't get any answer. Then Jim turned the doorknob and went in.

Victor was lying on his workout bench in the middle of the room, holding the bar of his big heavy metal with both hands. He lifted the weight, held it up for a few seconds, and then lowered it down. The metal bar banged against the holders, which were metal as well. It was quite noisy. Victor's T-shirt, light gray hair, and white beard were all wet from perspiration. The large drops oozed on his forehead, slid down his temples, and fell onto the leather bench beside his head. He was all shaky from tension.

"Hi, Victor," Jim said sociably. "How are you today? I heard that you have a cold. I guess you'll get better soon if you keep on doing what you're doing. My grandma always said that the best treatment for a cold is to sweat. When I would get a cold, she would give me hot tea with raspberry to drink, and she would cover me with a sheepskin blanket. I would get very wet, just like you now, and it helped right away."

Victor didn't answer, but Jim didn't really expect any response. He just felt drawn to this man, especially knowing his story, and tried to socialize a bit, hoping that maybe Victor would understand what he was saying. But it didn't happen. Victor continued exercising silently with the same speed, automatically, almost like a zombie. Only the sweat and his heavy breathing showed that he was a living creature, not a machine.

Jim looked around and saw an untouched meal on the table. Beside it was a little glass of water and an oval orange pill. *Victor begins working out early in the morning*, Jim realized. *He even didn't take a lunch break and still hadn't taken his medication.*

"Uh-oh," Jim said, full of care and sympathy, "it's not good. Maybe you didn't have an appetite because you're too tired and have a cold, but your medication . . . I think you need it, Victor. If you didn't take it at the right time, I think you'll feel worse. You'd better stop for a minute, please, and take it."

He took the pill with his two tiny fingers and the glass of water with his other hand, stepped toward Victor, and reached out to him. The pill was very slippery and so was the glass; it wasn't easy for Jim to hold them both, but he tried to force Victor to take them.

However, it didn't help. Victor banged his weight on its holders so hard that the impact dumbfounded Jim. He quivered, and his weak small fingers lost hold of the pill, and then the little glass of water dropped to the floor. The brown carpet was quite soft, so the glass didn't break, but the water poured out right over the pill, which dissolved in an instant and disappeared between the carpet fibers.

"Oh, gosh!" Jim exclaimed, bewildered. "Sorry, Victor! Silly me! I am so clumsy! Oh shit! What will we do now?"

Victor didn't react.

Jim bent over, picked up the glass, and put it back on the table. His first move was to go and call Rona or Andy and ask them to give Victor another pill, but then he remembered that Mona usually managed Victor's medication by herself, and that stopped him. He didn't want to cause another scandal with Mona and decided that it would be better just to keep silent. The empty glass was on the table—it must look like Victor had already taken his pill.

"Sorry, Victor," Jim repeated guiltily. "I'm really sorry. I only hope that nothing bad will happen to you if you miss a pill. You'll have it tomorrow, I promise. I'll come and make sure that you have it. But don't be angry at me, please. Okay?"

Victor continued his exercise silently, and Jim left the room feeling frustrated, forgetting completely what he had come for.

All evening, Jim worked on his symphony and didn't even walk outside. He didn't want to see Mona or to leave his room unlocked. And he still felt a little guilty about Victor's pill.

The next day, Mona wasn't at lunch once again, and Jim felt free to visit Victor once more and, this time, maybe to borrow the smallest weights from him at last. When Jim entered the room, he saw Victor on his bench exercising, his lunch and medication on the table, just like yesterday. It seemed to him that nothing had changed.

"Hi, Victor," he said, surprised to see Victor stop lifting as he sat up on the bench and looked at him. His deep brown eyes still were empty, but it seemed to Jim that a little sparkle of awareness flashed there for a moment.

"How are you today?" Jim continued. "No cold? I told you that sweating would help."

Victor eyed him attentively. His lips quivered suddenly as he quietly asked, "Johnny?"

"Oh!" Jim was so overwhelmed with surprise that he was silent and stood still. He felt sad, realizing that Victor had called him by the name of his little son who had been killed. The boy's name was Johnny, according to what Mona had told Jim as she showed him Victor's room and equipment for the first time.

Feeling uneasy, Jim at last found the power to hold himself in check, coughed a bit, and said carefully, "I'm sorry, Victor. I dropped your pill yesterday. Do you want to have it now?"

Surprisingly, Victor nodded, still gazing at him.

Jim took the pill from the table, very carefully this time; squeezed it in his tiny fist; and gave it to Victor. Then he took the little glass of water with both hands, carried it to the man very accurately, and handed it to him. Victor took the pill with two fingers, held it for a while in front of his eyes, and examined it. Then he whispered clearly, "Headache."

"Do you have a headache?" Jim asked.

Victor shook his head. "This is headache," he repeated what he had said a bit louder and suddenly dropped the pill into the glass. It dissolved rapidly, and the water turned a light orange color.

"Oh!" Jim moaned, again bewildered as Victor poured the water onto the carpet and returned the glass to him.

"No! You should take it!" Jim tried to protest, even if it was too late.

"Quiet, Johnny, quiet . . . shh . . . keep quiet," Victor murmured, looking straight into Jim's eyes. "Just . . . quiet." He lifted his hand and pressed his index finger to his lips.

Mesmerized, not removing his glance from Victor's eyes, Jim automatically stepped back and returned the glass to the table, not quite grasping what was going on. "You can talk," he noted, still astonished. "Maybe you can understand, can't you?"

Victor didn't answer. He only took a deep breath, lay on his back, and started to lift his weights again. Jim understood that the conversation was finished for today, but he tried to return to the point of his interest.

"Sorry to bother you, Victor," he said, walking around the room. "I actually came to borrow some little weights from you. I want to exercise to get stronger. Of course, I wouldn't be as strong as you, but I need to gain more muscle. Can I take this one?" Jim approached a set of dumbbells that contained five different sizes and took the smallest one. Even this little dumbbell was too heavy for him, so he took only one of them, instead of a couple, and held it with his both hands, instead of one like a normal person would do.

"I won't even ask you to show me how to use them," Jim continued, walking slowly to the door and breathing heavily because carrying the dumbbell was much more difficult for him than he had expected. "I'll find instructions on the internet. Thank you, Victor. I'll return it in a couple of months. Okay?"

Victor banged his weight onto the holders. "Be quiet, Johnny . . . just quiet," he repeated in a whisper to Jim from behind. Confused about what was going on, Jim left the room.

It seemed strange to him that Victor's mind had begun to awaken when he stopped taking his pills. Jim thought about it all night and wanted to know more. However, the next day when he peered inside Victor's room to see how he was doing, the room was empty. Victor must have been well enough to go to work at the factory with Ella and Todd.

CHAPTER 25

A week later, Mona finally appeared at the group home lunch table. She seemed to be especially elated as if she was celebrating some sort of victory; perhaps one more episode of her business life had been successfully completed. The events surrounding the bus robbery was almost over, and the police investigation promised to take a long time as there were no further leads. As a result of this story, the remuneration system at the group home was renewed. From now on, the workers' salary would be directly deposited into their bank accounts.

Another result was personal. Mona had gotten the revenge she wanted; Ramah was fired. A new bus driver had already replaced him.

Interestingly, Mona had added another diamond necklace to her collection. She had hidden it by now at Sharon's house, proving to herself and her daughter that she never failed. It was obvious that she had used the stolen money from the bus, but there was no evidence as always.

During lunch, from time to time, Mona glanced over at Jim inconspicuously. Once, as their eyes met, she held his glance for a moment, smiled playfully, and slowly licked her lips, showing Jim openly that she wanted him again. Jim felt uncomfortable in light of such open expressions of indecency. He felt that Mona was turning him on, something he did not want.

Jim finished his lunch, packed up what was left for later, and silently left for his room. He felt all shaky because of Mona's hints and took a cold shower right away, standing under the water for a few minutes longer than usual. However, as he walked out of his bathroom, wrapped in his little dark green robe, he found a porno magazine beside his computer. Jim grabbed the magazine, surprised at first, wondering what it was and how it had appeared on the desk in his room. He realized indignantly that only Mona could have left something like this in his room while he was in the shower. Her imprudence angered him at first, but soon the magazine had riveted him.

It was a very beautiful magazine and of professional quality. It contained pictures of teenage girls in enticing poses and a number of dirty short stories. Jim was a mature man but not as stoic as a saint. He wanted to throw the magazine away, but he couldn't.

He sat in his armchair and flipped casually through the magazine, surprisingly discovering immediate erection. Soon Jim couldn't help but flip through the magazine once again, slowly turning the pages one by one. Then he looked again, paying special attention to details. The feeling of lust that resulted was so intense that it began to resemble pain. It was impossible for Jim to tolerate it.

Since his last sex session with Mona, quite a lot of time had already flown by. Jim managed not to think about or concentrate on sexual thoughts and would take a cold shower if they came. The problem seemed to have been solved.

However, the dark, terrifying power accumulated gradually deep inside his little body throughout the month. He didn't know a thing about it and couldn't even imagine how sexually hungry he was. Finally, it built up inside him to the point where it began to overflow like a fountain. Jim took a look at the magazine, which left him with a sudden huge ejaculation. He couldn't resist its power. The complete relief that soon came was a great relaxation for him, but it was not what he wanted. All these things were like torture to him. The physiological function of the human body was the same as that of an animal. It was natural but wild and dirty. There was no spirit in it at all, nothing even close.

Jim realized that Mona continued to consider him a brainless little animal, a sex-obsessed rat, a slave overcome by physical needs that she could play with as she wanted. Her attitude toward him was extremely abusive and humiliated him. Feeling all wet, sticky, and full of disgust and hatred toward her, in anger, Jim threw the magazine across the room and went back to the shower. He turned on the warm water to wash up first and then turned it to cold. Then he repeated these warm-cold showers for about ten times until he finally calmed down and could leave the bathroom, lie down on his bed, and sleep for a couple of hours.

When Jim woke up, it was already evening, and he was as hungry as a wolf. He ate all the food he had, even what was prepared for tomorrow's breakfast. Finishing his meal, Jim was upset that he had missed his creative hours. Mona, still insidiously involved in his life, interrupted his work, ruined his plans and dreams, and tried to crush his soul.

Why? What is so attractive in me? Why doesn't she want to find another man and leave me alone? Jim despaired. *Where is her new bus driver anyway?* he thought. *It seems as though someone has already been hired and has begun to work since the guys had left for work on the bus this morning. But a new driver hasn't come for lunch. It's strange because Ramah usually did. Oh God, how I wish he is a handsome man and captures Mona's attention and lust so I can be free from her at last.*

Jim decided to make up for lost hours and continue his work late into the evening, but before he started, he wanted to put a definitive end to his relationship with Mona. He took the porno magazine and a big black marker and wrote the word *no* in huge letters right across the cover on top of a young girl's beautiful body. Then Jim walked downstairs, went to the Mona's suite, and slipped the magazine under her door.

Walking back to his room, he smirked sarcastically, imagining that Mona was now lying on her bed, naked, silver blue in the moonlight; wearing only one of her diamond necklaces; and waiting for him. Jim knew that she was sure her magazine would work, and he felt proud of himself that he could defeat her influence and the magnetic attraction of his sexual hormones. *I have proved to myself that my soul and mind are stronger than my body,* Jim thought, considering himself a winner in this last round of Mona's game. *I'm not an animal, not a slave, not a doll. I'm a spiritual being, and I am free.*

A few days passed quite regularly, and it seemed to Jim that Mona had finally left him alone. At least she was ignoring him during lunch now. He didn't talk to her or look at her. However, he knew well that Mona wasn't the type of person who could forget everything or forgive something. Jim felt that if she had a plan in her head, nothing would stop her from carrying it out. He was sure that she still had something in mind for him. Jim was on the alert, expecting a storm sometime ahead.

In this situation, Jim didn't feel safe and was unable to sleep well. Most of the time, he continued to be tense and nervous. That tension, along with a sense of hidden danger, pushed him to exercise with Victor's weights every morning and continue his orchestration work intensively and strictly on schedule. He even put in extra hours to finish it faster.

PART 2

LADA

CHAPTER 26

One nice afternoon in the middle of April, Jim was composing while lying on the floor as he usually did. The pages he would write on were quite big, and working on the table with them would be uncomfortable for him. Suddenly, something in one of the accords caught his attention. It looked as if one of the notes was wrong. He stopped writing and tried to hear the note in his mind and even hummed it a bit, but it wasn't enough. So he decided to play it on the piano.

Jim stood up, lifted the piano lid, climbed onto his high stool, and started to play. Correcting the accord only took him a few seconds. He quickly realized how horribly he missed his piano and decided to play more. He had no time to play last month, being completely busy with the orchestration, which required the work of his mind, his ability to hear sounds internally, knowledge of instruments, and skill in writing music. Playing piano wasn't involved in this procedure, and he had neglected it.

Jim slowly played the main part of his symphony, enjoying the beautiful melody. A part was performed by clarinets with the light tremolo of the first violins in the background. This music was supposed to express the theme of the first chapter of his symphony—the sunrise over the ocean. It was like a breeze over the silver, slightly pink ocean surface, and in Jim's imagination, it even smelled like the ocean.

He immersed himself fully into the music and didn't even notice when the door to his room opened. He suddenly noticed that it had gotten lighter in the room. Jim hated when residents or staff interrupted his piano playing. He abruptly turned to the door, ready to reprimand sternly anyone who would break his rules by entering while he was busy playing, but instead, he remained motionless, his mouth hanging open in surprise.

A young woman stood at the door, looking at him curiously. She burst out laughing but suddenly stopped herself, covering her mouth with her palm. But her mischievous green eyes stared straight on. "Hi," she said and paused, continuing to gaze at Jim, still not knowing if it was all right to laugh or not.

"I'm sorry, you just look so funny. Maybe it's impolite to laugh, but . . .," she murmured bashfully and then immediately found an excuse, "I don't know. I'm new here. I might do things wrong, which may seem rude to others. Sorry about that. You shouldn't feel offended. I didn't mean to hurt you. It's just my inexperience. Will you forgive me?"

Jim silently nodded, staring at her. The girl was so young, pretty, and innocent that Jim was left speechless by his excitement. He couldn't believe his eyes. Full of rapture, he held his breath, watching her and terrified that she was a ghost who could disappear in a wink—as sudden as she had appeared. It didn't really matter what she was talking about. Jim didn't listen to her words; he saw only her beautifully outlined lips moving, her eyes sparkling, her long wavy light brown, almost blond hair covering her shoulders.

She was athletic but not tall. Through the thin fabric of her short sundress (white with pink roses), Jim eagerly undressed her with his glance, grasping her ripe apple breasts, thin waist, and graceful hips with his hungry eyes. Her face, arms, and legs were well tanned, and she wore sandals on her feet. It didn't matter that it was still April, and the girl was holding a light wind jacket in her hand; she looked like she just came from Hawaii and even smelled like an orchard of fresh limes.

Jim couldn't say exactly whether this was the aroma of a perfume or a shampoo. He merely breathed it in, combining in his mind this bouquet with the scent of the ocean of his symphony, which he experienced right before the girl appeared. Altogether, these fragrances created the image of a hot, torrid ocean, washing the rocks of a volcano island covered with coco palms, lemon bushes, and orchids.

The girl was awesome. Her appearance seemed impossible here in the nursing home. She didn't match. She was from another world, an unknown world. She was a fairy who suddenly burst into Jim's life from a fairy tale and who unexpectedly opened his door without even knocking. Jim was quite sure that she had come into his room by mistake. If she wasn't a ghost and didn't disappear, she must be somebody's relative coming for a visit and accidentally opening a wrong door. "Who are you?" he mumbled so quietly that she could barely hear him.

The girl laughed carelessly and answered, "Do you hear that my accent is so horrible? That's why you are asking? I know my English is so bad. Sorry, but I can't help it. I've been here for about five years but still have this ugly accent. I'm an immigrant. Actually, I'm the new bus driver. My name is Lada. Do you want to shake hands to acknowledge our acquaintance?"

Still laughing, she entered the room, closed the door behind her, approached Jim, and reached her hand out. With uncertainty, he dipped his tiny hand into her hot and strong palm and noticed that her fingers were thin and long. "Nice to meet you," Lada said, smiling. "And what is your name, Mr. Little One?"

"Jim," he whispered, his lips shaking. "Jim Bogat."

"Oh, do you want me to call you by the last name? Mr. Bogat? It sounds Ukrainian to me. I am Ukrainian too. My last name is Meleshko, but I'm absolutely sure I don't want you call me Miss Meleshko. Lada is much better, isn't it?"

"Yes," Jim said with a sigh. "It's beautiful. I never heard it before. I have only heard of the cars called Lada. I read about them on the internet."

"Oh, that is a big problem. Somebody who was in love with some women many years ago gave their names to a bunch of cars, like Mercedes, Chevy, Lada, and now everybody only knows the cars. But it's not fair. The women's names were first. Lada is an ancient Russian Ukrainian name. Do you know what it means? The goddess of love and beauty, the same as the Greek Aphrodite or the Roman Venus. So you see, my name is quite old. I guess more than a couple of thousand years old."

Jim coughed lightly, confused, and then finally noted in a normal voice, "Certainly, by its meaning, that name perfectly matches you." He was even surprised by his own bravery to say such a thing, but she took the compliment with no objection and thankfully smiled back at him.

In spite of her good looks, it was clear that she had not been spoiled by admirers.

"Sit down, please." Jim pointed to the armchair across from him. "If you're not in a hurry, of course. Since you are a new employee, I guess you are taking a tour of the group home to meet the residents, aren't you?"

Lada sat into the armchair and shyly pulled her short skirt toward her knees to cover a bit more of her legs. "No." She shook her head, still smiling and continuing to gabble, "I've been working for four days already and have met all the guys who take the bus. Why would I need to meet the others? I'll meet everyone on a shopping day or when there is a field trip. You're probably surprised that I'm here in your room. It happened accidentally. I have never come into the house before, but today it was quite hot outside. On the way home from the factory, I wanted a drink but dropped my bottle. Oh, you know, sometimes I'm so clumsy. It doesn't even matter that my fingers are strong and agile because I play violin." Lada giggled confusingly and took a deep breath. "So I asked Mrs. Lainer if I could come in and have a drink. When we came in, she asked Nurse Sue to get me a drink, and then Mrs. Lainer left. While I was drinking, I heard someone playing piano, and I decided to take a look to see who it was. And it was you, Jim. Isn't it funny?"

He nodded, not wanting to remove his excited big eyes from her, but Lada didn't match his glance and curiously looked around the room instead.

"Wow," she commented, amused, observing Jim's stuff. "I'm going to have more than a thousand questions here. Do you play piano? How do you use the computer? Why is it connected with your piano? Why are the notes on the floor? Is it a score? Are you writing an orchestra piece? Are you Ukrainian? Can you speak Ukrainian? Who are the people in those pictures on the wall? What is this statue of? Why are you so little? How can your tiny fingers play music? Who taught you to play music? Oh my gosh, how can I stop? It's too much, isn't it? I'm too talkative, aren't I? How can you tolerate me?" She grinned contagiously and sincerely.

Jim couldn't help but laugh with her. "I'm going to answer all your questions and many more," he replied lightheartedly as they finally stopped laughing. "And I'm going to have *more than a thousand questions* for you. Who are you? How come you're here, in America? How come you're here at our group home? How come you're a bus driver? How come you play violin? Who taught you? Who is your family? How come you're so beautiful? And maybe we can speak Ukrainian."

"Who is your family?" Lada exclaimed happily, speaking Ukrainian. "Do you understand me?"

"Of course, I do, and I can answer too," Jim assured her in Ukrainian as well. "Do I have an accent?"

"Barely, just a small one."

"My grandma taught me because I was raised on a Ukrainian farm. But later, I took Ukrainian in university for four years. I also took English and French to be more educated and then Italian because my grandma told me that I have some Italian blood. In reality, Italian is supposed to be my mother tongue, but it didn't happen. My parents . . . actually, I lost my parents and was adopted by farmers."

"Gosh, that's so romantic. It sounds like a novel to me," Lada commented excitedly. "Such a mix of languages and nationalities. Unbelievable!"

"It's our American reality, you know. Italian is also related to music. Most of the musical terminology is Italian, and when I started to study music, my teacher told me that I had to learn it."

"You're so educated." Lada shook her head. "It's difficult to believe."

"Why? Do I look stupid?"

"Come on, Jim." Lada waved her hands. "I didn't mean that. Sometimes I do not express my thoughts clearly because of my poor English. I meant that, for me, it's difficult to believe that someone could study so much. I'm actually quite lazy. I'm studying music at the university here in Minneapolis. I play violin, but I'm not doing so well, being so lazy."

"You can be," Jim reassured her. "But I couldn't. You might have a lot of other things in your life, but I don't have anything else. All I have is my music. It was my only fun, my only business, and my only happiness. It was predestined by my birth. I'm really thankful to my fate that I was born in the twentieth century and not the Middle Ages. Back then, I would have been a jester and worn the funny, strange clothes by the court of some earl or prince and nothing else. Our society gave me the possibility of being a normal person, even if I was injured as an embryo."

"Yes, I know." Lada nodded with compassion before taking on an air of seriousness. "And I really appreciate that America is so democratic, so perfect, and so helpful. Only I could estimate the situation for you because only I know that in Russia or the Ukraine, you would be suffering no less than in the Middle Ages. You would be teased, hurt, and abused a lot and wouldn't have any help at all. I know that from my own experience. You see, I'm always laughing. It's because I'm happy here. I'm happy that I was so lucky to emigrate. In the Ukraine, which was at that time a part of the Soviet Union, my father was killed in the summer of 1991, right before the last communist putsch. He was a journalist, a military correspondent, and wrote an article about the Russians in Afghanistan. He wrote the truth."

Lada failed to speak because of the spasm in her throat. She stopped, bit her lip, and closed her eyes, fighting the tears back.

"I'm sorry to hear that," Jim said fondly with sincere sympathy toward her. "I understand that if politics interfere with one's life, it always brings something horrible. Thanks to fate, you're safe and free now. We'll return to this subject later, if you want to talk to me again. Now I suggest a little walk outside. Is that okay with you?"

Jim slid down from his high chair and approached her, adding bashfully, "If you're not too ashamed to walk with me, of course."

Lada wiped two little tears from her cheek and sniffled. "Why should I be ashamed?" she asked, shaking her head and smiling at him once again. "You're funny. You're really so little. You look like a child to me. You know, I've always dreamed of having a child, especially a boy. When I was twelve years old, I took a baby-sized doll, wrapped it into a blanket, and proudly walked around our district, showing the bundle I carried to the neighbors and telling them it was my baby inside, my son. Can you guess what happened next?"

"The people gave you presents for him—baby clothes and bottles? Or congratulation cards with best wishes? Or flowers?"

"It's a nice difference in mentality." Lada smirked bitterly. "You're lucky, Jim, that you'll never grasp it. The people got angry. They complained to my mom that I was a little prostitute because I was having a baby without being married, especially at age twelve. They blamed me and shouted that I ought to be ashamed. All of them hated me and my baby, and I hated them. It was horrible. My mom begged me to stop playing this game and to stop defaming our family, which already had enough problems. She took my doll and hid it away, saying that I was too big to play with dolls. So they killed my father, and then they killed my dream to have a son.

"You know, Jim, it's better for me not to remember my motherland because I always cry when I do. I don't cry from the nostalgia, like others, but because of the feelings of hate for my country and its mentality. That place broke my heart and abused me a thousand times, beginning in my early childhood. Sorry, Jim. I won't talk about it anymore. You'd better give me your hand and come for a walk."

"It's okay," he said peacefully, full of understanding and compassion for her story. Jim never thought about the mental difference between the countries in the East and America. He sensed now that this girl was like a winged bird—so helpless, fragile, and full of hidden pain. She was too young to carry such a burden from the past, but it was obvious that she did. Lada intrigued him and gave him some unusual information to think about but not yet, later. Now he was only enjoying her touch on his hand. "It's really good if we can be friends."

He was nicely surprised to see her mischievous smile and hear her say confidently, "We can, Jim. It's very interesting to talk to you. You're so unusual. You seem to be an enigma to me. And I'll solve it. Do you remember that you still owe me the answers to my thousand questions?"

He nodded, feeling flattered that she still remembered that. It was a perfect start. Jim was scared even to think about anything more, knowing well that Lada was a woman and that she was not for him. She was from heaven. He had begged for an ugly, sick, old, and handicapped woman, but to send him such a beauty was an odd twist of fate. He felt as though his condition was being scoffed at. This girl wasn't equal to him in physical qualities, and they didn't fit together as a couple. He knew that he had to forget even the slightest idea of a relationship. It was hopeless.

However, Jim was very glad to have met this girl who had such a deep soul and seemed to have suffered a lot during her life. This was the only thing about her that was comparable to Jim's situation. It was something that could possibly bring them closer to each other, but it was merely a possibility. For now, it was amazing just to have such a connection with someone and to talk so openly. Jim had missed this for so long.

Continuing to speak, laughing and joking with each other, they left Jim's room and walked into the empty hallway. It was about seven o'clock, and the nurses were bringing the residents into the rooms and preparing them for bed. "Let's go downstairs," Jim said to Lada. "I'll show you a trick."

He sat on the top step and slid down as he usually did. She gave him a thumbs-up and grinned. "Wow, I want to try that too!" she exclaimed jealously but then looked down at her short skirt and changed her mind. "Well, I'll do that tomorrow when I have my jeans on. It'll be better for sure. Would you mind teaching me?"

"I promise," Jim assured. "It's quite easy. You'll get it."

They left the house and walked through the garden in front of the building. Then they proceeded through a meadow and toward the forest. It wasn't easy for Jim to walk so far, but holding hands with her, he could manage.

The untamed forest intoxicated and roused both of them with powerful aromas of rotten old leaves and damp soil under their feet. There was the smell of fresh green leaves too, and the air was full of the scent of the first spring flowers—primroses, violets, yellow bells—and the wildly blossoming chokecherry trees. It was a dizzying mix of fragrant smells that aroused everyone and stirred all life nearby to awakening and kicking around. Spring was the time of renewal.

Holding hands, Lada and Jim walked, chatting about nothing, teasing each other, and giggling a lot. Lada broke a few thin branches off a chokecherry tree and intertwined them into her hair on the side of her head. "How do you like it, Jim?" She laughed, holding a provocative pose. "Do I look like a gypsy woman or a Spanish noblewoman?"

"Amazing," he answered, eyeing her, full of excitement, knowing well that it was only a game and that she was playing with him, just like she played with her baby doll at age twelve. He was absolutely sure that she didn't feel the same need for him that he felt for her; she merely wanted the admiration, and it didn't matter from whom.

Jim was an adult, and he was mature enough to understand the situation he was in. He considered Lada very womanly and saw that she was a girl who wanted love and admiration. Jim didn't even know if she had a boyfriend or not. It was impossible, in his opinion, for such a beautiful creature to be alone. He didn't dare ask or even hint about it.

He remembered what Grandma Cathy had told him. "There are some women in the world who can flirt even with a chair or wardrobe and can laugh even if you show them your index finger. It's because they're young, healthy, and full of energy. Life is brewing inside them. But mostly, they're not serious and are only playing with men." Now Jim was quite sure that Lada was one of them.

During their conversation in his room, she unveiled a bit of her soul and revealed the tragedy of her life; but while walking in the forest, she was in a good mood and seemed playful and lighthearted to Jim. Yet he saw another side of her too. Anyway, it was so exciting to walk with her, and Jim was overjoyed. He was ready to forgive her lack of seriousness. Lada was too young and too invigorating, and this was just perfect.

Inviting her for a walk, Jim had agreed to a game without knowing it. She would play the role of a princess, and he would be her admirer. Now they were both enjoying this game, feeling that it was exactly what they really needed.

However, it was time to go home. In the past, Jim had never ventured so far from home, even on the farm. It didn't matter that the biggest part of their walk had been spent sitting on the rotten log and chatting, but Jim felt tired. He didn't want to show Lada his weakness and helplessness, but he had no choice. It was better to walk home now than to later collapse and let his princess carry him. Jim had already survived this shame with Mona. With this girl, it would be even more shameful, and he didn't want this, so he suggested returning to the group home.

Jim didn't even know where he had found the strength to hold himself in check and walk, but he did it. He had captured Lada's attention by talking and was sure that she hadn't noticed how difficult the walk home was for him. He felt like a man and was proud of his own willpower.

In his room, they continued to chat and laugh until Lada finally saw that it was already getting darker, and it was time for her to drive the bus home. "Would you like to give me your phone number?" Jim asked before she left. "Maybe sometime we could chat again. Here is my cell number."

"That's nice." Lada smiled, taking the little yellow note from his tiny hand. She tore it in half and wrote her phone number on one of the pieces. "I didn't get all the answers to my questions," she reminded him. "I still have about half a thousand left. Right, Jim? Anyway, bye. See you tomorrow."

"Sure. Good night, Lada." He was quite positive that he wouldn't see her tomorrow or again at all. He didn't take the bus much, only on shopping days. Jim had the feeling that she would soon forget their walk and their friendly discussions and would never come to his room again. This girl still was a mystery to him. She wasn't easy to understand.

After she left, Jim lay down immediately, sadly realizing a normal life of dating and girls were not for him. Even the simple walk had left him exhausted. He would never be normal. He couldn't do any of the activities that healthy young people were accustomed to doing—walking, dancing, skateboarding, biking, playing ball, racing, and so on. Lying on his bed, he was overwhelmed by this thoughts and feelings, until suddenly he noticed Lada's jacket hanging on the back of the chair.

My God, he thought, startled, *she forgot it.* It was a perfect hook for him to hold on to. It was an opportunity, but for what?

Jim looked at the clock and could barely wait until an hour passed. It was just enough time for Lada to return to her house in the city. He reached for the phone two or three times with uncertainty, until he finally found the courage to make the call. Listening to the long rings, he felt sick to his stomach with fear of what she would think of his call. Then he heard her nice voice. "Hello."

"Lada," he said, his voice quavering, "sorry to bother you. It's Jim. You forgot your jacket here in my room. I only want to let you know that it is safe, and tomorrow you can get it."

"I know." She laughed. "I realized I forgot it about half the way to the city. There was no reason to return. I didn't worry, but thank you anyway, Jim. You know, your voice sounds so nice on the phone. I could have thought I was talking to a movie star or a famous singer. It's so impressive."

"Thank you."

"Has anyone ever told you that?"

"No, never."

"Just don't let it go to your head."

"I won't. I promise."

"What are you doing now, Jim? I'm already in bed. Are you sitting or standing?"

"I'm standing in the middle of my room," he lied.

"Could you sit in your armchair, please?" Lada requested.

"Of course, I can, but why?"

"We're still not finished talking. It might take quite a long time. Do you want to continue? About my questions? I don't really want to sleep yet. What about you?"

Jim was half dead from fatigue, but it didn't matter. "I want to continue," he said confidently. "I won't go to sleep yet."

CHAPTER 27

L ada was lying in bed, settled cozily, with the phone squeezed between her cheek and the pillow. She smiled as she looked into the gloominess of her room. She didn't know why, but she was in a really good mood tonight.

The light in her bedroom was off, but the rays of the lanterns outside in the backyard penetrated through the embroidered flowers on the lacy curtains and drew whimsical patterns on the walls. The shadows of the trees' branches, shaking from the light spring wind, added even more mysterious attraction to these miraculous drawings. She loved to watch them before sleeping and even in the middle of the night, if she woke up occasionally. Now she enjoyed them while listening to Jim's voice and feeling excited by his unusual life story.

"You described everything so well, Jim," Lada said dreamily. "It feels like I can see the farm, the birch grove, you sitting in an armchair under the trees and working on your computer. Then Grandma Cathy came to you and sat on her little squeaky stool beside you. You said, 'Look, Grandma, at what I composed for you today.'

"She looked in askance at your computer screen and shook her gray-haired head with a bun at its back. 'Oh, I don't understand anything of that anyway, darling.'

"'But you have ears, Grandma. Listen, please.' And you turned on your music. Wow, Jim, it was so romantic, so happy."

"Actually, not much romantic," Jim objected. "It was all quite casual. But it was quiet, calm, and full of love from both sides. It was real happiness, though I didn't appreciate it at the time being as much as I appreciate it now that I've lost it. But alas, nothing can be returned or changed. It is what it is now."

"It seemed good, and it was good, Jim. At least you had one person in your life who truly loved you."

"You were luckier than me. You had two, Mom and Dad, right?"

"Right," Lada said uncertainly. "And it seemed good, sometimes even perfect for outsiders, but it was horrible in reality."

"What was horrible? Politics?" Jim wanted to know.

"Oh, no." Lada took a deep breath. "I am not talking about politics, regime, and country problems. I was a child. I didn't understand such things, and I didn't care at all. My family . . . our family history . . . horrible things were hidden behind it. Actually, I never told anybody here in America a thing about that. It is all gone now, and there is no reason to remember our past in the Ukraine. But I don't know why . . . somehow I want to tell you. Maybe you're just a good listener. Okay, would you mind listening now to my life story in return?"

"Not at all. It's really interesting to me. Hearing about your world, I think it will help me understand you better, though I already know a bit about your father's death."

"There's more to that and much worse things."

"What could be worse than death?" Jim asked, not quite grasping what she meant.

"You will know. Actually, it's not *my* world anymore. It's my *former* world from which I escaped—luckily and strangely. Just listen, until I am in the mood. Just listen and don't say anything, please. Would you?"

"Okay. Will do."

Lada was born in 1980 in Kiev, the capital city of Ukraine, and resided there for most of her life until the age of seventeen. Her mother, Tatiana, was a Russian woman and a music teacher who was forty-four when she gave birth to Lada. Her father, Gregory Meleshko, was Ukrainian, a retired colonel of the Soviet Union Army, and became Lada's father at age fifty. He worked as a chief editor of a military newspaper in Kiev, the *Red Star* and was, of course, a member of the Communist Party, which every military man of the Soviet Union automatically was. Both parents were hardworking people, making quite good money; they created a nice, typical, well-provided communist family where Lada was a little princess—her aged parents adored her and tried to spoil her as much as they could.

The first serious problem occurred in Lada's life when she was six—the Chernobyl nuclear plant meltdown, a worldwide tragedy. It was very close to Kiev, and the whole radiation was blown by the wind right to the city. At the time when her father was actively involved with the whole army in turning off and burying under a mountain of cement the dangerously melting reactor, Lada and her mother were sent to stay for the summer in a small village by Moscow, the capital of the Soviet Union, where Lada's grandma, her mother's mom, usually lived during summertime.

The world was fuming, and everybody cried about the Chernobyl tragedy, but Lada felt quiet and safe and enjoyed picking mushrooms in the forest very much. Their hats were huge, the size of the family frying pan. Lada always brought them home, holding them with difficulty on both stretched arms. She wanted to show them to her *baba* and mom, knowing well that they wouldn't believe her if she just told them that she saw a mushroom of that size.

The dandelions that summer were as tall as the six-year old Lada. Her *baba* even took a picture of her standing between two dandelion plants, hugging them with each of her arms. Their yellow heads stood exactly at the level of Lada's curly blond hair. *Baba* even signed the picture, "My three dandelions." The black currants in her *baba*'s garden were the enormous size of cherries and clearly showed the presence of radiation even in Moscow, more than 1,000 km away from Chernobyl. But what could they do but just live their lives and keep laughing about these unusual growths of nature?

One more remarkable thing of this summer was that Lada accidentally overheard a part of a conversation between her mother and grandmother in the late evening when they had put her to bed and were sure that she was asleep. Her mother had shown some photos to her grandmother, and both of them were crying. "Oh my God," *Baba* said, sniffling. "He looks so grown up. It's difficult to recognize him. He looks like a mature man. Oh, my poor darling, I am pretty sure it was the right thing to do. I don't believe that it was wrong. Look at the house. Look at their happy faces. Could you leave one photo with me?"

"I can't, Mom. Sorry," Tatiana answered, sniffling as well. "I promised to return them. Otherwise, they won't give me the letter next time."

It seemed to Lada quite boring—they looked through photos and talked about some unfamiliar people they knew. However, one question stuck in the child's mind. *Why are they both crying?* Of course, very soon she forgot about that information; dandelions and mushrooms were much more interesting. She remembered about this crying scene six years later after her father's death.

In 1991, Lada cried relentlessly about her father for a couple of weeks; and then too desperate to calm herself down, she finally wrapped her doll into a baby blanket and walked outside, pretending that she was walking with her baby son. Subconsciously, she craved to have some manly figure to replace her father in her soul, though it was just a baby. When she returned home a couple of hours later, sobbing, she was all dirty from being beaten by thrown stones and apples, and there were rotten eggs and mud in her hair and her bundle. One of their neighbors had even run after Lada all the way to her home and, shaking her raised fists, shouted to Tatiana, who opened the door and stepped out to protect her daughter.

"Look, you stupid fucking bitch mother, what you brought up!" the woman shouted. "Your son is a motherland traitor! Your daughter is a little prostitute! What a disrespectful family! Intelligentsia! My husband, my son, and my daughter are drunk every day and beating each other, but they never would betray our motherland. In good Stalin's time, you would all be in concentration camps and shot! Our dear father Stalin was right to finish off bastards like you. But it's okay. We, his followers, are still alive and will annihilate you. We already started with your husband, you silly piece of shit!"

Lada was surprised that her mother didn't answer a thing, just locked the door after she stormed in; then the mother pulled her daughter into the living room, set Lada on the couch, hugged her, and cried. "Please go take a shower," Tatiana said, sobbing. "And then I need to talk to you. We have a serious problem here. You should know the truth, and then we will decide what to do because it is impossible to live like this anymore."

"Is this woman an idiot? Or did she mix us up with someone else?" Lada asked, still sniffling. "What is she talking about? 'Your son is a motherland traitor.' What stupidity is this? You don't have any son."

"Go, please, sweetie, go wash and change. I will clean your doll, and then I will show you something important."

When Lada returned from the shower and calmed down, with her hair wrapped into a towel, her mother placed a photo album on the table and put her hand on the top of it to show her daughter that they should talk first. "You know, actually, I have a son," Tatiana said. "His name is Boris. You have an elder brother."

"Do I?" Lada's eyes widened. "Adopted one?"

"No, your real brother in blood and flesh. Your dad and I had a son twenty-two years before you were born."

Lada was looking at her stonily; she couldn't pronounce a word.

"You don't know him and never saw him," Tatiana continued. "You were born later. When your brother was twenty, your dad cursed him and prohibited me from any contact with him. Your dad said, 'We don't have a son anymore. Let's have another baby and start our family from the very beginning, from ground zero.' And we did, and you were born. But I love my son unconditionally no matter what. So I contacted him secretly, behind your father's back. If my husband knew, he would probably kill me. But I had no choice. I love my son anyway . . . and some people helped me, gave me letters and photos from him."

"Is he in prison?" Lada guessed. "Did he kill somebody?"

"No, sweetie, of course not."

"If he is not a killer, what could be the reason to curse him and to exclude him from our life? It must be something serious, at least."

"He immigrated to the USA, and he lives in America now."

"Really? Unbelievable! It's amazing!" Lada jumped on her chair. "What's wrong with that?"

"Your father was a communist, and he had a very strong communist mentality, according to which each emigrant is a motherland traitor. Only last year did your dad change a bit. After this last communist putsch, he started to understand a bit who is who. But Boris emigrated twelve years before that, in 1979. It was a very harsh time, and very narrow-minded mentality blossomed then. Your dad was about to lose his job because of Boris's action. He was very angry at Boris, but he couldn't do anything, just stop immediately all contact with him to keep his military job.

"However, it was not only for his job. It was for his heart too. He really believed that what Boris did was a motherland betrayal. But it was not true. Boris did it for his love. He fell in love with his school sweetheart, a Jewish girl, Rita Berkovich, when he was eighteen. They were madly in love and very happy. Then her parents decided to immigrate to the USA. It was not comfortable for Jews here. They were humiliated and abused a lot. And Boris just followed his girlfriend and then married her. He couldn't live without her. But nobody wanted to understand this."

"For love? Wow, I would understand! Though I am only twelve, I am pretty sure I could understand!" Lada exclaimed, her eyes shining from excitement. "There must be his photos in the album, right?"

"Yes, his photos and his wife's, their children's, their house, their cars."

"Oh, Mom, I remember." The thought suddenly popped in Lada's mind. "Did you show them to *Baba* when we lived in the summer of 1986 with her in the village? I heard, one night, you both crying, and she said, 'Oh, he is so grown up.' I didn't pay much attention then, but I remembered her words."

"Yes, your *baba* loved Boris until the last day of her life. She mostly raised him while your dad and I were both working a lot. *Baba* used to live with us at that time, actually, until Boris emigrated. He was *Baba's* only beloved grandson. When you were born, your dad insisted that *Baba* move back to Moscow. He didn't want somebody tell you about Boris."

"Oh, damn!" Lada exclaimed angrily. "Dad robbed me of my family. He made me lose my brother, almost lose my grandmother. Why? What idiotic mentality! Was he obsessed with these stupid ideas? And finally, when he started to change his mind, they killed him. These ideas killed him."

"Yes." Tatiana's voice turned into a whisper. "You are right, sweetie, but keep quiet about this, please. These ideas are still alive in some people's hearts as you could notice from the woman who ran after you. During all these years, I secretly contacted Rita's uncle, Aaron Berkovich, who still lives here in Kiev. He is actually the principal of the music college where I had worked. Sometimes he received letters with photos from Rita and Boris and gave them to me. Now I notified Boris about Dad's death, and he sent us a letter. He wants to apply for sponsorship for you and me so we both could immigrate to America and live with him and his family. Let's look at the photos, and you tell me if you'd like to go."

"I will go! I am ready to go!" Lada screamed, jumping on her mother and hugging her crazily. "I want to see the pictures, but I don't need them to make a decision. It's already made. I am already happy to go, Mom."

Five years followed, during which all the emigration documents were finally accomplished, and US Citizenship and Immigration Services permission was received. Those were the years of happy anticipation but difficult at the same time because of the people's growing anger, blossoming crime, raising Mafia activities, economic instability, and lack of everything, even food. However, Lada was hopeful and patient. She walked to school, took her violin classes with her mother, hung out with her friends, and lived the normal life of a regular Ukrainian teenager but waited, dreamed, hoped.

Some days before their departure, at the age of seventeen, she was assaulted on a street by a group of young men. She didn't tell Jim exactly what had happened, just said that she spent two months in the hospital afterward and had three reconstruction surgeries because of this assault. Doctors were even surprised that she survived. This caused delay of their departure to America, but when they finally arrived, she was physically healthy again but still emotionally stressed, horrified, and shocked. Boris hired a psychologist and even a hypnosis professional to help cure her mentally and emotionally after all her experiences.

"So now I forgot everything and practically don't remember any details," Lada said, laughing. "I am completely happy with my life, Jim. Do you believe me?"

"Of course," he assured her. "Why not? And this is very, very good that you are having a new life."

"When my treatment was finished, I was enrolled into university music courses as a violin player. I also took a driving course and drove a school bus for three years. I discovered that it is delightful and exciting to have some of my own money, though we are living with Mom in Boris's house and not paying for anything, not even rent and food. Mom is cooking and working on our household. She is also watching my niece, Rebecca, who is fourteen and my nephew, David, who is twelve. Boris and Rita are both working full time, so Mom is a really good help.

"A couple of weeks ago, I noticed an ad in our university lobby that your group home is looking for a bus driver, and I decided to go because much bigger money was promised here than at the school bus company. You know, though I have everything, it still would be nice to sometimes buy something new, like a purse, jeans, makeup, perfume. You know, I am a girl after all."

"Yes, I know." Jim smiled, tired to death, sleepy, and weak but unbelievably happy.

"Okay," Lada agreed finally. "I think I am getting tired now. It is five in the morning already. I need to sleep for at least two hours and then get ready really fast and drive to your place to pick up the guys at eight-thirty for work. See you, Jim. I will come to pick up my jacket after three o'clock, when I bring the guys from work."

"Won't you come for lunch?" he asked hopefully.

"No. After I drive guys to work, I usually go to the university until two o'clock. Don't forget, I am still a student. Okay, sweet dreams, Jim, though it is already dawn. Bye."

"Bye," Jim whispered, listening to the beeping sounds after she had hung up. He slowly unglued his hot phone from his cheek and connected it to the charger. Its battery was almost dead. He had never in his life been on the phone for so long. Was it good or bad, or what? He had no idea what was going on in his life now. It was too much information. He was completely overwhelmed but had no power now to think about it; he just carelessly drifted to the dark abyss and fell asleep like the dead.

CHAPTER 28

Next morning, Jim woke up very late and almost missed lunch. He ran as fast as he could to the lunch table, not even washing his face and combing his hair, to have something to eat quickly; then he grabbed his portion for later and return to his room to lie down on his bed more. He was devastated after this sleepless night, and his composing schedule was ruined once again. In the past, he always blamed Mona for interfering into his work process and not letting him work on his symphony more productively and faster. Now Lada was to blame.

However, Jim didn't accuse her for his tiredness, weakness, and unwillingness to compose and found hundreds of excuses for her. She was too young, too light headed, and even too beautiful to understand his conditions and his need to be organized by proper schedule—sleep a decent amount of hours, eat on time, exercise daily, and make music every morning and evening. It was not Mona's fault nor Lada's; it was his fault. He was supposed to watch after himself and not dating women, just concentrating on his schedule. It would be ideal and proper for a handicapped, but his life would be boring and unhappy this way; it would not be life but existence, smoldering but not blazing. He obviously didn't want that. He craved a fire with passion for his music, for his creations, and for a woman, which had to inspire him. So to hell with the schedule; he could catch up later. To hell with tiredness and weakness; he would rest later.

He must concentrate now on Lada and her awful, unbelievable story that she shared with him. She trusted him. She wanted to be friends with him. He must make a step toward her and not breach her trust. He must respond, and it was what he did, listening to her confiding the whole night. The story, by itself, gave him a lot to think about, especially the story of emigration of Lada's brother.

Boris and Rita were inseparable friends during their school years and then started dating seriously on the first year of music college, but only after Boris proposed, Rita confessed to him that her family was in the process of emigration for already four years. They were almost done and ready to leave in about a month. To marry Boris now and to add him to the family file would mean to start the whole process again from the very beginning and spend additional four or five years in their awful country and lose more years of her life and opportunities. Then who knew what would happen later? No society in the world was more unstable than the Soviet Union. At any day, a new law could appear that might prohibit the emigration of Jews again, like it was before, and then they would be all stuck in this country forever. This risk Rita would never take.

Also, to emigrate with his newlywed wife and her family, Boris would need the written permission of his parents, and he knew that it would never happen. His mother would be okay with that, but his father would rather kill him than give him permission to leave his motherland. It was a dead end. Boris and Rita had no time to even cry together and to suffer. They had to come up with a plan. And so they did.

Rita left with her family and spent six months in Italy and then moved ahead to New York. Boris stayed in Kiev and continued his study in the music college as a violin player. He just got Rita's phone number from her uncle Aaron Berkovich and waited for his chance.

To bystanders, it looked like Boris forgot about Rita completely. Boris and Rita never talked on the phone and never wrote letters to each other because the phone calls would be listened to and the letters read by KGB. The young couple trusted each other in full and were loyal to each other to death, kind of Romeo and Juliet of the day. They both waited for a chance, and it finally came. The student orchestra of the college, where Boris played in the first violins of the string section, was supposed to go on tour around Japan for a week. Hugging Boris at the airport, his parents couldn't even guess that they were seeing him for the last time—for his father forever, for his mother for the next twenty years.

From Japan, Boris called Rita. She was as fast as lightning, bought an airplane ticket, and joined him in Tokyo in three days. They went to the US Embassy, got married, and applied for immigrant status for Boris as a husband of an American citizen.

For the Ukrainian orchestra, it was a complete shock. An undercover KGB agent on duty who traveled with each Soviet musician, dancer, or sportsman group came to the embassy building to talk to Boris. They were sitting at the opposite ends of a huge, long table and talking in the presence of two American security guards. "You are fleeing from the Soviet Union illegally," the agent said. "You are betraying your motherland. It will create huge problems for your family. Do you realize that?"

Boris nodded. "Yes, I do. But I love my wife. I can't live without her. There isn't any betrayal. My wife is my family now. It is absolutely normal. It is not my fault that my dad and you have different opinions."

"Are you sure that your motive is only personal? No politics involved?" the agent inquired suspiciously.

"I am absolutely sure, no politics at all. I just want to live together with my wife wherever she is. That's all."

"Okay, just remember," the agent warned, "if you will give some interviews to the media, don't even say one word about our country and our politics. Just one word, and you are toast. You will be killed right away. We are keeping our eye on you."

Since that day, about twenty-five years passed, and Boris was now forty-four, almost like a father to his younger sister, whom he loved dearly and for whom he served as a perfect family man role model. Lada worshipped him and admired him like crazy.

Lying in his bed and thinking of it, Jim felt that he was ready to admire Boris as well. What things he did for his love! It was fantastic. He was a real hero in Jim's eyes. But the whole story was very disturbing for Jim's heart and left him a lot to think about.

Another point of Lada's story that hurt and worried Jim was the assault on her some days before her departure from Ukraine. Two months in the hospital, three reconstruction surgeries? She must be injured really seriously. Where? At which part of her body? These severe injuries should leave some scars, but nothing was visible, at least at those parts that Jim saw—her face, neck, arms, and legs. They were absolutely fine. Was she also handicapped as he was, just in some hidden areas? Maybe this was why she felt such sympathy and fondness for him. Did she understand him perfectly because of that?

This thought made Jim worry about her and required more knowledge, more research from him. He craved to know everything about her; he cared about her sincerely. It was very important to him.

At about three o'clock, Jim went to wash rats and then spread his sheets of score on the floor and lay down on his stomach on the top of them with a pencil in his hand to write more music. He knew that the guys were coming from work usually at three, so Lada would appear in his room pretty soon to get her forgotten jacket. He didn't want to let her know how tired and useless he was this morning. He wanted to show that he was okay and did work on his symphony the whole day already. She was still a mystery, and he desperately tried not to bring her attention to his weakness and incapability. He tried to be a usual, normal, regular lad, whom indeed he wasn't.

Unlike yesterday, today Lada knocked at the door. "Come on in," Jim said, not even standing up from his score sheets.

She entered and looked very different today, wearing jeans and a raspberry-colored T-shirt. Her hair was done in a ponytail; only bangs hung down almost to the level of her eyes. But there was the same shiny smile on Lada's face as was yesterday, and she still laughed mischievously, looking at him. "Hi, Jim. Oh my God, you're still so funny. Sorry, sorry, sorry. I don't mean to be impolite. It is just very funny. You are writing on the floor as little kids usually do."

"It is just more comfortable for me," he said shyly.

"I know, know, I am sorry. This laugh is just bursting out from me somehow. I don't know what to do to stop it. What I love about you, Jim, is that you make me laugh. I never laughed so much in my life like I do with you."

"Is it good?"

"Yes, it's perfect. It's difficult to believe, but I am happy to see you."

"Me too. You can laugh how much you want. It doesn't hurt me. I feel that this is not a malicious laugh but a laugh of happiness. So it makes me happy as well," Jim agreed.

"Okay, Jim, what are we up to today?"

Jim stopped writing and sat on the floor, looking at her. Lada sat down on a little chair in front of him and gazed questioningly.

"You know," Jim confessed, "I didn't want to tell you, but I was thinking about your story the whole morning. There are many things that worried me and that I didn't understand completely. I need a bit more information."

"Well . . ." Lada got serious right away and put her finger to her lips. "Shh, Jim. Stop it, please. I told you that I didn't tell this story to anybody in America. You are the first and the last one. Now you have to forget about it completely. I actually forgot everything. My brother paid thousands of dollars for hypnosis sessions to make me forget. I am cured now. I have no other past than the past here in America. My past is how I was studying English in the beginning here, how I was enrolled into university courses four years ago, how I learned to drive, how I took a bus driving course and drove school bus for three years—no other past, no other questions except these. I did cut off everything about the Ukraine forever. Okay?"

"Okay," he agreed, having no other choice.

"You told me nice things from your past, Jim, like your life on the farm with Grandma Cathy, your studying music, your travels to the ocean, your ideas of symphony, your teacher Mr. Dangly from Juilliard. I could guess that you had some bad things in your life too, but you never told me about them, right?"

"Yes," Jim whispered, blushing, thinking about his sex story with Mona.

"Okay, let's leave it this way. Maybe sometimes, one day, we will tell each other not only nice things but the bad things also but not yet, please. We don't know each other well enough, and let's not spoil the impression."

"Wow!" Jim smiled, looking at her with admiration. "You are so young but so clever. It is amazing. I agree completely with everything."

"Well, let's talk then about your symphony. I remember you told me that you're stuck with this vocalization thing. Could you accomplish the symphony without vocalization?"

"I could, of course, but it will be too simple, too plain. About half of the impression will be lost. For me, a voice should be a sound of spirit here, Holy Spirit. Like in church chorales by Bach and Mozart—a voice of heaven."

"You told me that you didn't find a singer yet, right? But you composed the vocal line?"

"Not yet. But it would be easy. I can hear it in my ears all the time. I could do it at any time."

"Okay, then do it right now."

"Why?" Jim looked at Lada in surprise. "What's the rush?"

"I'm just trying to help and have some ideas, but the melody should be written."

"Okay. Would you mind passing me a clean sheet from the table?"

"Of course not." Lada stood up, took one empty music sheet, and gave it to Jim, who spread it on the floor right away and started jotting notes as fast as he could, which in reality was slow.

"I was just thinking," Lada said while he was writing. "Your voice sounds so beautiful on the phone, deep, sexy . . . I don't know, it sounds like a professional singer's voice. Maybe you could sing this vocal part by yourself."

"Lada, dear." Jim stopped writing and smiled coyly, looking up at her. "Didn't you notice that I am not talking loud, always in a hushed voice?"

"I didn't pay attention. Oh yeah, maybe. It was even sexier on the phone."

"Probably. But there is a reason for that. My lungs are a very small in size. I can't take in a lot of air, just very short breaths, which makes singing, shouting, and raising my voice absolutely impossible. Plus, I realized just now, while describing for you this vocalization, that it should be a woman's voice. It should sound like an angel who is spreading her wings in the beams of the sun over the ocean."

"Angels are men sometimes," Lada disagreed, "according to Renaissance art that I saw in museums and albums."

"Well, they could be. But my angel should be a woman. I got it. I feel it really clear."

"Okay, could I try to sing?"

"Of course, you can try. To tell the truth, you really look like an angel to me. But . . . do you have a vocal voice?"

"Absolutely not, quite the opposite. I always had trouble with solfeggio while studying in music school back in Ukraine. But once more, I really want to help you. And also, I am curious how it will sound with the symphony."

"Okay, take the notes." Jim extended his hand and handed to Lada the piece of paper where he just wrote some lines of melody. She took it, hummed a bit, explored the line of music, coughed, tried her voice timidly, and then began to sing nicely but very quietly.

Jim listened to her politely, suppressing the smile on his lips and making an effort not to laugh. She got his thought and stopped. "I know." Lada laughed over herself. "It is funny, isn't it?"

"No." Jim laughed now openly as well, seeing that she looked at the situation with a good sense of humor. "Not very funny. You are singing nicely for a regular person, not a singer. But . . . I wanted to suggest to turn on the music on the computer together with you and to see if it will match. But there is no need. I see now. You can imagine how the whole orchestra will sound together with this singing. They will muffle you not even 100 percent but 200, 300! Nobody will hear a sound from you, even with a microphone."

"I would look like a fish opening my mouth soundlessly." Lada grinned almost to tears, closing her mouth with both hands, bowing her head, and sitting back on her chair. "Oh boy! How funny I am really! Oh my God! Yes, I see now, Jim, that you need a real professional singer, opera singer. But . . . it's a huge amount of work."

"The learning of the vocal part and then about three months of rehearsals every day, two to three hours."

"You see, who would volunteer, even if you choose a singer? Not every singer is free and has so much time, and also, I guess nobody would work for free. Do you have money to pay a singer or musicians?"

"No." Jim shook his head. "No money at all. I am as poor as a church mouse."

"Do you have some income? I mean . . . pension?"

"Of course, I do. I even have a sponsorship, but all those funds are going to cover my living expenses here in the group home. Just very little is left for my personal needs, like . . . like one day I bought a pack of CDs, something like that."

"Wow." Lada sighed sadly. "I wish I was a millionaire. Then I would do that for you."

"Anyway, thank you very much for suggesting." Jim was really touched by her saying that. "It was a nice try."

"Okay, Jim." Lada stood up and grabbed her jacket from the back of the chair on which she was sitting. "I have to go now. I have a great deal of homework for tomorrow for my university class. I will have a test in harmony. But I have another suggestion for you. Please keep writing your vocal line and make as much as you could tonight. I will bring my violin tomorrow and will try to play this melody with your computer together. We should try to check if that matches."

"I think maybe not." Jim smiled coyly again and shook his head. "I hear it inside my mind."

"I know that you are genius." Lada chuckled. "But I am not. I don't hear it inside my mind, and I want to try. Okay?"

"Of course, it will be a pleasure."

She placed a fast kiss on top of his head and disappeared behind the door. Jim was left startled from its unexpectedness, but before he could think about it, the door opened a crack, and Lada's head appeared again. "Okay, and tomorrow you will teach me how to slide from the stairs," she reminded him, giggling. "Don't forget, please. Bye, I have to run."

CHAPTER 29

W asn't it an inspiration? What could be a better inspiration than knowing that this charming girl was trying to do her best for you, trying everything that she could and would continue these attempts until she finally could help you? Also, she wants to have a fun time with you, like sliding from the stairs. She definitely wanted to continue a relationship —friendship, acquaintance—and she wisely found an ideal point for that, mutual serious business and mutual entertainment.

Jim was pretty sure that Lada didn't think about these things consciously and didn't make up anything on purpose. She was a natural; she was born smart, tactful, and clever. This excited him even more than just her good looks. It was her inner beauty, and it was extremely important for him, much more important than anything else.

Full of this inspiration, Jim worked like crazy, unstoppable until late night. He finished the vocal line for the first part of his symphony and went to sleep finally, feeling completely happy and satisfied with this serious work done. Next morning, he started work on the vocal line for the second part of the symphony and, with just two short breaks for lunch and washing rats, practically finished it at about three o'clock, exactly when Lada was supposed to appear with the guys on the bus. However, she didn't come.

She called a bit later instead, already driving her bus back to the city. "Sorry, Jim," she said. "I have to apologize. I forgot yesterday that today I also have a rehearsal at five o'clock for my violin exam next Monday. I only remembered about the harmony test this morning. I am completely out of my mind. I am like a senior lady with Alzheimer's. Jesus! It's awful. I am angry at myself."

"It's okay, don't worry," he assured her. "It gives me more time to finish vocal lines for the third and fourth parts of my symphony. I understand that now it is time for spring exams, and you are just overloaded. No Alzheimer's, no old lady, just too much on your head to remember. Plus, I am sitting on your neck with my problems."

"No, no, no, Jim, don't say so. You are fun. If not you, I would probably be really pissed off. I found this job at the wrong time—exam session on the way. But it will be finished soon. Since May 1, 2003, I will be free of university until September and will work more for Mrs. Lainer and have more fun with you."

"Will Mona give you more work?" Jim asked worriedly. "What do you mean?"

"She said that my duty also included maintenance work and more driving—garbage disposal, bottle depot, sometimes bringing visitors for the guys, if they unable to drive. Now I am not doing all these because of my exams, but when the school year finished, I have to. So I will be there more, will come for lunch every day, and will see you more, Jim. Also, I will have more money then. Isn't it great?"

"Yes." Jim took a deep breath. "I know. The previous bus driver did all these. He also shoveled snow in winter. But . . . okay, we will talk about that another time. Now you have to concentrate on driving. It is not good to drive and talk on the phone at the same time."

"I know." Lada laughed. "I am accurate, believe me. I usually don't do that. I just wanted to let you know why I didn't come. To make you wait in vain would not be nice of me, right? These are the two worst things to do in the world—to wait and to run after. Okay, bye, Jim. See you tomorrow."

The discovery that he would stay alone this night didn't hurt Jim at all, quite the opposite. It would be nice to see Lada, but he also was happy to have more of his private time and to continue to work on the vocal line of the symphony. He decided to finish today the assumed singer's melody line in full and polish everything tomorrow morning, and he put all his efforts into it.

The thought that, starting in about a week, Lada would be here every day and they would have lunch together with other stuff was a bit disturbing to Jim. He knew that Mona would watch them; they would talk as if under surveillance. In his opinion, it would be dangerous for their relationship, which was just born, just started. If Mona noticed something, she would destroy everything and kill their friendship. He could easily lose Lada forever.

Actually, Jim couldn't completely understand why Mona hired Lada. After losing Ramah, this monstrous, sexually obsessed white rat should hire someone whom she could use as a new lover, some strong young man also capable of maintenance work, loading and unloading heavy stuff in the basement, and shoveling a lot of snow in winters. Lada didn't really match any of these purposes nor wild sex. Then what?

Wasn't there any other candidates? Or Mona wanted to use Lada as a lesbian lover, which Jim knew from Lily she was well capable of. She was a monster without border and never did anything without ulterior motive. What was her purpose there?

Jim felt that he was obligated to warn Lada about the danger. But how? He couldn't say anything bad about Mona without any serious reason. It would sound defamatory and would make an impression for Lada that he is the bad guy. The famous rule "If you can't say something nice, say nothing at all" was sitting in his mind. He remembered how indignant he was when Lily said a bad thing about Mona the first time. He didn't want to make Lada the same because he was pretty sure that Mona was obviously nice with her and acted like an angel as she usually did with new people. He didn't want to destroy his own image in Lada's eyes; he didn't want to spoil their closeness and friendship, which just started to develop.

What to do then? Jim took a deep breath and decided to forget about these thoughts for now, just keep working. He promised himself that he would find out the answers later.

CHAPTER 30

T he next day, while waiting for Lada to come, Jim was productive enough. He was lying on the floor on his stomach and kept working on the orchestration. He just finished the last accord of the first part of the symphony as she entered.

Lada appeared in Jim's room about ten minutes to four, though the bus with the guys arrived usually between three and three thirty. She was dressed today in light blue sweater, denim miniskirt, matching blue leggings, and sneakers. Her hair was done in a braid that hung over her shoulder to her chest. She looked a bit different but still sweet beyond measurement in Jim's opinion. "Hi, Jim," Lada greeted him, smiling broadly, and he noticed that she was holding her violin as she promised. "I am sorry. I am a bit late today again."

"It's okay," Jim answered, standing up and gathering his pages from the floor. "I had enough time to accomplish the score of the first part of my symphony when I was done with the vocal line for all four parts. So the first part now is done completely, even ready to perform." With these words, he put the pages into a folder on his desk and patted the top of it.

"Wow! Congratulations, Jim!" Lada beamed at him and extended her arm to shake his little hand. "It's excellent that I gave you some extra time. I just talked to a nurse a bit and waited until Mrs. Lainer will go to another room, and then I sneaked in here."

He looked at her, surprised. "Why? You don't want Mona to know that you are seeing me?"

Lada nodded. "The less bosses know, the better. It is an old rule. Before I start working here, my brother instructed me and reminded me about it. And you know, Boris is my life coach. I listen to each of his words."

"Well . . ." Jim laughed. This was a relief for him; however, there could be another obstacle. "So if I want to be your friend, I should deserve your brother's approval?" he asked curiously.

"For sure."

"Do you think he will like the idea of our friendship?"

"Of course. Why not?"

"Because . . ." He stopped, blushing. "Because I am living in a nursing home."

"So what?"

"My conditions are . . . special."

"So what? Oh, Jim, you are so funny at times. Why is it supposed to matter?"

"I don't know. Some people don't like the handicapped."

"I know. In the Soviet Union, everybody usually hated the handicapped enormously. They also hated Jews, they hated people from Middle Asia, from Caucasus, and they hated Americans. Jesus, they hated everybody, even themselves, believe me. That's why we are here, Jim. We are Americans now, and our psychology is completely different. It changed with the years. But my Boris, you know, he was different even there. He was brave enough to date a Jewish girl. He told me when I came here that nothing matters to him except real human values, like love, people's decent personality, people's soul, and talent, even while living in the Soviet Union. And he was right. You know, actually, Rita was a very talented girl. And now she is an amazing mother, a perfect wife, and also a great violin player. She is a concertmaster of the string section in the orchestra of our university. She also teaches violin there and sometimes plays personal concerts. I really admire her. I don't even know how she finds time for everything. Then again, our mom is keeping our household now. It helps Rita and Boris a lot. They have more time for children and for work. But . . . sorry, I am again too talkative. How could I stop? I am awful, right, Jim?"

"Not at all. I love to listen to you."

"Oh, you are too kind to me. Okay, it's better we talk about your symphony than me. Can you show me what you wrote for vocal? And we will try it. You see, I brought my damn subject of torture." Lada laughed and put the violin on his desk.

"I noticed." He nodded. "Here it is." Jim handed Lada a bunch of papers.

She sat on the chair beside the piano and put her nose into the sheets of music. She looked through the whole vocal line and hummed a bit, turning pages one by one. Her face got serious, her brows knitted, and she bit her lip, following her finger on the lines of music.

Jim observed Lada's face with admiration, excited by the changes she was capable of—from laughing crazy like a silly teenager to true seriousness and businesslike expression. This young lady had many sides, and most of her sides were still a mystery to him. They made him curious and attracted him more and more every day.

"Well, okay," Lada said finally, finishing her looking through the notes. "Let's play." She took her violin out from its case, tuned it for a couple of minutes, and then began to play, looking at the notes that were lying down on the table. There weren't many efforts on her face, she smiled with ease, and her violin sounded deep and beautiful; however, Jim realized right away that this wouldn't match his symphony at all. The violin sound would be completely lost between the orchestra sounds. There were too many violins in his score.

Usually, when a composer created a concert for violin with orchestra, he does it in a very different way; he eliminates the violin solos on a ground of the tutti or a ground of the string section; he makes the violin line separated or on the ground of a woodwind section or something else of contrast. It was not done in Jim's symphony. He didn't plan solo violin and didn't expect it here. He planned and expected a human voice, a woman singer's voice, and that was it.

Jim kept listening to Lada's playing just to enjoy her musician's ability and let her try to help him, but he knew already that the sound of the violin wouldn't match here in any way. As for his work, it was wasting his time now, but it was fun and something that made him and Lada closer to each other spiritually, so he let her play and listened to her, smiling joyfully.

However, Lada somehow grasped his facial expression and stopped her playing quite suddenly. "What's up?" she asked. "You don't look happy. I know I am not the best player."

"No, no, it's not that," Jim protested actively. "It is not your quality of playing. It is the quality of the violin timbre. It feels wrong. I actually knew that. Listen, Lada. Let me turn on the music on my computer for you so you could know what I had composed. Then you would know better what is a match over there. I am sure you will feel it too."

"Okay," she agreed obediently and put her violin away into its case. "Indeed, you know, Jim, it was our mistake from the very beginning. You should've gotten me to listen to your symphony first. I am maybe completely wrong in my imagination of what you wanted to hear there."

"No problem. We can do that now, if you are not in a hurry to go home."

"No, I am okay today. I need some time to relax from these damn exams." Lada sat down on the armchair and when the music started, she threw her head back and closed her eyes, completely immersing into the sounds.

Jim expected that she would like to see the notes and follow the music on the sheets, like Mona did, pretending that she was a professional in this area. Lada was professional in reality, and she could do that too, but she didn't. She just sat quietly and smiled a bit from the beginning and then got more serious, and the smile disappeared from her face. Jim watched her facial expression attentively. It was important for him to know how she understood his creation, how she felt his music. Her opinion and her feelings were what mattered to him the most. It was a base for their future relationship, and he was sitting quietly and tensely, greedily staring at her.

Jim noticed that somewhere in the middle of the first part, Lada's seriousness changed slowly into sadness. Then suddenly, she bit her lip and took a deep breath, and two little tears slid from her closed eyes, sneaking from under her trembling eyelashes, leaving rivulets on her cheeks, and ending up on her lips. She licked them nervously and then wiped her mouth with her palm and opened her eyes. They were so huge—excited, happy, and sad at the same time, surrounded by wet eyelashes that stuck to one another as bunches. He wanted to say something and to ask her why she was crying, but she closed her eyes again, and it was visible that she fully immersed back into the divine music that continued to drift in the air, refilling the whole room.

When the first part finished, Jim pressed the Off button and stayed silent, watching Lada questioningly. She opened her eyes, sniffed, and wiped her face with her palm. He gave her Kleenex from the box on his bedside table. She took it but didn't use it as it was supposed to be used, just squeezed it in her hand and took a deep, shaky breath. "It's shocking,

Jim," she whispered. "I see now why you wanted the voice here. It will make the whole thing holy. Like you told me, an angel is singing on the ground of silver-pink sunrise. Absolutely shocking . . . and so sad."

"I didn't consider it sad," he noted thoughtfully. "I wanted to express here much more than just sadness."

"I know. I know everything now, Jim. I mean, that you are a genius, supergenius, no less than Mozart or Beethoven. And it is so *sad* that you are . . . you know . . . let's say . . . handicapped. This is what's damn sad!" she exclaimed and banged her fist on her knee in despair. "Otherwise, you could conduct your symphony by yourself. You could conduct your own performance! Jeez! It's so unfair! It drives me crazy! Such a genius . . . and handicapped!"

"You know, Beethoven was handicapped as well," Jim said quietly. "He was deaf, which was even worse for music than my condition. However, he conducted his *Ninth Symphony* by himself, not hearing the orchestra. All was sounded in his inner mind. I don't care much about conducting myself. To me, it is much more important to finish all the orchestration and then to find a performer. And I would like to know if you like my music."

"Oh yeah, I love it—no, wrong word, I admire it—no, wrong word again, I really . . . really I am worshipping it, Jim. And to tell the truth, I am worshipping you too. It's unbelievable how you, being so . . . so restricted in your possibilities, could do that. It is so difficult for you. Everything is difficult, extremely difficult, even to write simple notes, even to hold a pencil. And you did it! You are a real hero, and I am . . . I am really excited that I met you. It is an honor for me to be your friend. Maybe one day you will be really famous—no, not maybe, wrong word again. For sure, absolutely sure, you will be famous because you deserve it, Jim." She suddenly began to laugh and clapped her hands. "Oh, Jim! And I could be famous with you, like Giulietta Guicciardi with Beethoven or Nadezhda von Meck with Tchaikovsky. Ha ha! It would be fun, Jim! Why not, right?"

"Yes," he agreed, smiling, noticing for himself that, yes, Nadezhda von Meck was a loyal and inspiring friend for Tchaikovsky, who was a gay in reality; but Giulietta Guicciardi was, on the contrary, Beethoven's first love.

"Come here, Jim, I really want to hug you!" Lada exclaimed, giggling and extending her arms toward him. He coyly approached her armchair, still smiling confusingly, and extended his little arms to hug her as well.

She squeezed him in a big bear hug, continuing to laugh; patted his back; and then kissed him affectionately on his cheek.

Jim blushed, feeling with a horror that this, her friendly move, turned for him in a very different way. He felt that a wild erection began to tighten his jeans. When you didn't have sex for quite a long time and then suddenly an amazingly attractive woman hugged and kissed you, what else could you expect? Just a mad explosion, which would be an awful shame in Jim's opinion. He would rather die than to let Lada see what was going on.

"Excuse me," he whispered worriedly, pushing Lada away by her shoulders. "Excuse me, please, I need . . . I'll be right back." He turned his back toward her as fast as he could, trying not to let her see his mounted front, and hobbled toward his bathroom.

"I will take a quick shower," Jim said, already inside the bathroom, turning back and looking at her from the crack of the door. "And then we could probably go outside for a walk."

"Okay," Lada agreed, giggling and not quite understanding what had happened. "But first, I would like to learn how to slide from the stairs."

Oh my God, Jim thought, completely amused by himself, *she is a complete child*. He felt hatred and disgust toward himself, like he did something absolutely awful, unthinkable, and criminal, producing sexual feelings toward a minor, though Lada wasn't one.

When Jim appeared from the bathroom fully dressed, he was pale with blue lips, shaking from cold after ten minutes of icy shower. Lada was standing beside the window, watching the backyard outside. "Oh my gosh!" she exclaimed, looking at him with big eyes. "You're freezing! Why? Is there a hot water out of order?"

"No," he stammered with shaking lips. "This is my regular exercise. I am doing it almost every day to get . . . hmm . . . to get stronger and healthier. I will warm up soon. Don't worry about me, please."

"Okay." She nodded. "I got it now. You want to be hardy, very smart and perfect. But at first, oh gosh, you scared me with these blue lips, looking like a frozen corpse. I understand now. This probably helps you survive."

"You're right. You can't even imagine how much it helps me survive." Jim laughed, feeling that the situation was a really funny one because Lada couldn't grasp the double meaning of his words, and he wasn't intending to explain it to her, never. It would be too shameful. But the wordplay was funny and enjoyable for him.

"Are you ready to go now?" Lada asked, taking her violin from his desk and heading toward the door.

"Yes, I am, if you'll hold my hand, of course."

"Oh, sorry, Jim. I keep forgetting that you need some little help to walk. I am so light headed. I am really sorry."

"You don't have to apologize, my dear. You're just living in another dimension. It's what it is, and I understand that, no offense taken."

Holding hands, they exited Jim's room and approached the stairs. The living room downstairs was empty. It was a nice sunny day, and the guys were rested and relaxed after dinner outside in the garden, not in the living room like it was usually in winter.

Lada put her violin on the floor beside the stairs and sat on the top step. "Now you show me how you are doing that step by step," she demanded, looking up at Jim. He sat beside her on the same step and put his feet on the next step down.

"I saw this trick done by a toddler when we went to the ocean first time with Grandma Cathy. We stayed in a hotel, and there were big stairs in the lobby. One day I saw a child, who was about eighteen months old, slide from the stairs this way. I couldn't repeat it at that time because I wasn't walking. I was in a child-sized wheelchair, but I was so excited about it that I printed it in my memory and promised to myself that if I would be capable of walking one day, I would do that too.

"However, we didn't have a stairs in our farmhouse. It was a bungalow. So only last year in November, when I moved into this group home, I started doing this on the stairs and was surprisingly successful right from the very beginning. It did not require any practice or exercise at all. Look."

He pushed his hands at the floor and slid his bum to the next step and at the same time slid his feet down to the following step. "See, it's easy. These carpeted steps are so soft. They don't hurt your bum at all."

They forgot one thing. This exercise required a person to have very short legs, like toddlers had and as did Jim. When Lada slid to the next step, following Jim, her knees came up to her chin because they were too long, and she was stuck. "Oh my God!" She chuckled. "Look at me. I am banging my chin with these knees. I can't move properly. Jeez! What the hell! It is not very comfortable. I can't do that. It's so funny." She laughed more and more, finally turned to her side, stretched her legs down, and slid down on her back, jerking her feet and howling from giggling. She sat on the living room floor, laughing like crazy with Jim, who slid successfully before and was now laughing beside her. "Oh my gosh! How clumsy I am! What fun!"

At that moment, Mona suddenly appeared beside them and looked at them with a haughty expression on her face, pursing her lips. "Well, well, well," she said, shaking her head with visible displeasure. "What's going on here? Miss Meleshko, what are you doing here? You should be on the bus, heading home, to prepare for your exams instead of lying down on the floor under the stairs with a mentally ill, handicapped person in our group home. Really, it is strange, isn't it?"

"Oh, I am sorry, Mrs. Lainer!" Lada howled, wiping her tears, still unable to stop her laughing, though Jim was sobered immediately and stood up silently, looking worriedly around and not able to decide what to do. "I just wanted to learn to slide from the stairs, like Jim is doing, but it's impossible. I fell down. My legs are too long, and it is so funny."

"It's nothing funny about that," Mona continued indignantly. "I hope you weren't hurt. But you should be more responsible about your duty. I was so kind to you. I allowed you not to do half of your job because of your exams, but I see you have enough time for horsing around with mentally ill patients over here."

"Jim is not mentally ill," Lada disagreed. "Right, Jim?"

"Oh my God!" Mona exclaimed, rolling her eyes up, and kept talking to Lada, completely ignoring Jim as if he wasn't here. "You are so inexperienced, Mis Meleshko. Don't you know that the first things that all mentally ill people are talking about are that they are not ill at all and they are absolutely normal?"

At some point, Mona was right. Jim remembered that Ella stated to him that she hated him and other cripples because she was absolutely healthy and "all guys around" were healthy too, meaning Maggie, Victor, and Todd. But as everything that Mona usually said, it was right and not right at the same time. It was her usual demagogy and manipulation. Lada obviously felt that and tried to argue a bit.

"Okay," she said, shrugging. "I am absolutely mentally healthy. If I am feeling that, does it mean that I am mentally ill too?"

"Come on, Miss Meleshko, you weren't hired to discuss mental health problems with me and to have fun with our patients who could be very dangerous sometimes."

"Jim is not dangerous." Lada looked surprised. "Right, Jim?

"You just don't know, Miss Meleshko," Mona insisted. "You absolutely don't know him, and I am warning you very seriously. If you continue to communicate with mentally ill Mr. Bogat, you could be easily killed at any given minute."

Lada looked at Jim uncertainly with huge eyes.

"Stop bluffing, Mona!" Jim barked suddenly and grabbed Lada by her hand. "Let's go for a walk outside as we wanted."

"Wait a second, Jim. I forgot my violin over there." Lada ran upstairs, picked up her violin from the top of the stairs, and returned down in some seconds. She was really confused but gave Jim her hand and followed him obediently, bowing her head. "I am sorry, Mrs. Lainer," she said timidly, turning her head back toward Mona before exiting the outside door.

"You don't know, silly girl, what his diagnosis is! Okay, you were warned!" Mona shouted at their backs. "No complaints, you both!"

They ignored her and walked out from the door to the little sidewalk that led to the bus stop and the big blooming garden behind it.

CHAPTER 31

"I guess you're fired now," Jim said sadly as they sat on the bench under the blooming lilac bush, and Lada placed her violin right beside her.

"Why? I don't think so." She smiled at him. "No, I feel quite safe here. I guess that Mrs. Lainer needs me much more that I need her."

"Why?" It was now Jim's turn to be surprised. "You aren't a perfect fit for this job actually. There are lots of heavy duties—loading grocery, boxes with bottles, garbage, shoveling snow in winter. It is sometimes about two meters high, wet, and very heavy. I can't imagine you doing all these. Mona is usually very reasonable in choosing her employees. Question is, why did she hire you?"

Jim looked around the garden. It was spreading from the house until the meadow with a forest following and was quite large. It was a nice sunny day, and his housemates obviously enjoyed this outing.

At the right side, about twenty meters from them, Victor was sitting motionlessly on the bench under a blooming chokecherry bush. He stared at one point at the distant flower bed full of multicolored tulips and daffodils, which smelled like honey and were homes to a bunch of bumblebees, humming over it. Beside Victor, Todd was playing solitaire on the rest of the bench. His ears, as usual, were plugged with earphones. At the left side from the bench, where Jim and Lada were sitting, quite far away as well, Ella was weeding another flower bed together with Nurse Rona. They were laughing and talking loudly. So it was quite safe for Jim to say something important to Lada. Nobody paid attention to them at all, and nobody would hear their discussion.

"Mrs. Lainer is the one who always used people around here, right?" Lada asked after some minutes of silence, instead of answering Jim's question of why Mona hired her.

"Yes." Jim nodded. "How do you know?"

"I am just observing her behavior. She definitely wants to use me somehow. I feel that, but I don't know how."

Jim felt feverish. His only guess could be that Mona wanted to use Lada as a lesbian lover, but it was so awful, so disgusting, and so scary that he pushed this thought away immediately. However, he felt excited how clever Lada was to notice Mona's core right away. She was ten years younger than him, but he was ten times naiver than her when he arrived to the group home last fall.

Lada looked attentively at his face. "Jim," she said, "you aren't mentally ill, are you? It's quite obvious. And you're not dangerous. I only know that Mrs. Lainer somehow really doesn't want me to be friends with you. She is saying all these about you . . . like your diagnosis . . . and other crap . . . just to make me scared of you and to push me away from you, right? The question is, why?"

Jim was pretty sure that Mona was just jealous. She knew perfectly that he was capable of sexual relationships with women, and being crazily sexually obsessed herself, she didn't want him to have anybody else. Mona promised him that he would never find another woman, and she wanted to prove herself to be right as always.

Jim thought that this was evidence that Mona had sexual intentions toward this naive, innocent girl, and this thought made him shiver. But he didn't say anything about it to Lada; he just shrugged and murmured, "No idea. Maybe she is aware that I will tell you something bad about her. I have known her for more than six months now, and I think I have good knowledge of who she really is. But it wasn't my intention at all. I wouldn't gossip about people around me without a reason. I don't like it."

"Yeah." Lada took a deep breath and squeezed her chin with her palm, thinking. "You know, this is quite strange," she said thoughtfully. "I noticed that Mrs. Lainer didn't want to hire me at the beginning when I came for the interview. Maybe you're right. I don't really fit this job, at least for its heavy part, which I am not doing now. But then during our conversation, she suddenly changed her mind—in a second, immediately. She told me that I am the best candidate, and I was hired right on the spot."

"What did you tell her?"

"It happened after I told her about my family, especially about Boris."

"Oh." Jim sighed with relief. He got it now. Mona decided to worm her way into friendship with Lada and then to use her brother as a lover. Quite a long-term plan, but if it was that, Lada was really safe for now from being fired and from lesbian attacks. "That's okay, I guess," he said. "Mona knows now that you have a protector, so you are safe. You are right, she won't fire you."

"It's not a 'protector' thing. It is something different. She had a big interest in him and asked about him a lot. Maybe he is the reason why I was hired."

Oh God, I was right, Jim thought with despair. "Well, let's leave it for now. Just try not to let her meet Boris. For example, if Mona invites you to come to a Christmas party and to bring your family with you, like it was last year, don't do it then."

"I don't think she wants to wait until Christmas," Lada noted uncertainly. "She already said that she would like to visit my family on one of the May weekends to know me better. She said it is a usual procedure. I was thinking what a nice boss she is to know the families of all the staff. It is quite amazing, isn't it, Jim?"

"It looks like that for a person who doesn't know her," Jim uttered slowly.

"Yeah. Now after talking with you, I changed my mind, not even because of what you told me . . . no, just her behavior with you. It was so rude. I was shocked. I didn't expect that she could be like that ever. I will be very cautious of her from now on. If she asks me to arrange this meeting with my family, I will tell her that Boris and Rita went to a tour around Europe for the whole summer or something like that."

"Do they really plan the tour?"

"Of course not. They both have a full-time jobs. They aren't even going on vacation. They are completely busy, believe me."

"So you will lie," Jim guessed. "You are so sincere. Do you know how to lie?"

"Don't worry." Lada laughed. "I am a woman from Eastern Europe. We survived a communist regime, which was 100 percent based on lies. People who didn't know how to lie were killed during seventy-three years of their rule. We all lied there 24/7, round the clock. Mrs. Lainer doesn't know whom she crossed with. I might look naive, but I am a great competitor for her. I don't really know what she wants, but I perfectly know what I want, and I also know that I will win anyway."

Jim smirked. Lada looked too self-confident for him. She definitely had no idea what an enemy Mona was. "And what is it that you want?" he asked curiously.

"I want to be your friend," she answered, making a funny face for him and then suddenly placed another affectionate kiss, this time on his forehead. "Mrs. Lainer also doesn't know how stubborn I am. If someone demands me to do something, I become angry and start doing the very opposite on purpose just to show that person that I do what I want but not what I am told to do. I am a free American woman now, and I am sick about that, Jim. Mrs. Lainer doesn't want me to be friends with you? Well, very well. This is what pushed me. I will be—on purpose."

Jim laughed happily. This amazing girl had a kind of character. He felt that he really won against Mona, at least for now. Being rude and defaming him in front of Lada, she made a big mistake. However, it all was a bit scary for him because he knew pretty well that Mona was unstoppable in what she wanted. The memory of Lily's death reminded him that she was even capable of murder, which Lada definitely wasn't.

They sat silently for some time, enjoying the hot sun beaming on their faces. Then Lada took a deep breath, hugged her violin, and said, "I think I have to go home, Jim. I should carry home my treasure." She jokingly kissed the violin case and stood up, pressing the violin to her chest. "I really have my last violin exam on Monday and have to practice more. Also, tomorrow is Saturday. I have to drive the guys to the swimming pool. Will you go?"

"I usually don't." Jim shook his head. "I don't like water. I love the ocean but not chlorinated water. Also, I can't swim anyway. My arms are too tiny and too weak."

"Oh, sorry." Lada sighed again. "Then I will see you only briefly, maybe just put my nose in your door to say hi."

"Okay," Jim agreed. "If you would like to talk, you can call me tonight."

"I don't think so. Tonight we are going to the movie with the whole family—Mom, Rita, Boris, and kids. Anyway, see you, Jim. Bye."

He watched how she was walking through the garden alley toward the bus stop, carrying her violin by her chest, hugging it like it was a baby. His eyes caressed her back, braid, and long legs. *God*, he thought, *I am turning crazy. I am almost ready to kiss her footsteps. I should be only friends with her. I have no right to fall in love.*

When Lada turned on the engine of the bus and drove slowly, circling the garden to reach the road, she waved to him through the open driver's window, and he waved back. Then Jim stood up and walked very slowly and accurately back home, steadying himself from time to time on benches or bushes along the way.

In his room, he wanted to keep working on his orchestration. The first part of the symphony was finished, and now it was time to start the orchestration of the second part. Before he started this job, Jim decided to check how he made the ending of the first part. The score pages were in the folder that was lying on the table. He climbed up on his chair, opened the folder, and was dumbfounded with his mouth open. The folder was empty.

CHAPTER 32

Jim stood still, motionless, but his brain worked a hundred miles per hour, trying to remember where he could have placed his score, if not in this folder. If lost, it won't be a dead end, of course, because he could quite easily remember his orchestration and redo it. But it was a month's work, and redoing it would take another month of a job done in vain.

No, he remembered absolutely clear that he put the score there. He was confident about this. So did then someone steal it? Mona, when they were sitting outside in the garden. *She knew that I was out of my room for a walk with a girl*, he thought. *Well . . .*

Jim exited his room, slid downstairs, and walked as abruptly as he could toward Mona's suite. Finally, it was time to confront her openly about all his previous suspicions related to his symphony and even to his earlier student works. Now the score disappearance lost the last drop of his patience.

He passed the kitchen and storage room, crossed the brightly lit hall with a hardwood floor, and banged at Mona's locked suite door with his tiny fists angrily. Nobody opened. "Mona, open the door!" Jim shouted, continuing to bang. "I need to talk to you immediately!"

"What's going on, Mr. Bogat?" He suddenly heard her indignant voice coming from behind. Jim turned right away to see where she was and was surprised to find out that she sat in her office with the door open. It was even strange how he passed her office door and didn't notice her inside. He was probably too angry and completely concentrated on the door of her suite, expecting her to be there but not in the office. "What happened? Emergency?"

Jim entered the office and approached Mona, who was sitting lazily in a leather armchair in front of her desk. "Did you enter my room?" he exclaimed.

Her eyebrows jumped up in surprise. "Your room? Why?" She shrugged, making a wry face. "I saw that you went for a walk. What would be a reason for me to go there?"

"The score of the first part of my symphony disappeared."

"So what? How does that relate to me?"

"Who else could take it?"

"My God! You keep being paranoid! It's absolutely awful to deal with you, Jim. Come on, calm down. You just put it somewhere and forgot where it is. Nobody here cares about your symphony at all, believe me. Nobody!"

"You always did."

"Only when I was your friend. I sacrificed on your behalf my spare time because I was really in love with you and really tried to help as much as I could." Sadness was ringing in Mona's voice, and she even sniffed a bit. "But since you were so rude and disrespectful to me and didn't appreciate my sincere care, I am not your friend anymore and don't care anymore about your hobbies." She took a deep breath and sadly dropped her hands on her knees.

"But who took it then? I left it in the folder on my desk, and when I came home after my walk, it was gone."

"Oh, Jim." Mona shook her head nonchalantly. "Are you still insisting on your point? Why? Why be so stubborn and not recognize that you just lost your pages? I am pretty sure that tomorrow you will find them somewhere in your room."

"Because I have a witness. Lada was in my room when I collected all the pages of my score and put them in a folder. She saw it."

"Oh!" Mona drawled, stretching her lips in a long *O*. "Are you that sure that she saw your score there? You mean, your guest? This new girl, bus driver? Miss Meleshko? This could be the change of the situation."

"Yes, she saw it, but she didn't take it!" Jim exclaimed indignantly, suddenly realizing with horror that it was exactly what could have possibly happened. Lada was already in his room, standing beside the door and holding her violin, when he picked up his last score pages and put them into the folder on his desk.

Mona slowly shook her head, noticing matter-of-factly. "It seems strange to me, Jim, that you—always so careful—allowed a complete stranger into your room. These immigrants, they all are thieves and liars. I really worry that I've hired her. I just had no choice. Other candidates were even worse. I bet you left her alone in your room, didn't you?"

"No."

"Not even for a minute, leaving for the washroom?"

Jim kept silent, remembering even with more horror that he took a cold shower, leaving Lada alone in his room for at least ten minutes or more. Mona didn't force him to answer but knew that she was right, reading his facial expression.

"Well," she continued thoughtfully, "it was enough time for her to put your score into her bag."

"She didn't have any bag," Jim retorted, agitated.

"Well, a violin case, it doesn't matter. The experienced thief would easily find a place where to put something."

"How do you know?" Jim teased her sarcastically. "Have an experience?"

"Yes, I do have experience," Mona answered sharply, pretending not to get his sarcasm. "I am working for twenty-five years with mentally ill people and with immigrants, with all these human garbage. I know them all quite well, believe me. They all are very cunning thieves. That's why I plan to visit her family soon and to check on her, to check what kind of people they are. We usually check the criminal records of our new employees. She is clear. But in reality, it means nothing. Also, she is a musician. And so is her 'famous brother.' She could be taking your score for him."

"Why?" Jim shook his head stubbornly. "What's the reason? She is a violin player, and so is he. Why do they possibly need the score of my symphony?"

"I don't know exactly." Mona shrugged, making a suffering face. "But her brother is not a violin player anymore. She told me. He changed his job some years ago because there weren't enough good possibilities for him as a violin player. Maybe your symphony could help him return to music. I am just guessing, of course, but . . . you know."

"I don't understand," Jim mumbled, remembering suddenly what Lada excitedly told him about her sister-in-law, Rita, being an excellent violin player in an orchestra and a violin teacher who was making personal concerts and so on but not one word about Boris's success in this area, not one word at all. He didn't pay attention to these details at the time, but now he realized that if her brother was a successful violin player, Lada would talk about him first, of course. Now it looked suspicious to him, really suspicious.

It appeared that Mona was telling the truth this time, no matter how mean she was. But Jim couldn't take away from her that she was very clever, intelligent, and experienced in almost all life situations. Jim stood, thinking hesitantly. He wasn't sure about anything now, but his thoughts kept working, jumping, and running through his head.

"You could check tomorrow," Mona continued, seeing his hesitation. "If this young lady will come to see you again, she will have a bag with her for sure. Leave her alone for a minute. Go to the washroom. Then do check your folder when she is gone. Your score will be there. I can guarantee you that."

"Why?"

"She will return it. She just took it to show her brother, I am sure."

"She could have asked me," Jim said. "I wouldn't see anything wrong with that. I would give her permission and give her the score. To ask would be easier."

"For some people, it's not, especially for liars."

Here, Jim remembered their conversation with Lada in the garden, when she convinced him that she was a perfect liar, and also how she hugged and kissed her violin, saying, "I should carry home my treasure." Gosh, it was unbelievable. The treasure was probably his symphony because before, in his room, she called her violin a "damn subject of torture."

"Do that tomorrow, and you will see that I am right," Mona continued, smiling. "Or a better idea, go and phone her right now. Confront her about stealing your score. Let her know that you are not so simple and easy to cheat. Just prove that you are a man, not a silly child whom everybody can take advantage of. Be a man, Jim, and take care of yourself. Good luck. I actually have a lot of things to do here and am quite busy. I did this small break to talk to you in respect of the sweet memory of our past relationship, which I miss badly, by the way."

Mona turned her back toward Jim, and when he walked away from her office, seeing that the conversation was finished, she suddenly said in a begging voice behind him, "I am just letting you know, Jim, that when you were outside with the bus driver, I was working with Basil, washed him, and made him ready for the night because Nurse Rona was outside with other guys as you saw. You could ask Nurse Andy. He saw me while he was working with Ali and Zahra next door at the same time. Ask him if you need witnesses for your investigation of my innocence."

Jim walked back into his room, not saying a word. He was too confused and messed up to say anything else.

CHAPTER 33

The whole night, Jim was thinking how he would confront Lada about his missing orchestra score and what he would tell her and not just that. There were also a lot of unclear moments about her, which he would be happy to clear up. What was she doing in her spare time? Did she have friends? Girlfriends? Boyfriends? What was her brother doing now? What profession did he have? Why did she come to work for the group home as a bus driver? Why didn't she stay on a school bus? Why did she need money if she lived in her brother's home and didn't pay rent and other expenses? He had a million questions that he was unable to ask her because she was preoccupied with the vocalization line of his symphony and completely took his attention away from the mystery of her.

Lada knocked at Jim's door at about 12:15 p.m. He jumped up, went to the door, opened it, and let her in, just standing in her way and not letting her to come further into the room. "Jim," she said, giggled, and placed a kiss on top of his head, "Good afternoon. I just sneaked in for a minute to say hi while the guys are loading into the bus. We're going to swim. It sucks that you are not going with us. I will miss you over there." She was wearing a sundress, and strips of her bathing suit were tightened around her neck. A big beach bag was hanging on her shoulder.

"Okay, okay," Jim said nervously, grabbing her hand. "Please leave your bag here beside the door on the floor. Then come here and sit on the chair."

"Why?" Lada looked very surprised but followed his orders. "Why? I actually have no time. I should run. I just have a couple of minutes to see you and say hi. On my way back from the swimming pool, I can stay as long as you want but not now."

"I would like to ask you something."

"Really, Jim, I have absolutely no time. Just give me a quick hug, and I should run."

"Can you show me what is in your bag?"

"Bag? This one?"

"Yes, this one." Not even waiting for her permission, Jim grabbed the bag from the floor by the door, opened it, and started digging in it. There were a bathing suit, towel, sunglasses, book, cap, rubber slippers, a little makeup bag, and nothing else.

"Jim." Lada looked at him in shock. "What are you doing?"

"Sorry," he said sadly, putting the bag on the floor. "I . . . I just was mistaken."

"Mistaken? About what? This is even not my bag."

"Not yours? But whose bag is it?"

"Mrs. Lainer's. She saw me going upstairs to your room and asked me to take her bag with me and give it back to her later on the bus. She said that she has to take care of Basil, and the bag was in her way, so she asked me to help with it. What's wrong with it? Why did you worry about that?"

"Sorry again." Jim approached her, took her hands, and looked at her, begging. "I really owe you an apology. I just messed up. It was a misunderstanding."

"Misunderstanding of what? You sound so secretive, so strange." Lada looked at him, completely confused. "Has something happened since yesterday? Something wrong?"

"Can I tell you later? I would like to talk to you when you come back from the swimming pool."

"Of course. I absolutely have no time now. I have to go."

"I will walk you to the bus. Okay?" Jim suggested.

"Okay." Lada giggled, still confused. "You are a mystery person, Jim. It is always fun to be with you, always something."

"I promise, I will explain," Jim reassured her apologetically. He opened the door. Lada took Mona's bag, placing it back on her shoulder; and together, they walked downstairs and out of the house toward the bus. Jim saw her enter the bus. She settled in the driver's seat and put Mona's bag on the front seat where Mona was usually sitting. He stayed by the door outside all the time. Everybody was already in the bus except for Mona and Basil.

"Is Basil going to swim?" Jim asked Nurse Sue.

"Yeah." She nodded. "He just had difficulty to be ready this morning. Mrs. Lainer is taking care of him. They will come soon."

A minute later, Mona appeared from the door, pushing Basil's wheelchair. Lada opened the lift, and Basil was successfully loaded. Then she waved to Jim and closed the door, and the bus slowly moved away from the driveway.

Jim walked back to the house. He hurriedly climbed upstairs, walked into his room, and grabbed the folder on the table that was empty one hour ago. His orchestra score was there, accurately placed in the proper order. Nothing was missing. The symphony was returned.

CHAPTER 34

J im was surprised but not in shock. Subconsciously, he expected something like that. He didn't realize at first how this happened. He sat on the armchair, held his head with both hands, and started thinking. "Calm down, relax, think it through," he told himself, taking deep breaths.

Lada couldn't do that, a hundred percent not, not at all. It was impossible. She had no bag. Mona's bag, which she held, had nothing out of the ordinary in it. She entered his door, sat in the chair, kept sitting there, stood up, and left through the door. She didn't approach his desk where the empty folder was. When they were talking and when he inspected her bag, he was in front of her, not leaving her unattended even for one second. So it was a setup.

It was an awful, mean huge setup organized by Mona on purpose—to destroy his relationship with Lada. Why? *Obviously from jealousy*, Jim thought.

He got angry at himself, really angry. How could he be so stupid to trust Mona even for a minute? How come he talked to her about his symphony disappearance and believed her scenario that she painted for him with her best acting ability, showing understanding and compassion and suggesting to check on Lada, suggesting not to trust Lada, and so on.

And he fell for it. *Jesus, it is unforgivable!* He didn't understand himself; he can't forgive himself.

Luckily, he didn't follow her scenario. *Lada will come with a bag. Leave her alone for a couple of minutes in the room, go to the washroom, and then walk her to the bus and see what will happen when you are back in your room. Your symphony will be back.*

Lada came without any bag; she left her bag in the bus. Mona obviously was waiting for her downstairs. Noticing that she had no bag, Mona asked her to help—take her bag for a while. She didn't expect Jim to check the bag. She was sure he wouldn't do that for a girl he liked. This was the moment where he went off her scenario.

Then he didn't leave Lada alone. When they left for the bus, Mona wasn't with Basil like she announced to many witnesses. She was looking from behind some corner and then ran to Jim's room and placed the symphony scores into the folder. Jim was pretty sure that the symphony wasn't the target at the moment; the goal was to destroy his friendship with Lada by planting suspicious thoughts into his head. Damn, she was successful for a while.

Now would come the most difficult part—apologizing to Lada, explaining to her what happened, telling her the whole story, and begging for forgiveness. Would she forgive him or not? How offended would she be? Would she understand his craziness and his nervousness about the symphony? To get it, she should know the whole story of his problems with Mona, the sad part of his life that he didn't want to talk about while telling Lada the story of his past. Now was the time to put all the cards on the table, to tell her the truth, except for the sexual part.

But why the jealousy then? How would he explain that to Lada? It was just that Mona was jealous of his composing, of his talent, of his symphony. But why did she want to push Lada away from him? It was just the normal tactics of a controlling abuser—to destroy the relationship of a victim with all friends, to leave a victim without any real help. Now Jim clearly understood this himself. So now he could convincingly explain this to Lada. That was his plan, which he came up with during the hours when his group home mates enjoyed their swimming pool trip.

When they were back, there was a lot of noise in the hallway, and then Lada knocked on his door and poked her head in. "Hi, Jim. Would you like to go for lunch?"

"No, I've already got an apple. You?"

"I had a couple of power bars on the bus, not much time for food. We have a lot of ground to cover, don't we? All these strange things from the morning, you owe me an explanation, right?"

"Yes, I do. Please come and sit. I will tell you the whole story of what happened after you left yesterday."

It took Jim about an hour to tell the long narrative of his history with Mona, with her stealing his first exercises in composing and then returning them, taking all his pages of symphony one by one supposedly to help him and then returning them again. And now he had the same story with the score of his finished first part of the symphony and so on. He told her of Lily's death, the unknown woman whom Mona claimed was Todd's mother, his appraisal of a diamond, Ramah's firing, Victor's pills, Maggie's lockout, and all that happened during his seven months of residing in Mona's group home.

Lada listened patiently, just shaking her head sometimes. "Wow," she said when he finally finished, covering practically all except for his sexual relationship with Mona. "Wow, it's a kind of mystery adventure going on here. Jesus, life is not boring in here as I imagined."

"It is not. But most important, I am begging you, please don't be offended that I distrusted you."

She chuckled. "After all this? Oh God, who would trust who? Of course, you haven't known me for long, less than a month. And now you checked me out and know that I am absolutely innocent, right?"

Jim nodded, holding his breath.

"Maybe an American girl would be offended by distrust," Lada continued, smiling. "But luckily for you, I am not offended at all. I'll tell you why. It is our mentality. We, the people from Eastern Europe, were raised on lies and distrust. It's kind of normal for us. I remember when I was a child, the first supermarkets were just opening in Kiev and Moscow. Most of the people began stealing right away, so cashiers were required to check the purses and pockets of customers. Some people were really offended that they refused to show their pockets and open their purses. Those were usually thieves. They scream about invasion of their privacy, their human rights, and so on. The police were called, they were handcuffed and searched, and a lot of groceries were found in their pockets, under their belts, and even in their socks and shoes. It was so funny and so disgusting at the same time.

"I never felt offended by this. Why? What's the problem with opening my purse and pulling my pockets inside out if I didn't steal anything? No problem at all. I went this way through the cashier, and it took me usually fifteen to twenty seconds. Those thieves who screamed about their privacy were given hours of rude search by police. I saved lots of time and, actually, a lot of dignity letting them look into my empty purse and pockets.

"It's the same here. You checked Mona's bag, which she gave me. You checked my movements in your room, and you know now that I am okay and worth your trust. So we are good, aren't we?"

"Yes, we are not just good. We are amazing. We are great!"

This girl was really special and really unusual, and Jim was full of excitement about her. A huge burden fell off his shoulders; however, some of his own doubts were still left unsolved. "It seems to me that sometimes you are contradictory," Jim added. "You called your violin 'my subject of torture' and another time 'my treasure.' I don't really understand. Do you like it or not?"

"Of course, I do." Lada laughed. "I love my violin and respect it. Actually, it is a real treasure because it is very expensive and also has sentimental value. My brother bought it for me when we came here. But you know my main quality—I am lazy. I love music, but I hate exercising for hours. It is torture for me. Jim, you are surprising me. You are a smart and sensitive guy. Don't you see it yourself?"

"Sorry." Jim felt confused now and ashamed of himself. "It was stupid of me to even ask and pick on some words. What kind of friend am I? I am pretty sure none of your friends ever asked you so many silly questions."

Lada smirked a bit sadly. "I don't have any friends except you, Jim."

"Why?" It was almost impossible to believe. "How come?"

"I don't know." She shrugged.

"Not even your classmates from university? Some coworkers? Neighbors? You are so social and so beautiful. Boys are probably hitting on you all the time. And girls, they want to be friends and have fun together, don't they?"

Lada shrugged again. "I know. I am very social and friendly with everybody, but this is just show. I don't feel close to anybody, except you, Jim."

"Thank you." His face subconsciously widened into a big and happy smile. He was really content to hear that. "But . . . you think it's enough?"

"For me, yes. I just don't have anything in common with girls. All discussions with them always turned to be about men, boys, boyfriends.

They all seem like they are sexually obsessed, but I am not. And boys . . . I don't know, I just hate men. I am not interested and never will."

"What?" Jim exclaimed. It was like a blow into his gut. "Why? You mean, you don't like men . . . like a lesbian?"

"No!" Lada laughed and shook her head. "No, I am a hundred percent straight. I really wanted to have a family of my own. I wanted to have a son as you know from my childhood story. I also wanted to have a husband one day. But then what happened, with this doll-son story, people stomped on my soul. And then with the assault before we left for the USA, they stomped on my body. I had this very serious surgery, I probably will never have kids, and I obviously never will love a man. I was killed inside, nothing left. It's just this beautiful shell outside."

Jim looked at her with wide eyes; he felt a shiver run down on his back. *Oh my God!* He realized suddenly, *She was raped! That's what I didn't get about her story before. Oh God, and she never overcome it in full, never cured completely in spite of these psychology and hypnosis sessions she told me about.*

"My gosh," he whispered. "Lada, I am so sorry that that happened. Can I give you a hug?"

"Of course." She smiled and opened her arms to hug Jim as well as he approached her. "It was my tragedy, but it all passed. I am absolutely okay now. I just know what it is, what I accept and what I don't. I love my brother very much. I practically worship him. He is a fatherly figure for me, actually because of his age as well. But I know for sure that there will be never a man in my life, I mean sexually, boyfriend or husband, not even just a man friend."

"But . . ." Jim looked at her, not understanding. "You said I am your only friend."

"Yes, my only friend, my closest friend, my very best friend because you are not a man. If you would be a man, I would never have come to your room and talk to you."

"Gosh!" Jim exclaimed. It was another, even bigger blow into his gut. "But I am a man."

"No, you are not." She laughed. "I don't consider you a man."

"But who am I for you then?"

"A child with a brain of an adult—a genius, a supercreature, someone who was sent by fate for me to save me, to cure me, to be my best friend forever, BFF as teens are saying now." And she laughed happily and mischievously as always. Her shadow of sadness was gone.

"My God!" Jim slumped on the armchair and covered his face with both hands. It was a dead end. He was in love with her, in love from the first glance, already a month. He knew she had friendly feelings for him, but he still had a hope that maybe it would change one day. Now it was clearly announced to him that it never would. Lada would always be his beautiful, sincere love and inspiration for his music like Grandma Cathy was, no more than that. Should he accept it or not? He had no choice; he had to accept it without a shadow of a doubt. Otherwise, he had no meaning in his life. Otherwise, his music couldn't exist; his soul couldn't exist. Otherwise he would be dead.

"Well," he said slowly, bravely fighting tears, "then BFF, okay."

"Good." She stood up, bowed, and kissed his hair on top of his head. "Then as friends, we need to talk seriously."

"It was already pretty serious," Jim noted.

"Now another topic, about your symphony. I know it means a lot to you."

"Not just a lot, everything. It's my life."

"I know. I mean, it's my life too now, and I really want to protect you. Mrs. Lainer's behavior looks obviously suspicious. I don't know about her plans for you, but according to what you told me, she is a dangerous person. So we should make our own protection plan."

"I tried," answered Jim and told Lada how he burned all his extra pages of music, how he hid all his DataTravelers and CDs on different shelves in his room among books, clothes, and towels.

Lada laughed. "Oh, Jim, you are so cute and naive. You did good job. It was better than nothing, of course, but still . . . it is pretty easy to find. It's just not safe enough. Don't you agree?"

"I know." He nodded. "But I didn't have another choice."

"Now you do. I am suggesting to take all your stuff home with me and save them there. We could leave here only the computer and piano versions of part 2 of your symphony because you will now start working on the score of it, right? First part, which so mysteriously disappeared yesterday and appeared today, is completely finished, right? I will take it too. And the computer versions of parts 3 and 4, which are waiting for later, I will take them as well, right? I hope you trust me on that."

"Yes." Jim nodded again. "I really do."

"And this also will give me a chance to show all your stuff to my brother."

"Mona said yesterday that you told her he changed his profession. He is not playing violin anymore," Jim started timidly.

"I lied to her." Lada laughed. "However, it is partially true. He is not teaching violin anymore. He is conducting a symphony orchestra at our university. I will try to persuade him to perform your symphony, to make your dream about the concert come true."

Jim felt his heart jump to his throat. It was one more blow today but an unbelievably happy blow. He almost lost his breath. "Oh my God! Is it really possible?"

"I don't know. It's pretty difficult. I was already thinking about it. I just didn't want to tell you anything about my idea until we clear our relationship. Now we're clear, right?"

"Yes," Jim whispered, nodding more.

"So," Lada continued, "there will be a lot of issues with finances, timing, finding a singer . . . but I will try. I promise, and if Boris agrees, I will introduce you to him as my best friend."

CHAPTER 35

What could be a bigger inspiration than knowing that light finally and suddenly appeared at the end of a tunnel on the way to your goal? Really, nothing. Jim felt so excited that Lada told him that she would try to show his symphony to her brother. The possibility of a performance—it was fantastic; it felt unreal, but at the same time, it was light, dream, hope.

They loaded together all his folders, pages, CDs, and DataTravelers full of his music into her beach bag, which she brought from the bus for that purpose. Jim suggested that she also take for safekeeping the beautiful marble statue of a sad woman—his present from Lily Donovan. He was worried that Mona would steal it because she showed quite a big interest in it before. After they carried all of Jim's treasure to the bus, Lada kissed him on the forehead and left.

"Wish me good luck," she said and waved to him, starting her bus. He waved back and sent a couple of kisses through the air to her.

Today was really the happiest day of his life in spite of some unexpected blows in his gut, but those were tolerable. He had learned already how to manage sex problems and how to live with that. It was okay. It was exactly what he thought long before—how people were living as monks in cloisters, how people were going on expeditions to the North Pole or to the Amazon jungles. They had no time and no place for sex; those people were serving a higher goal—God, faith, or science, depending on what was important to them, what they had chosen as their life meaning.

For him, it was his music that was important, his creations. It was the meaning of his life, and knowing now that the goal was approaching, he could live easily without sex and just be Lada's friend, if it was what she decided. It was still a bit hurtful psychologically that he was not a man for her. But this pain now moved into the background and became less of a problem. The number one issue now was to work hard and to finish the scores of all four parts of the symphony as fast as possible. What if Boris said that he liked it and wanted to perform it and Jim wasn't ready? It would be a shame. It could crush all his dreams.

The first part of the symphony was finished and gone with Lada. The vocal line for all four parts was also finished and gone, though a singer hadn't yet been found. Now came time to work on the scores of the second part. So Jim nestled on the floor with his big pages and wrote all night, until he finally fell asleep like the dead, with his head on top of his work still on the floor in the middle of the room.

He was so exhausted that, in spite of that very uncomfortable position, he slept soundly and almost missed breakfast. When he slid downstairs at the last minute to grab his food, Mona was already cleaning the table. "Oh, Jim," she said smiling slyly, "you overslept a bit, but it's okay. You can still have your breakfast. I hope it was a happy sleep."

"It really was," Jim said, smiling as well.

"You got her, that stupid immigrant girl? Did she return your symphony? Was it in your folder as I predicted?"

"Yes, it really was," he answered happily, chewing on his cereal. "I got it. You were right." Jim and Lada decided yesterday that they would lie to Mona from now on and coordinate their lies carefully to not make any mistakes and to keep her out of their hair and Jim's business.

"Well, I hope you appreciate my advice and my friendship now," Mona noted contently. "And we could be friends again."

"Just friends." Jim smirked. "I am sorry, I should run. I have a lot to do."

"I understand." Mona nodded. "Keep working. And sorry for all the noise. Don't pay any attention to it. Today is visitor's day. There will be a lot of people around."

"Okay." Jim grabbed the rest of his food and walked to the elevator with full hands, really impatient to keep working on the scores of the second part.

Lada didn't come at three o'clock as usual; she called him instead. "I am sorry, Jim, I can't see you now. I am outside, watching some kids. If you want to say hi, you can come out for a while."

Curiosity was a main characteristic of him. *What kids? Why?* In spite of being extremely busy with his work, he really wanted to know. And it was time to wash rats anyway, so Jim headed to the basement first and then changed his clothes because some water splashed on him downstairs, and finally, he was ready to go outside.

When he exited his room, he noticed that, a couple of doors to the right, Ali and Zahra's door was open. Over the threshold of their room, a little rag spread on the floor, and a strange figure in black clothes genuflected on it, probably praying. He couldn't see the face or even the head of the person because it was inside the room but realized that it was obviously a woman—a beautiful women's shoe stuck out from under black dress. *Oh, visitor's day,* Jim remembered. *Must be their relative.*

He went outside, and on the grass field behind the garden, he found Lada, surrounded by a bunch of children. "Hey, Jim!" she shouted and waved to him. "Come join us! We are playing soccer!"

As Jim approached, the children stopped running and looked at him in astonishment.

"Hey, let me introduce you," Lada said while hugging the shoulders of a boy and a girl who were clasped to her from both sides. "This is Jalal, nine years old. And this is Manal, eight. And those with the ball are Muaz, six, and Ahmed, four. And in the stroller is sitting Fedva, two. She is not playing with us yet. But she will be soon, right, Fedva? Maybe in a couple of years." Lada laughed and pressed the little girl's nose with her index finger. "And this is my friend, Jim, guys. He could probably play with us. Is it okay?"

The older kids nodded silently; the smaller ones screamed "yeah," ran to Jim, and hugged him. He hugged them as well; however, he felt confused because the kids were really nice and friendly, but he hadn't played ball in his life ever and obviously couldn't, especially soccer, which required a lot of running. "I think I better sit and watch," he suggested shyly.

"Oh, yeah, I am so sorry, Jim!" Lada exclaimed, slapping her forehead with her palm. "It was so stupid of me even to say that. I am really, really sorry. Jim can't run, guys, but he can stay with us and enjoy watching our game. You could sit here, Jim." She threw her jacket on the grass and helped Jim nestle on it.

"Okay, whose turn is it now?" Lada asked, throwing the ball to the kids.

"Mine! Mine!" they started screaming and running one after another.

They continued to play, and Jim was sitting and watching, surprised at how natural Lada was with kids. She understood them and felt them, and it was mutual. She was like an elder sister with them, like a child herself, happy, fast, light, and playful. It was a real pleasure to watch her and caress her with his eyes. It was exciting and sad at the same time.

My God, he was thinking dolefully. *She is so good with kids. She knows how to deal with them and obviously could be a great mother. It's such a tragedy, real tragedy, that she can never have her own children.*

It was a nice day, and there were many other people around coming and going through the front door. Visitor's day was in full swing. Jim already knew some of those relatives and friends after their Christmas party. He even noticed Todd's father and wanted to approach him and ask about Todd's mother to find the truth finally, but he moved pretty slow to stand up from the ground, and when he at last did, Todd's father was already gone.

Actually, it began getting too long for Jim. He didn't want to spend the rest of the day outside; he had too much to do, but he didn't know how to say to Lada politely that he would prefer to go home. However, being pretty sensitive, she noticed a confused expression on his face right away. While kids kept playing by themselves, she came and sat beside him, hugging his shoulders. "You are not happy, sweetie," she said, looking in his eyes with compassion. "Tired? Do you want to go home?"

"No, I am not tired. I just should keep working." He brought his main subject carefully. "What if Boris says, 'Bring me the whole symphony,' but it is not ready? It would be such a shame."

"I didn't talk to him yet, Jim. You still have time," Lada said. "Let me explain to you. It doesn't work too fast. It requires a special moment and a special situation. I need to find a proper time to sneak your score to him when he is not busy, not preoccupied, and also in a good mood. He is the boss in my life, but believe me, I know how to play him when it's needed. I may look naive and sometimes stupid, but I am pretty cunning also." She laughed mischievously. "And the main point is I will do everything for you, Jim. I am crazy about you and your music. Just be patient. Yes, go and keep working. And I will return these kids to their mom soon."

"By the way, who is she, and how come you're babysitting them?"

"Her name is Heyriah. She is Ali and Zahra's stepmother. I drove her and their father here already a couple of times. We talked, and we became kind of friends. You will be surprised. She is only three years older than me. She is twenty-five but already has five children and is now pregnant with the sixth one. However, she is very smart," Lada continued excitedly. "Being in America, during all these pregnancies, she graduated from high school and then attended a college, and now she is working as a math teacher in a Muslim school for girls. Could you believe it? It's fantastic. I am so poor in math, and I am so lazy, but she is so hardworking and so talented. Wow, I admire her really."

"Yeah," Jim noted. "When people here see women in black clothes and headscarves, they usually underestimate them."

"Pretty much so."

"And her husband allowed all this education? Usually, oriental men don't like their women being too smart."

"Come on." Lada giggled. "Their women know perfectly how to manipulate their husbands. They look defenseless, vulnerable, and submissive, but this is just a comfortable image for them. From her husband, Heyriah has only one condition—she must always wear a hijab and pray five times per day, but she is free to do what she wants. She has a nanny for the children, a cleaning lady, and a cook for the household. They also have a house in Hawaii where they reside every summer. They are actually very, very rich. You know, her husband owns oil sands in Saudi Arabia."

"Yes, I knew about that." Jim nodded. "The oil allowed him to pay for keeping his older handicapped kids here. Mona told me their story long ago. But I've never meet them in person before. I didn't even know that they are visiting. Today when I left my room, I saw them praying in Ali and Zahra's room."

"Yeah, Heyriah is pretty religious, in spite of being a modern and educated working woman." Lada shrugged. "But I think it is how they were born. It is more of a cultural tradition. And Saudi Arabia is a religious state ruled by Islamic high priests in reality more than by the king."

"Wow," Jim said, laughing. "You became an expert in Middle East culture."

"I learn." Lada giggled and tenderly slapped him on the shoulder. "See you tomorrow, sweetie. By the way, I will bring you something interesting that you will probably enjoy."

She helped him rise, picked up her jacket from the grass, and waved to the kids. "Hey, guys, it's time to get on the bus. Mommy and Daddy will come soon. It's time to go home."

CHAPTER 36

The next day, Lada brought a little black case full of CDs. "Here," she said, handing them to Jim. "This is a Christmas present that Boris gave to our mom—her favorite music from her youth. You should listen to it."

"Why?" Jim was surprised, looking through the disks. "Those are popular songs, groups, pop culture of the sixties and seventies. I know all of them. I listened to them hundreds of times. I know what you mean—I should look for my singer here, yeah? But it's different. Quality of voices and style of performance are really diverse. I need some opera singer, not a pop star. Look . . . Beatles . . . Beach Boys . . . Sonny and Cher . . . M. and Sandra . . . ABBA. It's not even a bit close."

Lada smiled and put her hand on his shoulder. "Sweetie, please. I talked to my mom, and it wasn't easy to persuade her to lend us her treasure. She is listening to these every day, so I took them with a promise to return them this evening. I brought them because, when I did listen with Mom, I noticed that Sandra's voice, when she did solo, is kind of what you want. I would like us to listen to this together, and I will bring your attention to that moment in her song."

"Okay." Jim nodded, feeling really flattered that Lada was so all into it, so full of his interest and his business. It felt exciting to be that close with her spiritually, emotionally, mentally, wholeheartedly. "Who do you suggest we start with?"

"This one." She pulled out one disk and gave it to him. "Don't read the story on the back now. Just listen to the song 'Sunrise over the Ocean.' Doesn't it remind you of something?"

"What? My symphony . . . name of the first part." Jim's jaw dropped in bewilderment. "I knew all their songs are about love."

"Of course, like all pop culture, it is about love. The lyrics of the song said that they wake up in the morning after their first night on the beach and were amazed by the beauty of the sunrise."

"Well . . ." Jim looked at the photo on the front cover of the CD and shook his head suspiciously. "Sandra is about fifteen or sixteen years old here, crazy makeup, huge glued eyelashes, sparkling minidress, almost naked, white hair standing up like an Indian warrior. How serious it could be?"

"I can say *well* too." Lada laughed, mimicking him. "But they sold 350 million copies of their albums in 1969. Doesn't it mean something?"

"Just that this style was popular at that moment, nothing else. This guy M. looks older than her but also difficult to say because of so much makeup. And those crazy ballet dancers in the back, dressed like flowers, kind of pretty cheap taste."

"Jim, don't be so judgmental and picky. Fashions and styles change with the years. You know that. Old-fashioned stuff often look like they are in bad taste or cheap. I don't care about that now. You should listen to the voices, especially Sandra's voice because you need a woman's voice for your symphony."

"Jeez." He chuckled. "She is probably dead long ago. Okay, okay, don't get angry, please. I am listening." He climbed on the armchair and sat comfortably while Lada inserted the CD into his computer.

The song was pretty nice, but the most important part was the vocal solo in the middle that Sandra did a cappella without the band, and then the beginning of the song repeated with both of them, M. and Sandra, and some choir. Then other songs followed, "I Will Never Forget," "Buy-Buy Italy," "Dancing in the Village," "Lonely Tears," and "Clouds on the Sun."

"What do you think?" Lada asked when the music finished. "Did you notice this vocal solo?"

"I did." Jim nodded. "I agree, her voice is beautiful. Maybe it's better to say *was* because we don't know what happened in all those years. I didn't hear about them lately. Maybe they are not into music any longer and changed their profession or even died. I really would prefer Maria Callas, but alas, she is dead."

"Okay, now read the back of the cover," Lada suggested, passing him the plastic box.

"'After phenomenal success of 350 million copies of their albums sold in 1969, the Soleys' career was abruptly ended. On September 29, 1969, Emmanuel was shot right on the stage during the concert by a maniac who wanted to become famous. Sandra did not perform after that by herself and moved back to Italy, where they were originally from.'" Jim lowered the box and sat quietly in shock for some moment. "Wow," he finally said. "It was exactly what I was looking for, what Lily told me, but I can't find the proper information anywhere. But . . . M. . . . the name . . ."

"M. is not letter *M* but Em, the short version of his name, how fellow musicians called him," Lada explained. "I read on the internet about this as soon as I got this CD from Mom. Emmanuel Soley—he was a very famous Italian singer long before he met Sandra. They moved together to America and made their career here, exactly like the Beatles. And Emmanuel was killed by a maniac, exactly like John Lennon, but eleven years earlier than Lennon."

"If she is gone, how could we find her and invite her to sing in my symphony, even if I like her voice?" Jim concluded sadly.

"I don't know." Lada shrugged. "I just was excited when I found out about this story because I knew that you were looking for it, right?"

"Yes, I tried. Lily was a backup dancer in this group as I understand now. She told me that I reminded her of someone who was killed on the stage. Probably she was thinking about Emmanuel. She just couldn't remember the name. And later, when she remembered, their scandal with Mona was about Emmanuel. And you know . . . my middle name is Emmanuel."

"Is it?" Lada exclaimed. "I didn't know that. Wow!"

"I just know that Mona really didn't want me to find out anything about this possible similarity, this discovery. She was screaming at Lily. She prohibited her of telling anything. 'To him' were exactly her words. It meant probably *to me* as I could guess now. She even killed Lily to silence her."

"Oh, come on, Jim. You don't know that for sure," Lada objected. "There wasn't any evidence. Mrs. Lainer, a murderer? It sounds funny. I can't imagine that."

"There was evidence. They cremated Lily the same day, and also, Mona washed all the cider bottles by herself."

"Those are kind of circumstantial. I know the word. I read some crime stories."

"I know too. It's obvious that I can't prove anything. That's why I didn't tell anybody, just you, my trustee and my friend . . . and even you don't really believe me. I think we should be very careful with this and not let Mona have even the slightest hint about what we had found. She could be a danger. She could kill both of us, like Lily. We should pretend that we're naive, stupid, and clueless about everything, right?"

"Agree," Lada whispered, making a facial expression of a conspirator.

"I just can't realize," Jim whispered back, "how could I remind Lily about Emmanuel? I don't look like him at all, not even close. He was tall, big, white hair, blue eyes."

"You know, the hair could be dyed. We should do more research. Your grandma Cathy told you that you have Italian background."

"It was her guess because my eyes and hair are dark. She was laughing about that and teasing me."

"Anyway, we should do more research, sweetie."

"Lada, darling, I have no time for that. I should finish my symphony."

"Okay, I have time. I will try to find Sandra."

"In Italy? If she is alive!" exclaimed Jim.

"And persuade her to perform your symphony!"

"You are crazy, darling. It's impossible. It's unbelievable. Why would she do something like that? I have no money to pay. Do you want to persuade her to do charity? Because I am a handicapped or what? I don't want this. It's kind of humiliating and hurtful."

"Sorry, Jim. I didn't mean to offend you. Don't get it wrong, please. I just wanted to find a way to make your dream come true."

"Some dreams are not real. Some dreams should stay dreams only."

"Stop it, please. If you do not believe in yourself, why are you composing then?"

"I don't know." Jim covered his face with both hands and shook his head. "I don't know."

Lada sat beside him in his armchair and hugged him. "What's going on, Jim?" she said in a low voice. "Are we fighting? I don't believe what I hear. Are you giving up when I almost found everything for you, what you dreamed about and lived for? Do you want to ruin everything right now? Why?"

"I don't know," he repeated, put his face on her shoulder, and suddenly began to cry. The huge tension of the past year and the stress of sudden discovery, which he tried to find out so unsuccessfully, finally exploded from his exhausted soul and heart.

"Oh, sweetie, please." Lada tenderly patted his back and shoulders, trying to comfort him and calm down his sobs. "Please, I understand. It's all approached so fast and so sudden. You were kind of waiting for this, but you weren't sure it would ever happen. And now it's almost here, so close that it scares you, right?"

Jim sniffed and nodded, still hiding his face on her chest. "I just . . . couldn't . . . believe it," he stammered. "Do you really . . . want to do that? To help me? To find Sandra Soley? Is it true?"

"Why not, if I can?"

"How can you? You are not a detective or investigator. You're just a girl who has a job, school, family, your own life."

"It is my life, Jim."

"You know"—he lifted his face and looked in Lada's eyes, still sniffing, swallowing his tears—"I am not religious, but I did pray for you. I begged God or fate or some universal high power to send you to me—to save me, to help me. Myself, I didn't believe that it would ever happen. I didn't expect this because I didn't get any answer for my prayers. But then some time passed, and here you are, my angel, who was sent to me from the sky."

"Come on, Jim." Lada laughed. "Don't overestimate me. I am just a regular girl, not really talented, not really smart, and it was just coincidence that I came to work here and met you. But you inspired me with your music, with your being so special, so unusual, so interesting. And believe me, it is getting more and more interesting every day. Now I have a job for my brother to do. Now I have a plan—to look for and to deal with some celebrity. Now I have Lily's murder case to solve. Jeez, my life is getting more and more unusual and unbelievable because of you.

"If not for you, I would be going to my university classes and then sitting at home, doing my homework. That's it. Boring, boring, awfully boring. Now with you, it's *life*. It's *adventure*. It's *fun*. You should understand how happy you make me. I am living life full of excitement because of you. So I am doing stuff for you, let's say for 20 percent, but I am doing the for myself for 80 percent. It's kind of selfish, but it's what it is. I am absolutely happy, and I have this happiness because of you. Did you get it now? That's why you should stop crying and never do it again."

"Okay." Jim smiled, wiping tears from his cheeks with both hands. "I got it. It's difficult to believe, but I do. And I am very thankful for you for all your efforts. It's not selfish. It's nice and generous of you. And I love you so much for that."

"I love you too," Lada said and gave him a warm, friendly big hug. "And I will prove it. I promise."

CHAPTER 37

Excited by the approaching goal, both Jim and Lada began working really hard because, in reality, that goal was still very far away, far beyond a visible horizon. Jim continued on the score of the second part of his symphony. It was much shorter than the first one, so he was almost finished.

Lada came every day after three o'clock, when she drove the guys home from work, but their meetings were very short—no dates, no walks outside, no listening to the music or talking heart to heart. They decided that they would postpone everything else until the work was finished. She just grabbed fresh pages of the score that were completed from yesterday. She hid them in her bag, gave Jim a kiss on the forehead and a fast hug, and ran home to do her own job on the matter.

The second part's score pages weren't left in Jim's room unattended even for a second. He went to wash rats or grab his food at the dining table only when Lada would leave with newly done pages. It was their best protection from Mona that they could think of. And they were right. Jim noticed many times that after he left for his duty in the basement or short walk in the garden, all the stuff in his room was disturbed and moved a bit. It was not really noticeable, but he knew right away that Mona was searching his room, looking for a continuation of his symphony, and got nothing.

The absence of the second part made her surprised, irritated, and angry. "Are you still working on your symphony?" she asked Jim once during dinner.

"Not really." He shrugged. "I kind of don't see a reason to continue. Anyway, it would never be performed. Why bother?"

"Oh no!" Mona exclaimed. "Why? You should continue. You are a genius. I can guarantee you that it will be performed. I can help. I will find a performer for you. Oh, Jim, you have to finish your symphony. It's the thing that is most important in your life."

It was a difficult moment to act. If Jim said that he decided to stop his work, Mona obviously won't believe him. He should be believable and a good actor and liar as Lada taught him. So he smiled enigmatically and said, "You know, I am working on it in my mind, in my head. I am thinking of each note, listening to them inside my soul. And then when I am ready, I will write everything down. Give me some time, please."

"Okay," Mona pronounced slowly and thoughtfully. "I could wait a bit, but I am so impatient, Jim, because I love you. Please don't forget that."

"Oh, I will never forget what we had." He smirked with a significant expression on his face. "Never."

"I am happy to hear that." Mona smiled. "We probably should continue with our love story. What do you think?"

"Oh, sure!" Jim exclaimed, pretending to be excited. "Just not now. We will celebrate in private when I finish my symphony."

"Good," Mona said and winked. "Do that faster, please. I can't wait."

Hmm, Jim thought. *I am turning into a perfect liar at last. However, it's okay if it makes me safe. Lada was right with her experience and her survival of horrible things. It's a white lie. It's a lifesaver.*

The following week, he even doubled his hours of working in spite of summer that was already almost there. The weather was great, and it was tempting to go outside, sit in the sun, and enjoy the beauty of nature. The flowers in the garden were blossoming, and their aroma even filled the rooms and halls of the group home, sneaking through the open windows. But Jim was steadfast and worked hard all evenings.

Lada did the same. She spent every evening in her room googling Sandra Soley's biography and trying to find her whereabouts. The information was not really clear and understandable and didn't help much in locating the singer.

After the death of Emmanuel, Sandra (obviously being in shock, horror, and depression as Lada guessed) moved to Italy. Then in 1970, she returned to America and was enrolled in Juilliard School to study vocal arts. She spent five years there and became an opera singer, and right after graduation, she got a contract for the next five years in the famous Italian Opera House La Scala. So she moved back to Italy and worked there until 1980. She never remarried and never had children, which she emphasized in many interviews, like in her well-known hour at *Larry King Live* and then with Oprah, Anderson Cooper, Katie Couric, and other famous journalists.

When her contract with La Scala ended, from 1980 until 1985, Mrs. Soley had another contract, this time with the New York Metropolitan Opera (back to America again). After that, she quit singing in theaters and concerts but turned to a teaching business. Now already seventeen years later, she was a traveling teacher who taught vocal arts in different musical schools, academies, and universities in multiple countries, working short contracts of two to three months. She was everywhere and nowhere at the same time, and her locations were practically untraceable. Of course, if you were an FBI agent, it would be easy to find; but unluckily, Lada wasn't.

There was no reason to go to the police or Interpol, and anyway, they wouldn't give away any information because of privacy law. How many crazy people in the world were looking for celebrities' addresses or phone numbers for different stupid and dangerous reasons? Protection was pretty strong.

So Lada kept digging by herself. She made a whole list of musical institutions in the world (which turned out to be thousands) and tried to go through their vocal classes' schedules whenever possible and find the names of the teachers. It was huge and tedious work, which was almost impossible to fulfill because not every school had a website. Not every school published their schedule or the names of their teachers. Her chances to find something were close to zero, but Lada still tried and spent all evenings in her room by the computer, instead of going outside and enjoying the beauty of the summer, exactly the same as Jim did.

But his work at least was successful. The score of the second part of the symphony was finished, and he turned to the third one. Compared with that, Lada's search, sadly, had completely failed.

One evening Lada heard a knock on her door. "Hey, kiddo, what are you doing on your computer?" her brother asked. "I hope you don't do anything stupid, like dating with sexual predators, do you? I know you are not a child and don't need a parenting control, but anyway . . ."

"Come on, BB." She laughed. "You know me better than that."

They both giggled. Lada called her brother that funny short name, which came from Big Brother or Brother Boris and sounded quite regular in America, where all kinds of abbreviations were very popular and accepted.

"Okay, then what are you doing?"

"Some research."

"I thought the school year is finished."

"It is. It's not for school. It's for my friend."

"Does your friend have a computer? Why couldn't she do it herself?"

"Well . . ." Lada turned the computer off and closed the lid. "First of all, it's not a she."

"Oh . . . a boy . . . that's what I suspected according to the intensity of your research," Boris noted sarcastically. "You are sitting here like crazy and wasting such amazing summer evenings for a boy's sake. Wow, must be a pretty special boy."

"Superspecial," Lada retorted.

"Do you wanna talk about him? I mean, why he isn't doing his research himself. Too busy, too lazy or what? Rita and I are frying hot dogs and marshmallows on the patio. Do you wanna join us?"

"I didn't hear any noise."

"The kids went camping with friends for the weekend. And Mama is playing cards at the neighbors."

"Oh, I got it now." Lada chuckled. "All your sources of disturbance are gone. That's why you're inviting me."

"Come on, kiddo."

"Okay, I'll go. I would like to take my computer with me."

"Couldn't you separate with this damn machine for a while?"

"I need to show you something. And maybe it will help us enjoy our evening."

"What is it?"

"Some music that you would probably like."

"Oh, that's okay." Boris nodded and held the door for her as she unplugged her laptop and carried it outside to the patio.

The backyard of their house was surrounded by blooming lilac bushes planted along the back fence. In the middle was a pretty large grassy space with a trampoline and an inflatable pool for children. It occupied only part of the area and also left some room to play ball or badminton.

On the patio, connected to the house, was a decorative metal firepit on tall legs full of burning pieces of coal. Above it, Rita held some sausages on long forks and put them on the dish when they were ready to be consumed. She was really a petite dark-haired woman, quite opposite to her husband, tall and blond Boris. Lada used to see her always looking a bit official, dressed professionally for work. However, now wearing an apron on top of her T-shirt and shorts, Rita reminded her of a cozy and comforting homemaker.

"Hey!" she exclaimed, turning to Boris and Lada. "Finally, I see you, sweetie. Where are you hiding? We're missing you over here."

"I know . . . was a bit busy lately," Lada answered. "Would you mind making some room on the coffee table for my computer? I brought an entertainment for us."

"Just a sec, just a sec." Rita fussed around, moving some plates out of the way. "Do you wanna show us a movie?"

"No."

"I thought we will talk about that *superspecial boy*," Boris reminded his sister sarcastically.

"Probably later," Lada said, ignoring his sarcasm. "But first, we'll listen to music."

"Oh." Rita made a wry face. "Professional cooks are not supposed to cook at home. Professional shoemakers always walk barefoot. We have so much music at work. Can't we have something quiet at home?"

"We can but not tonight," Lada said persistently. "I really need yours and BB's opinion about this."

"What is it?"

"Guys, I am serious. I won't tell you anything because I don't want in any way to influence your thoughts and feelings. Let's just sit and listen."

"Couldn't I chew a hot dog at the same time?" Boris chuckled.

"You could try, but I think you will stop eating probably while listening."

"Why?"

"You will be dumbfounded."

"Oh, come on, kiddo. I am so old and have heard everything possible and impossible in my life. Nothing could dumbfound me."

"We'll see."

"Okay, sweetie, let's do that." Rita calmed them all down. "I am ready." She sat on her chair and looked at Lada questioningly. Boris sat beside her and grabbed a long fork with a hot dog.

"You can chew. Just be quiet," Lada warned him as she inserted Jim's DataTraveler into the computer and pressed the button.

CHAPTER 38

After the guys on the bus arrived from work the next day, Lada didn't come to Jim's room but called him on his cell. "We need to talk," she whispered in a conspirator's tone. "Could you come outside and bring all the score pages that you wrote from yesterday? Wrap them somehow or hide them under your jacket. Mona is in the kitchen."

"Okay," Jim whispered back. "I will be there ASAP." It sounded serious, and he realized that something must have happened since yesterday.

He wrapped the pages into his jacket and walked downstairs in a careless gait, like he had nothing to do, and just walked outside to waste some time. Lada was sitting in the bus with the door open and gestured him to come close. Then she helped him in, drove about fifty meters out from the driveway, and stopped behind some hazelnut bushes by the turn to the main road that led to the highway. Nobody from the group home building could see the bus standing there. Then she moved from the driver seat to the bus bench opposite Jim and took his hands. She looked at him, beaming, and he breathed in the feeling of happiness that emanated from her and floated in the air around them.

"What's happening?" he asked carefully, scared to destroy this amazing aura of delight.

"I introduced your symphony to Boris and Rita yesterday night. They really enjoyed the music. They liked it, Jim, and we discussed what to do to perform it."

"Oh my God," he whispered almost breathlessly, not knowing what else to say. "Oh myGod . . . I can't believe it. I couldn't believe that it would ever happen . . . oh my God." He almost teared up.

"Yeah, it's happening." Lada shook his both hands in excitement. "But it will take time. BB already has a full schedule for his orchestra for the summer. He should think about what to change, discuss some stuff with his musicians, reorganize some things. The shortcut is they, he and Rita, want to meet you. So you are invited to come to our home next weekend. We will decide how to do things, and then you will stay for dinner, even stay overnight because there are enough problems to think of for two days, even more. You can return to the group home Sunday night. I will drive you."

"Oh." Jim just breathed out. "Um . . ."

"What?" Lada exclaimed heatedly. "Are you not sure? You don't want?"

"No, no, no." Jim shook his head vigorously. "I want, of course. I really want. I just . . . I'm kind of tied here. If I'm going somewhere, I have to tell Mona and get her permission. Otherwise, she will report to the police that I am missing. She has to count everybody when people retire to sleep. I am not sure she will give me permission to stay at your place for the weekend. Actually, I am pretty sure that she won't. You know that."

"Yes, of course. That's why I didn't come in today. We should pretend this whole week that we are not friends anymore. Mona doesn't need to see us together. And not only that, we need to invent a cover-up story, explaining where you're going and why."

"So lie again?"

"Yes." Lada nodded.

"Jeez, it's so difficult," Jim said unhappily. "I used to live with Grandma Cathy for thirty-one years, and she never lied to me, and I never lied to her. In the group home, I am only here seven months, and look at me now. I am learning to lie . . . I am trying . . . but I don't really want to turn into a skillful liar. It's kind of shameful and disgusting."

"It's a white lie," Lada concluded seriously, trying one more time to convince him. "There is nothing wrong with that. It's a question of survival. You know . . . let me give you an example. Did you read *Les Misérables* by Victor Hugo?"

"Of course. I did read almost all the French classics."

"Me too, actually. It was translated in Russian. It was one of my childhood favorite books. Then you probably remember the scene when Jean Valjean is hiding in a nun's room. The police came and asked the nun who was praying. 'Ma'am, are you here alone?' And she said, 'Yes, only I am here and God.' And she kept praying. So she lied to them in the face of God, being a very religious person, because it was a lie to save a life of an innocent man. She called it a 'holy lie.' Don't you understand? It's absolutely the same here. Mona is very suspicious, and you yourself tried to convince me that she is dangerous. We should use a holy lie all the time here. What's the problem with that?"

"No problem." Jim laughed. "I am just not experienced in that and not really good."

"Then practice, learn. You're smart enough. You will be good very soon. Inside your heart and soul, just give yourself permission to do it. Understand that not only villains lie but sincere, honest people, like that nun, do so sometimes too. It's a life, Jim, the life you don't know and haven't experienced until now. Your grandma Cathy kept you in a happy bubble without the knowledge of real life and struggle for survival. Here for seven months, as you said, you're learning what life is. It's not what you knew before on the farm."

"Oh, it's definitely not, believe me. I learned that already, even before I met you." Jim smirked. "Okay, I agree with everything you're saying. Let's think, what could I invent as a cover-up story?"

"Say . . . you have a doctor appointment," Lada suggested.

"Mona usually drives our people to doctor's appointments, or doctors come here."

"Well, we still have four days. Think of something, but don't tell her anything in person because she would obviously ask questions about details. Just say to some nurse that you are leaving and leave a note for Mona that you're going to such and such to do such and such and will be back on Sunday night. That's it. And please work as hard as you can. The more of the third part score you finish, the better."

"I think with how my work goes now, I will be able to finish the third part completely by the weekend," Jim said convincingly.

"That would be great. We will talk on the phone, but I will not come to your room these days. Every day you should wrap the new pages that you complete, go for a walk, bring them here, and hide them in this hazel bush. I will pick them up when I drive home."

"Jeez!" Jim giggled. "It's like a movie or spy book for teenagers. It looks like we're playing games here."

"Yes, we are." Lada clapped her hands. "And this is exciting. This is fun. That's why I am so happy to do this, Jim. That's why I love you so much."

When Lada left, Jim slowly walked home by himself. The whole evening, he worked on his scores and later, already in bed, started thinking about how to build a cover-up story for the coming weekend. A doctor's appointment? No, but he could pretend that he is having an appointment with his psychologist to whom Grandma Cathy introduced him about a year ago and with whom he had a phone consultation after a bad breakup of his love story. For that, Mona had no obligation to drive him; it was his private business.

Well, then who will drive him to that "appointment"? Mona could guess that it would be Lada if he didn't give her a reasonable explanation. Actually, it was possible to find that explanation. There were some people in Jim's farm life whom Mona didn't know about, for example, Nurse Edward, whom Grandma Cathy hired the last three years to accompany Jim on his trips to the Atlantic Ocean when she was too weak to travel with him herself. Jim and Edward didn't develop a friendship, but they had a good working relationship, and the nurse provided Jim with all the care that he was paid for, and as a result, the trips were pleasant enough.

I could say that Edward will drive me, Jim thought. *If Mona asks me how I could pay him when I have no money, I could say that Grandma Cathy already paid him for two more years ahead. It would be a kind of stupid explanation, but Lada was right—don't talk to Mona and just leave her a note. "I am going to my psychologist appointment and will stay in a motel overnight. My nurse from the farm will accompany me and drive me back on Sunday evening." No, there should be a reason. Okay. "I can't work on my symphony. I have a writer's block and decided to ask my psychologist for help. I made an appointment for Saturday. My nurse from the farm will drive me there." And no motel, again, because no money. "I will stay with the nurse overnight, and he will drive me back on Sunday evening." That would be better.* He *underlined that the nurse is a man so as not to make Mona jealous.*

All that sounded a bit artificial and not really believable, but Jim had four more days to discuss his version of the story with Lada and to make it believable. After discussion every evening on the phone with Lada and after many edits, a short and simple cover-up story was finally created. It said, "Dear Mona, I am leaving for the weekend to visit an old friend of mine from the farm who moved recently into the area close by. He'll drive me back Sunday night. Jim."

It took some time for Jim to write this note on the paper with big block letters. His tiny fingers were tired of holding a pen. He was surprised himself how much easier it was for him to write musical notes with a little pencil on the lines of score. It was absolutely different, but he finally managed to accomplish that task successfully. He folded the note and hid it in his pocket to make sure that Mona, while she is searching his room, looking for the symphony, wouldn't find it earlier than Saturday morning.

"Look, Jim," Lada said to him on the phone one evening. "Today Mona talked to me when I brought the guys home after work. She suggested that she will come to visit my family and talk to my brother this weekend."

"Oh my God!" Jim exclaimed. "What a coincidence! She is like a dog, sniffing my tracks. So everything is ruined?"

"No way." Lada laughed. "I told her that BB and Rita are leaving on a cruise to Alaska for a week."

"But they won't," Jim guessed. "Right?"

"Of course not, but it's partially true. From my family, my mom and children, Becky and Dave, are going to an Alaskan cruise to watch whales. BB bought them the tour as a present for the end of the school year. They are boarding a Princess ship in LA. So Saturday morning, I'll drive them to the airport and then pick you up after. You see, when I am lying to Mrs. Lainer, I am always using some true details to make my story more believable."

"You're professional." Jim chuckled. "I admire you. So did she believe you?"

"She has no other choice. I promised that she could visit them one weekend later when they'll be back, and she agreed."

"So we are safe."

"For now, yes. I am driving home. Are the new pages in the bush?"

"Yes, ma'am, as usual," Jim teased her.

"Okay, I'll pick them up. How much score left to do?"

"Three or four pages, about one day of work. I'm sure I will be finished by Saturday morning."

"Good. Talk to you later. Be safe."

"You too," Jim answered and added shyly, "Love you." He was expecting to hear it back.

"As always." Lada laughed and turned the bus ignition on.

CHAPTER 39

I n spite of the fact that the third part of the symphony was successfully finished on Friday night, Jim couldn't sleep. He was too excited about his coming visit to Lada's home. All feelings came together and overwhelmed him—being invited by a woman with whom he definitely was in love; meeting her family and the most important person in her life, her brother; having a small possibility that his symphony would be performed one day, maybe in some months. What was *never* before now turned into *possibly* and even *soon*. His whole world was turned upside down, though in a good way; but still, it was too much. It was almost a shock—happy shock, dream shock but still a shock.

Jim even started to work on the fourth part of the symphony's score and made a couple of pages but then decided to lie down, if not to sleep, at least to rest. Otherwise, he would be too exhausted tomorrow and couldn't possibly function well. That would make an impression on Boris that he was severely handicapped and may not be capable to be involved in rehearsals and the performance of his symphony. It was anticipated to be a huge job, which he very much craved to be involved in. So he forced himself to quietly lie on his bed for a long time until he finally drifted to sleep.

They agreed that Lada would pick him up at ten o'clock after she dropped her mom, niece, and nephew for their flight to Los Angeles.

Breakfast at the group home would already be finished and cleaned up, and Mona would be away from the kitchen and the living room. Jim didn't want to leave his notice on the table because it could be accidentally thrown away and lost, so he asked Nurse Sue, who was preparing medications on the trays, to pass it to Mona, and she promised to do so. Then he walked out of the front door, carrying his backpack with his personal stuff needed for the sleepover and also the last pages of the third part and the first pages of the fourth part of the symphony, which were accomplished last evening.

Lada was waiting in her car at the end of the driveway behind the hazelnut bushes. She took his backpack, put it into the trunk, and helped Jim settle on the passenger seat and buckle his belt. "Did somebody see you leaving?" she asked worriedly.

"Nobody was there, just Sue, but she is okay. She will pass my notice to Mona, and she usually doesn't gossip. I guess we're safe." Jim's hands were still shaking a bit. He wasn't used to this kind of adventure. He had left his places of residence a number of times in his whole life just for his yearly trips to the ocean or field trips at the group home. And today's outing was a very special and unusual event. He never visited someone's private home before.

Lada noticed his tenseness. "How was your sleep last night?" she wanted to know. "I actually was jumping all night like crazy, imagining that you couldn't leave and get caught."

"No, I didn't worry about that, but I was too emotional to see you finally after these five days of break and also to see your family. I just don't know how they will accept me. What if they don't like me? What should I do? If they ask questions, what should I say?"

"It's okay, Jim. I told them your whole story, everything you told me. So there's no need to ask you anything except about your creative work."

"That I can survive." Jim laughed. "It's not confusing at all."

During their forty-minute drive, they chatted a bit about nothing, joked and laughed a lot, and managed to relax and calm down all their worries. It was fun to see the surrounding nature and the city, which Jim practically didn't know at all. The two field trips to the Mall of America in Bloomington were definitely not enough to learn more about cities.

When the car stopped on the driveway by the house, Jim was pretty much shaky and exhausted from anticipation, but he made a huge effort not to show this to Lada. Even though he was not a man in her opinion but a kind of unusual creature, a *child genius* (which, alas, included the word *child*), he still considered himself a man and did not want her for a second to see him as a crybaby. So he gritted his teeth hard and jumped out of the car, not even waiting for Lada to help him.

"Wow, you're doing great." She laughed, noticing what he did while she took his backpack out of the trunk.

The house was about eighty years of age. It was bricks outside and looked almost like a palace, but inside, it was pretty old with oak hardwood floors and decorative wooden panels on the walls. They had renovated most of it but kept it purposely antique-style, which Boris and Rita were big fans of. Lada revealed this to Jim in a whisper, holding his hand while they were climbing the brick steps to the roomy porch with huge flowerpots on both sides, and then opened the stained glass door with an inlaid metal design of grapevine branches.

It was an unexpected shock to Jim when, suddenly, a huge ball of white fur rolled in from nowhere, pushed him onto his chest with two paws, and started licking his face when he plopped on his bum, losing his balance. "Sorry! Sorry!" Lada screamed. "Oscar, leave him alone!"

But the dog was visibly too happy and excited to greet the guest and didn't want to let Jim go, until Boris appeared from nowhere as well and grabbed his collar.

"Kiddo, you should let your friend know about this crazy dog over here. Don't worry, Jim, he is very friendly and obviously loves you. But it's enough greetings. Take him away, *bebe*," he suggested to Rita, who came out from the living room behind him.

"Oh, I am okay with that," Jim said, smiling confusingly. He turned on all fours and then stood up, wiping his face with his sleeve. "I grew up on the farm with lots of dogs, cats, goats, rabbits. Even horses sometimes were kissing me."

"So you're our boy." Boris giggled. "We also have two cats and a turtle. They are important company for our children, and even kiddo over here plays with them."

"Mostly, cats come to sleep with me, not much playing," Lada noted, a bit offended. "Come on, guys, let us enter properly and sit on the couch. Jim needs a rest."

She grabbed his hand and walked him into the living room slowly and accurately, and everybody noticed how difficult walking was for him. It wasn't her goal to show this to her family, but it happened unintentionally. However, when she helped him climb on the couch and settle comfortably, Boris and Rita couldn't help but stare at him, bewildered.

Lada told them that he was a midget, but he was really different from other little people whom one would see in regular life or in the movies, even in documentary series about families with similar disabilities. There was even one pretty famous Hollywood star in a dwarf condition, but he was still much bigger and stronger than Jim, could easily walk, also did sports, and performed in the films. The size of his head was in proportion to other body parts, which wasn't the case for Jim, and this was extremely unusual.

"Well," Boris said, trying to break the tension, "it is very nice to meet you, Jim. We've heard a lot about you, believe me."

"Same here." Jim chuckled. "Lada told me a lot."

"And we decided finally to meet you in person," Boris continued, "because this kiddo over here is head over heels about your symphony."

"Not exactly that." Rita stepped in, trying to fix his announcement. "We, Boris and I, had the privilege of hearing your symphony, and we were really impressed. It's not surprising that Ladochka decided to introduce it to us. And we are happy she did because it would be very engrossing, even honorable, for our professional career to perform it with our university orchestra. This would be a more proper statement, *bebe*, right?" She smiled to Boris apologetically. "We would be interested to know how you do compose. Ladochka said that you have a special program."

Jim already knew that *-chka* is a fond part of a word that people in Russia or Ukraine are adding to children's name to show how affectionate they are toward their kids. It was strange to him that Rita used it, but Boris didn't. He simply called his young sister "kiddo," probably feeling that he was more a fatherly figure in her life than just an elder brother.

"Okay." Jim smiled, feeling the conversation moving into his favorite direction. "You can see that I can't play piano properly, like many other composers do. Everything is in my head and my heart, maybe, even better, in my soul. I started to feel music as a child when I traveled to the Atlantic Ocean with my grandma. Somehow the view, the sound, and even the special smell of the ocean touched me and inspired me. I did hear it in my mind as music. But at that time, I had no idea how to write it down. Then I began to study notes and the whole music grammar on the basic school level, then on the college level, and then in Juilliard. A computer program was customized for me just to write down what I hear and feel.

"Sometimes I hear music, but I don't know how to start composing a song or a part of a symphony. Then I go to sleep, and in my sleep, I find a special note. I remember it, and in the morning, I start from it, like pulling the end of a thread, and the whole tangle is unraveling in front of your eyes. I read that Picasso usually looked at an empty canvas attentively before he began painting and used to find a place for his signature. Then he began his painting from there. It's kind of similar. I somehow believe that all art—music, literature, poetry, actually everything that people create—already exists somewhere above, somewhere in the universe's energy fields, and creators are only finding the end of this rope and pull it. And here it is, their creation. After that, I just write it down on the computer."

Jim chuckled and shrugged. "That's it. It sounds pretty simple. But I am doing my score manually. I can hold a little piece of pencil in my fingers. You did hear how my symphony sounded on the computer. I guess that the real score in live orchestra will be much better, much more alive."

"That's exactly what I said!" Boris exclaimed. "I knew it right away. And as we were told, you also want to add a vocal—"

"Yes, we're working on that," Lada interrupted. "Actually, I am working on it. Jim already did his part—wrote vocal lines to all four parts of the symphony."

"I saw you, kiddo, sitting like crazy on this damn internet all evenings. No luck yet?"

"No, BB."

"Well, I would try to talk to the dean of our vocal department. Maybe he could suggest some student singers, and you could try them, Jim."

"It's a nice idea." Jim nodded. "I would be happy. It could help."

"Okay, Ladochka, let's go prepare some lunch," Rita suggested. "Let the men talk about their music business."

While they worked on a Caesar salad in the kitchen, Boris asked Jim about his preferred orchestra settings. There were different shapes of stages—rectangle, square, circle, and crescent, the last two with a conductor positioned in the middle. From that, they turned to discuss practical problems—how long it would take to scan all Jim's handwritten score sheets into the computer and then to spread them into separate music lines for each instrument and print them out. Even with the computer program, which the university had, it would take at least one week of printing and giving notes to musicians before they could start rehearsing. For safety, they would give it two weeks. Would it be enough time for Jim to finish the score of the last part of the symphony?

These were serious business problems. Without solving them, the work on the symphony performance wouldn't be possible. It was an eye-opening experience for Jim. He had no idea how the business of music worked. He was a dreamer. Boris, on other hand, was a practitioner, and their talents combined together could give pretty good results, but it all required a lot of work, time, and effort.

They were engaged in this conversation, which continued until lunch, when some kind of disaster came. What was supposed to be a nice family gathering by the table and sharing of a meal appeared to be extremely difficult for Jim. He got used to the comfort of his furniture in his group home and his food, which were always served by Mona or the nurses properly cut on his plate. His utensils were usually plastic ones of tiny sizes designed for him to lift and hold easily by his wee fingers. Here, everything was made for people of normal size, and it was impossible for Jim to use.

Boris walked him to the washroom and showed him a little step stool to climb on to reach the toilet and the sink to wash his hands. It was used by their children when they were toddlers. Then it was kept for many years in the kitchen because Rita was a petite woman and couldn't reach the top shelves without it. However, even from this step stool, Jim couldn't reach the tub to turn on the water by himself. Lada came and did it for him and gave him soap and a towel.

Then this step stool was used by the table to help Jim climb on the chair, but when he sat, the table edge was above his forehead. So Rita brought a couple of really fat dictionaries from the living room bookshelves, and they were placed on the chair. But to sit on them, Jim should be lifted by Boris and settled on the top. He can't climb there by himself because the books were not really stable and could easily collapse.

Then it was discovered that the silver utensils were too huge and heavy for Jim to hold. Lada ran to the kitchen and found some plastic ones in the cabinet where they kept stuff for picnics. She also put on his plate a couple of spoonfuls of Caesar salad, and she cut long chicken breast strips into smaller pieces.

Everybody was helpful, nice, and full of care for Jim; but he felt awful, really ashamed, and humiliated by this care. It struck him in his heart, demonstrating clearly how incapable he was for normal life, normal family, and normal company. Instead of helping him, he would prefer that everybody just ignore his incapability and not notice it. But if that would be the case, he couldn't sit and have his lunch properly by the table with everybody. Help was absolutely necessary. The house wasn't designed for little people's needs. So settling for lunch, Jim felt confused and blushed. Everybody noticed and tried to turn the situation into jokes to reduce the tension. Finally, it worked, and he began to smile.

After lunch, the men continued to discuss their business because there was still a lot to cover, and they were extremely preoccupied. Not to bother them, Rita and Lada went for a walk with the dog and then cooked dinner together. This time, by the table, everything went smoother and more comfortable for Jim because all special preparations were left in place after lunch. Soup was easy for him to eat with the plastic spoon, and as for BBQ ribs, which Boris cooked on the patio, Jim asked to give him one rib only, so Lada cut it for him, and he ate it with both hands. Surprisingly, it worked very well.

"You see," Lada said, giggling as usual, "it required just a little bit of experience, and you will be good to live here forever." Jim blushed, realizing that it was a joke, though a strange and silly one, but he didn't say anything. Boris and Rita smiled but didn't comment either.

After dinner, Boris and Jim continued their business discussion. This time, Rita joined them. Lada, however, left to her room, saying that she would do more work on her computer.

In the evening, the whole family watched a movie, comfortably settling in the living room, Lada with both cats on her lap, Jim hugging the dog, Oscar, who lay down on the couch beside him and absolutely refused to leave. Boris and Rita positioned in deep and cozy armchairs.

Later, when darkness fell, they gathered on the patio and burned chopped logs in the firepit, having a good time. Everybody laughed and joked a lot, teasing one another while frying marshmallow and sausages on the long forks and enjoying the warm summer evening.

Boris, Rita, and Lada each had a half glass of red wine, but Jim insisted that his portion would be much smaller, so he just got a shot glass. Oscar, of course, was there, lying down on the floor beside Lada's feet, and both cats settled on Rita's shoulders. When it was time to retire for the night, Jim asked permission to sleep outside on the patio in his sleeping bag.

"Are you sure?" Lada asked, organizing pillows and blankets on the couch to find a room for his sleeping bag. "We have a raccoon sneaking around here at night."

"Stop teasing me." Jim laughed. "I always slept outside on the farm in warm days, even though there were wolfs, bears, and cougars in the forest. I was never bothered ever."

"Okay," she agreed, helping him zip his bag. "Then Oscar will stay here to guard you. Sweet dreams, sweetie." And she kissed his forehead before leaving.

CHAPTER 40

On Sunday night, Lada drove Jim back to the group home, but he didn't leave her car right away. They sat on the driveway behind the hazelnut bushes and talked for a while. It was such a nice, cozy, and exciting family weekend that both of them were quite reluctant to part with. They talked about everything, enjoying and rethinking all the events one more time.

"I didn't have any family time since last summer. I didn't even know how terribly I missed it!" Jim exclaimed passionately. "It was as good as the time when I was living on the farm with Grandma Cathy. I'm a bit jealous that you're blessed with a family like that. Your brother, sister-in-law, and I am sure your mom, niece, and nephew—they all are so kind, so warm, so understanding. The whole atmosphere of your house and family relationship, even dog, cats, all this—it feels like a miracle for me. I am so thankful that you let me experience that. I am not even talking about our music business with Boris. It's just really . . . really over the top. I don't know."

Jim covered his face with both hands. "It's so great . . . I don't know . . . I probably will believe in God now. I begged Him to send you to me, and He did, not right away, but He really did."

"I didn't beg for anything." Lada smiled. "But I am very happy to find a friend like you, Jim. For me, it was an absolutely unexpected surprise when I heard someone playing piano in a place like the group home. And curiosity pushed me to sneak in and check. It was so funny. But seriously, I am glad that we looked at the stars last night. I love them so much. For me, they are probably the same inspiration in life as the ocean is for you. It feels important to share them with you. And I have an idea. What if one day we go to the ocean together and sit at the beach at night and look at the stars? We'll feel and smell and hear the ocean, and we will see the stars."

In the middle of the last night, Lada woke Jim up, suggesting to look at the sky together. She knew the constellations quite well. Her *baba* taught her when she was a child, and she lived at times in the summer in her country house (*dacha* in Russian) near Moscow. *Baba* read books to Lada about astronomy and showed her the constellations in the late evenings when the sky was clear.

When Lada moved to the USA, she was surprised to find out that all the constellations were in different positions compared with their position in the Russian sky—much lower above the horizon. Being on the opposite side of the earth changed the view of it. But for her, it was still a sacred memory about her childhood, about her dear late grandmother, about the unbelievable beauty of the night sky full of stars, and she was pretty eager to share it with Jim. Somehow she had a feeling that he would understand. He absolutely did.

She put their sleeping bags on the patio floor, and they spent the rest of the night lying down on their backs, watching stars, and whispering almost until morning when the tiredness finally overcame and forced them to sleep. Rita found them at seven o'clock when she came out for a jog and started looking for Oscar, her regular partner in her early walks. The dog was sleeping on the patio floor in the middle, and Lada and Jim were on both sides of him, each hugging him. Rita whistled and patted her leg to signal Oscar that it was time to go, and he readily jumped up and followed her. Lada moaned something and pushed a pillow on the dog's spot, so they kept sleeping but now hugging that pillow.

You like him a lot, Ladochka, Rita thought. *Of course, how is it possible not to like this amazing genius creature with a kind, sincere, emotionally sensitive, open, honest personality? How could fate give all these beautiful qualities to such a poor sufferer! I just really don't want a rejection tragedy strike him and hurt him more. You shouldn't be so light headed with him. Boris and I need to have a serious talk with you later.*

Lada and Jim slept throughout breakfast and were woken up only by Boris, who came to the patio to cook the family Sunday brunch as he usually did. There were a lot of conversations about the music business during brunch again, and later in the day, they all drove to the city for some sightseeing.

The first destination was the Minnehaha Park. Lada wanted to show Jim the popular waterfalls and also the statues of Hiawatha and Minnehaha—the main characters in Longfellow's "The Song of Hiawatha," which she was sure he read and knew pretty well.

They walked through the park, had dinner at the Sea Salt Eatery, and enjoyed a live show at the Minnehaha Bandstand. Expecting Jim to be tired of walking, Boris put a child's seat on the bike that Rita used when she had toddlers, and now Lada rode Jim all the way around. There were so many new experiences, so much excitement and fun. Jim enjoyed it so much that he was even overwhelmed and couldn't talk. He couldn't stop smiling and just looked, listened, and sensed all the sounds, smells, and views that he missed during the last seven months in the group home.

"I don't know how I could thank you for this weekend," he said to Lada now. "I really don't know. Nothing would be enough."

He took her hand with his both hands and kissed it affectionately. "Thank you, thank you, thank you," he was whispering while he kept kissing it. "I love you so much. You deserve to be worshipped. You're my miracle."

"You're silly." Lada giggled. "Stop it, Jim. It tickles." But he noticed subconsciously that she didn't pull her hand away, and she let him kiss every finger. He brushed them with his lips and tenderly sucked a tip of every finger, gently biting them with his teeth while caressing her palm. Bit by bit, he became so carried away that it made him excited, and he was close to tears, feeling with horror that his erection started. Still holding Lada's hand with one of his hands, Jim grabbed a box of Kleenex with another and put it on his lap to cover the view and to make sure that she didn't notice anything.

She kept laughing and chuckling and brushed the fingers of her free hand through Jim's hair jokingly. "Jim, stop it. You're silly. It's funny. Oh my gosh! Please don't be stupid! It feels very strange!"

"I love you," he whispered, and tears dropped from his eyes right onto Lada's palm.

"Jeez, please stop it. It makes me ticklish, really. See, I am all shaking. Why are you doing that? And why are you crying? I love you too."

"No, you don't," Jim sobbed.

"I do, silly. We're friends, best friends, and friends love each other. It's normal. You can't be a friend with someone whom you don't love. Friendship is one of the sorts of love. Let my hand go, please. Jeez, look, now it's all wet from your tears. Give me a Kleenex, please. Why did you grab the box all for yourself?"

Breathing heavily, Lada finally removed her hand from his grip, pulled one tissue, and wiped it. Then she took another tissue to dry Jim's cheeks. "Oh, my sweet baby," she said, making a funny expression while wiping his face, "I am so sorry that I made you cry. I forgot that you're so sensitive."

Jim calmed down slowly as well. The moment passed, and his erection subsided. Lada returned him to the dead end—friendship and nothing else forever. He realized that he should hold himself in check better if he didn't want to lose her. "I didn't see much happiness in my life, especially in the group home," he tried to explain calmly in a neutral voice. "I become pretty strong, kind of numb inside, when I see disgusting and horrible things and people, but when I see real happiness, somehow it touches me so deep I just can't hold back the tears. I am so sorry. I didn't want to scare you. This happiness just burst out of me. Believe me, I am not a crybaby usually."

"I know." Lada affectionately kissed his forehead and then both his cheeks. "It's just funny. I felt butterflies in my stomach. It felt exciting and ticklish and stupid. Okay, let's forget about this now. I have one important question. How much time do you need to finish the score of the fourth part of your symphony? One week, two, or more?"

"I don't know. You wouldn't believe this, but I miss the ocean seriously. Every year since I was eight, I went to the ocean in June. Even the last three years when Grandma Cathy was weak, she hired a nurse to go with me. If I could stay by the ocean now, one week would be enough. It pushes me toward music. It forces me to create. It inspires me.

"But this year, such a trip would be impossible, and this thought is killing me inside. It's extremely important to me, but alas, this is a dead end. I should work here, and it could take much longer."

"You don't need a nurse. I can go with you," Lada suggested readily.

"Thank you for everything again, but this is out of your reach and mine as well."

"Why?"

"I told you already. I have absolutely no money. And you are working. You have family. You have no time to travel with me."

"And sadly, I have no money too." Lada laughed, making Jim wonder what was so funny about that. "Actually, I have some, but it obviously wouldn't be enough for a trip for the two of us. And I can't borrow from BB because they just spent more than ten thousand on this Alaska cruise for Mama and the kids. It all went from their savings."

"Lada, forget about this, please." Jim looked at her seriously and took her hand again but, this time, just held it strongly. "Even if you had money or your family had, I would never ever in my life take it from you. I have no right to borrow if I have nothing to return. I can't accept a present like this from the woman I love. You may be considering me as a child, but deep inside my heart, I feel like a man. And a real man should be responsible for money in a relationship with a woman. Yes, we're friends as you insist, but it is still a relationship, and my moral bone would never allow me to take money from a woman, even just a friend. A gift or a debt, it doesn't matter, never! Not in any circumstances!"

"Wow," Lada said seriously too. "You give me more and more reasons to respect and to admire you, Jim. But I am still confused. You have some pension. You have some sponsor. I know it goes to pay for the group home, but . . . are you sure that there's nothing left? Just some dollars to save every month? Little by little and maybe next year, it would be enough to go to the ocean"

"I don't know, no idea. I was told that that's it. I never checked my account. Oh no, wait . . . once, I bought a DataTraveler and a box of CDs during a trip to the mall. It was not expensive, something over twenty dollars, and there was enough money for this purchase."

"You see." Lada chuckled and clapped her hands. "We should check. Maybe we could find some money for you. It would be fun. Okay, it's getting late now. You should probably go home. I will not see you tomorrow because I have some work to do at home in the evening. But Tuesday after three o'clock I will come, and we will do this money thing."

"Yes, I would be happy to see you again."

They hugged each other and kissed goodbye, and Jim climbed out from the car and walked to the house while Lada drove away.

He was surprised to find the front door unlocked at that time. *Mona probably left it unlocked for me, and she is waiting inside to make a scandal about my absence without her personal permission,* he thought. However, he was wrong. Nobody was waiting for him. The living room was dark and empty, and he successfully climbed the stairs, entered his room, and locked his door. He was home, and everything for now looked calm and quiet.

Thank God, he thought quickly and went to shower and then to bed. In reality, he was completely exhausted from the happiest weekend of his life, full of unusual activities and strong emotions.

CHAPTER *41*

After a long time spent in the fresh air, Jim slept like a baby. He hadn't had as many outings during his life in the group home. It was especially difficult for him because, while living on the farm, he used to be outside a lot. In the summer, he even practically lived in the yard near their birch grove but rarely in the house. He slept many times in the bundles of hay and madly loved its smell of freshness. In the last seven months, those nice experiences were all gone.

But in spite of the calmness and contentment in his heart, he realized that there was a nightmare bothering him. He saw himself beside the ocean where a terrible howling storm was going on; a violent wind with growling waves cried and screamed with piercing voices. And there was a boat in front of him that began to sink, and some passengers on it were also screaming and crying like crazy. Those deafening screams finally woke him up.

He sat on his bed and listened for some minutes. It was all quiet, but just as he realized that it was only a nightmare that broke his sleep, real moans and screams began from somewhere behind his door in the hallway. It was obviously a woman's voice, and someone was also shouting angrily at the screaming woman, and he recognized right away that it was Mona. She was fighting with someone; the doors were banging, and even chairs fell on the floor with a thunder. Then it calmed down for some minutes but soon started again.

Jim slid from his bed and, in his pajamas, walked to the door, opened it a crack, and looked outside. Two doors on his right, across from the room of Ali and Zahra, the door of Maggie's room was wide open and brightly lit. Mona, fully dressed, was pulling Maggie in her nightgown out of her room. The poor girl didn't want to go, grabbed the furniture and the door frame, and screamed and howled madly. She was very fat and swollen, and her stomach was huge like a giant balloon.

They fought while Mona pushed her into the hallway, slapped her in the face, and hit her on the shoulders and back. Then she suddenly noticed Jim standing beside his open door and watching them in horror. "Oh, Jim, I am so sorry!" Mona exclaimed apologetically. "You are already home. I didn't know that. I didn't see when you returned because we have a situation here. Maggie is suffering a horrible attack of her mental illness. I am trying to force her go to the hospital. She doesn't want to, but it is absolutely necessary. I am trying to pull her downstairs."

"Do you want me to call the ambulance?" Jim asked.

"I already did. They are coming soon. I left the main door open for them."

"Oh," Jim said. He understood now why the door was unlocked when he arrived home. "It's so loud. You'll probably wake up all the guys here."

"It doesn't matter. They all are locked for their safety."

"I am sorry I can't help you pull Maggie," Jim noted. "She is about ten times bigger than me."

"It's okay. I will do everything myself. Go to your room and lock your door, please," Mona ordered in a harsh tone because Maggie, after a short break, suddenly started howling and wailing again, holding her stomach with both hands.

Mona grabbed her by the hair and pulled her toward the elevator. Finally, it looked like she was successful. Jim closed his door, returned to his bed, and placed a pillow over his head to block the awful screaming. It didn't help much, but soon the elevator buzzed; they went downstairs, and the noise ended. Jim didn't hear if the ambulance came, but there were no screams anymore. Everything got quiet.

He couldn't sleep for some time, feeling very disturbed by the scene he saw and pity toward poor Maggie. Mona was shockingly rude with her. *Why not leave Maggie in her room and let the paramedics deal with her?* he thought. *But well, actually, it's not my business. Now she is probably already on her way to the hospital and will get good care there.*

During breakfast the next morning, Mona wasn't there and Nurses Rona and Andy were serving. Jim guessed that Mona stayed in the hospital with Maggie. He tried to discuss it with his roommates, but Todd and Ella said they absolutely didn't hear anything. Victor, as usual, kept silent and stared sullenly into his plate.

After they left for work and the nurses began working with the bedridden handicapped who stayed in their rooms, Jim decided to check in the basement how the rats were doing without him washing them for two days. When he stepped out from the elevator, he was really surprised to discover that the room was unusually hot. Wood was burning in the fireplace, a mattress was on the floor beside it, and as a big shock, Mona and Maggie were sitting on it. Maggie was smiling and held a tiny baby wrapped in some piece of cloth in her arms.

"Bababa, bububu," she said happily, noticing Jim, and extended her arms to show him the baby.

"Jim, what are you doing here?" Mona exclaimed indignantly.

"I am sorry to interrupt," he mumbled confusingly. "I just wanted check on my rats. I see they are clean."

"Of course, I washed them during your weekend absence. Not like you, I am responsible. And actually, they are *my* rats."

"I know that. Sorry again. I didn't expect to see you. I just guessed that you were in the hospital with Maggie."

"No," Mona answered in an aggressive tone. "I misunderstood. It was not her illness attack. She was delivering a baby. Surprise! I didn't even know that she was pregnant. I thought she was just getting fat. When paramedics arrived, the baby was already here, and there was no reason to go to hospital. You know their bills are pretty costly."

"Don't you have medical insurance for the group home?" Jim asked shyly.

"Why do I hear this investigating tone in your voice again, Jim?" Mona almost screamed. "Nothing of it is your business. And please keep your talkative mouth shut. Nobody should know about this baby. It will be given up for adoption right away. We're not supposed to have any children here."

"I don't think Maggie is capable of making this decision."

"Jeez, it's not your business, Jim! Her family did it for her, her father, Mr. Senator."

"And how about the father of the baby? Is it Todd?"

"Of course, it is. Who else could even take a look at this fat piece of retarded meat? Only the schizophrenic."

"Doesn't Todd have a right to know? It is his child after all."

"Todd doesn't know and doesn't understand anything. He is just a horny animal! He doesn't care! And nobody is asking him! Do you understand that, Jim? So, just shut up!"

"But I still think you should probably talk to him today before the baby is gone."

"Okay, okay, we'll try together during the dinner," Mona suddenly agreed pretty peacefully just to get rid of him. "Now go, Jim, and work on your symphony. That is your business. And don't bother to come at three o'clock to wash the rats. I will do it myself again. Maggie and baby need rest, and I don't want to see any extra people here. Understood?"

"Yes, of course." Jim nodded.

He returned to his room, thinking that obviously Mona was lying again. She knew that Maggie was pregnant; she was experienced enough in life to know that. That was why she locked Maggie from the middle of March to make sure that nobody else noticed, at least the nurses.

But now everything seemed back to normal, and the problem was solved. Maggie survived childbirth and looked good and happy after all. The baby would go to some nice family, like he himself went in his time to Grandma Cathy and Grandpa Phil Bogat. So there was no reason to worry about them. Now he can really start to work on the scores of the fourth part of his symphony to finish it as soon as possible.

CHAPTER 42

R ight before dinner, Mona escorted Maggie in her room to rest and locked her door. Then she came to the dinner table, where all residents, including Jim, and the nurses were already sitting, and began serving food as usual like nothing happened. "I have very good news," she announced cheerfully. "After being on a very strict diet for some time, Maggie lost part of her weight and will continue losing more. Now she is healthy enough to go to work with you, guys, tomorrow."

"Oh, good, good." Nurses Sue and Josef nodded, but the residents once again had no reaction whatsoever.

"Todd," Jim said and pulled the big man's sleeve, "unplug your ears, please."

Todd waved him off like an annoying fly and kept listening to his music while chewing slowly. Mona laughed and winked to Jim. She approached Todd and abruptly pulled the earphones from his ears.

"What the hell!" he exclaimed and tried to grab them back.

"Todd, don't make me angry," Mona said in a harsh tone. "Jim wants to say something to you."

"Who is Jim? That child? Hey, merry Christmas, child. What do you want?"

"Todd, do you remember Maggie?" Jim asked.

"Who is Maggie?"

"The fat girl who always watched TV with me on that couch," Ella prompted, irritated.

Todd shrugged. "I don't remember any girls. I don't care about girls. I only like boobs."

"Oh, she had pretty big boobs," Ella confirmed. The nurses giggled, and Mona winked to Jim again.

Todd knitted his brows, trying to remember. "Girl with big boobs," he repeated pensively. "Oh, yeah, I like to grab them and squeeze. Jeez, it was fun. But she is gone. She was transferred to another institution a long time ago."

"What do you think, Todd, if you have a child? Would you like to have him or her in your life?"

"What the hell—child? You're a child. I don't wanna have you in my life. I hate children. They always interrupt card games and my fun. Why are you asking such a stupid question? Oh, yeah, children are always saying something stupid. But big boobs I like. Wait, if my child is a girl and she has big boobs, I will have her in my life. Oh, I will have her for sure! Ha ha ha!" He smacked his lips and neighed loud and rudely with a kind of dirty expression on his face.

"Okay." Mona gave him back his earphones. "Enjoy, my dear. Thank you. So . . ." She turned to Jim. "Are you satisfied, Mr. Bogat? You just had a very meaningful, serious, intellectual conversation with this guy, didn't you? I was right, wasn't I?" She smirked sarcastically.

"Yes, you were," Jim noted sadly, took the rest of his food, and walked to his room. The story was obviously finished, and the baby would be lucky to escape a parent like this.

Adoption is the only possibility in this case, Jim thought. *And Mona is right again, I should mind my own business.*

He looked through some pages of the score of the fourth part of the symphony, which he started to work on before leaving for the last weekend. Slowly, sounds of different instruments of the orchestra came back to him, and he began writing with his little pencil, as usual lying on the big sheets of lined paper on the floor. The work went smooth until late evening when Jim felt that it was getting hot in the room, and he definitely needed some fresh air.

He grabbed the main door key, went outside, and locked the door behind him. Then he sat on the bench in the garden and took some deep breaths, enjoying the amazing smell of mirabella and blossoming white and cherry tobacco plants. Then he looked at the sky, thinking that it must be dark enough to see some constellations, which Lada taught him. It would be nice if he could practice finding them by himself and surprise her next time.

The door of the house suddenly opened. A dark figure went out and walked to the driveway behind the hazelnut bushes, where Jim usually met with Lada in her car, not to be visible from the main porch. In spite of twilight, it was clear that it was Mona—her tall slim figure was very recognizable. She obviously didn't notice Jim on the bench. Behind the bushes, he couldn't see her either, but he heard that she stopped there, no more footsteps, probably waiting for somebody.

Jim's investigative mood woke up immediately, and he held his breath, listening intensely. Some minutes later, it sounded like a car slowly approached Mona and stopped beside her. The door didn't open, just a window went down, and Jim heard a woman's voice that sounded familiar to him. Of course, he realized a couple of minutes later that it was Maggie's grandmother, whom he saw a number of times at the Christmas party and also on visitor's days. *She probably came to take the baby,* Jim thought. *Maybe she will adopt it. That would be a really happy ending. The senator's family is pretty well off, and the child would live there perfectly.*

"Good evening, Mrs. Gordon," Mona said nicely.

"Oh, Mrs. Lainer, I would be glad to thank you for the amazing job you did," the new great-grandma said. "My son is very content and thankful to you for solving this scandal for him. He was so worried. It could completely destroy his campaign. The election is next month, and his competition really could use it against him. We are very devoted Catholics, and he relies on the same voters, so you could imagine— retarded daughter, out-of-wedlock baby from a schizophrenic! What values could he possibly preach to his electorate with the mess in his own family? He would never be reelected, ever! And thank God that He sent you to us. We're unbelievably thankful for your help. Here is your payment, exactly as you requested—a diamond necklace for $200,000. The receipt is there. You can check. It's very beautiful."

"I don't need to check. I trust you, Mrs. Gordon." Mona laughed.

"Just promise, please, that this never happens again."

"Oh, I can guarantee that, swear to God."

"Then okay, good night, Mrs. Lainer."

"Good night, Mrs. Gordon. My regards to Mr. Senator."

"Of course, of course." The engine started, and car was gone in a minute. Mona walked back to the house and locked the main door. The whole scene lasted five minutes, maybe even less.

Jesus! Catholics! She didn't even ask how Maggie is doing! Jim was shocked. He was lucky that he got the key for the main entrance with him when he went for his walk. This way, he didn't need to ring the bell, and Mona would not find out that he was outside and overheard this meeting.

He wondered if it would be quiet enough to sleep or if the baby, who was obviously with Maggie in her room, would cry. He knew from some movies and commercials and also heard from some neighbors' families on the farm that babies sometimes were very noisy at nights, and young parents could be suffering from lack of sleep. However, everything was absolutely quiet, and Jim slept actually pretty well.

The next day after lunch, Jim decided go to the basement to wash the rats earlier than usual to make sure that Mona wouldn't call him irresponsible anymore. When he stepped out from the elevator, a burning smell hit him strong. It felt like an inexperienced cook was trying to fry a steak and burned it badly. Mona was standing beside the fireplace, digging in ashes with a metal poker.

"Sorry to bother you," Jim said, feeling uncomfortable to bump into her again. "I just wanted to wash your rats." He grabbed the hose and made a step toward the cage but stopped, astonished, seeing blood on the floor where usually only the rats' droppings were mixed with pieces of carrots or other leftover vegetables from the residents' menu. Mixed with blood now were tiny pieces of baby's fingertips and nails.

"W-w-what-t-t's that?" he stuttered as his jaw dropped, and his hands subconsciously let go of the hoses.

"Here you are again!" Mona screamed. She dashed toward Jim, grabbed the hose, turned up the gushing water, and washed everything away in a second. "I have so much trouble! I have so many problems, and you, instead of helping me, always are in my way, always just irritating me."

"But . . . but . . .," Jim whispered still in shock. "It's . . . it's . . . some . . . fingers."

"Yes, Jim. It's a life of a person who is managing tragedies that mentally ill people are creating. After delivery and all this pain, poor Maggie was in distress, and she suffocated her baby. She is retarded, so she is not criminally responsible for her actions. We consider it as a tragic accident only. I gladly would organize a funeral and buy a plot at the cemetery for her, but her family strictly prohibited that. It could create some investigation that would destroy her father's election campaign. Her father is hiding Maggie here because of her look and conditions that will undermine his political image. You know, he is a senator, so I can't refuse. I have no right to refuse. I am just following his orders to get rid of the body.

"Actually, when we go officially, anyway, it would be cremation. So I cremated head and bones, but I decided to feed my animals some fresh meat. They usually have only vegetables here, but in real life, they are meat eaters. It's a bit difficult to understand, but I have to take care of everybody here, even my rats. They deserve treats sometimes for their hard work of cleaning garbage for us.

"You should keep quiet about this, Jim. Ethically, not everybody would agree with me, but it's okay. I don't care. It's nobody's business. It's my business. My residents are, sadly, retarded and can't understand anything. I am always fixing their problems. It's my job."

"I . . . I don't know," Jim whispered still in horror. "I don't know what to say. There is some logic in your words and deeds. You can't disobey the senator. You're also covering for Maggie because you care for her. The poor girl suffered enough. She needs your help, and you are kind of helping her in a way . . . but these rats . . . it's so scary. You could just cremate the whole body."

"Yeah, maybe it would be better. However, I am just a human. I make mistakes sometimes as everybody does. And you know, Jim, I was scared. I was very scared when Maggie did it. I felt helpless. I didn't know what to do. I panicked," Mona added in a crying voice, and Jim suddenly realized that it was all show like it was before, like it was always with him, *Mona-style show* for idiots.

"Are you lying again?" he asked, distrustfully looking at her.

"I am not lying!" Mona exclaimed, agitated right away. "Are you rude and ungrateful with me again? You know what, Jim. I don't need your help anymore. Give me the key for the basement. You are not coming here and washing rats anymore. I will do everything by myself. I will wash and disinfect everything here with bleach. Everything will be clean, and if you say a word about the whole story, I will insist that you are mentally ill and always have crazy hallucinations. Otherwise, why are you in this group home, eh? You have no evidence of anything. It's all your delirium. So go and shut up forever. Or you will be next in line for dinner to my animals. Your size is just as good for this cage as the baby's. Get out from here!"

"Well, okay," Jim mumbled through squeezed teeth and shrugged. He threw the basement key on the wet floor and stepped into the elevator to go back to his room.

CHAPTER 43

J im returned to his room so angry and agitated that his hands were shaking. He dashed around, grabbed some of his stuff, and began putting them into his backpack. "I can't do it anymore," he almost screamed to himself. "I can't live here. I won't stay here one more day. It's impossible. That awful monster has no morality at all, no heart, no soul, nothing! She is just a wild animal. No, the animals are even better. They have no mind, but this monster does. And she is using it to obtain money without any consciousness, without anything human! It's impossible to be in one house with her. These poor guys can't see that, can't understand what she is doing, but I can. And I can't tolerate this anymore. I am leaving right now!"

Finally, he dropped his swollen backpack on the floor, collapsed on his bed, and sobbed unstoppably, hugging his pillow for quite a long time, realizing that his situation was a complete despair. He actually had no place to go.

Slowly, the pain in his soul subsided a bit, and he started thinking more rationally. What could he do? If he could stop paying for the group home, $3,500 monthly, then he would be able to rent a small apartment and still have some money for food and other expenses, like internet, cell phone, printer cartridges, paper, and so on. But how could he do things for himself, like laundry, cooking, cleaning, buying grocery?

Well, groceries could be delivered as well as other stuff from Amazon, but this would increase the cost of everything a lot. And still, his hands were only capable of holding a little pencil, a plastic spoon, a kid's toothbrush, and a disposable shaving blade. Simple tasks like installing a new cartridge into a printer or pressing a button on a laundry machine or plugging in an electrical wire were absolutely impossible for him. All this was used to be done for him by Grandma Cathy, hired helpers, Mona, or nurses. He also needed special furniture, bathroom, kitchen, and laundry equipment of tiny size. Where was it possible to find an apartment with all these?

At Lada's place on the weekend, he wasn't even able to reach the tap at the back of the sink to turn on the water to wash his hands, even using a step stool. Everything so essential for a person needed to be special for him, really special, absolutely customized compared with stuff for regular little people with a dwarf condition.

The only chance to leave the group home, where all services were provided so perfectly, was to hire a caregiver, but this would be pretty expensive; and for that, definitely, he would have not enough money. And how to find a proper person who would be understanding and nice? Place an ad on Craigslist? Conduct interviews? Or ask Lada for help? It would be absolutely impossible. He already asked her for too much. He considered her the love of his life, not a maid to do his laundry, wash his floors, and clean his toilet. It would be extremely humiliating for him to ask her for more help, more than he already had, to ask for anything of household kind.

But how then could he leave this group home? What was his choice? Stay here? Live beside the monster, the murderer, and pretend that he didn't see or know anything about her deeds? Pretend to be an idiot? It was humiliating and also morally just murderous for Jim. There was nothing left to ease his despair, absolutely nothing, and that made him sob, realizing his weakness, his helplessness, his dependence. Mona was an emotional and spiritual burden for him. For Lada, he would be a physical burden; and he would never, in any circumstances, want that for her.

A quiet knock at the door sobered him up. It must be Lada. They had planned today to go to the bank together to check on his account. So Jim stood from his bed, wiped his face, and walked to unlock his door. To his deep surprise, it was Mona.

"Sorry, my baby," she said in the nicest voice imaginable. "I came to apologize. I was rude with you and said stupid threats. I really regret my words and my behavior. I was just too nervous and suffered so much with poor Maggie. I lost control of my emotions. It was wrong. I should be always nice with you in sacred memory of our past love."

"Mona, please go away," Jim begged. "I don't want to see you, and I don't want to talk to you."

"No, baby, this is not right," Mona continued, entering his room in spite of his protests. "Yes, we fought, but this is normal. This is what all lovers do. And then when the fight is finished, then love becomes even sweeter. We should try to do this once again and see. Maybe we will return to our love story." She tenderly put her hands on his shoulders. "I will give you a massage to help you relax."

"Please don't." He pushed her hands away.

But she was pretty adamant and persistent. "You need to calm down, Jim. Otherwise, how could you finish your symphony? It should be finished as soon as possible. My daughter, Sharon, already contacted her composing professor, and he promised to help find a performing orchestra for you. It is an amazing news, isn't it? Are you still writing your score?"

"No," Jim said angrily. "I have a writer's block. I can't do anything more."

"What do you need to overcome this block? I will do everything for you," Mona promised and sat on his bed.

"I need to go to the ocean. It would be my inspiration. I know that for sure. It happened before, and my grandma always let me go to the Atlantic Ocean to rest and to start writing music again."

"Oh, it's so sad that she died and can't do that again. But I will talk to my daughter. Maybe she will go with you. She is extremely poor and has no money for the trip, but maybe she could take a loan from a bank or something. I will try to help as much as I can. Come here, baby. I would like to hug you."

At that moment, the phone rang. "Sorry, but I need to take that," Jim said. He was sure that it was Lada and that she was already downstairs, waiting to come over to see him. He pressed the button.

"Hi, Jim, it's me." He expected right; it was her.

"Hi," he said, not pronouncing the name of the caller.

"Sorry, but I can't make it today—" Lada continued; however, Jim interrupted the conversation right away.

"I am sorry, but I can't talk right now. I have a visitor in my room. I'll call you back." He hung up abruptly and put the phone into his pocket, feeling more at ease that she was not coming and would not bump into Mona in his room.

"Who was that?" Mona asked. She was already lying down on his bed.

"It doesn't matter. What are you still doing here? I'm not hugging you. I'm not talking to you. I do not love you and never did. You didn't love me either. You were just teaching me what sex is, but that school is finished now. I've successfully graduated already."

"Obviously with the honor diploma." Mona giggled. "But some lessons are nice to repeat just for fun."

"Not in this case. Go away, please, right now, or—"

"Or what?" Mona smirked. "You will call the police and report that I tried to rape you?"

"Don't be stupid!" Jim barked. "Or I will go." He turned and left his room, slamming the door.

He went outside to the garden, sat on the bench, and called Lada. When she answered, he heard a lot of noise and laughter behind her.

"I am visiting with my friend Heyriah now and playing with her kids," she said. "They are leaving for Saudi Arabia tomorrow, and I just wanted to say bye. Anyway, evening is not a good time to go to the bank. All banks are probably already closed. Let's do it in the morning. I will come to pick up the guys for work, and you can go with us. We will drop them at the factory and then have a free time until two o'clock. It would be enough for us to do anything we want. Right, Jim?"

"Okay, sounds like a plan. But what reason should I use to go to the city?"

Lada laughed. "Say that you want to go with the guys to the factory because you want to see what they are doing. Say that you're thinking, maybe, to get a job there as well."

"It won't be believable. Mona knows that I am not capable of this job. I tried to get it already for real."

"Well, then say something harsh, like I'm going to the city because I want to, and I will do what I want from now on."

"That would be believable." Jim chuckled. "I just had a big fight with Mona, and this would be the proper answer now."

"Perfect, see you tomorrow then."

CHAPTER 44

Next morning after breakfast, when the guys lined up by the door, waiting for the bus go to work, Jim announced to Mona, "I am going for a walk. Will be back for dinner."

"Such a long walk?" she noted, astonished.

"Yes," he said and went out from the main door.

"You will be too tired!" she shouted at his back. "And you will miss a lot of time to work on your symphony!" But Jim ignored her and continued walking.

The bus was already beside the front porch. In a minute, Mona escorted Maggie, Ella, Victor, and Todd toward it and gave instructions to Lada to keep an eye on the new girl. They seated Maggie on the front seat by the window, Ella beside her by the aisle, protecting her from Todd's unwanted touches. Todd was on the very back seat by the opposite window, with Victor beside him by the aisle. This stopped him to get out too easily and to approach Maggie. However, Todd didn't pay any attention to Maggie and probably didn't even notice her. She was still pale and a bit swollen, but her stomach was getting visibly smaller. And again, nobody paid attention, only Lada, who didn't know how Maggie looked before.

When everybody was settled, the bus moved from the driveway and turned onto the highway, where Jim was already waiting for it on the corner, behind the hazelnut bushes as usual. Lada stopped, opened the door, and jumped out to help Jim in. "What the hell! Where is he going?" Ella exclaimed in surprise.

"We have two new people here today. Jim is going to work too," Lada answered for him and smiled. "Is everybody buckled up? Okay, let's hit the road." Nobody cared again, so their trick went pretty smooth for now.

After Lada dropped the guys at the factory, she drove to the Mall of America and let Jim out. They found a funny yellow plastic car connected to the shopping cart and, for fifty cents, unplugged it from a chain. Now Jim could be seated in it like a toddler and not get too tired from a long walk to the bank.

At first, Jim felt uneasy, recognizing the mall's surroundings. The last time, he left this building in March under horrific, tragic circumstances after having Mona's diamond appraised. He knew then for sure that the only love story of his life collapsed forever. Being reminded of that moment made him shiver. It was still too painful even now, almost three months later.

But Lada, who rolled him through the mall in this funny little car, chuckling and giggling almost to tears, returned him to a good mood. It was impossible not to laugh with her. She was his champagne, bubbling and sparkling; his sunshine; his fresh air to breathe; his beautiful angel to love. And it was happiness. It was fun.

At the bank, Jim gave his card to the teller and asked to check the balance on his account. They waited a couple of minutes until the computer opened the proper file, and then the officer announced, "You have seven thousand dollars left for now."

"What?" Jim and Lada exclaimed together, thinking that they probably misunderstood something.

"Seven thousand," the officer repeated. "But it will change in a minute. You wrote a check yesterday for this amount, and it was deposited into an ATM this morning, so it's now in process."

Confused, not quite understanding what he was being told, Jim looked at Lada questioningly. "Stop the payment!" she screamed to the officer. "Stop it immediately, please. It's a mistake. He didn't write any checks."

"Yes." Jim nodded. "I don't even have any checks at all, never did."

The teller looked at the computer attentively. "You opened this account on December 22, 2002. You deposited $ 2,000 at 2:34 p.m.

On the same day, during the account opening procedure, we gave you a checkbook, and you left a sample of your signature, which we have in the computer." The officer turned the screen toward them, and Jim and Lada could see his signature in funny big block letters right in the middle of the screen. "Is it yours?"

"Yes." Jim blushed. "I can write letters like that only. I have difficulty holding a pen."

"It's understandable," the officer said politely. "It's okay. Do you still have that checkbook of yours? I would like to see the copies of the checks you wrote over the last six months."

"I didn't write any checks. I never held this checkbook in my hands. Mona Lainer took it right away from you when we were here. She had it all the time, even now."

"She must have written these checks," Lada suggested. "To whom they were payable for?"

"To Mona Lainer," the officer answered. "Okay, let me make a stop payment on the last check, and then we will look at this problem more closely."

While the officer worked for some minutes on his computer, Jim looked at Lada with big eyes. "Wow," she whispered.

"What's happening?" he whispered back, shrugging. "I don't really understand."

"I do." Lada chuckled. "You're naive like a baby, Jim. Why did you allow her to take your checkbook?"

"I don't know. I didn't think I needed it. What for? I don't do any payments and don't write any checks to anybody. Why did I need it in the first place?"

"It goes automatically with the opening of a checking account."

"I didn't know that."

"Okay," the officer announced finally. "The payment on today's check is stopped. What else can I do for you?"

"Would you mind, please, printing out all his statements for this year?" Lada asked.

"Of course I don't." The officer nodded. "Be a few more minutes." He went to the printer, which was located somewhere in the back room, and waited there for a while. Jim heard quiet buzzing and clicking noises, and then the officer appeared with a stack of papers in his hand. "Here," he said. "If you'd like, we could sit together by the table, and I will navigate you through these statements."

Jim and Lada both nodded and followed him to an area of the bank where a small round table and chairs were settled cozily in the middle of the room.

"Okay, let's start from the opening day, December 22, 2002. You deposited $2,000 at 2:34 p.m. Next is a purchase at a jeweler's store in this mall at 4:18 p.m. for the amount $1,998. Two dollars were left in your account."

"Sorry, some questions right away," Lada interrupted. "Where did you get $2,000 to deposit, Jim?"

"I didn't. Mona did. She just got an investment from my sponsor for me. That's why she opened the account on my behalf."

"Who was that sponsor?"

"She refused to tell when I asked."

"Isn't it strange?"

"This question will be answered in the statement for the next month." The bank teller smiled. "Look here—"

"Wait a sec, sorry," Lada interrupted once more. "I'm not finished with December yet. What did you buy in the jeweler's right away, Jim, for almost two thousand? Or was it Mona who did it again?"

Jim blushed and bit his lips. It was the first time that he forced himself to lie to Lada. "I bought Christmas presents for people in our group home."

"For all of them?"

"Yes."

"You mean women, of course. You mean Mona, Ella, Maggie, nurses, cleaning ladies, right?"

Jim nodded and blushed even more, but Lada didn't pay attention to that.

"Well, okay then," she said. "It was very nice of you. It's so typical of you actually. You have such a kind heart. That's what I like in you." She laughed and placed an affectionate kiss on his cheek. The bank officer watched this with huge eyes, which were almost ready to jump out from his eye sockets.

Lada laughed and turned to him. "Sorry for the interruption," she apologized. "Now we can continue with January's statement."

"Okay." He looked at the next page. "January 1, 2003, deposit $500, pension from government. January 1, 2003, deposit $10,000 from charitable organization Voices of the Future. This must be your sponsor."

"Voices of the Future?" Lada exclaimed. "What does that mean? Did you hear ever about this organization, Jim?"

He shook his head no.

"We should look it up on the internet. Okay, thank you, Officer. Continue, please."

"January 2, 2003, withdrawal $3,500 for services of the group home Fir Forest. January 3, 2003, check no. 1 for $7,002 to Mona Lainer. Here is copy of the check with your signature, Mr. Bogat."

"Here it is. We got it," Lada announced happily. "You didn't even have that checkbook, Jim, right? So Mona wrote it herself and forged your signature. She even took the last two dollars that was left from your Christmas presents. Oh my God! How mean this is, isn't it? What greediness!"

"This kind of signature even a first grader could forge," the bank teller noted.

"Yes." Lada nodded, agitated. "Would you please mark in your computer that, from now on, any checks that come for Mr. Bogat's account will be processed in his personal attendance only? Like a warning or something. Do you agree, Jim?"

"Of course, I agree."

"Yes, it's possible to do," the officer confirmed. "We're doing that sometimes for customers whose home situation is not safe and some family members could potentially sneak into their account. I will do that for you, Mr. Bogat. Can we continue now?"

"Yes, please," Jim said.

"Nothing more in January, your account was empty. Now we're going to February. The same story—pension and sponsorship deposits, then a withdrawal for the group home services, and a personal check no. 2 to Mona Lainer for another $7,000."

"So she continued doing that, Jim. She was robbing you every month," Lada uttered sadly and hugged Jim by his shoulders. "Jesus! Poor you!"

He blushed again almost to tears, remembering that February was his happiest month with Mona. Their "love" and sex blossomed, and he was kissing her diamond before going to sleep every night after one more crazy session. He hoped that it would be his love story, but it was just robbery. He passed over that tragic disappointment later in March, when he discovered all of Mona's lies and broke up with her. But in February, he was such a happy idiot, and it was so shameful to realize now.

"March," the bank teller continued, "again, deposits for $500 and $10,000 and then a withdrawal for $3,500, but there is a difference. The usual check for $7,000 wasn't taken right away for some reason. Computer shows a purchase at the electronic store in this mall for $21.87 made at 3.47 p.m. on March 22, 2003. Then the very next day, March 23, 2003, comes check no. 3 for $6,978.13, again with your personal signature, Mr. Bogat. And here we go, your account is empty once more."

"Yeah, " Jim confirmed. "It was during last shopping trip when I bought some CDs and a DataTraveler. For some reason, Mona probably forgot to take this check earlier. So my purchase was successful, and I didn't notice and didn't suspect anything at that moment."

"And then she took everything that was left!" Lada exclaimed indignantly. "Even the last thirteen cents! It's unbelievable!"

Yes, she was extremely angry after the breakup, Jim thought but didn't say anything aloud.

"Okay, April," the officer continued, "same story, same deposits, same withdrawal for services and same check, no. 4 now, for seven thousand leftover. Then May, absolutely the same picture, and check no. 5 was cleared on May 3, 2003."

"So she stole from you thirty-five thousand for now, and we were accidentally in time today to save the last seven thousand," Lada concluded.

"Do you want to start an investigation and press charges?" the bank teller asked.

"Not yet." Jim shook his head. "I am still living there. She is cooking for me. She could poison me any day. Let us think what we could do."

"At least nobody will forge your checks from now on because I posted this warning on your account," the officer confirmed. "But I would suggest an investigation, especially if you think that this person is so dangerous. What else can I do for you, sir?"

"I have an idea," Lada said. "Would you mind, Jim, if we took five thousand cash right now?"

"Why?"

"You will need it. I will explain later."

"Okay, if you say so." Jim shrugged and turned to the officer. "Can you do that, please?"

"Of course, no problem," the officer answered but looked at Lada suspiciously, thinking, *Well, now here is another woman milking this poor handicapped's account*. However, he remained professional and didn't say anything, just went to his counter to do the procedure of withdrawing cash for Jim.

When they left the bank with five thousand in Jim's pocket, he asked Lada, "Do you think I will need this money to pay musicians of the orchestra for their work on rehearsals?"

"No." She laughed. "It is too early to talk about that. Boris is still printing each musician's part, and they have not discussed your performance yet. It's a long ride, Jim. And what is five thousand? It's a drop in the ocean. Even if one musician could accept it as a payment for working three months in a row, which is, by the way, too tiny an amount of money for that amount of work, there are eighty people in the orchestra. You should pay altogether $400,000 just for rehearsals, minimum."

"Oh my God!" Jim exclaimed with despair in his voice. "What should I do? Ask those sponsors again?"

"It's a big question, of course." Lada laughed in spite of the fact that it wasn't really funny. "I don't know who your sponsors are and why they care about you so much. But if they are capable of sending you ten thousand monthly, it doesn't mean that they could afford lump sum payment for almost half a million."

"So is my concert impossible?" Jim inquired in a shaky voice.

"Yes, unless BB will persuade the musicians to do that for free."

"Why would they do that? For charity? Because I am handicapped?"

"No, silly. Because you are a genius, and they, as professionals, would be proud of their task to let society know of your music. This is actually why my BB is doing this for you, not because I asked. And that's why I actually asked him, not because we're friends."

"Well . . ." Jim took a deep breath. "Your appreciation of my music makes me happy. Could I hug you as a thank-you?"

"Yes, not just hug but also a kiss." Lada giggled, squatting in front of him, hugging him and placing a kiss on his cheek the second time in the last twenty minutes.

"But then . . . why did we take this five thousand for?" Jim wanted to know.

"You'll see. I have a surprise for you."

"Okay. I want to do some little surprise for you as well. If we're in this mall anyway now, let's go to the jeweler's. I will show you something that you would probably be curious to see."

"Interesting," Lada agreed. "Let's do that. I was actually never in my life in a jewelry store before. I guess it would be fun."

CHAPTER 45

The jeweler's shop assistant recognized Jim right away not just because his previous visits here were quite remarkable but also because his appearance was very unusual and memorable too. "I am happy to see you back, sir." He smiled at him meaningfully, at the same time excitedly observing Lada from head to toe, "And you, Miss, nice to meet you finally."

Lada obviously didn't get the hint that Jim previously was buying a present for his girlfriend here. She said, "We're not buying anything now, sir. Jim just wanted to show me around because your store is so beautiful."

"Thank you. Thank you." The assistant nodded. "Of course, you're free to look around as much as you want. We're the best store in this mall."

"Wow!" Lada looked at everything, a bit astonished. "What did you say is interesting here, Jim?"

"I just wanted to show you the diamond necklaces that Mona has," he said as he pulled Lada to one of the counters. "I saw the one that was broken, and also, she showed me a couple of the others when we were friendly at the beginning."

"Wow!" Lada exclaimed once more. "They are unbelievably beautiful, like for a queen or a princess from a fairy tale, but . . . in real life, what are they good for? Even if I have them, I couldn't wear them at university, at work, at home, at walks and bike rides in a park, even visiting with friends or neighbors. You know, my friend Heyriah, she is the wife of a millionaire, but she doesn't have anything like that. She has just some gold—rings in her ears, chains on her neck, simple ring bracelets on her hands. For her culture, it's okay, though for me even that is too much. But these diamonds . . . what do you think, Jim?"

"I think Mona used them as investments because she can't have her stolen dollars in banks, and to keep them somewhere at home will not be safe. They can be burned in case of fire or just depreciate in value. Diamonds never will."

"So they are good for thieves?" Lada concluded. "Sounds reasonable. However, it's sad that such a beauty is serving dirty purposes. And what it is here that you bought for Christmas for your roommates?"

"Just some tiny charms." Jim was cunning enough to avoid a straight answer and pulled Lada to another counter where the rings were on display. "Look at these. Aren't they amazing?"

"Oh, engagement rings." She nodded. "Yes, Rita has one, though BB bought it for her much later. You know, they were married in the US Embassy in Tokyo, actually without any engagement and still okay, almost twenty-five years together. So no superstition."

"Do you want to try one just for fun?" Jim suggested.

"Yeah, why not? If I would be married ever, I would like to have one. But alas . . . you know, I never will. But to try for fun doesn't hurt, right, Jim?"

"Of course." He smiled. "Just for fun, nothing else."

The shop assistant grasped this game right away and winked at him, pulling from under a glass a big velvet plate full of rings. "Which one is calling for you, Miss?" He chuckled.

Lada bowed and looked attentively at the display. "My God, they all are gorgeous." She laughed. "My head would be spinning if I seriously should choose. I love stars more than anything else, you know, Jim. This one looks like a star. Can I put this on, sir?"

"Of course, Miss, of course." The assistant pulled out a ring with a small star on top. "It's absolutely charming, but alas, the size is a little big for you. Let me look for another one for you. I'm sure we have smaller sizes in stock. We definitely do."

"No, it's okay, don't worry," Lada assured him and shook her head. "We aren't buying anyway. Let me just try and see how this star looks on my hand." She pulled this quite big ring on and squeezed all her fingers together so as not to let it fall off, and then she stretched her arm and looked at the star, estimating it. "Wow, this is beautiful and not too much, unlike those necklaces. It's just beautiful, exactly as needed to confirm . . . what? . . . love? . . . devotion? . . . I don't know. It's just great. Thank you, sir." She took ring off and handed it back to the assistant.

"Thank you, Jim." She turned to him and smiled timidly and a bit confusingly. "It really was fun. Now I think we should go. We have a lot of work to do—"

"And a lot of things to talk about," Jim finished her sentence while the shop assistant winked at him again.

They left the store and sat in the armchairs in the middle of the corridor beside huge tropical bushes. Lada looked at her watch. "Twelve thirty . . . we still have a lot of time until two o'clock, when we should pick up our guys from the factory. Let's talk about this five thousand of yours."

"Okay." Jim nodded. "I am listening."

"Yesterday night, I didn't come to see you because I was visiting with Heyriah as I told you. That's true, but the reason for my visit wasn't just to say bye before their departure to Saudi Arabia for some months. I told her your story. I told her about us—"

"What do you mean *about us*?" Jim interrupted her, feeling tense right away.

"I mean about our friendship, about our mutual efforts to give a live performance of your symphony. I told her that you're stuck a bit now with your work because you need an inspiration. You need to see the ocean, which you did for many years, but now it seems impossible. So . . ."

"Oh no, you did ask for money!" Jim exclaimed in horror, feeling that he would burn from shame. "Did you?"

"You silly." Lada laughed. "Am I that predictable? No way, Mister. She suggested a much better thing. Look at this." She pulled out a key from her pocket and extended her hand toward Jim. "It's a key from their house in Hawaii. They are not using it this summer, and she suggested that we go and stay there for two weeks absolutely free. They have a couple of live-in caretakers there. She called them and said that we're coming. So they expect us. You wanted to see the ocean? There is one, Pacific instead of Atlantic this time for a change. How about that?"

"Oh . . . oh." Jim was absolutely dumbfounded. "We . . . you mean, we, together . . . going to Hawaii? I can't . . . get it . . . really."

"I know you can't digest it right away. But it's true. I will put your five thousand on my Mastercard, and tonight I will buy airplane tickets for us. The rest of the money will go for food and renting a car. Isn't it amazing? Aren't you happy, Jim? I myself am so happy that I'm ready to jump."

"Yes, yes," he whispered and covered his face with both hands. "I can't believe it. It's just . . . so much."

"My poor sweetheart." Lada sat beside him at the edge of his armchair and hugged him, noticing that he was shaking. "Baby, please don't cry. It's good, isn't it? You are happy, aren't you?"

"Yes," he murmured, sniffling his tears away. "Yes, I am happy. I just can't believe that you are doing this. Who are you really, Lada? A goddess? An angel? How come you're doing that all for me?"

She giggled. "I am a regular girl, you Mr. Silly. I'm a student, a bus driver, a daughter, a sister, a sister-in-law, an aunt, a friend, a fan of your music, nothing else. It is as simple as that."

"Will your family allow you to go to Hawaii with me?"

"Jeez, I am almost twenty-three years old. My birthday is next month. What are you talking about?"

"Will you ask Mona's permission to leave your work for two weeks?"

"Yes, I will, of course. I will lie about something, that somebody is sick, and I need a leave for medical care or something. Don't worry about that."

Jim squeezed his face to her shoulder and took several deep breaths to calm himself down.

"Okay," Lada said, getting businesslike and serious again. "Now we need to go to my bank and put your money there on my account so I could pay my Mastercard bill later."

"I just have one question." Jim stopped her. "When we came here this morning, you already had Heyriah's key with you, right? But how did you know that I have money for the trip on my account and we could go?"

"I didn't."

"So what if we weren't so lucky and Mona got her check before us and there would be no money left as usual? What could we do in this case, even with that free accommodation?"

"In this case, Heyriah would lend us some money."

"How could we pay her back?"

"After your symphony is a success, you will have enough money for everything, Jim, even to pay her if it would be needed. Luckily, it isn't as we now know."

"Do you really think my symphony will be a success?"

"No question in my mind, silly. Never even think any doubts. Okay, now we need to go to a store and buy me a second bathing suit, and we'll need some beautiful beach towels to lie down at night and look at the stars. Remember, I told you about my dream before. We are together by the ocean, looking at the stars. We're combining our two favorites, your ocean and my universe. Now I have a chance it will come true. So are you ready to go?"

"You know what?" Jim pulled out the envelope with the five thousand from his pocket. "I am really a bit tired. Would you mind taking it and going alone for all this shopping and so on? I would prefer to sit here and relax and wait for you."

"Okay." Lada took the envelope and kissed his forehead. "I'll be back soon. You may even have a snooze. See you in an hour." And she walked away with her light and swift gait.

Jim closed his eyes for no more than five minutes, and then he slid from his armchair and went back to the jeweler's. "Hey," he said to the shining assistant, "could you now, please, get me this star ring in a smaller size that you said you have in stock?"

CHAPTER 46

When Lada returned from shopping, Jim was snoozing in the same armchair where she left him. He looked very happy, content, and relaxed.

"Hey, sleepyhead." She pushed his shoulder tenderly. "It's not your bed. Wake-up time. We need to go really fast now to get the guys from work. Sorry, I even have no time to show you my new bathing suit and our towels."

"It's okay, I will see them soon in use anyway." Jim laughed. "It would be much more interesting."

"You're naughty." She giggled and lightly slapped him on his hand. "Come on, let's go." She seated Jim again into the yellow plastic children's car and put the bags with her purchases into the shopping cart connected to it. Then she almost ran, pushing it in front of her, to the exit of the mall where their bus was parked.

"When are we leaving for Hawaii?" Jim asked, already in the bus.

"As soon as possible. It depends on airplane tickets that are available. I will look at something for tomorrow, latest after tomorrow. We'll see."

"So soon?"

"Why wait, Jim? We're going for two weeks, and the scores of the symphony should be finished there. When we're back, BB would start rehearsals. He has these two weeks to get everything ready from his side—talk to musicians, reorganize schedules, print out all single instrument lines, check with the vocal department for singers, you know . . . all these things."

"Wow, you sound like a real businesswoman," Jim noted excitedly. "You're so young but already know everything."

"I have two best teachers—you and BB." Lada laughed. "And actually, I am not so young. In my age, many famous people already had their careers. I have none of my own. I am doing yours, kind of parasitic on your talent, you know, like this tiny fish on a big shark."

"Jeez." Jim wrinkled his nose. "Don't say that about yourself. It's pretty rude. You're my guardian angel, not a parasite."

"I know, just teasing." She chuckled. "Okay, how do you think we should come to the group home? Together on the bus, or you would like to exit earlier and go home on your feet, pretending that you're coming from a walk?"

"I'm actually pretty tired to walk from the driveway. Anyway, Mona will find out that I was in the bank when her check is returned as insufficient."

"Okay then, I will drive you right to the porch with the guys together."

When Jim's roommates loaded on the bus, he didn't talk with Lada anymore. She just asked the guys politely how their day was, but nobody answered except Ella, who barked, "Disgusting!"

"Oh, I'm sorry to hear that." Lada sighed. After that, they drove in silence.

Mona was waiting for them on the porch, which was quite unusual. Normally, she was fussing around the kitchen, preparing dinner and expecting the guys to come in by themselves or be led by the bus driver. Looking at her red and angry face, Jim got it right away—she knew all about his banking business.

Mona waved the guys in but stopped in front of Jim and Lada who followed him a bit behind.

"Who gave you the right, Mr. Bogat, to steal all my money from my account?" she almost screamed. "I got a phone call from the bank, saying that you stopped payment on my check. Why did you do that? What is happening with you? A sudden attack of your mental illness? You never in your life understood banking and never cared about it. You're an idiot who is not capable to do this. And now suddenly, you go to the bank and withdraw all my money! What the hell!"

"It's actually my money and my account," Jim answered surprisingly calm. "You got my checkbook and forged my signature on checks already for five months. Those are funds that my sponsor is sending to me."

"Your sponsor is my friend and is sending these funds to *me!*" Now Mona really screamed. "If not for me, you won't get a penny. I already talk to that sponsor, and your payments will be stopped too. You will learn how to live on your five hundred bucks' pension."

Maybe she was bluffing but maybe not. Jim felt confused and even a bit guilty. He didn't know what to say and looked at Lada for support.

"Mrs. Lainer," Lada said, "I think you should give Jim an opportunity to talk to this sponsor and find out why he is sponsoring him and whose friend he is."

"There you go!" Mona looked at her with piercing narrowed eyes full of hate. "Now I can see from where this wind blows! What the hell? This isn't your business, Miss Bus Driver. You should know your place as an immigrant in our society—cheap, dirty jobs. That's it! You have no right to put your nose into the health-care management business. You have extremely bad influence on my patients. That's why I don't need your services anymore. You're fired! Give me the keys for my bus!"

Lada smirked. "Okay!" And she threw the keys, which Mona caught.

"Get off my property!" she screamed even louder than before and pushed Jim toward the door. "Get in, Mr. Bogat! Immediately!"

"You have no right to scream at her or at me," Jim said confidently. "And Miss Meleshko is right, I insist on talking to my sponsor."

"You have no sponsor anymore. There is nothing to talk about. You're finished, Mr. Bogat. This month, your rent is paid. But starting from next month, you will be homeless. Then you'll probably learn how to appreciate it when someone is taking care of you as I did."

Jim turned to look at Lada, not knowing what to do about this situation. He was ready to fight, to protect her as much as he could, but she just nodded to him and made a gesture with her hand for him to follow Mona.

Everybody inside was sitting at the dinner table and eating, and Jim suddenly felt that he was very hungry. However, he didn't want to stay here and look at Mona anymore. He just grabbed some food and went to his room. But the story was not finished yet. She followed him, and while he tried to slam the door in her face and lock it, she still pushed it and entered. "Get out of my room!" he exclaimed, mocking her when she yelled at Lada. "Leave me alone finally!"

"I will go, don't worry," Mona answered, strangely calm. "I just need to clarify something with you, Jim. Tell me, why did you need the money so suddenly? What happened? Did she ask you for money? Did you sleep with her?"

"Hell no! She doesn't relate to this at all. Her role was only to drive me to the bank because I can't do that by myself as you perfectly know. I told you, I have this writer's block. I can't finish my symphony. I was thinking why, and I remembered that every year in June, I traveled to the ocean, and it was my inspiration. So I decided that I need to go now to get this inspiration again. I need money for my airplane ticket, for the hotel, and also for the nurse, Edward, whom my grandma Cathy hired the last three years to go with me."

"Understandable." Mona nodded. "I agree with that. To finish the symphony is a task of extreme importance. I already arranged a performer for you. My daughter, Sharon, will help you do that. You just need to give her the whole score when it's finished. But why didn't you ask me for money? I would pay for this trip. Why all these lies? 'I go for a walk.'" Now she mocked his voice. "'I will be back for dinner'?"

"I was ashamed to ask. You're doing so much for me. How could I ask for more? I decided to check my bank account, just in case. Remember, in March, I bought some CDs. There was money at that time. So I decided to check now. It was my idea. That girl is not related to this in any way. She drove me to the bank only. That's it." Jim was surprised himself of how smooth and calm he learned to lie, how nice his story flowed.

"When you are going? And for how long?" Mona wanted to know.

"After tomorrow, for two weeks. Nurse Edward will pick me up and drive me to the airport. He will leave his car there to drive me home when we return."

"Okay, sounds reasonable. I hope I'll have a chance to see this nurse, Edward, and make sure that he is driving you, not that stupid thief, immigrant girl."

"No." Jim laughed. "Don't be so jealous. After I confronted her about the disappearance of my score, as you taught me, she returned it, but we are not friends anymore—at all."

"Yeah, she must really be offended by your distrust," Mona concluded, smiling happily. Then she stood up from the armchair. "Well, Jim, I forgive you for stealing my money because I love you as you know. And I agree with your reasoning."

As soon as she left, he called Lada. She answered on the very first ring. "Where are you?" he whispered, worrying how she could get home without the bus.

"Here in the garden, sitting on the bench. BB is at work, so I called Rita. She'll come and pick me up. How is our monster? Not killed you yet?" She giggled.

"You hear my voice. It means I'm still kicking. You sound not too sad about losing your job," Jim noticed. "Don't you regret it?"

"Of course not. It makes everything easier. Now I don't need to look for an explanation why I will miss work for two weeks and create some stupid lies. I am free. By the way, I looked for tickets on my phone. We could catch a plane about noon after tomorrow. When I come home, I will book it and send you the itinerary. How are you coping?"

"Actually, pretty good. I concocted such a story you wouldn't believe. I surprised myself how perfectly I learn to lie now. And as you told me, half true, half lie with a lot of small details make it believable. Thank you so much for these lessons."

"You're welcome. I know, teaching you to lie is not the best that I have done for you. But, Jim, we should survive somehow, shouldn't we?"

"I agree. In this situation, we have no choice. You don't even know half the deeds of this monster."

"You told me a lot."

"Not everything, but I don't want to talk about it now. Let's just be cautious. So when can I see you?"

"When I come in my car to pick you up for the ride to the airport, we'll talk about the exact time when I've got the tickets."

"You know, there is a problem. Mona said that she wants to see Nurse Edward, who will pick me up and travel with me. What should we do?"

"Okay." Lada laughed mischievously. "Then BB will pick you up."

"You're a genius." Jim smiled.

"No, my sweet darling, you are," she answered, still laughing.

CHAPTER 47

T he next day, Mona called her daughter, Sharon. "Sweetie," she said, "I need one more favor from you. I fired the bus driver, and I need you to post an ad about hiring at the university on the noticeboard. But underline that this is a job for a man, not a woman. A lot of heavy duty included, but salary is very impressive. I want a young man—strong, tall, athletic, and virile."

"Oh my God! Again?" Sharon whined. "I hate it when you ask me to do these things. Always something wrong with your bus drivers, and it feels like I am at fault."

"No, no, darling, I never said that. It's my fault that I am so nice to them all, and they take advantage of my kindness. I hired this stupid girl because she mentioned during the interview that her brother is conducting an orchestra. I planned to give your symphony to him and have him perform it to start your success as a composer. But now as you already gave the first part of that symphony to your composing teacher, I don't need her anymore. Your teacher will do all that. That girl was stealing my money, and I can't tolerate that. So she is gone. Did your teacher already talk to the conductor?"

"Not yet. The last week, he was on sick leave. He just returned to work today. I'll push him to do that tomorrow."

"Not push, baby. Give him a nice, expensive present. Remember how well our presents worked with your piano teacher, Mrs. Thompson? You graduated successfully because of those presents. Now next step of your success—become a millionaire composer. I know that, in two weeks, my midget will finish the symphony, and he will give the scores to you."

"How could you persuade him to give it to me?" Sharon wanted to know.

"Easy. I know how to take from people what I want. So feel free to tell your teacher that you're finishing the last part of your symphony and will bring it to him in two weeks. And don't be cheap on the present. It will be worth it."

"I know, Mom. Don't be annoying. I'll call you tomorrow and tell you how this is going. And I'll post your ad, don't worry. I am just irritated because it's taking so much time."

During the same day, Jim packed his backpack and a small carry-on luggage for his trip and then talked to Lada on the phone for a long time. They decided that she and Rita would come to the airport in her car and park it there for two weeks. It would be used when Jim and Lada came back from Hawaii because there was no guarantee that Rita or Boris would be free to pick them up on the day of their return.

Tomorrow morning, Boris would drive to the group home in his car and pick up Jim, pretending to be Nurse Edward, and deliver him to the airport, where Lada and Rita would be waiting for them. Boris laughed a lot when his little sister expounded to him her plan, in which he was supposed to play the role of Nurse Edward. "Jeez! You're so cunning and inventive, kiddo!" he exclaimed. "Where is it coming from? I don't understand."

"Come on." Rita winked at him. "It's definitely running in the family. Don't you remember what you did to escape from Ukraine? Who was cunning then?"

"I did it for you, for our love. People do crazy things for love sometimes." He giggled.

Rita waited until Lada left the room and whispered to him, "Well, what do you think she is doing all these for?"

"I was told there is only friendship involved," Boris said, "and admiration for his talent probably."

Rita smiled meaningfully. "*Bebe*, you are not a child. Didn't you notice how he is looking at her? I'm sure he is madly in love, and she maybe knows that. She is kind of . . . not indifferent toward him . . .

friendship or not. I just feel pity for him. Knowing her conditions, we could expect a very strong rejection, and this will break his heart enormously."

"Yeah." Boris sighed. "I feel pity too. He is a nice fellow and obviously a supergenius. This level of talent comes once in hundreds of years. I'll probably talk to him, try to prevent a broken heart."

On the day of their departure to Hawaii, Boris—in his silver Mercedes—approached the group home porch while Jim was already outside with his luggage, waiting impatiently. He was almost shaking from anticipation of this adventure and of a chance to be with Lada alone, to see new places, to find his inspiration for music again, and to return to the ocean finally.

Mona wanted to check on Nurse Edward but was a bit late. When she appeared from the door, Jim was already in the car, and the ignition was on. She came to the car's open window, exclaiming in her nicest, sweet voice, "Have a good trip, Jim! Enjoy the ocean and come back as soon as possible. We'll miss you over here." While saying that, she was attentively estimating Boris at the driver seat. "Hi, Edward. I heard a lot about you. Please take a good care of our beloved boy."

"I will. I promise, Mrs. Lainer," Boris answered, laughing. "I heard about you a lot as well. Bye." And they drove off, leaving Mona suspiciously looking at the car as it moved away. In her opinion, it was too expensive a car for a nurse.

Lada and Rita arrived at the airport earlier than Boris and Jim. Driving time from the city was much shorter than from the group home, located far away in the forest. While they were waiting in the car at the parking lot, Rita said, "You know, Ladochka, I wasn't sure whether to tell you now or later, when you return home. I actually found something very interesting. More properly, the word should be *someone*."

"Who? A singer?" Lada exclaimed, knowing that Rita planned to visit the vocal department of the university some days ago to talk to the dean on Boris's behalf.

"Not yet exactly, but, I saw an ad on their board that Sandra Soley will teach a vocal course for three months this summer, starting July 1. You told me that you did look for her, didn't you?"

"Wow!" Lada shrieked. "How could it be? Coincidence? Unbelievable!"

"I don't think it's exactly a coincidence." Rita smiled. "It's more like the old Russian proverb 'An animal always runs toward a hunter' or 'Who is looking will find eventually.' You did work so hard on it, so your efforts have borne fruit true finally. But don't be in a hurry to tell Jim, until you talk to Sandra first. I asked the vocal department dean, and he said that he knows Sandra pretty well, and she is not really a nice person. She is quite haughty, arrogant, often becomes irritated and angry. It's not too easy to deal with her."

"I can imagine. If you have $350 million on your bank account, it could change who you are." Lada laughed. "But not everyone. I am sure that money would never change me from who I am now."

"Not just money," Rita suggested. "Could you imagine seeing your husband killed right in front of you? She probably survived a lot too. She lost him, and she practically lost her career at the same time. We can't judge what we don't know. But I think it's still worth it to talk to her. There was a sign-in list on the board for students who want to take her class. It says she would accept twenty people. Fifteen are already signed, so I signed you as number sixteen just to make it easier for you to get an appointment."

"Wow, Ritochka, love you!" Lada exclaimed, hugged her sister-in-law, and kissed her cheek. "So if she agreed to sing in Jim's symphony, I could tell him. If she refuses, I will not because it would be another hurt for him."

"Sure. And one more thing, for an appointment with Sandra we should prepare a very impressive folder about Jim. It will include his résumé, photo, CDs of the symphony, and all printed-out notes of his best works, starting from the earliest compositions—until now. While you're in Hawaii, I will go through all his pages that you left in your room and choose what is better to show Sandra, and you can make his résumé. While he is busy with the scores of the last part of his symphony, you should ask him sometimes when he was in college, when he started university, when he graduated, and so on, just dates like that. Knowing the dates, you could easily write his résumé. I'm sure that he is very capable to do that himself, but we don't need to take his attention from his job. We're kind of short on time here, so it's better if you help and do that for him."

"Will do, of course. God, I'm so happy." Lada giggled and clapped her hands. "So happy! It looks like we're on the right track finally. But what's going on? Where are BB and Jim anyway? We're already waiting for them for so long. Let's go look for them, or we could miss our flight." And she exited the car.

On the way to the airport, Boris and Jim were talking about their mutual business—the performance of Jim's symphony. But when they stopped at the parking lot, Boris said, "You know, Jim, you're going on this trip with our kiddo. We were thinking about that a lot because we did notice that you probably have feelings for her."

Jim blushed and bit his lip but didn't say anything.

"I'm not asking if it's true," Boris continued. "I just want to warn you that she is a very unusual girl. She survived what probably one girl out from a hundred million girls could survive. And she is damaged for life. It's a huge tragedy for our family because, otherwise, she is a very nice kid. You know she was assaulted there in Kiev one evening, when she was coming home from her girlfriend's house, from the birthday party of that girl."

"I know," Jim said quietly. "Lada told me about the assault."

"She didn't tell you half of it, I'm sure, because she herself doesn't know the whole story. Most of the time, she was unconscious. Also, in the former Soviet Union, doctors never told patients what was really going on with them. But they tell family, our mom, and that's how we all know now, except for Lada."

"Maybe I shouldn't know as well," Jim objected. "I'm not the family."

"But she is considering you her closest friend in the world. You're the man who will live with her together in somebody's house in Hawaii and the man who is obviously in love with her. We decided that you should know who you're dealing with because she is extremely fragile."

"I kind of guessed from what she told me that she was raped," Jim pronounced even more quietly.

"Worse than that."

"What could be worse?"

"Not just raped but gang-raped. Twelve . . . I can't say men . . . they were wild, disgusting animals. She was only seventeen years old." Boris's voice cracked a bit, like he was suppressing angry tears. "Luckily for her, they hit her on the head, and she lost consciousness. She didn't see and didn't feel anything. Later in the hospital, she didn't even know what happened to her. She thought a car hit her."

"Lada told me that she had three surgeries. She knows something." Jim pressed his palms to his cheeks, feeling that horror beginning to accumulate in his gut. "I don't know how could I help here. What could I do?"

"Just listen. The Soviet gangs had their own tradition—when they are done with a girl, they shove a glass bottle into her and break it." He squeezed his fists with hatred. "It took the doctors eighteen hours of surgery to remove all pieces of glass and to sew back what was damaged and then another surgery in a month to fix some scars that did not heal properly the first time.

"Plus, those animals infected her with an STD. Luckily, it wasn't AIDS but something curable. However, it took two more weeks in hospital on IV with very strong antibiotics. And in two months, when everything was finally healed and looked good, it was discovered that she was pregnant. Nobody wanted a rape baby from a drugged and drunk gangster, so they did an abortion. Lada doesn't know about that. She was told that it was another reconstruction surgery. And there were some complications after the procedure, so the doctor told her that she wouldn't have any sexual feelings. She couldn't have a relationship with a man and wouldn't ever have children."

"I know, she told me about children," Jim noted in a shaky voice. He sighed deeply to calm himself down after what he had heard. "Did the police ever catch those criminals?"

"Yes, quite soon, actually, just some days later. They are in prison, probably even now, but how could it help us? An amazing teen girl was robbed of her ability to have the normal life of a woman, to become a wife, a mother, even grandmother one day later in her life. Our mom was robbed of a chance to have more grandchildren. Rita and I were robbed of a chance to have nieces and nephews. Together, we all lost so much happiness that could be in our family. Nothing can compensate for that. Even if those monsters were executed, it won't help at all.

"Luckily, everything was healed during the last six years. Now Lada is physically a perfectly healthy girl," Boris continued. "With the help of hypnosis, she mostly forgot about what happened and about the doctors' warnings. But what is left, probably forever, is the fear of men and a total absence of sexual feelings. She is pretty adamant about that."

"Why should I know about that?" Jim whispered with shaky lips.

"Because it's visible that you love her. I mean . . . you're a man. If you make a move, she will reject it very harshly, and we don't want your feelings to be hurt. You and Lada both could be hurt because she doesn't want to lose you as well, but she will if she'll realize that you're a man. You're her only friend, not counting that Muslim woman with a bunch of kids. Lada is very attracted to her family too and pretty often babysits them. I guess that, psychologically, it compensates somehow—to not have her own kids but to be with kids a lot. Subconsciously, she probably has a craving for children. So if you really love her and don't want to lose her, please don't touch her even with one finger."

"She told me that she is not considering me a man at all," Jim uttered with pain. "I agreed for a friendship because I treasure her a lot. I don't want to lose her, of course. But about touching . . . you noticed that we're holding hands while walking. Lada is helping me. Sometimes she helps me climb on the chair or on the couch, and to do so, she kind of hugs me, and I hug her neck to hold on while being lifted. There are some touches involved and not with one finger but with both hands."

"But those are caring and friendly touches of help as I understand," Boris concluded. "Okay, then let me paraphrase the point. Could you promise me not to touch her with, let's say, sexual intentions? It is very serious, Jim. Everything here is at stake—your relationship with her, our relationship with you, even the performance of your symphony. Do you realize that?"

"I do," Jim whispered. He took a deep breath and closed his eyes. "Okay, I promise not to touch her with sexual intention, not even with one finger. That's what you want to hear?"

"Yes. Thank you, Jim." Boris nodded. "Let's shake hands on that. We made our contract. I trust you."

At that moment, Lada banged at the passenger side car window. "Hey, guys, what are you doing here for so long?" she yelled. "We're waiting and waiting, and you're stuck here. We could be late for our flight! What the hell are you guys talking about?"

"Just regular guys' talk." Boris laughed. "You know, beer, cars, football, women."

"As far as I know, none of you is interested in none of those things," Lada retorted.

"Come on, kiddo, I love beer. And I have four women in my life— Rita, Becky, Mom, and you."

"Me?" She was surprised. "I hope you didn't talk about me. Did he, Jim?" Usually, Lada could read Jim's facial expression perfectly; and looking now how pale and obviously nervous he was, she grasped immediately that something was wrong. "What did he tell you, Jim?"

"Not a word," Jim answered quietly, bowing his head and not looking her in the eyes. "We just had some contract to discuss and some decisions to make. And we did it successfully."

"Thank you, Jim," Boris said and put his hand on Jim's shoulder. "I knew you were a good sport."

CHAPTER 48

When Jim and Lada arrived at the house in Hawaii, a caretaker couple was in shock to meet them. Heyriah told them that her girlfriend will come with a boyfriend, so they expected a young, strong, and beautiful oriental couple but found on their porch a blond European, Lada, with a very strange little "creature" holding her hand.

The caretakers expected that their guests would go surfing, boating, swimming, fishing, dancing in the bars, and enjoying different kinds of activities in Hawaii, which young people usually do. Instead of that, Lada spent a couple of hours with them arranging the furniture and other household settings for the needs of a midget. There were many step stools placed everywhere; luckily, they had a lot of them, intended for a bunch of Heyriah's little kids. The house was big and beautiful with six bedrooms and had an adjoined patio overlooking the ocean and also a private beach where guests could be alone and enjoy their privacy. It was surrounded by a high fence with a line of blossoming oleander bushes along it.

While Lada was organizing for his comfort in their vacation home, she left Jim to sit on the beach, on her new beach towel, and get adjusted to the place. He was never in a tropical climate before, so all the surroundings were new and unusual for him, especially the plants and flowers, as well as the birds and the cute little green lizards, geckos, running around. And the ocean itself, of course, was overwhelming. Jim was breathing deeply, drinking with his lungs the amazing smell of salt water and seaweeds, listening to the murmur of waves caressing the white sand and rolling back to the endless vastness of the water. He was so happy, felt like in seventh heaven, and realized pretty soon he was ready to write music again. He climbed on the patio, spread his paper sheets on the floor, took his tiny pencil, and began to work.

Their schedule slowly formed out on its own. Jim was writing his scores usually in the middle of the day, and Lada was sitting beside him with a notebook and made her notes for his résumé, which she was working on, and also researching his sponsor—a charity called the Voices of the Future. Dinner was served by the caretakers on the patio at about six o'clock, and then the servants left for the night, and Jim and Lada stayed later by themselves.

At night, they were lying down on the beach, watched the stars, and listened to the ocean. Lada's dream really came true, and she felt unbelievably happy about that. Sometimes they talked in a whisper so as not to destroy the quietness of the sleeping nature and talked almost till morning. Then they went home and slept till noon, woken up by the caretakers, who served their breakfast.

Jim and Lada didn't leave the property even for an hour during the first week. They worked hard, and this intensive work was rewarded—the symphony was accomplished successfully and ready to be performed. The goal of this trip was reached, and now finally came time to rest and relax.

Lada's work was done as well. The full and impressive résumé was written. About Jim's sponsor, she discovered that it was a nonprofit organization that opened the music schools in almost every inner city in America for children from low-income families. Absolutely free, those kids could learn the basics of music theory, play different kinds of musical instruments, dance, and sing in choirs. If someone was blessed with a beautiful natural voice, he or she could have vocal classes on top of it all, free as well.

The internet didn't show the name of the founders of this charity, but now it was clear to Lada and Jim that Mona was bluffing. The people who did these things for poor children from the kindness of their hearts couldn't be friends of Mona Lainer ever. They probably found out about Jim through some musical area and decided to sponsor him. So it was a lie that Mona called them and canceled Jim's sponsorship. It gave some hope that maybe the money for him would keep coming, and he would be able to rent an apartment, to move from the group home, and to hire a caregiver.

Lada put the notes of her research and Jim's résumé in the folder and packed it together with the symphony. Then she rented a car, and they started driving for excursions around the big island of Hawaii. They went to the volcano and visited the city of Kailua, where Lada bought a bunch of souvenirs for her family and leis of Hawaiian flowers for herself and Jim. They took lots of pictures, laughed unstoppably, and had a great time.

One night while they were looking at the stars, Lada sat up on her towel and said, "Jim, I want to talk to you about something . . . something very important to me."

"Okay," he agreed. "I am listening."

"Do you remember that weekend when you visited my family?"

"Of course."

"Do you remember, when I drove you home and we were sitting in the car and talking, you told me that you're so thankful that I gave you this experience?"

"Y-y-yes," he pronounced slowly, not really understanding where this conversation was going.

"And then you took my hand and started kissing it . . . and it turned kind of crazy. You were kissing my fingers . . . I don't know . . . like sucking them, and I couldn't stop you."

"I am sorry," he whispered, blushing, and was glad that she couldn't see it in the twilight. "I'm so sorry. I just lost control for a minute. I promised you that it will never happen again. Please don't be angry at me."

"I'm not angry." She giggled, a bit confused. "Quite the opposite. I had a very strange feeling then, which I did not completely understand. I need to check it to realize what it was. Could you do that again, please?" She extended her arm, almost touching his lips with her fingers.

Jim rose and sat on his towel too. He didn't know what to do. It was like another blow to his gut. "Listen, Lada, sweetheart," he said finally, taking a deep breath. "I am sorry. But I can't do that now."

"Are you not feeling well? Then when? Tomorrow?"

"No. By the word *now*, I don't mean a time. I mean . . . I can't touch you anymore."

"Why?"

"I have no right. I promised."

"You promised what? To whom? I don't understand what you're talking about."

"I gave my word to your brother that I won't touch you for . . . I don't know for how long. I didn't get what he meant . . . during this trip . . . or forever."

"Why? It's stupid. I don't understand how BB is related to this."

"He loves you, cares about you, and worries about you. He wants to protect you. That's all."

"He told you that? Oh, Jeez! It's not his business. I'm not a baby! I really will give him a hell about that! Did he force you to give him a word, knowing that you're such an honest person who will keep the word? It was so mean of him. Idiot! He is a sick idiot!" Her lips trembled. Then Lada turned away from Jim; fell on her towel, covering her face with both hands; and began to cry. She was all shaking and sobbed with such despair, so pitifully, that Jim couldn't listen to that without pain in his heart. He realized how deeply he hurt her and felt absolutely brokenhearted himself.

He moved closer to her and lay on his stomach beside her, hugging her neck, caressing her hair, and kissing her shoulder and her ear, trying to comfort her, to soothe and to calm her down.

"You . . . don't . . . understand me . . . Jim," she stuttered trough her sobs. "I was . . . thinking . . . that you are . . . the one . . . person in the . . . world who . . . understands me, but . . . you don't."

"I'm sorry."

"Stop apologizing all the time." She sniffled, irritated. "It's not your fault. You just don't know what I survived and what's going on with me now. I was told hundred times by doctors, by psychologists and other professionals that I won't have any sexual feelings. It was true. I really didn't. But then when you kissed my fingers with such a passion, I felt something . . . something strange. It's important to me to get it. It's very important to understand myself. I should know. I need to know. It's my life. It's my future. It means everything to me. What does this stupid BB know about that? And why are you touching me right now if you are so honest and so adamant to keep your word?"

Jim felt a hint of sarcasm in her voice. "I can explain," he whispered. "I'm just soothing you as your friend, and these touches are friendly, not sexually excited at all."

"So you're allowed to touch me friendly? Did BB give you permission for that?"

"You're sarcastic again, but that's true. We can have friendly touches all the time. It's not a problem."

"Then what's the problem? Oh boy! You both are two sick idiots!" Lada sat on her towel, wiped the tears from her wet face, and suddenly began laughing. She was swinging from side to side and giggled almost to tears again, making Jim confused, not understanding what was going on with her. "Jeez, you men are idiots!" She chuckled, and Jim was really surprised to notice that she used the word *men*. So was he considered a man now? Or did she just misspeak?

"Tell me, what was your agreement with BB?" she asked as she finally stopped laughing, crying, and shaking.

"I promised not to touch you even with one finger with a sexual intent."

She took a couple of deep breaths. "It's okay. Remember, I told you, if somebody ordered me to do something, I became stubborn and do the opposite on purpose."

"But he didn't order anything to you. He ordered me."

"Yes, he knows me. I see now. He is as cunning as I am. He is really my brother, the same family, the same blood. Well, let's turn it this way. You keep your real man's word. You're not touching my hand even with one finger. You're touching it with your lips. And you're kissing my fingers without any sexual intent. It is a scientific research intent—to help me with my psychological and physiological understanding of my inner condition, to help me understand myself, to understand my feelings. So now please kiss my fingers . . . friendly, same as the last time you did." And Lada extended her arm toward his lips again.

"This won't be friendly," Jim objected shyly. "Your fingertips are too sensitive as are my lips. Even if it starts friendly, it will turn sexy soon anyway. I'm not sure I can hold myself in check for a long time. You do not really understand me either. I love you so much, and to tell the truth, I want you so badly that I'm like walking on the edge of a razor here. I can't guarantee what will happen if I kiss your fingers."

"Okay." Lada laughed mischievously as usual. "Let's try to do it friendly anyway. Seriously, I need to analyze this feeling, if I have it again."

"Could you promise to stop me if I lose control?" Jim asked, desperately grabbing at the last straw in an attempt to keep his real man's word.

"Okay," she agreed, smiling happily. "What do you want me to do? Slap your cheek or pull your hair? Or I can do both?"

CHAPTER 49

The kisses with *scientific intent*, as Lada invented, turned out even much crazier and more unpredictable than Jim expected. He obviously lost control in a couple of minutes, but Lada didn't stop him at all. It appeared to him that all doctors' warnings were completely evaporated now, almost six years after those surgeries, and she developed very strong sexual feelings, not knowing anything about it herself. These feelings were hidden somewhere deep inside her and waited, like Sleeping Beauty, for a special Prince Charming to wake them up with a kiss. And there it was—his kiss of her fingers when she drove him home after the nice family weekend. However, she still wasn't sure then. She wanted to test it, and it looked like the test now proved her guesses.

Jim was thinking about that, lying down on the beach in Hawaii, squeezing his stomach into the sand to hide his erection from her, but Lada wouldn't notice it anyway. She was too concentrated on her own feelings. Her thoughts were floating somewhere in the sky, losing the sensation of reality. She forgot who she was, where she was, why, with whom. She just threw her head back, breathing heavily, a little shaky, and bit her lips, moaning sometimes with pleasure.

Jim kissed her fingers in a friendly manner as he tried at the beginning, but then as he brushed them with his lips, sucking, licking, and biting them tenderly, Lada started to react. Jim just pushed away the thinking and continued his kisses from her hand to her arm, moving up along it to her shoulder, neck, and ear and then all the way down the back. To him, it felt much more than *friendly*, but he still tried desperately to keep his word. He even was the one who made an attempt to stop her, whispering affectionately, "Sweetie, please, that's maybe enough for the first time. Let's stop it."

But she shook her head and almost cried, "No, no, no, please, please don't stop . . . ever."

Jim hugged her by the waist, put his head on her chest, and fondly blew some air on her hot face, murmuring, "Shh . . . calm down, baby. That's enough, my love. You're okay. You're really, really good now. You have your feelings. I see that. Do you understand it yourself now?"

Lada stubbornly was shaking her head no, but then slowly, she calmed down and was lying on her towel motionless, quiet, exhausted, and weak. Jim held his breath. He didn't know what to say at the moment, except that he loved her and would love her forever, if she would want that. The discovery that she had her sexual feelings back scared him to death. He realized that being a beautiful young woman in normal health conditions, she easily could turn her interest to another normal young man. Compared with him, anyone could be a successful competition.

Then Jim noticed that she fell asleep. It soothed him. What was the reason to worry about the future? That night, she was with him in his loving arms; she belonged to him, not fully sexually yet but spiritually and emotionally for sure. And it was real happiness. He nestled his head on her shoulder and, finally, slept too.

He was woken up by Lada, brushing his hair with her fingers and kissing his forehead. "Jim, wake up," she whispered into his ear. "You should see this."

He opened his eyes, rubbed them to push away the sleep, and sat on his towel. "Wow" was all he could say, astonished by the beauty opening in front of him. The sun was rising over the ocean, coloring the completely still water surface with silver-pink tinges of light purple, the same as the sky.

"You see," Lada whispered, putting her head on his shoulder, "it is the sunrise over the ocean, the name of the first part of your symphony, also the name of Sandra's song. Remember? They woke up after their first night on the beach and saw the sunrise, it said. And look what's going on with us now? Did you get it? It's fate, Jim."

"I actually never saw it," Jim whispered back. "Even when I traveled to the ocean, I never was on the beach that early in the morning. We usually slept in hotels. And the Atlantic is known not to be that quiet as the Pacific. Mostly, it was quite stormy over there. But it was what I always imagined, how sunrise over the ocean should look like. I saw it in my mind, felt it in my soul, and here it is. I see it the first time in reality. And I see it with you, my love. Oh God! I never was happier in my life."

"Me neither." Lada nodded and tenderly squeezed his hand. "Me too, Jim."

"Okay," he said as a sudden thought came to him. "I know what I should do now."

He dug in the pocket of his jeans that were lying down beside him on the sand and pulled out a little velvet box. "Lada," he said solemnly, "I want to give this to you, but don't be scared, please. It's not an engagement ring. It's just a promise ring. I promise to be your friend for the rest of my life. If you could promise that too, you'll accept it." He opened the box, and she looked in big surprise at the star ring that she chose at the jeweler's and liked so much.

"Oh my God," she whispered in excitement. "Jim, you're crazy but in a beautiful way. You're amazingly crazy, and I love you so, so much. Of course, I accept it, my cute little star, and I swear to God I'll be your friend until my last breath." She laughed, hugged him, and kissed his cheeks while tears were streaming down her face. "Sorry." She sniffed. "I didn't believe ever that people could cry from happiness, but look at me. Here I am now."

"Even if one day you'll love another man and marry him, I'll be the friend of your family forever," Jim added, putting the ring on her finger and kissing her hand.

"What?" Lada exclaimed, giggling. "That was the stupidest thing I've ever heard! I was right when I said that you men are idiots! Don't even think anything like that ever, Mr. Silly." And she slapped him on the cheek but pretty tenderly and more jokingly than angrily. "I love you, and you couldn't even guess how much. Are we clear?"

"Yes." Jim nodded, smiling happily. "I could apologize, but you ordered me to stop doing it. So I'm not sorry now."

"The best apology would be if you do that again—I mean . . . you know . . . our scientific research." She blushed, a bit confused by her own suggestion. "But first, let's watch the sunrise a bit more until it is finished, and the sun will be completely up."

CHAPTER 50

During the last four days of their stay in Hawaii, Lada insisted that *the scientific research* continued more and more. Jim sincerely tried to object, but she was very persistent. "You know that scientists do not come to a conclusion on the basis of only one experiment," she explained to him convincingly. "They are doing hundreds, maybe even thousands of experiments to prove something. I need proof that I am psychologically and mentally healed and that I have these sexual feelings now, which normally any girl of my age would have. Don't you agree, sweetie?"

Jim saw and knew that she was feeling extremely sexy from kissing her fingers and arms. She had multiple orgasms every time and pretty intensive and crazy ones. She played a game and enjoyed it enormously, but she didn't understand obviously what it cost him. "Darling, you can't really imagine what a torture it is to me," he said once finally.

"Torture? Why? I was thinking that you're enjoying that too, aren't you? You turning insane sometimes too. Isn't it a pleasure for you?"

"It definitely is, but it's extremely difficult to hold myself in check. Sometimes—well, I don't really want to talk about that. I don't know how to explain that . . . if you don't know how a man usually functions."

"I know. I'm not a baby," she objected indignantly, but it was absolutely visible to Jim that her experience was on a level somewhere about zero. "Okay, if you don't want to kiss my fingers anymore, we could leave these experiments alone for now. Let's talk about something else. Did you ever kiss a woman? I mean, other than your grandma Cathy on the cheek with a Christmas present?"

"Oh God," Jim moaned.

"It means yes." Lada giggled. "If it was no, then you would just say no, right?"

"Right." He blushed almost like a tomato.

"How was it? Did you like it?"

"Actually, I did . . . a lot," he said slowly, thoughtfully. "It was the best thing that ever happened to me before I met you."

"What happened with this woman? Did she dump you?"

"Yes." It was his only chance to avoid this conversation.

"Oh, she is stupid," Lada concluded and passionately hugged his neck. "You're so handsome, Jim. Are you looking in the mirror sometimes?"

"Only when I'm shaving."

"Then look once at another time. Your lips are so beautiful. They are outlined so clear—you know, like one Egyptian pharaoh I saw in a movie. And you know, I never kissed a man. It does not count, of course, kissing my dad as a child or kissing BB and my little nephew, Dave, on the cheek while giving them presents on their birthdays or at Christmas. No, I mean a real kiss, like in the movies."

"Jeez, you saw a lot of movies." Jim chuckled, anticipating with some fear where this conversation was going. Kissing was his thing, and he knew that if it came to that, he definitely wouldn't be able to stop himself if needed.

"I would like to kiss you, Jim, but I don't know how. Could you teach me, please?"

"I have no right! Sorry! It would have sexual intentions."

"Really?" Lada laughed mischievously. "I would consider that *educational intentions*. I need to learn something, and you're the one I want to teach me."

"You're teasing, right? Is that what I am supposed to tell your brother?"

"No, that's what you're supposed to tell yourself if you want to feel proud that you're keeping your word as a real man. You don't need to tell BB anything at all. It's not his business. And actually, he never would find out anyway."

"I don't know. I won't be able to look him in the eyes if I don't keep my word."

"Then don't look him in the eyes. Gosh, Jim, sometimes I admire you, but sometimes I hate you for your honesty. Please, don't you love me?"

"I do." He nodded, thinking that *educational intentions* actually sounded pretty reasonable because he missed real kissing so badly that he really can't resist. "Okay . . . but I have one condition. I can do that if I am lying down on my stomach on the sand only, no other way. You lie on your towel beside me on your back, turn your head toward me, and I will kiss you from above. That's it."

"Sounds strange, but it's okay if you insist that it's more comfortable for you," Lada happily agreed and rolled momentarily as he instructed. "I still don't get why you want it this way, but it doesn't matter." She hugged his neck and pulled his face close to hers. "So teach me, please, now."

"There's actually nothing to teach," Jim whispered. "I'm just touching your lips with mine, and you do what you want, what feels right. Be creative and trust your instinct. Do anything that you feel is needed to give you those butterflies. Do an experiment to find out what makes you excited."

"Okay," she whispered back and outlined his lips with a wet tip of her tongue.

He shuddered, murmuring, "You're a hell of a student." And after that, they didn't talk anymore for the whole evening.

CHAPTER 51

On their flight from Hawaii to Los Angeles and then to Minneapolis, Jim was practically sleeping all the time. The last three days of these *scientific experiments* and *educational sessions* were so exhausting for him that he wasn't sure he would survive them. While Lada was blossoming, beaming, and shining with happiness and satisfaction, he lost huge amount of vitamins, minerals, energy, and power, which were draining with the ejaculations three, four, or sometimes more times per day from his tiny body into the Hawaiian white sand. If not for the beautiful fresh suntan that covered his face and made him look even sexier and more attractive in Lada's opinion, he would be extremely pale with dark circles around his eyes.

She was also well tanned and looked like a model in her short sundress. Her dark blond hair had faded in the bright sun and appeared almost white. All these turned a lot of heads in airports and on the planes. Noticing her engagement ring, people were guessing that her fiancé must be somewhere behind the picture at the moment and that she was traveling with a little handicapped because she was working as a caregiver or a nurse on duty.

In spite of his tiredness and weakness, Jim was happy beyond belief. It looked like all his dreams came true. His symphony was completed, the performer was found, the ocean was visited, and the sunrise over the ocean was seen for the first time in his life. Also, his ring was accepted, Lada's love was confirmed, and her sexual sensitivity was healed and proved to be a great deal. What else in the world could he wish for? It was total bliss.

Before their departure from Hawaii, Lada hugged him and said, "I hope we will continue this at home, right, Jim? I really, really love our sex."

"We didn't have any sex practically." He smirked.

"We didn't?" She looked surprised. "Then what is it that we're doing?"

"I could say a foreplay," he suggested uncertainly, "even just the first part of it, the very beginning of the foreplay."

"You mean there is more to it?"

"Oh, believe me, much, much more."

"Wow," she said. "Then I am looking forward to that *much more* foreplay, though I couldn't even guess what else it would possibly be. To me, it looks like we did everything imaginable."

"Well . . ." He laughed. "Your imagination is kind of restricted."

"Then you'll improve it, right?"

"I will try." Jim shrugged, flirting. "But I don't know how we could see each other now if you're not working as our bus driver anymore. Where could we meet? And how? Also, it would be a very busy time ahead to work with Boris on the symphony rehearsals. I don't know. I'm a bit confused of how our life will continue from now on. We also didn't find a singer yet."

"Don't worry," Lada assured him. "We'll figure out something. It will all settled by itself, I'm sure."

Now on the airplane, he was daydreaming quietly, knowing that she was with him, that she would definitely figure out what should happen after they arrived home and lead him in the proper way, and he was ready to follow her forever.

When they arrived to the group home, it was already after seven o'clock. All the residents and both nurses of the shift were in the garden, enjoying the fresh air before retiring for the night. Only Victor was inside, sitting motionless in his favorite armchair in the living room, and Mona was still in her office, doing something on the computer.

As usual, none of the wards paid attention to their arrival; just Nurses Rona and Andy waved from the farther bench and shouted, "Hi, Jim! Welcome home!" He waved back to them.

Lada took out Jim's luggage from the trunk of her car. Before giving him his backpack, she pulled out the folder from it—the pages that he wrote in Hawaii, the score of the fourth part of his symphony—and locked it into her trunk. All her works went there as well. "Safety first." She laughed. "You don't take that stuff inside here, right, Jim? I am giving them to BB so he could finish spreading them to his musicians."

"Of course." Jim nodded. "Now we should say our goodbyes. Let's sit on the porch for a minute."

They climbed on the stairs. Jim sat on the very top step, Lada three steps down so their faces were on the same level. "Bye, my love," she said and hugged his neck. "I'll call you as soon as I come home tonight."

"I'll wait," he whispered. "Love you. Last goodbye kiss?"

Lada looked around fast. "Nobody is watching, and nobody cares anyway." She laughed, and then she kissed him deeply on the lips. He hugged her as well, and they stayed in this kiss, forgetting again everything in the world around them.

Just at that time, Mona came out from her office to the kitchen to finish cleaning and organizing some stuff. She was sure that nobody was at home and was surprised to see Victor, sitting in the living room. "Hey, darling, why are you sitting here?" she inquired. "Go outside. Enjoy the evening. We have one more hour before sleep."

Victor stood up and walked to the door quietly and meaninglessly as usual, like a zombie. He opened the door, stepped on the porch, and stopped there, confused and not knowing what to do. Lada and Jim were sitting on the stairs, hugging and kissing passionately, completely blocking his way down the steps to the garden. He stood there and watched them for some moment and then turned around, went back inside, and sat on his armchair in the living room again.

"What the hell!" Mona screamed at him. "I told you to go outside. Why aren't you listening to me? Go right now!"

Victor didn't move, didn't even look at her, and kept sitting silently where he was. Mona came to the door and looked outside, trying to realize why he wasn't going to the garden; and then she saw them, Jim and Lada, kissing on the porch. Her first instinct was to run outside, screaming like hell, and kill them both, but she stopped herself—too many people were around. She didn't need any witnesses, so she just squeezed her fists and growled quietly like a dog, preparing to attack. Then she took a couple of a deep breaths and stepped outside with a charming smile on her face.

"Jim, darling, welcome home," she pronounced quietly. "Let me carry your luggage inside. And you, Miss, get out from my property immediately, or I'll call the police and have you arrested for trespassing. Get lost, you little fucking bitch!" She hissed the last words slowly and calmly, not giving anybody in the garden a chance to hear or notice anything.

"Excuse me," Jim said confidently, turning to her. "You're not talking to Lada like that. Watch your mouth, Mona."

"It's okay, Jim." Lada stood up and helped him stand up as well. "I've heard worse in the Ukraine. I don't care. I'm leaving anyway. Bye." She bowed, kissed him on forehead, and ran from the steps to her car.

"It was rude of you," Jim insisted, following Mona into the door. "Next time you see her, you should apologize."

"Of course, of course, sweetie!" Mona exclaimed pretty loud, making sure that this time everybody in the garden could hear her. Then she closed the door, dropped his luggage, turned to him, and hit him in the face with all the might she was capable of. It was so sudden and so unexpected that Jim lost his balance and fell to the floor. Mona grabbed him by his arm with one of her hands and by his hair with the other and pulled him like a rag doll through the kitchen, storage, and the little hall into her suite.

"I'll kill you, you fucking bastard!" she screamed in uncontrollable anger. "I'll show you how to cheat on me, how to fuck stupid girls, you disgusting, ugly cripple, you debauched piece of shit. I'll show you who you are supposed to sleep with."

Jim tried to kick her with his sneakers and his tiny fists but was unsuccessful, of course. She pulled him into her suite, slammed the door, threw him on her bed, grabbed the neck of his T-shirt, and tore it in half, leaving his now well-tanned chest bare. Then she tore off her dress and fell on her bed, pulling Jim on the top of her. She kept screaming profanity, every word in the book, while slapping him really strong on the cheeks, pulling him by his hair and squeezing his face to her breasts. "You'll do what I order, you stupid idiot! Love me now! Suck me now, you freak of nature!"

Mona was absolutely insane in her unstoppable angry rage. Tears of despair almost suffocated Jim. He felt that his arms and legs were useless to fight her. The only weapon left for him were his teeth. So he bit her, not even knowing where, somewhere on her naked body, as strong as he could and felt with nausea that his mouth was suddenly full of her blood. Mona howled and wailed in pain and, with angry madness, pushed him away. He rolled over her bed and ended up on the floor. She jumped up and started beating him everywhere with her shoes—on his stomach, his chest, and his face. He curled up subconsciously into a fetal position and covered his temples with both hands, trying to protect them somehow so as not to get killed. She continued to hit him on his back.

Luckily for Jim, his bite was pretty powerful, and the blood that was leaking now from Mona's wound took her attention. She left him alone and ran to the washroom, where her medicine cabinet was, to tend to the wound. On her way, she stomped on his phone, which fell from his pocket during the fight, and then grabbed it, broke it in half, and threw the pieces at him. "You'll never talk to her on this phone again, you fucking biting wild animal!" she growled. "You'll never see her again!"

When Mona disappeared into the washroom and turned the water on, probably to wash her wound, Jim combined all his willpower and might and, with the greatest effort, stood up and walked out of the suite. He tried to run as much as he could, but in reality, he just slowly dragged himself toward the kitchen and then the living room, on the way spitting Mona's blood from his mouth. Finally, Jim bumped into Victor, who was still sitting in his armchair, motionless. Feeling complete helplessness, Jim grabbed Victor's legs, pushed his bloodied and bruised face to Victor's knees, and sobbed breathlessly.

Then Mona appeared from the kitchen, holding a medical bandage by her wound. She searched the room with her angry eyes, looking for Jim. She saw that Victor put his hand on Jim's head and mechanically patted his hair, trying to soothe him and calm him down. The witness, even catatonic, still was a witness. Mona decided that it wasn't safe for her to approach in this situation and retired back to her suite, not saying a word.

Jim sobbed, still shaking from horror and pain. It looked like he was incapable of calming down and stopping from crying ever. Then Victor looked around askance, and seeing that nobody was there, he bowed his head and whispered into Jim's ear, "Midnight . . . my room . . . we need to talk."

In bewilderment, Jim sobered in a moment. "You can . . . talk . . . better now," he stuttered, choking on his tears, and looked at Victor with his wet eyes, one of which had a huge purple bruise under it.

Victor pointed with his eyes and a light nod toward the door of Jim's room and breathed out almost inaudibly, "Go." And he lightly pushed him by his shoulder.

Inspired by this absolutely unexpected protection, Jim gathered the rest of his strength and power, climbed on the stairs, entered his room, and locked the door behind him right away. He went to the washroom, brushed his teeth, and rinsed his mouth with Listerine three times in a row to get rid of the disgusting taste of Mona's blood. Then he took a shower, washed all his scratches and bruises tenderly, and put an antibiotic cream on them.

He heard a loud bang outside when Mona threw his luggage and backpack at his door. He gave her some minutes to go away and then opened the door very cautiously and pulled his stuff inside. Both luggage and backpack were open and searched through. All his belongings were turned upside down and inside out. Mona was obviously looking for the scores of his symphony and, again, didn't find anything. This doubled or even tripled her anger.

Jim put his pajamas on, climbed into his bed, and lay quietly, thinking how he could now contact Lada. Nobody in the house had cell phones except Mona and him. He really had a privileged treatment over here before. The internet was only in Mona's office and his room, but as he tried it, it was already disconnected. The first thing that Mona did after he escaped was to unplug the router in the office. Now he found himself in a prison.

What could be his choices? To walk away through the main door? Mona probably set a security alarm already, which she sometimes did, though not always. But tonight there was no question about that. To walk away through the back door in the basement? But he didn't have the key for the basement anymore. And where could he go? To the highway, sitting there until the morning and wait for an occasional car to pass by and ask people for help? In this forest area, it probably would never happen.

Jim was completely lost and scared. The pain of all his bruises tortured him and didn't give him a chance to fall asleep in spite of the awful heavy exhaustion. He lay there and watched at the clock on the wall, counting minutes until midnight.

It was a strange surprise that Victor could talk. He probably managed somehow not to take the pills anymore since Jim dropped Victor's pill accidentally at the beginning of April. So did he just pretend to be a zombie? Why? And what did he want to talk about now? Did he need some help, or did he want to suggest help for Jim? Even feeling almost dead from the tiredness and pain, Jim still was anxious and curious and still had his investigative mood. Five minutes to midnight, he slid from his bed, opened his door, and soundlessly tiptoed through the long hallway toward Victor's room.

CHAPTER 52

ada drove into her driveway about 8:30 p.m. and called Jim right away. There was no answer. *He must be tired after our long flight and went to sleep right away*, she thought. *He said he will wait for my call, but well, it's okay.*

The house was quiet. The only one who jumped out to greet her was the dog, Oscar. Then his happy bark and whine got the attention of Lada's mother, Tatiana, who returned from the cruise to Alaska with the children a week ago when Lada was absent. Now she came out from the living room, where she was sitting and knitting. "Ladochka, my darling!" she exclaimed, hugging her daughter. "I'm so happy to see you. Boris and Rita are working a concert tonight until very late. The kids are already in their beds with their phones, so I'm alone here. Come, sit with me and tell me everything about your trip. Oh, your suntan is so beautiful. And I see you bought yourself a new ring."

Lada sat on the couch with her, and they chatted a bit like people usually do when someone returns from a trip, talking about the flight, weather, ocean, accommodation, and so on. "I'm pretty tired, Mom," Lada finally said. "I need to go to sleep. I will see everybody at breakfast, and then we'll talk."

First, she went to Boris's desk and left the folder with the last part of Jim's symphony for him. Then Lada went to her bedroom, took a quick shower, and tried to dial Jim once more. Again, there was no answer. "Well . . ." She took a deep breath and got under her covers to sleep. The cats appeared from nowhere and nestled beside her.

She overslept a bit and came downstairs in the morning when half the breakfast was already consumed. The whole family was sitting at the table. Becky, her fourteen-year-old niece, was in her usual spot beside Boris. She was big, tall, about three times bigger and one head taller than her mother, Rita. She was also blond and looked a lot like Boris and definitely was a daddy's girl. A stranger would think that she was in her twenties, but in reality, her very childish face with big pink cheeks gave away her real age.

The nephew, twelve-year-old Dave, was quite the opposite—tiny and slim with curly dark hair and deep brown eyes with long eyelashes. He was looking much younger than his age and was so cute that it would be possible to think he was a girl. However, if someone said that, he would be really offended. He was a mama's boy and was always sitting beside Rita.

Lada sat next to her mother across from Boris and Becky and, at the beginning, answered nicely at the regular morning greetings and small chat, but it was noticeable that she wasn't in a good mood. She tried to call Jim before going downstairs and wasn't successful again. This started to worry her. But that wasn't the main reason. "Business first," she said finally. "BB, the symphony is finished. I left it on your desk yesterday night."

"Thank you. I saw it already. So the trip was not in vain. Jim got his inspiration from the great Pacific. Very well."

"But I wanna tell you, BB, I am angry as hell at you."

"Oh my God, Ladochka!" Tatiana exclaimed in horror. "Watch your language! It's not the way to talk to your brother!"

"Why did you ask him to give you his word?" Lada inquired, ignoring her mother. "Why did you force him to give you that idiotic promise?" She was getting more and more agitated, already almost screaming.

"He told you," Boris noted matter-of-factly with a sigh.

"Yes, of course, he told me. We tell everything to each other. And you have absolutely no right to put your nose into my sex life—"

"Wow, wow, wow, let me stop you right there," Rita interrupted abruptly. "Kids, it's time for Oscar to go for a walk. You've already finished your breakfast. Chop-chop, go fast."

"Mom," Becky whined. "I'm okay. I had sexual education class last year. I know everything."

"I hadn't yet." Little Dave giggled. "But I know everything too."

"Class or no class, I said you're going for a walk," Rita answered in a very strict voice. "And you're going immediately."

"I don't know where his leash is," Becky kept moaning, trying to buy some time.

"Mama, please help them find the leash and make sure that they are gone." Rita turned to her mother-in-law, who was shaking her head in disbelief of what she had heard from Lada.

"Yes, Ritochka, of course." Tatiana stood up and walked from the room, followed by the children, who were lazily dragging their feet, still hoping to hear something forbidden and, because of that, especially interesting.

"Listen, kiddo," Boris said. "I know that you hate it when men are hitting on you. I just wanted to protect you."

"I'm a grown-up woman. I don't need a protector, especially from Jim."

"But mostly, I wanted to protect him," Boris continued calmly. "He has enough on his plate. And he's obviously in love with you . . . and he's also a thirty-three-year-old man. I thought that if he would make a move on you, you'll go berserk as usual and will kick him away. Then he would be heartbroken. Rita and I, we both like him very much, and we plan on working with him, so we don't want extra suffering for him."

Tatiana returned to the room, nodded to Rita that the kids left, and sat on her previous spot by Lada.

"So you did care about him! But did you care about me?" Lada screamed with tears. "Did you even guess the position you put me in? I was crying, I was begging him to kiss me, and he absolutely refused because of that stupid promise that you manipulated him to give you. Could you even guess how humiliating it was for me? It was a shame! It was abusive to me, and you did it all!"

"My God, Ladochka," her mother whispered, pressing her palms to her cheeks. "You don't behave like that with a man. Who is this man? Rita, do you know him?"

"Yes, yes, don't worry, he's okay," Rita whispered back to her.

Boris answered to Lada, "Sorry, kiddo, I really couldn't ever guess that you would want to kiss him. It would never come to my mind. You were always so adamant about men. And I . . . I really can't imagine . . . what kind of relationship could be . . . there."

"By the way," Rita noticed, "is that an engagement ring?"

"No, it's not. It's a promise ring. I promised to be his friend. That's all."

"Well, it's an engagement ring," Rita established the fact. "A promise ring should be simple and cheap, no diamonds."

"He said it's a promise ring!" Lada yelled. "Why don't you believe me?"

"You see!" Boris exclaimed indignantly, lifting his palms. "He manipulated her to accept his engagement ring. Jeez, he's cunning."

"*Bebe.*" Rita put her palm on top of his hand. "Calm down. Don't be too harsh on him. He's a man in love, and you all are cunning when it comes to that. Don't you remember how you manipulated me when you wanted what you wanted?"

"I married you. But she can't marry him." Boris shook his head. "Look at her! She is a kid! And I'm sorry to say, but he doesn't need a wife. He needs a nanny and a caregiver."

"You're talking about me like I'm not here!" Lada shrieked. "You, stupid BB, have no right to make life decisions for me!"

"Why does he need a caregiver?" Tatiana whispered to Rita.

"He is handicapped from birth."

"Oh my God!" now Tatiana yelled. "Ladochka, you're such a beauty! Couldn't you find a normal man? Why a cripple?" She covered her face with both hands and began to sob.

"Because he's the best in the world!" Lada yelled back. "And I love him. That's why!" She was crying too, sniffling and choking on her tears.

"Kiddo," Boris said, almost ready to cry as well. His mother and sister were breaking his heart. "You just get one thing, please. We have nothing against Jim personally, but if you'll marry him, your life with him won't be normal because of his condition."

"Normal?" Lada screamed and jumped up. "What was normal in this family ever? Was it normal that my father was killed? Was it normal that people threw rotten tomatoes at me when I was playing with my doll at age twelve? Was it normal when she"—she nodded toward Rita—"was practically kicked out of her country because of her nationality? Was it normal that you, BB, escaped illegally just to marry the woman you love? Was it normal that your father condemned you for the emigration but also, let's be honest, for marrying a Jewish woman? Was it normal that I was born as a substitute for you, as a second choice for my parents? Was it normal that I was robbed of my relationship with you until our father died? Was it normal that I was almost killed right in the middle of the street and people were passing by and nobody cared, that nobody even called the police? What was normal with us ever?"

"Kiddo, you're talking about the former Soviet Union, about the communist's mentality. You drew a very good picture, explaining why we all emigrated from there," Boris confirmed sadly.

"This mentality is still alive!" Lada shrieked. "Look at her!" She nodded toward Tatiana. "I'm too beautiful to marry a cripple! Do you listen to yourself, Mom? How dare you say that to me? We're living in America now, and there is a different mentality here. There is nothing wrong in loving a handicapped, in marrying a handicapped, in living with a handicapped. People with disabilities are respected here. They're getting help. They live a normal life. That's what is normal here. And if I hear from anyone of you even one word against Jim ever, I'll marry him tomorrow!"

Lada ran to her bedroom upstairs and slammed the door. There was silence for a long moment. Then Boris shook his head. "Hmm." He turned to Rita. "*Bebe*, it's a good thing that you sent the kids away. It's not just about sex. It's kind of much more."

"Yeah," she agreed thoughtfully. "Kids aren't mature enough yet to understand."

"Nobody here understands immigrants." Tatiana sniffed, wiping her tears. "What should we do now? Let her marry a cripple? Boris, I'm begging you, please don't allow her to bring him into your house and live with him here. I'll have a heart attack just looking at him! I can't imagine my sweet little daughter with a cripple! My God! How bad is he disabled?"

"Pretty bad." Boris sighed. "Much more than you could imagine."

"Oh my God!" Tatiana sobbed again. "My poor girl! Where did she met him? I guess while driving that bus? She shouldn't go to work in this place where the cripples live!"

"Actually, he's not just a cripple," Rita objected. "He is a genius. He is much above the level of a so-called normal person. And I think it's my turn now to go and talk to Ladochka."

At that time, in her room, sobbing into her pillow in despair, Lada dialed Jim's phone again. And again, there was no answer.

CHAPTER 53

R ita, knowing that she wouldn't hear anything in response except for an angry "go away," still knocked at Lada's bedroom door. She was a person of ethics and never broke her ethics code, even when their family circumstances were unusual. She knew that the response would be directed not to her but to Boris. So in spite of the "go away," Rita just opened the door and entered the room. "Ladochka," she said calmly, "I brought you the folder that I collected for Jim while you were in Hawaii. Do you want to take a look at it?"

Lada turned on her bed, lifted her wet and red face from the pillow, and looked at Rita. "For Sandra Soley?" she asked.

"Yeah." Rita sat on the edge of her bed and put the folder beside her. "Because Sandra is a singer, I tried to choose most pieces that Jim wrote for a vocal performance. I wrote dates on them because some works were done when he was a child or teenager. You know, just in case, if she decides that some pieces have a childish approach to the music, she will know that it was really a child who created it. I included in that folder also the vocal part for the symphony. I hope that vocal music will be more attractive to her. I put the whole symphony there too because we assume that Sandra would sing it, and she should know what to expect from the whole work. Right?"

Lada nodded, smearing the tears on her face.

"Here is a Kleenex, Ladochka," Rita suggested and gave her a tissue. "How about his résumé? Did you prepare it?"

"Yes." Lada sniffed. "Look in the folder on my desk."

"Good." Rita took the papers and read them attentively while Lada sat on the bed and moved closer to her to see together what she was reading.

"Very well, you did a good job," Rita concluded a couple of minutes later as she finished going through the papers. "And you took a very nice picture of him, beautiful portrait. He's actually a very handsome man. And the CDs are also included. I hope Sandra would be impressed and agree to work with us. Oh, I almost forgot, Mrs. Soley already arrived in Minneapolis and started her interviews with the students. She has about two weeks to choose whom she'll keep in her class. I signed you for an appointment tomorrow at ten in the morning."

"You're the best." Lada hugged her affectionately. "Thank you. I love you so much, Ritochka. And I'm sorry that I screamed at your husband. It was probably hurtful to you."

As much as Rita tried to turn Lada's attention away from the family scandal, she was forced to answer now anyway. "You'll figure out that with him," she said. "Just remember that he loves you very, very much, and you will always be a little sister for him, a young child. I know it's wrong, but it's what he feels. So sometimes he goes a bit overboard. But we're sorry. We just didn't think that you have such deep feelings for Jim. Now we know."

"And Mama . . . I don't understand her. She sounded so silly and rude with me," Lada complained, still tearful. "It looks like her brain is stuck at fifty years ago."

"Ladochka." Rita hugged her by the shoulders. "She is a senior. She is a woman from another generation. In the Ukraine, when we were young and in love, she was the best one to cover for us and to understand us. She had a very democratic and modern mentality at that time. It was great then and there, but today and here, it's definitely not enough. You know, many seniors, even after emigration, aren't capable of changing. Just keep it in mind and don't talk to her about sensitive subjects."

"So . . ." Lada smirked sarcastically. "Just household, weather, playing cards with neighbors, her favorite old songs, knitting—that's all that we're supposed to talk to her about?"

"Yeah, pretty much," Rita agreed, "if you want to keep peace in the family. When we live together with seniors, we should be diplomatic.

Maybe it is good for you that Jim has no mother. Sometimes not having a mother-in-law is just great."

Lada looked at her questioningly. "You mean . . . you and BB will accept if I marry him?"

"It's up to you, Ladochka. Only you can decide that. No one knows your feelings as you know. Well, let's talk better about another subject that is much closer. Did you think about how you will start your conversation with Sandra Soley? You should be ready, especially because, as you know, she's quite a difficult person. Think about that." Rita stood up, ready to go. "I'm leaving my folder here on your desk," she said.

"Okay." Lada nodded, and then she took her phone and dialed Jim again and again—there was no answer. "Damn, what the hell!" she exclaimed.

"What?" Rita asked as she stopped on her way to the door. "What happened?"

"I wish I knew. Jim's not answering his phone, not yesterday night, not today. I should probably go there."

"Maybe he just forgot to charge it."

"He never does. He is kind of crazy about our phone calls. Normally, he would have already called me a dozen times. I worry that something happened."

"Nothing can happen in a group home." Rita soothed her. "They are usually very well managed and very safe places."

"Not there." Lada smirked. "He told me a lot."

"He's very sensitive and sometimes maybe overreacting," Rita suggested.

"I don't know. Should I go today? What do you think?"

"Wait until you talk to Sandra tomorrow morning. Then you can go and maybe bring him the good news. That will be an extremely important meeting for Jim and for all of us, if we want success for his symphony. I agree with Jim's opinion—Sandra's voice would sound perfect there. So you need to work on your speech today to impress her."

"Okay." Lada sighed. "I'll wait until tomorrow. Tell BB that I love him and kiss him for me."

"He just left for the university with the rest of Jim's work. The three parts of the symphony are already printed, but this one needs to be spread to lines on the computer and given to the musicians as well. And don't worry, everything is now back to normal at home. I know you don't like this *normal* word. But it is what it is. Everything has calmed down.

Before I came to your room, your mama was cleaning the table after breakfast, and the kids returned from their walk with Oscar. They are playing now in the backyard with friends. We, you and I, are preparing for your tomorrow's meeting with Sandra. Look, everything is okay, and there's no reason to be upset."

"Okay." Lada laughed. "You convinced me. I'll stay here and work on my speech all day."

When Rita left, Lada lay back on her bed and closed her eyes, trying to imagine how Sandra Soley would look like. *She must be about fifty now*, Lada thought, *so . . . old. But celebrities are usually good at hiding their age.*

In the evening, when Boris returned from the university, he asked Rita to come to his office in the basement and closed the door. "I want to tell you something important," he said in a quiet voice. "Where is kiddo? Are you sure she couldn't hear us talking?"

"No, she is upstairs, in her bedroom."

"Well, something extremely unusual happened today at the university. While I was printing the scores in our computer lab, the composing teacher, Mr. Erikson, approached me and showed me some pages. He said that a couple of months ago, he got a new student, Sharon Lainer. She graduated this May as a pianist, not the best one, by the way. But she began composing recently and showed an unbelievable talent in her works. He wanted me to look at them and possibly perform her symphony. And you would never guess what. It was Jim's symphony."

"What?" Rita exclaimed in disbelief. "How is that possible? I don't understand!"

"I was in shock at first too," Boris continued. "Then I told him that I already have this symphony to perform. We did talk a pretty long time about that story. I think someone stole it from Jim and is trying to get all the benefits from his talent. Mr. Erikson said that he is suspicious a bit too because he gave his students an assignment—to write the variations on the exact theme, which he created himself. And you know what? That Sharon Lainer couldn't do that at all.

"She complained that she has a headache or some other health conditions. Anyway, she begged him to help perform this symphony immediately. And also, guess what? She has only the first part of it in the scores. She said that she is working now on the parts 2, 3, and 4. But we already have them here. Jim finished the second and the third parts a month ago and the fourth one in Hawaii. And kiddo brought them here right away. So they can't be stolen from him. That's why this girl doesn't have them."

"Wow!" Rita exclaimed. "Should we call the police? Or a lawyer for the author's rights?"

"I decided with Mr. Erikson to observe a bit more, to collect more evidence. I just wonder, should we tell kiddo about that?"

"Yes, we definitely should but not today. She is nervous enough after all that . . . you know. And she's also preparing herself for a meeting with Sandra Soley tomorrow morning. Let's tell her after that meeting, okay?"

"Well then, I'll just go there and give her a good-night kiss."

When Boris knocked on Lada's bedroom door, there wasn't an angry "go away" anymore. She answered calmly, "Come in."

"Hey, kiddo," he said, entering. "How are you hanging?"

"Okay." She sighed. "BB, I'm so sorry that I screamed at you. I was very angry. I love you so much."

"It's okay, kiddo. I was actually wrong to cause you that pain. And I love you too, of course. So we're good now?" He sat on the edge of her bed.

"Yes, we are." Lada chuckled, hugged his neck, and kissed him on the cheek.

"By the way, do you know a girl at the university named Sharon Lainer? She was in the piano department."

"No. Why?"

"Just curious. I've heard something about her today."

"No, we don't have much contact with pianists usually, very different classes. Or maybe some harmony . . . or music history . . . but there are almost a hundred people from all the departments. I can't possibly know everybody. But . . . wait . . . that last name, Lainer, sounds familiar. Oh . . . wait . . . wait . . . I remember . . . Mrs. Mona Lainer, my former boss, is the manager of Jim's group home."

There you go, Boris thought, standing up and heading to the door. "Okay, we'll talk about that tomorrow. It's not important now. Sweet dreams, kiddo."

CHAPTER 54

The next morning, at five minutes to ten, Lada was already in front of the door of the auditorium, which their university designated for Mrs. Sandra Soley to conduct the voice trial of her potential students. The internet research about the singer showed that she was a classy person. So Lada tried as much as she could to dress up not as regular teenager would but in her best classy way—dark blue English suit, white blouse, and high-heeled shoes, which she borrowed from Rita. She also made her hair into a bun, which was sitting low at the back of her head, almost on her neck. It was Sandra's style as well. Lada hoped that her appearance would be attractive to the singer and that she would be nice and understanding to her.

At exactly ten o'clock, Lada politely knocked on the door and entered the auditorium, holding Jim's folder in her hands. She was very tense and all shaky, so she didn't even hear if someone inside said "come in" or not. The auditorium was pretty spacious. Sandra Soley was sitting at the desk at the very end of it. A bunch of papers were in front of her on the table. She seemed to be busy and did not even lift her eyes from the papers to see who came in.

However, Lada noticed that she looked exactly like her picture from the internet—slim, pretty tall even in a sitting position, well tanned with dark brown hair made into the same-looking bun that Lada herself was wearing now. She didn't dare come closer without an invitation and stopped by the door. "Good morning, Mrs. Soley," Lada started politely.

"Name?" Sandra asked indifferently without any pleasantries, finally lifting her eyes from the papers. Her voice sounded deep and beautiful, obviously an opera singer's voice.

"Meleshko," Lada said.

Sandra looked back into her papers, probably to verify the name and time of appointment, and marked a check with a pen. "What do you want to sing for me?" she asked next.

"Mrs. Soley, unfortunately, I am not singing. I came to see you for another reason."

"I'm not seeing people for other reasons," Sandra answered abruptly and pointed at the door. "You can go now."

Lada felt the anger begin slowly brewing in her gut, and as usual, she did the opposite of what she was told. She walked some steps toward the table and announced in quite a harsh voice, "Mrs. Soley, I'm not going anywhere until you listen to me. My appointment is twenty minutes, so I still have time, and I will tell you what you need to know."

"What? I don't need to know anything from you if you're not singing." Sandra looked at the young lady in front of her like her eyes were ready to jump out from their sockets. "What's going on here? What do you want? An autograph?"

"No."

"Then what? Money? I'm doing enough charity, much more than any other singer had ever done."

"I don't need money. Just listen," Lada continued forcefully. "I came here on behalf of one genius composer, a real genius. He is like Mozart or Beethoven or Wagner of our century, on the same level, no less. Here are some of his works." She extended her hand, holding the folder. "He likes your voice."

"How flattering!" Sandra smirked sarcastically. "Some amateur composer likes my voice. Oh my God! Go away, please. Your appointment is finished."

"No, it's not," Lada said loud and clear and came closer. "So he likes your voice, as I said already, and he wants to invite you to sing a vocal line in his symphony. It will be performed at the beginning of September. Rehearsals will start next week. You have some time to learn your part."

"Who the hell are you?" Sandra exclaimed as her face turned red with anger.

"I am a student of the orchestra department of this university. And I am his fiancée."

"Of course! If you're his fiancée, he is the genius for you!"

"Not just for me. My brother thinks that too."

Sandra exploded with a malicious laugh. "You, your fiancé, your brother—what is it, a small family business of some kind?"

"It's a very big business, even a huge one, Mrs. Soley. And this composer is not an amateur. He is a highly educated professional. He graduated from Juilliard, exactly like you. Not just us but his composing professor, Mr. Dangly, called him a genius too. Did some of your teachers in Juilliard addressed you as a genius ever?"

Strangely to Lada, Sandra ignored her sarcasm, maybe not even noticed it. The reference to the Juilliard School and to a composing teacher well known to every musician cooled down her irritation a bit. Like most celebrities, she was tired of people chasing her for autographs and begging for donations. She hated the paparazzi eager for photos of private moments in her life; she disrespected nosy journalists perverting the facts and writing gossipy articles for cheap magazines, representing tragedies as dirt just for popularity and fun. She hated those people and, deep in her heart, was scared of them, which made her lash out in anger. Not sure if Lada wasn't one of them, Sandra lifted her protective barriers immediately.

"I hope," Lada continued, "if you are a real professional, you will look at his works and understand and appreciate his level of talent. You will realize that to sing in his symphony would be the most interesting experience for you. Our orchestra is quite well known in this country, and my brother is a very serious and gifted conductor. All our musicians are experienced people, amazingly creative, talented, and devoted to music. It would be a pleasure for you to work with us and, mutually, for us to work with you."

"Hmm." Sandra smirked and shrugged with uncertainty. "I will teach the vocal class here. I have no time for anything else."

"If you fell in love with his music—and I know you will—you'd find the time," Lada concluded. "So now I urge you not only on my composer fiancé's behalf but also of the whole our orchestra and the whole university, Mrs. Soley, to please take this folder and look at its contents. Then you decide."

"Hmm." Sandra shrugged again. "What is his name? If this composer was such a genius at Juilliard, I should have probably heard of him."

"I doubt it. He was there almost twenty years later than you. I won't tell you his name now." Lada smiled enigmatically while approaching even closer to her desk. She tried to increase Sandra's interest. "Everything is in this folder—his résumé, his photo, and some of his works. You could listen to his music on these CDs. There is also a vocal part of his symphony that you're invited to sing. Take it, please."

"I don't know." Sandra made a wry face. She took the folder and threw it scornfully on the far end of her table. "Maybe I'll take a look at it, if I have some time... eventually... God knows when."

"Please do that, Mrs. Soley. Hundreds of people are waiting for your decision and depending on it. It is very important. It's extremely important, actually. Anyway, thank you for your time, Mrs. Soley. Now I can go."

As Lada headed for the door, Sandra suddenly called at her back. "Wait a minute, where is this genius composer? Why didn't he come to see me himself? Is he in prison or something?"

"No." Lada laughed. "Not at all. He just doesn't know that I'm here. He felt that it's not worth his time to talk to you because you'll refuse anyway. But I decided that it's worth my time. I knew that you're a very nice person and that you'll understand and appreciate his music."

"It's not worth his time to talk to me?" Sandra exclaimed indignantly. "How rude! Who the hell is he really? What arrogance! What a bastard! Now he sounds like a true genius. Most of them have absolutely disgusting characters. Well, I can't promise anything, but I'll let you know . . . if I'll find a time for that . . . ever." And she gestured for Lada to go.

When the door of the auditorium closed behind her, Lada sat on a bench in the hallway and giggled. "Sorry, Jim," she whispered to herself. "Sorry, my love, that I described you for her as a bitch, but it looks like it worked. She is such a bitch herself that she could only understand fighting fire with fire."

Then she dialed Jim's phone one more time and again—no answer. *Oh my God! I am turning insane*, she thought, running to the parking lot and starting her car. *I'm going there right now, and nothing will stop me. I don't understand what happened with you, Jim.*

After forty-five minutes of crazy, irrational driving, when Lada was already about a mile from the group home, her phone suddenly rang. She looked at the display. A number was unfamiliar, and it showed the name of an unknown caller—Josef Romado. "Gosh! It's probably some person from a hospital or police! It must be about Jim!" she exclaimed and parked the car at the edge of the highway as soon as she could.

"Hello!" she screamed into her phone.

"Lada, darling, it's me."

"Jim! Oh my God! Finally!" With a deep sigh, Lada dropped her head back on the headrest. "Where are you? What's happening?"

"I am okay, sweetie." It sounded to her like Jim was whispering. "I just broke my phone accidentally. I dropped it. I'm sorry I couldn't call you earlier. Nobody here has phones. Mona does not allow nurses to bring their phones to work. I begged them to give me a chance to call you, but they all are scared to lose their job. So everybody refused. Finally, Nurse Josef brought his phone for me today. We're now sitting with him in his car behind the garage, pretending that we went for a walk."

"Oh God, Jim, I was so worried. Why didn't you send me an email?"

"My internet is not working for some reason too. I don't know. Maybe there was a storm, and trees fell and broke wires." Jim really didn't want to worry her more, but she grasped immediately the inconsistency in his voice.

"You sound suspicious. Is there something else?" Lada asked nervously. "Please just don't lie to me. Has something serious happened?"

"Lada, I can't talk about that at the moment. You should understand I'm here with Josef. By the way, he's saying hi to you."

"Say hi to him too and a big thank-you for letting you use his phone. It's very nice of him and probably very risky as well."

"Yes, I'll tell him that from you. Now please, Lada, buy me a new phone. Is there some money left for that?"

"Sure. The leftovers from Hawaii are about fifteen hundred. It would be more than enough for a phone and to pay a bill. I will go back to the city now and get you a new phone right away. Give me about three hours. Wait for me by our hazelnut bush as always."

"Okay. In three hours, I'll be there. See you." He hung up.

Jim was alive, but Lada didn't calm down much. She felt caution with a tingle of despair and fear in his voice. It warned her that something did happen in the group home, something extraordinary and a lot more important than just his broken phone. She started her car and turned toward the city.

PART 3

THE CONCERT

CHAPTER 55

"**O**h my God . . . Emmanuel . . . no, no . . . it's impossible. Please, God, help me." Sandra Soley was whispering while tears were sliding slowly from her eyes to her chin and dropping onto the papers in front of her. She didn't wipe them.

She was holding Jim's photo in her trembling hand and shaking her head. "No, no, it's absolutely impossible. Oh my God . . . that name . . . James Bogat . . . James Emmanuel Bogat . . . yes, that was the name in the adoption contract. I remember . . . I will always remember it . . . but who is he really?"

Sandra was confused. Was he a genius composer from Juilliard as this cute girl, his fiancée, tried to convince her some days ago? Or was he a malicious, uneducated, mentally challenged cripple as was said in the letter that a defiant woman sent her in November last year from some group home? There were a couple of photos enclosed into the envelope with that letter then, but Sandra didn't even look at them. She just read the letter, which demanded two hundred thousand for keeping her secret. Full of disgust, she threw it into the fireplace with the envelope and photos altogether. What a blackmailing monster!

What could Sandra do? She believed the despicable woman about the conditions of that person, James Emmanuel Bogat. If her letter wasn't true, why in the world would he be in a group home for mentally ill people? And how could he be normal anyway after what she did, trying to get rid of him during her pregnancy?

That person, that scary and probably ugly person—she couldn't ever pronounce the word *son* or *child*. She never saw him. When she gave birth at home in her palace in LA, the midwife and the adoption lawyer—both older women—were the only people who attended. They took the baby right away, and when she asked in a weak, tired voice, "Can I see him?" the midwife answered dolefully, shaking her head, "You better not, ma'am."

"Why?" Sandra insisted. "Is there something wrong?"

"It doesn't matter, ma'am," the lawyer said. "He's going to the farm in a deep forest right away. He'll be on the flight to Pennsylvania tomorrow morning. Don't worry about him and forget that anything ever happened."

Receiving that blackmail letter from the group home in November last year, thirty-two years after her delivery, Sandra just yelled from horror and sorrow. She asked her personal driver to bring her to the Fir Forest Group Home a couple of weeks before Christmas. Yes, she brought a bag with the requested money and threw it in the face of that awful woman, warning her that it would be the first and also the very last time. However, she agreed to continue the monthly payments of $10,000 for the services, which she did already for thirty-two years anyway, sending that money to Phil and Cathy Bogat's farm in Pennsylvania.

After this troubling encounter, everything went quiet again. The awful woman didn't bother her anymore, and she was sure that the story was finished and completely forgotten. Phil and Cathy Bogat both died during these long years as did the adoption lawyer and the midwife. Her secret had been buried deep into the sand.

What was happening now? Where was all this coming from? How could this *person*, if he was that awful, have such a nice, pretty fiancée with a surprisingly strong character and attitude? Obviously, that beauty loved him and cared about him deeply. Maybe he really was a genius composer. He actually could be as he was Emmanuel's son. He could inherit not just the facial features but the composing talent as well. Emmanuel was very good in writing original songs, more than good; he was brilliant, $350 million brilliant. But that person—he couldn't be normal after what she did, not a chance.

However, he looked very handsome on that photo, exactly like Emmanuel was. And he also had a very high education, according to his résumé—college degree, three university degrees, the Juilliard degree. Unbelievable!

Sandra couldn't understand. At the moment, she was sitting in her hotel room and crying for hours and couldn't stop herself. Her whole life unfolded back in her aching mind, the whole tragedy that she couldn't overcome ever.

Sandra Montini was born in Italy, in a small fisherman's village not far from Napoli, on the coast of the Tyrrhenian Sea. She started singing at the age of eight, which wasn't a big surprise for anybody in her family or in the village. Most of the Italians were blessed with beautiful natural voices. Nobody there took that ability seriously; it was too casual, just some entertainment for fun.

Every day after school, little Sandra walked to the coast and was singing there for hours, sitting on the rocks while watching the endless water. The sea inspired her to dream. She loved it madly and, in her mind, called it "the ocean."

Instead of admiring her talent, her parents were quite irritated and not happy about it. They would prefer if she helped at home with cooking and sewing for her mother or fixing fishing nets for her father, which most of the villagers' children did. The parents called her a lazy girl and sadly shook their heads, showing that they were worried about her future. Who would marry a young lady without useful household skills?

Her parents were a little proud only on Sundays when Sandra sang at the church, which they all attended regularly, being very devoted Catholics. All the parishioners admired her voice there. But come on, every girl in the village was singing at the church in turn. It wasn't such a big deal. And again, who would marry a girl who was only capable of singing at the church and not serve a good dinner at home? In their mentality, any girl existed only to get married and produce children, and they knew that their parenting duty was to prepare her for that. And they felt, sadly, that they were failing this responsibility.

At school, Sandra was a friendly and social girl. She always had a lot of friends and liked to hang out with them sometimes. They all loved singing and dancing, listened to a lot of popular music, and all were secretly in love with the most famous Italian rock star—Emmanuel Soley. They all kept his photos under their pillows and sometimes traveled on the bus to Napoli if he had a concert there. They all were dreaming that maybe he would notice them while they were screaming in excitement, jumping from happiness, waving their arms in the first row of the concert hall, and he would autograph his photos for them. But alas, that never happened. Sandra was praying every evening and asked God to help her meet Emmanuel in person. She was praying really hard for two or three years, and unfortunately, God didn't answer her prayers until, one day, something absolutely unbelievable happened.

She was singing by the sea as usual, sitting on the rocks. Above her, on the highway that led to Napoli, she heard the sound of a car stopping and then some men's voices discussing a problem—a flat tire. There were three or four men at least. Sandra quit singing for a moment and listened to what was being said there.

She heard when they took some tools out from the trunk and began working on the tire, joking, laughing, and teasing one another. They obviously were friends and not teens but very grown up. And in spite of the tire mishap, it felt to her that they were having a very good time. Probably, they were a bit tipsy, maybe coming from a bar. So there was nothing interesting to pay any attention to, and Sandra began to sing again.

She just finished the first couplet of "Sola mia" when small rocks and sand started rolling from the trail above, and she realized that someone was coming down toward her. She stopped singing, looked at the trail, and lost her breath. There he was, sent by God—a very handsome tall man with wavy dark brown hair and big deep blue eyes, not typical for Italy at all. He was about thirty years old and looked exactly like his photo, which she kept under her pillow and kissed every evening after her prayers.

"Hi, little one," he said, smiling. "I guess you know who I am."

Sandra nodded breathlessly. *Thank you, my God!* she thought. *You heard me!*

"It looks like you don't believe your eyes." He laughed. "Let me confirm. Yes, I am Emmanuel, and who are you?"

"I am Sandra," she whispered.

"Please don't be scared and don't lose your voice from horror. I do not bite, absolutely sure. Why did you stop singing? You sounded amazing. Would you mind continuing for me?"

She blushed. A compliment about her voice from Emmanuel? Not one of her friends would ever believe her. Or maybe they would because they all knew that God could create miracles.

"Come on, don't be shy, baby." Emmanuel laughed and sat on the big rock beside her. "I'm listening."

Sandra coughed a bit to clear her throat, which became husky from the huge excitement she felt, and began the second couplet of "Sola mia." Emmanuel listened attentively, nodding with the rhythm of the song; and when it came to the third couplet, he started singing with her. They finished the song and were both silent for a moment. Then he said, "Wow, we're good together, aren't we?" And he laughed again.

Sandra was thinking feverishly what to do next; ask for an autograph now or later? How could she prove to her friends that she was singing with Emmanuel? No one would believe her ever. She was a village girl, only fourteen years old. And such an unheard-of privilege! Such an honor!

Her thoughts were interrupted by one of the men shouting from above, "Hey, Em, we're done here! Let's go! Hell, you can't miss a girl ever, even a child!" His friends all giggled and waved him to come up.

"Okay." Emmanuel looked straight into her eyes. "Darling, we should go to our studio right now and record that. It was too good to be lost. Do you want to go with me?"

Sandra was confused but for no more than a second. She knew, of course, her parents' nagging "Don't go in a car with a stranger," but it was not an unknown stranger. It was Emmanuel, the one well known to everybody. And if they would have a record together, it would be the best proof for her friends. She would be the most popular girl at school after that forever.

"Yes," she said. "Thank you for an invitation. I would like to go."

"Excellent, baby!" Emmanuel laughed again.

Oh God, what a charming laugh he had! Sandra thought.

And he took her hand to help her climb up the hill toward the highway where his friends, actually the members of his band as she found out later, were fussing and giggling around their car. When Sandra found herself in a car with four adult men, she got scared for a moment, but Emmanuel was sitting right beside her, holding her hand, and very gently caressing her finders; so she calmed down and felt protected, safe, and confident about her voice and her ability to make a good record with him.

Obviously, God was watching over her—they really came into Emmanuel's studio, and they worked on the record for at least two hours together with the band. The record came out just perfectly. All musicians recognized that, and all congratulated her on her first success.

Then the band left, and Emmanuel started kissing her and brought up the whole standard set of statements that a thirty-year-old rock star would give to a fourteen-year-old girl fan. "You're so beautiful. Your voice is fantastic. I've never heard anything so divine in my life. I fell in love with you at first glance. I'll love you forever. I'll make you a famous singer. We'll be together forever. I'll marry you," and so on.

And then there was wild sex, in which little Sandra lost her virginity not in a palace, not in a hotel, not even in a bed but just on the floor in the middle of the recording studio. She was scared and in pain, had a lot of bleeding, and shed a lot of tears. But Emmanuel convinced her with all of the above statements that everything would be okay and drove her home at night.

She cried at home all night, terrified that her parents would notice something and that God would punish her for her sin. But she was confused—Emmanuel was her idol, her hero, and maybe he would really love her forever as he said. In this case, there would be no sin but a happy marriage. Finally, she decided to let God determine if it was a sin or not. If not, Emmanuel would not forget her and come back tomorrow as he promised. Sandra was afraid even to believe what she was dreaming about.

But to her surprise, Emmanuel really came next day. They met on the rocks by the sea, drove to his studio again, and worked all day on recording another song together. He suggested that they start writing original songs. The lyrics would be on her, and he would compose the music. She was pretty good in writing poetry and usually had A marks for her assignments at school. Emmanuel also proved to be not only a star singer but also a talented composer, and in a week, they created five beautiful songs and recorded them.

With this hard work on songs, Sandra had no time to go to school. At first, she lied to her friends that she was sick and then lied to her parents that she got a job in Napoli busing tables in a restaurant. She promised that she would bring home some money soon, and with that, her parents approved. Every night before sleep, she prayed more and more, begging God to forgive those lies because they were done for a higher goal—to help Emmanuel, the love of her life, make a new album of twenty of their songs.

She didn't know how and to whom Emmanuel sold some songs. He even gave her some money. She brought it to her parents as evidence that she really had a job in Napoli. They were very glad about that and gave her permission not to attend school anymore but keep working—at least there was some use in the household of this "lazy girl" now. So Sandra was left without finishing grade six.

Emmanuel and his agents were working restlessly on different kinds of promotions. He obviously had some goal in mind, which Sandra had no idea about. She was busy with her part of the work—writing lyrics, singing for records, and providing crazy, unstoppable sex every night. She did not understand it, did not like it, did not feel it but just tolerated it, knowing subconsciously that it was a big part of the deal. She was madly in love and kept worshipping her idol no matter what.

Finally, the day came when Emmanuel got a phone call from his agent in the USA. Their last album was noticed. The agent suggested that he sign a contract. Emmanuel and his band were screaming from happiness, hugging one another, laughing, and jumping like crazy teenagers. The contract was for three years for thirty million dollars and came automatically with a green card for the whole band.

There was a lot of discussion about the details of the contract on the phone with the agent almost every day. Emmanuel was told that the US visa would be eligible only for him but not for Sandra.

"We can provide a visa for you and your family because you're famous," the agent said. "If you had a wife, no problem. But for a rookie cosinger, sorry, no. You can always find another cosinger here if needed."

"What the hell!" Emmanuel screamed in anger. "Are they, those Americans, crazy?" He knew perfectly well that all the success of the last album was because of Sandra, though he didn't tell her that and didn't want her to know. In their business, he was supposed to be the sun around which all the planets turned; but day by day, it came out that she was the one, and he knew that. If he would come to America to sing alone, there would be no success; the contract could be easily canceled along with all the millions of dollars.

"Well, baby"—he turned to Sandra—"let's go and get married."

His bandmates began laughing and screaming, "You, a married man? Gosh, it's unbelievable! Would you be married ever?"

"The thirty million to tolerate this inconvenience! To hell with it! Are you ready, baby?"

"I am fourteen," Sandra said sadly.

"What? Jeez, why didn't you tell me?"

"You didn't ask."

The bandmates began giggling and screaming more and teasing him that, instead of the USA, he would go to jail for child molestation and get registered as a sex offender. They were laughing almost to tears, but

Sandra got really scared that he would agree to move to America without her and leave her forever. She had no idea that she was the heart and core of this union. She couldn't imagine her life without him anymore. But he couldn't imagine his success without her anymore.

"Okay, let me think how much it would cost," Emmanuel said as he finally stopped laughing.

He made some phone calls, talked to an agent, and asked him to give some bribes; and a couple of days later, they went to the city hall where Sandra got her new birth certificate and passport showing that she was two years older. Sixteen was the official age when marriage was allowed at that time, and right there, right away, they got married. Now the US visa and the contract were safe. There was no ceremony, no white dress and veil, no father walking his daughter on the aisle, just a couple of bandmates who served as witnesses and an agent who brought the rings, which he bought on the way to the city hall. They had no time for frills; they should apply for the family visa immediately and then start packing their luggage for a new life in America.

When Sandra told her parents that she got married and was going to move with her husband overseas, they didn't believe it at first until she showed them her marriage certificate. And then much to her surprise, they approved. "At least you are a married woman now, and there is no danger that you will live in sin and sleep with someone out of wedlock," her father said.

Her mother added, smiling happily, "And you got yourself a very rich man. Good for you, my sweet child."

That was all. Sandra, who expected their protests in anger, even a scandal, was a bit disappointed. It looked like they were happy to get rid of her because she was "useless and lazy" anyway. If they loved her, they would be offended not to be at her wedding and also by the absence of any wedding in the first place. But they showed some kind of indifference, and it was very hurtful for her. She felt that her parents betrayed her.

However, her friends at school were very happy and excited, many were jealous, and many did not believe her until she showed them photos of her and Emmanuel exchanging rings at the city hall. In the end, they all asked for those photos with Emmanuel's autographs, and that made them absolutely content and satisfied. They all promised to write her letters as often as possible and begged Sandra to send hers and

Emmanuel's new records as a Christmas present in the future. That was how the fourteen-year-old Sandra, Mrs. Emmanuel Soley, moved to America, not knowing a word in English and not having the slightest idea what was waiting for her over there.

CHAPTER 56

J im was sitting on the grass under the hazelnut bush and waiting for Lada to bring him a new phone. He was seriously considering what to say when she saw his bruises. Lie that he fell from the stairs and broke his phone? He finally learned to lie to Mona for self-defense but to Lada, no, never. He truly loved her and knew quite well that real love shouldn't be based on lies. It could destroy the relationship, which he treasured more than anything, maybe even more than his music and his life altogether.

But then what? Tell the truth about Mona's assault and about his visit with Victor? It would make Lada too nervous and too worried, even scared for him, and he didn't want those feelings for her either. The problem had no solution. He put his palms on his temples and was thinking, thinking, thinking, trying to figure out what to say and analyzing every detail of events that happened two days ago.

As Jim tiptoed at midnight to Victor's room, he didn't want to knock or make any noise. He just pushed the door, it opened, and he entered, knowing that Victor probably expected him to come and wouldn't sleep. He was right. The light was on, and Victor was sitting on his workout bench at the far end of the room with his elbows on his knees. And he was smiling. That fact alone was pretty surprising. During his seven months at the group home, Jim never saw any expression on his zombielike face.

"Hi, Jim," Victor said. "Nice to meet you. Let me introduce myself—Special Agent John Delany, FBI." And he extended his arm to shake Jim's hand.

"W-w-what?" In shock, Jim plopped on his bum on the floor.

"But for you, only Victor—forever. Remember that. I am working a case here, undercover." He rose, approached Jim, and helped him stand up. "You can sit here," he said, pointing at the small step stool beside the weight-lifting bench.

Noticing that Jim looked at the step stool in bewilderment, not understanding why it was here in the first place, Victor explained, "I am using it to step up and down while holding weights on my shoulders."

"Well . . . oh . . . so you always pretend . . . those catatonic . . . conditions," Jim mumbled, shaking his head in disbelief.

"Not always. I've been here a year already since last July. From the beginning, this Mrs. Monster really poisoned me with those pills. They started working a couple of days after I swallowed the first one. They kind of paralyzed me mentally, gave me a little headache, not strong, tolerable, but it was buzzing in my brain all the time like a tiny beetle, and I couldn't react to anything. Thanks to you then, in April, you gave me one pill to dissolve."

"Actually, it was the second one," Jim prompted. "The first one I dropped and dissolved myself accidentally. Then the next day, you already got better. You said 'headache' then and dissolved the second pill. I guess, after that, you somehow evaded taking them."

"I just flush them into the toilet if they leave them on the table, but if a nurse or the monster is giving them to me and watching, I invented a trick. Look. My fingers are pretty big. However, the pill is small. I take it, squeeze it between my thumb and the next finger, and then move them inside my mouth. Pretending that I had dropped the pill inside, I drink the water from the glass that I'm holding in another hand. I am making it look like I swallowed it. I keep holding the pill between my fingers until those people are gone, and then I flush it."

"Wow," Jim said. "I didn't guess that your job required you to be such a good actor."

"Yeah, undercover always. Sometimes we're acting like drug dealers, bank robbers, drunks, druggies, even terrorists. Hell knows who. The main point—you should be believable. Otherwise, you're dead."

"It's funny that you're calling Mona 'Mrs. Monster.'" Jim giggled. "We, my girlfriend and I, call her the same. It's actually a really good match for all that she is doing here."

"I know," Victor said. "I saw some things during the last couple of months since I cleared my brain. Just yesterday morning in the kitchen, she was kissing the new bus driver."

"Is somebody already hired?"

"Yeah, as soon as you left to Hawaii, a very handsome African American guy about twenty-five, maybe twenty-seven, tall, strong with pretty good muscles, not worse than mine." Victor moved his chest and shoulders, playing with his muscles, and laughed quietly so as not to make much noise at night.

"That's okay." Jim laughed too. "Now she will be happy and not that angry."

"I wouldn't say that if I were you and looked in the mirror. You had quite a fight this evening. I was worried that she'll kill you. Sorry, I just couldn't interrupt. You understand that. It looked to me like she was jealous and turned berserk after she saw you kissing that girl on the porch. Did you have something going on with Mrs. Monster as well?"

"Yeah, but it's finished three months ago." Jim nodded, a bit confused. "It was a big mistake on my part. When I came here, I was very naive, like, you know, grandma's boy, experience zero. She manipulated me easily. You too?"

"No. She saw that I'm catatonic. What could she expect from a zombie? She did not even try. Jeez, I was kind of surprised about the new guy. By the way, his name is Jason. He is a nice fellow and only here one week, and she is already doing him."

"I was here only three days when she made her move on me." Jim chuckled. He felt good about this conversation with Victor. It was very friendly, funny, and manly, like a couple of guys would socialize over a glass of beer, sharing their experiences about women. He didn't do anything like that before ever. It gave him a chance to feel like a regular man. The possibility of having another man as a friend seemed very attractive to him as well.

"Last summer during my first days here, before she started feeding me those pills and I lost my mind, I saw her with Todd," Victor continued, "and with the previous bus driver, Ramah. After that, I didn't get anything at all in my head anymore. So I didn't know about you, Jim."

"I didn't know about Todd." Jim smirked. "What the hell! But I knew about Ramah for sure. She fired him because he got married and also because she lost the possibility to steal money from his father's grocery store. Actually, you know, Victor, I don't care much about her sex adventures. To me, it is more important that she is stealing money from me, the same as from everybody else here."

"And she is stealing your symphony too. I heard her talking on the phone with her daughter about that while you were in Hawaii. They are really waiting for you to finish that last part."

"They'll never get it. It's already gone to my girlfriend for safekeeping. But I don't understand why they need it."

"To make some money on it also, the same point again."

"So she is having sex for fun, stealing my symphony for money," Jim concluded, "and murders for money as well."

"Murders?" Victor lifted his brows.

"Yes. She poisoned Lily, a woman with the multiple sclerosis, which was in the room where Basil is now. You were catatonic at that time, so you didn't know anything about that. And now some days before I went to Hawaii, Maggie gave birth, and the monster killed her baby because a senator, Maggie's father, paid her to do so."

"Gave a birth?" Victor knitted his brows, now trying to remember. "That's what all the screaming that night was about? Are you sure that she murdered the baby?"

"I'm absolutely sure, but she said that Maggie did it. Could you arrest the monster for that finally?"

"Unfortunately, I can't yet." Victor shook his head. "I'm working here on another case about her connections with the Mafia. I can't tell you any details about that case now, but about those murders, as you said, you could be a good witness for us later, Jim. So be careful. She probably knows that about you witnessing as well."

"She does. That's why I plan to move out from here if I'll get money for that next month. I'm not sure about that yet," Jim said and then remembered. "Oh, about Mafia, she told me your story."

"What story?"

"I don't want to hurt you for saying this . . . but . . . your family was recently killed . . . and you became catatonic because of that . . . I'm very sorry . . . or was it a lie too? She is actually lying all the time."

"Partially true." A shadow run over Victor's face, and he sighed. "It happened about twenty-five years ago, when I was in business. That event forced me to became a policeman and then a detective. I didn't stop until I solved my own case. Those villains are on death row already for many years. Then I moved to the FBI. This case here is different, not related at all."

"So she was lying again," Jim concluded.

"I was working inside the Mafia, undercover," Victor continued. "But then I just disappeared for the bureau. My colleagues have no idea where I am today. They might even be thinking that I was killed a year ago. The Mafia placed me here as their member and hired Mrs. Monster to watch me and to keep me catatonic until they need me. I guess that they were suspecting I could be a cop. I heard her talking to them on the phone. They'll probably come here for me sometime in September. There's a big chance that they will try to kill me."

"Wow," Jim said. "What can you do about that?"

"That's why I'm talking to you, Jim," Victor added seriously. "I need help."

"But I'm kind of useless. You saw how I was fighting today. I was helpless even against a woman."

"Not that kind of help, Jim. I need a gun."

"Hmm." Jim lifted his palms, not knowing what to suggest. "We have some money left after Hawaii. I don't know if it would be enough for a gun."

"It's not about money." Victor shook his head. "The bureau would reimburse the money. The problem is we couldn't go to the store or order one on the internet. None of us could. We need an outside helper for that. I saw tonight that you were with this girl, kissing, and I thought maybe she could help if you ask."

"I . . . I don't know." Jim bit his lips, thinking gravely. "I really don't know. I don't even know how to ask such a thing. I don't want to scare her."

"Just try to explain to her that, with a gun, I could protect myself and you and other people too if something happened. Otherwise, I also would be useless. If she could buy a gun and ammo and bring it to you, you could meet her outside, put the stuff into your backpack, and bring them inside. And then at night, like today, pass it to me."

"Where will you keep it?" Jim wanted to know. "You can't carry it in your pocket. It would be visible. And in the room, the cleaning ladies will find it anyway. They clean usually very deep, at least in my room."

"I know. I already made a little hiding place under the carpet and put my very heavy weight-lifting equipment on top of it. They are cleaning all the way around, but they never lifted it. They just can't. They are too small and too weak for that. So it would be okay."

"Well," Jim said finally, "I will talk to Lada, I can promise that. But I can't imagine how she will react. I can't promise that she will agree. And I won't force her. So I can't guarantee you anything. Sorry, Victor. And just a simple question, why don't you call the bureau and ask them to bring you a gun?"

"If they knew where I am and also that I'm in danger, they'll come and rescue and remove me from here immediately. It's our code of ethics, our policy, not to leave a friend in danger ever. But I don't have enough evidence yet for the lawsuit to convict Mrs. Monster. Most of what I have is circumstantial, same as you have. She's quite good in hiding her deeds.

"If I was removed from the case and stopped now, all the work, which was done for years, would be in jeopardy, just in vain. Then Mrs. Monster and the Mafia will keep doing what they are doing and blossoming in it and laugh at us that we're useless. I can't lose all that I achieved. I don't want all my sufferings from those damn pills to be for nothing. It's too early to stop the investigation now. So please try to talk to your girl about a gun. If she refuses, it's okay. Then we'll think about other ways. At least you have tried. But there is one more point, Jim. I also need some help from you."

"Well, I would be happy to do something for you, but you know that my skills are very limited and are mostly those of a musician. I will do what I can do."

"You have a very sharp brain, Jim, and not only about music. I heard that the monster was screaming at you sometimes that you have an investigative mind. It's true. You have learned a lot during your time here, and you're good at noticing small details, comparing them and analyzing results of the comparison. It's a kind of detective work."

"I read everything about Sherlock Holmes in my childhood." Jim smirked.

Victor smiled, nodded, and continued, "You know I am going to work at the factory five days a week. I would like to ask for your help while I am at work. Before, you were busy with your symphony. Now you said that you already finished it, and it has gone to a safe place. So you have some free time, I guess. Would you mind doing some surveillance for me—to watch, to observe, to listen, to find out what the monster is doing and what she's talking about on the phone? She's conversing with the Mafia every second or third day. It's important for us to know what they plan to do and when we should expect it. It could save our lives, and it could help collect more evidence for the court. It would give us a chance to arrest Mrs. Monster and to convict her properly."

"I would be happy to do that, Victor, without a shade of a doubt," Jim said. "She killed Lily, who was kind of my friend. And she killed this poor baby and fed it to the rats in the basement. When I saw baby fingers and blood under the cage with her rats, everything turned upside down inside me. She's not human." His voice quivered with tears. "I don't know . . . they could have just given the baby up for adoption . . . and she got a necklace worth $200,000 as payment for this murder." Jim covered his face with both hands. He couldn't hold himself in check anymore and suddenly sobbed.

"Wow," Victor said and put his hand on Jim's shoulder to comfort him. "Are there rats in the basement? I suspected something like that, but I wasn't sure. Nobody ever went there. I was surprised when I got off the pills and my mind returned that I saw you going there at the end of April and in May. What did you do there?"

"She gave me the duty to wash the rats daily with a hose." Jim sniffed. "And wash away their droppings under the cage. That's where I saw the baby's fingers. She confirmed this, and she said that her animals deserved a treat—fresh meat. The baby was not human for her but just meat for the rats. Maggie didn't kill it. She was so happy she was laughing and shining when she showed me her baby." In despair, Jim sobbed even more; and Victor, seeing that, sat on the floor beside him and hugged him.

"Calm down, please," he said, patting his head. "I promise you, Jim, I'll do everything I can to combine a strong case against that monster."

"And I promise you, Victor, that I'll help you as much as I can," Jim uttered, lifting his face and looking at Victor with his wet eyes, full of devotion.

Now the sound of a car stopping in front of him returned Jim's mind to today's surroundings. He realized that he was sitting on the grass under the hazelnut bush and couldn't suppress a happy smile, seeing Lada jump out from the driver's door, run to him, and hug him.

"Here is your new phone, my love!" she exclaimed happily, giving him a small box. "I put it on my plan. For the phone company, you're a member of my family now." And she giggled mischievously as usual. But then she noticed the bruise under his eye.

CHAPTER 57

While Sandra was packing her small luggage for moving to America, she took a break to visit her maternal grandmother for a last hug and farewell. The old woman was over eighty, and she lived by herself at the far end of the village, with only a black cat as a companion. Usually, little Sandra came to sing for her at times, and Grandma told her fairy tales in return. They had a pretty strong bond for years, but it got weaker since Sandra grew older. She preferred to hang out with her friends. But now she felt a big need to see her granny before leaving forever.

The old woman hugged the girl. "You know, sweetie," she said, "life is not always a cakewalk. There could probably be some sorrows and difficult moments as everybody has at times. I want to give you something that could possibly help."

She took from a shelf a small gray marble statue of a very unusual shape. It was a naked young woman in a sitting posture. Her legs were hanging down, and her arms were crossed on her knees. Her head was lowered, so her face was not visible, but her long free hair hung down to her feet in front of her figure. Her body and hair created a circular shape. It was a masterpiece. The marble seemed to breathe as if it were alive, and the entire statue radiated an overwhelming sadness.

"This statue was in our family for generations," Grandma said. "We're calling her the Lady of the Sorrows. If you have some troubles or sufferings ever, just hug her, squeeze her to your chest, and hold tight. The marble will get warm, even hot. It will suck in all the bad things and feelings, and you'll be happy again. Everything bad will go away."

"Thank you, Granny," Sandra said, carefully taking the beautiful statue. "I don't think I'll ever need it. I am unbelievably happy. But it would be nice to have it anyway as a memory of you." She wrapped the statue in a soft scarf and placed it in her handbag, not putting such a breakable and emotionally memorable thing into her check-in luggage. In America, she always kept the statue on her bedside table in any house or hotel wherever she lived.

Against all her expectations, life in America turned out to be extremely difficult for Sandra. She discovered here two very important things about her new husband, whom she knew only for two months before marrying him. First, he was a workaholic. In combination with a great deal of composing talent, strong vocal experience, and really beautiful voice, it wasn't a bad thing. Quite the opposite, it was a sure ticket to big success, which came pretty soon because of his qualities.

But the amount of work required for this success was almost unbearable for a fourteen-year-old child, whom Sandra in reality was. However, it seemed that Emmanuel didn't care about that at all. He did not allow her to have a teddy bear to hug in bed, but she secretly hugged her grandma's Lady of the Sorrows every night when her husband slept after sex and wouldn't notice. The hot marble gave her the power to cope somehow and to survive.

Right away, Emmanuel hired a private teacher for Sandra, who didn't know a word in English, and she was obligated to take classes daily and to do homework nightly before sex and sleep. He even insisted that she speak to him in English only. It wasn't a bad thing either because she knew that knowledge of the language of the country where they were living in now was the main point of survival and was extremely important. But again, the amount of work got even bigger.

Every day at nine o'clock, they were already in the studio, recording songs with Emmanuel's bandmates, who all got green cards as well. It usually lasted until lunch or sometimes later, depending on how work was going. Then until dinner, Emmanuel and Sandra were working, just the two of them, in private, creating new songs. From five o'clock, Sandra had her daily English class for one hour, and after that started the rehearsals on stages or concerts, which lasted sometimes until midnight. Then she was supposed to do her homework in English and then to satisfy her husband with sex. By that time, she was usually exhausted, almost to death; and quite often, she just slept deeply during the session. Then when he was done, Emmanuel finally allowed her to sleep, if she wasn't asleep already. That permission usually was received at two or even three o'clock. Wake-up time was at seven o'clock to have a small breakfast and to get ready for the work in the studio again.

Emmanuel was extremely persistent with this routine for Sandra and did not allow any exceptions ever. The four or five hours of sleep were definitely not enough for her young and still developing body, and the nightly hour of sex was too much. But he absolutely didn't care. Practically, he exploited her amazing natural voice and her body viciously, but she didn't get it. She thought it was her fault that she was sleepy all the time and exhausted and could barely hang on, but she tried hard, desperately wishing to make him happy. She also was very thankful for him for making her, as he promised, a famous singer, and she tried to be grateful for that.

The enormous work wasn't in vain. The money was falling in their joint bank account like a mountain waterfall. In just two weeks, they passed the first million-dollar level. Emmanuel used a lot of the money to increase the business. He hired some more singers as a choir and about a dozen ballet dancers for background. It helped. The flow of money got even stronger.

But money had no use for Sandra at all. She had no time to get any pleasure from this money ever. Emmanuel never invited her out for a good dinner in a beautiful restaurant, for example. They usually ate burgers and fries, pizza, or Chinese takeout during the short breaks in the studio, together with the band, from paper plates and plastic forks, sitting on the floor. Those were not the typical lunches and dinners for millionaires.

Sandra always wore T-shirts and jeans during studio work and rehearsals or special bright, shiny costumes and makeup for performances. She didn't even have one beautiful dress or other outfit nor a pair of normal dress shoes, like other teens. Emmanuel thought that she didn't need them; where could she wear them anyway? And she silently accepted her practically slavish life conditions. They didn't travel anywhere except for concerts and tours, but those were all for business and didn't provide any sightseeing or entertainment—no pleasure, no rest, no relaxation, no beautiful experiences, just work, work, work.

At fourteen years old, Sandra was completely robbed of her education, her school, her friends, her chances to go for simple walks, to ride a bicycle, to play ball outside, to dance or swim with friends. She was thrown from childhood straight into adult life, skipping the teen years. Her charming, incredible idol and hero, Emmanuel, literally robbed the cradle, and she became the victim of that robbery, having no idea of what was happening to her.

But all these problems weren't the worst. The second discovery that Sandra made in America was that her beloved husband was a big womanizer. In spite of the fact that they were married now, he didn't miss any woman whom he saw. Sandra had heard some hints about that from his band members even while being with him at home in Italy, but she didn't get them at that time and actually didn't care. She was too excited and too much of a little girl. She believed wholeheartedly all those standard statements that he used with her just as with every woman he ever met. She loved him and was sure that he loved her too. What more proof did she need? He married her. Wasn't it enough proof?

Only after a couple of months in America, Sandra discovered that he slept at least once with every producer, tailor, makeup artist, assistant, dancer, and musician who worked with them in their business, even with her own English teacher, who was a serious lady far over fifty. There wasn't any age range for him. He even invented his own proverb. "Every woman younger than eighty is a beauty, so why not?" His devoted bandmates admired, approved of, supported, and always giggled about it. Sandra even guessed that they all probably laughed at her for being his stupid little blind wife.

However, to her own surprise, this discovery didn't hurt Sandra a lot. Of course, it was not a nice feeling, but she disliked sex so much that when she noticed that her husband was absent sometimes at night, she got really happy. It was her chance to finally have a break from him and have a good sleep for more hours than usual. Then he began appearing at home at night less and less often.

When Sandra confronted him about that, he answered pretty defiantly, "What am I supposed to do, baby? You're a child. You cheated me right from the beginning, not revealing your age. You're not a woman yet and don't have any feelings at all as I see. I don't like to fuck a dead body. I am not a necrophiliac after all." And he really laughed.

She got very angry and yelled at him defiantly as well, "Do what you want! Just don't bring me an STD, please!"

"Oh, no." He giggled even more. "Don't worry about that. I always have a pocketful of condoms. Never in my life have I had sex without them."

"You did with me all the time!" she screamed, angrily stomping in despair.

"Jeez, I knew you were a virgin. There was no danger at all. And now you're the devoted, faithful wife. I appreciate this. So calm down, please, baby. I still love you very much."

"Go to hell," she concluded, surprisingly calming down. "And do what you want. I don't care."

"That's my girl." He chuckled happily and would have given her a high five had she not already run to another room.

Sandra wasn't really jealous and probably told him the truth that she didn't care. His behavior was disgusting, but she knew that there was nothing to worry about—all those women meant nothing to him, only some kind of entertainment. He used to have fun before he met her. It was his regular lifestyle.

She was much more important for him. She was his legal wife, business partner, cosinger, cowriter of his songs. Without her, his business would collapse; and his business, his music, his songs were what Emmanuel loved and treasured more than anything in the world. They were his life, the meaning and the core of his very existence. Nothing ever would force him to break up with her, to dump her, to leave her as long as she could sing and write lyrics for the songs. And Sandra knew that she'd sing forever and write forever. So there was no danger unless he fell in love with another woman, real love, true love, the kind of love for which people kill, commit suicide, leave family with little children, destroy their own business and their own life, practically become crazy.

But even being a child herself, Sandra already perfectly understood that these kinds of things could never happen with Emmanuel. It was not in his character. He was too light headed and too much of a fun lover. True, mad, obsessive love would be too serious for him; and for that reason, it would never happen. God, if she only knew how wrong she was.

CHAPTER 58

"What happened, Jim? Who hit you?" Lada screamed, hugging him and looking attentively at his bruise, which already started to fade but became even more multicolored, though a bit paler. "Why? It's absolutely unacceptable!"

Jim felt relieved that she didn't see the dozens of other ones that were hidden under his clothes. She would be even more shocked, and he didn't want that for her. "Mona," he answered, blushing. "She got very angry that we were sitting on the porch there."

"Yeah, I noticed." Lada shook her head and sat next to him, still not moving her eyes away from the bruise. "Unbelievable! She obviously was angry at me that I came on her property. But why hit you? Why not me?"

It was clear to Jim that she didn't get the jealousy point and absolutely didn't suspect about his previous affair. That was another big relief. His past was extremely shameful for him now, and he didn't want Lada to know about that ever. It was dirty and disgusting, but Lada was too pure and too sacred for things like that, he was sure. Mentally and morally, this discovery would kill her love for him. He believed this truth should stay unraveled forever.

"She has no right to hit her patients," Lada continued indignantly, "absolutely no right. We should go to the police, Jim, right now. She should be fired."

"She can't be fired. She owns that business," Jim stated.

"Well . . ." Lada grabbed his hand and stood up, pulling him to stand up too. "We'll think about it. Let's go to my car."

"Okay," Jim agreed, "we really need to go to your car because it's about time for the guys to return from work on the bus. They and the new bus driver could see us sitting here and tell Mona. Let's drive about a mile ahead on the highway and stop somewhere in the forest. We won't go to the police now. I need to talk to you very seriously first. Something happened here that you need to know."

"I felt that, Jim. That's why I was worried like crazy about you when you didn't call," Lada said. "Okay then, maybe not the police, but we should start looking for an apartment for you right away. You need to move away from here immediately. It's not safe and not a nice place for you anymore."

"Yes, my love, just listen to my story first, please."

Lada stopped her car in a small clearing about half a mile past the group home on the highway and killed the ignition. "Okay, Jim, I'm listening." She hugged him, kissed him on the cheek, and put her head on his shoulder. "Tell me everything, please."

He skipped the fight with Mona, letting Lada think that it was only one slap on his face and nothing else, and concentrated on Victor's story. She listened very quietly, not interrupting, not asking any questions, not even looking at him. She stared somewhere at the side. As he finished, she shook her head like she was still in disbelief and took a deep sigh.

"So all these mean that we're not going to look for a new apartment for you, Jim," were her first words when he finished the story. "You must stay here now and do some work. You must help Victor. Actually, it would be a great revenge to Mrs. Monster for this bruise of yours. I'll never forgive her for hurting you. Now do you remember, Jim, I told you that I'm living an adventurous life because of you?"

"Yes, I do. I remember every word you said to me ever."

"So I think it is time to prove that it is really adventurous. I don't know if I'll be allowed to buy a gun, but I guess why not? I'm an adult, not mentally ill, no criminal record. And after buying a new phone for you, there is still about one thousand dollars left on my Mastercard. I expect it would be enough for a gun, maybe not a big one nor a fancy one but just something regular. I'll try. And . . . probably I'm not supposed to tell anything to anybody about that, like to BB or Rita, right?"

Jim nodded. "Yes," he said. "I trust them, of course, but when many people know some secret, it always somehow comes out anyway, maybe even by accident. Victor's life depends on us now. It's a big responsibility. It's better when no one knows, just you and me."

"Yeah, Victor." Lada nodded thoughtfully. "I remember him pretty well. He was always on my bus, always motionless and speechless, like a real zombie. I started working here in April, so he was already off his pills. God, he's really an amazing actor. He should go to Hollywood."

"We joked with him about that," Jim said. "So seriously, please make sure that we're keeping his secret. Could you promise that to me?"

"Okay," Lada agreed and added, "I'm sorry that I'm so quiet, Jim, not laughing, not kissing you. I am kind of overwhelmed right now and can't even almost say anything. It's just so different from the life that I live regularly—I mean, at home with family, kids, Mama, dog, cats . . . university, music, orchestra . . . I don't know. I am still in shock a bit. And the other part of my life is with you—your symphony, our trip to Hawaii, your kisses, our dreams about your success, that ring you gave me . . . and you yourself, looking so little and weak, but now you're a kind of FBI agent, and I am helping you with this. Unbelievable! Oh my god! How could it happen?" She covered her face with both hands.

"Please don't cry," Jim requested quietly, putting his hand on her shoulder.

"I'm not crying at all. I am just thinking and trying to digest everything. Today I was sure that I found the biggest surprise for you, but yours surpassed mine a million times. I love you, Jim, and I'll be beside you always. Even if you go to the battle on barricades, I'll go with you."

"I don't think there will be a battle." He laughed. "And even if there would be, I don't expect us to be involved. At the end of September, we will be at the university, preparing for our concert, but not here. Victor will deal with his gun by himself. And what was your surprise? You are very dressed up today. Did you go to some special event?"

"I had an interview this morning."

"Looking for a new job?"

"No." She shook her head and finally laughed for the first time during this meeting. "I did something for you, Jim, but I still won't tell you until I get results. My surprise is not ready to be revealed yet, but I hope it will be soon."

"I can wait. It's okay." Jim smiled too. "But for now . . . do you want another *education session*? I'm anxious to kiss you. I missed you during these past two days like crazy."

"I missed you too. But surprisingly, I don't want our education session now." Lada giggled. "I'm not in the mood for kissing. I am still digesting what happened and kind of all shaking inside. I'm more in the gun mood. Let me drive you back to the group home, and I'll go and make my research on the topic—where you could buy a gun. And also, how could you love the smallest-in-the-world FBI agent with a big bruise under his eye?"

They both laughed and continued laughing as she started her car and laughed all the way to the group home.

CHAPTER 59

During the first year of their hard work and successful tour in the USA, Emmanuel and Sandra passed the level of $180 million in their bank account but didn't get much happier. He kept dashing from woman to woman, pretending that he was having fun and enjoying his life; however, it was obvious that something was seriously missing in his soul, in spite of his obsession with singing and composing new songs. Sandra, on the contrary, slept alone almost every night, hugging her Lady of the Sorrows and whispering her prayers in hope that God would forgive her husband and that they would be a happy and devoted family one day.

Then she noticed that something really changed in Emmanuel's behavior. He stopped giggling and laughing all the time and became quieter and thoughtful and, at moments, extremely angry. He mostly started sleeping at home again, but it wasn't good for Sandra. He attacked her with pretty wild sex that felt rude and revengeful, and when he was done, he often squeezed his fists and bit the pillow in despair and, once, even sobbed. She thought that he probably was drunk; however, it wasn't a usual characteristic of him. Normally, he never drank, smoked, or did drugs so as not to harm his voice.

Sandra felt such pity for him at the moment that she hugged him and tenderly patted his hair on the back of his head while his face was dug into a pillow. "What's happening, darling?" she whispered fondly.

It was like the last straw that made him explode. Emmanuel abruptly sat on the bed, hugged Sandra, and suddenly cried desperately, like a child on the chest of his mother. "She is a stupid idiot! She doesn't understand. I love her, I want her, and she doesn't understand!"

"Who?" Sandra inquired in shock.

"This fucking dancer . . . Lily."

"Oh God," Sandra whispered. She understood perfectly now.

From the twelve background dancers in their group whom Emmanuel hired at the beginning of their American tour, three were men and nine women. Emmanuel slept already with eight of them, but one still stayed a mystery and proved to be very stubborn and harsh. Her name was Lily Donovan, and she was a lesbian.

Lily didn't hide that fact; quite the opposite, she was very proud of it. Everybody in their business knew that and accepted that without any problem. Emmanuel was the only one who was sure that being a lesbian was just a stupid habit and that she would easily cancel it when he made his move on her. Of course, he was so charming and amazing. Not one woman in the world had refused him ever. It would be impossible to reject him. It would be unthinkable. Lily was the first one who did it.

She was petite with small breasts. Her hair was cut very short, about one centimeter long, and dyed almost white. From a distance, she looked like a twelve-year-old boy. Something was very unusual in her, especially her enormous deep blue eyes, similar to the eyes of aliens in Hollywood movies. However, she was really beautiful in her specialty and uniqueness.

In contrast to Emmanuel, Lily drank cider all the time and smoked cigarettes and marijuana. She didn't need to care about her voice, and those habits did not affect her dancing at all. She was eighteen, just three years older than Sandra, but a hundred times more educated and more mature mentally, morally, and spiritually, though she didn't pray and didn't go to church.

Lily came from a very rich and educated high-society family. Her father was one of the most famous researchers and academicians in the USA and also a devoted Catholic. When Lily announced to her parents, at the age fifteen, that she was a lesbian, they literally threw her on the street and prohibited her from coming back home ever. So she made her way in life all by herself. She saw, experienced, and survived a lot and, because of that, matured early. At the age of eighteen, she sounded almost twice her age.

For Emmanuel, it was a pleasure talking to her after she surprised him once with her knowledge. "Shame on you, Em," she said. "You're an Italian, and you don't know the history of your own country and nation? Let me tell you something about ancient Romans, which is so common that everybody should know, especially every Italian."

That was how they began talking. For him, it was so unusual, interesting, and intriguing. He started coming every day to the dance studio where Lily did her daily stretching exercises to watch her and to talk to her heart to heart. Emmanuel himself was surprised at how talkative he became with her. He told her everything about himself that he hadn't told anyone in the world ever—about his father's death, his mother's illnesses, his difficult and poor upbringing, his work as a fisherman during his teen years, trying to save some money and take care of his younger brother, who died later in a car crash. Then he talked about how he started singing unexpectedly, even for himself, sometime after nineteen; about his tense relationship with his dying mother; about his feelings of disappointment toward church and religion; about his first girlfriend, first music teacher, first concert, first original song he composed.

His first song, "The Endless Water," happened accidentally on the boat. Emmanuel was staring at the horizon of the sea and felt that his heart was literally melting. The beauty of the water was unbelievable, endless, unspeakable. Something clicked in his brain, and he suddenly began singing. The fellow fishermen were surprised because he never did it before. "Hey, Em, what is that song? I never heard it!" one of them shouted.

"I don't know. It's like buzzing in my head, like it sings by itself, just pouring out from my throat. Maybe it's mine . . . I don't know . . . original?"

That evening in the bar that they frequented, Emmanuel got some beer for bravery, climbed on the stage, and sang this song. The host band slowly began playing along with him. He was very nervous and not confident but unexpectedly got a standing ovation from his accidental audience. It was the beginning of his career, though later that evening he even cried backstage from uncertainty—he craved to sing more, but he couldn't leave the fishing boat. He needed money and also needed to see, feel, and smell the vastness of the water farther from the coast, where it was really endless.

He told this story to Lily and even sang her "The Endless Water." "It was your first song?" she screamed. "Jeez, you're a fucking genius, Em. Why didn't you include it in your concerts? It should be in all your albums, you silly. It's so good that I would hug you if you were a woman, Em. Hell, I would probably even have sex with you if you were a woman."

He suspected that his first song wasn't good enough, but Lily's opinion meant everything to him. "The Endless Water" was renewed with Sandra and was included in their next album. It alone brought them an extra twenty million dollars.

Emmanuel didn't know why, but he really opened his heart to Lily. He gave everything to her that was hidden somewhere deep in his soul. Then he suddenly realized why. He was in love with her, absolutely, crazily, madly in love—so in love that he was ready to die for her if she wanted. This discovery shocked him. He understood that he physically needed her, craved her, and wanted to own her forever and have unstoppable sex with her right away, immediately, right now.

During their conversations, Emmanuel was usually sitting on the floor by the wall, watching Lily while she was practicing the splits, rolling through the room there and back, or jumping high, almost flying in the air. She was unbelievably flexible. He was always thinking that she would be the same in bed. He was anxious to try.

"Why are you staring so intense?" she asked once.

"I'm just wondering how God could create such an amazing beauty."

"Come on, Em, cut the bullshit." Lily laughed in her husky voice. "You do know that I'll never sleep with you, don't you? Save your meaningless standard statements for other women."

"If you just drop your stupid habit—"

"It's not a habit! Go to hell, you idiot! It's who I am. And it will never change, not in any situation and any circumstance."

"What if I just hug you and kiss you, and then we'll see?"

"If you approach me in less than one meter, I'll kill you," Lily warned him seriously. "You know, I have a gun in my purse to protect myself from idiots like you."

Yes, Emmanuel knew. He saw her gun already. But he still had hope and believed that she would change her mind one day. He also didn't understand himself why he permitted her to talk to him in such a disrespectful tone while he was her boss and could fire her at any given moment.

"Well," Lily continued, "I don't understand you, Em, why you behave like that and why you are always pretending to be such a shallow person. You're a very spiritual guy in reality and have a very deep soul. I can see that, and I feel that in all our conversations. Just think about it and don't sell yourself that cheap. You're humiliating yourself."

"So you appreciate me?" He smiled happily.

"Yes, I do. I practically haven't had such interesting and spiritual discussions with a man ever as I did with you. And I love you very much as a friend."

"So you love me too?" he exclaimed.

"Just as a friend, emotionally and spiritually, yes, of course. Otherwise, I wouldn't talk to you."

"So you agree that we love each other?"

"Yes, we do," Lily confirmed harshly, a bit angrily. "But it's not what you mean. And what you mean will never happen. Remember, please, that word, *never*. Never! And stop talking about that. I'm tired of these stupidities. You're a very smart person, Em. Then stop pretending to be silly."

He did stop talking. From now on, he was just sitting silently, hungrily watching her every movement, and undressing her with his eyes. Then he usually came home and poured out all his passion and unsatisfied sexual desires on his naive and uneducated fifteen-year-old wife.

Sandra was scared and didn't know what to do. Her prayers didn't help. Finally, she decided to talk to Lily, though a bit cautiously because Lily was pretty well known as being very harsh. However, it turned out unexpectedly nice. Lily gave her a friendly hug and confirmed that she'd never take her husband from her.

"You know, Sandy," she said, absolutely calm, "actually, I am in love and in a relationship right now with a woman. Her name is Bertha. She is much older than you and me. She is in her forties, a university professor, very well educated, and clever. She loves me too, and at the same time, she cares about me, almost like a mother I don't have anymore.

"You probably did hear that our gay and lesbian community is fighting for our civil rights. We sent a petition to the government, demanding our right to get married. It was refused, of course, but we keep fighting. And if one day in my life same-sex marriage is allowed, I will marry Bertha without a shadow of a doubt. I love her forever. So I swear that you're safe with Em. I don't want him and don't need him at all, just for friendly chat sometimes. Don't worry, he'll be with you forever too. He told me your voice means the world to him."

"Just the voice?" Sandra whispered with tears. "Not me."

"Don't worry, he'll be back to you emotionally too. I'm sure," Lily reassured her. "He's just obsessed now with power and control issues. I guarantee that he doesn't love me either. He is just suffering because he can't suppress me and own me, like he did with the other women. I'm not hurting him. His own powerlessness does. He always used to be a God, but with me, he feels like he's nothing. It's a pain for him, but it will pass.

"Actually, I have an idea what I can do for you, Sandy. I'll just go, move somewhere to another city far, far away. Yeah, I'll talk today with Bertha about that. She and I, we both should find new jobs and a new place to live because Em is getting really annoying."

Sandra became much happier after this conversation. It calmed her down and soothed her worries.

However, some days after, Emmanuel turned even much more insane. Probably, Lily told him about her plan to leave. The crazy attacks of mad sex poured on her head again and became more and more awful. Every night after that, the hugging of the Lady of the Sorrows became extremely important for Sandra. But when one evening she pulled her arm to take it from the bedside table, she was shocked to discover that the statue was missing.

"Where it is? What happened?" Sandra exclaimed in horror. "It fell down? Broke? Oh my God, what would I do without her?" Crying, she looked attentively everywhere, searched the whole place, and then decided to ask Emmanuel. He was somewhere in a bar with friends and was probably drunk, but still, it was worth to ask anyway. She took a taxi and appeared in the bar unexpectedly.

"Where is my statue? Did you see it?" Sandra screamed, approaching him. "Did you touch it? Where is it?"

Everybody around became silent and looked at them. That was quite a surprise for their bandmates. No one ever saw Sandra mad like that. She was mostly very shy and quiet all the time.

"Come on, baby, what the hell?" Emmanuel answered, pretty agitated by her behavior as well. "You don't need it. I gave it to Lily as a farewell present to remember me."

"What? You have no right to do that! It's mine. It was in my family for generations. My granny gave it to me! It's my treasure."

"Well . . . not anymore." Emmanuel laughed defiantly as he always did before. From his anger and despair of losing Lily, he was obviously turning back to his usual self now. And what was new, he even started to drink.

Sandra swung her arm and slapped him in the face so strong that the red prints of her fingers got clearly visible on his cheek. Emmanuel jumped up and swung his arm to hit her back, but one of his band members stood up in front of him and covered Sandra. "What the hell, Em!" he yelled. "Are you crazy? Do you want it to be in every newspaper tomorrow? Don't be an idiot! We don't need this kind of fame! Shut up before someone calls the media. Let's go, Sandy. I'll drive you home." He hugged Sandra by her shoulders and walked her out from the bar.

"Thank you, Doug." She sniffed, still crying. "But not home, please. Let's go to Lily's hotel first. I will take my statue back from her."

But when they arrived in the hotel, they were told that Miss Donovan left this morning without leaving a forwarding address. Nobody had any idea where. Sandra's family's treasure, the Lady of the Sorrows, was gone forever.

The next morning, Sandra discovered that she was pregnant.

CHAPTER 60

During the next three days, Lada didn't appear at the group home. She was busy with her research for an affordable gun. Also, Boris asked her to help a bit at the printing lab, trying to finish the spread of Jim's last scores into lines for the orchestra musicians. It was a long and tedious job, and it didn't go fast enough in his opinion. He had a lot of other work to do, so his little sister's help would be very useful.

However, Lada and Jim talked on the phone a lot, two, three, or more times per day. For Jim, it took a while to get used to his new phone. It was more modern and developed technologically than the old one, but in time, he finally figured out how it worked.

Boris told Lada about Sharon Lainer's attempt to introduce Jim's symphony as her own, and she warned Jim, but he already knew that anyway and wasn't very surprised. One night he discussed that with Victor, and they decided to wait a bit and to collect more evidence to arrest Mona and her daughter together, maybe closer to the concert or even at the concert.

Jim and Victor invented their own secret source of communication. When Victor needed to say something important to Jim, he coughed a couple of times during dinner. When Jim needed to discuss something in private with him, he dropped a spoon or fork on the floor, pretending that it happened accidentally. In these cases, Victor didn't lock his door at night, and Jim came for the next orientation sessions.

Not working on his symphony, not washing rats, and not having the internet anymore, Jim had a lot of free time. Now he was spending most days sitting in the living room in Victor's favorite armchair while Victor was at work and reading available books. At the same time, he was watching Mona's every step and listening to her every word but so far didn't get anything of importance.

Jim talked on the phone with Lada only in his room, and when he was leaving the room, he usually hid the phone under the mattress. He never took the phone out, worrying that Mona might notice it and break it again. It all turned out to be fun and adventurous as Lada considered, and Jim agreed with that now. Some feeling of danger that Mona could poison him still nestled deep in his brain, but he suppressed it by drinking only from sealed cans or bottles. Also, he was only eating something, mostly soup, that he took out from the big bowls on the dinner table that were designated for everybody—the patients, nurses, cleaning ladies, bus driver, and Mona herself—to make sure that there wasn't any poison for him.

For now, everything was safe. Mona ignored him, and he paid the favor back, but they managed to coexist in the group home somehow. He wasn't sure, but it felt like Mona was waiting for something from him. What for? He didn't know. It was just his guess.

During these days, Jim had a chance to make the acquaintance of the new bus driver, Jason. It would be impossible not to agree with Victor's opinion that he was a pretty nice, helpful fellow and a very handsome one. It was sad that Mona grabbed him right away for her own use. But it was up to Jason. He was an adult and was capable of making his own decisions and taking care of himself. If he fell for it, then it must be his choice and not Jim's business at all.

Finally, Lada called and said that she had a gun and ammunition and obtained a permit to carry it, and she would bring it tomorrow morning. Jim took his backpack and went outside to meet her, as usual, under their hazelnut bush on the corner from the group home's driveway to the highway. It was a very hot day, and the sky was completely clear, piercing blue, and endless. The birds were singing, especially a little skylark that was flying around, above the field of wheat that spread far away behind the bushes. The wheat was very tall and bright yellow already. It could hide Jim completely. Even if Lada walked there, only her head would be visible. *It's actually a great place for us to sit*, Jim thought. *We could talk in the middle of that field, and no one would hear or see us ever. And this lark is so cute and is singing so beautifully.*

When Lada appeared, he suggested that they go for a walk into the field. "Okay," she agreed. "Then I should park my car a bit farther at the edge of that field. I don't want to leave it too far out of my sight because, on the back seat, there is a folder with your scores of the last part of the symphony. I was helping BB print it out, and we are finally finished, so he asked me to take it home. But I'll do that later. I missed you so badly, Jim. I didn't want to waste our time driving home first and then here."

She took his backpack to help him carry it while they were walking. Then they made a bit of free room, bending some stems of the wheat. Jim pulled out one of their Hawaiian beach towels, spread it on the ground, and sat on it. Lada took a package from her purse, unwrapped the cover, and handed the gun to him. It was brand new and smelled like metal and grease. The ammunition was packed into two long plastic boxes.

"I don't know how good it is," she said apologetically. "If Victor wants some exact brand, he should have given you instructions about that. For now, I got this one, and I hope he'll be glad."

"Thank you, my love." Jim smiled happily. "With that, I think our job is done for today." He put the boxes of ammo on the bottom of his backpack and the gun on top of them and moved it aside from the towel. "Now an education session, please."

Lada laughed. "You know, Jim," she said, "I was thinking a lot and analyzing what was going on inside me. When I am picturing your face, your lips . . . I don't know, I am turning crazy. It's like everything is burning inside here." She put her hand on the lower part of her stomach. "It's not just butterflies. It's intense, almost like a pain. It's unbearable. It's probably what you men are saying with the words *I want you.*"

Jim nodded, blushing a bit and biting his lips, guessing where she was going with this.

"I accepted your ring. I love you, and I know that you love me. I think I'm completely ready if we make love. The only point is you know that I am not a virgin because of that awful assault, but in reality, I am a virgin mentally. I absolutely don't know what to do and what to expect. Of course, I saw in the movies—"

"I know what to do," Jim interrupted her and put his hand on top of her hand. "Is that what you mean? You're not sure that I know?"

"Yes," she whispered, blushing as well. "Did you ever have sex?"

He nodded again silently. He was really dreading the next question.

"Was it the same girlfriend who taught you kissing and then dumped you?"

"Well, Lada, I never forced you to tell me any bad things from your past. You told me only what you wanted and when you wanted to tell. For now, please, I really don't want to talk about my past story and maybe never will. It's our time. It's very sacred to me, and I am begging you, please forget about anything other than us."

"Sorry, Jim, but I'm struggling, I'm just trying to understand. I'm scared. I don't know what it would be like. Was it bad with her?"

Jim took a deep breath. "Yes, the relationship was very bad," he answered as he felt that he was yielding a bit.

"And the sex?"

"So-so, tolerable. Sex couldn't be good if there is no love."

"Then why did you do that if there was no love?"

"I was stupid. I was naive. It was a mistake. Please stop it." He covered his face with both hands. "I can't talk about that anymore, please!"

"Okay." Now Lada took a deep breath. "I'm sorry, Jim. I'm very sorry. Please just know that you are the only one with whom I can talk about these things. I can' t talk to my mom—she is too old fashioned and judgmental—or to BB, of course, or even to Rita. You're the only one I have in the world, and I love you. So please help me with that."

She was almost ready to cry, and Jim completely gave up. He pushed her fondly on the shoulder to lie down and began to kiss her with all the passion he was capable of. "Don't be scared," he whispered between the kisses. "I know everything, and I promise you, everything will be good. I love you more than anything in the world, and I would never hurt you in any way, I swear. Just close your eyes, relax, and concentrate on your feelings. And listen to this bird that is singing above us. It's our love song that we'll remember forever."

Lada didn't say a word, just answered his kisses, and the little lark in the sky kept singing and singing for them, flying very high in circles.

CHAPTER 61

T he discovery that Sandra was pregnant made her really happy. She knew many people in their village in Italy who weren't faithful to their wives, but as soon as a baby was born, they became very devoted fathers and family men. The tiny, little creature changed them with its irresistible charm and cuteness. It could be a good chance for her to return Emmanuel to their little family. After the loss of his obsessive passion to Lily and the scandal in the bar, he practically wasn't home at nights anymore. He didn't talk much with Sandra before, only about business during work on albums and rehearsals. Now he didn't talk to her at all.

However, she wrote on purpose lyrics for two new songs about his love for Lily and palmed them off on him at the studio, implying, *Hey, write the music to that.* Those became "The Lonely Tears" and "The Clouds on the Sun," their most popular songs ever. Emmanuel was sobbing while working on them in the studio. Even performing them onstage, he was really crying, which everybody thought was high-quality acting. Only Sandra and he knew that it was what he truly endured at that time. He even said to her, "Thank you, girl." And he gave her a little hug. Sandra finally felt proud of herself and appreciated by him. And she found the nerve to tell him about her pregnancy at last.

But in spite of her expectations, it turned out really bad. He didn't get excited at all, just shrugged. "What the hell. Let's go to a doctor and get an abortion immediately. We don't need these obstacles in our life. It is unbearable enough even without screaming babies."

"No!" Sandra yelled angrily. "Never!"

Point one was that she was Catholic and knew that God prohibited killing any life. But most importantly, the baby was her dream. She craved to have someone who would love her unconditionally and whom she would be able to hug every night to warm up her soul. She needed the baby to calm herself down, to replace her lost Lady of the Sorrows.

"Jeez, Sandy, we're still on contract," Emmanuel explained to her at first almost calmly. "You can't go onstage with a bloated tummy and look like a balloon. You also could lose the beauty of your voice. Even temporarily, it would not be acceptable. We have no right to take any breaks in our touring. It's absolutely impossible. Forget it."

He even forced her to see the doctor, who confirmed her pregnancy but explained that it was too early for the abortion. "You could come in about three to five weeks from now," he suggested.

Every night Sandra was sitting and thinking of what to do. She didn't care about their contract, about their touring, about their singing and writing lyrics for his new songs anymore. She cared only about her baby. The only chance to keep it was to dupe her husband and to lie to him that the abortion was already done. Why not? He was cheating on her unstoppably. Why couldn't she do it at least once for a holy purpose—saving her child's life?

"Okay, Emmanuel," she pretended to agree. "You're right. I will go to this doctor and do this procedure for sure. And I'll do it alone. I'm your wife, and I'm listening to you."

Being almost a child herself, Sandra didn't give much thought to what could happen later, when her stomach would get bigger and when the pregnancy would become noticeable to everybody. What would she tell Emmanuel then? Confess her lie? Or just run away and never see him again? *I'll think about that later*, she decided. *For now, I should be just a good actress and play my role.*

After several weeks, she chose the day when Emmanuel was extremely busy with some business problems and obviously couldn't go with her and said, "I'm taking a taxi and going to the doctor . . . you know . . . for this procedure."

"Okay, okay, good luck." He just waved his hand at her to leave and kept doing what he was preoccupied with.

My God, she thought, *what support from a "loving husband"? What if I really would do that? Is it how he will support me and help me?* It was the first time in the two years of their marriage that Sandra realized that she began hating him. Yes, everything that she was doing felt right, no doubt. He really deserved to be lied to.

In the evening, when Emmanuel appeared home for a short moment, she was lying in bed, crying, pretending to be sick and in pain after the procedure. "Did you get rid of this garbage?" he asked fast, on the go.

"Yes." She sniffed and added in a crying voice, "I wanted you to be happy, so I did it for you."

"Very well." He waved his hand again like she was an annoying fly. "I am happy. Thank you. See you in the studio in the morning." And he left for the night as usual.

Sandra felt proud of herself again—how cunningly she duped him. She just didn't expect one thing—pretty soon the morning sickness began torturing her daily, and she didn't know and didn't understand what was going on. She decided that it was punishment from God for her lie, and she thought that she was dying. Luckily for her, its attacks were usually happening early in the morning before she had breakfast. At that time, Emmanuel never was at home, so he didn't notice anything at first.

Her sickness continued for a couple of weeks, but then instead of disappearing, it got worse. When she threw up a couple of times in the studio during recording and then a couple more at evening rehearsals, many band members realized what was going on. Finally, someone told Emmanuel, "What the hell is happening with Sandy? Does she have stomach cancer, or what? You should use condoms, bro. Look at her. She is going to break our contract."

When Emmanuel came home to talk to her, Sandra got really scared. He looked so bad, almost unrecognizable. His face was distorted with anger and also, surprisingly, with despair that all his life, all his success, all his fame, all his business that he lived for was collapsing because of her. And after that collapse, the money would be collapsing as well later.

"What's going on?" he asked, narrowing his eyes. His voice was not loud but shaking with malice and hate for her. "Are you pregnant again? It's impossible. I didn't fuck you since Lily left. And I'm sure you're not fooling around. So you probably lied to me and didn't do that abortion. What the hell! You shouldn't do that. We were quite organized together. We were blossoming in success. I never lied to you. Why are you doing this to me and to yourself as well? Why destroy all that we built together?"

"You never lied to me?" Sandra exclaimed through her tears. "You are the one who is fooling around all the years that we're together!"

"But I never lied. I always told you that you're a freaking child but not a woman to satisfy me. I tried to be a good husband at first, believe me. I tried very hard. Maybe I was even in love with that divine voice of yours, but it didn't last long. You're silly and not educated. I simply can't talk to you. We have zero in common. I can only sing with you and nothing else. What are we talking about being in this kind of relationship? What family? What babies?"

"Then why did you sleep with me at all and make this baby?" Sandra was helplessly crying, covering her face with her palms. Her shoulders were shaking while she sobbed more and more.

And then he finally said what she already suspected but was too terrified to admit to herself. "I didn't make this baby with you. I wanted Lily to have my baby. I loved her, and every night I closed my eyes and imagined that I'm fucking her, only her! Every cell of me was in her! I still love her with all my heart, and I will love her forever. You don't understand that and never will, but I'm dead inside now. Everything died in me when she left. And she left because you stupidly tried to save your family, to keep your husband, and you possibly persuaded her to leave."

"I didn't," Sandra protested, crying softly but endlessly, like a never-ending rain shower.

Emmanuel was also crying now, but he sobered up quickly and held himself in control again. "Well," he said matter-of-factly, "I decided what we'll do now. We'll continue our work and life as it was until now, like nothing happened. You'll sing and perform until your stomach will be visible. And then we'll break everything. I'll leave you and hire a private investigator to look for Lily. I'll find her, or I'll die. I can't live without her anymore, and I won't live without her."

This was the end, but Sandra still desperately tried to do something. "If we are pretending that nothing happened"—she sniffed timidly—"would you be sleeping here tonight?"

"No, it won't work. I am having an affair now with a married woman. Her husband is on a long business trip. When he'll come home, then maybe I'll return here for some time. You see, I'm completely honest with you. As I said, I never lied to you. Enjoy your baby, you silly baby yourself." With that, Emmanuel left.

Sandra clearly remembered the last moment she saw him in private. The picture of him was imprinted on her brain forever as he turned at the door to look at her for the last time, tall, athletic, very handsome with his wavy dark brown hair, big blue eyes, perfectly outlined lips, and charming dimple on his chin—the picture of a beautiful, talented genius so unbelievable, so special, and so unhappy, her one and only beloved husband, whom she hated madly from now on for what he did to her.

A couple of weeks later on September 29, 1969, Emmanuel Soley was shot and killed in the middle of the concert right on the stage, right in front of Sandra and all this friends, the band members. The husband of his last lover returned home from the business trip and found out what was going on in his home while he was absent. The police got the killer the next day.

It cost Sandra and the band a lot of money to falsely inform the media that Emmanuel was killed by a maniac who just dreamed to become famous. They didn't want to smear Emmanuel's reputation, opening the truth and presenting him to the public as a womanizer and an unfaithful husband to Sandra. His fans adored, admired, and worshipped him, and his fans were the whole country, maybe even the whole world. His happy and shiny image from the stage should stay in their memories forever.

Emmanuel's popularity made a huge burst because of his sudden and unusual death, and more albums were sold in the following months. Sandra was left alone in that world. She was a pregnant sixteen-year-old widow with about $350 million on her bank account.

CHAPTER 62

J im woke up first. He carefully climbed out from under the towel with which he covered them both so as not to get burned while sleeping under the midday's sun. He got dressed and lay down on his stomach on the ground and enjoyed looking at Lada sleeping deeply. She was completely exhausted after the enormous amount of sexual pleasure she experienced for the first time in her life.

Because of their *educational sessions* in Hawaii, she was fully prepared for real lovemaking, though she claimed that mentally she was a virgin. Her mind didn't know what to expect, but her body knew perfectly how to react with Jim's touch and kisses and how to convulse with strong orgasm from even one small caress of his fingers. Her body knew what to expect and craved it. She was now absolutely healthy sexually, physically, and mentally and readily immersed into her new sexual life, normal for a young woman of her age. Tomorrow was her birthday, and she was about to become a twenty-three-year-old.

Jim gently moved aside a lock of hair from her cheek and watched her face, enjoying her blissful and relaxed expression. Barely touching, he traced his finger to outline her slightly open lips. While not waking up, she still felt it. She shuddered and moaned quietly. Her eyelids shook and lifted for a second and then closed again.

Oh God, he thought, *she is enjoying every touch even while sleeping, even subconsciously. Jeez, she is so sensitive sexually now. I don't know what I did. I wished for it, but . . . be careful what you wish for.* Jim was scared to death to lose her. He was afraid even to think about that possibility and threw these thoughts away immediately. He just kept watching her calm face, soaking in all the beauty and peacefulness of it, being happy almost to tears.

Then a sudden, loud bang coming from the side of the highway shook the air. It was like an explosion with the sounds of crashing metal and breaking glass smashed into smithereens. Lada woke up and sat on the towel, bewildered. "What's happening?" she whispered sleepily.

"Probably a car crash," Jim said. "It's over there. Sounds like it is on the highway."

But then came another blow and another and one more and more, until finally the car's alarm began beeping loudly in protest. "Oh God, it's my car!" Lada exclaimed. "I know its voice. It's my car. It's parked there."

She threw away the towel and feverishly pulled on her clothes, which was lying beside them. "Take the towel, Jim!" she shouted to him, grabbed his backpack, and ran toward the highway. The loud blows continued. It was obviously something different from a regular car crash. Jim stood up, rolled the towel on his shoulder, and walked after her as fast as he possibly could. He was helping himself walk by grabbing the tall wheat stems on both sides of the trail that Lada left behind on the field.

Then the wailing alarm on the car abruptly ended because the honking device was probably destroyed. Lada jumped out from the wheat field and stopped in her tracks. In front of her was Mona with a baseball bat in her hands, beating and thrashing her car.

All the windows were already gone. Then Mona threw aside the bat, lowered her hand into the back window, and opened the back door of the car. She grabbed Jim's scores folder from the back seat, turned around, and began walking toward the group home, but Lada was already behind her.

In a second, practically not thinking, just by impulse, she unzipped Jim's backpack, grabbed the gun, and screamed at Mona, "Police! Freeze! I'll shoot you!" It was exactly like she used to see in the movies.

Mona stopped in bewilderment, turned around, and saw Lada holding the gun with both her hands, her arms stretched in front of her, again exactly like in the movies. "You're not the police!" Mona laughed with malice. "You're a stupid little girl . . . a bus driver! I'll call the police now, and you'll be arrested for an illegal possession of a weapon."

"Drop the folder!" Lada shouted. "Drop the folder, or I'll kill you."

"If you shoot me, you'll go to prison," Mona answered, calming down a bit. She realized that Lada was just a child against her, almost nothing.

"I'll go to prison, but you'll go to a casket and into a grave. What is better?" Lada screamed. "Drop the folder right now! Leave Jim's symphony alone. I will never forgive you for hitting him."

"Oh, that is what this is all about!" Mona realized. "Now it's your turn to fuck this debauched little freak of nature. Look what he did to me! He bit me, and I was forced to hit him in self-defense." She lifted her T-shirt and showed Lada the crescent red bite on her stomach, the print of Jim's teeth.

"Cut the bullshit, Mrs. Monster! Drop the folder. I'm shooting now! The safety is off!" Lada yelled and loudly clicked a cocking peace, preparing to pull the trigger.

Mona had no chance to know that the gun was unloaded, and the sound convinced and even scared her. "Okay, okay," she said, giving up finally. She threw the folder on the grass, lifted her hands, and slowly began moving back slowly. "I'll go, but I'll call the police immediately about that attack of yours."

"Cut the bullshit," Lada repeated, approaching the folder and picking it up from the ground while still holding her gun in one hand, pointing to Mona.

At that moment, Jim appeared from the wheat stems and saw the whole picture. "Jeez, you're watching a lot of movies, my love." He shook his head and plopped on his bum on the ground, laughing. Lada lowered her gun, still following Mona's back with her eyes. Then she sat beside Jim, laughing too.

"Why did you fight so much about my folder?" Jim asked. "You said that we don't need it practically anymore. All copies are already printed out, and the whole symphony is in Boris's hands, ready to go. Why not just let the monster take that folder?"

"I don't know." Lada shrugged when they both finally stopped giggling almost to tears. "I just hate her so much. I don't want her to have anything of yours."

"But they already have the first part of my symphony anyway. Well, thank you for protecting me that fiercely, my love." He placed the gun and his folder into his backpack and zipped it.

"Do you think she will really call the police?" Lada inquired.

"Not a chance ever. She is the one who is scared of the police more than anybody else. The psychologist explained that to me long ago when I consulted with him about my confrontations with Mona some months before."

Lada nodded. "I, by the way, have my license for the gun, so I'm not worried about that. And this thing was unloaded, not even cleaned from the storage grease yet." They laughed some more but then finally stopped and got serious.

"Let's go see what damage is done to the car," Lada said. "It looks like it is not drivable anymore. Not just the windows but also all the lights are smashed. I don't know what to do. Call the insurance probably? Or the tow truck? Or an auto shop? I need my car. How would I come here to see you, Jim? And tomorrow is my birthday. We should go to the city and celebrate. How could we do that now?"

They stood confused for a while, observing the wreck, and then walked in circles around it, sadly shaking their heads and comprehending what to do first. Then they heard the sound of the bus. It came from the driveway of the group home, turned to the highway, and moved toward them.

Lada grabbed Jim and jumped over the little ditch that separated the road from the wheat field to protect the both of them in case it was Mona driving the bus with the purpose of running them over. However, the bus stopped; and the new driver, Jason, stepped out from the door. "What happened? An accident?" he asked worriedly. "Is someone hurt? Do you need help?"

"No, thank you, Jason," Jim answered. "No injuries here."

"Wow," Lada whispered, staring at the guy in surprise, astonished. "Are you the new bus driver here?"

"Yes, ma'am." Jason nodded, looking at her with sparkles of excitement in his eyes as well. "Is it your car?"

Lada nodded.

"What happened with it? Just vandalism? It looks completely wrecked. Do you know who did it? Did you see?"

"Your boss, Mona," Jim answered again as Lada reminded silent, just smiling at Jason.

"With that bat?" Jason laughed, pointing at the baseball bat that was lying on the grass. "It's crazy, but I can believe it. Mona can get angry sometimes. I already noticed that. And she is also an extremely passionate woman." He smirked meaningfully, which only Jim could understand.

Then Jason continued, "I was in the basement, loading the boxes with bottles into the bus, so I didn't hear anything. We're actually here, pretty far from the building anyway. Damn, those boxes are so heavy. They accumulated so many bottles here during the last four months. The previous bus driver ignored this part of job and probably was fired because of that."

"I'm the previous bus driver." Lada chuckled. "And believe me, I was fired *not* because of that."

"Oh, a colleague." Jason smiled even more broadly. "Nice to meet you. What's your name, by the way?"

"Lada. And you are?"

"Jason."

"Nice to meet you too, Jason." She extended her hand, which he shook.

Jim looked in silent shock how her little palm disappeared in his big and strong light brown hand as they both laughed and kept looking at each other with visibly growing excitement. Jason held her hand for a couple of seconds longer than it would be appropriate in Jim's opinion, and to his surprise, Lada allowed it, glowing.

Then still shaking his head at the wild car damage, Jason said, "How could I help here? Actually, I have an idea. I'm going now to the city, to a bottle depot, anyway. So I can give you a ride, Lada. I could help find a tow truck and send it here. We could also make an appointment in a shop to do the repairs. It would take probably a couple of weeks to fix all these, but they could give you a courtesy car for that time. I know one very decent shop where we could stop before I pick up the guys from the factory."

How many times did he use the word we? Jim noticed nervously.

"Oh, that would be great!" Lada exclaimed. "Thank you very much, Jason. You're my lifesaver. Otherwise, I would be stuck here forever."

Jason walked to the bus, and Lada ran after him. He stopped by the bus door and gave her his hand, like a real gentleman, to help a lady to climb on the steps, and she accepted it, smiling flirtatiously.

"My God," Jim whispered to himself in horror, "she was working on that bus for more than two months and never needed any help climbing on the steps. And now she suddenly needs it?"

Then Jason turned around and asked, "Jim, do you want me to drive you to the porch, or you'd prefer to walk home?"

"I can walk," Jim answered, not wanting to emphasize his weakness.

"Okay then. Bye." Jason waved and climbed into the bus.

"Bye." Lada, who was already inside, waved to Jim too.

In a few seconds, they drove away, leaving him to comprehend what had just happened. *If Jason didn't say bye, she would forget it,* Jim thought. *Not even a little hug, not even a kiss goodbye, nothing. It is not like her. It's not like her usual self at all. It's like another person momentarily emerging as a handsome guy appeared.*

He felt droplets of a cold sweat sliding down his back. What he dreaded the most was now unfolding right in front of his eyes, and he couldn't do anything about it. He just fell on the grass and lay motionless for a long moment. Then he finally found the inner power to collect himself; stood up; took his backpack that was now heavy with the gun, ammo, and folder; and dragged himself very slowly with huge difficulty toward the group home.

CHAPTER 63

The music was deafeningly loud, and the crowds in the huge stadium were screaming and wailing in ecstasy, jumping, waving arms, whistling, catcalling, clapping, so practically almost nobody heard a gunshot. Emmanuel had just finished the first couplet of the song, and it was Sandra's turn to begin the second one when he suddenly fell to the floor on his back. His friend Doug, who was with a guitar right beside him, even thought that it was some new trick that Emmanuel probably invented for fun. He expected that Emmanuel would roll around and jump up in a second as soon as Sandra started singing, so he kept playing.

Sandra had just begun her line as she looked askance at Emmanuel, who was supposed to be on the right from her, but he wasn't there. He was on the floor with arms spread wide and blood oozing on top of his shiny silver jacket. She choked on the words of the song. "W-w-w-what?" And she stopped in the middle of a sentence. Doug turned to her to check what was happening but saw Emmanuel at the same moment and dropped his guitar. The music abruptly ended, and a silence fell above the stadium but for just a few seconds. Then the screaming of the crowds exploded a hundred times louder and crazier than before. Now it was pure panic.

As a loving and devoted wife, Sandra was supposed to run to her husband, hug him, cry, and yell for help. But she didn't do any of that.

She just hugged her head with her arms and sat on the floor where she stood a second before and rocked slowly back and forth. She knew that Emmanuel was dead. After their official breakup two weeks ago, she prayed for God to punish him, and here it was—the punishment, the end of everything. There was no reason for her to cry now. She already cried all she could, no more tears left. Emmanuel was already deceased to her forever during the last two weeks. Now it was just the materialization of his death, just the legal end.

The backup dancers, instead of her, ran to him, shook and hugged him, and cried. Some of them were probably in love with him but not Sandra. She felt abused and hurt by him so much that she was almost ready to smile with satisfaction that her prayers were finally answered. These feelings scared her. She didn't know what to do and just kept rocking, sitting on the floor in silent shock.

She didn't hear or understand what was going on around her. There were so many people fussing on the stage—security, paramedics, ambulance, police, the whole of their business group, even some fans. For everybody, it was panic, a shock, a mess, horror, and it all mixed up in Sandra's eyes. The strange multicolored silhouettes flashed around her, she felt someone shook her shoulder, and someone else talked to her, but she couldn't concentrate and understand anything. She just felt suddenly very nauseous and began to throw up, and then everything went black for her as she collapsed on the floor beside Emmanuel, unconscious.

Her strange behavior at the moment of her husband's murder alerted the police. It looked suspicious to them as they had found out that their marriage was not the happiest one, Emmanuel had no relatives, and Sandra was the only inheritor of his $250 million. The other about $100 million in their bank account was her own money, which she earned with the group for her singing, recording albums, and writing lyrics to the songs.

The police questioned Sandra for quite a long time, but luckily for her, the killer was arrested the next day. He didn't even try to hide and took full responsibility for Emmanuel's murder. Such a fast success in police work, solving that special, extremely important case, saved Sandra. She was acquitted from the suspicion that she was the one who hired a hit man to assassinate her husband.

What should she do now? She locked herself in their house, sitting alone on her bed in a dark room with closed windows and thinking. Sandra couldn't stop imagining the last picture of Emmanuel that was imprinted in her memory. He—tall, strong, handsome but very sad—was standing by the door, his hand on the doorknob just seconds before exiting and leaving her forever. His last words to her were about Lily. "I'll find her, or I'll die. I can't live without her anymore, and I won't live without her." It was already the end. His decision was made deep inside his heart. It was obvious that, even after being found, Lily would refuse him again. He openly told Sandra that he would commit suicide in this case. He was already practically a dead man.

Could she expect something like that from him? Absolutely not, ever. It was not in him, not in his character, but it was how he changed. It was what unrequited love did to him, and it forced him to rave.

But what did his damn love do to her? What in the world could be more offensive and hurtful for a woman's soul than the knowledge that her beloved one, during sex with her, imagined another woman? That all his passion was directed to another woman? He even dreamed of making a baby with that woman, not with her at all. And now what? Not that other woman but Sandra herself was left with this pregnancy, not with her own baby but Emmanuel's and Lily's baby. Was she a surrogate, a substitute for him? It was such an unbelievable disrespect to her. Such an offensive and unbearable pain! It was not forgivable.

After clearly realizing the deepness of that wound in her heart, Sandra hated Emmanuel and his baby so much now that she became obsessed with the idea to get rid of them both. Though fooling around with dozens of women, many of whom were married, Emmanuel obviously played with fire, and his behavior invited one of the jealous husbands to kill him. During the last two weeks, he knew that it would happen one day, but he was okay with that. He was on the edge of killing himself anyway, at least very close to that edge. But Sandra was sure that it was God who answered her prayers and helped her get rid of him. Now God should help in freeing her of his baby.

She prayed and prayed, but nothing was happening with the baby so far. Then she thought that probably it would be better to ask for help from that doctor to whom Emmanuel introduced to her earlier. Maybe it would work faster. She wanted to finish everything as soon as possible and forget all of her tragic past forever.

Many times, Emmanuel reproached her for being silly and uneducated. But who the hell took her from school, snatched her from the sixth grade, and didn't allow her to even get an elementary education? He told her that he loved Lily because of her very wide knowledge of almost everything, her brilliant education, and her sharp mind. He convinced Sandra that a woman's brain could attract men sexually no less than a woman's body but sometimes even more.

Well, Sandra would get her education. She would sharpen her brain. She would increase her knowledge. She was free now, and she would compensate herself for all she lost because of him in her teen years—school, friends, fun, lightheartedness. It was not too late. It was all possible. She just had to get rid of his damn baby, who was designated for the other woman.

When she talked to the doctor now at the beginning of October about an abortion, he strictly refused to perform it. "Ma'am, you are already four months pregnant," he said. "It is absolutely impossible to terminate this pregnancy at that time. It would be extremely dangerous for your health, and there is a big chance that you will die. It's far too late. I am very sorry for the loss of your husband, but his baby is destined to live. It's probably fate. You don't have any other choice."

Sandra was absolutely devastated by the result of that visit. But then she thought a bit and decided not to give up. Usually, Emmanuel was adamant in everything that he wanted. She was the shy one who always gave up, not anymore. Now was her time. Now she would be adamant in everything that she wanted. If America was not helping her, there was another place on the earth where she would go—Italy. There, she would know what to do.

Sandra remembered that, in her village, she heard some stories about girls who had unwanted pregnancies sometimes. They were all Catholics, so abortion was prohibited by the law, but miscarriage wasn't. There were witch doctors, old women who made their own concoctions from some herbs. Those girls were given a drink, and oops, the baby was gone.

The next day, she bought an airplane ticket to Napoli, not saying a word to anybody where she was going or why. While their whole band of friends, musicians, coworkers, and almost the whole country of America mourned her star husband, she went over the ocean to see a witch doctor.

CHAPTER 64

Jim didn't know how he even found the power to reach the group home and then his room. He dropped his backpack on the floor and collapsed on his bed. He would lie motionless until the evening and miss dinner because he didn't want to go downstairs and see Jason. But he had a duty now—to make a sign for Victor that he would come at night and bring the gun.

So he went and had his dinner and dropped a spoon very realistically—his hands were shaking because Jason wasn't at the dinner table today. He delivered the guys back from the factory and left immediately. Why? Did Lada invite him for dinner? Or what?

Not knowing what happened between Lada and Jason during their ride on the bus gave Jim some hope—maybe nothing, though they both were obviously smitten with each other. He remembered what he told her in Hawaii while giving her the ring. "If one day you'll love another man and marry him, I'll be a friend of your family forever." Her answer was "That was the stupidest thing I've ever heard."

At that time, they laughed, but now he realized that it was really the stupidest thing to say. He wouldn't be their family friend; he would just die. Lada was already much more than just a friend; she was his woman, and if he'd lost her as his woman, there would be no question about any friendship ever. He wouldn't live without her. That was it.

Where did he get it, this crazy obsession? Where did it come from? He would never have guessed that he was capable of something like that. He was never jealous in his life before. But what did he have to be jealous about?

At some point, Jim chuckled, remembering the famous French writer Alexandre Dumas in his book *The Vicomte of Bragelonne: Ten Years Later* describing the three levels of jealousy in people: (1) love and not jealous, (2) love and jealous, and (3) not love and jealous. Jim was thinking all the time of himself as the first one but suddenly realized that he was the second one. The third one was the worst, angry and hateful without love whatsoever. It was obviously Mona.

What is jealousy for me? Jim thought. *Just pain, unbearable pain in my soul, and the horror of losing her, which is really a horror of death because I won't live without her. It was decided once and for all.*

Lada called him in the evening. "Jim, why didn't you call me during the day? I was terribly busy, running around, preparing for tomorrow, plus talking to insurance, arranging repairs for my car, and stuff. Are you okay?"

"Of course, I'm okay. Why wouldn't I be?" He didn't want to show her any jealousy or control ever. She should always feel free while being his girlfriend, but it wasn't that simple with Lada. She knew him very well, and that gave her the master skill of reading him with excellence.

"Because your face was pale from horror and crooked when I left on the bus. Don't you think I know you, Mr. Silly? You do really want to ask now how my ride was with Jason, don't you?"

"Maybe I do. So what? You're a free woman."

"I'm not. I'm your fiancée, and I belong to you, and I want you like crazy all the time now. So are we clear on that?"

"I . . . I don't know . . . I wish we were."

"Well . . . do you love me, Jim?"

"Of course, I do."

"Then we are clear. And never question that again ever. Now I can tell you about my ride with Jason. He is actually a very nice guy. He noticed my ring right away and asked if I am engaged. I said yes. He asked when my wedding is. I said tomorrow."

"You were kidding, of course." Jim almost laughed.

"No, I was not. It is my birthday, and you're giving me that birthday present. We are going to the city hall tomorrow and get married. What the hell, Jim. I love you, and I want to have sex with you every day, with you as my husband. Do you want it or not?"

"Oh, Jeez, of course, I want it. But, Lada, are you serious? What kind of husband could I be? You will have to take care of me all the time like a nanny."

"So what? I'm doing that already anyway. I am used to it." She giggled. "It's actually kind of fun."

"But you deserve all the best in the world. What could I do for you in return?"

"What you did on that wheat field this morning. It was the best in the world, wasn't it? I was almost dead. To have sex together all the time, isn't it what marriage is about?"

He loved her, but God, how childish she was at twenty-three. "Partially yes, mostly yes," Jim said, smiling. "But there is much more to it—legal issues, financial issues, responsibilities, household, children . . . a lot. What if you, for example, get sick? How could I take care of you? I am practically not capable of anything, just composing music."

"Then you'll compose music, and we'll hire two caregivers for both of us. That would be even more fun!" She laughed almost to tears. "So listen to me, Mr. Silly, please. I took Rita's car today and went to the mall, to the same jeweler, and bought us wedding bands. I've got mine already. Yours is a tiny one and requires customizing, so it will be ready tomorrow morning. Jeez, Jim, you'll be a married man. Don't you get it? Just a simple legal proceeding for now, no wedding yet, but we will have a big wedding after your concert. It would be your triumph and my triumph with you as your wife."

"Okay, but what about Jason?"

"Oh, about Jason. He told me he is a student in our university. That's where he saw an ad on the noticeboard about the bus driver position, exactly like I did before. He is in the physical education faculty. He wants to become a gym teacher and also a football coach. He likes to work with teens.

"And then it was very funny, you know. He didn't ask me who my fiancé is, but when he drove me home, there was BB in our driveway, washing his car. Jason asked, 'Is it your dad?' I answered no. Then Jason said, 'Don't you think that such a big age gap with your husband is a bit too much?' I laughed like crazy. He thought that BB was my fiancé. Isn't it funny, Jim? So I introduced them to each other, and BB invited him for dinner."

Here it was, the blow into his gut that Jim was waiting for during every minute of this conversation.

"But then our mother came out, and she looked so upset that Jason politely refused dinner. He said that he is in a hurry to go home because his girlfriend is waiting for him for dinner. Actually, you know, he is engaged as well. His fiancée's name is Lucy. She is a rookie policewoman. I asked where he met her, and he said that they were classmates. I guess it means high school sweethearts, right? I asked when their wedding will be, and he said in a couple of years because Lucy needs to establish her position in the police department and concentrate on that."

"Lada, darling," Jim begged, "it's too much information, which I don't need. I don't care about Jason and his fiancée problems. Please stop talking about that. Let's talk about us."

"Well . . ." She got a bit confused. "But it was your question. 'What about Jason?' you asked. I'm just answering it. Sorry if it was too much. About us, okay, here is the plan for tomorrow. I'll pick you up in the morning at ten in Rita's car, and we're going to the city. BB and Rita will wait for us at city hall. They will be our witnesses. Then we'll go to a restaurant to celebrate my birthday and our marriage. And then I'll drive you back to the group home in a courtesy car that the auto shop is giving me tomorrow afternoon. Now are we good? Can you promise me that you will sleep happily tonight and forget about any stupid jealousy?"

"Yes, I can," Jim assured her. "No more jealousy, but I'm not sure about a good sleep. You know that I need to see my friend at night and pass him your present."

"Sorry, I forgot about that, just too much of everything. Good luck and say hi to him for me."

"Will do. I love you, Lada. Sweet dreams."

"I love you too, Mr. Fiancé or Mr. Groom . . . I don't know what you'd prefer."

With that, they hung up.

"Oh God!" Jim pressed his palms to his temples and laughed for a long moment. He remembered one funny anecdote that he heard long ago on the farm from one of the workers: There was once a very good man, and God decided to give him a prize. He invited that man into his place and said to him, "Ask anything you want. I'll do anything for you."

"Okay," the man said. "I would like you to build a bridge for me from LA to Hawaii."

"Wow," God said. "It's not easy, even for me. It will go through the deepest places in the Pacific. Can you imagine how much cement will be needed to build poles that tall to hold this bridge? Maybe I better do something else for you."

"Okay," the man said. "Then teach me how to understand a woman's soul."

God went silent for some minutes and then said, "Well, back to that bridge. Do you want two lanes or four?"

Jim laughed when he heard it at first, not really knowing what it was—a woman's soul. He knew only one woman then, his grandma Cathy. And her soul was pretty easy to understand—kind, loving, full of care, nothing else.

Now he understood much more about the topic and could laugh at himself like a man. How wise this tale was! How could he understand Lada? With Jason, she was flirting like crazy; and now right away, she wanted to marry him. Really, even God wouldn't be capable of getting it.

Lada didn't tell him just two things. Tomorrow afternoon, their marriage and her birthday celebration with her brother and sister-in-law would be secret. Then she would drive him back to the group home. Only after that would they celebrate her birthday at home with her mother, the whole of her brother's family, and some neighbors and family friends. Lada and Boris decided to do so because their mother, Tatiana, made quite a fight with her daughter after she saw Jason. The old communist mentality and typical Russian racism were obviously alive in her mind.

"Ladochka, my dear, beautiful daughter," she sobbed, "what's wrong with you? First, a cripple, then a black ass. Couldn't you find yourself a normal man?" That was what made Lada, as well as Boris and Rita, worried.

And Lada didn't tell Jim that she gave Jason her phone number.

CHAPTER 65

During the two and a half years of her absence from her home village in Italy, Sandra wasn't forgotten. All the villagers watched the concerts of her group on TV and were buying their group's albums. She was a real pride for her parents now, not a lazy girl anymore. It looked like everybody was happy to see her, but she noticed pretty soon that all people were in reality most interested in her money and nothing else.

It occurred that, suddenly, everybody around her had problems. Someone lost a job, someone got sick, a spouse died, a house needed repairs, a car broke, a store was robbed, a wallet was lost, a wedding was coming, or a baby was born—and all of them needed money. Even knowing well that she just lost her husband in such an unusual and tragic situation, everybody still asked, "Oh, I'm so sorry for your loss, but . . . did you inherit his money? Did he have other family, or is everything yours only?" Nobody, luckily for her, knew the exact amount that was in her bank, but they easily guessed that it would be pretty significant, much more than she needed, and they all felt free to ask.

At first, Sandra felt pity for these people. She carelessly gave checks for $1,000 to all her friends at school, the teachers, the neighbors, practically everyone in the village, including her parents. But she was really surprised that, instead of being thankful, people got unhappy and angry with her. "What a greedy girl! Couldn't she give some more? What is this, just one grand? It's practically nothing." Such an open ungratefulness made Sandra feel surprised, at first, and then sad and disappointed in people she knew all her life. It was so hurtful that she began crying every night again. She wanted to be nice to people, but they definitely weren't very nice to her.

Nobody asked why she came home or if she needed some help. What help could a rich person need? But she really needed serious help—to find a witch doctor.

It occurred not to be a difficult task. Most of the girls knew where the witch doctor lived, and with some more gifts from her, they escorted Sandra to the house. Knowing who Sandra was, the witch doctor requested $2,000, though normally she charged the village girls in Italian lira, the equivalent of $20. It wasn't important to Sandra. If needed, she would be ready to give a million just to get rid of her problem and to make her revenge on Emmanuel at the same time.

After getting the witch doctor's concoction, Sandra drank it right away; and about fifteen minutes later, the reaction in her body started. But it wasn't like she was told it would be—"oops, and the baby is gone." There was such a pain in her abdomen that she stayed in bed for some days and cried. With that came nausea, vomiting, dizziness, weakness, headache, and some bleeding from her womb, but what was coming out definitely wasn't a baby. She couldn't eat at all, just had a sip of water from time to time and lost a lot of weight during that week.

Finally, her friends helped her reach the witch doctor again and complain that there wasn't a proper result. The baby was still there inside. "Probably, it's a big baby," the witch doctor said, very surprised. "Let me give you some more."

Now with horror, Sandra got another portion of the drink for another $2,000. The result was the same. She was even sicker and in more pain, but the baby still didn't come out. Sandra felt that she would probably die from this awful sickness created by unknown herbs, but the baby was still alive and even began moving inside her. It was the right time for that—exactly four and a half months of the pregnancy.

Sandra was really adamant; she learned that from Emmanuel. She bought the third portion that almost killed her but not the baby. It was like an undeclared war between them. Who would survive, her or the baby? And to her big surprise, they both survived.

"Why aren't your drinks working?" Sandra complained to the witch doctor. "Look, it is even jumping inside, getting more active instead of dying."

"What?" the witch doctor exclaimed in shock. "How pregnant are you, girl? Why didn't you tell me how far along you are? My drinks only work during the first or maximum of second month but not later. You're crazy. You could die easily. Get away from here and never come back."

Sandra was pretty sure that she told the witch doctor what term of pregnancy she had. It was obvious to her that the old woman also decided just to milk some money from her, like everyone else in the village. And it was so extremely hurtful.

Sandra came home in tears again. She lost her fight. *Probably it is Emmanuel's spirit from the sky who is protecting his child*, she thought. What could she do now? The last possibility left for her was to give up that baby for adoption and forget about it.

Her parents were happy that she overcame her strange illness and could stay with them for Christmas. She did, but it wasn't a happy time for her at home. To console herself somehow, Sandra returned to her childhood routine—every day she went to the coast, sat on the big rock, and sang while looking at the vastness of the water. There was something very special and sacred for her in the whisper of those waves coming and going, the tenderly moving sand, and the little rocks on the beach, bringing the empty seashells out from the depths of the ocean.

She knew that Emmanuel was also obsessed with the ocean, no less than her, but this knowledge didn't push her away. It was the only thing in which she was always in complete agreement with him. Music, singing, and the ocean created their unbreakable bond of souls, which still stayed in her, in spite of everything bad that happened later in her relationship with him, in spite of the death of her love story, which ended so tragically.

Her usually jumpy and active baby always got quiet while she was singing by the sea. Probably her voice was soothing and sounded like a lullaby for it. She was told by someone that science proved now that unborn babies could hear what was going on around their mothers and especially could hear music, so it was good to sing for them. But Sandra didn't sing for the baby; she sang for herself. It was her farewell with her childhood, her village, her home, and her big rock on the coast, where she saw Emmanuel in person for the first time.

Leaving for America at the beginning of January 1970, Sandra left a check for one million dollars to her parents. She didn't love them now but still was respectful and thankful to them that they gave her life and didn't try to get rid of her with the help of any crazy concoction. She felt guilty of her own behavior but still adamant about what she would do next.

Luckily, the media didn't know that she arrived back in Los Angeles from Italy. Nobody saw her tummy, now already seven months along. With no noise and no gossip, all went smoothly and quietly.

Sandra locked herself in their palace again and, first, found herself a lawyer, who advised her to create a charity foundation that would be a great help to take care of her money. They discussed what this foundation could be, and then Sandra decided that she wanted to help children in music education. She didn't get it herself in her time of childhood, and she felt that she really missed it. The lawyer prepared all the documentation. They named the charity the Voices of the Future.

Then Sandra found an adoption lawyer, a senior lady, kind and experienced. They had two months to find adoptive parents for the baby, but it should not be in LA, where it would be noticed by the media and would create a dubious reputation for Sandra as a malicious and a heartless woman. It should be somewhere really far away in terms of distance and also of the level of society so nobody would suspect anything and find anything, even if they tried.

The lawyer proved to be good and inventive. She found a couple of poor childless Ukrainian farmers in Pennsylvania, deep in the forest. Those people were pretty old and sick and in a big need of money for their farm, which was on the edge of bankruptcy. Nothing could be a better match. They signed a contract momentarily as they were told that they would receive $10,000 monthly from the charity foundation the Voices of the Future for the care of a child. It wasn't important in this situation who this child would be or if it would be healthy or handicapped.

Now Sandra was just sitting at home and waiting. However, she made herself very busy, not wasting her time. She started working hard on her education. In these two months, she took academic upgrading classes with a private teacher; and when the baby was finally born and moved to Pennsylvania, she successfully passed her exam and got a high school diploma.

Sandra was also seriously thinking about her career. She knew that she would sing all her life. This was her talent and her passion and her only ability. Writing lyrics for songs, which she did with Emmanuel, could be now a fun hobby and maybe one day could be combined into a small book of poetry. But singing was the dream career for her.

However, now she despised Emmanuel's style—no more pop, no rock, no huge crowds and stadiums. There was big money there, but she didn't need it, and it wasn't her taste anymore. She decided to go to Juilliard School in New York and get an education in classical style and level, which seemed more attractive to her. She decided to become a professional opera singer.

Sandra had no doubt that she would be accepted. There was no question about that. She knew now the value of her voice and her stage ability. She grew up a lot, and she learned a lot about herself. She gained real self-respect and self-esteem now and was very confident and proud of herself. And this really worked out well. She was accepted into the Juilliard School and, in five years, graduated successfully.

Then her career rolled up smoothly, without any problems whatsoever. The only difficulty was to lie on interviews that she never had children.

CHAPTER 66

At that night, Jim came to Victor's room and brought him the gun and the ammo. He also shared the story of Mona destroying Lada's car to get at his folder with the last part of his symphony. Then both men laughed, imagining the brave Lada with the gun, protecting it. "Wow, I really regret that I didn't see it. It would be fun," Victor said. "You, Jim, have gotten yourself a very special kind of girl. Thank her a lot for me for the gun. I'm sure that it will be very helpful. I'm feeling much better already. But I am thinking . . . this folder is with you now. Why don't you give it to the monster yourself? Anyway, they have part 1. Now give her part 4 and then get from your girl parts 2 and 3. Let Mona and her daughter have the whole symphony.

"Then the daughter will bring it to her teacher, who has been alerted already. It would be a big help when we arrest the monster and her daughter together. The teacher could be a useful witness and all four parts of the symphony, which we will confiscate from him, will be the evidence. It could be a good catch. At least we will have something material finally.

"Another point—you didn't get any news from Mona about my case. I guess she didn't trust you and did not talk with those guys on the phone where you could hear. She did it in front of me all the time, knowing that

I'm catatonic and couldn't understand anything. But with you hanging around, she is pretty cautious. If you give her the symphony, it could improve your relationship. Pretend to be, if not friends again, at least a bit more friendly."

"Maybe it's a good idea," Jim agreed. "But I won't sleep with her under any circumstances ever."

"I'm not asking for that, Jim. Just think about my idea."

"I will." Jim nodded. "But Lada and I are actually going to city hall tomorrow to get married. So I'll be pretty busy with that."

"Wow!" Victor exclaimed again. "As I said, you've gotten yourself an unbelievably special girl. Congratulations! You're a lucky guy, Jim."

In the morning right after breakfast, before Lada picked him up, Jim—holding the folder in his hands—approached Mona, who was cleaning the dining table. "I usually keep my promises, Mona," he said timidly. "I did promise to give my symphony to your daughter when it is finished so she could find a performer for me as you promised in your turn. Here is the last part. I'll give you parts 2 and 3 soon in a couple of days."

He placed the folder on the table. Mona looked at him, bewildered. "What happened, Jim?" she asked, knitting her brows. "Yesterday your fucking little bitch almost killed me for this folder. What changed now? Did she dump you?"

"I think yes," he said in a very sad voice he only could muster. "She found another man."

"I'm not surprised." Mona laughed. "She is an immigrant. They all are prostitutes. And you are not a Hollywood star either for her to fuck. It's understandable, and I'm the only one who could appreciate you. I regret that our friendship broke."

"But I still remember that we were friends some time ago and that you promised to help with my concert. So would you accept the folder and give it to your daughter?"

"Of course, I would. I'm keeping my promises as well, Jim. So when will other missing parts be available?"

"As soon as I can. I'll try my best. Now I'm going for a walk and will be back for dinner."

"Why for so long?" Mona inquired suspiciously.

"I would like now to add one more part to the symphony," Jim explained. "It requires a lot of thinking. I'm better in that while I'm walking."

Mona shrugged. "Well, good luck with that, my friend."

Three hours later, when Lada put a tiny wedding band on Jim's little ring finger, she felt that she was the happiest woman in the world. The ring looked so cute on his hand that she was laughing from excitement and happiness. Boris and Rita were a bit worried, watching her. It appeared to them like she was not serious enough and was just playing dolls with Jim. But they didn't show any disapproval, trying not to hurt her nor Jim.

"I still think that you're a bit too young to be a responsible wife," Boris said, hugging her and then Jim. "I know that you are twenty-three, and please stop pushing this fact in my face all the time. In spite of your age, kiddo, you're still very much childish."

"BB, you got married when you and Rita were twenty."

"We were much more mature and serious than you, kiddo."

"No, you weren't. You eloped to Japan like two teens."

"And I think Lada has now a very serious and mature husband, who is thirty-three," Jim noted, stretching his arm and observing his ring with a very broad smile on his face. "Though we eloped too from my group home."

"And from our house with Mom," Lada finished the sentence for him and giggled, jumping and clapping her hands and hugging him.

"We know that you love each other, and we really support your feelings," Rita said. "But we are a little concerned where and how you'll live as a married couple now."

"We will rent an apartment," Lada announced. "By the way, Jim, I did check your bank account. The money from your sponsor is already there. It arrived yesterday. So Mona was lying again. She has no power to cancel your sponsorship. Now we can easily afford rent. But I'm letting you know, BB, that we will not move together until after the concert. Jim has some work to do now at the group home."

During their lunch at the restaurant, which was supposed to be Lada's birthday party and their wedding celebration, Jim apologized, "Sorry, my darling, I didn't get you a birthday present yet."

"It's okay." Lada giggled. "I'll buy myself something I like and then show you later."

Boris and Rita looked at each other, surprised. Their little kiddo, being married only a couple of hours, already bravely managed Jim's account and behaved like a very experienced wife. And Jim absolutely didn't care and allowed her to do what she wanted without a shadow of a doubt. Probably, they were really right for each other and could have a very happy life together. Maybe she wasn't as childish as she looked and behaved but a true adult as she claimed.

At that time, Sandra Soley was sitting in her suite in the Fairmont Hotel, still holding Jim's photo in her shaky hand. The tears were sliding from her eyes to her cheeks and chin, but she still didn't wipe them. The tragic story of her youth, which she remembered and relived already for some hours, ended now with her baby's adoption.

She didn't cry for the past thirty-three years. There wasn't any reason to cry after she got free from Emmanuel and his child finally. Her life got very interesting, beautiful, full of success and creative work. She was happy all those years, dedicating herself to her singing, teaching, traveling, and writing some poetry for fun.

Sandra was friendly with most of her coworkers and students and had some friends, though not very close ones. The only thing that she refused boldly was love and sex. She never remarried, never even had a lover or boyfriend. She was so overloaded with the amount of sex that she got from Emmanuel from the age of fourteen until sixteen that it was enough for her for the rest of her life. Deep inside her heart, she didn't trust men anymore and was even afraid of them. Also, maybe she wasn't sure herself; but just possibly, she still loved Emmanuel and would love him for the rest of her life.

However, he wounded her so deep that, subconsciously, she was scared now. She thought that if she would have sex with a man, he would close his eyes and imagine another woman, like Emmanuel did. And she would never forgive that and never agreed to experience this pain and humiliation again.

So Sandra was a strong, successful, hardworking professional. But she was restricted, cold, and distant with many people, especially with men, even harsh and tough sometimes. This was her reputation.

Everybody knew that she survived the tragedy when her husband was killed, but nobody guessed that this tragedy was much deeper and painful when he was alive. Today thirty-three years later, she was crying again, remembering everything that happened with her, and wondering who was this guy, James Emmanuel Bogat, whose symphony was now playing from the CD player in her hotel room.

The Symphony of the Ocean was the title on the disk cover. The names of the parts of the symphony were "Sunrise over the Ocean," "Sparkles of Waves," "The Colors of the Calm," and "The Ocean's Twilight."

So he was as obsessed with the beauty of the endless water as she and Emmanuel were. He definitely inherited that from them.

The music was divine; it was impossible not to recognize that. His little fiancée, that girl with an attitude, was right. He was a genius, a real genius; and he inherited his talent, not just his facial feature, from Emmanuel also. The only difference on that photo was that Emmanuel had blue eyes, but this guy had dark brown eyes, actually her eyes. Now Sandra knew perfectly who he was but still can't find the nerve to pronounce, even silently in her head, the word *son*; she was still thinking about him as "this guy."

Her baby was adopted to the farm in Pennsylvania. How come this guy was here in Minnesota, in the group home in the faraway forest? What was wrong with him as he was living with assistance? What kind of damage did she do to him while he was her unborn baby yet? Maybe not much if this pretty girl became his fiancée, maybe just a little, nothing serious.

How did he become a composer of that level, being raised on a farm by an almost illiterate senior couple? Where did he get that perfect knowledge and deep feeling of the vocal line that he wanted to add to his symphony and suggested her to sing? Just by intuition because of his talent? Or he got a special education? Or both? That girl mentioned something about Juilliard School. How could a farmer's boy get there? It was something absolutely unbelievable.

There were so many questions yet no answers. Finally, Sandra calmed down a bit and wiped her tears. She was curious to find those answers. She looked at the résumé in his folder and got the phone number, which was Lada's in reality and dialed it.

I will ask him, "Who the hell are you, Mr. James Emmanuel Bogat?" Sandra thought. *I will demand an explanation before I agree to sing for him, if I'll agree ever.*

Lada and Jim, with Boris and Rita, were in the middle of their celebrating lunch when Lada's phone rang. "Kiddo," Boris said, disapprovingly shaking his head, "even if you're a married woman now, the rules in our family are still the same, no phones at the table."

She looked at the display and jumped up from her seat. "I need to take it, BB!" she screamed. "I need to take it!" And she ran out from the restaurant to the lobby.

Boris and Rita looked at each other questioningly. "Do you know what's going on here?" Boris asked his wife.

"No, but I could guess." Rita opened her eyes wide. "You do know, *bebe*, for whom I did that folder while they were in Hawaii, right? Do you know, Jim?"

"No." He shrugged. "Lada told me some days ago that she is expecting some surprise for me. But I have no idea."

While in the lobby, Lada pressed the button on her phone and almost yelled, "Hello, here is Lada Meleshko."

"Why are you answering this phone, Miss Meleshko?" Sandra was surprised. "It should be your fiancé's number as it written on top of his résumé. Or is he still thinking that to talk to me would be a waste of his time?"

"No, no, no, I'm sorry, Mrs. Soley!" Lada exclaimed passionately. "It's just . . . he has no phone. I can pass the message, please."

"Well . . . I was listening to his symphony . . . maybe I'll sing it but with one condition only. I would like to meet the author in person first."

CHAPTER 67

In anticipation of the meeting in person with "this guy," James Emmanuel Bogat, Sandra was very anxious. She craved to see him, and she was afraid at the same time. She wasn't that sixteen-year-old girl anymore who was always scared. She was a mature and very confident woman, but she was almost shaking like that unhappy village girl thirty-three years ago.

The million different feelings were overwhelming her. Most of all, it was guilt for what she did to him as an innocent tiny baby. Was it revenge of the deeply wounded sixteen-year-old to Emmanuel? It sounded so stupid now, so childish. She couldn't understand herself—why did she do that?

When, during their conversation on the phone with Lada, Sandra said that she would like to invite Mr. Bogat for dinner in her suite in the Fairmont Hotel where she was staying, Lada answered, "Thank you. We will be there."

"I am inviting him, Miss Meleshko, not you," Sandra retorted, irritated by the impudence of this girl, who obviously was holding the whole situation in her hands.

"I'm very sorry, Mrs. Soley," Lada answered politely. "But Jim couldn't come alone. He needs assistance. Also, ask the room service, please, to provide a high chair for a child and couple of step stools in your suite. They could be needed too."

What's going on with him? Sandra thought. *If he is a handicapped, he should be in a wheelchair. I could understand that, but what are these things needed for? It's so strange. I can't comprehend.*

When they knocked at the door and entered the room, Sandra subconsciously moved a couple of steps back and pressed her palms to her mouth in silent shock. She could anticipate anything but what she saw in front of her now. Lada was standing by the door and holding the hand of a strange creature that looked like a three- or four-year-old child by the size of the body but had a head of a normal man. And it was Emmanuel's head with Emmanuel's face.

Sandra slowly moved backward until she plopped on the couch and covered not just her mouth but also her whole face with her hands. The couple entered the room. "Good morning, Mrs. Soley," Lada said, smirking at Sandra's reaction. "Let me introduce to you my husband, Mr. James Emmanuel Bogat, that genius composer I was talking about. You had the privilege to listen to his symphony, and now you can make an acquaintance of him in person."

"I'm really sorry if I scared you." Jim blushed. "That wasn't my intention."

My God! Sandra shook her head in another shock. *It is unbelievable. When he's talking, his voice sounds exactly like Emmanuel's.*

She removed her hands from her face and looked at Jim attentively with tears in her eyes. "Could you sing?" she asked unexpectedly.

"No, I can't take in enough air for singing. My lungs are pretty small for that."

Sandra closed her eyes. "Please say something else to me," she begged.

Jim shrugged. He didn't understand what she wanted or why. "Okay," he agreed politely. "I can tell you my story if you want . . . if you'd be interested actually."

"Yes. Please sit." She gestured toward the living room. The couple came closer. Then Lada lifted Jim and placed him on the armchair across from Sandra and sat herself on another one.

"Well, where could I start?" Jim smiled. "I'm afraid that it's too long of a story and you would be bored, Mrs. Soley. But anyway, thank you very much that you found time to listen to my symphony. It's really flattering for me."

"Thank not me," Sandra answered. "Thank Miss Meleshko, this crazily persistent fiancée of yours. Or what did you say? You're already his wife?"

"Yes." Lada giggled happily. "I am not Miss Meleshko anymore. I'm Mrs. James Emmanuel Bogat. You can call me Lada, though. We just got married three days ago."

"Wow, congratulations then." Sandra shook her head in disbelief. "Sorry for the question. Do you really love each other so much?"

"Much more than you can imagine." Lada laughed. "So can we let the man tell his story finally?"

"Yes, of course," Sandra agreed quietly. "But please do not feel offended if I listen to you with my eyes closed. It's not that I don't want to see you. I just really need to concentrate on the sound of your voice. It is extremely important to me."

Lada and Jim looked at each other questioningly as Lada rolled her eyes. "Of course," Jim said, "if it is more comfortable for you. I'll probably start from my childhood at the Luhoway Farm in Pennsylvania with my grandma Cathy."

He told the story of his life, making a more detailed presentation of the moments that were related to music, how he started composing, his education, the huge influence of the ocean on him—everything until Grandma Cathy's death and moving to the group home. Then he discussed his work on his symphony in every detail. Then he related how he was looking for a singer and had a big surprise when Lada finally found her, Sandra.

"I think that your voice, Mrs. Soley, would make a great match with my idea, with my feeling of the spirit of the ocean, which I am trying to share in my symphony." Jim ended his narrative. "I would be really happy if you would agree to perform in my concert."

Sandra listened motionlessly and silently, not interrupting, not even asking one word. Then she opened her eyes. "You probably don't expect that, Jim," she said, finally throwing away the official name, Mr. Bogat. "But we're talking here not about the performance of your symphony only. We're talking about things of much, much more importance than just a concert."

"Sorry, Mrs. Soley," Jim interrupted. " But there is nothing more important in my life than that."

"Yes, there is, Jim." She nodded toward Lada. "Your wife, she is probably more important, isn't she?"

"I don't know." Jim blushed. "It's not exactly comparable. Those are very different feelings. Lada and the symphony, they both are my life, of course, in a sense."

"I used to have both too." Sandra smirked sadly. "The love of my life, Emmanuel, and another love of my life, singing and performing on the stage. And I lost them both in a blink of an eye when I was sixteen and pregnant."

Lada and Jim looked at each other again, and Lada once more rolled her eyes and soundlessly mouthed to him, *What? Wow!*

"It's obvious to me that you're extremely talented, Jim, and it is worth my time to be involved in your creative work and your concert," Sandra continued. "But before I officially agree for us to work together, I would like to tell you my story. Because there will be an important decision to make on your part. You think that you know who I am, but in reality, you don't. And before we make a determination about the symphony and the concert, you need to know whom you're going to be implicated with."

"Of course." Jim nodded. "I would be happy to know you better. I just didn't dare ask about that. I considered it kind of impolite of me. You're famous enough for everybody to know everything about you. But if you would like to share more with us, of course."

"Okay then, listen very carefully, please."

Sandra started her story, exactly like Jim before—from her childhood in the Italian village to her crazy love of the sea, which she liked to call "the ocean"; her singing on the rocks by the water; her first meeting with Emmanuel; and their first songs together. Then she related their marriage with the huge age difference; she was fourteen, and he was thirty. She narrated their move to America, concerts, albums, touring, band, and friends.

She purposely skipped Emmanuel's infidelity and fooling around but told all what she knew about his mad obsession with the brilliant dancer of their group, the lesbian Lily Donovan. She didn't notice that Jim's facial expression changed at that moment. He bit his lips and widened his eyes toward Lada. She opened her mouth in shock and couldn't close it but pressed her palms to the bottom of her face.

Then Sandra told them about the scandal at the bar after Emmanuel gave to Lily her family treasure, the sacred statue, the Lady of the Sorrows. She confessed that Emmanuel was on the edge of committing suicide because he told her openly that he couldn't live without Lily, but there was absolutely no chance that they would be together ever.

Jeez, Jim thought, *it's so crazy. It's exactly like what I am feeling about Lada. I'm lucky that she is with me. That poor guy Emmanuel, if it would be possible to use the word* poor *about a rock star with $350 million on his account. What a paradox of life!*

Then Sandra's story came closer to the point and, because of that, got scarier—Emmanuel's murder, her pregnancy, her dream of revenge for his love to Lily, her trip to Italy, the attempts to get rid of the baby with the help of concoctions created by a witch doctor, her return to Los Angeles, the childbirth, the adoption contract, and then her lies on interviews about not having children because she was afraid to confess what she did to the baby. And with the adoption contract came the names of the Pennsylvania farm, Luhoway; Cathy and Phil Bogat; and James Emmanuel Bogat, who in reality should be James Emmanuel Soley.

As she finished, Sandra bowed her head on her hands and took a deep breath. "Now it's your turn, Jim," she said, "your verdict. All is up to you."

There was silence for a long moment. Lada was shaking her head, still not capable of closing her mouth. Jim stared at the floor and breathed heavily. "It means," he slowly pronounced finally, "that I am . . . I am . . ."

"Yes." Sandra nodded, combining all her inner power together to hold herself in check. "It means, Jim, that you are my and Emmanuel's son. I knew that right away when I read your résumé. Your name was too well known to me. I remembered it for thirty-three years. And when I listened to your symphony, your level of talent only confirmed it. You have obviously inherited it from Emmanuel. For too many years, I was scared that my secret would come out. I was even blackmailed for it and paid big money to that disgusting woman in your group home."

"Oh Jeez!" Jim exclaimed suddenly. "It was you! I remember before Christmas, you came to the group home and gave a bag to Mona. The mysterious woman in a black car, with a driver wearing white gloves! I was watching from behind the corner of the building. I was curious. I felt some excitement and attraction toward you. I felt some strange connection, but Mona convinced me that you were a mother of another man there and brought presents for him."

"Lying as usual," Lada prompted sarcastically, finally able to close her mouth and then talk.

"Now," Sandra continued, "I realized, Jim, that you're not a person to hide. You're a real genius composer, and I should be not scared but proud to announce the truth to the world. But"—she turned to Lada—"would you mind, my dear, to give me some time in private with my son?"

"Of course not." Lada stood up. "Just a couple of words to my husband, please." She came to Jim's armchair, bowed, and whispered something into his ear. He nodded. "Are you thinking what I am thinking, Jim?" Lada asked.

He nodded again.

"Okay, I'll be back in about one hour," she said and left, smiling enigmatically.

When the door behind her closed, Sandra stood up and approached Jim. She knelt in front of him, took his hands, and kissed them. Then she let them go, covered her face with her hands, and lowered it on Jim's lap. "Jim, my son," she whispered through her tears, "can you ever forgive me for what I did to you? For the attempts to kill you . . . for destroying your life completely . . . I was a silly girl, abused and hurt. I was out of my mind . . . I understand now that those are not excuses for what I did to you. But maybe . . . just maybe . . . could you find the power in your soul to forgive me ever?" The sobs shook the whole of her body; she could not hold her tears inside anymore and let them stream out freely.

Jim put his hand on the back of her head and slowly petted her hair. "You know," he said quietly and pretty calmly, "I already forgave you long ago. I did have problems with that first time when I was about eight or nine, when I realized that I am not a normal person, and then maybe at twelve or thirteen, when I found out that the adoption contract was sealed, and I never would be able to find you. I was very angry at you and hurt a lot. I was even thinking about suicide. I didn't want to live like that, betrayed by my mother. The only thing that saved me was the ocean, the water, which gave me the sounds of music and forced me to compose and to live for that. But it was then. Now looking back, I am actually really thankful for what you did to me. If I was normal, I guess that I would be more like my father."

"Yes." Sandra sniffed. "You would be exactly like Emmanuel—tall, handsome, talented, brilliant in everything, irresistible."

"But what did all these things bring him? Was he happy? Look what happened to him," Jim continued. "Because of what you did to me, I actually was really blessed to be raised by Grandma Cathy. It was happiness and a privilege of my life to know her and to be loved by her. She was a real angel—old, sick, almost illiterate, but she possessed so much wisdom. She taught me everything, explained to me everything that she knew about life. She gave me education. Of course, I understand now—with the help of your money. But she never took a penny for herself. She gave everything to me. She was the best mother in the world whom one could just dream of. And I am very thankful to you that you passed me to her to grow up with.

"Then about my disability, if you didn't use those concoctions, I wouldn't have ever ended up in the group home after my Grandma Cathy died. And I would've never met Lada, another angel of my life. I can't imagine being happier than I am with her now. And this happiness I've got again, thanks to you. So what would be my reason not to forgive you? Of course, I did. Even more than that, I am thankful to you a lot for everything you did."

"So you will accept me, in spite of everything you know now, as a singer for your symphony?" Sandra asked, lifting her face and looking in his eyes.

Jim took her hand and kissed it—now was his turn. "It is another point of my happiness—your voice and my music combined together," he said. "Of course, I'll accept you. How could I not? It is my dream coming true, Mrs. Soley . . . Sandra . . . Mother . . . Mom. I don't know. What should I call you now?"

"Maybe Mama, in Italian *mamma mia*," Sandra said and stood up as they both laughed. "Now I think it is time to order that dinner. Where is that wife of yours, Jim?"

When the dinner was delivered and served in the dining room of the suite, Sandra lifted Jim and sat him into a high chair at the table. "Well, now I am doing what I was supposed to do with my baby." She laughed. "No offense, Jim."

"None taken." He laughed as well. "I like it when people laugh, even at me. It's better than them crying, looking at me. Laughing is much healthier."

At that moment, with a polite knock on the door, Lada came in, holding a wrapped package in her hands. "Oh, dinner is here!" she exclaimed happily. "Good, I'm hungry as a wolf. But first, Mrs. Soley, this is for you. It comes back to its lawful owner finally." She unwrapped the package and placed a marble statue on the table. It was the Lady of the Sorrows, which she kept for the last two months on the bedside table in her bedroom after Jim gave it to her for safekeeping.

CHAPTER 68

After the July 4 holiday, Boris invited the orchestra members for an orientation session on the new business. The rehearsal hall, where they were gathering now, was connected to the concert hall but was much smaller. The stage here had the same width but pretty low, just couple of inches above the rest of the floor. The audience place was also smaller, just the size of a regular auditorium, with a couple of rows of chairs lined up at the far end of the room.

The rehearsals were always a public event, and any of the university staff or students had the right to attend, if they would like to. Today there were already some people at the back row, and one of them was Lada. Beside her sat Sandra Soley. Lada suggested that they would come to the presentation together because, after the meeting, she planned to introduce Sandra to Boris and Rita as her new mother-in-law.

Boris invited his musicians to listen to Jim's symphony, all four parts of it, on the computer; and seeing that they were really impressed, he started his presentation. "I know, guys, that we have our schedule full for the summer," he said. "But this piece is unbelievable, don't you agree? I think it would be a real pride for us to play it and also a big benefit for our professional future. We could get all the credit as the first discoverers of this genius composer. This concert is planned for the end of September, so we have a little less than three months for rehearsals. I know, it's a bit tight, but your lines are already printed out, and you could get them right now." He tapped on the pile of papers lying in front of him on the table.

"A couple of days later," he continued, "we will add a singer and a vocal line to our symphony. We're working on the contract with the singer now. So these would be very special rehearsals as we never did them before with vocals. Professionally, it will be a great experience for all of us."

"Are we still playing our regular university programs?" one of the musicians asked.

"Yes, we're working for the university as usual."

It meant actually that their work hours from 10:00 a.m. until 3:00 p.m. every day would continue. However, Boris didn't say that. He was careful, trying not to focus their attention on the amount of work time, but they got it anyway.

"Well," another musician said, "then when do you want us to work on this new symphony? In the evenings?"

"Yeah, I guess after dinner, also on weekends. This way, we could do both, the regular program and the new one."

"Boris, are you crazy? Don't you know that we all have families?" someone started, and then protests began shooting at their conductor's head like bullets.

"It's summer. Kids are out from school. We would rather spend weekends with them on the beach."

"Your wife is here with you, but my wife is working full time. When would I see her if I'm working here all evenings?"

Rita was playing in the orchestra as well. She was the concertmaster of the first violin section, but nobody ever pointed this out as a privilege for Boris. Now it happened for the first time.

"You're suggesting that our working days be nine to ten hours long?"

"Who will pay overtime?"

"And how much?"

"I am afraid it should be volunteer work," Boris said. "But it is extremely important. We have to do that. We don't have a choice."

"What is so important in it?"

"For whom?"

"No, you're crazy, Boris. Volunteer work is usually one day per week, no more than that."

"It's impossible!"

"Don't you know that we have bills to pay?"

"I did talk with our administration, and they refused to finance this concert because the composer is unknown to them and not famous yet," Boris said. "But come on, guys, it's impossible not to see the quality of this music. It's absolutely clear that it will be a phenomenal success, which will be beneficial for all of us. We'll probably repeat this concert every week after the premiere, and it will bring us more and more money with each and every performance. A little investment that we could do now will be paid off double, maybe triple. It is really worth a try."

"Sounds good," one of the musicians agreed. "But we still have to pay bills. I, for example, have a second job on weekends. Do you want me to lose it?"

"Who would volunteer every evening? Nobody!"

"I would," Rita suddenly said, loud and confident.

"You're just supporting your husband!"

"Easy for you to say, Rita, when you have a grandma for your kids at home. I don't have any."

"And I can't pay a babysitter for evenings if I am not earning anything here."

"No, it's absurd, Boris."

"Don't even think about it."

"Pretty stupid suggestion on your part."

"Guys," Boris said very seriously, even a bit angrily, "I am not joking here. You'll understand that later and will thank me that I pulled you into this work. I am so sure about the success of this concert and the profit of our investment into it that I would sell my house and pay you for rehearsals. Just tell me how much you want."

The musicians laughed.

"It's not funny. I'm not joking," Boris continued persistently. "I can easily see through this music. I'm sure that, as professionals, you could as well. You're just scared of financial problems and some family difficulty, but it is all solvable. Tell me, for how much each of you will agree to work every evening and every weekend for three months?"

"Boris, aren't you scared to sell your house?"

"Where would you live with your family then?"

"Ask Rita, if she agreed." Someone giggled.

"I'll sell the house now, but I'll buy a palace after!" Boris exclaimed. "Who will laugh then?"

"No, you're obviously crazy."

"You're out of your mind!"

"Rita, say something." The violin players from her string section turned to her.

Rita, still calm and collected, smirked a bit sarcastically and noted, "I actually agree with that. I trust Boris's intuition. He knows what he is doing . . . usually. And this music, guys . . . I'm a pretty strong person, but I really was crying when I heard it the first time. I noticed that some of you had tears as well. I'm sure it will be a big success."

"Just tell me how much you want," Boris repeated heatedly. "Guys, let's move ahead. We're wasting time. How much?"

The musicians started turning to one another, whispering, discussing their potential salary. Many were shaking their heads in disbelief; many got thoughtful, calculating hours in their minds. They discussed money in each section separately and then collected their results together. This reminded Boris of a jury discussing a verdict, especially after they chose the concertmaster of the woodwinds to announce the results.

"Okay, we have reached our verdict," the stocky gray-haired flutist said finally, and everybody laughed. "Three thousand per month would be good, even though we still have to discuss the problem at home with our families. For three months, it will be nine thousand per person, and there are eighty of us. So if we included some other expenses that might appear during this time, like advertising, for example, and also your salary, Boris, altogether, about eight hundred thousand. Can you be sure that your house will sell for that much?"

"I think so." Boris nodded.

"And how fast could you sell it? Sometimes it takes many months or even years!" someone else shouted.

"I will try to do my best. I'll start with a realtor tomorrow morning," Boris confirmed.

At that moment, Sandra rose from the back row and walked to his table. She stopped in front of the musicians. "Ladies and gentlemen," she said, "during your work on this symphony, there could be some more unexpected expenses as well. I am suggesting I will pay you one million altogether. I hope you trust Mr. Meleshko to share this money as salary for all of you equally." And she put the check, prepared beforehand, on the table in front of Boris.

Everybody went silent, looking at her in astonishment. For the musicians, it was a complete shock. For Boris and Rita, it was as well. They had no idea that Lada invited Sandra to the presentation.

"I myself will work for this symphony as a volunteer," Sandra continued. "I am the singer whom Mr. Meleshko was talking about."

"Mrs. Soley!" one of the musicians screamed. "I know you. I was playing in the Metropolitan Opera in New York when you were starring as Aida there. I remember our orchestra working with you."

Sandra smiled. "I don't remember you, sorry. But yes, I was singing *Aida* there for three seasons."

"But why do you want to pay for this symphony, Mrs. Soley? I saw your interview with Larry King. You told him that you're doing a lot of charity. But why this one? Are you as sure as our Boris here that it would be a success?"

"The author of this symphony is my son," Sandra said quietly, "and also the son of Emmanuel."

"How come? I remember you said to Larry King that you never had children."

"It was not true," Sandra answered, suppressing a spasm in her throat. "When my son was born, I was only sixteen. I gave him up for adoption when he was three days old, and I feel that I owe him for that now."

CHAPTER 69

The following three months until the concert were extremely busy for everybody. Sandra Soley was teaching her vocal classes in the mornings, and at evenings and on weekends, she worked with Boris and his orchestra on rehearsals of Jim's symphony. She suggested that the concert would be dedicated to the memory of Emmanuel and would be held on September 29—the day of Emmanuel's death thirty-four years ago. The musicians approved. The idea even made everybody excited, and Boris was sure that it would be great for their advertising.

Jim was already introduced to the musicians of the orchestra as the author of the symphony and Sandra and Emmanuel's son. He decided to compose a little piece for a ten-minute introduction—variations on Emmanuel's first song, "The Endless Water," in memory of his father, whom he sadly never had the chance to know. It should be a perfect match for his symphony.

Lada, unexpectedly for Jim, proved to be an excellent manager. She ran around, preparing and organizing everything for the concert—announcements in all the newspapers and on local TV and radio stations, printing fliers and programs for distribution to the public before the concert, delivery of fliers by mail to most parts of both cities Minneapolis and Saint Paul, and so on. She also ordered a huge sheet with Jim's portrait printed on it. During the concert, it would be rolled up and hung on the ceiling by the back wall of the stage. At the end, it would be rolled down and represent the author's appearance on the stage.

According to Victor's advice, Jim gave Mona scores of parts 2 and 3 of his symphony, which he took back from Lada's safekeeping. It looked like Victor was right—after that, Jim's relationship with Mona got a bit better.

A couple of days after that, Mr. Erikson—the professor of composition—came to see Boris again, holding folders of the scores of all parts of Jim's symphony. "My student Miss Sharon Lainer brought these to me yesterday," he said. "She is claiming that she finished all scores and that they are ready to be performed. What are we going to do about that, Mr. Meleshko?"

"You know," Boris answered, "we were thinking about that for quite a long time. Jim consulted with some authorities. He didn't tell me with whom exactly—police, lawyers, or someone else—but they plan to arrest Sharon Lainer and her mother for theft right at the concert. So it is important for us to make sure that they will attend, and at the end, during the ovation, Sharon will come out on the stage, pretending to be the author. For that, we will need your cooperation along with the orchestra. My guys need to know what's going on here."

"So how can we do that?" Mr. Erikson asked, shaking his head in disbelief of the whole story. For more than thirty years, he had been teaching young composers in the university and never seen such an unusual and unlawful situation.

"I think that Jim, you, and I should talk to my musicians," Boris said, "and let them know the whole story of the step-by-step stealing of Jim's work. He is living in the group home owned by Sharon's mother, Mona Lainer. She found out that he is composing, that he is talented and also naive and trustful like a child. And she obviously decided to use his work for her daughter's benefit. During Jim's residence there, about nine months, she took his work page by page and made copies. Then she gave them to Sharon to bring to you."

"Yes, I did notice that all Sharon brought to show me were just copies," the old teacher said. "I was surprised by that, but she convinced me that she kept the originals at home as she is scared that they could be lost or stolen if taken out. It was a strange explanation. However, I didn't have any other choice but to believe her. The scores of the first part of the symphony were copies as well. But these, what I have now—parts 2, 3, and 4—are originals written with a pencil, not a pen, which is very strange. How could this happen?"

"Jim's tiny fingers are only capable of holding a short piece of pencil. Any pen is too big and bulky for him, so he is always writing with pencils. He gave the originals of the last three parts to Mona Lainer because the authorities advised him to do so. They need evidence to complete the case," Boris explained. "Let's go, Mr. Erikson, and talk to my orchestra."

After Boris revealed to his musicians Jim's story, everyone was bewildered. None of them had heard anything like that before. They knew that sometimes lawsuits happen between composers in regard to copyrights, but this usually occurred with short songs or even some lines in the songs but not the whole symphony. It was huge. It was even difficult to believe.

The musicians consulted one another and discussed in groups the possibility of tricking Sharon and participating as witnesses in the coming lawsuit. Then they reached their verdict, exactly like the last time when it was about money. The announcement was made by the concertmaster of the woodwinds group. "We agree to be introduced to Miss Lainer and to pretend that we are believing that she is the author of the symphony. But we need to be more than 100 percent sure about her fraud. So we would like to meet her and ask her the same questions about the symphony and the procedure of her composing, which we already asked Mr. Bogat. He gave us a very clear answer for every question. We would like to hear what Miss Lainer would say. We think it would be fair to give her an equal chance to talk and defend her work."

To compare Jim's and Sharon's knowledge and experience in composing seemed to be laughable for Boris, but this request sounded fair; he couldn't disagree with it. So Sharon was invited, together with her composing professor, to meet the orchestra and its conductor. The old Mr. Erikson promised that he would just listen silently and would not be involved in the questioning.

They did not invited Jim, Sandra, or Lada to this meeting. Sharon should assume that Boris and the orchestra didn't know them and never met them. And then the meeting started. The first question was "Miss Lainer, you told your teacher that you're composing with the help of a special customized computer program," one of the musicians said. "I know this program. It was designed for a person who, for some reason, is not capable of playing a piano. You're a professional pianist. Why do you need to use this program?"

"Just because it is new technology." Sharon shrugged. "It is always beneficiary to use newer concepts."

"In what year was it installed into your computer?"

"I don't remember."

"What's the name of the company who did this program for you?"

"I don't remember."

"Every composer in the world is writing scores with a pen if they do this manually. The manual job is actually very seldom nowadays. Most modern composers prefer to use computers. Why are you writing with a pencil?"

"Because I want to."

"The reading and especially the writing of orchestra scores are very professional skills. There is a course in Juilliard for three years to get these skills. You just started composing some months ago. How do you know how to write the scores of the whole symphony?"

"By intuition." Sharon shrugged. "Because I am a genius obviously."

The whole orchestra exploded into a thunder of laughter. Sharon smiled shyly.

One man said, "I am playing the clarinet. In the second part of the symphony, in the main line, you used very high notes. Why did you use them there? Do you know what the clarinet's range normally is?"

"I don't remember now. If I'll start composing, I will remember, though."

Another burst of laughter followed this stupidity.

"Maybe this is enough acquaintance with Miss Lainer, ladies and gentlemen?" Boris asked.

"No, no, no, we're having fun here!" someone shouted.

"Let us enjoy some more, Boris."

"Why did you name your work *The Symphony of the Ocean*, Miss Lainer?"

"I don't know, just because I want to."

"Why did you decide to add a vocal line to it?"

"I never did. Vocal shouldn't be in the symphony. It is an instrumental only."

"So there will be no singer performing on this concert, Miss Lainer?"

"Of course not."

"Do you want to add an introduction before the symphony? Like a famous song or something?"

"No. It's a strange idea. Of course not."

Some musicians teared up with laughter. It was great fun for them, but Boris made a serious face, urging them to stop it and make it more believable for Sharon. "That's enough, absolutely enough, ladies and gentlemen," he insisted. "We already know Miss Lainer and her composing ability well enough to agree to perform her symphony. Don't you think so?"

"Yeah!" everybody screamed while still giggling.

"So, Miss Lainer, we will start working now on the rehearsals to be ready for your concert," Boris said as he tried to end the comedy show. "It is scheduled for September 29 at 7:00 p.m. You will be very welcome to attend and to bring one guest. There will be special seats in the audience prepared for you as VIP guests. I am sure that the performance would be successful, and you'll be very happy about the quality of the job we will do for you."

"When could I receive my royalties?" Sharon asked. "And how much would it be?"

Everybody in the room held their breaths. Jim never asked anything like that.

"It depends on how many tickets are sold for the concert," Boris answered. "We can't say anything about that now. But you don't have to worry. We are doing a great deal of advertising, and there is no question that you'll get big money. Congratulations, Miss Lainer! Your work is accepted for performance."

Boris politely saw Sharon to the door. When she left, he turned to his musicians. "Guys, are you satisfied now?" he asked with a smile. "No questions about the author anymore?"

"No!" everybody screamed, laughing like crazy.

"It was a shame to me," the composing professor said sadly. "I don't know how I should continue teaching my class with her after that."

"Mr. Erikson, with all due respect," Boris said, "for the sake of justice, you should help us, please, and continue your classes with her, pretending that everything is okay and that nothing suspicious happened here. You saw Jim. You understand his level of talent and his vulnerability. To steal the work of his life from him is a serious crime, but more than that, it is a huge moral crime, and this is absolutely unforgivable. When you see Sharon, please be very cautious. Don't let her suspect anything that may happen at the concert. This is your citizen duty and also the duty of your conscience."

"I know," the old teacher answered. "I promise, Mr. Meleshko, I will do my best."

"All that I said to Mr. Erikson," Boris continued, addressing the musicians, "is the same to all of you, guys. No one says a word about the coming arrest at the concert. Sharon is still in this university. She has friends, classmates. If even one word leaks somewhere, the whole police procedure could be ruined, and justice may never be served. Swear to God for me, please, that you will be silent about this whole story until after the concert."

Everybody nodded and shouted their approval and their promises.

"I trust you, guys, and I believe in you." Boris ended his speech. "Now back to work, please. Sandra will be here in five minutes. Let's start our rehearsal."

CHAPTER 70

In spite of the pretty hectic time during the months before the concert, almost every day, Lada found the opportunity to meet Jim and have sex with him, which she was now crazy about. Usually, she drove to the group home after three o'clock, when the guys arrived from the factory, and Victor took over from Jim the duty to watch Mona. Then Jim was free to go where he wanted.

If the weather was nice and sunny, Lada and Jim walked to their favorite wheat field and enjoyed the memory of their first lovemaking. They listened to the little skylark singing above while loving each other madly until completely exhausted, and then they always slept for a while. For the days when the weather was cold and rainy, Lada made a little unofficial contract with Jason to drive Jim to the city after dinner. She knew that Jason was going home to the city on his bus anyway. Then Lada and Jim would go to a hotel for their date, and in the evening, she drove him back to the group home.

During his rides with Jason, which occurred at least a couple of times per week, Jim still felt hesitant to develop a friendly relationship, though Jason really tried. One day Jason asked, "Hey, Jim, you have been here for a long time already, aren't you?"

"Nine months," Jim answered.

"Could you tell me something about Mona? What have you learned?"

"Why? You're the one sleeping with her now, and you should know," Jim retorted.

Jason was surprised. "Why do you think I am sleeping with her?"

"I have my eyes. I saw something."

"No." Jason laughed. "You didn't see anything ever."

In reality, Jim didn't see anything by himself; he just repeated what Victor told him. He had no right to betray Victor, but he also couldn't suppress the wish to be sarcastic with Jason. He still had difficulty overcoming his jealousy. "I saw your bus staying overnight by the garage many times," Jim said, though in reality he didn't. "And in the mornings, pretty often, you do not arrive on the bus to pick up the guys, but you come out from Mona's suite." It was again what Victor had told him.

Jason giggled. "Okay then, it's part of my job."

"Yes, it may be. The previous bus driver did the same thing."

"The previous bus driver was Lada as far as I know," Jason objected.

"No, another guy, Ramah, who worked here before Lada. But he was at least single, and you have a fiancée. It's a shame. Why are you doing that?"

Jason shrugged. "As I said, it's part of my job. How do you know I have a fiancée?"

"Lada told me."

"Oh." Jason laughed again. "Of course, she is your wife. She is telling you everything." Jim felt a hint of sarcasm in the last sentence, especially as Jason emphasized the last word. It warned him a bit; however, he didn't say anything more.

"Now," Jason continued, "back to Mona. I am not asking about anything private that you assume I should know myself. I am asking how she is with other people here. Did she ever hurt somebody or steal something from somebody? Those guys are so vulnerable and defenseless. I feel pity for them and kind of worry a bit about them."

"Well, if you're sleeping with her," Jim said, irritated, "you should see her diamond necklaces. She is always wearing them in bed. This fact alone could tell you everything."

"How do you know about that, Jim?" Jason winked at him. "Did you go down that path too? Hello, brother! How many necklaces are we talking here about?"

"I saw at least three," Jim confessed, even more irritated at himself for talking about that.

"I saw six so far. And this is what forced me to ask, what do you think about Mona? She is obviously hiding money from the banks. So they must be stolen, I guess?"

"You know, Jason"—Jim shook his head—"I don't want to say anything about a woman I was involved with once, long ago, when I just came here. She is a monster, that's for sure, but she is still a woman, and it's kind of dirty for us to talk about that."

"Actually, I agree." Jason nodded. "Sorry about that, Jim." After that, they just drove in silence and never returned to this topic again.

One time the rainy and cold days continued for a week, and Lada said to Jim, "You know, I'm actually tired of these hotels. It feels disgusting, like we are hiding something. I feel like a thief. Let's go home. You're my lawful husband, and I want to sleep with you all night in my own bed. It was kind of stupid decision on my part to hide our marriage from Mom. BB and I decided to do so because we just wanted to keep peace in the family, but this hiding can't continue our whole life. It will come out anyway someday. So why not now?"

Jim called Mona and warned her that he would stay overnight with a friend in the city. Their relationship became a bit better lately, so Mona gave him permission.

When they came to Lada's home, nobody was there except for the dog, Oscar. He greeted them, jumping happily and licking their hands and faces, where he could reach. Lada pulled Jim in her bedroom right away and locked the door. "Here we are safe," she said, hugging and kissing him. "Gosh, I miss you so much, Jim. I am dying without you, though we just did it yesterday."

"Okay, please relax, darling," Jim whispered between kisses. "Relax and calm down. And enjoy. It will be okay, even in this new place, I am sure. I feel it already."

Now with their experience, he knew perfectly her every wish and desire and what would make her especially happy. As for Jim, he was happy with everything, absolutely everything, that they did together. In the past, with Mona, sex was always exhausting and almost killing him. He was afraid of it and hated it. It was repellent to him because she was aggressive. Lada was quite the opposite. She wasn't aggressive at all and did not request Jim to do anything.

He did what he felt was right to both of them. In bed, she always appeared weak and vulnerable and clearly related to the very wise old proverb "The power of the woman is in her powerlessness." She was just immersed in her own feelings so deep that it didn't matter to her what Jim was doing. Anything was perfect for her, and any touch gave her orgasm after orgasm. She felt so sexy that practically every millimeter of her skin was now an erogenous zone. When she was lying beside Jim, absolutely spent, almost dead from the enormous amount of pleasure, she was so weak and powerless that it gave him an unbelievable feeling of being a strong, powerful, and confident man who owned her completely. And it was exciting; it was real satisfaction and happiness for him physically, morally, and emotionally.

Afterward, they slept for a while as usual to restore their strength and then were woken up by the noise downstairs. The children came home from hanging around with their friends in the park. "Okay, I'll take a shower, and then we'll go there, and I'll introduce you," Lada said.

However, Jim decided that he felt confident enough to try to do it himself. He got dressed and quietly walked out from the bedroom door. On the landing, he sat and slid from the steps of the stairwell as he usually did in the group home. The children were in the living room.

"Wow," little Dave said, seeing him. "It's quite a trick. I would like to do that too."

"Who are you?" Becky exclaimed and began laughing, exactly like Lada did when she saw him the first time.

"I'm actually your new uncle," Jim said, laughing too. "I am the husband of your aunt Lada. My name is Jim. Nice to meet you, guys."

"Husband? We didn't see any wedding. Aren't we invited? Why? Show me your ring."

"We just got a marriage license in city hall," Jim explained, extending his hand toward Becky to show her his ring. "Our wedding ceremony will be after the concert at the end of September. Then you'll be invited for sure."

"Such a cute ring!" The girl nodded in approval. "Okay, I am Becky, and he is Dave. Nice to meet you too, Uncle Jim." She still kept laughing. "Oh Jeez, you're so much shorter than Lada. Now she can't wear high heels when she goes with you somewhere. Why are you so small? Didn't you eat well while you were a child?"

"I was born this way," Jim said calmly. He wasn't offended at all. Kids are always learning, and they ask questions. He did it all the time with Grandma Cathy.

"We were kind of expecting that you were handicapped," Dave said. "I overheard something. The adults were fighting over this a couple of times. But you are kind of too small. We have a math teacher at school. He is handicapped too. He is in a wheelchair, but he is much bigger than you."

"Much, much bigger," Becky confirmed. "Do you have a wheelchair?"

"I did when I was a kid. But then I did exercise a lot. And from age fifteen, I can walk myself."

"I still would like to learn this trick on the stairs," Dave repeated his request. "Could you teach me?"

"I don't think you can do that." Jim laughed. "This is for toddlers. My legs are the same size as a toddler's, but yours are too long. Lada tried it once, and she tucked her knees to her chin and then fell down. I remember we were laughing like crazy then."

"You know, you're kind of cute," Becky said. "I like your dimple on the chin. It's a kind of rare thing. And your hair is so beautiful. Actually, you remind me of someone. I can't remember exactly, but I guess I saw your picture somewhere."

"I know where," Dave prompted. "Do you know Grandma's CD collection? Her favorite songs . . . there is one guy on the CD box. He was probably a singer. I think you look a lot like him."

"I know. I was told many times. Actually, he was my father, Emmanuel. My parents were singers in the group called M and Sandra," Jim said, feeling surprised that he could say that aloud for the first time in his life.

"Wow!" Becky exclaimed and clapped her hands. "If I tell my friends, they would be all pissed off that I have the son of M and Sandra as my new uncle. Jeez, right away, I will be the most popular girl at school!"

At that moment, Lada appeared at the top of the stairs. "Hey, guys." She chuckled as usual while walking down and joining them in the living room. "I see you already got to know one another. I can see that you like my husband, right?"

"He is kind of cute," Becky repeated her previous statement. "Do you know, Lada, who his dad was?"

"I do." Lada nodded. "Jeez, were you already bragging, Jim?"

"No, it's just jumped out accidentally."

"Well, I would like Jim to stay with us today for a sleepover, guys. Any objections?"

"No." Everybody giggled, and then they heard the sound of a car coming into the garage. Their grandma returned from grocery shopping.

CHAPTER 71

Wile Lada was thinking of what to say or do, how to eliminate the problem with her mother, and whether to send the kids to their rooms or let them stay, Dave solved her puzzles, not even noticing it himself. He ran to the garage to help his grandma carry the bags of groceries, screaming, "Grandma, Grandma, we have a new uncle here, Lada's husband, Jim!"

Then Becky joined him, yelling, "Grandma, he is so funny but kind of cute!"

Lada took a deep breath and whispered to Jim, "We better sit on the couch." She lifted him from the lower step of the stairs, where he was still sitting after his slide from the second floor. She placed him on the couch and sat beside him.

"Don't worry," she whispered, squeezed his hand, and kept holding it, tenderly caressing it with her shaky fingers.

Jim wasn't worrying at all; he guessed that she said this much more for herself than for him. He felt that she was extremely tense and even scared. They obviously had fought about this before as Dave already let the cat out of the bag.

Jim knew that the reaction to seeing him for the first time would be surprising for Lada's mother. It always was for everyone, and he got used to it. He didn't care. To appreciate who he was, people were supposed to talk to him and get to know him better slowly. And he was always open to conversation with anyone.

Lada's mother, Tatiana, and the children entered the kitchen together from the garage door, carrying the bags and putting the groceries on the counters. The kids were jumping and giggling from the excitement of the news, which they shared with their grandmother. Then they came into the living room all together.

Tatiana looked at Jim with huge eyes and shook her head. "Ladochka, you did it," she said matter-of-factly. "Why?" And then she sobbed, covering her face with both hands while lowering herself in an armchair.

"Grandma, don't cry!" the children began shouting and hugging her. "Why are you crying?"

"Guys," Lada said in a very harsh voice, "please leave Grandma alone and go to your rooms for a while. We need to talk here, and it will be an adult talk. I'll call you back later when we are done."

"Okay, okay," the children mumbled, pouting, knowing pretty well that if they didn't listen to Lada, she would call their parents. So nonchalantly, they left. Lada wasn't sure that they wouldn't eavesdrop somewhere from behind a corner from curiosity, but that wasn't her business anymore.

"Mama," she said, still trying to be calm, "why are you crying? What happened? I married the man I love, and I am happy. What's wrong with that?"

"Ladochka, I was begging you not to bring this cripple here ever." Tatiana sniffed. "Don't you deserve a normal man, not this tiny monster, which is impossible even to look at without throwing up?"

She was speaking in Ukrainian, and Lada felt the awful horror, knowing that Jim could easily understand. "Stop it!" she screamed in Ukrainian as well. "Nobody here is asking your opinion. Have some respect if not for my husband, at least for me. I am an adult woman, and I deserve to be happy finally."

"How happy would you be if you will produce the same terrifying freaks of nature instead of normal kids?" Tatiana yelled back, agitated. "I don't want to have grandchildren who look like that."

Jim, to her huge surprise, suddenly said to her in Ukrainian as well. "I am sorry, ma'am. I didn't want to scare you. You don't have to worry. Our children won't be looking like me. It's not a genetic disorder. It was just a tragic accident that happened with my mother. That is what made me become a midget."

"How do you know Ukrainian?" Tatiana exclaimed, bewildered.

"I was raised by a Ukrainian family, and I also took a language course at the university. Now if you're not happy with my presence in this house, I will leave and never come back. Sorry." Jim slid from the couch onto the floor and look at Lada questioningly, not being sure that she approved of what he just said. She jumped up from the couch as well, grabbed his hand, and pulled him to the door.

"We're leaving, Mama!" she screamed. "And I'll never come back, and you'll never see me again until you apologize to Jim. He is an angel, my real angel, and the love of my life. I'll never forgive you for hurting him. Remember, you don't have a daughter anymore!"

Lada slammed the door behind them, lifted Jim, and ran from the steps of the porch down to the driveway, where her car was parked. Breathing heavily and shaking from anger, she settled him in the passenger seat. Then she walked around the car, got in the driver's seat, and turned on the ignition.

"Where to?" Jim asked very quietly. Now he was pretty shaky as well and could barely talk from a spasm squeezing his throat.

"To the hotel again," Lada answered abruptly and suddenly sobbed almost hysterically while starting to drive. She turned to the street from the driveway, went a couple of blocks, and then stopped, dropping her head on the steering wheel and choking breathlessly on her sobs. She couldn't drive anymore in this condition.

Jim unbuckled his belt, climbed up on his seat, and stood on it, now the same height as Lada. He hugged her and put his head on her shoulder, trying to soothe her; but instead of that, they cried together for a while, holding each other tight.

"What's happening with us, Jim? Look, everything is turned upside down," she repeated and repeated many times in a row. "Now you have a mother, and I don't. I don't understand how could it happen."

The whole night in that hotel, Jim didn't sleep but caressed her unstoppably, trying to soothe her and calm her down. It ended up in affectionate lovemaking. They fell asleep only in the morning, exhausted almost to death and feeling like their hearts and souls were beaten up badly.

When Boris and Rita returned home from the rehearsal at about eleven o'clock, nobody was sleeping there as they expected. Tatiana was crying on the couch in the living room, and the kids were sitting in the big armchair across from her, hugging each other and crying as well. "What's going on here?" Boris asked in a strong voice. "What's happening? Is somebody hurt, sick, or dead?"

"Lada brought her husband to meet us, and Grandma doesn't like him," Becky complained.

"He knows how to do the funny trick on the stairs." Dave joined her. "I would like to do that too."

"Yeah, he is very funny, but I think he's also kind of cute," Becky continued. "And you wouldn't believe who his father is."

"Okay, okay, okay." Boris stopped her. Realizing right away what happened, he turned to Rita. "*Bebe*, please take the kids upstairs and talk to them while they are getting ready for sleep. I will deal with the rest here."

"Yes," Rita replied while trying to keep smiling to reduce the tension. "Let's go, my sweethearts. It's already long past your bedtime. You will tell me the story up there." She hugged the children by their shoulders and led them to the stairs.

Boris sat in the armchair across from his mother. "Calm down, Mom," he said. "Stop crying and explain to me properly what happened."

"I begged you, Boris, to not give her permission to bring this cripple here. The kids can be scared."

"They don't look scared at all."

"Yeah, maybe, but he is disgusting. It's not normal for children to see someone like that."

"Mom, stop pretending to worry about the children. They are just fine," Boris retorted, quite irritated. He and Rita had an eleven-hour working day and were tired, but instead of finally resting and relaxing at home, he was forced now to deal with this stupid problem about nothing. "What do you really want?"

"I want Ladochka to be happy."

"And how is it working for you? Did you make her happy?"

"No, she is stubborn, and she doesn't understand that she is beautiful and absolutely capable of finding a normal man. She probably still has that complex, fearing normal men."

"Mom, listen to me, please, and stop crying. It's annoying. Jim is much more than any normal man could be. He is a genius composer. He is highly educated, more than any of us, actually. And he has a very honest, open, kind, and warm personality, very big soul and heart. This is why Lada loves him, I am sure. This is what attracted her at the beginning, when they just met."

"Big soul and heart?" Tatiana retorted sarcastically. "Maybe he also has a big penis."

"I don't know about that." Boris smirked. "You remember at that breakfast after Hawaii, she screamed at me that I have no right to put my nose in her sex life. But in spite of his appearance, I can see clearly that he obviously knows what to do in bed. Look at her. She is beaming, blooming, glowing, blossoming. She is not walking but flying around. I never, in the five years that you are here, did see her that happy.

"You know, Mom, we always had problems with Lada after her tragedy—all those surgeries, treatments, her fear of men, her social awkwardness, her inability to find friends, her absence of feelings. Jeez, how many psychologists, psychiatrists, and hypnotists I did spend endless money on with no results! And Jim fixed all her problems effortlessly, just like that." Boris snapped his fingers. "She changed dramatically. She is a different person now—absolutely healthy physically and mentally and emotionally and absolutely happy. We, our whole family, should be thankful to him even for that alone."

He continued, "Then Jim gave us the privilege to perform his symphony, which will be a huge burst of professional success for Rita and me and the whole orchestra. And this is no less important for me than the health and happiness of my little sister. We really should bow our heads in front of Jim and thank him wholeheartedly, and don't be as ungrateful to and defiant with him as you are, Mom.

"This is already the third scandal here in the last month. Our family never was like that after my father died. The scandals always were with him only. You remember how mad he was about my emigration? And how that ended? He just lost me as a son, you lost me for eighteen years, Lada lost me as a brother for twelve years of her life, my grandma was sent away from Kiev to Moscow. She lost me as a grandson and practically Lada as a granddaughter. Jeez, the whole family was destroyed for one stupid reason—my father didn't want me to do what I wanted to do. And he was angry that I did it anyway.

"Do you get it, Mom? It is exactly what's going on here now. You don't want Lada to do what she wants to do. It never works. You should never ever interfere with your child's choice of a partner. When my kids grow up and choose their partners, I, as a father, would never object to their choices, and I am sure Rita wouldn't as well."

"I agree, if they will find a nice partner." Tatiana still sniffled a bit. "But what would you do if Becky, for example, brought home a drunk, dirty, druggy, uneducated loser who doesn't want work and will be mooching on her? Would you permit that? Wouldn't you blame her and prohibit that?"

"It would never happen in the first place because I am raising her to understand certain standards of what a family should be. Rita and I, we are role models for our kids, so I am sure their choices would be decent and acceptable. And this dirty image that you trying to draw for me is a hundred percent not related to Jim. He is not a bad guy, not even a regular good guy. In reality, he is a superman with all his moral, mental, and spiritual quality. I am happy and proud of our little kiddo that she made that excellent choice."

"You sound convincing in theory, son, but I am still confused," Tatiana said thoughtfully. "I don't know what I should do now."

"I know what you should do." Boris stood up, went to the sound center beside the TV, and inserted a CD into the player. "Listen to this music first, Mom," he said, "to understand who Jim is. Then you will know why Lada fell in love with him. I am going to sleep now, but we will talk about this tomorrow."

CHAPTER 72

The next morning, Lada and Jim went to look for an apartment and, by noon, already rented a one-bedroom suite. They decided that Lada would settle there alone for now, and Jim would visit her for dates until the concert. Then after the concert would be their big wedding, and finally, he would leave the group home, and they would move together and start their own family life.

For now, they just bought a new mattress and the whole bedding set to put together on the floor and also some kitchen stuff, like kettle, coffee maker, and so on. Lada planned to order customized furniture for Jim's height, like the one he had at the group home. It should be ready in a couple of months when Jim would move in.

All these preparations would be very exciting if they weren't darkened by Lada's conflict with her mother. Tatiana's behavior was really undermining their good mood. Boris and Rita talked to her a lot, gave her a chance to listen to Jim's music, and revealed the story of Sandra and Emmanuel—her favorite rock group from her younger years. They explained what happened to Jim and convinced Tatiana that there was no danger for her future grandchildren, if they actually were ever to be born, knowing Lada's diagnosis. Finally, Tatiana agreed to apologize to her daughter and her husband, but it turned out that Lada and Jim both refused to accept her apology.

They discussed it once and for all, sitting on their mattress in their apartment, holding hands, and looking into each other's eyes. Lada was pretty adamant and said that she would never forgive her mother for hurting Jim. He persuaded her to soften up a bit.

"My love," Jim said very calmly and quietly, "you know that forgiveness is a very spiritual moment. We should do that. We have to forgive your mother. It is important for us much more than for her. We don't need to keep anger in our hearts. I am sure that she is not a bad person at all. She just can't change her mentality and points of view as simple as she changed her country of residence. For some people, it is easy to change, for some not.

"I could understand that she would worry about our future children. I could understand everything, and I forgive everything. But one thing hurt me the most—she called me a monster. It is how we're calling Mona, jokingly, of course. But that is what she really is. She is not human. She is a real monster. But me . . . only because I am small . . . this puts me on the same level with Mona. I forgive that as just a stupid word, but I really don't want to have your mother in my life. I am sorry, but I don't want to see her coming to us and apologizing. We don't need any apology. Just tell Boris to pass the message that we forgive her, and that's it."

"I agree." Lada sniffled a bit but held her tears bravely. "Okay, I am not angry anymore. I forgive her too, but I don't want to see her or listen to her apology because I am sure it wouldn't be sincere. I love you, Jim, and BB loves you, and Rita loves you, and the kids love you, and Sandra loves you, and the whole orchestra loves you, even the dog, Oscar, loves you. And I don't want to have a person in my life who doesn't love you deep in her heart and never would, apology or not. Yes, I will tell BB to pass the message from us that we forgive her, and that's it. Promise, my love, we will never talk about this again."

With that decision, the burden fell off their shoulders. The happy anticipation of the concert and of their future life after the concert became the main topic of their conversations from now on.

There was still so much to do. Almost every day they came up with new ideas. It was decided unanimously that Lada would be the host of the concert.

At one of the city's TV stations, Lada found a ninety-second old commercial advertising Emmanuel's group in 1969. The commercial presented him standing on a sailing vessel, wearing a white suit, holding the sailing canvas with one hand, looking at the open sea and the big waves ahead, and singing his first song "The Endless Water." His thick, wavy dark brown hair was flying in the wind. Sixteen-year-old Sandra, in red bikini, was sitting on the edge of the deck beside him, looking with excitement at him and at the waves ahead. She was singing too.

The commercial was beautifully done, though a bit faded with age; but they discussed it with Sandra, Boris, and the orchestra and decided to show it at the very beginning of the event. For that purpose, Lada ordered a big movie screen to be placed on the back wall behind the stage. Jim's musical introduction—the variation of the same song—was supposed to follow. Then there would be a small break for about twenty seconds, when Lada would announce the symphony.

The time before the concert was really exciting, but also exciting for Lada and Jim was the anticipation of their wedding and honeymoon. Sandra's contract for three months of teaching in Minneapolis was coming to an end on October 1, 2003, and she planned to go home to Italy for a vacation. She invited Jim and Lada to come with her for their honeymoon. She wanted to show them her birth country, museums, the opera theater La Scala, her village, her former school, and the memorable places of her childhood, especially the big rock by the sea where she was singing a lot and where she met Emmanuel. She wanted them to know her family history, which was now theirs as well. They accepted the invitation with great excitement and couldn't stop talking and dreaming about it almost every minute.

The coming concert was a huge milestone for their life, which was separated now in two parts—before the concert and after the concert. Before the concert, many things could still happen that could change something or change everything unexpectedly.

One day at the very end of August, Jason called Lada and invited her for coffee. Lada and Jim were in bed at the moment when her phone rang. They didn't make love, just talking, and Jim was lying right beside her. "I would like to talk to you about something important," Jason said. "But please don't tell Jim that you'll meet me."

"Okay," she answered, not quite understanding what he wanted. "Why?"

"I'll explain to you in person."

"Okay," she repeated slowly. "Then tell me where and when."

It seemed quite strange to Lada to keep some conspiracy from Jim. But she got curious. Jason must have a serious reason for that for sure. She listened silently while he arranged a time and place of their meeting, and then she finished the conversation abruptly with "okay" again.

"Who was it?" Jim asked.

"It's about business, one of my orders," she explained, blushing a bit. She felt very uncomfortable lying to him, but curiosity forced her. However, it came out well. Jim didn't notice anything wrong with her conversation and kept hugging her and smiling. But Lada still felt angry at herself.

The next day, when she met Jason at the downtown Starbucks, this anger came out. "What the hell!" she exclaimed as she entered and saw Jason waiting for her with a cup of coffee in front of him.

"Whoa, whoa, whoa!" He laughed. "Where is your usual polite hi? Sorry, I didn't get a coffee for you because I didn't know what you'd like. But I will right now as soon as you tell me."

"A small cappuccino," Lada said, calming down a bit. "Hi then. I'm very upset because you forced me to hide something from my husband. I never did that before in my life."

"Your married life is how long? Three weeks? A month?" Jason giggled and walked to the counter to get her coffee.

"Two months already!" Lada proudly shouted at his back.

"Okay, let's be serious," Jason said as he returned and placed on the table in front of her a white porcelain cup with a beautiful picture of a leaf on the foam. "I would like to talk about Mona. I don't want Jim to know because I already tried to ask him. He told me a few things, but he refused to tell me more. He said that it is kind of dirty to gossip behind her back.

"I appreciate that your husband is a man of ethics and very high moral standards, and I respect that. But the monster is possibly a danger for the whole group home, and I worry a bit about those challenged and vulnerable guys. I noticed some things. I know some stuff of what she is doing, but this is not enough, you know . . . to report. I am sure Jim told you a whole lot about her, didn't he?"

"Oh yes, he did, of course. And you got the right person here. I am not hesitant to gossip. You couldn't imagine how much I hate her. She hit him in the face when we came back from Hawaii. You probably saw this bruise under his eye."

"Yes." Jason nodded. "But I didn't ask. I assumed that he fell down accidentally or something."

"She was stealing his money for half the year, and she murdered one handicapped woman in her care, Lily, in January this year and also Maggie's baby recently."

"Murdered?" Jason put his elbows on the table and leaned toward Lada. "Really? And Jim knows about that? Why didn't you report it to the police?"

"Because there is absolutely no evidence. She is brilliant at hiding all her deeds. Nobody would believe anything without evidence. She said to Jim that she will present him as mentally ill with hallucinations if he tells something about her to anyone." Lada was getting more and more agitated with this ongoing discussion. "She threatened him. She fed Maggie's baby to the rats in the basement, and when Jim saw that, she said that he would be next in line to feed her rats."

"Wow!" Jason knitted his brows, trying to absorb the information.

"There is not as much ethics on Jim's part, as you think, but a fear of her," Lada continued. "I am sure he is just scared that's why he is not talking. Also, I am not even speaking yet about her stealing his symphony. We kind of dealt with that. Jim reported it to someone—I won't tell you to whom—but let's say to some authority. They plan to arrest her and her daughter at the concert for theft and fraud, but those are pretty small charges. They are nothing compared to what she really deserves."

"Why is Jim still there? Why doesn't he move in with you yet?" Jason asked, confused.

"Because this is not the end of the story. Mrs. Monster is also working for the Mafia, and together, they are planning another murder in the group home."

"One more murder?" Jason exclaimed, widening his eyes. "Really? Whom?"

"I can't tell you now. But Jim is watching Mona, trying to get more information, maybe some evidence so we could report it."

"But this is extremely dangerous for him, Lada." Jason shook his head. "He is not a professional to know how to do a proper surveillance. This is crazy. Jeez, you guys are playing with fire here."

"Maybe, but Jim is really adamant that he wants to do that. He can't forgive her for the baby's murder. He was in such a deep shock when this happened. It was before we left to Hawaii. You weren't working there at that time, Jason. So you didn't hear Maggie screaming in childbirth and

Mona beating her. And then she was paid for the baby's murder with a diamond necklace. Jim saw everything."

"Gosh!" Jason pressed his palms to his temples. "It's unbelievable! I didn't know anything about that. Yeah, I started work there when you were on that vacation. Mona was sure that Jim went with some man, but when she saw you, she realized that you're together. She told me about that, and then she hit your car in anger." Jason kept shaking his head, still in disbelief of everything that he heard. "Okay," he said finally, "I have one request for you. Please persuade Jim to tell you everything that he knows one more time, even every very small detail, and record it on a tape. And then give this tape to me. It could be really needed if you seriously want justice."

"How could you help here?" Lada asked. "You're just a bus driver exactly as I was. I saw a lot too, but I wasn't capable of doing anything. Oh, maybe your fiancée, Lucy—she is a policewoman, right?"

"Well . . ." Jason laughed. "Maybe my fiancée, Lucy . . . right. So please, Lada, I just need that tape and as soon as possible."

"Okay, I will try my best to persuade Jim to do that. But I also have one request for you, Jason. When you drive Jim on the bus again, please don't tell him ever that we met for coffee and for this conversation. You didn't want him to know about this meeting because he refused to talk to you about Mona. I don't want him to know for another reason."

"What is your reason?" Jason smiled. "Could I guess?"

"No need to guess, I can tell you. Jim is very jealous of you. I know that he wouldn't say anything to me or to you . . . yes, because of his ethics and moral level, as you call it . . . but he would suffer a lot silently. Believe me, there has been enough pain in his life. I don't want to add more. I love him very, very much, and I really care about his well-being and his happiness. I want to protect him from his own jealousy."

"Hmm." Jason smirked, shrugging, and then pronounced slowly, "I actually don't see any reason for him to be jealous. We're not—"

"Stop it," Lada interrupted, giggling flirtatiously. "Tell the truth, Jason. We are . . . kind of . . . like each other, and this is pretty obvious, isn't it? I even see right now how you look at me. Stop smiling! Your eyes are sparkling . . . and you probably see how I am looking at you as well. You're a damn handsome guy, Jason. I am sorry to recognize that. Your fiancée, Lucy, is a very lucky girl."

"Well . . ." He chuckled flirtatiously as well and lifted his palms. "She is . . . if she really exists."

"What?"

"Nothing, nothing, just kidding. Come on, married woman. I am very happy for you and Jim honestly. And of course, I won't tell anything. Don't worry. Just please make sure that I get this tape."

"I will. I promise," Lada said. "I understand the importance of this business well enough."

CHAPTER 73

There was one month left before the concert. On weekends, when Victor wasn't working at the factory and Jim was free from his surveillance of Mona, Jim and Lada quite often went to the concert hall to listen to the rehearsals. It was very interesting for Jim to hear and to see for the first time in his life how a beautiful full creature, his symphony, appeared from pieces, short cuts, and separated and unrelated lines into one living organism of orchestra work. Lada wasn't a novice in this procedure because she attended Boris's rehearsals of other different classical works many times, but Jim enjoyed it immensely. The unbelievable feeling of pride for himself lifted his soul. He finally did it. It was his symphony.

Of course, there were moments when he didn't like something in a musician's performance or disagreed on how Boris interpreted some line. Then Jim asked them to stop, and they seriously and calmly discussed the problem and always found a mutual solution pretty fast. It was an amazing process of creative work of many people, and Jim felt absolutely excited to be the epicenter of it.

Sometimes after the weekend's rehearsals, Jim and Lada went for dinner with Boris, Rita, and Sandra. Those were also very beautiful and inspiring moments for Jim. He enjoyed the company of people very dear to him and the conversations they had together about the most important coming events of his dream—the concert, the wedding, and the trip to Italy.

Sandra loved these dinners as well. They gave her the feeling of closeness of a family. It reminded her of the same feeling that she had as a teen while working with Emmanuel and his group. They were a family at those times too, family united by one work, one goal, and one happiness, until everything collapsed. She hoped, this time, everything would stay nice, loving, and exciting much longer, maybe even forever.

At the group home, Mona noticed Jim's wedding band, of course, and he confessed that he got married. She laughed like crazy about that news but then gave him permission to stay in the city with his wife any time he wished without reporting to her every single time. It looked like she didn't care much about him anymore, and he was free to go in and out when he wanted.

That gave Jim and Lada a chance to spend many nights together in their small apartment. In the mornings, Jason usually picked Jim up and drove him to the group home. Jim had breakfast there with his roommates and then was left behind when it was time for Jason to drive the guys to work at the factory. For several days in a row, Jim went to his room and was working on the composition of his introduction— variations of Emmanuel's song "The Endless Water." It was a very sacred time for him emotionally—his composing ability and those of his father were combined together.

Though he never knew Emmanuel, he was warned about his character and behavior from Sandra's narrative. In spite of that, Jim felt that somewhere deep in his heart, he now loved his father very much. Sandra tried her best not to say anything bad about her late husband and to eliminate any mention of his unstoppable fooling around, but the facts were talking by themselves—seducing and practically raping a fourteen-year-old girl, exploiting her talent, leaving her without education, and then dumping her for crazy unrequited passion for another woman. Did all these facts draw the proper picture of that genius composer and rock star singer?

Jim felt something deeper under the surface. He felt that Emmanuel was very unhappy in spite of all his success and money, and he was messing around in painful and unsuccessful attempts to find happiness and himself. He was lost, he didn't know what to do with himself, and Jim felt pity and compassion toward him. It was very good luck that Emmanuel was convinced that alcohol or drugs could destroy his voice.

This idea prevented him from using drugs, like what happened with many other stars probably for the same reason—to be a glowing and happy star in public and to be a lonely sufferer behind closed doors.

Jim felt that he had a lot to do with the introduction's song. It was not an easy task to turn a rock-band-style into a classical-orchestra-style. He never did it before; he always created his own music without any prototype, but now he had to do that out of respect and love for his father. The schedule was also quite tight; the scores of this piece should be printed out on lines for the orchestra and rehearsed by the musicians as well. To be sure that he would be done on time with this work, Jim tried to spend as much time on it as he could. Sometimes he even sacrificed his night with Lada and asked her to drive him to the group home late in the evening so he could start his work very early the next day.

One evening Jim came to the group home at about ten o'clock, and being sure that everybody was sleeping, he tried his best to be very quiet. He opened the main door with his own key, stepped into the small lobby, and then pulled the second door to enter. When the second door opened just a crack, he suddenly heard a piece of sentence that Mona's voice pronounced. "Who cares if he is a cop or not? It doesn't matter. He is a zombie anyway."

Jim stopped in his tracks, holding his breath. Finally, he caught something. He looked through the crack between the doors. Mona was sitting at the table in the dining room, her back toward the entrance door, holding her phone by her ear, and listening to what her partner in conversation was telling her. She couldn't see or hear Jim. Obviously, she was sure that he was spending the night in the city.

"I know you already paid, but it was more than a year ago. You don't need to repeat that a hundred times . . . all the money is already spent . . . hell, you don't care. Of course, you don't care, but I do. I am not working for free. To eliminate him, I can easily do an overdose, but I want my money first."

Jim felt his knees getting weak from tension and horror. He sat on the floor and put one of his sneakers into the crack to keep the door open a bit to hear better.

"No," Mona said in an unhappy voice, "I don't approve you attacking the house. It could break windows and doors, cause a lot of damage. I don't want to spend money for renovations afterward . . . insurance? . . . I know better than you about insurance. Fuck off . . . don't put your nose in my business . . . yeah, the bus may be better . . .

you can make an ambush in the forest or something . . . it would look like regular robbery . . . no, don't worry, there is just garbage on the bus, the black driver and four retarded idiots . . . Who cares? . . . the collateral damage . . . yes, he would be one of those idiots . . . though the overdose would be much simpler . . . no, I won't do a thing until I get my money."

Jim was thinking with horror what he should do now. If Mona noticed him, he was a dead man. Should he go outside and stay all night in the forest? Or call Lada from the garden? She had probably not driven really far away and could return to pick him up. Or should he stay and warn Victor somehow?

"Okay, let's agree with the bus," Mona continued. "No . . . not right away. I still have some preparations to make. It's not as easy as you think . . . yeah, let's say the first of October. I still need my bus until the end of September, but then you can burn it with all the garbage together. When will you deliver my money? . . . why do you need to think? There's nothing to think about . . . do it as soon as you can . . . and don't even think about threatening me. I can threaten you too. I can stop giving him the pills, and in a week, he will be a normal cop for you. Ha ha! Then we'll see how happy you'll be . . . okay, I'll call you tomorrow at the same time, and you'll give me the exact day to get my money."

Jim finally came up with his decision of what to do. He pulled his sneaker out and the door closed quietly. Then holding the door, he stood up, stepped back to the main outside door, and slammed it very loud, pretending that he was just coming in. Then he opened the inner door and said in a cheery voice, very loud again, "Hey, Mona, good evening! I'm home. Are you still awake? It's actually pretty late."

She hung up immediately, put the phone on the table, and turned to him. "Oh, hi, Jim," she said sweetly. "You are pretty late tonight. Don't you want to spend the night with your wife?" And she winked, smiling. "I am not sleeping because I was talking with my daughter. She is very sick, and I am really worried about her, so I am checking on her almost every hour."

"I hope she'll get better soon. Good night, Mona," Jim answered and climbed the stairs to his room on the second floor. Now he had the opportunity to think about what to do for the whole night.

CHAPTER 74

In September, the new school year should start at the university, which was supposed to be Lada's last year before her graduation. However, she went to the administration office and did all the paperwork required for a leave of absence for the whole year while still keeping her place as a student. The news caused a burst of tears from Lada's mother, Tatiana, again—her beautiful daughter not only found a freak for a husband but also lost her education forever. Boris wasn't very happy about it as well, but Lada gave him a pretty detailed explanation. She wanted to concentrate on the preparations for the concert and then for her wedding, to make a trip to Italy, and then to do all the arrangements on their apartment and completely settle into their new life. It all required a lot of time. She didn't want to be sloppy in her university classes now, so she decided that she could start them in a year with her full attention, when all her life should be completely settled.

Lada also started thinking about taking business management courses next year, together with her music course. She liked all that she was doing now, organizing things for Jim's concert. Also, she was so good in doing it that it could be her profession in the future. All that sounded reasonable to Boris and Rita, and they both finally approved of Lada's decision.

Sandra Soley actually approved it right away without any questions. She knew well from her own life experience that education could always be postponed and then renewed, but family life and love was not. She tenderly hugged Lada and sincerely thanked her for her love for her son and her excellent care for him. This proved to Lada that a mother-in-law was not always a problem for loving young couples. Sometimes she could even be a better helper and supporter than her own mother.

There was one more important point in Lada's decision that she didn't tell absolutely anyone—she suspected that she might be pregnant. She wasn't completely sure yet but wanted to be ready if it happened. If the doctors was wrong that she lost her sexual feelings forever, they might be just as wrong about her possibility of having a child. So the last month before the concert for her was busy, exciting, and full of anticipation.

When Jim called Lada in the morning from the group home and said that he wouldn't come to the city today and maybe even tomorrow, it wasn't a big surprise for her. She knew that he was working hard to finish his introduction for the concert, and it was going a bit slow. "Okay, sweetie," she said. "I hope that in a couple of days your work on the introduction will be finished. I have a lot to do here as well. But call me anytime, and as soon as you can, come with Jason to the city. We need one very important thing to do here together."

"I guess that there are hundreds of important things that we need to do immediately when I arrive." Jim laughed. "Love you, darling." He didn't tell Lada anything about Mona's conversation that he overheard last night. He didn't want to worry her.

After thinking the whole night about what to do next, Jim came up with a plan. He couldn't go to see Victor that night because he wasn't present at dinner the previous day, and they didn't exchange their usual signals. Victor probably was sleeping and his door locked. Jim didn't want to knock and make noise, so he postponed his visit to the following night.

Jim decided to dedicate this day to his musical work and finish it immediately. He wanted to be free from it finally. There was only a small part of the introduction's scores that was left unfinished, so Jim started working on it right after breakfast and continued until dinner.

At dinner, he dropped a spoon and apologized to Mona for his clumsiness. Victor coughed not right away but at the very end of the dinner, so it would be impossible for anybody to relate their signals to each other. Then Jim walked back to his room and continued his musical work, which now went smoother and faster because he finally calmed down—the meeting with Victor was arranged successfully.

At about nine o'clock, the scores of the introduction were finished. Jim packed the papers into a folder and put it into his backpack to be ready for tomorrow. Tonight, though, before seeing Victor, he had one more important thing to do.

Last night, he overheard Mona say to a mafioso on the phone that she would talk with him again the next evening at the same time. Jim needed to know if they had reached an agreement about the money. If they did, Mona would need a couple of days to get this money, and then she would begin the work. Victor should know about that immediately and be ready to act and fight for his life.

During dinner, Jim said to Mona that Lada would pick him up tonight and that they would go to the city. So after this scenario, in the evening, Jim went outside, sat in the garden for half an hour, and then very quietly went back inside. As he did the night before, he unlocked the main door with his key and then very cautiously pulled open the inner door a crack. Oops! Unlike last night, Mona wasn't in the dining room with her phone. The living room was empty. The nurses from the afternoon shift were gone home long ago, and the wards were all locked. Everyone was sleeping.

Mona must be in her office, Jim guessed. *What should I do? Try to sneak there or not?*

He walked very carefully through the kitchen and then through the storage room behind it. Lights were off everywhere, but in the back hall with a hardwood floor, Jim noticed a line of light under the office door. Mona was there. He came closer to the door and listened. Yes, she was on the phone but not with the mafioso but, this time, really with her daughter. Her voice was muffled a bit by the closed door, but the words were still recognizable.

"No, sweetie, I don't work for free," Mona said. "I know they paid last year. But it was only half a million. I bought you a car and a necklace for myself, and that's it. So nothing's left. And now they want me to do another job for them for this old payment? Unbelievable! . . . no, don't worry, I know how to trick them . . . I gave them a date, October 1, to attack my bus, but it won't ever happen . . . yes, I know about insurance. I did it already in April, pretending that the bus was robbed. I hung it on the former bus driver, Ramah . . . no, nothing happened to him. Police didn't find any evidence to accuse him . . . yeah . . . I just kicked him out . . . no . . . only five months passed since. The insurance company won't believe the second robbery. Now I have a better plan . . . just one second, sweetie, it's getting stuffy in the office. Let me open the door."

She stood up from her chair and headed to the door. Jim quickly dashed back into the dark storage room and squatted behind the big box of paper towels. Mona opened the office door wide and returned to her armchair. She didn't bother to look outside into the hall, knowing well that nobody could be there. She felt safe and confident in her house.

"I'm back, sweetie," she continued on the phone. "You know, for my group home, my insurance is not bad. . . about ten million . . . you remember, we talked about that last week . . . yeah, I want to carry out my plan. And when those bastards, who don't want to pay me, come here, they would find out that I screwed them. Let them wait in their ambush for the bus."

She laughed angrily. "Gosh, it's the first time in my life that someone decided to dupe me with money. Ha ha! No way, idiots. You know, sweetie, it's getting pretty late. I still have to finish up some things in the kitchen. Call me when you receive the confirmation from the concert hall that they will give us not two but three VIP seats. I want to show off my young and handsome boyfriend. Yes, I want him to sit together with me. And don't pout. You, Sharon, should be happy for your mother. I am not only smart and rich but also an attractive fifty-four-year-old for a man twice younger than me . . . okay, sweetie, love you. Good night."

Jim realized with a horror that Mona hung up and now would go to the kitchen as she said. He didn't think of this possibility before. He was sure that she would go to her suite to sleep after the conversation.

To get to the kitchen, she needed to pass through the storage, where he was now behind a box. If she needed to take something from the storage and turned the lights on, she would see him right away. This would be his doom. But to stand up now and walk to the kitchen ahead of her and then to the living room and then try to reach his room, that was out of question. He was too slow. She would walk in the same direction as him and see him right away.

Jim lay down on the floor on his stomach and crawled under the bottom shelf where he found Mona's diamond almost ten months ago. He moved the box of towels a bit closer to cover himself from her view and held his breath. Mona passed very close to him and entered the kitchen. She did something there for quite a long time. Jim heard the sound of water running into the sink and some dishes and utensils clinking. Then she fussed for some time in the refrigerator, organizing stuff over there.

Jim felt almost dead under the shelf, his legs became numb, and he wasn't sure that he would be able to get out of there ever. He was very cold. In horror, he feared that his teeth would chatter and make some noise, which could give away his presence. *What if dust tickles my nose and I sneeze?* Jim thought. *I don't want to die today.*

He had Lada, he had his symphony, he finally had his mother. He now had so many things to live for. Shaking from cold and completely terrified, he remembered what always helped him in the past—his ocean and his music—and he begged them to come for help once more. He began to imagine that he was in the water, swimming, sinking, listening to the sounds of the waves.

He didn't even notice when his fear started to subside; he became calm and content, and now music sounded in his head. It was not his symphony; it was Emmanuel's song "The Endless Water," but it was Sandra who sang it. Her voice—beautiful and strong but calm and kind at the same time—soothed him and forced him to forget everything bad, scary, and dangerous. He enjoyed listening to her lullaby until he finally fell asleep.

CHAPTER 75

Jim woke up in absolute darkness and couldn't understand at first where he was. He stayed lying down on his stomach, slowly returning to full consciousness, until the events of the last evening came back to his mind. He remembered listening to Mona's conversation on the phone in her office while he was hiding in the storage a couple of meters beside the office door.

Now everything around him was quiet. Mona probably finished her business in the kitchen and went to her suite long ago. Jim had no idea how much time passed while he was sleeping under the shelf. He shuddered, realizing that if he made a sound during his sleep, he would be dead already. But no, he was alive, so he must have slept like a baby, soundlessly.

Jim moved the box of paper towels aside and started massaging his hands, his fingers, and then his legs, trying to return them to life. Then he did a little exercise for his feet, moving them back and forth, getting rid of little sharp pinches of numbness. Finally, Jim climbed out from under the shelf and very carefully moved to the kitchen, stretching his arms forward so as not to bump something and create any noise accidentally. In the kitchen, there was more light than in the storage; the bright green numbers were shining on the stove and on the microwave oven, showing the time. It was two o'clock already. He was late for his meeting with Victor. In the living room, there was even more light—above the stairs to the second floor, the little lamps were on.

Jim climbed up and walked to Victor's room right away, not wasting time to stop by his own room. When he opened the door, Victor was lying in his bed but not sleeping. "Sorry, I couldn't sit anymore and wait for you, Jim. Just got tired," Victor said, raising and shaking Jim's hand. "Was something holding you for that long?"

"Yes, actually, a lot," Jim answered. "I am sorry for the delay, but I finally got some information for you. I understand now why we didn't get anything for so long. Mona changed her time of conversations. She is now contacting those people in the late evenings, when everybody here is sleeping. I was also sleeping usually, or I was in the city with Lada."

Jim told Victor the whole story of his accidental late return home and hearing Mona's conversation in the living room. Then he spoke about her conversation in her office and about his time spent under the shelf. Victor was shocked.

"Jim, before I thank you for your bravery and for the importance of the information you've got, I would like to say that you're absolutely crazy. It's enormously reckless, even—I am sorry for the word—*stupid* to risk your life like that. Promise that you'll never do that again."

Jim blushed and nodded confusingly.

"Just understand, please, that for justice to be had, we need you alive as a witness," Victor continued. "If you were to be killed, there would be no witnesses to anything, and any lawsuit would be unsuccessful. Mona will get away with everything. So treasure yourself, if not for your life, for your music, for your family but at least for justice. Are we clear on that?"

"Yes, we are clear." Jim blushed even more. "I am sorry. I really wasn't thinking. I wanted to do my best."

"And you did, and a big thank you for that. Now we know that Mona wants insurance money and that she'll do something to this building. I don't know exactly what is possible—a gas explosion or fire? And we also know that it will be before October 1, maybe September 30, not earlier because on September 29, you have a concert, and Mona wants to attend and to cheer her daughter as the author of the symphony. She also wants to show off Jason as she said. Wow! what a career for a young bus driver!" Victor smirked sarcastically. "However, at the same time, it is strange that she called him 'garbage' with all four of us together and 'collateral damage' in case of the attack on the bus."

"But in reality," Jim objected, "she duped those mafioso, and there would be no attack on the bus. It was just blah-blah-blah on her part."

"You never know. There are still three weeks until the first of October. She, as well as they, easily could change their minds and invent something else. Anyway, thank you very much, Jim. I got that all these plans were mostly to eliminate me. I'm just wondering, how did they find out that I am a cop? I was very cautious and believable while I was with them. Did I do something wrong? I will think about that more attentively later.

"So," Victor continued, "it would be quite a big burden on me to try to save all our vulnerable guys here in case of an explosion or fire. Who else would be capable of doing that if not me?"

"I would be with you. I will help you," Jim suggested bravely.

"Jim, no offense." Victor laughed. "But you won't be much help in the emergency situation. You will just give me an extra guy to take care of. You already did what you could, and it is a lot. Thanks for the warning. It was very helpful, Jim. You probably saved a lot of lives here with your bravery—stupidity. That's it.

"However, I think that you should do one more thing, Jim. Get a tape recorder and record everything that you know about Mona's deeds during these past ten months that you had been here. Remember everything, even the tiny details that may seem useless, but they aren't. If something happened, like it was last night when you possibly could be killed, this tape could be used in the lawsuit against Mona. I know it would be considered a circumstantial evidence, but it depends on the prosecutor. We'll use the best one, who could make that tape to be acceptable in the court. And if the jury would hear those stories, especially about the baby's murder, they would consider it for sure."

"Okay, I'll do that as soon as I get back to the city, maybe even tomorrow," Jim agreed. "Do you want me to give this tape to you?"

"No, it wouldn't be safe here"—Victor shook his head—"knowing now that we are possibly expecting a big battle. I would need my hands free for saving people, not the stuff. You better ask Lada to hide the tape somewhere, to give it to her brother for safekeeping or, maybe even better, to rent a safety-deposit box in the bank. Discuss it together."

"When could I see you next time?" Jim asked.

"When you have other information, otherwise no need. Just concentrate on your concert. I would be really happy to listen to it, but alas, I probably won't this time. Okay, Jim. Thanks again for everything."

They hug each other friendly as a farewell and Jim left.

Now there was one more trick for him to do—to convince Mona that he was in the city the whole night. He went outside and slept the rest of the night on a bench in the garden. When in the morning Jason appeared on the bus, Jim walked into the group home with him, pretending that he just came from the city. Then they had breakfast with the wards. While the guys loaded into the bus to go to work, Jim grabbed his backpack with the notes of his last creation—the introduction of the concert—from his room and went with them.

"Jim, did you just come from the city to have breakfast?" Mona laughed. "Couldn't your wife make breakfast for you?"

"Not just that." Jim shrugged. "I'm also moving my stuff to the city slowly. Have a nice day, Mona."

He didn't trust Jason at all but just hoped that the young bus driver wouldn't betray him and tell Mona that he found him in the morning at the garden outside the group home. But for now, everything seemed to be okay. In the city, Jason dropped him in front of their apartment with Lada, not saying a word, except for "Bye, Jim."

The first thing Jim and Lada did, of course, was to make love, which they both were missing like crazy. Then later that day, Lada showed Jim the new tape recorder, which she bought, and said very carefully, expecting that he would possibly refuse, "You know, my love, I was thinking that after our concert, when Mona will be arrested on small charges, we could try to make them bigger and give the police more information about her deeds."

"Do you want me to record everything I know?" Jim got it right away. "Of course. Victor suggested I do the same thing. I know, it could be very important, no doubt. Let's do that."

The procedure of taping Jim's narrative proved not to be as simple as they thought it would be. It took much more time than they expected. Especially, the problem was when Jim came to the moment of the story when he helped Victor get off the pills and become a normal man again. Jim and Lada discussed that a lot. Should this be mentioned or not? Also, the fact that Victor was an FBI agent—should it be revealed to the police or not? If the tape got in the wrong hands, it would be a betrayal of Victor and his whole business, which he trusted them with. It would be a huge danger for him. And they both felt responsible for his life and his goal as well.

They decided finally that the tape would go to the police, and the police and the FBI often work together, especially on such complicated cases as that of Mona's crimes. And Victor would be involved in this case for sure, so his identity and his role in it would be revealed anyway. It would be reasonable for Jim to tell the whole truth as he knew it.

Another point was that the tape would be used only in case Jim would be dead or seriously wounded and couldn't attend the lawsuit in person as a witness. Otherwise, he would be there. Both Lada and Jim hoped that it would never happen and that the tape never would be used. They did it just to feel safe, just as a kind of warranty or insurance that this information would not disappear without a trace.

The recording took about a week of their evenings because they were very busy with other things as well. It took not one cassette but a full six. However, finally, it was accomplished.

Lada made copies of all the cassettes and placed them into a safety-deposit box that she rented from the bank. She wrapped the originals together in one package, and then, one day, when Jim was at the rehearsal in the concert hall, she called Jason and met him again in the same coffee shop to give him the tapes.

Having coffee, Lada and Jason talked for a while, joked, flirted, and laughed a lot and had a very good friendly time together. The only little shadow that darkened the situation for Lada was the feeling that she was hiding something from her husband. She hated that because it made her very uncomfortable. She liked Jason very much and would be happy to continue the friendship with him forever if not for Jim's insecurity and jealousy about this guy, which Lada considered silly. Jason took the tapes and thanked her. As they parted, they gave each other a friendly short hug.

A few very busy days passed with preparations for the concert, until Lada finally found some time and bought a pregnancy test in the pharmacy. Yes, it showed that she really was pregnant. It was an unexpected, unbelievable, and happy surprise for her, which she decided to hide temporarily until the concert. Everybody was now so preoccupied with the coming of Jim's symphony performance that her surprise would be diminished in its importance and not that noticeable as she would like it to be. She imagined how excited Jim would be after the concert, when she would tell him about that.

Some more days passed, and then one day Jim asked Lada, "My love, where did you put the tapes that we recorded?"

"In the safety-deposit box at the bank," she said but also added a bit of a lie to that. "And copies I gave to BB for safekeeping."

"It's okay, "Jim said. "I was a little worried that they accidentally could somehow get into Jason's hands."

"Why?" Lada looked at him, surprised and cautious. What a hell of intuition he had!

"I heard today at the rehearsal that Sharon and her mother ordered three VIP sets, two for them and one for Mona's boyfriend. I assume that would be Jason. He is coming with them to the concert. He is sleeping with Mona. He could easily give the tapes to her."

Lada felt her knees go weak and soft like cotton, and she almost collapsed on their mattress. Jim looked at her questioningly. "I am sorry, sweetie, I just have a headache," she whispered as she covered her face with her hands.

There were six days left until the concert.

CHAPTER 76

Lada was crying all night, devastated by the feelings of guilt and shame of what she did. She was hurt and offended. The sorrow and pain all mixed together. How could she trust Jason? How could she get so easily duped? She was very disappointed in herself; she even hated herself.

What might happen now if Mona got the tapes? Lada couldn't even imagine that. Victor could be killed by an overdose immediately; Jim could be killed as soon as he came to the group home. The other guys there might likely be killed by a gas explosion, and Mona could receive ten million dollars from the insurance and get away with everything. Justice would never be served—not for Lily, not for Maggie's baby, not for anyone. Even at the concert, Sharon would show up as the author of the symphony. It would be the end of the world, and all that would be her fault.

In addition to all this horror, Lada started throwing up. That continued the whole night with tears and convinced Jim that she really was sick. He tried to take care of her, but what could he do? He just gave her a cup of water, hugged her, kissed her, or caressed her. None of that seemed to help now.

In the morning, Lada stood up abruptly and said to Jim that she was going to see a doctor. She called Rita and asked her to do her a favor— pick up Jim and take him with them to the whole orchestra working day to listen to music, even not his music, on the first part of the day. At least he would be occupied with something while she had her time alone.

Rita was surprised by the unexpected request but promised to help. When Jim was gone, Lada called Jason and said that she needed to see him and that this was very urgent. They arranged a meeting at the park after he dropped off the guys at the factory. While talking to him on the phone, she tried to hold herself in check as much as possible to make sure that he didn't notice her condition and didn't know what to expect from their meeting. He was surprised, of course, by her call, which he absolutely did not expect, but he was kind of flattered and sounded happy at the idea of seeing her.

When Lada came to the park, she didn't look her best after the sleepless night. She was pale and had dark circles under her eyes, and her eyelids were swollen from endless crying. She was as angry and mad as a devil.

Jason was sitting at the bench and smiling as he saw her approaching, but when she came closer, his smile disappeared. He felt her nervous condition but still had no idea what it could be about. *Maybe Jim suspected something about our two secret coffee meetings, and this caused a jealousy scandal in their family,* Jason guessed.

Lada came to him and stopped, and even before he had time to say hi, she suddenly extended her arm and slapped him on his cheek as strong as she could. "What the hell!" Jason shrieked, jumped, grabbed her by both wrists, and held them tight in front of her.

"You're a bastard! You're a villain! You're the worst jerk in the world! I hate you!" she screamed in his face. "I trusted you! I liked you! I believed you! And what did you do? You betrayed me and Jim. You betrayed everybody!"

"What the hell did I do?" Jason exclaimed back, still holding Lada's hands. "What happened? I don't understand."

"You duped Jim and me to record those tapes. You gave them to Mona. You're a traitor! You want to protect her from justice because you're sleeping with her!"

"Gosh! Where did you get that from?"

"Jim told me," Lada answered a little quieter but still in a very agitated voice.

"Why in the world would Jim tell you such a thing? This is crazy."

At that moment, Lada suddenly felt that she could be wrong. She could interpret something wrong here. She remembered her first coffee meeting with Jason and remembered his face, the sadness in his eyes, when she told him all the horrors about Mona. She remembered his reaction, his facial expression, the gesture when he pressed his palms to his temples. It was all sincere; it was all real. Jason wasn't acting. She felt that then, and she was sure about it now.

A person who was feeling things like that couldn't be Mona's lover who would be ready to warn her, to save the monster from justice, and to betray for her sake a dozen of innocent, vulnerable people. He did talk about the group home wards very fondly and compassionately. A man who would be on Mona's side wouldn't talk like that ever. Lada felt suddenly so ashamed of herself for what she did now that she couldn't hold the tears, and they streamed from her eyes in that moment. "Please . . . let . . . my hands . . . go," she whispered through her crying.

"Well, if you promise not to hit me anymore," Jason said, and she felt in his voice that he was really offended by her crazy, mad, and rude actions and words.

"I promise. I am sorry, Jason. I am so sorry. You know, I am getting insane. Please forgive me." She suddenly hugged him by his neck and pressed her face to his chest, still crying and making his T-shirt wet with her tears. "I don't know what happened with me. I completely lost control. It's probably hormonal because I am pregnant."

Jason hugged her back and slowly patted her hair, soothing her like a child. "Okay, okay," he repeated peacefully, calming her down slowly. "It's okay that you're pregnant. Jim is probably in seventh heaven."

"He doesn't know yet. I want to surprise him. I will tell him after the concert."

"Okay then, who knows? Your brother? Your mom?"

"No, no one. I didn't tell anybody."

"So I'm the first one to know?" He sincerely laughed. "Usually, women tell these things first to the most important person in their life."

"You are a very important person in my life. Now please stop hugging me."

"Well . . ." Jason moved his arm away from her. "I swear to God it was just a friendly hug to calm you down."

"I know," Lada wiped the rest of her tears. "It was friendly on your part. But for me, it is a bit scary. I can't . . . I kind of have butterflies . . . you know, I have a problem now. I have too much feelings. I was emotionally dead for many years. Jim woke me up. And since that happened, I am reacting to every touch, even accidental, even a friendly touch. That really turns me on without any reason actually. I am sorry about that, Jason."

"I did notice that you hugged me first." Jason smiled. "Jeez, what a story. Jim is a really lucky guy to have such a sexy wife, believe me. And he has a really big job to do at home, I guess. But I still don't understand how all this is related to me. Why was all this screaming about Mona and the tapes? Why should I give her something? I hate her no less than you and Jim."

"Jim said you're sleeping with her."

"Damn, where did he get that?"

"I don't know. He said that you told him."

"I didn't tell him anything like that. He's simply overreacting and exaggerating. I just said that it is part of my job, which sadly couldn't be avoided. Lada, please, let's sit and talk seriously."

She nodded in agreement, and they sat on the bench beside each other, Jason still hugging her by the shoulders. "Please don't hug me anymore," she begged. "You don't understand. It's difficult for me. I like you much more than I should. You said that we must talk seriously, but I can't be serious if you don't move your arm away from my shoulders."

"Sorry, sorry," Jason agreed, removing his arm fast. "Are we okay now?"

"Yes," Lada said and then asked, "Did you listen to the tapes?"

"Yes, I did."

"Where are they now?"

"In the evidence box, in a safe, in my office."

"Do you have an office?"

"I do." Jason nodded.

"Are the tapes safe there?"

"Hundred percent."

"Is there some other evidence in this box about the monster?"

"Not so much, but there are photos of all of Mona's diamond necklaces, which I took with a hidden camera. They are actually here as well in my phone. If you want, I can show them to you."

"I saw some of them. Jim showed me the equals at the jewelry store. He knows them pretty well."

"And he complains about me." Jason smirked. "For me, it's at least part of the job."

"What?" Lada didn't understand.

"Nothing, just kidding."

"Why do you have a hidden camera?"

"It's a part of my job."

"No, it's not. I was a bus driver at the group home too, and I didn't have anything like that ever."

Jason turned on the bench to look straight in her eyes. "Lada, my girl," he said in a very serious tone of voice, "you're really pushing me into a corner. I like you very much, maybe even much more than you could guess. I am trying to be a decent person here, not one of the beautiful names with which you called me when you came here this morning."

"I am sorry, Jason." She blushed. "I did apologize for that, and I should probably apologize a hundred more times."

"No need for that. I forgave you for today as an exception. But anything like that will never happen again. Are we clear? Can you swear on it?"

"Yes." She nodded. "I do swear."

"So I know that you're a married woman and that you have a very happy family, which now will get more populated." He winked, smiling. "That's why I am trying to be friends with you, just friends. And friends should be open with each other, I guess. You're too curious and too persistent. You keep pushing and pushing me into a corner. I don't want to lie to you. It's extremely risky for me, even prohibited probably, but I will tell you the truth. I am working in this group home undercover too, not like Victor, of course, which I knew now from Jim's tape. I am from the Minneapolis Police Department just as a regular cop."

Jason took out from his pocket his ID and badge and put them in Lada's hand. "Here," he said, "if you still don't trust me."

"I do trust you," she answered but looked curiously at his stuff. "Sgt. Jason Halls, MPD. Wow."

"Victor's case is much more complicated," Jason continued. "Mine is pretty simple. I am investigating what the monster is doing because we had a couple of serious complaints about her. The last straw that forced MPD to start this investigation was a complaint from Senator Gordon's mother, Maggie's grandma. She complained that Mona didn't do her job properly and was neglecting the wards. Mona didn't pay enough attention to what's going on with Maggie and didn't protect her from being sexually abused. And then Mona also forced the Gordon family to pay her with a diamond necklace that cost $200,000. MPD gave serious attention to this complaint because there is a senator involved, and they placed me there to check on the situation.

"Also, there was another reason to place me in the group home—the investigation about Mona's bus robbery in April wasn't finish yet. There was not enough evidence. Now from Jim's tape, we know what happened. So I did my job pretty successfully, didn't I?" Jason laughed. "Thanks to Jim and to you, my girl."

"Gosh," Lada whispered. "You could arrest me for assault on a police officer on duty."

He laughed even more, shaking his head. "I consider what happened here today as our personal relationship, not related to my work at all. So now can you be sure, finally, that Jim's tapes are safe and are in the proper place?"

"Yes, I am sure. Thank you, Jason. But how about your sleeping with Mona?"

"Jeez, you keep pushing." He giggled a bit, confused. "You know, Lada, when you do undercover work, sometimes you have to do things to obtain information. Mona is an ugly, disgusting, and really mean person, but she kind of attacked me during my first week here, and I thought it's a perfect way to get evidence. How could I get the photos of her necklaces otherwise? She is wearing them only in bed."

"Not exactly," Lada protested. "She did show them to Jim when he was friends with her at the beginning."

"Well, okay." Jason smirked. "If this is what he told you. He is your husband, and you should, of course, listen to what he is saying to you. Your family relationship is not my business. My business here is—first, could you promise not to say a word to anybody in the world, including Jim, about me and my work? My life is depending on your silence. If Mona found out, she could easily kill me too. Second, as Mona's boyfriend, I am going with her and her daughter to the concert. In reality, I am going because I am the one who will arrest them there."

"Victor told Jim that he would."

"Maybe he would as well. I think we both would be happy to help each other. And I would be happy to shake his hand on that. For now, I am his bus driver, and he doesn't know who I am. To me, he is my catatonic patient, though I know who he is. Tricky, huh?"

"Yes." Lada giggled as well. "Do you have a gun or handcuffs or other police stuff on the bus?"

"Of course, I do."

"Where are they?" she asked, returning to him his badge and ID.

"Under my driver's seat."

"I always used to put my purse there when I was the bus driver." She smiled. "Last question before I go, aren't you hurting your fiancée, Lucy, by . . . hmm . . . working with Mona?"

"What is it? Women's solidarity?" Jason chuckled. "Do you want to protect her rights, my funny girl, my silly Lada? That fiancée doesn't exist. There was one girl in my class at the police academy called Lucy, but we weren't even friends, just classmates. I invented the fiancée to shield myself from your mom when she came out from the house and was very unhappy to see me. I was just kidding."

"I am very sorry about my mom, Jason. She hurt Jim a lot as well. Please keep in mind that she is very different from my other family. None of us is accepting her judgmental behavior."

He shrugged. "Don't worry, I don't care. I actually got used to this and learned how to ignore these reactions. Much more important for me is that you like me."

"I do. I really do," Lada said, standing up from the bench. "Jason, I swear to God, your secret is safe with me. Thank you for trusting me. And once again, I am very sorry that I let myself turn crazy for a moment and slapped you. As an apology, could I kiss that cheek that I hurt?"

"Of course, you could." Jason laughed, a bit confused. "But no butterflies, please. Let's be honest for Jim's sake."

There were five days left until the concert.

CHAPTER 77

In the morning of September 29, all other orchestra works were canceled, and the time was dedicated to the general run-through of the evening concert. The whole concert hall—1,400 seats—was sold out mainly because the event was in memory of Emmanuel Soley, and Sandra Soley would be singing. Those names attracted a lot of their former fans, who were now mostly aging people. Nobody knew of Jim's name yet, and also, it wasn't announced anywhere for a very special reason—to convince Mona and her daughter that everything was going their way.

The final rehearsal was done in an almost empty hall; just some university staff and students were allowed to attend, altogether no more than fifteen people. Jim was sitting in the middle of the aisle at the center of the hall on the VIP seat when the composing professor, Mr. Erikson, approached and sat beside him. "You know, Jim," he said, "I was thinking. I remember now that I saw some of your previous works long ago. I knew your teacher from Juilliard, Mr. Dangly. We weren't friends, but we knew each other as professionals, and sometimes we exchanged news about our interesting students. He sent me your Little Fantasy for Camera Orchestra. Also, I remember a piece of the Italian Violin Concerto. He was very proud of you, and I liked those works too. They were very remarkable."

"Thank you." Jim smiled. It was nice and flattering to hear.

"Did you ever think about the possibility of performing those works?"

"No." Jim laughed. "I was just a farm boy at that time. I didn't even imagine how they could be performed. I was just writing what I was feeling. But now I am thinking this may be a good idea. I will talk to Rita after the concert. Maybe she could play my Italian Violin Concerto. I know that she is playing solo violin concerts sometimes. Thank you, Mr. Erikson."

"My pleasure, Jim. I wish you good luck for tonight."

The run-trough was ended at about one o'clock. Right after that, Lada started fussing around, completely busy because some small things weren't finished yet, and only six hours were left before the concert to accomplish them.

Jim decided to go to the group home on the bus with Jason to dismantle his customized piano and computer system to pack it into boxes and to bring them to their apartment in the city before the concert. This was the only stuff of his that was left in the group home. Those things were very important and extremely needed for his future work as a composer. Jason picked him up on the way while delivering the guys home after work at the factory.

"So are you ready for your concert, Jim?" Jason asked sociably.

"You will see yourself tonight. You're a VIP guest," Jim answered with a little tinge of sarcasm.

"Yes, I am." Jason smiled broadly. After that, they drove in silence.

At three o'clock, they arrived to the group home and, as usual, had dinner, together with the nurses from the evening shift, Sue and Josef. There were also the cleaning ladies, who just finished their work and were supposed to go home after dinner. Then Mona said to Jason, "My darling, I need your help to pack some of the stuff into the boxes and load them onto the bus. Those are actually my daughter's things and my former husband's. He lives with Sharon in her house for about ten months. As our divorce is finalized, he now wants his belongings back. I have already prepared everything for you to do this."

Mona continued, "Also, I would be happy if you, my love, could help Jim unscrew his piano and computer from the wires and pack them into the boxes as well. We will help him and deliver his customized music system to his new home in the city. Right, Jim?"

"Y-y-yes," Jim said uncertainly. "I need help undoing everything and packing, but to drive my stuff to the city . . . no, Lada will come and take my equipment and also me before the concert."

"Not much time left, Jim," Jason said, almost forcing every word, like trying to convey some hidden message to him. "Only three hours until the concert. Lada must be very busy now. You better go to the city on the bus with Mona and me. And of course, I can take your equipment."

"No, my sweet boy, we don't need him with us." Mona used her most charming voice and smiled. "Let him wait for Lada. We'll just take his equipment."

"Okay, darling." Jason smiled back at her. "Let me start with Jim's stuff, and then I will load everything from your suite that you want."

Jim climbed on the stairs to his room, and Jason followed him, carrying the empty, folded boxes that were prepared in the living room by Mona. To do all the unscrewing and dismantling didn't take Jason too long. Then he put everything into the boxes, sat on the armchair, and looked at Jim seriously. "Hey," Jason said quietly, making sure that nobody could hear him in the hallway. "I did promise Lada to take care of you."

"When did you promise her that? And how? I didn't see you talking to her."

Jason was confused a bit. Lada called him after today's run-through and begged him to look after Jim while they were together in the group home. But he didn't want to tell Jim about his and Lada's practically daily communications on the phone. "Okay, it doesn't matter when, where, and how. I did promise her that you're going on the bus with me and Mona. And do not question anything. Just do as I said."

"Who the hell are you to order me around? You're not the boss here!" Jim exclaimed heatedly and made a wry face. "I did call Lada, and she said that she will come and drive me to the concert." It was a lie, of course. Lada was too busy to do that before the concert, and that was the reason why she asked Jason for help.

"Are you sure that you're safe here to wait for her, Jim? I am not joking. I am responsible for you," Jason insisted.

"If you drive your monster lover away from here, everything should be safe," Jim retorted. "I don't want to sit on the bus with you and watch for the whole hour how you are hugging and kissing with Mona. It's disgusting. I am not talking with you anymore. Thank you for your help. Just carry the boxes downstairs. That's it."

"Your choice." Jason shrugged and then opened the door and carried the boxes one by one into the hallway and then downstairs into the living room.

Before going to Mona's suite and carrying her stuff out, Jason said to her, "I need to move the bus closer to the door for loading." And he walked outside to the garden to call Lada.

"Hey, girl," he said on the phone, "Jim refused to go back to the city on the bus with me and the monster. I could protect him from her easily if we were all together. But he says no. He will stay here and wait for you. Did you promise to come and pick him up? Is it true?"

"Of course not," Lada answered. "He is lying. You can imagine how hectic it is all around here at the moment. I haven't a free minute. But let him be, Jason. I am sure that he wants to go with Victor. He just isn't telling you that."

"But Victor doesn't have any transportation," Jason objected.

"He is resourceful. He'll find something. Maybe borrow a car from the nurses or something. I am sure he has a plan."

"Okay, your choice, girl. Then I'll just follow the monster," Jason answered. "See you at the concert. Good luck."

During this time, Mona escorted all the patients into their rooms and locked their doors not with just simple, regular locks but with padlocks that were used very seldom. She only left unlocked the doors of those who were bedridden and couldn't get out anyway, Basil's and Ali and Zahra's. However, she didn't lock Jim's door. He was still sitting in an armchair in his room.

Then Mona ordered Nurses Sue and Josef to go to the city to buy groceries using both their cars. They were surprised at this strange request. "Couldn't we go together in one car?" Sue asked.

"No. Pay attention, Sue. Look at this list of groceries. It's for two months. It's so huge that there would not be enough room in one car for all those bags. Normally, I would send the bus for this shopping, but today the bus is going to carry my stuff to my daughter's house before the concert. So you're going in two cars, separated from each other."

"Who would watch the wards with us gone shopping and you gone to the city?" Josef asked.

"Nurses Rona and Andy will come and stay here, until you return with groceries."

"But they worked today on the morning shift. They just left before dinner," Sue objected.

"That's okay," Mona explained patiently. "I persuaded them to come back and work a bit of overtime for extra payment, of course. By the way, you and Josef would get some overtime today as well. Usually, you finish at eight o'clock. But today because I am going to the concert and will be back very late, you should stay until I return. I will pay double for these extra hours."

"Okay, sounds nice," Sue agreed, smiling. "Then let's go, Joe." They went to the garage at the back of the house, where their cars were parked, and left.

Jason, during that time, was in Mona's suite, packing and gluing the boxes with tape, making them ready for loading, so he didn't see the nurses leaving. Then he started carrying all the boxes out to the porch and then loaded them onto the bus. Mona went outside and put a small package on the grass beside the porch, and then she said to Jason, "My sweet boy, we both are working so hard now. We're getting all dirty and sweaty. You know, because we're going to the concert tonight, we should be dressed beautifully. I bought an evening dress and shoes for myself and a very nice evening outfit for you as well. When we get to my daughter's house, we should take a shower together and get dressed before going to the concert hall."

"Oh, thank you." Jason smiled. "I guess it would be fun—I mean, the shower." And he winked at her, thinking, *Hell, can I be more believable than that? I really deserve to win an Oscar.*

When everything was loaded, including Jim's boxes with the piano and computer system, Jason sat in the driver's seat and Mona in the first passenger bench. "Let's go, my sweet baby," she said as Jason turned on the ignition.

The bus slowly moved from the driveway toward the exit to the highway when Mona suddenly exclaimed, "Oh, my darling, stop, please! I forgot my evening dress in my suite. Please stay here and wait for me. I'll just grab it very quickly. I'll be back in a minute."

"Okay." Jason stopped. *I hope there would be no time left for that shower because of this delay,* he thought. *Please take your time, Monster.* He opened the bus door. Mona jumped out and ran back to the group home.

Jim was sitting in his room in the armchair and thinking. Almost eleven months of his life was spent here. It was kind of melancholy in his soul parting with this room forever. There were some bad things that happened but also some very good and happy ones. Here, he accomplished the goal of his life—his symphony. Here, he met Lada. It was sad to say goodbye to all those memories, but now it was time to move on to a new life. And he felt happy and content about that.

He was waiting for Mona and Jason to leave, and then he wanted to walk to Victor's room and knock on his door. They would decide together what to do next. Suddenly, the door of his room opened wide, and Mona walked in very fast and abrupt. "Let's go, Jim," she said in a very agitated voice. "This is the day of my daughter's concert. Her symphony would be performed. It's time."

"Time for what?" he asked, surprised, not understanding what was going on.

"Time to feed my rats."

She grabbed Jim by his arm and hair as at their last fight and pulled him like a rag doll again into the hallway and then toward the elevator. He was so shocked by the unexpectedness of this attack that he didn't even understand at first what was happening.

Then he tried to fight back and screamed, "Help! Help!" He hoped that someone, probably nurses, would hear him. Holding him tight, Mona walked along Ella's door, which was the closest one to the elevator, and then lifted Jim a bit and hit his head on the corner of the wall. The hit was so strong that Jim stopped screaming and passed out. Everything went dark in his eyes, and he didn't fight anymore.

The elevator went down to the basement. There, Mona locked it in a position with the doors open, so nobody could use it. She opened the cage with rats, placed Jim inside, and locked the cage again. Then she opened the back overhead door, grabbed the bottle of gasoline that she put there beforehand, and went out, closing the door behind her. The pieces of firewood that she placed at night along the back and the side walls of the house were still there. She ran beside them, pouring gasoline on them, and then dropped the bottle and her rubber gloves into the garbage bin at the corner. She clicked on a lighter and threw it at the end of the stringlike tiny line of gasoline that now surrounded half the building. A small fireball rolled on this line toward the overhead door of the basement.

Mona grabbed the package with her evening dress that she left beside the porch and ran to the bus. The whole procedure took only six minutes. "Sorry, my love," she said to Jason, breathing heavily from her running, "I didn't want you to wait too long for me. Here is my dress, see?" And she showed him the package, covered with a clear plastic. "Now we should go really fast because we could be late for the concert."

"Yes, ma'am. It's a beautiful dress, by the way." He laughed, started the bus, and turned onto the highway while gaining speed.

There was one hour left until the concert began.

CHAPTER 78

The smell of smoke caught Victor while he was exercising with his heavy metals lying down on his workout bench. He stopped for a moment, sat on the bench, and sniffed a few times more. "Hell," he said to himself, "did she do it today? Damn! I didn't expect anything until tomorrow."

He planned to go out from his room after his exercise and to find transportation to the city anyway. His intention was to be in the concert hall by the end of the concert and arrest Mona and her daughter on the charges of fraud and theft over $5,000, meaning Jim's symphony. Solving the problem of transportation wouldn't be difficult. Victor would borrow a car from one of the nurses or take Mona's car, which was left in the garage. He heard during the dinner that she wanted to go to the city on the bus with Jason, so her car would be obviously left here. The fire could change everything. It still would be possible to follow his plan, but it would be much more difficult.

Victor's room was the last in the hallway, right above the basement overhead door. He went to the window and looked outside. The whole wall under his window was on fire. He ran to the door, opened the simple lock, and tried to push the door but realized that it was held by a deadly strong padlock. "Fuck!" he screamed, understanding now that Mona left him and all his roommates to burn alive. There was no time for reckoning. He should do things really fast. Every second counted.

Victor grabbed his dumbbells, moved them aside one by one, opened his hiding place under the carpet, and pulled out the gun. It was good luck that he had prepared it before—cleaned off the grease and loaded the gun. He poured out the rest of the ammunition from the boxes and thrust them into his pockets, and then he turned to the door and started shooting out the screws that held the lock panel. In a couple of minutes, which felt like an eternity, the lock fell off. The door was open, and Victor jumped into the hallway.

He expected to see the nurses, scared by the sounds of gunshots, but nobody was there. The hallway was empty. He tried the doors on other side of the hallway—Todd, Maggie, Ella, everyone was locked inside. The smell of the smoke was already penetrating into the hallway.

On the same side of the hallway where Victor's room was located, every door was unlocked—Ali and Zahra, Basil, Jim. The bedridden guys were in their rooms; Jim's room was empty. Victor knew that he couldn't save everybody on his own; he needed help. So he started shooting at the lock on Todd's door first. In a short time, it was open.

Todd was sitting in an armchair with earphones in his ears as usual, humming a song and clapping his palms on his knees rhythmically. "What the hell!" he exclaimed, looking surprised at Victor. "Why are you shooting?"

"Listen, Todd," Victor said, pulling out Todd's earphones. "The house is on fire. Don't you smell it? We will all die in ten minutes. We should get out immediately! I need your help right now!"

Todd looked confused. "How the hell are you talking, zombie?" he asked, looking around in uncertainty. He stood up from the armchair, sniffing the air. "Yes, fire." He nodded. "Should I run? Where? How?"

Victor grabbed him by the arm and pulled him into the hallway, which had already more smoke than a few minutes ago. "Look, Todd!" he shouted, forcing the guy to Basil's door. "Do you see this cripple? He can't walk. You are a big strong man. Grab him, put him over your shoulder, and carry him downstairs and out of the door to the garden. Got it?"

"And you? Why not you?" Todd tried to object but then shut up, seeing that Victor reloaded his gun.

"Just do it!" Victor screamed. "I'll free the girls. Then I'll take the others. Go, Todd! It's an order!" And he started shooting into the lock on Maggie's door and then on Ella's.

Both women went out into the hallway very scared, more by the shooting than by the fire. When they smelled smoke and felt that it was already difficult to breathe in the hallway, Maggie began crying and Ella screaming and swearing like crazy.

Victor pushed them to the door of Ali and Zahra's room. "Girls," he said as normally as he could, trying not to scare them more but to calm them down, "it's an emergency. No panic! You see, I'm taking Ali. He is bigger. You two grab Zahra by her arms. She is slim and small. She is not heavy. Lay her on the floor and pull her downstairs. Follow me! Fast!"

He grabbed Ali from his bed, threw him over his shoulder like a sack of potatoes, and ran into the hallway toward the stairs and then down to the living room, jumping over two steps at once. It was almost full of smoke there. Todd was already downstairs, walking ahead of Victor, carrying Basil over his shoulder, and opening the main door.

Both men went out, ran as fast as they could about fifty meters from the building, and dropped Basil and Ali on the grass. "Stay with them!" Victor shouted to Todd. "I will help the girls." And he ran back into the house.

Maggie and Ella lowered Zahra on the floor from her bed and tried to pull her into the hallway, but the smoke was getting quite thick there, and Maggie start coughing. She covered her mouth with both hands and let Zahra's arm go. Ella pushed Zahra, but she couldn't do that alone and was stuck at the door of the room. "Help! Help!" she screamed. "You fucking men, where the hell are you?"

"I'm here!" Victor shouted, jumping up two steps on the stairwell. He lifted Zahra from the floor and threw her over his shoulder, like he did with Ali before.

"Run, girls," he ordered. "Ella, pull Mag! Follow me!" And he ran downstairs.

Ella grabbed coughing Maggie under her arm and pushed her toward the stairs and then down into the living room, where there was almost no visibility because of the heavy smoke. There, she also started coughing. Todd came to the main door from outside and held it open for them. In a minute, Zahra was on the grass beside her brother and Basil. Then Maggie and Ella, reeling from the smoke, slowly walked out to the garden and sat on the bench. The whole house was now engulfed in fire.

"Where are the nurses?" Victor asked as his hands were still shaking from tenseness.

"I heard Mona sent them shopping," Ella answered.

"Both?"

"Yeah, in the two cars."

"Fuck!" Victor angrily narrowed his eyes. "Where is Jim? Does anyone know where Jim is?"

Everyone shook their heads silently.

"Answer me!" Victor screamed. "Where the hell is Jim?"

"Who is Jim?" Todd asked, confused. He felt very uncomfortable without his earphones.

"Damn! The little one! Midget!"

"Oh, that child! I remember him." Todd nodded. "I once carried him on my shoulders. He was asking stupid questions. He asked if I like Maggie. How is it possible not to like her? Look at her boobs!"

Maggie was still crying on the bench, and Todd sat beside her and hugged her.

"Did you see Jim?" Victor kept yelling. "Did he leave on the bus?"

"I don't think he left on the bus," Ella said suddenly. "He bawled for help two times when Mona pulled him to elevator along my door."

"Hell! He's in the basement!" Victor exclaimed. He reloaded his gun once more. Then he tore off the terry towel that was around Basil's neck and thrust it into barrel of the rainwater that sat beside the bench in the garden for watering the flowers. "I'm going there! You all stay put!"

"Wait! It's too late!" Ella shrieked. "There is fire already in the living room!"

"I'll go get him!" Victor ran up on the porch. He wrung out the towel and pressed it to his face with his left hand while holding his gun in the right hand. Then he opened the door and entered the blazing house.

At that moment, only fifteen minutes were left until the beginning of the concert.

CHAPTER 79

The concert hall was almost full already. The people were arriving at the main entrance from the parking lots located on three sides of the building. The big line moved steadily like a parade.

At the entrance, a ticket collector was checking the tickets and names on the VIP list. Aside from Mona, Sharon, and Jason, on the list were several other special guests—the president of the university with his spouse and three Nobel Prize laureates in mathematics, physics, and chemistry who were working at the university as professors, all with their spouses as well.

The usherettes were giving away glossy programs featuring a picture of Emmanuel's beautiful memorial, which Sandra built in Los Angeles some years after his death. The lines under the picture declared that the evening was dedicated to the anniversary of Emmanuel Soley's murder on a stage thirty-four years ago. Inside the program was noted that the evening would consist of

1. a short film commercial from 1969;
2. the orchestra introduction, the variation on Emmanuel's song "The Endless Water"; and
3. *The Symphony of the Ocean*, which consists of four parts, "The Sunrise over the Ocean,"

"The Sparkles of the Waves," "The Colors of the Calm," and "The Ocean's Twilight."

It would be performed by the Symphony Orchestra of the Minneapolis University, conducted by Boris Meleshko. The starring guest singer was Mrs. Sandra Soley. The host of the concert was Mrs. Lada Bogat. The name of the author of the introduction and the symphony would be announced at the end of the concert was written in most of the programs. But three of them were different, stating that the author of the symphony was a young genius, a composing student of the music faculty of the university, Sharon Lainer. They were purposely printed separated from others and given, according to the VIP list, to Mona, Sharon, and Jason only.

They arrived just a couple of minutes before the beginning of the concert and were led to their VIP seats by the special usherette in a Paladin Security uniform. Mona was wearing a long black evening dress, and as an exception to her usual rules, she wore one of her diamond necklaces. It was a very special day for her—the triumph of her daughter as a composer—and for an event of this importance, it was worth it to break her own rules.

Sharon was wearing a very stylish dark blue evening dress and another diamond necklace from her mother's collection. He hair was done uniquely and beautifully. She was supposed to look as a striking star when she appeared on the stage at the end of the concert. Her exterior was designed to correspond to her new status as a celebrity. Mona prepared a camera in her purse to take pictures of her daughter on the stage.

Jason was also looking very special. Instead of his usual T-shirt and jeans, he was wearing Mona's gift—a light gray suit, a white shirt with thin dark blue stripes, and a blue tie. When they arrived at Sharon's house, he insisted that he and Mona take their showers separately and very fast, no more than five minutes each, because time was extremely tight. They were almost late for the concert and didn't even unload the bus. It was left for after the concert, like the shower together with Mona.

She agreed to postpone the fun because Jason promised that, tonight, he would make her "especially happy like never before." While Mona was in her quick shower, he went to the bus and took his equipment that was needed for the evening from under the driver seat—two pairs of handcuffs and his gun. He thrust the handcuffs into his outer suit pocket, his badge and ID into an inner pocket on his chest, and the gun into the holster above his ankle. When Mona was ready to go, he was ready as well.

Sharon drove them all in her bright red Aston Martin Vanquish S. "Wow," Jason said as he saw the car. "It's a kick-ass piece."

"If you satisfy me good tonight," Mona whispered tenderly into his ear, "I'll buy you the same one shortly as soon as I get the insurance money."

"Insurance for what?" Jason asked.

"Wrong question, baby." Mona giggled. "You're supposed to ask, 'To satisfy how?'"

"Oh, I don't need to ask that." He laughed as well, still thinking of what he knew from Jim's last tape. *What the hell does she mean with the words* insurance money? *Attack on the bus? No, the bus is here in the city. Then . . . attack on the group home? Hell, that stubborn Jim is still there. The only hope of saving anyone now is Victor.*

Then Lada walked out on the stage in a long sleeveless red evening dress and high heels. A simple gold chain was on her neck, and her hair was done in a low bun Sandra-style, sitting on the back of her neck. This time, Lada copied the style not to show off, like on her first interview with Sandra, but because of her sincere love and admiration for her new mother-in-law. Just a small difference in the hairstyle was one spiral blond lock hanging from the top of Lada's head along her left cheek.

Lada announced the start of the concert. She greeted the public and thanked them for coming. Then she told the story of M and Sandra, the popular group in 1967–69, and suggested that a short film commercial be shown to remind the fans of the singers how beautiful they were looking and sounding together. This was supported by applause from the audience. "Years passed since Emmanuel was dead, but his songs were never dying and never will," Lada ended her speech. Then she pressed the remote, and the commercial started.

"What the hell, Mom," Sharon whispered to Mona's ear. "Why do I need this pop music beside my symphony? Why did nobody consult with me on how to build this program?"

"Shh, sweetie." Mona calmed her down. "We can't do anything about that now. After the concert, you could talk to this fucking conductor and give him hell."

"But why is your former bus driver, this stupid immigrant girl, hosting the concert? I don't understand."

"Because the conductor is her brother. He just gave her the work to make some money. Don't care about that."

The musicians of the orchestra began entering the stage and taking their seats. Boris came out and gestured for them to stand up, and the public started clapping to greet the orchestra. Lada announced the introduction to the symphony, the variations on Emmanuel's song "The Endless Water," and the music started.

At this time, Victor jumped through the fire in the unrecognizable blazing place that was left from the living room of the group home. He ran into the second smaller living room—the winter garden, where he liked to sit in the armchair under the palm tree long ago, being a zombie on the pills. The glass roof and many of the glass plates in the walls were already broken from the heat. The live plants that filled the room became yellowish and crooked, ready to burn.

As he jumped through this inferno, Victor's jeans and jacket caught fire. He fell on the floor and rolled around to put it out. His long hair and beard were also mostly burned, but he wiped his head and face with the wet towel and stood up again. It was easier to breathe in this room because a lot of smoke went out through the broken glass.

There were two doors before him, the door of the elevator, which wasn't usable now, and the door of the basement. It was locked, of course, but Victor reloaded his gun and shot at the lock again, and in a few minutes, it opened. The electricity was off because all wires were burned, and there was no light in the basement. The big refrigerators and boilers weren't buzzing anymore. But the blazing overhead door gave some illumination and a chance to see. It was covered with some plastic before the fire and now the smell of burning chemicals was absolutely suffocating, combined with clouds of smoke from the fire.

Squeezing a wet towel to his face, Victor walked down the cement stairs. A big cage was hanging on the left wall, and there was a dark puddle on the cement floor under it. In the middle of the cage was a pile of swirling white rats, but many of them also were lying dead around there from inhaling smoke and chemicals. Victor saw Jim's sneakers sticking out from under the pile. A big padlock was hanging on the door of the cage.

"Jeez," Victor moaned through his towel. During his professional life, he saw a lot of awful and horrible things but nothing like that ever. He shot the lock from the cage, opened the door, and brushed off the rats, which ran down to the floor. Victor thrust the gun into his pocket to get a free hand, grabbed Jim's foot, and pulled him out of the cage.

Jim was unconscious but still had a weak pulse. Luckily, he was fully clothed, so the rats did not have lots of places to bite him. Most bites were on his hands and face, but the worst was on his neck at the carotid artery, where blood was streaming from.

Victor grabbed the towel from his face and pressed it on Jim's wound, trying to stop or at least reduce the bleeding; but without the towel, he couldn't breathe himself. So he ran up the stairs with Jim as fast as he could while holding his breath, afraid to lose consciousness himself. The winter garden with broken glass walls and roof was the only place where it was possible to breathe. It was also a chance to get out by breaking more glass. He put Jim on the floor, pulled out the gun from his pocket, and started beating the glass walls to make the opening bigger for him to walk out, holding Jim in his arms.

As soon as Victor, carrying Jim, escaped through the hole in the glass, the burned door between the two living rooms fell off. A huge fireball from the main living room rolled into the winter garden, burning the hardwood floor and the big armchairs with all the plants. Victor ran around the building, not even having a chance to notice that and realize how lucky he was to be alive and to pull Jim out of that inferno. *Jim needs to be in a hospital* was one thought that pushed Victor. *He needs a blood transfusion. How could we get there?* He came to the garden where Ella, Todd, and Maggie were sitting on the bench and put Jim on their laps.

"Hold him, girls," he ordered. "And you, Todd, press the towel to his neck and keep it tight. I'll go get the car."

"We need to call 911," Ella said. "But where the hell can we find a phone?"

Victor ran to the garage and shot the lock off. That was actually his last ammunition. The gun was empty and useless now, but he still put it into his pocket—it should go into an evidence box first and then would be returned to Lada.

Mona's car was in the garage, but the keys were nowhere to be found. So Victor broke the glass on the driver's door with the gun—one more use for it—and opened the door from inside. He sat on the driver seat and spent about five minutes hot-wiring the car and then drove backward from the gate, stopped in the driveway, and jumped out from the car.

"Get in, guys!" he shouted, running to his roommates. "Fast, chop-chop, you lazy asses! Todd on passenger seat beside me, girls on the back!" He held Jim in his arms, waiting until they settled in the car. Then he put Jim on Maggie's lap. "Hold him, sweetie. And you, Ella, keep pressing the towel on his neck. Got it?"

"Yes! Fucking yes!" Ella barked, irritated that her hands were now all smeared in Jim's blood.

"Quiet!" Victor barked back. "We're saving a life here. Nothing else counts. Let's go!"

He turned onto the highway at such a speed that the wheels screeched deafeningly, and they headed toward the city. While Maggie was holding Jim's head on her left arm, with her right hand, she was tenderly petting his hair, repeating quietly, "Ba-ba, bo-bo, be-be-be." Tears were sliding down on her cheeks. Then she bowed and kissed his forehead.

"Look at this hell." Ella smirked. "She is singing him a lullaby. She thinks he is her baby."

"She is probably remembering that he was the only one who saw her baby," Victor said.

"Which baby?" Todd asked. "Where are my earphones?"

"You'll get them when we arrive at the hospital," Victor answered. "Now shut up, guys. Let me concentrate on driving. Never in my life did I speed that crazy." Mona's car was almost flying.

At the concert, the introduction was finished; and after the long applause, Lada announced *The Symphony of the Ocean*. Sandra Soley walked out on the stage in a long dark silver dress with long sleeves and turtleneck. The small diamond studs in her ears were her only jewelry. It was her usual classy style. She stopped beside the conductor's stand; folded her hands together, the fingers to her chin as if in prayer; and closed her eyes. She was preparing to sing, but no one knew that she was really praying at the moment for the life of her son.

CHAPTER 80

A s Nurses Sue and Josef approached the group home in their two cars full of groceries, they were shocked to see a huge cloud of smoke in the sky. The blazing flame was still engulfing the rest of the carbonized carcass of the building. They stopped at the far end of the driveway, jumped out from their cars, and ran closer, guessing in horror what happened with their patients.

Surprisingly, they found Basil, Ali, and Zahra lying down on the grass in the garden in their usual condition but not hurt by the fire in any way. "Oh, God, thank You for saving them!" Sue exclaimed, hugging Zahra, her favorite. "Where are the others? Do you see someone, Joe?"

"No," Josef answered, walking around the garden and approaching the house at a safe distance because the heat would not allow any closer. "Jeez, I hope they are alive. But where are they?"

"It's so bad that Mona prohibited us to have phones." Sue sighed. "We can't even call 911. The only hope is that someone with a phone will pass on the highway and will notice the fire. But the chance of that is very slim. Gosh, we're in such a secluded location."

"What should we do with these guys now?" Josef reckoned.

"You know, it's getting late. It's seven thirty already, and the grass is getting wet from the dew," Sue said. "They could catch a cold. We should put them into our cars and drive them to the hospital. There is a phone there, and we should call 911 from there and report the fire. And there are social workers who would help find a new accommodation for the guys."

"And also a new workplace for us," Josef added, shaking his head, still in disbelief.

"Jeez, Joe, we're not thinking about that yet. Let's do what we have to do now," Sue insisted with a trace of indignation in her voice. "Let's put Basil in your car."

"How could we do that? He is pretty big," Josef complained but pulled the seat release handle and let the passenger seat in his car turn into the semilying backward position. "You know I am a short man. And it is one thing to turn him to the side in bed and to change him and another thing to lift him."

"Hell, Joe, you're strong enough!" Sue exclaimed. "Look at me. I am smaller than you and also twice as thin, but I am a strong and persistent woman. Okay, now grab him under his arm, and I'll do that from the other side, and let's pull him in your car. If we leave them here now and drive to reach a phone somewhere and then wait for an ambulance, it will take a couple of more hours. The guys can't stay on the grass for that long. Don't you get it?"

They finally pulled Basil into Josef's car, in spite of the all difficulties, and then pulled Ali into Sue's car the same way. For Zahra, Sue freed the back seat of her car of groceries, and they settled her there, though without a seat belt but still pretty safe. Then they drove to the nearest gas station to report the fire and also called the hospital and requested to prepare some spots for the three bedridden handicapped.

The first part of Jim's symphony ended, and there was a small break of about fifteen seconds before the second part began. There wasn't supposed to be any applause during that break, but the audience probably wouldn't applaud anyway. Everybody froze silently in shock from the divine beauty of the music they had just heard.

Jason wasn't a fan of orchestra music. He never listened to it and absolutely wasn't interested. As a regular teenager of the nineties, he was accustomed to rock, pop, jazz, or any other music that was popular in those years between friends of the same age. Now for the first time in his life, he attended a symphony concert; and he was as surprised, enchanted, and impressed as the other people. Jason knew that music mostly was for dancing. He never expected that music could be such a concentration of spiritual feelings and deepest emotions imaginable. He was just sitting there with his eyes closed and couldn't suppress the feeling that this music was written for Lada. It stated in the program that it was about the ocean, about the beauty and endless power of the water. But for him, it felt like it was about this weak, fragile girl who hugged him last week in the park and was crying helplessly on his chest because she liked him, wanted him, and couldn't overcome her feelings and also couldn't fulfill them.

It was now clearly visible to Jason through this music how much Jim loved, admired, and worshipped Lada. His music was breathing with this deep, endless love. And Sandra's voice sounded with the orchestra like the voice of an angel coming from paradise to bless this love. *No, Jason thought, no, no, no! I shouldn't interfere with their life and their love anymore. If I stay here, I won't be able to stop myself from seeing her, and I won't be able to stop her. I don't want to do that to this poor guy who really is a supercreature, a supergenius. She is the meaning of his existence, and I have no right to hurt him.* He decided that, tomorrow, he would talk to the MPD chief and ask for a transfer to another city, as far away as possible.

Then the second part of the symphony ended, and within seconds, the third part started. The name of it was "The Colors of the Calm." The sounds became colors, and the colors became music. It was an unheard-of and unthinkable combination of the beauty and holiness of the spirit; it was so deep and touching that Jason felt even more doomed. This music gave him understanding not of why and how Jim loved Lada but of why and how Lada loved Jim. And he sadly realized that it was eternal, endless love. It was forever. Jason folded the program and put it into his pocket. It should go into the evidence box as well.

At the hospital, Victor left Mona's car running in the parking lot and ordered Todd to stay in the car. He himself burst into the emergency room, carrying Jim in his arms. Ella and Maggie followed him as they were told.

"I am John Delany, FBI special agent," Victor almost shouted, agitated. "This is Jim Bogat. If he does not make it, he will be a homicide victim. Huge blood loss, smoke inhalation, and lots of animal bites. He needs surgery. His carotid artery was bitten. Also, I got him out of a fire. Give me your phone. Where is your phone? I need to call the police."

The triage nurses were scared and uncertain for a moment, looking at him. They thought he was a brain-damaged hobo. He was wearing almost burned clothes, all covered with blood and ashes. Not only were his hair and his beard burned but also were his eyebrows and eyelashes. However, the nurses put Jim on a stretcher right away and called a doctor immediately. Victor enlightened the doctor about what happened to Jim, and after some short tests and IV connection, Jim was rolled into an operating room for urgent surgery.

"Listen to him!" Ella screamed, seeing distrust toward Victor on the nurses' faces. "He pulled all of us out from fire. Our house was on fire. Look." She lifted her bloody hands and stretched them toward the nurses. "I was holding Jim. I pressed this fucking towel to his neck for him not to die. I need to wash my hands now."

Victor finally was led to the phone at the reception desk while Ella grabbed Maggie by her arm, and they disappeared together behind the washroom door. At first, Victor called 911 and reported the fire at the group home Fir Forest, eighty-two miles west of Highway 212. He explained that there was a danger—the fire could spread to the surrounding forest area. It was an obvious arson, so he suggested that they send the police there as well. He also requested that they send an ambulance to the same place because three bedridden handicapped were left there outside. They were safe from fire but needed medical attention. The nurses listened to his call and was now inclined to believe Victor.

The second call he made was to his partner from the bureau, Bob Pauls.

"Hey, Bob," he said, "John Delany here . . . no, I am not calling from the grave, not there yet. I am calling from the general hospital. Just brought a homicide victim here. Listen, I need your help. I am now going to the concert hall at the university to arrest the suspected killer who is at the concert at this moment. I need you to call security there and ask them to let me in. I am kind of dirty. They probably would think that I am a homeless person."

His partner started to ask questions, and Victor answered, trying to convey the story in general. There wasn't enough time for the details. Still, it took some time. "Okay," Bob said finally, "I'll call Paladin Security, but I myself will also go to the concert hall right now. Meet you at the main door, John. See you there. I will bring your credentials. Damn, we did miss you here, brother. How long were you hidden in this nursing home? More than a year?"

"Fourteen months," Victor answered. "Just don't enter the concert without me, Bob. I know the exact moment when we should get her . . . yes, see you there. And thank you."

While the nurses were listening, one of them went out and returned later with a bunch of clothes. She stood beside Victor and waited until he finished his conversation with Bob. Then she said, "Sir, here are some clothes from our hospital's thrift store. They are secondhand, but at least they are clean. If you'd like, you can take them and change."

It was a great help, so Victor thanked her and went to the washroom, carrying the clothes with him. After he washed up a bit and changed into clean clothes, he made one more call—to the hospital social workers. He explained the situation to them—the handicapped from the burned nursing home were waiting in the hospital ER lobby for help. They needed to be taken care of and placed in some new facility for residence. And it should be done immediately because it was already evening, and they needed a place to sleep and also their medications.

At that moment, one of the assisting surgeons came out and approached Victor, and he realized by the doctor's face that the situation wasn't good. "We're trying our best, sir," the young doctor said. "But he lost too much blood from his tiny body. Though the transfusion is in place now and the artery fixed, the chance is very slim that he will make it. If he has any family, please inform them to come as soon as possible if they want to see him before he goes."

"Thank you, Doc. Will do," Victor answered.

Very briefly, he said bye to Ella and Maggie and thanked them for their help and cooperation and told them to stay put and wait for the social worker. Then Victor ran to the parking lot, where Todd was waiting in Mona's still running car. "Thank you for your patience, Todd," he said. "Now I will guard the car. You can go inside to the washroom. Just really fast, please."

"Why the hell do I need it?" Todd giggled. "I leaked already behind the bush right there. I thought you're dead there, zombie. Why was it so long? Where is the child?"

"Jim is still in surgery. We need to go right now."

"Where?" Todd wanted to know. "To get me new earphones?"

"To the concert hall. I'll have some business there, but you will find Lada and bring her here."

"Who the hell is Lada?"

"The young woman, your former bus driver."

"Jeez, you make things so complicated, zombie! It was easier to understand you when you weren't talking."

"I'll explain all that to you when we get there," Victor promised, turning from the parking lot.

At the concert, the last part of Jim's symphony just started.

CHAPTER 81

The last part of Jim's symphony was designed to be calming and soothing—a sunset, the rest of the day, the moments before the evening coming to a peaceful end. But Jason felt that it moved him even more than the previous parts. He saw Lada's face imprinted in his memory as she came out to the stage, announcing the concert today. A spiral lock of her hair hanging along her cheek attracted Jason as a magnet. He wished he could wrap that lock on his fingers, hold her face in the palms of his hands, and kiss her endlessly. He knew it would never happen in reality, but at least for now, with this music, it was such a joy to imagine that and to dream about it.

While working in Hawaii on his symphony, Jim wasn't thinking of conveying those feelings in this part, but it was written when he kissed Lada for the first time and when he gave her the ring. Those were the happiest moments of his life. Somehow his symphony absorbed them and now gave them away to the audience. Jason noticed many couples around him held hands, so they must be experiencing the same emotions. Even Mona moved closer to him and whispered into his ear, "Hug me, baby."

"Not now," he almost growled through his teeth. "But I promise to do that as soon as the music ends." He wanted to make the process of putting the handcuffs on her easier because he knew that she was strong enough and capable of fighting.

"I'm waiting," Mona whispered and put her hand on his knee, but Jason removed it right away, saying, "Be patient, please." He was really happy that this part of his undercover work was coming to an end. Mona was getting more annoying, and he got sickened of her more every day.

When the music ended, there was a pause for a few seconds while everyone was still holding their breath under the spell of the divine sounds. Then Boris put his conductor's stick on the stand, gestured his orchestra to stand up, and turned to face the audience. It was the end of the concert.

At this point, the whole concert hall of 1,400 people exploded with an enormous storm of applause. The audience stood up, screaming in excitement, clapping their hands like crazy, whistling, catcalling. Finally, this wild squall of excitement somehow combined into an almost well-balanced chanting. "Author! Author! Author!"

"Sweetie, it's your time," Mona said, smiling to Sharon. "Congratulations, my darling. You have to go on the stage now." She pushed her daughter gently on the shoulder.

Jason, however, who was standing beside Mona, attentively watched the public, trying to see if Victor would approach on the aisle that led to the middle of the concert hall from the main entrance. Now he slid in behind Mona and Sharon and hugged Mona by her waist, holding her tight. With his other hand, he grabbed Sharon by her arm, preventing her from walking toward the stage.

"Don't you touch me, you Mama's fucking black-ass lover." She hissed at him, trying to free her arm and go, but Jason held her tight.

At that moment, he finally saw Victor, followed by two security guards who were coming close to them. Jason let Mona's waist go while pulling handcuffs out from his suit pocket. "Let me introduce myself," he said. "MPD sergeant Jason Halls. Sharon Lainer, you are under arrest for fraud and theft over $5,000 of Jim Bogat's symphony." With that, he clicked handcuffs on Sharon's hands behind her back.

Sharon froze with her mouth open from astonishment.

"What the hell!" Mona screamed. "Stop this silly joke, Jason. It's not funny."

"I agree," Jason confirmed. "It's not funny at all. Nice to meet you, John." He addressed Victor, who was already in front of him and Mona. He handed Victor the second pair of handcuffs, which he took out from his pocket as well. "Daughter is mine. Mother is yours."

"FBI special agent John Delany," Victor said as he clicked handcuffs on Mona's hands in front of her. "Mona Lainer, you are under arrest for eight attempts of premeditated murder and arson."

"Fuck!" Mona uttered angrily and then maliciously laughed. "They were right that you could be a cop! They were right, and I didn't believe them! I regret that I didn't poison you when I had a chance. I will call my lawyer." After that, Mona and Sharon didn't say a word.

The other people from the VIP section of the hall looked at them in surprise, but most of the audience didn't notice anything because the noise was deafening. They kept cheering and clapping. "Thank you for coming in time, John," Jason said to Victor. "It would be a bit too tough for me to arrest them both on my own."

"Jeez, I never expected that, Jason," Victor answered as they shook hands. "You were good. How do you know about me?"

"From Jim's tape."

"Yeah, it's a big thank-you to him. He persuaded Lada to get me a gun. If not that, the eight people would be dead today in the fire."

"Did she burn the group home?" Jason asked, nodding toward Mona. "You look like you are scorched, John."

"It was quite an inferno," Victor confirmed. "Let's go book them. I have the guys from the bureau waiting outside, just in case."

They walked Mona and Sharon along the aisle to the exit of the building while the applause and chanting of the audience continued. "Author! Author!"

Lada appeared on the stage and pulled a string. A huge canvas with Jim's portrait rolled down along the back wall of the stage. She came close to the stage's edge, stopped beside Boris and Sandra, and said into her microphone, "I am happy to announce that the author of the symphony is Mr. James Emmanuel Bogat, the son of Mrs. Sandra Soley here and her late husband, Mr. Emmanuel Soley. Here, you can see the author's portrait. He may be a bit late tonight because of some trouble with transportation, but I am sure that he will be here very soon."

Lada stepped backward to the back of the stage, letting Boris and Sandra do their bows. She looked around, a bit worried that she still didn't see Victor coming with Jim. At that moment, she heard a strange voice from the side wing. "Psst, psst, hey, bus driver."

Lada turned to this side and, to her huge surprise, saw Todd waving at her to come closer. She knitted her brows and approached him. "Todd? What are you doing here? How did you get here?"

"Zombie brought me. He said he has some business to do, but he asked me to let you know that this child, you know, the midget, Jim . . . he is in the hospital. Docs said family to come. Who is his family? You know?"

"What?" Lada grabbed Todd by his shirt. "What? Why is Jim in the hospital? What happened? Car accident?"

"No, car is okay. We left car on the parking lot. Zombie said it will go as evidence. You know, he broke the glass with the gun . . . Midget is probably dying. You need to take me to the hospital with you. There is Maggie—you know, the girl with boobs—and the other girl who always swearing. I forgot her name."

It was quite difficult to understand Todd's incoherent words, but Lada got the point that something horrible happened to Jim. She felt like a knife was thrust into her gut; she got lost for a moment and didn't know what to do or say.

Boris, on the stage, already agreed with public requests to play another piece as encore. He decided to repeat Jim's variations on Emmanuel's song "The Endless Water," which was played at the beginning of the concert. There was no vocal line in this piece, so Sandra didn't need to sing anymore. She walked from the stage to the side wing where Lada was standing with Todd. "What's going on, my dear?" Sandra wanted to know, noting Lada's face was as pale as a corpse, and beside her was quite a strange man whose pockmarked face was also covered with scars, making him look scary. "Who is this man?"

"It's Todd. He is okay. He is okay," Lada repeated, all shaky. "Victor sent him to pick us up."

"Who is Victor?" Sandra asked, even more surprised.

"Jim's friend, our friend. Jim is . . . I . . . I don't know . . . Jim is in the hospital for some reason. I don't even remember where I parked my car. Oh my God!"

"Okay, I am calling my driver to get the car to the back entrance," Sandra said, grabbing her purse from a chair where she left it before the concert and dialing the number on her phone.

"Which hospital, Todd?" Lada yelled.

"I don't know, big one. There is sign 'Emergency.'" It wasn't very helpful, but Lada and Sandra decided to start from the general hospital and call the others on the way from Sandra's car.

Lada pulled Todd by the sleeve, and they ran together toward the back exit from the stage of the concert hall. Sandra followed them, asking Todd on the way, "Why is Jim in hospital? What happened?"

"There was fire," Todd tried to explain as best as he could, breathing heavily from the run. "She locked him in the basement. Zombie shoot the locks. Zombie pulled child out—I mean, midget. Everyone would be dead."

"Okay, don't listen to that!" Lada shouted. "Let's just go. We will find out at the hospital."

When they were already in the car, Lada texted Rita to let her know that something happened with Jim and that she was going to the hospital. She knew that Rita would not answer right away because she was still on the stage, but she wanted her and Boris to know why she left the concert hall so unexpectedly.

Realizing that Lada was gone somewhere for an unknown reason, Boris announced that the orchestra would play an encore, the introduction to the symphony, the variations on Emmanuel's song composed by the author of the symphony, James Emmanuel Bogat, the son of Sandra and Emmanuel Soley. Then he turned to face his orchestra and lifted his stick from the conductor's stand. The audience sat back on their seats in silent anticipation. The music started.

CHAPTER 82

As soon as Sandra's black Mercedes, with the driver wearing white gloves, turned into the parking lot of the general hospital, Todd recognized the place. "Here!" he screamed. "I told ya. See? 'Emergency.' And here is the bush where I leaked."

"Who is this man?" Sandra asked Lada with a touch of disdain.

"He is Jim's roommate from the group home," Lada answered.

"Did Jim live with that for eleven months?"

"Yes, and I worked there as a bus driver for two months."

"Oh my God," Sandra whispered. "I will never forgive myself. It's all my fault. I shouldn't have paid that despicable woman who blackmailed me. I should have gone to the police right away in November. Then it would never have happened."

"Please, Sandra, don't say that," Lada begged, making a big effort to hold back her tears. "Then I would never have met Jim. It is all fate."

"I know it's fate. It's my fault again. We shouldn't have done Jim's concert on the day of Emmanuel's death. Emmanuel was thirty-three when he was killed, exactly like Jim now. Oh my God." Sandra closed her eyes and began to pray.

The driver stopped the car right at the front entrance. Lada and Todd jumped out and ran inside, and Sandra slowly followed them, still whispering a prayer.

In the lobby, Maggie and Ella were sitting with social workers and the nurses Sue and Josef. Basil, Ali, and Zahra were lying on three stretchers. Everybody from the group home was here, safe and sound. The problem of finding new housing for all the former residents of the Fir Forest was discussed at the moment. "Bu, bu, wa, wa!" Maggie shrieked as she saw Todd and stretched her arms toward him.

"Come here, my booby girl." Todd giggled and hugged her. They seemed very happy together. The social workers and nurses laughed in approval. Everybody liked happy scenes, which were not normal in emergency departments.

"We're the family of James Bogat," Lada said to the receptionist. "I am his wife, and this is his mother. We need to see him."

"A wife?" the reception nurse lifted her eyebrows in surprise. Nobody expected that such a tiny and strange creature could have a beautiful wife who appeared in the ER wearing a red evening gown and also a quite young-looking, stylish mother in even more spectacular shining evening dress.

"Yes," Lada confirmed in a very agitated voice. "Where is he? We want to know what happened to him. We need to talk to his doctor."

"Okay," the receptionist said, checking her computer. "Mr. Bogat just came out of surgery. You can go to room 317. The elevator is in the hallway on your left. I'll call the doctor and say that you are with the patient. He will come and see you there."

When Lada and Sandra reached Jim's room, the doctor was already there, waiting for them outside the door. "Ladies," he said with a very sad expression on his face. "I am very sorry. We did everything we could. Your husband and son had a huge blood loss and for quite a long time. It is not replaceable, even with a blood transfusion. The surgery didn't solve the problem. He absolutely couldn't make it. You're lucky to catch his last minutes to say goodbye. We were worried that you might be too late even for that." And he ushered them into the room.

"What? What? Jim!" Lada screamed and dashed to the bed. Sandra silently walked to the opposite side of the bed, sat on the chair, and took Jim's bandaged hand. She sat motionlessly, petrified from grief and despair.

Jim was lying in bed with a lot of tubes and wires connected to him, and his face was also bandaged. Only his eyelids and lips were visible between white fabrics. His eyes were closed.

"Jim!" Lada shrieked, hugging him and sobbing unstoppably. "Jim, please. Darling, please. My love, please do not die on me. Jim, I am begging you. Don't die on me. Your symphony was a triumph today. It's great, Jim. It's a success, Jim. It is your dream come true, right? Do you hear me, Jim? I love you. I love you so much. I am pregnant, Jim. I wanted to tell you after the concert. Please don't leave me, Jim. Please don't go. Please stay with me."

Jim opened his eyes for a moment and whispered barely audibly, "Thank you . . . love you, Lada." And then his eyes closed forever. Her name was the last word he pronounced in his life.

"No, no, no, please, Jim. Please don't leave me. No, no, I don't want you to go. You will be with me forever. Please, Jim, please, my love." Lada continued crying and sobbing hysterically, holding him tight for a long time until she finally lost her consciousness and collapsed on the floor beside his bed.

The doctor and nurse ran in, lifted her, and seated her on the chair. The doctor was holding her by the shoulders to prevent her from falling again until the nurse rolled in a stretcher, and together, they put Lada on it.

Sandra was still sitting pale and motionless, holding Jim's hand. Tears were sliding down her cheeks, but she didn't make a sound. She looked like she was really petrified.

"Poor girl," the doctor said. "I understand her grief, but why did she lose consciousness? Is there something wrong with her?" He turned to Sandra. "Do you know, ma'am?"

"She is pregnant," Sandra said quietly. "She is my daughter-in-law. That baby . . . it is everything that is left for me from my beloved husband and my beloved son. It will be my only blood relative. Is there a danger that she could have a miscarriage from a nervous breakdown? Please, Doctor, do everything to save this pregnancy. Any treatment, any care, any expense—everything is on me. I will do everything imaginable for this girl. I don't want her to repeat my mistakes. That baby should live."

"Yes," the doctor said. "Better be safe than sorry. A miscarriage is very possible in these circumstances. She requires to be checked. We can give her a room now and keep her here for some time to make sure that the baby is safe."

"Please do that," Sandra begged. "I will stay with her all the time. I want to be sure that she has all that she needs. I am sorry, but I can't do anything more for my son. I can only save his child."

She rose, bowed to Jim, and kissed his forehead. "I know you will meet your father now, Jim," she whispered fondly. "And he will be very proud of you. You did great today in respect of his memory. Your symphony, your variation of his song—they were brilliant, as brilliant as he was. You were a genius, Jim, as he was.

"It was all my fault from the very beginning. I shouldn't have gone with Emmanuel as a fourteen-year-old girl. I shouldn't have tried to get rid of you while pregnant. I shouldn't have given you up for adoption. And this is my punishment from God for my sins. Both of you were taken from me in the age of Jesus, thirty-three years old. Both of you were taken while at the top of your blossoming careers.

"I know, Jim, that you forgave me. But I am not sure that I could ever forgive myself. The only good thing that lets me forgive myself was both of you left a child in this world."

CHAPTER *83*

The situation with Lada's health proved to be much more complicated than the doctors expected. At her checkup, it showed that the baby was okay, and there wasn't any danger of a miscarriage, but her current mental state didn't allow her to go home from the hospital. She absolutely couldn't accept Jim's death. She cried and sobbed hysterically, unstoppably, demanding that Jim be returned to her. Giving her a sedative shot was the only way to stop these outbursts. After that, she would fall asleep for some hours; but as soon as she woke up, the attacks started again.

Sandra was patiently sitting beside her bed all day. For the nights when she went to her hotel to get some sleep, she hired a special nurse just to stay beside Lada and watch her. Boris and Rita came right after the concert to see Jim for the last time and to say their farewells, as well as to try to soothe Lada, but it was absolutely impossible to do. She became practically insane.

Sandra, with Boris and Rita, organized a beautiful celebration-of-life event for Jim. They repeated most of the concert—the introduction and the symphony—with the whole concert hall full of people who loved and admired Jim. Then there was a beautiful huge funeral where—in addition to Sandra, Boris, Rita, and their children—the whole orchestra attended, along with some professors and students from the university, some officers from MPD, some officers from FBI, and even all Jim's roommates and nurses from the group home.

Sandra arranged for a high-ranking Catholic priest to come from the Vatican in Italy to conduct the funeral of her son. There were tons of flowers and oceans of tears, and the only person who was missing at the funeral was Lada. She was still lying in the hospital, unconscious, sleeping all the time, or sobbing and screaming, "I want my Jim back! Give me my Jim! I won't live without him!" Then she got her shot and slept for many hours again. It looked like this would never end.

There were some visitors who came to check on Lada. Boris and Rita came almost every day when they could, and they brought their children sometimes. However, Lada strictly refused to see her mother. When Boris suggested to her that her mom can come and stay with her, she screamed madly, "I don't want to see the only person in the world who would be happy that I lost Jim!"

"She is still your mother," Boris tried to object.

"No. My mom is now Sandy," Lada sobbed. "Jim forgave Sandy. She blessed us. She is my mother and the grandmother of our child now and will be forever. And leave me, please. I want to be with Sandy alone, alone, alone." Then once again, only a sedative shot stopped her outburst.

One day the FBI special agent John Delany, Victor, came to visit Lada, though she was sleeping at the moment. He shaved his burned beard and got a proper military-style haircut. That made him look much younger, in spite of the gray. His eyebrows and eyelashes started to grow back slowly. "I want to thank your girl," he said to Sandra, who was at the bedside as always. "She is basically the saver of seven people's lives. She was brave enough to buy a gun and bring it to the group home. She did it on the very unusual request on my part, despite that it may be even scary for her. She is a music student who is really far away from any policing or military business. But she did it for Jim, I am sure. I think you should be very proud of your daughter."

"She is not really my daughter," Sandra answered. "I am Jim's mother."

"Oh, Jim told me a lot about you, Mrs. Soley. I am sorry I didn't recognize you. No offense, I was never an opera fan. But I was a crazy fan of your group when you were singing with Emmanuel. I was fifteen at that time."

"Same as I." Sandra nodded. "But you are right, sir. Yes, Lada is my daughter now. You know, it is kind of strange. I didn't have any children for most of my life, but then I found my son, and now I've got a daughter. And I will also have a grandchild in a few months."

"I am truly happy that Jim left a child," Victor said. "I am not much into music, though I've heard from other people that Jim was a genius. But I knew him mostly as a person and, I am proud to say, as a friend. He was so sincere, open, kindhearted, even selfless, sometimes crazily brave. He was the most amazing person that I ever met. And thank you very much for giving life to that great human being. I consider it a big honor to be friends with him. He will always live in my memory and in the hearts of the people who had ever known him."

On another day, Jason came to the hospital. He wasn't confident to come earlier. He felt somewhat guilty that he couldn't save Jim and didn't force him to leave the group home on the bus with him and Mona. He knew that Mona would never allow that, and it would have created a big problem. Maybe even the chance of arresting her and Sharon at the concert would have been lost. Maybe even his whole undercover work would be lost and destroyed, but at least Jim would still be alive now.

Jason was completely concentrated on his task at that moment. Mona manipulated him very successfully so as not to notice how she implemented her plan to get rid of Jim before the concert. What happened to Jim wasn't really Jason's fault, but he felt sometimes that it was. He didn't know if he would ever be able to look Lada in the eyes. But he knew that he had to see her. He needed to understand where they were in their relationship at this point.

When Jason came, Lada was sleeping. He introduced himself to Sandra as Jim and Lada's family friend who wanted to check on how she was doing. "You can try, of course," Sandra answered. "But I can't guarantee a success. Sometimes she doesn't want to see anybody and talk to anybody. Also, you should wait. Nobody knows when she will come to. She is unpredictable. And be ready for a lot of screaming and crying when she does wake up."

"It's okay," Jason accepted. "I can wait as long as needed. But I won't go anywhere until I talk to her. If she says that she doesn't want to see me and kicks me out, then okay, I will go. But I should hear that from her personally."

Hmm, Sandra thought. *This is quite a persistent statement for a family friend, and it sounds much more than just friendly.* But she didn't say anything. She had no idea who Jason was and how he was related to the whole story.

Jason sat on the chair at the other side of Lada's bed opposite Sandra. He looked comfortable, like he was settled there forever. Sandra was surprised and a bit confused but didn't say anything about that either.

They chatted a bit about Jim's funeral, which Jason actually attended. Sandra told him that she intended to add Jim's image to Emmanuel's Los Angeles memorial, which was created by a world-famous sculptor. She wanted them—the father and son, the only two loves of her life—to be immortalized together in this memorial forever. She also planned to add Jim's symphony to the sound circle of Emmanuel's songs that were repeating there at the memorial 24/7.

"That would be great." Jason nodded. "I'm sure Jim would love that."

Then Jason asked her about Lada's condition and mentioned that he was a bit worried how she would manage to live now as she was pregnant. "How do you know that she is pregnant?" Sandra asked, surprised.

"She told me a couple of weeks ago."

"Wow!" Sandra was almost shocked. "She didn't tell Jim . . . or me . . . or her brother."

"It happened accidentally," Jason explained. "She just misspoke. And she wanted to surprise Jim after the concert and also to surprise the whole family."

"I see, you were kind of very close friends," Sandra noted cautiously.

"Not really." Jason shook his head. "Lada just helped me conduct the investigation about Mona and her daughter's crimes. I am actually a policeman, though not a detective yet, but I was assigned to this group home case."

"Oh, I got it now." Sandra smiled with relief. "You scared me a bit with that."

Jason laughed sincerely. "It's okay. It was just a friendly conversation that I had with Lada at Starbucks. There is nothing to worry about, I swear to God."

Then Lada moaned, moved her head, and opened her eyelashes a bit. "Jason," she whispered, blinking her eyes in disbelief. "Jason, did you get the monster?"

"Yes, I did," he confirmed. "We did it with Victor. We're working her case now, together as well."

"You know, Jason," Lada murmured, "she took my Jim. I want my Jim back. Please bring him back to me. You're smart and strong. You can do everything. You are the only one who could bring my Jim back to me. Please help me. I want my Jim back." She turned on her stomach and started to sob, beating her fists at the pillow. "Where is my Jim? Where? Where? I want him back!"

"Here you go." Sandra sighed sadly. "I warned you. Maybe you better go now."

"No." Jason shook his head. "I would like to try a bit more." He sat on the edge of the bed and put his hand on the back of Lada's head, petting her and wrapping her matted locks around his fingers. To Sandra, it looked like he was caressing her.

"Lada, girl," he said quietly and fondly, "the monster will get a life sentence without parole, maybe even the death penalty. It will take a couple of years, but she will get the proper justice. It is what Jim dreamed about, isn't it? I am not a God. I can't return Jim to you, but you could do it yourself. You should calm down, my girl. You should take good care of this little Jim, who is inside you now and who will come to you very soon and will stay with you forever."

There is much more here than just help in an investigation over coffee at Starbucks, Sandra thought. *Oh my God, she stopped crying. It's a miracle.*

Lada froze motionless for a while, listening to Jason, and then turned and looked at him. "Do you think it's a boy?" she asked barely audibly.

"It doesn't matter if it is a boy or a girl. It is your Jim anyway. And if you continue crying all the time, you could lose this baby, and there would be no Jim anymore. Do you get it? The life of this little Jim is dependent on you now, on your health, on your nerves. Jim's life is in your hands. So calm down, my dear girl, please. Calm down and save your Jim yourself."

"Oh God, it's a miracle that you know what to say," Sandra pronounced aloud with tears in her eyes.

"Didn't anybody ever say that to her?" Jason asked as he stood up from the edge of Lada's bed.

"I did many times, but she didn't listen. You have such a talent, young man. You should be a priest, not a policeman," Sandra answered.

"No." Jason laughed and shook his head. "A priest could do that for anyone, but I can only do that for her."

Weakly, Lada requested, "Jason, please give me your hand."

He extended his arm toward her, and she grabbed his hand, hugged it,and squeezed it to her cheek. "Don't go anywhere, please. I won't let you go. You are returning my Jim to me. You're the only one in the world who is capable of returning my Jim to me. I always knew that. I always felt that." And she started crying again but softly and quietly, hugging and pulling his arm toward her so strong that Jason was forced to sit again at the edge of her bed so as not to fall down.

When Lada finally fell asleep after another sedative shot, he freed his hand, stood up, and said to Sandra, "I guess you need some rest after the tragedy of losing your son, Mrs. Soley. It was pretty demanding for you to stay here all this time. Thank you very much for your help. I'll go now to the chief of MPD and do the paperwork—an application for vacation for two weeks at least. Tonight I will come back and stay with Lada 24/7 until she is completely healed and her little Jim will be a hundred percent safe."

CHAPTER 84

The hospital placed a cot for Jason in Lada's room. He sat beside her all day long and slept on the cot at night. She was a bit confused at first. "I don't know, Jason. I don't want you to see me without any makeup. And wearing this hospital gown . . . I don't want you to think that I am not attractive," she claimed a bit flirtatiously.

He laughed. "You're looking like an angel, my girl. I can tell you when you were not very attractive. It was when you came to the park that day, swearing at me, and slapped me in the face. That was really not attractive. You were disgusting then. But we already passed that, didn't we?"

"Yes, we did." Lada sniffed apologetically. "And you forgave me, didn't you?"

"Yes, I did."

They were talking a lot but not like Lada used to talk with Jim. She didn't tell Jason a word about her tragic Ukrainian past. For him, her life started here in America, five years ago, and the experiences she shared with him were all from here. Also, she didn't tell Jason the story of Boris and Rita's immigration and their tricky escape from the communist regime for their love. What she told about them was just their house, work, family, children, dog, travels—life here in America.

Subconsciously, Lada crossed out all the past because it was a tragedy she shared with Jim. It belonged to her and Jim. It belonged to their love only. It didn't matter how nice and caring Jason was, how handsome and sexy looking he was, and even how badly she was attracted to him and wanted him sexually; he still was not Jim. And he couldn't ever be Jim.

Jason, quite the opposite, shared with her absolutely everything about his life and upbringing. But there weren't any tragedies, like in her life and Jim's life. His life was more a picture-perfect story of a middle-class American family.

His parents were nice, educated people, his father an electrical engineer, his mother an English teacher in high school. They were happily married for thirty-three years and were in good health. Jason had one elder sister, Melissa, who was already thirty and well educated and had a full-time job as a paralegal. She was also happily married and had three children. Her husband was a police officer who actually studied with Jason at the police academy, which was how they met.

Nobody in the whole family ever had cancer, died, divorced, or used drugs or too much alcohol or was killed or injured in car accidents, robbed, abused, or bullied at school. Nobody ever fought. Everybody was loving and caring. That was where Jason learned to be like that. He and Melissa were mostly grade A students and always had a lot of friends and a lot of fun, decent and happy fun.

Jason's uncle, his father's brother, was a police chief in Portland, Oregon. It was where Jason learned a lot about police work and heard lots of stories as a teenager while he and Melissa spent some summers with their uncle's family on the Oregon coast. That determined his decision to go into the police academy after his high school graduation.

Somehow even racial storms passed around Jason's happy family, not hurting them. Their house was located in a pretty diverse and decent area, where all their neighbors and friends were as multicolored as only possible in America. His own mother was half African, half Mexican and father half African, half German. Melissa's husband was a white Irish. Both Jason's best friends at school were East Indian, Ramesh, and native Cherokee, Bill. Even the two girlfriends with whom Jason had previous relationships and used to live for about a couple of years each were Chinese and Filipino girls. Their relationship ended quite amicably and not because of their skin color.

Of course, Jason's parents and uncle gave him proper lessons on how to behave as safely as possible as a black young man in America. "Do not jog on the streets and in the parks ever, where the white policemen could think that you are a criminal running away. It's better to exercise inside gyms and sport clubs. If you ever were stopped by white officers in traffic, keep quiet, calm, and polite, even if it seems to be an unfair stop. Tell them to search your pocket and to take out your ID and badge to prove that you are a policeman too. Don't ever try to do it yourself by putting your hands in your pockets. They could think that you want to take out a weapon. So just be cautious, and you will be okay."

Jason learned these habits well. He was stopped a couple of times in traffic and pulled out from his car and searched, but then his credentials were found, and the white policemen let him go, even apologized. He actually wasn't offended by that, just considered it as a joke and a funny story to tell friends. He was a really a "glass half full" man, very optimistic and happy by nature.

That was why he agreed to go undercover, to observe and investigate the group home where abuse of handicapped people was suspected. That was where he met Lada—half Ukrainian, half Russian—whom he now would be interested to add to his really diverse family as he said to her, laughing, pretending that it was also a joke.

Lada was listening to the beautiful story of his life with envy. She never heard about any happy families in her country of origin. "How come? I don't get it," she asked in disbelief. "Sandra had so much tragedy in her life as Emmanuel, Jim, and my family, which by the way I don't want to talk about. Is it European-style to have a tragic life, or what? Or is it fate? I am trying to understand. You're such a lucky duck, Jason. You're spreading around so much positive energy because of your upbringing. It's amazing. It's what I really need now. And you know what? I want a hug."

"I am always happy to help with that." Jason laughed again and opened his arms for her.

Lada climbed out of bed, came to him, and sat on his lap. She hugged him by the neck and hid her face on his chest. He hugged her by her back with his left arm, and with the right hand, he was petting and wrapping her hair around his fingers. It was something that he really liked to do. Somehow her long blond hair aroused him, together with the warmth of her body that he felt through the thin fabric of the hospital's gown. She snuggled up to him like a child, longing for protection on a mother's chest, and held him tight as if she would never let him go. They were sitting silently for a long moment, both enjoying the feeling of closeness to each other.

"You know, Jason," Lada whispered finally, "when I was a little girl, I was sitting like this with my grandma sometimes when I needed to be comforted. It felt so peaceful, warm, calm, quiet, safe, protected. It was so good. Now with you, I am feeling like that, like you are my grandma."

"Thank you." Jason smirked sadly. "Very sexy."

"Oh, about sexy . . . you remember I told you in that park when we had a fight that I didn't have any sexual feeling for many years? I was numb and dead inside, and then Jim unexpectedly woke me up."

"Yes, I remember," he said, a bit uncertain where this conversation was going.

"I have pretty bad news. I feel like those feelings died with Jim, and they are gone. I am scared that it is forever. I don't know what to do."

Jason kept fondly caressing her hair and then answered slowly, "You know, my girl, the hospital is not the best place to work on returning those feelings to you. We probably better do that at home. At least we can try. What do you think about this idea?"

"Which home, mine or yours?"

"I think mine would be better. My apartment is fully equipped. Yours is practically empty, just a mattress." He didn't add that it was the mattress on which she had sex with Jim. He let this thought go.

"Okay," Lada agreed. "If you would like to help me with that, I can tell you what Jim did."

"No, no, no, please don't. I respect Jim's memory very much, and I admire his music, but I absolutely don't want to know what he did with you in bed."

"It wasn't in bed. It was in my car."

"Jeez, it's even worse."

"Sorry." Lada laughed. "You misunderstood, silly. It wasn't what you think." She only wanted to tell how Jim kissed her fingers in the car when she drove him back to the group home after the weekend with her family—that was where she felt those butterflies the first time. "I am sorry. I just said it wrong. Let me paraphrase this sentence. Okay, here it is—I can tell you what I like."

"Oh, Jesus, please don't." Jason pouted. "I don't want to hear this either."

"Why?"

"Because I want to find this out myself."

"Well, how could you find out if I am not telling you?" Lada objected.

"There are many options for that."

"Tell me at least one."

"Do you want to turn me crazy right here in the hospital? You're playing a dangerous game, my girl. Well, okay, as soon as we come home, let's say, I could kiss you from head to toe, and it would be very clear what you do like and what you don't."

"And what we will do with places which I don't like?"

"We will forget about them forever."

"And what we will do with the ones that I like?"

"We will stay on them forever. Jeez, I can't do that anymore, Lada. Please stop it, and let's tell the doctor that you are ready to go home. There are two more days left from my vacation."

"Okay." She laughed happily. "I think that I am ready to go home now."

During those two weeks that Jason spent with Lada in the hospital, Sandra and Boris with his orchestra signed a contract for a tour in Europe for three months with the performance of Jim's symphony. It included fourteen countries. They were supposed to leave at the beginning of November and perform on Christmas and New Year. Then another tour at spring next year was arranged through the American states on the East Coast.

The unbelievable success of Jim's symphony skyrocketed Sandra's and Boris's professional success as well, though they were successful enough before that. But it was still interesting work for them to do. They were happy about that and very proud to immortalize Jim's life through his music by opening it more and more to the world.

Sandra, Boris, and Rita were a bit worried about Lada, imagining that it would be pretty difficult for her to live alone while carrying the child. Boris suggested that she return home, where her mother would stay with their children while they were on tour, but Lada strictly refused. Sandra, in her turn, suggested that she would rent a two-bedroom apartment for Lada and hire a live-in caregiver/homemaker to help her with daily household needs.

"I have a better idea," Jason said while he, as a family friend, was attending these discussions. "I will rent a two-bedroom apartment where Lada would live as a roommate with me. We could hire a walk-in housekeeper for the times when I am at work. Otherwise, I would take care of Lada."

"I still would like to pay rent," Sandra insisted. "My grandchild would be living there."

"No way." Jason laughed. "I can easily afford the rent. A housekeeper could be on you, okay, because it would be for Lada and her child, but the apartment would be mine."

Sandra looked at him suspiciously. "Jason, you said that Lada would be a roommate only. Am I right? In this case, she should pay half the rent, right? So half the rent still would be on me."

"Okay," Jason finally agreed, trying to show to Lada's family that this would really be a roommate agreement only. However, everybody suspected that it wouldn't be but didn't say a thing.

Before leaving for the tour, Sandra brought her Lady of the Sorrows statue to Lada. "You know, my dear daughter," she said, hugging her, "this lady was in my family for generations. I'm thankful that Jim and you found it and returned it to me. It helped me overcome the tragedy of losing Jim and survive through these awful times. But now as you're having his child, it would be a true inheritor of the statue. It would be my only descendant. I don't have anybody else in this world, just you and Jim's baby. So you keep that lady, please, and pass it to my grandchild and to the next generations ahead. Love you, Lada."

"I love you too, Mama Sandy," Lada answered and hugged her. Then she pressed the statue to her chest, smiling. She felt that the marble was getting warmer and warmer with every minute, and a happy feeling of comfort enveloped her completely.

PART 4

EPILOGUE

FIVE YEARS LATER...

The investigation on Mona Lainer's crimes took more than three years. Jason Halls and John Delany, a.k.a. Victor, worked on this case together and became close friends. Mona was charged with three counts of first-degree murder of Lily Donovan, the baby of Maggie Gordon, and James Bogat and also with seven counts of premeditated murder attempts, arson, bribery, money laundering, her own group home's bus robbery, abuse of the handicapped in her care, and so on. The list was pretty significant.

After long discussions between the lawyers, Jim's tapes were accepted and considered as evidence during the investigation. Jason and John were also valuable witnesses themselves. The prosecutor insisted on the death penalty, but Mona took a plea in exchange for the sentence of life without parole. However, Jason and John were a bit worried about that. They knew that she was smart enough to possibly manipulate some guards, present herself as a helpless victim, make a sexual love story, and use this as an advantage to escape from prison. For that reason, they persuaded the judge to decide that she should be placed in a strongly guarded facility.

Her daughter, Sharon, received a light sentence—$50,000 fine, one hundred hours of community service by picking up garbage along highways, and three years of parole, during which she was not allowed to do anything that was related to music. So she was forced to change her profession. Her house; her red car, the Aston Martin Vanquish S; all of Mona's twelve diamond necklaces; and Jim's piano and customized computer system that were left packed in the boxes on the group home bus, still parked beside Sharon's house, were confiscated. Some of these were used as evidence during the investigation.

Boris and Rita went through all of Jim's works, which were kept in their house as he gave them to Lada for safekeeping. They combined a big and beautiful program from these works, which included much more than just his last symphony. They performed it with their orchestra, as violin solo concerts, as chamber orchestra concerts, or as some vocal cycles with Sandra Soley and other singers, making Jim's music more known everywhere in the world. Some of Jim's works got included in other famous performers' concerts, like André Rieu, Yanni, and so on. Lada, as the author's widow, received all the royalties from those performances.

As a result of this huge effort and hard work, Boris got a big promotion. He was invited to take the position as the general conductor of the Philadelphia Orchestra—the most famous in the USA and also in the whole world. So he and Rita sold their house in Minneapolis and moved to Philadelphia with the children and the grandmother, Tatiana.

Sandra Soley got a new contract as an opera singer in al the Theater La Scala in Italy for three years, starring as Violetta in the well-known, brilliant opera *La traviata* by Giuseppe Verdi. She temporary left her vocal teaching business, still thinking about returning to it as her contract would be finished.

Lada and Jason got married in February 2004 while she was seven months pregnant. Her family and some friends were thinking that it seemed like a rush and showed to everybody that she forgot Jim way too fast. But this wasn't the case. Jason wanted a small wedding just with their closest family members and some friends to respect her pregnancy. He only insisted to get married before the child was born to make sure that it would have his last name. It would be much easier than going through the whole adoption process later.

Lada, on the contrary, wanted a very big wedding. In addition to Jason's extended family, Boris's whole orchestra was invited, as well as many MPD officers and FBI officers, some of Lada's teachers and classmates from the university, and even the whole staff from the burned group home, Fir Forest. The nurses also brought former patients who knew both, Lada and Jason, pretty well:—Ella, Todd, and Maggie. The last two were living now in another group home and shared the room as a couple after having a sterilization procedure.

John Delany, whom Lada still called Victor, was the best man for Jason at their wedding, together with Boris and two of Jason's school friends, Ramesh and Bill. Lada's bridesmaids were Rita; her daughter, Becky, Lada's niece; Heyriah, Lada's friend who finally returned home to Minneapolis from Saudi Arabia; and, of course, Sandra Soley. Lada's mother didn't attend the wedding. She didn't approve of her daughter's choice of a husband again, but Lada didn't invite her anyway.

For the wedding, they decorated and adjusted the university concert hall, turning it into a kind of dinner theater. The tables for the guests were placed between the rows of seats, covered by garlands of white roses. While Jason's father, Tyrone, walked Lada down the aisle, the orchestra was playing the potpourri that Boris and Rita combined from the best classical pieces of wedding music.

A Catholic priest took the vows and married the young couple. During their exchange of rings, Sandra was singing "Ave Maria," accompanied by the orchestra, which was accepted by a standing ovation from the whole audience. Many had tears in their eyes, touched by the beauty of the ceremony.

Sandra, unlike Lada's mother, really approved of this marriage, absolutely excited about the great help that Jason did for Lada and her baby at the hospital. She thought that it would be impossible to find a better stepfather for her grandchild than Jason. Sandra also understood the rush. She herself got married to Emmanuel after two months of their acquaintance, and the rush there was also for other reasons, not related to love itself.

Lada and Jason prepared for a honeymoon in the Caribbean. Both the airplane tickets and the hotel accommodation were already done and waiting for them. When they came to their bedroom for the first night of their married life, Lada looked at herself in the mirror. She saw herself wearing the amazing white dress, special hairstyle, and veil. She just experienced the wedding of her dreams, and suddenly, instead of being happy, she realized what was happening to her.

"This should be my wedding with Jim," she said quietly to herself and then repeated loudly, "After the concert, it should be my wedding with Jim. We wanted to go to Italy with Sandra for our honeymoon. We . . . we . . ." And then she fell on the bed and began sobbing hysterically.

Jason was in such shock that he got lost for a moment and didn't know what to say or do. Unexpectedly, it turned out to be their only night when they didn't have sex since they moved together. After they got undressed from their wedding outfits, Lada spent all night sitting on Jason's lap, hugging his neck, and crying unstoppably, almost to insanity. He didn't say a word, just held her silently, hugging her back and caressing her hair, like he had done in the hospital.

What could he tell her? There was an unbearable sharp pain in his soul as he began to realize what he got himself into. He knew now that for the woman he loved more than anything in the world, he was a second choice and always would be. He felt doomed. It was obvious to him that she agreed to marry him only to have a protector, comforter, and father for her child and to satisfy the sexual feelings that were awakened inside her with his help. Could the combination of those reasons be named love? He wasn't sure. She never said this word to him.

Jason closed his eyes, squeezed his teeth, and with huge difficulty held himself in check, prohibiting himself from crying with her. He knew that he should be strong. Everything would pass. They would survive this together, but for now, it was torture.

Close to morning, Jason finally said, "My girl, it's enough crying, please. Did you forget that you can hurt the baby?" He only hoped that it would work. And it actually did.

"Sorry," Lada whispered, still stuttering from sobs. "You're right . . . I forgot . . . completely. Let's lie down, please. Hug me, Jason. Kiss me, please. I need you."

"We have maybe a couple of hours to sleep. Then we are going to the airport. We're leaving for our trip," he reasoned. "Did you forget that too?"

"No, I didn't forget that. But I can't go anywhere . . . it should be my honeymoon with Jim . . . my trip with Jim . . . no, no, no, I can't." Her tears came again.

Jason lifted her and put her into the bed. He did lie down beside her and whispered tenderly, moving away her hair from her face, "It's okay. If you don't want, we are not going anywhere. Just tell me, what do you want, my love? What should I do to calm you down?"

"Hug me. Kiss me. I want you. I want you so, so much, please."

"That's okay. I want you too always," he agreed, though at this moment he wanted her to stop crying much more than to love him.

The two weeks of the honeymoon, instead of being a beautiful and exciting trip with a lot of interesting and memorable experiences that could make them spiritually close, turned out to be two weeks of unstoppable sex at home. Lada didn't let Jason leave her for a minute.

She was clinging on him like a sinking person grabbing a safe buoy. She was begging him for more and more endlessly. He truly loved her, so he enjoyed it as well. It was giving him a little illusion of happiness, feeling that she wanted him, exactly him, and no one else, until he realized that she just used sex for healing, like a sick person using medication or like people using alcohol or drugs to forget, to get away from the pain of reality.

Jason had no idea what Jim did in bed or how their sex life evolved, but it obviously was very different from what it was with him. At least what he had with Lada now belonged only to him. It was his. Actually, he knew well that his personal sex appeal was the main thing that attracted Lada to him from the very beginning when they met.

During their sex now, Jason himself was in her thoughts and in her rapturous moaning. She never mentioned Jim anymore, and Jason convinced himself that everything had finally calmed down during these two weeks and came back to normal. However, a bit of insecurity was still left sitting inside his head and quietly buzzing inside his heart.

As a wedding gift, Sandra gave to Lada and Jason half the payment for the new house. Jason refused at first, considering this as too huge a present, but Sandra insisted. "You know, Jason," she said, "I am doing that for my grandchild, who will live in this house. The money really does not mean that much to me. Since I got married to Emmanuel, I always had huge amounts of money, but don't even ask me if I ever was happy. I got happy only when I found Jim, but . . . how long did it last? You know that. I think we understand each other pretty well, don't we?"

"Yes." He nodded sadly. "I would like to confide something to you, if you don't mind. I have a bit of a problem with Lada. I told her hundreds of times that I love her. And I really do, but she never says it back. You probably noticed that, even in the wedding vows. Maybe you could give me some advice. Do you think it is possible that she still loves Jim?"

Sandra smiled as she talked to him in a very caring, even motherly tone. "I never had another man in my life after Emmanuel's death. Could you guess why? Look at me, Jason. I am not an unattractive woman. I had many admirers, and many of them did seriously love me. But I didn't love anybody except Emmanuel ever. Those Soley boys, Em and Jim, they both set the bar very high with their specialty and their brilliant talents. It is very difficult to surpass them."

"If I don't have a talent in music, I don't deserve to be loved?" Jason objected, agitated. "Is that so?"

"No, my dear. I didn't mean that, not at all. I am just trying to explain to you what is going on here as I understand that situation with Lada. You're an amazing person, Jason, and you're younger than Jim was, and you are also a strong and very handsome man. Of course, you are easily surpassing him physically and—I don't know for sure, but I could guess—sexually. And it is obvious that Lada is extremely attracted to you. She did marry you. Doesn't it prove that? But spiritually, she still loves Jim, of course. She treasures that special bond they had. Really, not that much time passed since his death. I am sure she will get over it. I am even sure that she loves you now but is just scared to say so, seeing it in her mind as a betrayal of Jim. Just be patient. Everything will be okay. That will pass with time."

"Thanks," Jason said and hugged her. "You're so kind. I love her so much. I will wait."

However, five years passed, and two children were born—Jim's son, Emmanuel James, at the beginning of April 2004, and Jason's daughter, Sandra Maria, in May 2006. The second name of the little girl was actually that of Jason's mother. They called the baby girl San-Marie for short. The young family looked picture perfect, but Lada still kept silent and left a mystery for Jason of what she was feeling.

Jason and Lada, while being very close friends, usually agreed on everything and were always happy looking and madly craving for each other sexually, but Jason can't stop feeling that she was holding something back, something really important and sacred in her soul. In sex, Lada actually was the same as she was with Jim, weak and vulnerable, almost dying in waves of her endless orgasms, but it felt to Jason like she wasn't with him, like she was somewhere else. She just enjoyed herself and didn't give anything back to him. He enjoyed her body, her pleasure, her vulnerability, but he wanted more. He wanted to feel her soul, her heart loving him back, but there was nothing. It was kind of offensive, like he was in his moments of highest passion on his own but not with her. And his thoughts were again the same—she still loved Jim.

One day two years ago, when little Sandra was born, Boris and Rita, with the children, came for a visit. And Jason find the nerve to ask Boris for advice about what could be going on with Lada. He asked very carefully, a bit ashamed and confused, "What do you think, Boris? Is it possible that Lada still loves Jim?"

Boris shook his head thoughtfully. "I don't know. She doesn't say anything about Jim ever. But they had a huge spiritual bond based on their tragedies. They returned each other to life. You know, there was a very wise English guy, William Shakespeare." Boris laughed. "You probably studied his works at school as far as I know about the English literature program, which my kids are taking now. In the Ukraine and Russia, his plays were all translated, but we didn't learn them at school. I actually know his *Otello* as the opera by Giuseppe Verdi, but the quote is the same anyway. He said there how he and Desdemona fell in love with each other. I am quoting, 'She loved me for my sufferings, and I loved her for her compassion for them.' In this case, with Jim and Lada, it went both ways. They both had unbelievable tragedies, and both had compassion toward each other. It made it a double bond and double love."

"I can imagine Jim's tragedy as he was born . . . you know . . . in his condition. But what tragedy did Lada ever have?" Jason exclaimed.

"Hmm." Boris lifted his eyebrows in surprise. "Didn't she tell you?"

"Not a word."

"Sorry, in this case, I probably have no right to tell anything as well. But you should ask her. You need to open her emotionally and open her soul. I think it could help if you ask. It would make you closer spiritually."

"I don't want to repeat anything that Jim did," Jason said, agitated.

"You wouldn't. Jim never asked her anything. She told him things mostly by herself. I got involved once, but she gave me hell after that, so I am not putting my nose in her life anymore ever."

After this conversation with Lada's brother, a couple of more years passed, but Jason still didn't find the nerve to ask Lada about this topic. He was afraid that this could break everything he had now and that he would lose her completely if something went wrong. He loved her and the children more than anything in the world and didn't want to take a risk. The half-full glass was still better than none at all.

He even consulted with a psychologist who spread some light on the problem. "You think that your wife loves you sexually, but in her soul, she loves another man," he confirmed after Jason told him the whole story. "I can tell you, with my experience with my patients, it is a pretty common case. It happens with thousands of men. You are at least much safer than any of them. Your wife can't leave you for him because he is dead.

The psychologist continued, "Try to find the way through the child. Become the best friend and best dad for him. It could bond her more strongly to you."

"I am best friends with him, but she insisted that he call me Jason, not Dad. He knows that his father is another man and that he is dead.

I don't know if the four-year-old child is capable of getting the concept of death, but at least he knows that his father is not with him but somewhere . . . I don't know . . . maybe in heaven . . . or something."

"It doesn't matter what the child calls you. The most important thing is if he loves you," the psychologist concluded.

"He does. He obviously does." Jason nodded. "Sometimes it looks like he loves me even more than his mother. We're really best friends. And Lada actually appreciates this. I know."

Then Jason told the psychologist about the tragedies aspect that Boris explained to him, which could create a spiritual bond of mutual love in a couple. "What do you think? How is it my fault that I didn't have any tragedy in my life ever? I don't deserve to be loved because I was raised by a nice and loving family and had a happy childhood?" he asked, really hurt by the idea.

"There is no one person in the world," the psychologist said, "who passed through their life without any tragedy at all. Look at yourself. Why are you here? What you are experiencing now is a real personal tragedy. It is torturing you, it is killing you inside, and you absolutely have to tell all this to your wife. It really could help. If she understands you, you will clearly see that she loves you."

Jason wasn't sure that it was the right time to start this conversation with Lada. She was six months pregnant again with their third child. But something forced him. The ultrasound showed that the baby was a boy, and she announced that he would be named James Emmanuel, not even asking Jason's opinion. That was the last drop of his patience.

On an evening before the weekend, Jason stayed a bit longer than usual with little Emmanuel, putting him to sleep. Instead of the usual one, they read two books together in turn. He wanted to give Lada more time to settle in bed for the night and to wait for him. Then he came to the bedroom and lay down on his side of the bed, but instead of hugging, kissing, and caressing her right away as he always did, he turned on his stomach, hugged the pillow, and hid his face into it, not saying a word. It never happened before in years of their marriage, and Lada was very surprised.

"Jason, what are you doing? Has something happened?" she asked fondly, moving closer to him and hugging his shoulders.

"Yes," he mumbled into the pillow. "We need to talk."

"Okay," she agreed, guessing that maybe something went wrong at his work. "Yes, I am listening. Tell me."

"No, I am listening this time," he said abruptly, suddenly turning to her and looking straight in her eyes. "You tell me."

"What?"

"Everything. We have been married for five years now, and I still don't know anything about you. You're hiding something. I want to know you, your heart, your soul, your true feelings. I am tired of being a sex toy or a sex machine. Don't you understand that I am a person as well? A human being who loves you madly and who needs to hear it back from you and to feel it back from you? How could we raise our kids, how could we be a family if we are not on the same page? Not one item? I want the truth. Do you still love Jim? Or do you love me finally?"

Lada stayed silent for a moment, and then she dropped her head on the pillow and sniffled a bit.

"No, no, no, no tears," Jason continued, agitated. "I am the victim here. I love you more and more every day. I never expected that it will grow so obsessive with years. Every cell of my body, every particle of my being is melting and dissolving in you. I love you to insanity, but I never hear anything from you ever. This is like a hell of a tragedy. It's torturing me for five years already. You have pushed me to the point where I don't know what I should do better—to kill myself or to dump you. But I can't live like that anymore. Please answer my questions—right now."

To his surprise, she suddenly said very calmly and quietly, "I am not crying at all. You are just pushing too hard. Do you want to hear it? Yes, I love you both. It's like a very religious woman who can love God above everything and also love her husband."

"So Jim is the God?"

"Kind of. He was always crazily jealous of you because he felt that I love you too. Now you're jealous of him? Too late. He does not exist anymore. I am all yours. I belong to you, and of course, I love you. I just didn't want to use these words because I used them so much with Jim. I told him that I love him many times per day, sometimes many times per hour. These words are all gone with him, all died with him. But the meaning is here, I swear. And my feelings for you are here for sure. Believe me, please. I very, very, very much love you, if these are the exact words that you really want to hear." She hugged his neck tenderly and placed her head on his chest.

"Thank you, my girl," Jason whispered with tears in his eyes and kissed her forehead.

They stayed silent for a long moment, holding each other tight. Then Jason took a deep breath and said quietly, "I want also to tell you one more thing that hurt me badly—the name." He tenderly put his hand on her abdomen. "Our boy's name. You do know that he will be a bit brownish and won't be even close to Jim in any way. For Jim, we have already his blond, blue-eyed Emmanuel—a carbon copy of him and Emmanuel Soley. I think it is enough to memorize him. Em is his living memory and his living blood. I want another name for my son, anything—Nick, Mike, Tom, Rick . . . anything but Jim. There's enough of Jim in our family. To put a period on this story, I did today something very important for Jim's memory for the last time, much more important than just gluing a label with Jim's name on my child."

Then he continued, "Did you ever notice what Em is doing while he is sitting on the floor and playing with his cars or trains?"

"No." Lada shook her head. "Talking . . . smiling . . . cooing . . . like every child does?"

"No. He is singing, quietly singing to himself. I guess that he is maybe feeling some music inside his head. He is just too little to express it. So I bought him a small violin."

"Did you? Oh my God! Jason, you are amazing." Lada almost jumped in bed and kissed him affectionately. "I will start teaching him to play tomorrow. Where is it?"

"In his room, beside his bed, waiting for him to wake up in the morning. I would like to see his reaction. It would be very interesting. And about the name of our baby boy, period, we are finished with that forever. Are we clear on that?"

"Okay, I will think about it, I promise," Lada whispered, hugging him tight.

"Now let's start creating our damn spiritual bond," Jason suggested a bit sarcastically. "It's time finally. About my hell of a tragedy, I told you already. And I don't want to repeat this ever. Tell me now about your past in the Ukraine, about a tragedy that happened there."

"Did BB say something to you? How do you know?"

"He didn't say much. He suggested you tell me yourself. Why did you hide it from me in the first place?"

Lada sighed deeply. "Because it was scary and disgusting. I wanted our life to be pure and beautiful. I was afraid that you won't touch me anymore ever if you had known."

"Jeez, my silly girl." Jason laughed. "Is that how you know me? First, I'll never stop touching you in any circumstances. You're my magnet, as attractive as honey for a bear. Second, I saw so many awful and disgusting things during the years of my work that nothing could surprise me or push me away ever. I've got a kind of immunity in my brain."

"Okay," Lada quietly and obediently agreed and took a deep breath. "Then listen."

They talked all night, hugging each other, sometimes crying together, and then talking again and hugging again. When the story was finally finished, Lada whispered, "Now let's go outside. I want to show you something that is very sacred to me." She grabbed the blanket from the bed and pulled Jason to the patio behind the house.

They spread the blanket and lay down on it, looking at the sky. The night was bright, and the dome of the universe shone with billions of stars above. It was so deep and so endless that the sense of understanding of eternity somehow enveloped their whole existence.

"This is my dream, my heart, my soul, my love," Lada whispered. "You did want to see it. Here it is. Just lie silently and watch. Catch those stars with your eyes and with your heart. Sense them. Embrace them. Then you will know and feel how much I love you, Jason. I love you forever."

They went to sleep only in the morning, and at lunchtime, when Sandra came to visit, they were still sleeping. A nanny was playing with little San-Marie, alone in the living room. Sandra kissed the little girl on the cheek and took her in her arms. The child was looking like a brownish angel with deep black eyes and a halo of African curls around her head. She was absolutely charming and adorable.

"Hi, Grandma," San-Marie said and kissed her back on the cheek too. Sandra showed her the coloring book that she brought for her. They sat on the couch and colored for a while together. Then the nanny took San-Marie outside to play in the backyard and to have a picnic lunch on the lawn between flower beds.

"Where is Emmanuel?" Sandra asked.

"In his room, ma'am. He didn't even come out for breakfast this morning. I brought him something to eat there," the nanny answered. "It looks like he is busy."

Sandra went to her grandson's room and knocked on the door. He didn't answer, so she just opened the door and entered.

"Grandma!" Em shrieked happily, ran to her, and hugged her legs. "Look! Look what I've got! This is a violin. Jason left it here for me yesterday night."

Sandra hugged him tenderly and kissed his forehead, petting his curly very blond hair. "How do you know, Em, that it was Jason who gave you that violin but not your Mom?" Sandra asked.

"He left the note. Here it is." Em gave her a piece of paper on which was written with big block letters "From Jason," and also, a happy face was drawn beside the letters.

"Do you already know how to read?" Sandra asked, surprised.

"Yes, Jason showed me the letters when I was little, like San-Marie. And now, Grandma, sit down and listen. I want to play something for you."

"You should take music lessons first," Sandra suggested, "to learn how to play violin."

"I kind of figured it out by myself. I did practice the whole morning. Listen, Grandma. I would like to play for you the song that I composed this morning."

"Is it about the ocean?" Sandra asked with tears in her eyes.

"No. Why? It is about the stars on the night sky."

CPSIA information can be obtained
at www.ICGtesting.com
Printed in the USA
BVHW042208100121
597445BV00004B/6